GOOD GIRL

~BOOK 1~

BLENDED

GOOD GIRL

Copyright ©2013 Erica Chilson

Wicked Reads
PO Box 29
Nelson, PA 16940

www.ericachilson.com/wicked-reads

Printed in the United States of America
First Printing, 2017
ISBN-13: 978-0-9979899-1-5
ISBN-10: 0-9979899-1-2

Dedication

To my own personal Devon. You said you'd be my best friend forever, and I yours. You lied. Your best friend will always be your mistress– addiction brought on by mental illness. I couldn't help you because you refused to help yourself. I couldn't suffer witnessing your slow suicide while putting my own safety at risk. I've forgiven you and released the guilt, but you've altered who I am at my core. In your stead, I created someone willing to take the help being offered. You bled me deeper than anyone before, deeper than anyone ever will, and I thank you for the education. The loss of me is your ultimate consequence.

There aren't many options for a girl who falls in the middle. I wasn't an athlete or a geek. I wasn't an artist or a musician. I didn't shake my pom-poms along with my butt. I was just a good girl who got good grades and kept her mouth shut. I didn't date my high school sweetheart and promptly get married the second I was handed my diploma. I'm not shiny enough to attract notice, nor dark enough to be a problem.

I don't have a tragic sob story. My daddy didn't leave us destitute, and I'm not a victim of a bad neighborhood. I am a middle-America, middle of the road, middle class girl with both parents fussing over their youngest daughter, who has no aspirations or goals. I've had every opportunity to succeed– supportive parents, stability, and a strong upbringing. I'm wayward, and everyone looks at me like I'm an alien.

My philosophy: how should I know what I want to do with the rest of my life the day I graduate? How am I supposed to know the second I turn eighteen what I'm destined to become? One moment you're a disillusioned seventeen-year-old with the world at your fingertips– the next? Congratulations! You're eighteen, and you're on your own.

CHAPTER ONE

"Mr. Kline," I greet my boss as I whirl into Revamped. The eclectic store is warm and cozy, a happy welcoming. But the winter chill followed me in, along with a healthy dose of snow. I flash a wide grin as Mr. Kline visibly shudders at my greeting, and then his eyes narrow at my wintery entrance.

"Don't worry– I'll clean it up," I grumble as I bounce toward the counter, leaving wet footprints across the vinyl tiles.

"I don't give a shit about the snow, Willow." Mr. Kline chastises me, then releases his patented sigh of disappointment. My boss is perturbed, as he always is when I call him by his surname. "Me– Auggie. You– Willow." He says this caveman-style, pointing at his chest, then mine.

I can't help but trail a giggle at his idiotic display, and his answering deep, hearty laugh makes him look like a gigantic teddy bear.

"It just feels strange calling you by your first name, sir." I sigh dramatically, acting all put out, as the heavy weight of my puffy jacket is lifted from my shoulders. Mr. Kline tugs it down my arms, then stows it underneath the counter next to the '*thank you*' plastic bags.

Mr. Kline has activated his alpha-male-caregiver-mode. I pretend I hate it, when we both know I secretly love it. Nimble fingers comb through my ponytail, righting the messy strands while brushing off the snowflakes, followed by a brotherly teasing tug.

I've worked at Revamped for a couple of months, basically since I graduated high school. There aren't many options for a girl who falls in the middle. I wasn't an athlete or a geek. I wasn't an artist or a musician. I didn't shake my pom-poms along with my butt. I was just a good girl who got good grades and kept her mouth shut. I didn't date my high school sweetheart and promptly get married the second I was handed my diploma. I'm not shiny enough to attract notice, nor dark enough to be a problem.

I don't have a tragic sob story. My daddy didn't leave us destitute, and I'm not a victim of a bad neighborhood. I am a middle-America, middle of the road, middle class girl with both parents fussing over their youngest daughter, who has no aspirations or goals. I've had every opportunity to succeed–

supportive parents, stability, and a strong upbringing. I'm wayward, and everyone looks at me like I'm an alien.

My philosophy: how should I know what I want to do with the rest of my life the day I graduate? How am I supposed to know the second I turn eighteen what I'm destined to become? One moment you're a disillusioned seventeen-year-old with the world at your fingertips– the next? Congratulations! You're eighteen, and you're on your own.

In a deep, growly tone, "Don't call me sir," Mr. Kline says with another shudder, practically cringing out of discomfort. He really hates it when the '*sirs*' pop out my mouth. He always winces in pain.

"Sorry! Sorry!" I rapidly spit. "I can't help it. It's hard to break eighteen years of conditioning. I see an adult, and they're automatically sir or ma'am. I still can't believe that I'm an adult– it's surreal."

I just barely stop myself from doing a celebratory dance while pissing my pants in fear. No doubt Mr. Kline would kick my ass if my Chucks left any more dirty snow marks on the tile floor. I try to let the pressure roll right off my back by acting indifferent, but days like today make it impossible. It's unfathomable– I feel no different than yesterday... or the eighteen years of days before.

Smirking at me like he can read my mind, Mr. Kline shakes his head, ginger curls flopping around. I know he's laughing *at* me, not *with* me.

I was hired to man the store so Mr. Kline wouldn't be bothered nonstop by patrons. An apologetic smile twitches my lips for my boss. "I'll get to work– go on. Create." My hands seek out Mr. Kline's broad back and forcefully shove him into the rear of the store where he spends his days. His warm laughter bubbles up his chest and vibrates against my palms. I rub the pleasant sensation away on my jean-clad thighs.

Mr. Kline. Auggie is an illustrator. He creates vivid, lifelike images with just the stroke of a pencil. He had goals and aspirations when he graduated. He was the geek, the jock, *and* the artist when he was growing up. He opened Revamped when he was only twenty with the money he earned selling comics at conventions.

Augustus Kline isn't wayward like me.

Revamped is like me. It's a quirky store filled with used everything: books, movies, old magazines, records, CDs and video games, comics, toys, and eclectic whatnots. We buy and sell anything that appeals to Mr. Kline. We also offer new items that are exclusive to local artists. Front and center, the best of friends, my brother's artistic masterpieces sit next to Mr. Kline's illustrations.

Robin Prynne– my brother isn't wayward, either. He's your quintessential tortured artist. Robbie makes my parents proud. He's the middle child and I'm the baby. Every family dynamic is the same: the oldest is a type-A personality, the middle child is artistic and emotional, the youngest is labeled lazy and uninspired as they live in their parents' basement and mooch... I don't actually live in the basement, but it's a pretty accurate description.

My sister is seventeen years older than me, and Robbie is ten years older than me. I was a menopause baby– a huge freaking surprise for my parents. After raising my siblings, my parents didn't have the energy to inspire me. I grew like my namesake– a willow tree flowing in the wind. My sister is as strong and resilient as her namesake– Clover. Nothing kills that shit in the lawn. No weed killer is strong enough for the force of Clover, and neither were my parents. Clover thinks she's my mother, and she's a massive thorn in my side.

My parents, Dave and Mary Prynne, are what most would call hippies. Dad may own a small business, but he's a certified tree-hugger. I'm thankful I won the lottery of names from nature. Poor Robbie– Robin... yeah, he got beat up a lot.

And that is where Mr. Kline came into our lives. My boss is Robbie's best friend, has been since their first day of Kindergarten. The only reason I got this job is because Mr. Kline has known me since I was born– a shadow of a surrogate brother.

I didn't even earn my position here at Revamped. I didn't even have to apply. It was handed to me when I graduated, just like everything else in my life. I'm good at it, though, simply because I don't want to disappoint. Just because I didn't earn it doesn't mean I'm not appreciative and thankful enough to try my damnedest to do Mr. Kline proud. It's not like it's all that difficult– a monkey could do it. I'm not a complete dipshit, no matter what my family and the town of Fairport, Massachusetts thinks.

Even with the excitement of the day, my mind still dwells on the fear of being lost in life. Sighing heavily, I drag myself from my destructive thoughts by deciding I better earn my paycheck.

A slacker's haven. It's not too early in the day since Revamped doesn't open until eleven a.m. and we close at six p.m. Mr. Kline is a night owl and doesn't crawl down here from his loft until just before opening. But that's not a big deal since there isn't a huge market for the kind of stuff we sell. I think we buy more than we sell– inside the store anyway. Mr. Kline is allowing me to do online auctions for some of our more valuable merchandise.

See– I told you I'm not a moron.

Mr. Kline put his trust and belief in me, even if no one else expects me to achieve anything out of life.

After grabbing a CD at random from the bin of CDs I've yet to test, I slide it into the player with a little prayer. The last batch of CDs were scratched to hell and unplayable. Auggie wasn't too happy from the lost revenue, saying we paid the schmuck for the right to dispose of his trash. Hey, I didn't do the transaction, so he was basically pissed at himself. I sigh in relief when its digitalized sound floods the store.

"Good choice," Mr. Kline's deep voice resonates from the back of the shop. He chuckles, and it's a nice sound– happy and sweet. "Isn't this before your time?"

"You know I'm a random selector," I volley back at him while laughing. I don't know who is singing, but the lyrics are a trip– *cat scratch fever*… what the hell is that? Is it a real thing?

When I should be tidying up the store instead, I find myself swaying to the tunes as my eyes keep track of an auction ticking its time away on the screen of the laptop resting on the counter. It's hypnotic and completely distracting. I busy myself with a rag and manage a half-assed attempt at cleaning off the counter around my obsession. I barely dust a square inch before I refresh the browser to see if the bid went up. Snapping the laptop shut, I growl at it in frustration.

My sneakers had left tiny puddles of melted snow from the front door to the counter. After grabbing a hand towel, I crabwalk while crouching to swipe the mess up, all the while humming that ridiculously infectious song.

"Ow!" I hiss as the front door beans me in the head– its bell dings for an eternity. Sitting on the heels of my Converse, I rub the goose-egg that's forming.

"Oh, shit! I'm sorry," a husky male voice spews in a panic. "I didn't see you down there." Eyes wide, I wonder if I'm seeing shit as I stare up at the boy who accidently hit me. His voice twists with annoyance, like it's my fault he hurt me– which it is. I was being a dumbass. "Why the hell are you on the floor in front of the friggin' door?"

"Oh… no…" I breathe out, words all shuddery.

I want to melt into the puddle of dirty melted snow beneath my feet– anything but this. My life just turned into a ridiculous cliché. Leaning over me is the blond and blue-eyed crush I've had since grade school. The boy every girl wants. The type of boy who never gave me the time of day in school. I'm ashamed to admit that I've always had a thing for the quarterback– that's where the cliché comes into play. I know he's probably a dickwad with the conversational skills of wet cotton, but he is a fantasy. Kieren Mason is a gorgeous, boy-next-door fantasy brought to life. Who cares whether or not Kieren's a buffoon when he fills out a t-shirt to perfection?

At eighteen, I'm not looking to pick out curtains. Vapid thinking or not, I just want a hot view– minus the mortification, that is.

Kieren flashes me a panty-wetting grin. The type of grin that's slightly naughty– a little bit angelic and a little bit evil. A grin that promises he's selling something I don't need and can't afford, but I'm going to want it anyway, and he's the only one who can give it to me.

Serial killers and car salesmen wear a similar smile.

"Isalright," slurs together. I meant to say "*it's alright*", but whether from the hit or the gobsmackage, I can't form a complete sentence. I shuffle to my feet, looking like a goob. I stare at the gray specks on the commercial-grade vinyl tiles, willing the embarrassed flush to drain from my cheeks.

"Willow?" Kieren says like he's never seen me before, his eyes tracking over me from my grubby sneakers to my barely combed hair.

I look like hell because I've perfected my wayward appearance. I may not know what I want to do in life. I may not know what patterns should go on the top versus the bottom, or what designers are in style. I don't even know how to apply makeup properly. But what I do know is that I want to be comfortable. So I'm in ratty jeans, a faded sweatshirt from our local university, and sneakers. My thick brown hair is in a ponytail– I'm pretty sure I combed it this morning, but it's hard to tell, which is probably why Mr. Kline was fixing it earlier. What I do know is that I don't look good.

Actually, I always look like a messy preteen boy. So I know Kieren isn't impressed by me. It's not as if he hadn't seen me look a lot worse in gym class as I flailed around like a fish flopping onshore. I shrug– *whatever*. It's not like I have a lick of pride or anything.

"I didn't think you'd be here," Kieren says in honest surprise. His grin ratchets up a few notches from charming to devastating. I get lost in that smile, as if it's only meant for me. His blue eyes begin to glitter in pure amusement, rendering me stupid for a few stolen seconds… and then I get smart.

Oh, so that's what that look meant. I'm such a loser that Kieren didn't think I had a job. My back bristles up and I try to mask the annoying hurt that flashes across my face.

"What can I do for you, Kieren? What brings you to Revamped?" I say with a saccharine, sweet voice– a voice so false I wince.

My natural voice isn't the whiny brat or cheerleader *yay* that Kieren's accustomed to. It's gravelly. I always sound like I'm getting over a cold, or like I've smoked five packs a day since kindergarten. Which is pretty accurate– the smokes, not the cold.

My best friend loves to tease me that I'd give good phone sex– not that I've ever had phone sex, or had sex, or even been kissed. All of which is probably due to the fact that I look like a little boy, and smell like the grubby floor of a bar. Eau de toilette, the scent of cigs, weed, and booze.

"I…" Kieren hesitates, looking embarrassed as he grips the bag he's holding– a plastic shopping bag that he's practically hugging to his well-formed chest.

Whether Kieren's comment was meant as a dig or not, I decide it's high time I looked professional. Obviously he came here seeking Revamped's services, not mine. I go around the counter to stand behind the cash register– ya know, make it look like I actually work here.

Hooding my eyelids, I take in the sight as Kieren's ball-catching hands flex on the bag. Unbidden, my thoughts begin to wander. I nip the corner of my bottom lip with my teeth as I wonder what those hands would feel like flexing on other things. Lower things.

Smirking at my naughty thought, a split-second later I get beaned in the head again. "What?" I whine in annoyance as I rub my new owie.

Mr. Kline looks at me with pissed off amusement, like he knew the naughty direction of my thoughts. I was so caught up with Kieren that I didn't notice my boss coming out the back of the store to see who made the front door's bell go ding-a-ling.

"NO!" is a low command said from between tightly drawn lips. Glaring, Mr. Kline points a rolled up comic at my face– the comic he used to hit me in the back of the head. My boss treats me like I'm a naughty dog who pissed on the carpet and was punished with a few swats to the ass with a rolled up newspaper.

Imploring, I give my boss big, brown, innocent eyes, just as I always have since I learned the manipulative power of my gaze. Returning my look, Mr. Kline stares at me in a way he never has before, just as Kieren did moments ago, like he's never seen me. Mr. Kline's view of me is suddenly different. I barely stifle a shiver.

"Mr. Mason, what can I do for you?" Mr. Kline sounds oddly formal as he speaks to Kieren, when they're practically family.

With a forceful nudge of his wide hips, Mr. Kline pushes me away from front and center. Hand slipping up my spine, over the nape of my neck, and up the back of my skull, he finds the bump on my scalp. His fingers tap around it in a weird manner, causing my mouth to fall open and goosebumps to pop on my skin. I shiver and snap my jaw shut on a whimper. Mr. Kline keeps this up all the while he conducts his business. Unable to do anything but endure his soothing, my upper body slumps to the counter with a thump. I become Mr. Kline's shuddering ragdoll.

"Ah– these are in excellent condition, Kieren. How much are you asking?" Mr. Kline sounds professional, not at all like he's playing phrenologist on my scalp.

Kieren's shopping bag was filled with action figures that Auggie is lovingly appraising. Kieren's face is bright red with embarrassment and his eyes are downcast, avoiding my direct gaze. Now I understand why Kieren didn't want me to know why he came into Revamped. He's selling what constitutes as playing with dollies. For some reason it only makes Kieren cuter in my eyes. A man who is manly enough to play with toys, and admit it, has a huge set of balls in my opinion.

"I'm trying to raise money to get my truck fixed. The four-wheel drive went out on it last night, and I have a lot of driveways to plow. Those parts are a bitch to replace and expensive. So whatever you can get me will be great. I…I was just holding on to 'em. It's not like I played with them or anything," he mutters bashfully as a crimson flush pinks his cheeks.

Like hell, Kieren doesn't play with them. Mr. Kline and I play with all the toys in the store, and we'll play with these after Kieren leaves.

"How about two hundred and sixty bucks?" my boss negotiates, voice eager when it's usually drier than a popcorn fart.

I raise a brow Mr. Kline's way, because he's way over the retail-value of the action figures. Not waiting for the boy to respond, my boss quickly pulls the cash from the drawer, then slides a waver across the counter. I stare into his manly face, trying to figure out what the hell he's up to.

"So… Willow, you still jailbait? Rumor has it you finally joined us in the land of legal adulthood?" Kieren asks with a smirk in his voice while he fills out the paperwork, his full lips curling up at the corners. With his eyes on the paper, Kieren doesn't see Mr. Kline's face transform from its soft, pleasant features to those of a raging bull. Auggie's face is so red with anger that his freckles disappear.

I try to step away, but strong fingers tighten in my hair. I move back to where I was, but that isn't good enough for my boss. Mr. Kline pulls me into his side and places a possessive hand on the nape of my neck. Fingers pulsing every few seconds, he causes my body to break out into a sweat.

"Um… just this morning, actually." I stammer as my eyes rove over Mr. Kline's angry face, looking for clues on how to react.

Today is my eighteenth birthday– no longer jailbait as Kieren so crudely called it.

Mr. Kline's hand pulsates on my neck in silent warning. Scowling up at him, I bite my tongue. He's my boss, but I have enough people telling me what to do. I'm finally an adult today, after all. I stomp my foot in a small version of a tantrum and accidently hit Mr. Kline's sneaker. He winces and squeezes my neck tightly in silent punishment, green eyes narrowed with a grimace gnarling his large lips.

"Well, maybe we could go out sometime. Maybe to celebrate your birthday?" Kieren's smooth, causing my eyes to bulge out of shock– I must look like a cartoon character from the 1940s. Kieren's lips quirk up into a smirk, then he winks in my direction.

Judging by the way Mr. Kline rolls his eyes exaggeratingly, he doesn't appreciate how smooth Kieren Mason truly is.

It got mighty hot in here all the sudden. Hotter than Hades.

"Willow will let you know." Frosty, my boss replies for me as if I'm too stupid to accept or deny the date offer I'd been longing to hear since junior high.

"Hey," I grumble, angry how Mr. Kline is now acting like a possessive father. Is Augustus Kline my boss, friend, brother, or father? He's confusing me with his bullshit.

My plea gets ignored, as per usual. "Good luck with your truck. Tell your dad I said hello and I'm looking forward to seeing him Saturday night." Mr. Kline's words are pleasant, but his voice is frigid, sharp and stinging.

"Sure thing, Auggie." Kieren conspiratorially winks at my boss, all the while blushing. "I'll stop in again and see ya real soon, Willow." Kieren doesn't look at me as he says it. He stares at Mr. Kline, and it's said in a way that's mildly threatening.

Mr. Kline makes a throat clearing noise that means *mmm-hmm*, *yeah sure*, and *buh-bye* all at the same time. I feel like I was the item being negotiated on, not the actions figures.

As soon as the bell dings, solidifying Kieren's departure, Mr. Kline breathes in deep, releases it in a gust, and his hand drops from my neck. Distancing myself from the strange aura Mr. Kline is giving off, I pick up Darth Vader and march him around the counter toward Aquaman. The action figure disappears just as Darth was about to pummel him.

"Hey!" I yell in annoyance. "Aquaman sucks anyway," I whine.

Darth disappears from my hand and is softly cradled in Mr. Kline's big paw. He practically coos at it, lips sliding into a satisfied smile as an awed expression softens the angry lines marring his handsome face.

Ah! It was Darth Vader that my boss was coveting. Now I understand that hefty chunk of change he paid for a handful of shitty action figures. I watch in amusement as Mr. Kline tucks his baby into an airtight display box, then disappears into his backroom.

I take my aggression out on Mr. Kline's toys since I can't punch or yell at the big brute. I transform Bumble Bee from his car into the mighty Autobot, then continue my assault on the lame Aquaman. He doesn't stand a chance. I may have even made sounds to go along with my assault, but I'll deny it.

"Are you through?" Mr. Kline asks in amusement– yet again laughing *at* me. Leaning his tall body on the doorframe to the back of the store, he gazes at me from beneath hooded eyes. I can tell he's been watching me for a while.

Blushing fiercely, I quickly pick up Kieren's dolls. "It's your fault," I mutter wryly. "You put me in a store with all this stuff when it obviously wasn't a very bright idea," I gesture all around me. "I only had Robbie's toys to play with growing up. Clover's dolls didn't survive to be handed down to me. My parents thought a toy was a toy, so I had action figures that were a decade old. Working here is the equivalent of a junkie cooking meth."

Big palms deftly grip my hips and plunk me on the counter. I'm five feet tall and weigh just under a hundred pounds– a twelve-year-old boy with a ponytail. A manly beast, Mr. Kline towers over me by a foot and a half and more than doubles my weight. When I'm in trouble, my boss puts me on the counter like a bad toy so he doesn't have to bend down as far to yell at me. I've known Mr. Kline as long as I've known my brother, just as long as I've known my entire family. My ass is well-acquainted with this countertop and Mr. Kline's verbal assaults.

My first memory is of Mr. Kline and Robbie playing horsey with me– I was the horse and they were my handlers. I would neigh and crawl around the yard, chasing after a carrot. No matter how well I took direction, Mr. Kline would never let me have the carrot. When he was done playing with me, he'd crunch it between his teeth while laughing at me. He also wasn't Mr. Kline back then– he was just Auggie. When Auggie graduated from high school, he told me to call him Mr. Kline. See why I'm confused now that Mr. Kline wants me to call him Auggie again?

"No Kieren." Mr. Kline commands, brooking no room for argument. "Do I make myself clear?" He towers over me and leans into my personal space. Anyone looking in Revamped's front windows would see a mammoth of a man eclipsing a child, but I'm not afraid– he'd never hurt me. Intimidate me? Oh, hell yes!

"Yes, sir," I say but I don't mean it. I've always wanted Kieren, and now's my time to have him, even if it's just for a little while. What's the big deal?

Mr. Kline manages to pull off a wince at the sir, mixed with a look of disappointment that has me strangely feeling guilty. I never feel guilty, and I don't like the emotion one bit. I manipulate adults or steamroll over them, and they either get out of my way or suffer the consequences. Not Mr. Kline, apparently.

"Auggie," Mr. Kline points at his chest again. "Never, sir. That term isn't to fall from your lips again, Willow."

I nod my head and keep quiet. I almost said *yes, sir*... again.

"We need to have a talk now that you're eighteen," he says in a parental sort of way that is at complete odds with the flexing of his large fingers on my hips and thighs.

"I have enough daddies and mommies, Auggie," I mutter snidely, causing him to roll his eyes at me. "Clover is enough parent for a school of kids, just ask my niece and nephew."

"Your parents and Robbie are too lax and Clover is too strict. It's created a monster known as Willow. A very sheltered, naïve, innocent Willow monster, and it worries me." Auggie murmurs in concern, and then he tugs my ponytail to lessen the insult.

Yeah, I admit I'm a little shit. I deserve the monster title.

"Of course, I'm innocent," I purr sweetly, allowing the words to roll off my tongue. "I haven't perpetrated any crimes today, but give me some time and I can fix that– today's the first day that it would matter anyway." I tease, and Auggie gazes at me like I've grown a second head. "I know what you mean, Auggie. Jeesh, I was joking." I laugh, but it doesn't soften Mr. Kline's face like usual. I know I'm in trouble bad this time when he doesn't fall prey to my manipulations.

"I saw that womanly look you gave Kieren," Mr. Kline says pointedly, causing me to blush out of mortification. "You don't realize what a look like that is offering– too much for you pay."

"I'm not a fucking kid, Auggie!" I snarl, hating how small everyone makes me feel, not measured in inches, pounds, and years.

"I know you're not a child anymore," Auggie whispers kindly, fingers flexing on my body. "It didn't happen at midnight when you became a legal adult. It's been happening for a while. The problem is that since you were too good of a girl, you will now become a target."

"I've had the sex talk a billion times. The first time was when I was four– I was eavesdropping when Mom and Dad gave it to Robbie. I've been lectured by my parents, Clover and Robbie, and even once from you. I survived high school and Essie's exploits. My body may be innocent because I look like a fucking child, but my mind isn't."

Struggling to get down from the counter, I'm so done with this humiliating shit show. I may be a virgin, but I'm not stupid. It's extra embarrassing, because having my parents and siblings give me the talk is normal, everyday bullshit, but having my boss give it to me on my eighteenth birthday while I'm at work– humiliating.

"This isn't the sex talk." Auggie adjusts me on the counter until I have to look him in the eyes. He even bends down slightly to get in my line of sight– there's no avoiding the freckled alpha now. "Trust me, sex isn't difficult. Any idiot can do it," he draws out roughly, voice sounding deeper than usual.

"Even an idiot like me?" I mutter begrudgingly underneath my breath. "I've gathered sex isn't all that challenging– the act, that is. I assume it's a difficult task to find a friend who isn't skittish about grinding body parts with someone they aren't attracted to," I mutter flippantly, pretending tears aren't prickling my eyes.

"Willow–"

"So what's this actually about, Auggie?" I stop Auggie from continuing, causing him to shift around as if uncomfortable while convulsively clearing his throat.

"This is a different kind of talk." More throat clearing, with freckles vanishing beneath a crimson kiss. I'm happy to see Auggie's as uncomfortable as I feel.

"I know you've had a crush on that little shithead for a long time. Believe me, Kieren knows it, too." A private smirk plays along Auggie's lips, making me wish I could reach inside his head and yank his thoughts free. "You don't know men at all, Willow. We're despicable creatures whose motives can't be trusted."

"You said I could trust you and Robbie and my dad," I point out how Auggie's advice is flawed. "You've said for eighteen years, if I had a problem, I was to go to one of you or Clover." Sighing heavily, my heart aches with loss. "Sam was the best at this stuff," I whisper beneath my breath, praying Auggie didn't hear me. But I know he did when an intense look of sympathy crosses his face.

Auggie's expression twists my heart– I try to ignore the agony pounding with each and every beat. Sam should've been here on my eighteenth birthday. They say time heals all wounds... I say they're lying bastards because the mourning never ends.

"I'm sorry, Willow," Auggie murmurs gently as he smooths his palm down my hair in a comforting gesture. "I'll do my best to say this without hurting you, but this conversation is important. Sam would want you to hear it. Okay, honey?"

"Okay," I mutter in defeat, because Auggie's not above manipulation either. Everyone uses Sam as their trump card against me.

"Men or not, you're to trust us not to harm you. Your family will never touch you like that, but a horny boy is a different matter." Face warping from mentor to alpha, Auggie's voice drops into a growl. "All a boy wants is a warm, wet hole to rest his prick in."

"Ew! Gross!" I try to push my boss away, but Auggie's chest is as solid as a brick wall. "That's nasty, and it can't be true."

"Trust me, it is." Auggie's usually deep voice warps into a husky rasp. "And the need never really goes away. We men hunt constantly."

"I so did not need to know that." I twist the words out, grimacing.

Ignoring me, Auggie speaks right over top of me. "There are two types of men. One type is like your brother and father– like Kieren's dad. Loyal, focused solely on those they love. The other type is like me and Kieren. The difference is that my type is broken into two parts: the protector and the predator. Kieren is a predator. His dad is trying to make sure the dumbshit stays off the playground. Now that Ren's older, he's stalking the fringes of the playground so he won't get arrested."

"I don't get it," I mumble in confusion, eyebrows scrunching in the center. "What does this have to do with a playground?"

Mr. Kline's full-bodied laugh fills the store. Green eyes glittering with amusement, Auggie hitches his head backward and laughs to the ceiling. It takes several seconds before he calms. Scowling up at him, I feel inept and more confused than ever.

"Yeah, you need a keeper." He sighs heavily, rubbing my hip. "Kieren didn't have a girlfriend in high school, right? He didn't exclusively date the head cheerleader like every other quarterback in the history of our nation. No, Kieren had conquests– one girl after another, and they all had one thing in common... and once it was gone, Kieren was gone. His stalking ground is getting narrower, and he'll start doing bad things. I don't want you to be hurt by him."

The look of confusion on my face has Auggie shaking his head at me in frustration. "Goddammit, Willow." He growls while giving me a little shake, fingers clasping over my upper arms. "I didn't want to actually say it out loud. The fact that I have to proves my point."

"What point?" I mutter, eyes never leaving his.

"Just how innocent you truly are. You're a virgin. Kieren only likes virgins. The sad truth is that you're his perfect prey. Kieren will play you, lure you in, have sex with you, and then he'll leave. It doesn't matter who the girl is, this is what he does."

"Thanks for the talk, Auggie. I feel so special now. No guy will ever want me except to deflower me. Great, I feel so much better." Guts clenching in pain, I mumble sarcastically while looking inward in horror. "And I love how everyone knows everything about me." I hop off the counter, grumbling a litany of curses underneath my breath. "Once I'm a skank, I guess I'll lose my appeal."

Auggie roughly yanks me back with his huge hands and plunks me on the counter with a thud. "We're not finished until you understand this." His growly-bear grunt stuns me into compliance. "You're susceptible to Kieren's manipulations. He will try to charm you, pretend to be your friend, date you, and then he will get what he wants and move on. It isn't about every guy, just him. Pick another one, and I will let you know if it's a good idea. I want you to date. I want you to have fun. I'm not lecturing about abstinence. Go ahead and fuck ten guys as long as you want them, it's about self-respect, and you're safe. But Kieren will either lie to get into your pants or take it. Kieren has to grow up and deal with his shit first before I allow him anywhere near you, Willow."

Anger flashes across Auggie's face and ignites his green eyes into fiery emeralds. He gives me a frustrated shake and growls deep in his chest. "I promised Sam! Dammit." A rough shake has my head lolling on my neck. "I don't want you to get *raped*."

Once the word has been spoken and out in the open, Auggie looks like he's going to be sick.

"Is that clear enough for you? You're eighteen now, and Kieren can't go to jail for fucking you. Forced or not, no one would believe you because everyone knows you've wanted Kieren forever. And this isn't Kieren's first rodeo– or his tenth. You got it now, Willow?"

Auggie's entire demeanor is different than I've ever see it. His eyes are usually a happy seafoam green, with his expression relaxed and pleasant. Rage-filled and terrified, he's my teddy bear no more.

My skin blazes in embarrassment so fierce that it prickles. Hiding behind my palms, I try to will it away. I'll leave Kieren alone for Auggie– Sam trusted Auggie, and so do I.

"Okay, no Kieren," sounds muffled from beneath my hands.

"That's a good girl," Mr. Kline praises me with a brilliant, toothy grin.

My hands drop. "I thought you said that being a good girl was bad. You called me a monster," I mumble sullenly as my bottom lip quivers.

"Yeah, it's bad for someone like Kieren." Auggie's eyes never leave my mouth, and it creates a confusing buzz in my belly.

"Who's it good for then?" I ask in all seriousness. If I can't play with Kieren, then who?

Auggie's gaze leaves my mouth and quickly darts to my eyes. He groans in frustration and runs his fingers through his reddish-brown curls. "Yeah– um… I'm not answering that one. Not touching that subject for nothin'. I've got to go to the post office. Yeah, the post office is where I need to be. I'll be back in a few minutes." He grabs his keys from the hook, then practically runs for the front door, his large stride eating up the space between the door and me.

"Well, men flee from you, Willow," I murmur as I jump to the floor. "You sure do know how to clear a room, birthday girl."

I quickly check the appropriate pricing for Kieren's dolls, tag them, and place them on display. Being spiteful, I mark Aquaman as free with purchase. I manage to clean up the store and check my auctions fifty times, and Mr. Kline still hasn't returned from the *post office*. I even sold a few things and told a woman to come back in an hour with her consignment items.

Worrying I've run Mr. Kline from his own store, I load another CD into the stereo and allow the music to melt away my insecurities.

CHAPTER TWO

"*He's a one-stop shop... makes my cherry pop... He's a sweet talkin' sugar-coated candyman... A sweet talkin' sugar-coated candyman... oh, yeah.*" I sing with Christina and bop my way around the shop, swinging my ponytail in time with the beat of the music.

"*Well, by now I'm getting all bothered and hot. When he kissed my mouth, he really hit the spot. He had lips like sugar cane... Good things come to boys who wait.*"

Random and cheesy from the tester box, music always motivates me to work harder– it seeps into my soul and I lose myself. It never matters the artist or the genre. If it has music notes, I enter my happy place where every chore becomes cathartic.

"*Sweet, sugar candyman,*" whispers salaciously from my parted lips. "*He's a one-stop, gotcha hot, making all the panties drop.*" I whisper again, "*Sweet, sugar candyman.*" Hopping in time with the lyrics, I let myself look like a moron. "*He's a one-stop, got me hot, making my uh pop... Sweet, sugar candyman... He's a one-stop, get it while it's hot, baby, don't stop.*"

Improvising, I grab Aquaman and use him as a microphone. I open my mouth and barely breathe, "*Sweet sugar–*"

"Hmm… is that what the good girl dreams about at night, the candyman?" Auggie purrs smoothly, surprisingly not looking as if he's making fun of me this time.

Lost in my idiotic karaoke act, I never even heard the front door bell ding. "Holy fuck!" I yelp, covering my face with my upraised hands. The prickling from earlier returns to a full-fledged burn. I doubt my skin will ever return to its flesh tone. I'll be forever red with embarrassment.

"Do I need to get a shotgun to keep this '*Candyman*' fucker from making your cherry pop? Hmm, Monster?" Auggie purrs in a way I've never heard from him, he almost sounds… seductive?

I'm struck dumb– speechless.

"Update, and then let's play some *Perfect Dark*." Auggie continues to laugh at me as he strides across Revamped to join me at the counter.

After groaning in mortification, I take a deep breath and soldier forth. It's not the first, and it surely won't be the last time I'm embarrassed. "I... um– priced Kieren's action figures. I made two sales. A lady will be back shortly. She has some stuff to sell. One auction is bombing, two are on the retail mark, and one is quadruple the price we paid." I rapidly reply to cover my embarrassment.

"And you were doing a perfect rendition of *Candyman*." Auggie hasn't stopped laughing, even while I was giving him an update. His cheeks are rosy from the cold and snow, or maybe from my ridiculous karaoke act, and his green eyes are twinkling as he loads the N64.

One of the perks with working at Revamped is that we don't actually work– we play constantly. I spend most of my time checking out the items people sell Auggie: listening to the CDs, playing the video games, and cleaning the objects. We can't sell as-is merchandise that is broken. If someone pulls a fast one, Auggie just leaves the store and tracks their asses down.

Fairport isn't that large of a town, and the offender is easily apprehended. They cough up the cash when they get a visit from my brute of a boss, who usually tries to make them eat their broken items. If they don't have the dough, he threatens to shove their shit back up their asses. Auggie has a very persuasive air about him.

Old game systems are our favorite and the most consigned type of item. Boys of all ages visit Revamped when they're in need of some cash. More often than not, they're back rebuying their shit before we manage to sell it to someone else.

Today's video game that we have to test is Perfect Dark on the N64– one of our favorites. Perfect Dark is a first-person shooter. Basically, we run around shooting at each other. I always customize my Joanna Dark, yet Auggie will make his exactly like mine. Last time I was Elvis the alien– a short, tiny body with a huge head begging to be sniped. When Auggie created the same avatar time and time again as mine, I finally asked him why, because you're a fool to use Elvis. Mr. Kline's response was that it's only fair if we're the same character– so much for individualism. Today I'm Joanna Dark again, wearing a *Datadyne* catsuit.

"Have you ever noticed how the CMP150 icon looks like the word calypso? I know it truly doesn't. But that's what I see and that's what I call 'em." I ramble to distract Auggie, because I want him to think the CMP150 pistol is my only weapon, which is one of the weakest weapons in the game.

Holding my snicker in like a poker player poorly hiding his tell, I maneuver my avatar near Auggie's. I sneak up behind him to stick a proximity mine on the wall next to his avatar. I make my Joanna run away, and I giggle when I hear the explosion.

"Oh, that was cold," Auggie drawls. "You're no longer a good girl. We're back to calling you Monster. Watch out, Monster, I know that dirty little trick now." Auggie chuckles good-naturedly, the happy sound making me feel warm and fuzzy.

I live to entertain Auggie.

Totally focused on having my avatar and its minions track down Auggie and his, the front door bell dings, effectively ending our fun as a customer enters Revamped. I snap off the ancient console television set and shut down the N64.

"I guess Tom Dillard's game is good for sale, eh?" I mumble more to myself than him. I'm competent enough to make that judgment call.

Fun-time over, we get into the peaceful groove we've adopted over the past five months. I take care of customers, with Auggie popping out of his office if they need to sell something. He doesn't trust me with that type of transaction yet, unsure if I can properly appraise the items. I don't blame him since I'm uncomfortable doing that kind of thing, worrying I'll mess up big time.

Since my auctions won't close until tomorrow at midday, my work here at Revamped has concluded for the day. The door dings again just as I finish closing out the cash register, triple checking that the receipts and wavers match the register tape totals.

You know the joke, '*a man walks into a bar*'? Well, '*a woman walks into a store*'… that is the only way to describe her– *woman*. My itty-bitty-titties invert in shame when I gaze upon the creature that is striding across the worn vinyl tiles.

Revamped's newest inhabitant has to be at least six foot tall– larger than life... or maybe not, she has on wicked spiky heels. I mean *spiky*– they are six inches of sharp, pointy, metal rods that would be an effective weapon, or maybe an incentive as they spear on horny, thrusting men as the spikes leaves perfect indents in the flesh of their asses.

The lady vamp in Revamped stands silently before me, posing, dark tresses draped perfectly over one shoulder, as if people check her out on a continual basis. Perhaps they do. Her tight jeans encase shapely thighs. I don't have a snowball's chance in hell of getting my legs to ever look that juicy, no matter what exercises I do. My jaw pops open when I see her perfect breasts peeking out of her tight sweater.

This woman bleeds sex– she has my innocent mind spinning fantasies within a nanosecond.

Envy.

Recognizing the suffocating sensation roiling through me as envy, my eyes finally roll up to her face. Pale skin is showcased by red-glossed, full lips, eyes as black as midnight lined in kohl, and perfect inky black hair. A younger, hotter version of Elvira. If her name is actually Elvira, I think I will swoon.

I want to grow up to be this woman.

Big fingers snap my lower jaw up to meet my upper jaw. I almost bite my tongue. I may have even drooled a little bit. I don't even care that Auggie is witnessing yet another instance of me acting like a buffoon today.

"Isis," Auggie says in greeting, but it sounds more like a warning.

Yeah, Isis is an even better name than Elvira. Somehow I manage not to faint. Even her name is perfect. I dab the corner of my lips where a spot of drool pools. I'm in awe– sweet baby Jesus, she's gorgeous!

Prowling toward my boss, long legs rolling at her hips, Isis stalks her prey. The sharp clack of her heels on the tiling reverberates down my spine, a tone of foreboding. Isis wraps herself around Auggie, reminding me of a snake around a tree trunk. Her fingernails dig into Auggie's back before they make a path toward his rear end.

I watch in shock as Isis kisses Auggie. Those vibrant, red lips part to give way for a pink tongue that snakes its way into Auggie's mouth. Her dark eyes pin me as she gives a sultry moan when his tongue connects with hers.

I'm naïve.

Innocent.

Isis is educating me.

Educating me in what, I have no fucking clue other than I want to learn more.

My jaw falls open again, and I just let it hang out down there– it's worthless to me right now anyway.

Auggie looks different next to Isis. He doesn't seem like a geek, like my big brother's best friend. He's no longer my boss. Auggie looks like a man– a manly man that Isis likes very much, judging by her red-tipped talons flexing on his muscular ass.

I've seen kissing. I've watched porn with my friends. I've even watched my friends make-out. Worse, I've watched Essie blow more dudes than I can count. I've always been happier getting wasted so I didn't have to think about how no one would ever want to fuck the body my brain and heart reside in. But I've never seen this potent intensity before. Teenagers fumbling around while drunk and high pales in comparison to real lust. The chemistry between Isis and Auggie boils the air around us, tightening my body with longing for something I'll probably never experience.

This new, strange buzz in my lower belly turns into a screeching alarm. An alarm that feels warm and pleasurable. I look at my shoes, blushing, trying to ignore the smacking noises that flash fire down my spine.

"That was inappropriate, Isis." Auggie chastises the goddess with a deep, husky voice I've never heard before. He always talks to me in a calm, kind tone, or a frustrated one. I have to look up to make sure Auggie didn't poof and was replaced by a sex god with lust infusing his voice.

The hungry look Auggie gives me creates a heavy weight in my belly along with that warm buzz. I flush deeper and his eyes widen in alarm. I look to the floor again, knowing Auggie caught me. I'm in trouble– Auggie's going to kick my ass. Thinking naughty thoughts about Kieren Mason got me into deep trouble, thinking naughty thoughts about Mr. Kline will get me skinned alive.

I anxiously step from foot-to-foot as I stare at the gray speckles on the tile floor. I'm not flushed from my boss… watching the vampire lady eat at Auggie's mouth didn't turn me on– nope!

"Augustus, won't you introduce me to your little *friend*?" Her rolling lilt slides down my spine to pool in my nether regions. Not once have I ever thought of a woman in a sexual light, but with Isis that is an impossibility. Isis is pure sex. She isn't a smooth flow of seduction– she's like a bolt of lightning to my beating heart… and lower. Isis lights my libido on fire and leaves nothing but ash in her wake.

Isis said *friend* weird, like it meant something else entirely. I'm naïve, but not *that* naïve– she didn't mean it in the bed-buddy sense of the word either.

My boss shakes his head no. Auggie's not going to introduce me to the seductive lady. Now, that's not very nice. Feeling like a rebel, my jaw moves to allow me to introduce myself. Feeling like a coward, no sound expels as my lips flap like a dying fish on land.

Begrudgingly gesturing toward me, Auggie mutters, "This is Rob's baby sister, Willow… as you well know. I'm pretty sure you had an alert set on your cellphone for Willow's eighteenth birthday, along with the rest of your fucking family." Auggie actually rolls his eyes. "Willow isn't for you to toy with," Auggie warns cryptically. "Rob would kill the pair of us, Isis."

Isis's answering smile is as brilliant as it is scary. I'm surprised her teeth aren't sharp and fanged by the feral quality she possesses. Not so much fear but anticipation flashes down my spine, jolting me. I back up a step, then yank my coat from underneath the counter. Auggie caused hot sparks to blaze in my body, but Isis's expression flashes ice water through my veins, like I'm stepping into something I'm not meant to be in.

"Rob speaks highly of you, my dear," Isis purrs. "I hear today is your birthday." Her voice is lulling, rolling off her poisonous tongue.

Said the spider to the fly.

"No!" Auggie shouts. I wonder if he smacks Isis with rolled up paper, too.

"Rob said Willow is just like him. I just want to see if he's right," Isis hisses in annoyance. She bites her pouty bottom lip– the lip that was just mingling with Auggie's moments ago. "Don't get pissy with me, prick. Willow isn't meant for you, either, might I remind you. Which is precisely why you're acting like a possessive bastard– don't think I didn't hear about what you were doing this afternoon. For Lord's sake, I just want to chat with Rob's sister. I've waited long enough."

"No!" Auggie commands again, looking like he's about to lose his shit– auburn hair suddenly looking like angry flames licking at his skull with green eyes glowing back at me with rapidly building panic. "Willow, get your stuff and get your ass in my truck. I'll drive you home," he grumbles after regaining his control. "Isis can wait for me here."

Feeling like a toy being fought over by two selfish toddlers, a toy I can't figure out why they'd want to play with, I mutter hesitantly, "Sir, you stay with your guest. I can walk. It's not far." I start for the front of the store, but I'm yanked back by a hand grabbing my ponytail, fingers painfully wrapping around the strands.

"Willow, don't say that word ever again," Auggie barks a panicked warning as he pats my hair back into place, trying to soothe the sting.

Too late, Isis laughs, sharp and wounding.

"Aaaahhhh," Isis draws out. "Now I understand. I'm not allowed to play with Willow because she's already your pet," Isis says in disappointment while flashing me a strange look. Isis is the third person to look at me in that peculiar manner. Today. What the hell does that look mean, anyway?

"You're in deep shit, Ugg. Deep, deep shit–"

"I hate it when you call me Ugg," Auggie growls. "You say a fucking word, and I'll take your only toy away. Forever. One word from me– just one word. You don't own Robin– never forget who does." The threat was meant for Isis but it wounds me, strangely pierces my heart and I have no idea why. I have no idea what shit I've just stepped in, but obviously I wasn't meant to meet Isis. Judging by Auggie's seething demeanor, I wasn't meant to meet her ever.

With rough, jerking movements, Auggie pulls my coat up my arms and starts buttoning it in a hurry. I smack his hands away and say, "I'm not a baby. I can dress myself," underneath my breath. He ignores me, hooking the last of the buttons.

Auggie pushes me from the store, and I run to his truck because he looks like he will forcibly move me if I don't get away from Isis fast enough. Confusion making me compliant, I let Auggie lift me in and buckle my seatbelt. Seconds later, we're making the half-mile drive to my house.

I'm young, maybe a bit naïve, but I'm not stupid. I know Isis holds Auggie's secrets, but I also know they're none of my business. I'm curious enough to ask Auggie what he was so frightened of, what was Isis going to tell me, but those words don't manifest.

"I could've walked home faster than it took for you to start your truck and drive me," I mutter in annoyance, and I barely get an entire sentence out of my mouth before my house comes into view.

Mood shifting to lighthearted now that we're away from Isis's sharp, forked tongue, Auggie grins at me, pulling out the charm with just the twist of his lips. "But it's cold out, and birthday girls should get chauffeur service on their special day," Auggie croons as he pulls up to the curb. Flashing me a roguish smile, his teeth glow white in the dim of the streetlights.

Maybe the most important question I should be asking Auggie is if he's bipolar.

By the time I unbuckle my seatbelt, he's already at my door, wrenching it open. Auggie's fingertips bite into my thighs, turning my body on the truck seat until we're face-to-face with my feet dangling. Auggie leans over me from where he stands in the open truck door. His expression is starkly sober, worried and filled with compassion. With just one look, I'd do anything he'd ask.

"Isis is another type of person you need to avoid. She's worse than Kieren Mason. Far worse. Just think of Kieren as a junior-Isis-in-training. Just stay the hell away from both of them."

"I don't understand, Auggie," I mumble out of confusion.

"I'd explain, but I don't want you to understand." Eyes flick away, as if Auggie's worried I'll read too much in his gaze. "Willow, my wish for you is to keep whatever naïveté you have left for as long as humanly possible. Childhood is priceless, and once you're jaded, you can never get your innocence back."

Auggie bites his lip in indecision, drawing my undivided attention. I want to smooth the indents left behind by his teeth with my tongue. I rapidly shake my head at the thought, clearing it away. Never has my mind wandered to Auggie in a sexual manner.

Green eyes track across my face and widen when they read my shameful thoughts. Leaning forward into the warmth of Auggie, I hide my face against his chest out of embarrassment. Uncomfortably laughing at the situation, Auggie murmurs how it's okay and he understands.

Auggie gives me a bear hug, and my arms barely go around his back and my knees don't part far enough to let him hug me fully. Solid and strong, I feel safe in his embrace. I bury my face into the crook of his neck and inhale, groaning in pleasure at his comforting, woodsy scent.

Time stills as Auggie holds me on my eighteenth birthday, shielding me from the chill of the wintery night air. This isn't the comforting hug you give a child, or the platonic embrace of friends. There is a charge in me that was never present before, as if something in Auggie calls to a dormant part of my being that was lying in wait for him to ignite.

For the first time in my life, I feel like an adult.

A woman.

"Please be careful tonight when you go out with your friends. Be a good girl," Auggie whispers in my ear. The vibrations tickle my skin, causing me to shiver. He pretends it was from the cold and tightens his hold on me for a second longer.

Reluctantly stepping away from me, Auggie speaks. "Here–" he pulls a box from his coat pocket, and I gladly take it with a smile.

"You got me a gift?" I say in surprise while cradling the small box to my chest. "You didn't have to. It's so unexpected."

The gift is a small box with a polka-dot bow on top. I wiggle the lid off the box, then peer inside. Shiny silver catches my eye as fingers deftly pluck my present from its tissue paper nest, then settle it around its new home. After Auggie hooks the necklace around my neck, I realize it's a choker by the tight fit. I finger a small charm dangling from the center, wishing I could see it better in the dim of the truck cab.

"Thank you," I whisper reverently into the dark. My voice is raw with emotions I can't name. Those same unnamed emotions are echoed in Auggie's tortured expression.

"I'll see you in the morning. Ya better hurry up and get inside. It looks like everyone is waiting on you." We both look at the long line of cars. I groan, causing Auggie to belt out a hearty laugh. Pulling me from the truck cab, he gently sets me on my feet.

Walking on numb, rubbery legs, I turn to wave goodbye when I get to the porch, only to find Auggie's pickup truck pulling away from the curb. I watch his taillights until they fade in the distance, no doubt heading back to Isis at Revamped. I wait until I no longer hear the rumbling of his engine before going inside.

Suddenly I feel lost and alone, when waiting on the other side of the door is my entire family– the only safety, security, and happiness I've ever known. My family: my past and my present.

What the hell is my future?

It's impossible to ignore the restless sensation after eighteen years– the icy chill of premonition that weaves up my spine. I don't belong here– I never have and I don't know why.

Before opening the door, I finger the charm on my necklace and curse underneath my breath. Yeah, having a good girl crush on the boy-next-door is a bad idea, having a monster crush on your boss is even worse.

CHAPTER THREE

"Happy Birthday, Willow," Violet deadpans the moment I open the door. Her glare is the first thing I see every night, like a resentful dog greeting its master. Coming to my defense, Seth, Violet's twin, pushes her for being nasty to me. This is my usual homecoming, minus the happy birthday salutations.

My niece acts exactly like her mother– a miniature, more volatile version of Clover. The twins are thirteen, and I'm pretty sure Violet loathes me. Violet is jealous because her mother seems to think she birthed me too, which isn't a reward. It's more like a lifelong punishment to have Clover riding my ass. I'm sure Violet's jealousy stems from the fact that her twin treats me like I'm his big sister. Violet wants complete and total control over Seth. I'm his biggest influence, and he's my biggest fan.

I hate Violet too, so I guess we're even. Our ages are inversed. She looks eighteen and I look younger than her thirteen. Violet has a nice body, curvy in all the right places and slim in the others. Plus, I'm jealous that she's tall. Violet is everything I'm not: poised, popular, pretty, perfect, and any other *P* word that is the total opposite of me– precious?

Violet and I share the honors of pigheadedness, pissy, and postal.

My counterpart nephew, Seth is adorable and still boy-like: round face with a button nose and tiny chin. Big, brown, puppy dog eyes, and an angelic grin that hides his wickedness. He even has my chain-smoker voice. Seth and I look just alike, even though he's the exact replica of his dad. *Sam.* Yeah, that's why Violet hates me– I'm Seth's real twin. But the real reason is because Sam loved me like I was his daughter too.

Nearly the same height, "Happy Birthday, Willow," Seth repeats in a cheery tone, then kisses my cheek. I place a big smacker on his chubby cheek as I give him a tight squeeze.

"Thanks, brother," I say loudly, making sure Violet heard me. Her glare could kill, but Seth looks pleased as punch.

"Behave, children," Hester warns as she barrels toward me, pushing Seth out of my orbit. Essie is twenty years old and my best friend and cousin. Well, Hester is *our* cousin: Violet and Seth's and mine. I'm sheltered, extremely so to my developmental detriment. My only friends share similar DNA to mine.

Nudging Seth with a hip, Essie orders, "Let's get this over with. I have a surprise for you later." We share a conspiratorial look, our own secret language only best friends speak.

And if that just doesn't make smoke billow out of Violet's ears, I don't know what would. We're a tight-knit group, and jealousy runs rampant in our family. I could deny that I don't enjoy them squabbling for my attention, but that would be a lie. I stick my tongue out at Violet to be a brat, and Seth rumbles a husky laugh.

Hester– Essie isn't much taller than me, but she was blessed with killer curves. I'd offer up my first born to have breasts like hers, not that I'll ever have kids since I can't lure a man into procreation without a set of tits blinding him to my other faults.

I've wished on the past eight birthday cakes for those breasts. They started to grow when Essie was only ten years old and continued to grow until a year ago. I've even begged to touch them just so I could vicariously experience what it meant to truly be a full-grown woman.

Essie let me. Yep, neither of us have any shame, she let me grope her.

Thank God, I have another birthday wish coming up! I need to become a woman.

At least I wasn't named Hester. Clover, Robin, and I resent my parents for our nature names, but not nearly as much as Essie despises her father for her moniker. I stitched a letter **A** patch during Home-Ec for Essie's sixteenth birthday and attached it to her sweater. I made her wear it to school when she was reading the *Scarlett Letter* for English Lit.

"There's my baby girl," Uncle Will sings to me as I enter the kitchen behind the rest of the kids. It won't matter if we're ninety, Essie, Violet, Seth, and I will always be kids to them, at least until we give them some new blood to cuddle and coddle.

Uncle Will is my dad's baby brother– Essie's dad. His name is William Prynne. Yeah, that wicked sense of humor runs in our family.

"Let's get this show on the road, Daddy. We have somewhere we need to be." Essie impatiently whines, acting fidgety.

Wallflower that I am, I begin to worry over Essie's rampant excitement. We may be best friends, but we don't have much in common. Frankly, Essie's idea of a wild night makes mine look like preschool. I'm more of a '*sit in the dark and get baked*' kind of girl, where Essie is a '*sit in the dark and get knocked up*' kind of girl. Huge difference, shadows aside.

I blame Essie's large tits, or my lack thereof, on the major difference in our nightly activities.

Adoration stares blindingly at me from multiple sources, not one gaze less potent than the next, and I don't deserve the unconditional love they bestow upon me. How did a wayward fuck-up like me get a suffocatingly affectionate family? Since Sam's passing, I've been horrific and they still shower me with attention.

My entire family is scattered around our cramped kitchen: a dopey-eyed Mom and Dad– otherwise known as Dave and Mary Prynne –a beaming with pride Uncle Will and Aunt Ana, a glowering Clover and Violet, and my partners in crime, Essie and Seth. Even Sam's mom, Margaret Webster, blessed us with her presence on my birthday. When I see Margaret my heart bleeds for a billion different reasons. But mostly because Margaret's appearance solidifies Sam's void.

But we're missing a family member. Robbie is AWOL. I try not to let my face fall, because it feels wrong that Robbie's not with us, especially on my eighteenth birthday. There's never been a celebration any of us have missed for the others. We're in this together. Always and forever.

We lost my grandparents a few years ago, and a little over four years ago we lost Clover's husband to pancreatic cancer. My grandparents' absence is painful... Sam– I'll never be whole without him with us. One person missing from our small family gathering is a big deal. We're all we have. This is why we're so sheltered and smothered.

Where's my Robbie?

"I wanted to make you a nice dinner, but Essie has been relentless all afternoon." Mom tries to clear the storm clouds crossing my face, knowing why I'm sad all of the sudden. "Essie said she made dinner plans for you tonight."

"Thanks, Mom. You know how Essie is. She always gets her way," I say with obvious affection. If Essie gets her way, then so do I. I follow her lead. After all, Essie has two years of living experience on me.

"Ridiculousness," Grandma Margaret snidely hisses. "Clover, why couldn't you get off your lazy ass and make this dear child dinner?"

Grandma Margaret is the type of woman a man would call a tough broad. She's younger than my folks by a good dozen years, and acts bitter after the loss of her husband and then her only son. There's a part of Grandma Margaret that mirrors the dark seed in my soul– we both lash out and say things we regret later.

The old broad forces me to call her Grandma Margaret, even though we're not blood related. But, at the same time, she demands that Violet call her Margaret– note the absence of Grandma before her name. Grandma Margaret dotes on Seth and me, ignores Violet– oh, and she passionately detests my sister, Clover. Grandma Margaret has verbal combat skills, and she deploys them on her widowed daughter-in-law every chance she can get because they're too much alike.

Ignoring the dig as always, refusing to engage her bitter mother-in-law, Clover presents me with a cake befitting a chocoholic. Five layers of chocolate decadence with raspberry jam filling: dark chocolate, milk chocolate, and even a few white chocolate curlicues. My mouth waters the instant my eyes light on it. My sister's only positive is her food. Whether savory or sweet, it's all mouth-watering deliciousness.

My cake is lit up with eighteen crackling mini-candles. They're spread far and wide by the family sadist, making wish-fulfillment nearly impossible. While the Prynnes and Websters sing a round of *Happy Birthday*, I draw in a huge breath and blow. As I play fire extinguisher on my cake, the whole time I'm thinking to myself *'make me a woman. I want to be a woman!'* I fiercely beg as I blow all eighteen candle flames out.

A cheer erupts from my family.

I flash them all a shit-eating grin for my accomplishment. Yeah, extinguishing flame is not a big deal for most people outside of firefighters, but I don't accomplish much, like ever.

"You won't get into trouble tonight, or I'll punish you until you're thirty," Clover scolds me as if she's my mommy and I'm not a legal adult with a full-time job. Her icy blue eyes are scalding me with contempt and utter disappointment.

Clover doesn't like how I turned out. She wanted another clone, like Violet. Since Clover prides herself on being my mother figure, I tell her often that it's her fault I'm wayward. I get slapped every time I say it, and it's on the tip of my tongue right this second.

"Don't!" My sister shouts at me in disgust, knowing the direction of my thoughts.

I smirk at Clover as she walks away, fed up with my bullshit. I didn't ask for Clover to be a controlling bitch. I will rebel as long as she treats me like I'm a two-year-old child. If Clover was a man, I might have changed my tune. But her boney ass can't take me, so she can't be in control of me. I know I sound sexist, but it's how I feel.

Either trying to save me or his mother, I don't know which, Seth eagerly hands me a gift to distract me from baiting Clover any further. A budding warmth blooms in my chest as I hold the present in the palm of my hand. I know Seth picked it out and wrapped it himself. I smile at my nephew– a real, genuine smile. Inside the funny pages paper is a pebble. It sparkles in the light as I turn it side-to-side. Seth knows I love it, and his round face brightens in delight.

Everyone else looks at us like we're freaks. They don't get us– our connection. Seth and I take walks all the time. Not so much since I've been working, but we manage one or two a week. We've done this since I taught him to walk when he was a toddler. Seth's first memory is of me and him collecting interesting pebbles on these walks. It's sentimental and mushy, and I love it.

Taking the attention from her twin and placing it firmly on herself, Violet hands me a pretty, purple package, in case I could forget that her name is Violet. Inside is a bottle of expensive nail polish, also purple. I look at my jagged, stubby nails that are colored in with a *Sharpie* and sigh.

Clover is next, and the gift is a pink dress that a baby-doll would wear. Clover and Violet are the same– their gifts are passive-aggressive hints. I'm not good enough being me– I need to change to meet their ideal on what makes a woman a woman. I need pretty buffed nails and a frothy dress to be a lady. In actuality, I'd look like Seth playing dress-up.

It must be my night to receive necklaces. Grandma Margaret presents me with a birthstone necklace in the shape of a **W**. I draw a blank at its meaning as I mutter my thanks. Must be the **W** is for Willow. Margaret flashes a satisfied smile in Clover's direction, and I just catch my sister looking slightly ill before she flees toward the sink, where she pretends to get a glass of water.

Drawing attention from the mother/daughter-in-law bitter rivalry, Uncle Will hands me the next gift, and I can tell by the look on the faces of Aunt Ana, Uncle Will, and Essie that I will love it. The long, narrow box is torn into with my jagged nails. My high-pitched screech fills the air as soon as I see the concert tickets. There are three inside, and they had to have cost a fortune.

Revolutionary Road was Sam's favorite band, something he and I used to do together before he got too sick. The gift is bittersweet, but I feel closer to Sam now than I have since he left us. For some reason, his loss was the hardest on me, and no one argues that fact.

I quickly hand a ticket to Essie and one to Seth, and I don't feel badly about it. Violet would have hated the music anyway–she's a Pop Princess who just wouldn't understand the subtlety of Indie Rock. She would've complained about her eardrums the entire time.

Essie draws Seth and me into a hug and the three of us jump giddily up and down, squealing like stuck pigs on crank.

"Oh, my God! Thank you, guys, for all the awesome gifts!" I clap and hop on heels. "Thank you, thank you! I love it all, and I love you all!"

"Okay, that's about enough gushage. I think I'm getting a cavity from the saccharine sweetness. They can tell you appreciate their obligatory offerings." Essie simultaneously makes light of their gifts and makes me feel like shit, as if the gifts were given because they must and that my response was faked. "We've got places to be, people to see, and trouble to find."

"Go on and get ready for your night. I'll divvy up the cake for everyone." My mom starts mutilating my delicious chocolate cake before I even have a taste. I sadly watch as she mashes it. I wait until Dad takes the weapon out of her hands and tries to fix the mess before I flee the kitchen. I lunge up the stairs to my room with Essie hot on my heels.

CHAPTER FOUR

"No," Essie warns, seeing the direction of my gaze as I contemplate burning before we head out. "Tonight is not a mellow occasion, no matter how nervous you may be. You have to feel it to appreciate it. No numbing yourself dumb."

"Fine," I mutter wistfully, tearing my eyes away, then the biggest motherfucking grin spreads my lips. "What's the plan?" I yelp excitedly as I yank my sweatshirt off. I have a tank top on underneath, and that flutters to the floor next. I toe my sneakers off and wiggle out of my jeans. My pants are getting too tight. They're my favorite pair– worn white from years of wear. I've had them since I was thirteen. I guess I've finally grown a bit since I have to peel the suckers off.

Standing before my floor-length mirror, I just stare at my body in silent horror, and the visage of a preteen boy minus a pecker stares back at me. The only discernable difference between me and a boy is a triangle of peach fuzz on my mound and the absence of boy parts hiding beneath my underwear.

Tears prickle my eyes, my bottom lip trembles– a sob builds. I don't speak my shame aloud, but I think it. *Why doesn't my body match my mind? I feel like a woman on the inside, no matter that the outsides screams I'm not. No guy will ever want to willingly touch this. Maybe I can find a nice bisexual boy, one who wants to look at a guy but is okay with touching a pussy.*

I live in a place called reality, where fictitious boys do not dwell.

My birthday wish didn't come true since I didn't instantly develop breasts. I try my damnedest to mash my itty-bitty-titties together and make some cleavage, but I literally come up empty-handed. After a minute, I give up.

Essie is grinning at me in the reflection of the mirror, and it's a nasty kind of grin– one where she could be laughing *with* me, or *at* me. Hell if I know which. I scowl back at her, and then grimace down at my breasts, or lack thereof.

"Not fair," I pout. "Do you think a pushup bra would help, or maybe a padded one? I look like a little boy. I'm pretty sure

Seth's chubby pecs are bigger than my nonexistent tits. Even my nips are flat."

"Willow, you've never even worn a bra. Implants are your only option. But, Chick, they would look ridiculous, like plastic softballs glued to your chest." Essie tries to sound serious but ends up choking on her suppressed laughter. "Willow, just accept the fact that you have no tits and you never will." Voice turning wistful, "You have a perfect ass, though. I'd kill for it."

I turn to the side to look at my butt in the mirror. A bit of cheek sticks out the bottom of my boy shorts. I smack my ass, then grin when the flesh jiggles enticingly.

"It does balance out my huge rack nicely, don't ya think?" My tone is serious, causing Essie to crack up, then I join her in making fun of my stunted body. "Well, if you'd give me half your boobs and I'd share half my ass, we'd make a normal sized girl." My chain-smoker husky voice deepens as my eyes covetously drink in Essie's double D assets.

Reaching out quicker than a rattlesnake, Essie plucks my nipple. Yelping in shock, I jump a good foot in the air. My nonexistent nipple gives an unimpressive showing. Then she tries to find something to grip, and comes up empty-handed too. Finally, Essie just rolls my nips in between her fingertips, twisting painfully hard. Eliciting a reaction, I flush, embarrassed.

"Well, at least they work. I was worried about that. Even your mosquito bites are tiny," she teases, giving another tweak before she sits back on my bed.

"Bitch." I smirk at her.

"Slut," she retorts with affection.

The gift Essie got me for my birthday is lying on my bed. I run over and pull on the shimmery, silver tank top and the black lace overlay. Essie knows that I don't wear a bra, so I have to wear a tank or an undershirt, so this combination is perfect. The tank is really tight and the overlay bares one of my shoulders. I change into a fresh pair of undershorts– black ones to go underneath the pleated skirt. It's a good thing I have the shorts, because the black skirt barely covers the tops of my thighs.

Essie tosses me a pair of fishnets, then kicks my boots out of my closet. I follow her lead as per usual. I know jack about dressing, and even less about what her plans are for the evening.

It turns out the stockings are thigh-highs, so I have to roll the tops over several times since my legs are short. I feel like a little kid playing dress up, that is if little kids played pretend street walker, pole shiner, or mattress tester.

Shoving my ass in my vanity table chair, Essie tries to pull my hair up into pigtails, and I balk at that. "Hey! I'm celebrating my newfound adulthood. No pigtails." She does it anyway, wrapping the length of my hair into two messy buns atop my head.

"The one thing you have going for you is the naughty little girl. No tits, a perfect ass, and the face of an angel– the guys will eat that shit up."

"Where are these guys? No one's been eating that shit up for me," I mutter to Essie's reflection in the mirror.

"Guys like two things: a woman who knows what she's doing and one who doesn't. I don't have a fucking clue what I'm doing, but I have to pretend since I'm shaped like a porn star. You're lucky since you don't have to pretend to be innocent and you fit the part. Even after you've had an education, make sure you don't lose the innocent expression on your face. Always bat those puppy dog eyes, and you'll get whatever you want."

Essie schools me in the interworking of male/female relations as she applies my makeup, since I don't know how to do that either.

When I was twelve, while the rest of my peers were learning how to apply makeup and giggling about boys with their moms and sisters, I was learning how to pick the seeds out of our weed and how to properly pack a bowl. Mary Prynne wasn't much on mother/daughter bonding time, not in the traditional sense anyway. When he wasn't organizing protests, Dad was teaching me how to wield power tools. Robin was teaching me how to drive, putting my library books beneath my ass so I could see out the windshield. Essie was teaching me about blowjobs. I was extending all this knowledge to Seth, while Violet ignored us. Clover was too busy at the time dealing with Sam's fatal illness, when she wasn't punishing me for kidnapping her twins and driving us all over hell and back. My formative years were more free-ranged, like a chicken being raised for slaughter.

Because of Sam, Seth, Violet, and I were allowed to do anything we wanted while Clover was distracted. If I asked, I received– still to this day. Smoked pot with Mom, built shit with Dad, learned how to take off with the twins via Robin. All that knowledge was funneled into the rage I felt over Sam's death, so I never learned what most girls did.

The only one who had a problem with any of this was Clover. Hence why we're oil and water. Clover longs to educate me, with Violet, about the softer things in life, but that's not happening.

Anything remotely girly: clothing, makeup, hot guys, sex advice, and malicious high school gossip, it all flowed from Essie. I trust Essie in all things fashion, hair, and makeup– Essie grew up to be a professional cosmetologist, after all. She has the diploma, student loan debt, and a job to prove it.

I'm the only slacker in the family.

"What's this? Who's AK?" Essie asks, fiddling with my choker.

"What?" I swallow in confusion as she hands me a compact mirror. The charm on my necklace says *Willow*. "What about AK?"

Essie turns the round tag over so I can read the inscription on the back: *AK's Good Girl.*

My face flushes bright red and the buzzing in my belly erupts with a vengeance. I clench my thighs against the terrible ball of ache forming at their junction. I bet this is what took Mr. Kline so long this afternoon– I knew he wasn't at the post office.

"Who's AK?" Essie bites out in accusation, like I've been holding out on her.

"Mr. Kline– I mean Auggie. He gave this to me for my birthday," I murmur bashfully, heart beating wildly in my chest. "He put it on me when he dropped me off tonight."

Essie's blue eyes turn into wide saucers. "You know what this is, don't you?" An awed expression fills her pretty face.

"It's a necklace," I mutter with a shrug.

"OH. MY. GOD." She shrieks in astonishment. "I'm not going to tell you. Holy fuck, Willow! Auggie's fuckin' hot."

"Hey, now, don't talk about him like that. Auggie has a girlfriend– I think. Her name is Isis, and no one could ever compete with her, believe me." I warn Essie off from getting any ideas into her pretty little head.

I don't think I would enjoy watching Auggie kiss Essie like he did Isis tonight. I don't know why I enjoyed watching him kiss Isis in the first place, but I did. Auggie and Isis just looked right together. I rub my tummy since it's threatening to cramp, all the while Essie watches me with an amused expression on her face.

"I feel funny and achy," I whine.

"I just bet you do," Essie knowingly purrs but doesn't explain. "We'll get that taken care of tonight." Her voice is rough, like what mine usually sounds like, but her natural voice is very girly.

"Let's go, birthday girl. You have a wild night ahead of you."

CHAPTER FIVE

Guilt returns, an emotion I despise. I feel bad about the gift my parents gave me– a freaking car. I ran down the steps to say my goodbyes, only to find the house empty. I found half of my family on the front lawn with Clover and the twins on their porch next door, and all of them were wearing ecstatic grins.

A big bow was on the hood of an old VW Beetle.

I cried with shame, not happiness. It made me sad how my parents cared that much about me when I have no true direction in life. Since Sam, I've been an asshole with a bad attitude, taking them all for granted. I was a mediocre, and sometimes shitty, student in school. I know I'm only eighteen, but the rest of the graduates have gone off to college or work here in town at jobs where they have a future.

Dad owns a business, is antiestablishment, and huge with volunteering. Mom grows pot and distributes it to the elderly population and cancer patients, on the down-low, after watching Sam fade away in inexplicable pain where we were all utterly powerless to help. Uncle Will has an important job, close to retirement, and he's only in his fifties. Robin has sold painting in galleries in Boston, and has more money than all of us combined. Clover's raising two kids, owns a home, and works as the mayor's personal assistant, doing it all alone because she's a widow. At twenty, Essie already graduated from cosmetology school and works at the local salon. They all chose their paths, were born to do these things.

What was I born to do?

Essie's driving my birthday present since she knows where we're going and she won't tell me where. I'm not even allowed to drive my own present– not fair. I said as much, but was ignored. Essie's just as pushy as everyone else in my life. If it wasn't for the fact that she pushes me toward fun shit, I'd be wicked pissed.

We pull up to the curb in the residential part of Fairport, just a few streets over from my house. I look around in confusion.

"Um… what?" I gesture to the maple-lined street in question, a place where no fun is to be had.

This neighborhood is a little bit nicer than my own– not by a lot, but it's noticeable. The yards don't bleed over into the neighbors' front lawn like ours does. On my block, we literally have three feet separating our houses. Like solving a difficult puzzle, it's fun when trying to mow the lawn or work on the house, but we make the most of it. One advantage to the close proximity is how Seth and I often use our bedroom windows for transport. When I get the munchies, Seth hand delivers Clover's baked goods from his bedroom window to mine. On this street, the houses have nice big yards for children to play with the family pet and a good fifty feet separating the sides of their homes– lucky ducks.

"We're picking someone up, and then we're going to grab a bite to eat." Staring into the rearview mirror, Essie applies a third coat of lipstick on her already flawless red pucker.

Movement catches my eye in the side mirror. I'm struck speechless as a blond, blue-eyed fantasy comes to life in the form of tight jeans, a polo shirt, and a leather jacket… and then I remember a promise I made this afternoon.

"Holy fuck," hisses between my clenched teeth when my brain finally registers who is strutting up to my car. "Mr. Kline is going to kill me, or maybe you… but most definitely him." I point at Kieren Mason as he strolls up to the car with a huge shit-eating grin plastered on his flawless face.

"Ladies." Kieren's greeting is all charm as he flashes me that *'used car salesman/serial killer/you know I have what you want'* smile.

Frozen, I just sit like a doofus as my body becomes hyperaware. Butterflies assault my insides as I simultaneously marvel over a wish come true while worrying about disappointing Mr. Kline with said wish-fulfillment.

Kieren opens my car door, causing me to look around for where he's going to sit in my two-seater Beetle. Essie laughs at the frantic expression on my face.

"Kieren gets the seat, and you get his lap." Essie chuckles sinisterly in the face of my wicked blush. Our eyes flick down to Kieren's lap, and we both giggle like dumb-shits.

I slide from the car, trying not to flash anyone my ass, and wait until Kieren gets settled in the seat. Feeling awkward and inept, I try to slide into his lap without putting any weight on him.

I've had a crush on Kieren Mason since elementary school, and I can't believe I'm sitting in his lap with his big hands resting on my thighs– it's surreal.

Happy eighteenth birthday, Willow!

I'm just relieved that it's dark outside, or else everyone would see how embarrassed I truly am, and that would be even more embarrassing.

"How's the birthday girl?" Kieren whispers near my ear, eliciting a shiver to roll down my spine. His arms automatically embrace me, trying to warm a fevered-chill that isn't cold related.

"Fine," I reply bashfully, blushing to the point I swear my flesh catches fire.

"I love the new ride. Someone took really good care of this vintage Beetle." Kieren shifts me on his lap and my skirt rides up to the top of my fishnets. His hard body cushioning mine, I can feel the power coiled in his thighs and the heat of his breath on my neck.

Shuddering, suddenly breathless, I can barely think straight, let alone speak coherently with the scent of Kieren's skin wafting into my nose– warm like oiled leather and spice, with a metallic tang.

"Thanks, it's been fun so far," I say as I pull my skirt down an inch in modesty. Kieren shifts in the seat again, and we do this routine for a few minutes until I give up and leave my hemline where it lies, barely covering my thighs.

Mr. Kline cautioning me to be a good girl echoes in my mind, along with his warnings over Kieren and men like Kieren– predators. I almost wish Auggie hadn't told me the truth. Now how am I supposed know if Kieren likes me for me or for my innocence? At least before I was ignorant. Now I'll just assume every guy is seducing me to play me. It kind of takes the fun out of being a teenaged girl on the prowl.

Feeling pessimistic versus optimistic, paranoia settles over me. Ignorance lost. Fantasy dissolving into thin air. What would have been fun yesterday lost all appeal in the light of Auggie's lecture.

I'm a woman in a boy's body. No way in hell would Kieren Mason ever want me for anything other than to use me up and throw me away. He's a walking wet dream who can have any girl of his choosing, way hotter girls than me. I'm just a conquest and nothing more.

Auggie thought to help me, protect me, but all he accomplished was to make me feel like shit, hopeless and worthless, and to doubt myself and the motives of every cute boy around me.

Thanks, boss.

I know Essie means well. She went to school with Kieren's older brother, Devon. I know Devon better than Kieren after countless parties I attended at Essie's whining request. The bad thing about hanging with the older crowd is that when they graduate, all your friends are gone. For two years, I was left with those in my class, and none of them acknowledged my existence, Kieren included. I don't blame Essie. She knows I've had a wicked crush on Kieren for years. But after being ignored until now, I don't feel special– I feel like the last dregs.

I'm also scared Mr. Kline is going to kick my ass when he finds out I disobeyed him. Auggie is a mammoth man who could put a serious hurting on me. He's also my sole source of employment since I have no job skills. My job pool is pretty narrow, as in only Auggie would ever hire me.

We pull into our local no-name diner. Fairport only has one restaurant, and it's actually called the No-Name Diner since no one ever got around to naming it. The food is barely edible, and it's all fried in ancient oil. Fairport is sorely lacking in the amenities. Don't even get me started on our bakery. The Bakery is worse than the No-Name Diner.

Popping my car door open, I shuffle off Kieren's lap, trying not to touch him too intimately. I don't want my first trip to second and third base being by accident. Kieren's hand surreptitiously grazes my side. If I had boobs, he would've copped a feel. I snort at his poor attempt. He'll find nothing here worth seeking, the sneaky bastard.

We settle in for burgers and Cokes, and engage in small talk. I was worried that Kieren would be boring, wet cotton, but we have a lot in common. It isn't exactly comfortable, but it's not forced either. Essie's a huge help at keeping the conversation flowing, chatting about mutual friends– gossiping about the juicy morsels she overhears at the salon. When the conversation wanes, I simply push a fry into my mouth and try to look hungry.

"How's your brother?" I ask Kieren conversationally to keep the flow. Essie looks at me in surprise for asking of Devon.

"Fine," Kieren curtly replies, effectively ending that line of questioning. *Mmm-kay.*

"Did you get your truck fixed?" I ask of Kieren's broken four-wheel-drive.

"Truck?" He asks in confusion, then I realize Kieren lied about why he sold Mr. Kline the action figures. It's none of my business, so I drop it.

"Oh," Kieren exclaims as he remembers his lie. "It's working great now." He smiles grandly, pouring on the charm.

"You'll have to tell me the name of your mechanic. He's a maniac if he works that fast," I mutter sarcastically, and underneath the table Essie kicks me in the shin to shut my ass up.

"Oh, he's definitely a maniac, all right." Kieren smirks at his private joke.

Now I refuse to play the wilting flower for Kieren. I may be a tiny girl, but the only difference between me and a guy is ovaries, a uterus, and a vagina. My bullshit detector is screaming.

I may be uninspired, but that doesn't make me stupid. I notice Kieren covertly checking out Essie and the wait staff. Kieren stares at Essie's cleavage like he's starving, all the while his hand tries to sneak up my thigh, tugging on the top of my stocking. No doubt he's pretending my thigh is Essie's, or her tits are mine– either way, it's disgusting.

Sad to say, I believe Auggie is right about guys.

Ridiculous, I roll my eyes at Essie. I don't blame Kieren for looking, and there is something strangely honest that he does it so blatantly. It's not like my cousin isn't trying to gain my date's attention. It makes me wonder if Kieren is my date or hers. Essie dressed up like she was on the prowl, and there are only three of us sitting here, and two of us are me and her. Obviously she wanted Kieren to check her out. Essie has a pushup bra on and the ladies are overflowing her blouse. The top few buttons couldn't be fastened and several are threatening to snap open. I give that thread another hour before it frays and that button pops an eye out.

Kieren is being honest with his ogling, but what the hell is my best friend up to? The more I dwell on it, the more offended I become.

If I hadn't had the lecture from Auggie earlier, I would've been flattered by the attention Kieren is giving me now. I would've turned a blind eye to his roving eye. I wouldn't have seen the signs for what they are– disrespect. I get Auggie's lecture now. I'm a conquest, and someone like Essie is who

Kieren would choose to date and have sex with. Essie seems oblivious to the fact that she would just be used, and I wonder if Mr. Kline shouldn't give her the same lecture too. She's not a virgin, but almost as naïve as I am when it comes to boys.

What Essie isn't oblivious to is her effect on the opposite sex. I don't want her to hide herself so I'll look more attractive. I just don't want her to seem so desperate. We can see Essie's tits in anything she wears, but we don't literally have to *see* her tits. It makes me want to run into the bathroom and scrub my makeup off.

Why can't I just be me? Why can't Essie just be Essie? And why can't Kieren stop staring at every pair of tits in the vicinity?

With every second that passes, the worse my night becomes. I just want to go home, sit on the back porch and burn until the haze descends, then spend some quality time with Seth and my birthday cake. Hell, I'd enjoy Violet's company over this visual inspection and finger-probing examination.

"I have your real gift in the car, girlfriend." Essie winks at me, and Kieren's eyes glaze over in excitement. He knows what the evening holds. I just hope Kieren understands that I'm not on the itinerary.

CHAPTER SIX

Uncomfortable and no longer feeling embarrassed, I shuffle around Kieren's lap in the cramped confines of the car, trying to get away from his roaming hands. I love what my dad had in mind. He made sure I could only have one passenger at a time by removing the backseat of my car– sneaky dad. But the lack of passenger seats is a real problem tonight. I'm sure Essie thought I'd like the close quarters of Kieren's hard lap.

I'm so over Kieren.

I may be over Essie, too.

Kieren's smarmy, clumsy hands paw at my ass in a poor attempt to mask it as helping me sit in his lap. That same hand keeps brushing my side, trying to find my nonexistent breasts, and then makes a circuit down to my hip to pull my skirt up. My shorts and the tops of my stockings are now on full display.

I pretty much feel compromised and violated, and not at all sexy. Unless sexy involves the scalding contents of a hot water tank and a bar or three of Dial Antibacterial Soap.

Kieren's hard-on is digging into my ass cheek, and I feel cheated because I'm pretty sure that constitutes as third base, and I'd like to have had a choice in the matter. Maybe if I wasn't so pissed I'd enjoy it– Kieren does seem quite endowed. I have no idea what's turning him on, but he's more than ready and willing. He probably thinks I'm a sure thing and it's revving him up.

I can't wait for this night to be over. It's my birthday, and I feel like I'm being held hostage. The small car shrinks with every caress of Kieren's nimble fingers. I close my eyes and breathe through my nose, praying for patience. When a pussy-seeking finger slides underneath the edge my shorts near my inner thigh, I almost grab the door handle and jump out of the moving car, risking road rash and possible death by a VW Beetle tire.

As soon as the car pulls into a parking lot, I hop from Kieren's lap and out the door before it slows to a complete stop. I walk-run to avoid toppling ass-over-teakettle, and then slow to a standstill. I rest on the pavement, dragging the cold December air into my lungs.

"Willow?" Essie calls as she hurries around the car after me. Kieren's arrogant smirk turns my stomach. Does he not see that I'm not interested, or does he just not give a shit?

I need a smoke– a potent one –and a drink –a half dozen shots! I grab Essie's hand and yank her a hundred feet away, leaving Kieren to guard the car.

"What's wrong?" Essie looks worried.

"Can we drop him somehow? Kieren's being handsy and I hate it," I grumble, trying not to whine and sound like a baby. I hold back the nausea that threatens to overpower me. The alarms are going off inside my mind again. It's not the same kind as before with Auggie, these are similar to the warning alarms Isis elicited.

I just wish Auggie would've kept his lecture to himself. Some things you just have to learn through example– i.e. mistakes, and this is one of them. With my ignorance lost, so was my innocence and my ability to act like an idiot teenager. Now I'm looking over my shoulder like a convict trying to spot cops, only my issue is hot crushes who seem to be crushing me back– it should be a wish come true.

Thanks a fucking lot, Mr. Kline!

The naïve Willow who woke up this morning would've been thrilled to screw Kieren's brains out in her new car. I'm not a girl holding on to my virginity for romantic reason. For real, I would've fucked Kieren, and not only never regretted it, I would've seen it as a victory.

I could've added *'orgasm-bringer'* to my list of accomplishments, directly above blowing out all the candles on my birthday cake. It would've been a good tale to tell the grandkids. This new, worldlier Willow worries over every little thing, and whether or not I can live with the consequences.

Adulting takes the fun out of life.

"It's okay, sweetie. It's only weird at first." Essie says with pity filling her soft eyes. "It might hurt a bit– Kieren's not exactly a tiny guy."

"It's not about sex," I hiss, momentarily distracted by Essie's comment. *Not a tiny guy*? How does she know that?

My fingernails indent the flesh of Essie's wrist, causing her to wince. I let go and try to put my feelings into words the best I can. "It's that it's Kieren. I may not have any experience, but I'm not losing my virginity to some little douche who watches my best friend while trying to get his fingers into my panties. I'm not that desperate, and you shouldn't be either. He's like a hormone-crazed date-rapist-in-training or some shit."

"Ooooohhhh," Essie draws out, eyes widening as a smirk twitches at her lips. "OH!" Her fingers pluck the charm on my necklace. "I get it. We'll lose Kieren in the club. Come back to the car and I'll get your gift."

Essie's mention of a club makes me take stock in my surroundings. I was so absorbed with my escape that I hadn't realized where we were.

Fairport doesn't have many businesses, aside from Revamped, our shitty diner and bakery, two gas stations, and a grocery store. There's no nightlife entertainment in Fairport other than Rush. We have no theaters, no shopping malls, no dive bars, but we have a church for every denomination and a civic center pumping out kids with religious and political aspirations. Because of this, Revamped gets a lot of trade by bored housewives looking for some shopping and men and kids of all ages looking for some fun.

Fairport is a small town where the city-haters dwell. Within a half hour's drive in any direction, you can get anything and be anywhere. The conservative middle class flocks to the gossipy, religious community known as Fairport, Massachusetts, where they create overachieving children and rebellious loners in droves– obviously I'm in the latter category.

The bane of Fairport's existence is Rush. Fairport is surrounded by dry towns and has the honor of housing the only liquor license in the county.

Rush.

It's indoctrinated into us from an early age by our parents, *'don't go to Rush'*. So for every rite of passage, we try to find our way into the establishment. The only true adult entertainment in a thirty square mile area, Rush is pumping tonight, as it is every night. The parking lot is filled to capacity, with cars parked along the street as well.

Rush is a warehouse on the outskirts of Fairport. Gray metal and cinderblocks, and only three doors– each one heavily guarded by a beefy guy.

A bit of plastic is tossed in my direction. I catch it out of reflex before I realize what it is. My birthday gift is a fake ID. As of tonight, I'm twenty-one with my actual birth name. It's flawless.

"I don't want to know, do I?" I murmur in awe.

"Nope, you sure don't." Essie reluctantly passes an ID to Kieren, and I can see her wheels turning. She wishes she hadn't gotten him one too, then we could've left him in the parking lot where he belongs. Essie and I share a look, a best friend way of silent communication.

"Why did we even need fake IDs? You're twenty, and Kieren and I are both eighteen. I thought you could get into clubs at eighteen. You just have to wear a little kid hand stamp so you won't be served." I follow Essie to the club through the packed parking lot, veering around cars that aren't in a spot.

Kieren sneaky fingers grab my ass, and I have to bite my tongue so I don't lash out at him with a scathing remark. I swat his hand away, and his response is a snicker and a full-on ass grab, fingertips gouging into my flesh. Lesson learned: ignore Kieren, because if you tell him no, he'll do something twice as worse. It's so outrageous that I swear he's testing the limits of my patience.

After a half a dozen steps, Kieren finds out how difficult it is to grope a moving ass cheek. His hand slides away as he falls into step beside me. Boundary testing completed without his desired results, Kieren finally behaves himself. The comfortable companionship returns between the pair of us, and I wonder which side is the real Kieren Mason– lecher or laid-back guy? Either way, I figure him for an ass and tit man. Judging by the way his eyes are glued to my ass, lucky for me, I'd say he's more into *A* than *T*.

"It's not that kind of club. No one under twenty-one is admitted. A girl I work with told me about how the owner decided no one underage can enter Rush. Keeps the narrow-minded residents of Fairport happy." Essie says over her shoulder, "Do you remember Bethany?"

"Yeah, I liked Beth," I reply, vaguely remembering a sweet girl who was in Essie's graduating class. When we were younger, Essie and Beth were thick as thieves, and I was slightly jealous. But somehow Essie started rationing her time, keeping Beth and me apart socially, until she had a best cousin and a best friend. I always hated being relegated to '*best cousin*' status, but it made sense with our age-gap.

"Oh, you're in for a shock, Willow." Adding another facet to his personality, Kieren includes antagonist to the mix with cad and casual. "Robin is in there tonight, as he is most nights– every night." Kieren says in an anticipatory way that makes me cringe, but I don't take his bait.

"Robbie's here? At Rush? What?" Essie gasps in shock, giving Kieren the desired reaction he was looking for from me.

I stare blankly ahead, feeling more alone than I ever have. My only brother abandoned me for a night at Rush, and for some reason Kieren is entertained by this.

"I'd wondered why Robbie wasn't at the house tonight." Essie tosses me a look of pity that I pretend not to intercept, but a best friend always knows what you're feeling, even when you wish they didn't.

"Robin is most definitely here, along with a few others," Kieren baits. "You'd be surprised to know who owns it, I bet," flows cryptically from his annoyingly perfect lips.

I don't give Kieren the satisfaction by asking who. If I was meant to know who owns Rush, I'd already know. It does hurt to know my brother went to a club instead of wishing me a happy birthday. I haven't seen Robbie in a week, and he didn't even send me a birthday card. I know I'm not the center of the universe and that he has more than one sister, but I only have one brother.

It takes two seconds to send a goddamn text message or Facebook post.

"Hey, darlin'," The cutie at the door purrs at Essie while ogling her tits.

I notice that button finally popped off somewhere between here and the No-Name, and now Essie's bra is completely hanging out. The button is probably hiding in my car, where I wish I was, preferably driving toward home where my cake is waiting. "I don't need to see your ID tonight. You've got, what, a handful of months until you're twenty-one?"

"Rory," Essie giggles. "There's no fooling you. I guess I wasted the money on the fake ID. Had I known you'd be working the door, I wouldn't have bothered."

"Yeah, fringe benefit of the job." Rory blushes, eyes glittering with lust. "You can't fool me, I remember you being beneath me in school with our Bethany, and I never forget when a gorgeous girl is beneath me."

The innuendo is so thick, I groan for the poor guy. It doesn't matter though, because Essie eats it right up. Glowing from the attention, she twirls her hair around her finger.

The smile slips from the bouncer's lips when he sees Kieren. "Mr. Mason, you're a day early. Are you sure you're supposed to be here tonight?"

"I don't know, Rory, am I?" Kieren counters, flashing that wicked grin of his– a grin I've since learned is a precursor to something unpleasant. "Should I yell really loud and find out? Pretty sure I have an all-access pass to Rush."

"During daylight hours, assmunch," Rory growls, clearly having a personal relationship with '*Mr. Mason*'.

"Hmm… I wonder what would happen if you didn't let me in. Do you like having a job, Rory?" Kieren is clearly an antagonist with a death wish.

"Someday…" Rory trails off, fists clenching at his sides.

"Yeah, it will be my pleasure," Kieren states sarcastically, looking feral with anticipation.

"What?" I grunt at my companions, drawing attention to myself.

"No way– this is even beneath you, Ren." Rory shakes his head in utter disbelief, not realizing the gut-twisting insult he just leveled against me. "You're like, what, ten or twelve or something?"

Rory just said I was beneath Kieren, and not in a good way. Not in the way he wants Essie beneath him.

I hate how the bouncer's eyes gloss over my body and glue to my face, like if he truly looked at me he'd be a pervert. I'm an eighteen-year-old grown woman, and here is a twenty-something-year-old guy looking at me like I'm in elementary school and should be at home playing with my Barbie dolls.

Proof of my superhero invisibility, this guy doesn't even remember me– doesn't remember going to school with me. Even way older than Essie, Rory was in my circle– the older crowd I first hung out with because Essie did. I guess Essie's tits eclipsed everything else, including her pitiful little friend, Willow. Rory had no problem smoking my weed and being on my team during Beer Pong and Flip Cup. I guess through sober eyes I look even younger– the fucktard!

"Just no– go home. Don't come back for at least six or seven years. Enjoy your childhood while you still can. Rush is off limits until you grow up, sweetie." Rory is so compassionate and earnest in the face of his insults, to the point I almost turn around and run back to my car to bawl my eyes out.

Fingertips pluck my ID from my hand while their owner has a hearty chuckle at my expense. "Rory, she's good. Read the name if you're in for a laugh."

Rory's eyes flick from the photo to my face, and then light on my name. "Willow Prynne, you say? Hmm… Willow, you do know Fairport isn't a very big place, right?"

Dejected, I sigh deeply, worrying that the bouncer will call this into the police. A trip to the clink is just what I need to end the evening. Clover is Mayor Ross's personal assistant. It would take less than a second before she flayed my ass for embarrassing the family.

"He needs his head examined. Seriously?" Rory turns to Kieren and gives him an indescribable look as he bends my birthday present in half, then pockets it.

"Who?" Essie voices for me, causing Kieren to choke on a snort.

"This is going to be good," Kieren chirps. "Priceless."

"You're a sick fuck, Ren." Rory looks disappointed but resolved. "Well, if it was up to me, I'd send your asses packing, except for you, beautiful," he murmurs to Essie. "But it's not up to me."

"No, it's not. Open the fucking door," Kieren orders. "My nuts are freezing, and the pet is off limits now that we're at Rush. Personally, I would've never come here tonight. I had other plans for me and Willow, plans of entering a tight place. But after this afternoon, I decided we needed some truth. I hate lying bastards, even if it's by omission. Open the door, Rory– open Willow's personal Pandora's box," Kieren says ominously.

"You have a serious death wish, bud," Rory mumbles underneath his breath as he opens the security door, allowing us entrance into Rush.

CHAPTER SEVEN

Music bashes me in the face the moment I enter Rush. Loud, pounding violence, and it's more intoxicating than the finest bud. The bass fills my ears and permeates my soul until the only thought I have in my mind is to dance.

The crowded club reminds me of a concert– packed bodies gyrating to loud music, with the sweaty tang of excited flesh flavoring the air. A huge grin spreads my lips as I intertwine my fingers with Essie's. Like a mosh pit, I fear I'll get separated from her and get trampled. Essie pulls me through the crowd in a strange zigzagging pattern until I realize we're losing Kieren to the mass of bodies.

"You're a fucking genius," I shout at my cousin.

Essie leans in close, teeth glowing white in the flashing strobe lights as she smirks at me. Essie presses her lips to my ear so she doesn't have to shout and be overheard. "Since you don't wanna play with little boys, we'll find you a man. Kieren doesn't have any skills anyway. He's always with virgins and it's stunted him. Trust me," Essie admits, voice warping.

Essie's last comment makes me really look at her, and we communicate with our eyes. Essie silently conveys how she was one of Kieren's virgins. Essie wouldn't tell me who she was with, only that it wasn't a very good experience. I was thirteen at the time, living vicariously through Essie, and I begged and pleaded with her for the details, details she refused to provide. After that, she had no issue telling me every detail about her sordid encounters, and at parties I witnessed them firsthand… but that first time has always remained a mystery.

I squeeze Essie's hand, letting her know that I understand as I try to ignore the vicious sting of betrayal. My best friend, my cousin, lost her virginity to the boy I was crushing on– the boy I called dibs on when I was in third grade. Kieren had pulled my ponytail and pushed me down on the playground, giving me a scuffed knee. I've proudly carried that battle scar for years.

Whether Kieren is worth the fight or not isn't the point. Isn't there a girl code against that kind of shit, stealing your best friend/sister/family member's crush and then lying about it? And then telling her on her eighteenth birthday while you make the guy tag along to add insult to the injury…

Maybe Essie's uncomfortable, shitty first time was Karma's way of biting her in the ass over the betrayal.

I'm beginning to realize I'm Essie's best friend, but perhaps she isn't mine. That '*best cousin*' bullshit is reality, seeing as how my only competition for the position is a pair of thirteen-year-old twins.

"Let's celebrate!" Essie pulls me through the mass of bodies and squeezes us up against the crowded bar. Using her blinding beauty, she collars the bartender and orders us a round of drinks.

I didn't fuck my way through school because I drank my way through it. Junior high was when I became a pro at sucking back alcohol while Essie became a pro at sucking cock. I down the shot without a thought and wait for Essie to pop hers back. I can't handle much alcohol because of my size, but I'll have a few drinks to loosen up.

Three shots of Patrón later, the warmth is radiating up from my belly to my limbs. I'm feeling dreamy as I sway on my feet to the rhythmic thump of bass. Essie and I share a giggle as the buzz infuses our bodies and eradicates our inhibitions, allowing me to momentarily forget past betrayals.

We join the swarm. We dance, sing, laugh, and shout, overcome with the freedom of youth. A few girls join us, and I recognize the one who graduated with Essie. Bethany, the friend who works with Essie at the salon, the one who told Essie about the club– the one who's actually Essie's best friend, because clearly I'm not.

No doubt Essie invited Bethany to this shit-show, thinking she'd be a third-wheel on Kieren's and my *date* and would need her BFF to entertain her tonight. I want to be an asshole to Beth, but it's impossible. She's a sweet, caring girl, with intelligence blazing from her eyes, and I'm instantly drawn to her. It's Essie who's the asshole, so I won't hold a grudge against Beth because of it– I won't hold a grudge against Kieren, either.

The sister code is between Essie and me, no one else broke it but her.

Another three drinks later, while keeping an eye out for Kieren, we're sweaty and bright-eyed and feeling damn fine. I'm buzzing higher than a bee and trying to stay in the moment. It's a difficult struggle to stop my downward spiral into self-deprecation.

Every few minutes, a new guy materializes to flirt with Essie and Bethany. Beth's more reserved, smiling and talking the entire time– friendly enough to appease bent egos, but not so much she encourages anything more. But Essie giggles and flip her hair, then presses her tits into the guy's sides, backs, or arms.

I refuse to abase myself like that for a stranger, and that's why I'm the only wallflower of the bunch. I'm here for the music and dancing, not mating rituals. Song after song, the girls around us partner up with hot guys, and I remain unnoticed. I pretend it doesn't bother me. After how Rory saw me, I can't really take offense because I know I look like a kid playacting with real women. I wouldn't pick me either, fearing a statutory rape charge. Eventually all the women around us branch off with their guy of the night, leaving Essie with her suitors and me alone.

In a surprising act of kindness, Essie takes their numbers but doesn't leave me.

"If I go home, you'd be free to play with those dudes. That one guy was freaking hot." I fan my face and grin.

"Not a chance, Willow. It's your birthday, and I'd rather hang with you." I know Essie means it, and it makes me feel that much worse. I feel bad that she has such a loser for a cousin. I'm holding her ass back, as usual.

"Kieren alert! Kieren alert!" Essie covers her mouth with a palm, trying to contain her giggles.

Sure enough, Kieren's blond head is weaving through the crowd. Athletic and tall, Kieren easily flows through the mass of dancers. From a few feet away, he makes eye contact with me. I groan at the victorious smirk he tosses my way.

I'm yanked so hard that my arm almost gets dislocated. "Jesus, Essie!" I grunt. "Did you forget your strength?" Stumbling over my feet, bumping into a few people who push back, I can barely keep up with Essie as she tows me through the crowd.

"Sorry, we don't want Kieren to catch up with us, do we? Unless you've changed your mind, because I'll take you to him if that's the case. But trust me– he sucks in the sack, and not in a good way."

"Don't be vulgar," I half-shout over the music. "I'm not that desperate… *yet*."

"At least Kieren's cute and charming, and can carry a conversation. He's smart. You could do a helluva lot worse." Essie smirks at me over her shoulder as she blindly tugs me down a dark hallway into the private area of Rush. "As I told ya earlier, he's a big guy."

"Girlfriend, I draw the line at your sloppy seconds. The instant I learned Kieren Mason had been inside your body, I lost any and all interest I've ever had." I do my damnedest not to scowl. I don't want Essie to know how much her betrayal hurts me. I'm just thankful she saved me from being used by that asshole.

"Don't be such a baby, Willow," Essie reprimands me. "Fairport is a small town. You'll eventually end up having someone's sloppy seconds. Do you plan on only being with virgins for the rest of your life? Or sticking with the first virgin you find? Past partners are not the business of the current partner."

Essie pulls us down a dark hallway and into another hidden hallway. Turn after turn, it's like a labyrinth. There's no way Kieren will ever find us in this maze. I highly doubt we'll find our way back out without a breadcrumb trail.

"Whoa…" Essie breathes in awe, coming to a standstill. I grunt when I hit her back, face-first.

I'm not articulate enough to say *whoa* because I'm speechless. Essie and I wandered into a den of hedonistic activities, and I'm awestruck. At least twenty people are engaged in every act of debauchery imaginable. Many of the twisted, contorted positions I didn't know existed outside of the Kama Sutra. The room and its contents escape me because the people hold my captive audience.

Feeling more naïve than usual, which is saying a lot, I realize porn soundtracks do not accurately describe the true sounds of sex: the repetitive slap of flesh on flesh, the fierce pound of a thrust, the wet slurp of lips sucking cock, and the heady moans of men and women in the throes of passion. Unlike a dirty movie, no one is faking their orgasms within this scene.

Guttural. Animalistic. Primal.

My eyes flick around, seeking, searching. I recognize every single person in the room but my mind doesn't register them… and then my vision lights on *him*.

A glorious back has me frozen in place, feet refusing to move. My neck muscles stiffen, making sure I cannot look away.

My mouth dries up because my jaw has dropped open. A flash fire engulfs my entire body until I throb with ache. My belly feels heavy, and the weight settles between my thighs. My heart beats to the buzzing heat that floods my system and wets my panties.

A beast of a man is the canvas for the most epic tattoo I've ever witnessed. It's too dark to figure out what the magnificent design is. I don't give a damn anyway, not with the sight of his muscular ass flexing before my very eyes. Kneeling before the man is a small woman worshiping at his cock. Thick fingers twist in her dark hair to yank her face back and forth in a fierce rhythm. Awed, I watch as the cock disappears in a sliding motion, in and out of her eager, gaping mouth, leaving behind a wet trail of saliva mixed with semen.

I've seen more than a few blowjobs in person, usually Essie's mouth working her flavor of the month. But this act is a display of pure power– owning, controlling, commanding pleasure from another human being who willingly submits. I want to be on the floor in front of this man, mouth parted to take him in, throat milking until he spills hot.

Engrossed, I don't see or hear anything that isn't *him*. Gravity, chemistry, whatever it may be, I cannot look away. I want to drop to my hands and knees, crawl toward him, fight the girl for the right to pleasure him, and *beg*.

I don't even know why I want to beg, or what I want to beg for. All I know is that I want to serve him. I *must* serve him. I hunger to be the girl at his feet, worshipping that thick cock while my fingernails dig into that impressive, virile ass.

A sharp sting to my cheek is so inconsequential in *his* presence that I brush it off. The next is harder, sharper. I whimper '*Ow*' while rubbing my pained cheek. Slowly my name filters into my ears, sounding warped and muffled. Ears tuning to my name, I still watch the beast take his pleasure from the beauty. Another sting and my name is roughly torn from Robbie's throat.

"What?" I mumble groggily to my brother, never moving my gaze from the man before me.

The Beast freezes when I speak. He half turns his face until I can see his whisker-stubbled cheek, leaving the rest of his features shadowed. I wait for him to look at me over his shoulder. Instinct trills, and I know I've captured his complete attention, just as he has mine. He watches me from his peripheral, and nothing could tear my eyes away from his partial gaze. The beauty at his feet doesn't let up and his body starts to quake uncontrollably, bucking in jerking waves.

All the strength I possess flees as the man finds his release, as if my strength is somehow connected to his. The need to drop and crawl to him is essential to my being. I begin to lower in slow-motion when a hand grips my upper arm in a relentless vise-like grip. The one who viciously clenches my arm walks between me and what I covet. I groan in frustration and numbly push at my blockage. The villainous laugh finally filters through my obsession– Isis.

"What?" I ask again, only this time it's in a coherent, pissy voice.

Reality filters back in and I finally notice the people surrounding me. Essie's eyes are glazed and her mouth is hanging open as she looks at me in shock. I guess my visceral reaction is unexpected, seeing as I've never been aroused before– not at this level. Robbie is seething, face flushed with barely leashed anger.

I absentmindedly rub my cheek, realizing that someone smacked me. It wasn't Robbie, because his hands are clenching Essie's upper arms. I flick my glare at Isis.

"Why'd you smack me?" I slur, pulling my chin up to act tough. Right now I feel like a superhero. I'd take on anyone who got in the way of my line of sight.

"We tried talking to you, but you were otherwise engaged. He's quite the sight, isn't he?" Isis gloats, her tone taunting and proprietary.

"Why don't you move? I wasn't finish watching," I say sweetly, trying to get on Isis's good-side. "Move, and I'll forget that you smacked me three times."

"Isis, please, Willow's just a child. Help me get my girls from this room." Robbie pleads. "I don't want Willow looking at him like that, and I don't want to see lust etched in her expression. I think I'm going to be sick."

I meet my brother's tortured, brown eyes, and I cannot fathom why he's so upset. All I want to do is watch the beast of a man with the magnificent tattoo. Where's the crime in that? I won't touch unless he invites me. Clearly he wants to be watched.

"It's far too late for that, Rob… way too late," Isis says ominously. She wheels me around, but I wrench my head, trying to catch a glimpse of my beast. Robbie sidesteps, effectively blocking my view of the man. My impatient whine tears a sadistic laugh from Isis, and the sound radiates down her hand to vibrate my arm.

The labyrinth of hallways flash by in a blur as I'm led by Isis. Robbie is next to me, pulling a shocked Essie down the hallway. We're both going to have bruises tomorrow. I don't know why Robbie is so wicked pissed. I'm an adult. Why can he play in there and I can't? I just won't look at him.

I'm shoved against the cinderblock wall with an audible thump, head jarring backward. Isis leaves fingernail crescent indents in my flesh, an everlasting reminder against trespassing in her territory. Essie and I are propped against the wall like criminals. Clad in only a pair of jeans, Robbie stands a few feet in front of me, glowering, clearly disappointed and miserable.

The sharp clack of Isis's metal stilettos wounding the tile floor causes me to flinch with every step she takes. Pacing, Isis looks like a caged predatory cat. Mr. Kline said I should avoid Isis, too. I think Mr. Kline is always right.

"Essie, I swear to God, I'm going to beat the living shit out of you for this," Robbie threatens our cousin, and then turns his attention to me. My brother inspects me, and a split-second later he bares his teeth in a silent snarl. "What the fuck is that on your neck?"

My hand flies guiltily to my choker, instinctively hiding the tag. Isis swats my hand away. Her blood-red talons turn the tag over, and she doesn't look surprised by what's on the other side. She merely arches a perfectly manicured black eyebrow at Robbie and waits for his reaction.

"That wasn't on her neck earlier tonight when I met her at Revamped," Isis states unemotionally, as if it doesn't matter when the necklace was placed on my throat, but it's somehow Robbie's business. "I told you he'd deviate from the plan. The prick is getting cold feet and using baby girl as a scapegoat."

My brother looks at the tag and explodes. Robbie literally sucks in air and forcefully blows it out in a torrent. I'd thought Robbie was pissed before, but I have no idea what to call the level of anger radiating off of my usually pleasant brother now.

Emotions rapidly flash across his round features: betrayal, pain, loss, torture, anger, and misery. Not one single emotion is pleasant to swallow.

"Hmm… I like you all protective. It turns me on, Rob. It's a side of you I didn't know existed." Isis purrs seductively as she runs her talons up and down my brother's bare chest, leaving marks in their wake. I don't know what she's talking about– it goes right over my head. All I know is that Robbie is well acquainted with those scary-ass nails. He shivers and holds Isis's hawk-like gaze.

"Whose idea was this?" Robbie spits out. I don't know if he's talking of the club or the choker, but his brown eyes return to my throat.

"It's for Willow's protection, I'm sure. Where else do kids go for rites of passage? He knew she'd eventually end up here tonight. Come on, Rob, let your girls have fun in the club. I'll put my employees on notice. They'll be treated like pampered guests."

"I want them to go home," Robbie mutters while his eyes track over Essie and me. "I should fetch Essie a t-shirt to cover her missing buttons."

Laughing, Isis gives Robbie a commanding shove to get him moving. "They're grown women, Robin. Leave it alone." Isis returns her gaze to me, and I cower against the wall. "Don't stay out too late, ladies. I'm sure Augustus would be pissed if you got into too much trouble." Isis's warning is layered in threat. Threat of what Mr. Kline would do to me if I got into too much trouble– any trouble… I'm already in trouble.

I'm fucked, and not in the way I want.

I watch my brother's back as he stalks away from me in a cloud of anger. Robbie never even said happy birthday to me. Tears prickle my eyes and my bottom lip quivers.

"Ah, don't get upset, Willow." Isis tries for words of comfort. I know she means them, but coming from someone who can only be described as scary-sexy, it sounds disingenuous. "Rob will get over it soon enough. It's hard to see you for the real person you are. I know all about that, baby girl," she grumbles and rolls her onyx eyes as if she's been in my shoes. Somehow I highly doubt that.

"Robin can't keep you as a child forever, even in his mind. Come back again when he isn't here and I'll let you in the Playroom. You can watch. I know there's someone back there you'd watch forever. You're perfect." Isis flashes an anticipatory smile as she runs one long, crimson fingernail along my quivering bottom lip.

"You're so innocent, Willow. It's intoxicating," is the only warning Isis provides.

I hiss when Isis kisses me full on the mouth. She takes advantage of my shock, penetrating between my lips, her tongue mingling with mine. Moist and sweet, her flesh slicks against mine. I shudder, too confused to compute what emotions are firing in my brain.

Isis rakes her fingernails over my chest, hitting a nipple. I finally feel what Kieren didn't make me feel earlier because I was blinded by fear– fear Auggie placed in me. The sensation of fire leaps from her fingernail to lick upon my budding nipple. I ignite for Isis because she scares me, makes me ache. I moan into her mouth and lean my chest into her sharp nails, trying to get more sensation.

I fall limp against the wall when Isis pulls away from me. My eyes refuse to focus as my lids rise. Groggy, I'm confused by my reaction to Isis. I've never been attracted to a girl before, and I'm not now either. Isis is scary-sexy, but something about the way her fingernails drew pain turned me on. It hurt, but it flashed lightning directly to my crotch.

"So sweet," Isis purrs into my ear. "I can see why he's distracted by you. You taste just like Robin– almost. Sugary sweet, but my Robin has an edge of pain that's a bite to the system. But then again, I'm partial since I've been addicted to him since the day I met him."

"Umm…" I grunt out an unintelligible word as Isis's tongue connects with the base of my throat. Slowly, in a wet line, she slicks her tongue along my flesh until she's teasing the rim of my bottom lip. I just stand against the wall and endure Isis, all the while quivering out of a mix of fear and excitement. It's as good of a high as I've ever experienced, and I've been getting higher than a kite since I was twelve.

"Just a friendly word of advice between women: protect your heart." Isis licks the tag on my collar, tugs it with her teeth, and then says, "That one isn't playing by the rules, and he won't be the one who gets hurt." Straightening to her full height, I watch as Isis's eyes clear of whatever high she was experiencing. "Heed my words, Willow."

"I…" I want to say, '*I don't understand*,' but no words exit my mouth.

Unaffected, Isis holds a conversation like she didn't just eat at my mouth. "Essie, come back again real soon, too. Willow and

Rob are cut from the same cloth. But you, baby girl, are just like me," Isis says with pride.

Isis prowls down the hallway, luscious hips swaying like a pendulum. When she catches up to where Robbie was resting against the wall, Isis smacks his ass to get him moving. The thwack sound fills the hallway and reverberates in an echo. My brother doesn't make a noise, but I know that had to have hurt badly.

CHAPTER EIGHT

"We should probably go now." Essie sounds panicked. Her voice cracking from shock accentuates her nervousness.

"Are you okay to drive? You seem out of it," I slur, lust more intoxicating than the six shots I digested earlier.

"Willow, how did that not affect you? Better yet, how come it affected you in the way it did? Jesus Christ, I thought you were going to get on the ground and crawl."

While laughing in awe, I whisper, "Fuck," beneath my breath.

"Who were you so intent on? I couldn't see him because the second we got into the room Robbie was on me, covering my eyes and holding my arm. It took Robbie, Isis, and me a minute or two to get your attention."

"I'd go back in there in a heartbeat if Robbie wasn't in there," I murmur, voice filled with intent. "You're right. I would've crawled to him and done whatever he wanted."

"Who?" Essie huffs out.

"Hell, if I know. He was a beast. I'll never forget that ass for the rest of my days. His back, ass, and thighs were magnificent. You haven't been giving blowjobs right. No, the guys have been lazy. Fuck, I wanted to suck him. I want to know if the cock matched the rest of his huge body. I bet it does," I murmur in a daze, voice slurring. "And I bet its taste is addicting."

"Willow?" Essie shakes me, hard. Her fingertips bite into the bruises Isis left as a memento. "Are you in there? This doesn't sound like you at all."

"I think I found my true calling." I laugh, shocked that I finally found someone who made me feel like a woman, and I have no idea who he was. I start walking down the hallway toward the main room of the club. I say over my shoulder, "We're coming back as soon as we figure out when Robbie isn't here. Isis said she liked you. I'm staying away from her, though. She's a scary bitch."

"She kissed you," Essie says in awe as she falls into step with me.

"Yeah, with the same mouth that was tongue-fucking Mr. Kline earlier." I groan– the heat in my belly is back, and I don't think it's dissipating anytime soon. I have no idea how to relieve it. "That alone made it worth it."

"Oomph," is expelled from my chest when I run head-long into a solid body. Possessive fingers grip my hips and draw me forward into the cage of his embrace. I'm trapped.

"Let go, Kieren. I'm sick of you touching me like that. I haven't given you any indication that I want to be groped!" I try to push him away but he tightens his hold. As I learned with Kieren earlier tonight, if I tell him no, he intensifies his efforts. I fall lax, not fighting him.

Kieren's eyes hold a feral glint– aggressiveness. He doesn't look like the blue-eyed, blond-haired boy-next-door anymore. He's more like the predator-next-door. I try not to panic, but I involuntarily flail around as he stares me down with blue eyes gone cold.

"I see you found the Playroom, and I see you liked it." Kieren's fingers grip both of my ass cheeks and squeeze– blunt nails biting into my soft flesh. Proof positive Kieren is one hundred percent an ass man. I try to fight him off, but one of his ball-catchers bracelets both of my wrists and traps me.

I turn to Essie for help, but she's gone.

Shit!

In preparation, I open my mouth wide while puffing out my chest, I drag in a mass of air so I can scream. Diverting my efforts, Kieren presses his palm over my mouth, fingertips lightly curling around my cheek. I try to bite, but my teeth slide on his saliva-slickened skin.

"Don't bother. It's just you and me, Willow," Kieren murmurs calmly. "Go ahead and scream if it will make you feel any better, but no one will hear you over the music." Kieren removes his hand from my mouth, and I unleash an epic, eardrum-piercing scream. My deep, husky voice echoes down the halls, the horrific sound vibrating the floor beneath our feet.

"Told ya, no one would hear if you screamed." Kieren acts like I'm trying his patience. "I'm not going to hurt you, Willow. Jesus, calm your ass down. What do you think I'm going to do? I just want to talk with you."

Voice raw from screaming, I swallow a half dozen times to wet my throat. "I don't want you like this, Kieren. You're pushing it. I'm not a toy you play with and throw away when you're done. I don't want to be used. Please, don't do this," I plead, but I only manage to turn him on more.

"God, Willow, you're just begging for it. I can smell your arousal. I'll give you what you need, Smokey. Just kneel before me and beg like the little bitch you are. C'mon, kneel," Kieren coaxes as he points at a spot by his feet. He presses my shoulder with his palm, trying to push me to the floor.

Kieren's eerily calm now, and that frightens me. The evil glint in his eye has turned to a calculated lust. But I fear that glint even more than his crazed expression.

"No, I won't do it. I don't know what it means, but I know I don't want to do that for you." I shove Kieren's hand away and quickly find out it does me no good. Kieren's built like a tank. I can't budge him an inch.

"You'll kneel for that arrogant bastard but not for me? You've had a crush on me for as long as I can remember. I finally want you back, and you deny me. What does he have that I don't?" Kieren's handsome face scrunches in confusion, revealing an underlying insecurity that I shouldn't find enticing but I do.

"Who? Who was the guy I was looking at?" I demand out of desperation.

"Are you a dipshit? Is that why you didn't go to college, you're too stupid?" Kieren hisses out of frustration-fueled anger.

I stand stunned, eyes watering. "I…I'm not stupid. I just don't know what I want to do with my life," I cry out, lips quiver as a sob rises from my chest. I stop both by biting my lip until I taste the coppery tang of blood.

"Willow, damn it! That's not what I meant, and if you'd pay attention you'd realize this. I'm never going to lie to you. Don't you see what's going on? Are you blind? I had Essie bring us here for a reason, and your mind is glossing right over that shit."

"What are you talking about?"

"Seriously? You've liked me since what… second or third grade? On the day I ask you out, you start treating me like I'm a freak. Do you wonder why? Because I sure as hell know who poisoned your feelings toward me. I'm not going to rape you in this hallway, so stop acting like I'm going to assault you. You've let that prick brainwash you with just a few well-placed words."

"I trust Auggie," I hiss defiantly. "I've known him my whole life and he wouldn't hurt me."

"What do I have to gain by lying to you, Willow?" Kieren says, sneering and shaking his head back and forth out of disgust.

"Fucking me– fucking me and fucking me over." I growl as I test the limits of my capture, finding out I can't move.

"I could have done that at any point between the time I got my first hard-on and this afternoon." Kieren doesn't sound arrogant because we both know he's right. "Contrary to popular belief, I asked you out because I like you. Now you're treating me like shit. Thanks a fucking lot, Willow."

"I'm not going to apologize," I whimper, feeling hella confused.

Kieren's eyes zero in on my trembling lip and he lets out a frustrated groan that shoots a strange sensation down my spine. Before I can blink, his mouth presses hard against mine, knocking our teeth together. In less than ten minutes, two separate people kiss me without invitation.

Fed up, every time Kieren tries to force his tongue between my lips, I bite him. He decides it isn't worth the fight after I draw first blood. Abandoning my mouth, he goes for a territory that can't bite back. Kieren feasts at my neck instead. My pummeling fists are useless as he presses me to the hallway wall, lips travelling up the column of my neck, teeth nipping my flesh, tongue dampening my skin. I try and fail to ignore the warmth radiating out from Kieren's kiss. Defeated, I pretend I'm not enjoying his touch as I struggle to make myself say no.

"Kiss me back," Kieren breathes against my neck. "Just one kiss. Kiss me back. Let me show you that the attraction you felt for me for the past ten years wasn't false."

"Kieren," I warn. "Don't do this."

"Just one kiss," he coaxes, kissing my throat tenderly. "Let me prove it to you. I won't hurt you. I promise I'll try to behave."

No time to accept or deny, Kieren's mouth descends on mine and captures my lips in a searing kiss. I don't have the ability to kiss him back; I'm merely a passenger to his ministrations. I groan as my body writhes, no doubt mimicking the movements of struggling but it's pure ecstasy that has my muscles spasming. I've never been kissed so thoroughly. I can feel Kieren's need, his passion for me.

My body disconnects from my mind, willingly opening my thighs to give way to a leg pressing into their juncture. Kieren rhythmically rubs his thigh against my panties, causing me to cry out in surprise. Hands that I used to fantasize about, but earlier tonight disgusted me, are now the object of my desire as they cup my ass and squeeze, pressing me closer to the heat of his body.

"Willow," Kieren breathes my name like a prayer on the wind. "I think I could come for you. My God, I know I could. I want to come inside you," he whispers in a voice dripping with lust and desperation, and it frightens me.

Still Kieren's passenger and not an active participant, I find my legs wrapped around his waist with the bulge in his jeans pressing and releasing against me in a rhythm befitting a sexual act. My neck arches as a moan is torn from my chest.

Two hands clench me, an ass cheek in each palm, as Kieren roughly rasps out, "I need inside you."

Kieren makes a move as if he's going to make good on his voiced thoughts, causing ice water to flush the heat out of my veins. I'm not losing my virginity standing up against the hallway wall of Rush with my brother nearby... and most definitely not to Kieren Mason after he's done his damnedest to manipulate me and place me into a situation Auggie promised Kieren would place me in.

No way.

I struggle to find my voice through Kieren's pleasurable assault— my voice to say no when my body is clearly ready for sex, judging by the way I'm salaciously, albeit unbiddenly, rocking my crotch against the impressive bulge in Kieren's jeans.

I acknowledge how I'm giving mixed signals here, when even I don't know which part of me I should be listening to, so how should Kieren know.

"My God, Willow," Kieren reverently breathes, shuddering. "I can't imagine how tight you are. Your pussy would feel like a hot fist gripping my cock. I want you to come so hard on me that my dick almost breaks from the pressure. I want your cum dripping down my balls as I fire deep inside of you." Kieren chants as if possessed, no longer in reality.

One of the hands gripping my ass slips underneath my shorts and heads straight toward a place no man or woman has ever touched before, as the other hand moves to unfasten Kieren's jeans.

Pure terror finally has me finding my voice, "No," I breathe out but Kieren doesn't hear me, too lost in his passions— deafened by his lust. This panics me, and I start to flail around: arms worthlessly hitting, feet kicking, head thrashing, voice shouting... all without avail.

"Kieren, no!" I cry out– the sound of a zipper lowering is scarier than a gunshot from pointblank range. Petrified, self-preservation kicks in. In my struggles, I manage to wedge my knee between his thighs and thrust upward with all my might, which isn't much. Kieren howls in pain and slaps me across the face out of reflex. I'd rather be slapped than have his dick invading between my thighs.

Kieren's weight disappears, and the first thing I see is Essie's panic-stricken face. She's crying, and I'm not sure why. *"What's wrong?"* I mouth at her, but I don't hear Essie's answer because Auggie's sudden appearance gains my undivided attention.

Auggie's holding Kieren against the wall with just one hand, his bicep bulging under the strain. The boy's feet dangle in the air, kicking. Kieren can't reach Auggie because his arm is almost as long as I am tall, and the distance between them is too great of a span.

"I warned you twice today: once after you came into Revamped and again when I got here tonight. Did you forget what I said? I said stay away from Willow. I said it in English, and I said it politely. Now I find you violating Willow in the hallway mere feet from me. This is the most blatant display of disrespect I've ever witnessed. I won't punish you because your father is more inventive than I could ever imagine. Isis is fetching him right now, in fact."

Kieren starts snarling and kicking in earnest, wild with frustration and anger. Auggie stands calmly with Kieren in his grasp, while looking around to make sure everyone is safe and sound. He tries to meet my eyes, but I drop mine to the floor out of shame.

I'm a bad girl– a monster.

"I see you didn't know your father would be here tonight, either. Such a happy surprise," Auggie says with a flare of sarcasm I didn't know he possessed. His voice is different again, deeper and commanding. It's the same as when he spoke to Isis at Revamped. It's a voice you cannot deny.

"Rob, take your cousin home," Auggie demands, and I finally see my brother lingering near me. It just goes to show how distracting Auggie is when he's this commanding. "I expect you to give Hester a thorough talking to about why tonight was fucking idiotic. It's too late now, since we can't have the girls unsee the Playroom."

My brother approaches me like I'm a wounded animal, hands out to his sides in a show of patience. His brown eyes are held wide with compassion and fear. Robbie looks as traumatized as Essie. I guess it was far worse to watch than experience. I was about to get the upper hand over Kieren.

I stand up straight and meet Robbie halfway. "I'm fine. I was about to kick Kieren's ass some more when Auggie intervened. Well, kick his balls in again, I mean." My voice is heavily laced with bravado– Auggie trills a laugh in response, but no one else does.

"I didn't know what else to do. Kieren looked at you wrong, so I ran." Essie whimpers, her voice breaking in panic.

"That was perfect, Essie. You did the right thing. It was better than you getting hurt, too. You and Willow don't know the rules, but Kieren does. He will pay for breaking them, I promise." Auggie speaks calmly to us as if Kieren's throat isn't gripped in his palm, with Kieren's fingers wrapped around the thick wrist holding him.

Kieren's stopped thrashing and trying to snarl something, and his face is as white as a sheet.

"What rule?" curiosity tears the question from my mouth.

"You never touch someone else's property without the consent of their owner. Isn't that right, Mr. Mason?" The tendons in Auggie's arm tighten, and Kieren blanches. Seconds later, Kieren's face turns beet red, and then Mr. Kline's muscles relax.

"I didn't see the collar, sir- honest," Kieren blubbers, and I feel bad for him when I probably shouldn't.

"Sure you didn't. Not when you sat next to Willow while eating dinner, or while riding in the car with her on your lap, or when you were sucking on her neck an inch from my collar. I'm sure you forgot me explicitly telling you that Willow was mine and that I am the only one with a say in who she dates. I must have misspoken when I informed you in no uncertain terms that you were never to sniff around Willow again. It seems you turned momentarily deaf during both those conversations today."

"I give up. You win," Kieren murmurs, not sounding defeated in the least. "But I honestly didn't see the collar." Rage fuels his words, "Because if I had, I would've torn the fucking thing from Willow's throat."

"How gracious of you to admit defeat. I'm sure it's a comfort for Willow to hear," Auggie murmurs sarcastically while flexing his fingers against Kieren's throat, as if he's imagining himself squeezing the very life out of Kieren.

"Fuck you, Auggie!" Kieren snarls, somehow finding renewed strength enough to put up a fight against Auggie. "You're a lying piece of trash. Willow isn't a toy, a pet, or a playmate. You can't own a person–"

"Let's go, girls," Robbie orders as he roughly grabs my arm– yet another bruise for the collection. The convenience of his interruption isn't lost on me. Everyone else may think I'm stupid, but Kieren has been trying his damnedest to say something, even before when we got sidetracked by grinding against the wall.

Kieren's been silenced since he entered Revamped this morning.

"No, Willow stays with me," Auggie commands.

"What?" my brother screeches, then his voice warps into rage as he realizes his best friend is being serious. "Auggie, this isn't the place for Willow."

"Take Willow's car and drive Essie home. Talk to Essie on the way, please. As soon as Malcolm gets his son, I'm taking Willow with me. She and I have a long talk ahead of us. I'll bring her home after work tomorrow. Go–" Auggie points to the end of the hallway toward the club, acting like he can just order his best friend around and Robbie will listen.

Robbie listens.

"Happy eighteenth birthday– you're no longer our sapling, Willow," Robbie mumbles despondently near my ear.

For the first time, I notice the choker circling my brother's throat. It's not like mine, with the exception of the round tag. Robbie's collar is leather with two large snaps, fitting it tightly to his throat. I finger the tag: *Robin*. The reverse side says: *Property of Isis Mason*.

Rule: you don't touch someone else's property without the consent of their owner.

Isis owns Robbie.

Mr. Kline owns me.

Robbie flashes me a sad smile before he places a soft kiss to my lips, and then turns to take our cousin home. I watch as they disappear down the hallway, Robbie's arm around Essie's shoulder with his hands rubbing her upper arms in comfort.

"Ah, I guess I finally figured out why everyone kept saying Robbie and I are alike." I snicker as I get comfortable against the wall. No one laughs as I expected as a tension breaker. "Nah, I guess I don't. But I get the concept on how we share a similar personality."

Auggie releases Kieren, and the bad boy falls several feet to the ground. A painful noise bubbles from Kieren's throat when he forcefully lands. I'd like to feel bad, but after a night of Kieren's grubby hands clenching on me, I rather enjoy the sound of his pain.

I smile at Auggie in thanks, and he gives me a look in return that says I'm as much to blame as Kieren. It wipes the smug right off my face, it does.

A scary man barrels down the hallway toward us, so I hide behind Auggie. With my fingers twisting in his sweaty t-shirt as an anchor, I bury my face against his back. He leans into me, and I instantly feel safe.

"Boy, what the fuck is going through your head? You and Auggie have been locked in this alpha male bullshit for far too long." The man's shoes stop moving an inch from Kieren's legs.

"You're all wrong," Kieren forces out from his raw throat, still defiant. "Auggie's wrong, and you fucking know it, Dad. But you always take his side in all things."

"Jesus, Ren, yesterday Willow was still a minor. I honestly don't know what I'm going to do with you. The girl has a right to choose for herself."

"Choose? She doesn't even know what that collar signifies. Auggie brainwashed Willow against me, with a bunch of bullshit lies," Kieren breathes, looking betrayed by his own father.

"Let. It. Go." Kieren's father is an older, bigger version of Kieren. Their eyes are the same shade of blue, but Mr. Mason's hair is dark and wavy. He's a mix of both his sons: Devon and Kieren.

"I can't." Defiant, Kieren lunges to his feet. "This isn't over, Auggie."

"Can it, kid," Auggie warns.

I draw in a breath to intervene, knowing something far deeper is going on beneath the surface, but Auggie somehow senses I'm going to speak. He silences me by pinching my leg in reprimand. Confused, I clamp my jaw hard enough that I bite the inside of my cheek.

"Sorry about this, Augustus." Mr. Mason's voice is soft, genuine, truly sounding concerned. "I'll give an apology to Robin when I see him next, and I'm sure Ren will come around."

"Willow, Robin, and Essie will get my apology, but he never will." Kieren points at Auggie, resentment and hurt resonating in his voice. "This ownership horseshit–"

Wrapping an arm around his son's shoulder, Mr. Mason sighs in defeat. "You crossed a line, Ren. Willow said no, and you were out of your head. We've been over this, and no one understands better than I do."

"I was gonna–"

"*Oh*," Mr. Mason and Auggie mutter in unison, understanding dawning. Whatever that signaled, a truce is met between Auggie and Kieren as they share a look. I have no idea what's going on, or why, but I can tell it's not about me whatsoever.

"Have Willow step out and let me have a look at her." Mr. Mason's voice is pleasant and friendly, coaxing.

Unsure, I press up against Auggie as tightly as I can, because something about the guy leaves me feeling transparent and raw beneath his gaze. Both men laugh at me in a deep rumbly sort of way that zing down my spine.

"Be a good girl, Willow," Auggie coaxes, chuckling, and I realize they're close friends. It's how Auggie knew Kieren had a problem with girls– I should always listen to Mr. Kline.

I step out from behind Auggie to stand at his side. Pulling my clothes back into place, I gaze at the floor, wishing I was wearing a hoodie and jeans, with my hair in a ponytail, not dressed up as an Essie wannabe.

"Willow is the spitting image of her father." Mr. Mason sounds like it's physically paining him to look at me for some bizarre reason. I don't really look like my dad at all. Robin and I look a lot alike, but it's Seth who's my doppelganger. "Bet she acts just like her mom," he mutters wryly to himself. "Auggie, under the circumstances, you know why this is difficult for me, right? You haven't um– you know?" I watch his hands move in the air, but I don't look up. "Jesus, please tell me you haven't."

"Does your gun still have bullets?" Auggie laughs humorlessly, with Kieren's ironic laugher flooding the hallway. "Besides, today is Willow's eighteenth birthday. You know me, Malcolm. I'm not at all like your father. They have to be able to vote before I touch 'em."

"Then how did you collar Willow?" Mr. Mason doesn't sound accusatory, merely curious. "This wasn't as we discussed– my boys, not you. She's just a kid, and he wouldn't want this life for her."

I peek at Kieren from beneath my eyelashes while they talk about me like I'm not even here. Slumped against the hallway wall but highly alert, Kieren misses nothing, not me or the men's conversation. Kieren has a ring of bruises blooming around his throat, and I swallow thickly in sympathy.

"The boys wouldn't know how to tame her. Willow definitely takes after Rob, but far worse– sheltered, naïve, and innocent. Far too curious for sanity's sake. Just like Rob, she's in desperate need of a keeper. Your plan would be a failure because she has needs we didn't anticipate. I know what I'm doing." Auggie speaks in a code only he and Mr. Mason understand, and they do that rumbly laugh again– definitely buddies.

Kieren hides a pissed off smirk behind his palm because he knows what they're talking about. If I wasn't so uncomfortable being alone with him, I'd drag Kieren off somewhere and force him to spill it.

Staring at the scuff on the tip of my left boot, I want the floor to swallow me. As if I'm an inanimate object, they're talking about me like I'm not even here. Kieren catches my eye, and I can tell he's sorry. I try to communicate that I don't believe that bullshit quest for virgins story Auggie fed me– there's something else going on.

Chancing a glance, I notice Mr. Mason isn't scary now that he's no longer pissed. He's handsome in a fatherly sort of way, with unruly, black curly hair and kind eyes. Malcolm Mason is a big dude, but not in an intimidating way. He's a lot younger than my dad, but Dad was in his late fifties when I was born. I realize with a start that Mr. Mason is close to Clover's age.

"It's a good thing I came to unclog the drain in Isis's apartment. What happened here tonight?" Mr. Mason commands, voice kind but authoritative, and I realize he's speaking to me. There's an interrogative edge to him, like he'd know the instant I tried to lie. With that scrutinous, narrowed gaze, I bet Mr. Mason is a cop or a lawyer.

"I used to hang out with Devon at parties, but I went to school with Kieren since kindergarten. I've um… I've had a crush on him forever," rambles out my mouth unbiddenly, causing a fierce blush to bloom. "My cousin surprised me for my birthday tonight by asking Kieren to join us. I disobeyed Auggie by going along with it anyway."

"Willow?" Mr. Mason calls to get my attention, because I was holding Kieren's gaze instead of his. Eyes flicking up, I instantly connect with Mr. Mason. It must be some type of internal lie detector test he possesses. "It's your choice– Auggie's not your father or brother, but you should listen to his advice if you trust him.

Realizing Mr. Mason isn't like Auggie, I relax slightly, words flowing without thought. "Kieren kept touching me, but I never said no." Closing my eyes, I admit the truth. "If tonight had happened before Auggie lectured me, I wouldn't have pushed Kieren away."

"You're such a dick," Kieren whispers, no doubt in Auggie's direction. "And a bald-face liar. You should go play with your own friends and quit sabotaging mine."

"Ren," Auggie issues as a warning, so I cut him off before he goes postal again.

"Anyway, Kieren was relentless, not listening to me– being pushy. I found out a crush is different than reality. I couldn't take any more pawing, so Essie and I lost him in the club, but he found me again. I take half the responsibility tonight, because I should've either listened to Auggie or listened to what I wanted. But Kieren has to take responsibility for not listening to me when I said no."

"I'm sorry, Willow." Voice rough, Kieren turns his face away from us, hiding his expression. "It won't happen again."

"I'm sorry for kneeing you *there*," I mutter with a furious blush blossoming on my cheeks. "That had to hurt."

Unbidden, my eyes seek out '*there*'. Humiliation flashes over my entire body when I see what I left behind. It would be pretty to think I turned Kieren on enough to make him cream his pants, but the heavy bulge pointing in my direction says otherwise. Kieren is cocked and loaded now that I'm staring *there*. The large, wet spot on the front of his jeans was all me. The evidence of the moisture is still dampening my panties and trickling down my thighs to moisten the tops of my hose. I left Kieren an embarrassing memento of our time together on the front of his jeans.

Gratefully the men share a laugh over my ball-kicking admission, distracting me from my mortification. Kieren mouths *'thank you'* at me. I mouth back *'do it again and I'll cut your nuts off, asshole'*. He nods in understanding. We're copasetic– Kieren wants to keep his testicles and I want girls to have a say in whether or not he gets between their thighs.

"Night, brother– have fun with Ren." Auggie's hand grips the nape of my neck, steering me down the hallway while I try to avoid tripping over my own feet.

"You too, Augustus. Don't have too much fun with Willow's punishment," Mr. Mason says with wry amusement, causing Auggie to snort when I shudder.

CHAPTER NINE

Twisting my fingers into the hem of my skirt, I try to dry the dampness that beads on my palms. The ride home feels even longer than the ride to the club. That's saying something, considering I was about to bolt from my car to get away from Kieren's roaming hands.

"I'm sorry," I whisper to Auggie in the dark truck cab. It flows so quietly, I doubt he can hear me.

"For what, exactly?" He asks with equal quietness, but where my tone quivered with cowardice, his is eerily calm.

"You said not to see Kieren, and I did it anyway. In my defense, I didn't know he was coming tonight. I did mean what I said to Mr. Mason about how I was leading Kieren on by not saying no outright." I try to appease Auggie by admitting it was partially my fault, but his long-suffering sigh informs me it's not good enough– too little, too late.

"No excuses, Willow. You must own your actions." Auggie sounds disappointed in me, and the guilt I hate feeling rises with a vengeance. "Every choice you made tonight was a turning point in your life. You have freewill, and you failed to use it properly."

"I don't understand," I grumble, trying hard not cry.

"I know, and that's the problem."

"I can't help what I don't know, Auggie. I'm so fucking sick of being called stupid." I can't hold back the tears that have threatened me all night.

Happy birthday, Willow, you stupid, ignorant bitch!

"I don't blame you for anything you haven't learned, Willow." Auggie whispers in the dark truck cab, but his frustration makes it sound deafening. "I'm disappointed in the things you do know but choose to ignore. That is the difference between ignorance and irresponsibility. I don't think you're stupid. I think you're highly intelligent, but young and naïve. You need to live and learn, that's all."

Auggie hands me a hanky, holding my hand for a second before releasing it. He sighs heavily while I wipe the tears away that I didn't think he could see in the dark.

"You believe that the decision was taken out of your hands because Essie invited Kieren. But instead of saying no, you sat on his lap and went to dinner. At the diner, you could've called it off, yet you didn't. You then rode to the club, which was another mistake, and still you didn't say no. I don't mean to Kieren– in general. You made another poor judgment call by using a fake ID to get into Rush. It's not twenty-one and over because of alcohol or any legislative law. It's because of the *illegal* Playroom in the back."

"I'm sorry–"

"You put yourself at risk by being around Kieren. At the same time, you curtailed the progress Malcolm and I were making with the Ren's issues. Then you compromised Rush by being underaged and entering during hours of operation. Ren is allowed to be there whenever, without my say so. You allowed Essie to take the control out of your hands because you wanted to do these things without taking full responsibility for your actions. *Essie told me to do it. Kieren forced himself on me.* Willow, every step was *your* choice, and neither Essie nor Ren are worthy or strong enough to take your power away– you *gave* it to them."

"I didn't mean it," I whisper.

Ignoring my interruptions, Auggie keeps lecturing me in a chanting tone. "Just so you know, I love Ren like he was my own blood." The fierce protectiveness in Auggie's voice steals my breath.

"Kieren seems to hate you, though," I mutter underneath my breath, earning a hopeless chuckle as a response.

"I know you like Ren, but he's not ready for the type of friendship you and he both need. My advice was more for him than you, even if I had to fudge the truth so it was in terms you could understand. As for Rush, I knew the instant you guys arrived tonight. Rory called and said I had a pet wandering the club. He wouldn't have allowed you in otherwise, because no way in hell could you ever pass for twenty-one when you don't even pass for fifteen. Choices, Willow. It's all about your poor choices. You can't blame them on anyone but yourself."

"You're right." I sniffle, trying to hide it behind the hanky.

"Let's record that for later playback, shall we?" Auggie teases, voice trying for levity.

Fuck you is on the tip of my tongue. I bite it back, but just barely. "What was so wrong with going out with my friends on my goddamn birthday, Auggie? What was so wrong with wanting to go on a date? My *first* date, for fuck's sake!"

"Nothing, which is why I let you drink and dance while inside Rush tonight," Auggie admits reluctantly. "I sent Bethany over to keep an eye on you and Essie."

"You sent Beth?" I mutter in confusion, but Auggie doesn't answer me.

"It was because it was with Ren, as I explained earlier today and then thirty seconds ago. The Masons have some issues they're dealing with, issues that are none of your business. You promised me. He promised me. You both broke that promise."

"Maybe it wasn't right of you to make us promise that in the first place, Auggie. I'm not–"

"Yeah, and your interrupted date-rape is the perfect example of why I was right. I don't care how much you were into it, Willow, I don't want that little fuck's prick inside you. Not while he's not healthy."

"Healthy?" I ask, but Auggie's on a possessive roll that can't be stopped.

"I don't care if you walk around in a perpetual state of arousal over Kieren Mason. I'm not blind– I saw Ren's jeans, Willow. You *drenched* him. You better not have gotten off on him. First times don't belong in hallways of seedy clubs, not for good girls."

"Maybe I'm not so good," I remind Auggie how he keeps calling me Monster.

"I'm warning you, Willow. If Ren touches you or you touch him before I okay it, he loses a dick. That's an order you'll both obey." Auggie viciously snarls, proving this isn't about me at all– there's something major going on between Auggie and Kieren.

"Ah… the unfortunate incident with the Playroom is all my fault. Fuck!" Auggie pounds the steering wheel out of sheer frustration. "I didn't think you'd find it. I thought you'd dance and get drunk like every other idiot teenager on the face of the planet. But, no, my monster finds a sex den and watches in enthrallment. I saw your face, Willow. There was no hiding that visceral reaction. Isis said she had to slap sense into you, and Rob was in hysterics." Auggie mutters in mystification, "Robin actually punched me. First time ever."

"I'm sorry," I whisper again, knowing it's not enough. "You didn't hit Robbie back, did you? He isn't as big as you."

"Oh, I know how much damage Rob can take, believe me." Auggie sounds beyond cryptic. "No, I didn't hit Rob. He was defending your honor. I would've been disappointed in him if he hadn't punched me. Robin was upset about the collar and you being in the Playroom."

"I'm not sorry about the Playroom, Auggie," I admit defiantly. "I liked it in there. But I am sorry about everything else, though."

"Well, at least that's a start. I know you're sorry, as I am. But if Malcolm is finally able to get through to Kieren, it'll be worth it– the boy may have had a breakthrough. As for Rush, it's a third your fault and two-thirds mine."

"It makes sense when you say it. It never felt right tonight. When I saw Kieren, I thought of your warning. All night I kept thinking to myself: *Mr. Kline is right. Always listen to Mr. Kline.* I wasn't even comfortable going out with Essie. I had a nagging suspicion because she wouldn't tell me what we were doing. I went along with it because I felt bad that Robbie missed my birthday and my parents got me a car I didn't deserve." Realizing I'm whining, I change the subject. "Nothing felt right until–"

"Until what?" Auggie asks when I stop mid-sentence. I shake my head no, finally taking note that we're parked behind Revamped. I have no idea how long we've been sitting here. A strange intimacy descends on us as we sit silently in the shadowy truck cab.

"You'll tell me eventually," Auggie says with confidence.

"What do we do now?" I gulp out, because Auggie's right as usual– I will tell him. Eventually.

"We get out of the truck and go into my warm apartment. We get cleaned up. You get your punishment, followed by that release you've been begging for. Then we'll talk some more, maybe grab a bite to eat. Talk more, and finally sleep. We get up in the morning and go to work, because once a punishment is given and words are spoken, all is forgiven. As long as you don't repeat stupid shit, all will be forgotten as well. Up we go…"

CHAPTER TEN

Auggie's apartment is the space directly above Revamped. It's a loft without any interior walls, offering absolutely no privacy. With no true bathroom, it's just a sink, toilet, and small shower installed against one of the walls. I would be mortified to use the toilet if it wasn't for the shower stall hiding it from view. The kitchen is a refrigerator and a serviceable island with a microwave and a hot plate. Auggie's environment is bare bones because it was never meant to be an apartment. It was originally the storage room for Revamped, and many of the items stored are still packed against the outer walls.

Sometimes I regret having my head shoved up my ass, never noticing any details of the people around me. Now that I'm officially an adult, I'm going to try better. I have absolutely no idea where Auggie lived his entire life. He was just always hanging around Robbie. I never thought to ask any questions if they didn't pertain to me.

After being at Rush, seeing Isis, Mr. Mason, Auggie, and Kieren interact, there's a connection there I'm missing but too cowardly to ask about.

I've been up in the loft a few times to clean or grab something real quick for my boss. Auggie has some eclectic, antique pieces that people bartered at the store and not much else. Basically, it looks and feels just like living in a storeroom. The place is tolerable at best if you're by yourself, but its total lack of privacy would be uncomfortable if you had a roommate.

"Go wash up and get comfortable. I'll give you some space." Auggie's husky words echo around the space. He stays on the farthest side of the loft away from the bathroom area, but on the same side as the bathroom so he can't see me. Settling onto a floral-patterned armchair, which belongs in a grandmother's house instead of a bachelor's loft, Auggie grabs a book and gets comfortable. It's almost comical seeing such a large man with a tiny book in his huge paws as he lounges in an ancient girly chair.

Running the water in the sink, I make sure Auggie can't hear me pee. Nature was calling something fierce after all the drinks I downed at Rush. I strip down to my boy shorts and tank top. It's not like Auggie hasn't already seen me in a bikini on countless occasions, and well… there is nothing to see anyway. I scrub my face free of makeup, and I'm thankful I'm not a hysterical type of girl or I would've bawled and had mascara running down my face. There's just a smudge of black from where I silently cried while Auggie lectured me.

I pull the pigtail buns out and let my hair lay naturally. I have thick, chestnut hair that falls perfectly straight to the center of my back. I like my hair, but it doesn't age me at all. Essie's hair is the same as mine, but she hacked it off at chin-length and she looks older because of it. If I tried the same thing, I'd look like a child trying too hard to look like an adult.

"Sit directly in the center of the bed, facing outward," Auggie orders the second I shut off the tap, authoritative tone brooking no room for argument.

I don't look at Auggie as I walk across the loft, then crawl up and onto his bed as I was told. The king-sized bed is almost three feet high, so it's a bit of a struggle for me. After settling in the middle, I sit cross-legged and wait.

"I'm going to get cleaned up now," Auggie quietly murmurs, not looking at me either.

As I watch Auggie unlace his boots, I realize I'm in perfect view of the bathroom. I should move, but he had to have known what and where I could see from this very spot. He sleeps here every night.

It's weird how Auggie strips from the bottom up. Most people do it the other way around. When Auggie is down to his underwear and t-shirt, he looks at me over his shoulder, green eyes more wounding than armor-piercing rounds. Holding my gaze in silent challenge, Auggie abruptly yanks his t-shirt from his body.

My surprised gasp is so loud it echoes throughout the loft. Feeling lightheaded from what is revealed, my chest tightens and my thighs clench against the electric buzz that emanates from between my legs and radiates throughout my entire body. I gulp in air, trying to teach my lungs how to breathe again.

"Who'd you think you were watching, Willow? No one will ever elicit such a strong visceral reaction from you as me." Auggie's voice drops low and trembles as he speaks.

Auggie doesn't take his eyes from mine, waiting for a response. I'm captivated, frozen by his predatory gaze. I lick my suddenly dry lips and nod my head in agreement.

Yeah, I should've known it was him. I know everyone else did. I think Essie was too scared to tell me the truth. It explains a lot of what Kieren was snarling, how he asked what Auggie had that he didn't. It's also why Robbie punched Auggie– probably for being the first man to tempt me. The first man to make me feel like a woman.

It had been a struggle to make my mouth form the *no* I gave Kieren. If we had been anywhere but that hallway, I doubt I could've mustered it. It would've been an impossible task if Auggie were to ask the same of me. I would've submitted without thought, without regret, without remorse, and never looked back. No doubt this is what angered both Robbie and Kieren– fear.

I'm lost in life without a true direction. Auggie said Essie and Kieren weren't worthy or strong enough to handle having power over me. That isn't the case– I could exercise freewill and say no to them. Whereas Auggie may be promising me sanctuary, a path without obstacles to harm me– there is comfort in feeling safe and protected –I'm not sure I can learn anything if Auggie is commanding every one of my actions. I'm powerless to say no to him. No freewill. No choice. Does he realize this? I don't know, but I have a feeling I'm about to find out, whether I want to or not.

I close my eyes as my beast pulls his underwear down and flashes that amazing ass. A deep, husky laugh permeates my being as he steps into the shower. Auggie put me here because he wanted me to watch. His show and tell was because he didn't know how to tell me he was the man in the Playroom. Auggie was the one I almost dropped to my knees and crawled toward.

Auggie was the one I longed to worship.

Auggie was the beast I wanted to suck– to fuck.

Auggie was the man I wanted to own me.

I don't know if I should feel shame or elation over this revelation. But I do know I feel very, very afraid.

I try not to watch, but my eyes keep radiating back to him. My geeky, artistic boss, the guy who's known me since I was born, is not the man I thought he was. I've always known Auggie was huge and built because he couldn't hide his virility beneath clothing. Auggie's love of everything in stock at Revamped clouded me to his actual personality: his commanding presence and the body of a sex god hidden beneath concert tees and threadbare jeans.

Graduation couldn't do it. My birthday couldn't do it. Dealing with Kieren couldn't do it. But knowing that I hadn't seen Mr. Kline clearly finally ages me into an adult.

I've always seen my siblings as my siblings. My parents were never people in my eyes– they were the people who birthed me and cared for me. They were my family: neither male nor female, child nor adult– simply people who were placed on this earth for my wellbeing. I realize now that each and every one of them is a person and has a personality beneath the title I've bestowed upon them. They all have dreams and fears and pains that have absolutely nothing to do with me and everything to do with being my fellow human being. I've been blind, and it leaves me feeling sick.

I understand Auggie's reasoning now, of why I was to call him Mr. Kline when he turned eighteen, but as of today, I was no longer allowed. When I was eight, Auggie was an adult. Today we are both adults– equals. I'll never call him Mr. Kline again.

My eyes feast on the sight of soapsuds concealing Auggie's body. He holds no shame or modesty as he washes in perfect view of me. I feel his eyes leveled on me, even though it doesn't appear as if he's watching me. The angle of his face is the same as it was at the club. I can see the curve of his cheek and the slope of one brow, but I know he can see as much of me as I can see of him.

I bite back a moan as Auggie's hands caress his taut body. He lingers in areas that I want revealed to my eyes. The suds block my view better than clothing ever could. I sit in awe because Auggie is allowing me to watch him in a personal and intimate moment. I never thought in a million years Auggie would be comfortable enough to allow me to watch him shower, let alone see him naked. I never thought I'd be comfortable enough to watch him without diverting my eyes or blushing. Well, I am blushing. My entire body is enflamed and my belly aches something fierce.

"I wanted to wait until you were less innocent, have you date and mess around a bit. But your sole focus was on a broken kid who can't give you what you need."

One day, I'm going to figure out what all this cryptic shit about Kieren means. Auggie said it was none of my business, so I'm not going to push. *Yet*. Curiosity killed the cat, they say.

"I knew this would happen eventually. I just didn't think it would happen so fast. I won't lie. I was hoping you'd enter the Playroom, because now there is no turning back. It's too late for that. You saw me, and I saw your reaction to me and the atmosphere, and neither can be unseen. In the truck, you didn't need to tell me why nothing felt right until you entered the Playroom. You didn't need to finish that sentence because I already knew your answer. You still need to say it out loud for yourself, though."

As Auggie steps from the shower, my eyes drink in every inch of flesh. He wraps a towel around his wide hips, failing to dry off, then he walks across the loft to dig around in the top drawer of his dresser.

"Augustus." I try the word out, and it rolls right off my tongue, sounding right.

Hearing his birth name, Auggie turns to me, smirk spreading his lips. He runs his fingers through his dripping curls, then playfully shakes his head like a dog, raining water on everything.

"That's so much better than Mr. Kline. I was beginning to feel like a school teacher," he teases. "*Mr. Kline... Mr. Kline... Mr. Kline.* I was waiting for you to raise your hand and act all eager for my attention. Perhaps asking to go to the potty, or to tell me that two plus two equals five, or that Lincoln was the first president of the United States."

"I'm not *that* bad at history," I mutter, offended. Auggie chuckles at my perturbed expression. "I'm actually pretty good at math. I enjoy it– the black and white rules. It's one of the only things I'm good at."

"Don't cut yourself short, Willow. You have many hidden talents." Auggie's voice is usually calm or playful, now he sounds like me– a husky chain-smoker.

Facing away from me, Auggie drops the towel. My breath hitches in fascination as his ass tightens and relaxes as he pulls on a pair of pajama pants. I try to ignore the fact that I can see *HIM* dangling heavily from between his thighs. The parts I threatened to cut off of Kieren, I'd never harm on Auggie. They're too perfect to be marred. They're so beautiful and ripe that my mouth waters instantly.

Dazed, I decide Auggie's tattoo is the safest place to rest my gaze.

"It's one of my illustrations," Auggie answers my unspoken question, somehow sensing where I was looking, which means he probably knew where I was looking a second ago. I hide my crimson face behind my sweaty palms. "It was the first of my works that was commissioned by a buyer. It was also my first major sale. I started a nice nest egg from this piece. It was difficult to part with it, so I had it tattooed on me."

"It's magnificent," I rasp breathlessly. I'm not sure if I meant Auggie's ass, back, thighs, or testicles. But the tattoo is incredible too. Auggie snorts, sensing the direction of my thoughts.

"How do you do that? Know what I'm thinking?" I ask out of curiosity.

"Body language... and I can feel your eyes on me. Your eyes betrayed you when you responded. They fell south of my back." He smirks while turning to face me. "Plus, your cheeks are flushed, your eyes are dilated, and your nipples are trying to wave hello." He gives a little wave at my chest, then snickers at my mortified reaction. "Why, hello there, sugar tits."

I gasp and cover my breasts out of embarrassment. My nipples never respond to the cold, so I always feared they were broken. My nipples didn't really bead when Essie was tugging on them earlier, but they could cut glass right now. Hell, it feels like I've grown boobs, too. Not big boobs– just ones that have something to squish. It no longer feels like skin covering my chest bones with miniature unresponsive nipples sitting on top.

"Put your arms down, Willow. I think it's only fair since you've been ogling me ever since you watched a woman suck cum outta my cock in the Playroom." Auggie's voice is deeper and raspier than usual, filled with challenge.

I instinctively licked my lips when he said suck, all the while replaying the scene in my mind on repeat. The beauty kneels before the gigantic beast with the lifelike tattoo moving with every flex of his hips. I can even hear the sounds Auggie made as he got off with me watching.

I drag in a deep, fortifying breath, then drop my arms. I'm afraid to know what my body language is betraying right now.

"You seem surprised about how your body is responding to me," Auggie murmurs, sounding more curious than anything. "I thought you'd at least have had a kid feel you up properly. I know Ren was doing a piss poor job earlier, but his hands were most definitely groping your tits and ass. I could lie and pretend that I didn't hear what he said to you, that his ultimate goal wasn't filling your cunt with his demon seed." Auggie snarls, and I swear he whispers beneath his breath, '*Oldest trick in the playbook. Kid's gotta do better than that to best me.*'

"Are you gonna piss on me next?" I growl, causing Auggie to toss his head back and release a laugh that has me quivering in delight. "Stop it!"

Auggie arches an auburn eyebrow in challenge. Stalking over to me, the towel is gripped in his hand, shielding the heavy weight that's swinging like a pendulum inside his pajama pants. I glare at the towel, willing it to fall.

"So… is there anyone else I have to geld for touching you before me? Has a guy groped your tits or not, Willow?"

"Yeah, as the running joke at parties, but there was never anything to feel up." The shame in my voice is so thick I'm choking on it. "I'm not totally innocent. I've had guys paw at my chest and ass. Sometimes our drinking games would turn into sexual stuff and the losers would have to make-out with me. Kissing on me was like making out with a kid. I had nothing to offer. But I never counted that as real. Not a real first kiss. Not a real first touch."

"Ah– virgin boys and virgin girls are such a disaster together. It's the blind leading the blind. My monster's not so flat right now, is she?" Auggie points at my swelling buds and smiles. "It's called being aroused, Willow. Kieren didn't do this for you earlier, did he?" He asks, gloating.

Wanting to wipe the smug from Auggie's face, I sting his ego. "You saw what I did to Kieren's jeans," I readily admit. "But I wasn't comfortable with what was going on, or else I wouldn't have said no. There was a strange edge to Kieren's actions tonight, like he was desperate. It was kind of a mood-killer. Your '*boys only want a wet hole*' lecture really ruined the experience. The whole time, I kept trying to figure out Kieren's motivations, whether or not he actually liked me."

One shoulder lifts in a shrug as a reply.

Understanding dawns, making me sick to my stomach. "Is that what you wanted, Auggie? Did you want me to doubt myself? Doubt Kieren? Were you sabotaging me? Is that why he was so angry with you and handsy with me? Kieren said you were brainwashing me, that he had no reason to lie to me."

"Doesn't matter either way, does it? You're sitting on my bed right now, not Kieren's." Auggie sounds unrepentant, and immediately changes the subject to one I cannot ignore. "Did you like watching me in the Playroom? Did it do this to you?"

Impatient, Auggie roughly grabs my breast and kneads, fingertips biting bruisingly into my swollen flesh. Auggie's gaze pierces me, holding me captive while he rolls my nipple between his thumb and forefinger so forcefully that I bite out a wince. A low moan spills from my parted lips, and the ball of ache between my thighs turns into a raging storm of need.

"Yessss," hisses out when Auggie pulls hard on my nipple, paining me, and I quiver in delight. "I want to watch you again."

"Rub your breasts– tug your nipples. See how much the mere sight of my body swells them, how much my touch arouses you. I'm not some virgin skirt-chaser. I know what I'm doing. Your body will be my instrument, Willow… let me play you with fine precision until your crescendo."

Auggie's voice is intoxicating and coaxing, luring me into being his puppet. His voice is the string from my hand to his request. My hands eagerly cup my breasts– cup them for the very first time. My birthday wish was granted. Tears start to fall rapidly from my eyes as I rub my tits in a combination of wonder and pleasure.

"Good girl. You only needed to become aroused. They may be tiny, but they're still tits. All straight men like female parts, but we all like something different. You wouldn't do well with a breast man for obvious reasons. But I'm not a breast man, so it doesn't matter. My opinion is the only one that matters– *ever*," Auggie commands.

At this moment, I agree with him. I'd agree with anything Auggie had in mind as long as he kept touching me. After years of being stunted, watching and listening to my peers and never joining them, never experiencing sexual excitement, I'd do anything to draw it out.

I'd do anything for Auggie because he finally makes me feel like a woman.

One of Auggie's large hands mounds both of my breasts. We both gaze at the sight of his huge fingers pushing my breasts together. I'm breathing heavily, but not nearly as badly as he is. I can feel the force of Auggie's breath down the extension of his arm to his hand. Auggie is panting at the picture his hand on my body paints, and it makes me feel proud that I have this effect on him.

Auggie sits next to me on the bed, large body completely taking over. He leans back a bit, rolling his glorious stomach muscles. Turning slightly, he looks me in the eye, judging my reaction to his nearness. The air around us heats with possibility. We're no longer boss and employee, or child and mentor, or Auggie and Willow. We're just two adults attracted to one another.

A feverish heat spreads across my body, causing me to shiver and quake. I don't understand why this intelligent, talented, gorgeous man wants me. I have nothing to offer him— nothing. It's unfathomable. Long moments pass as Auggie makes me wait for what comes next.

"It's time for your punishment." Voice drowsy, Auggie slouches on his bed with his feet dangling to the floor. "Monsters get punished. Good girls get rewarded. Lay your body over my lap." His voice is serious and solemn, tone making it sound as if it physically hurts him to punish me, as if it's only for my own good. But there's a wicked gleam in Auggie's eye, showing the pleasure he's getting from me being his monster.

Having a good idea of what comes next, I reluctantly crawl across the bed. Auggie tugs me across his lap, arranging me where he wants me. Auggie's lap is very wide– when talking to him, I forget just how huge he really is. My cheek rests on one thigh with my hips on the other.

I freeze like a startled rabbit when Auggie's fingers deftly roll down the waistband of my boy shorts, exposing my bottom. Something hard flexes beneath my nipples. I think it's Auggie's thigh– it has to be.

My parents coddled me, never punishing me. Clover would beat me because threats and punishments never worked with me, and I'd hit her right back. So I've never been spanked, but there is no doubt that I am about to be. Not scared, a thrill runs up my spine, radiating down my limbs, until the electrical sensation pools between my thighs and ignites my budding nipples.

I need Auggie to punish me. After disappointing Auggie and myself, I want the guilt to dissipate over my poor actions and judgments. I don't care that it's my birthday– I've screwed up, and I need to be punished to feel better.

The cold air caressing my ass doesn't chill me– it flashes fire throughout my body. Scalding hot waves radiate up and down my spine in anticipation of what's to come. I tense, and the ache in my belly grows to a painful hunger I've never experienced. I whimper from the level of arousal that swarms me.

Auggie shushes me while stroking my hair soothingly, hand smoothing down my back. But the comforting action doesn't dampen the fire building between my thighs, it enflames it.

"You're about to see what type of man I am," is a warning, quickly followed by the obvious answer. "An ass man." Auggie purrs hypnotically, voice an intoxicant clouding my mind, drugging me into compliance.

A shrill scream is torn from my throat before the pain registers in with my brain. Auggie's huge palm smacks my ass and thighs in one hit. Hip to hip, tailbone to thighs, his palm covers my entire bottom. Flames licking along my back and legs, I have to pant through the pain as it radiates from Hell and back.

"Why are you being punished, Willow?" Auggie asks in the voice I associate with when he's Mr. Kline. It's a tone that means he's either aroused or won't be denied.

"I'm a monster. Good girls listen to Mr. Kline. Monsters ignore his sound advice." I robotically answer while breathing through the pain licking flames along my ass and thighs.

"What do monsters get?" Auggie asks, voice thick with anticipation.

"Puni–" *P...u...n...i...s...h...e...d...* I scream long and loud as Auggie whacks me three more times in quick succession. Tears dampen his thigh as I release my guilt right along with the pain. I want to rub the burn away, but I instinctively know that would be a huge no-no. I accept the pain as penance for my bad behavior. I will never forget to listen to Auggie. Whatever he says is law.

Whatever *that* is beneath my nipples isn't a thigh. Underneath me it bucks and pulses to an unknown beat. It can't be *HIM*. It spans from one breast to the next, and then some.

"What do good girls get?" Auggie growls deeply as both palms massage my flaming ass cheeks. I squirm around in his lap, loving and hating the attention. His touch soothes the burn, but manages to intensify it into another unnamable sensation.

"Rewarded," I sob.

"Masturbate for me, Willow." Auggie orders in a sluggish voice. "I want you to associate this type of pain as pleasure."

"I don't know how," I mumble underneath my breath, fearful my ineptitude will disappoint Auggie, and then he'll start thwacking me all over again.

"You've never touched yourself?" Leaning down, he whispers near my ear, sounding mystified.

"No," I answer with all honesty. "I've watched Essie do it before while she went down on a guy. But I've never tried. I... I've never really been turned on before, and I never felt like a girl. I just didn't bother."

"What do you mean by that?" Auggie asks softly, and I feel a flutter over my hair like he's petting me.

"I get the concept. But if you don't find yourself remotely attractive, how can you get turned on enough to get off? I'm disgusted by my little boy body," my voice twists in misery. "I may think and feel like a woman, but I don't look like one."

"I never want to hear those words from your mouth again." Auggie smacks my ass in reprimand. A scream is torn from my throat from the intensity of the pain– my skin retracts, pulsing as if it's throwing off its own throbbing heartbeat.

"Remove those negative thoughts from your mind." Auggie orders with another swat. This last spanking only makes me hiss between clenched teeth, because it falls across my thighs.

"I assure you, you're all woman. You've been hornier than hell all day." Auggie's whisper turns into a comical sound. "I'll show you how to get off. But from now on you'll masturbate before you go to sleep and when you wake up– until you come – every day."

"Yes, sir," I agree. I'd agree to anything as long as I didn't get another swat.

Auggie fists my hair roughly, wrenching my head backward, forcing me to meet his heated gaze. He releases a feral growl, the endless rumble vibrating from his chest.

"You have no idea how horny that word makes me. Every time you say *sir*, I get as hard as a rock. Some days I felt like I would go fucking insane. Yesterday I masturbated eight times– rubbed my cock raw. I swear to God, every time I came out of the backroom fresh from whacking off, you'd call me sir again, and I'd get harder than the previous time. Today I denied myself release, and you decided to be a horny little monster with your hungry eyes eating me alive."

Unbidden, my back arches into Auggie's touch as he grips my ass in both hands and squeezes violently, grinding his palms into my raw flesh. I writhe in his lap, unsure if it's pleasure or pain as the pressure mounts to a crest.

"I almost sheared Nina's tonsils off tonight when I came–"

"Nina?"

"The woman you watched suck me off," Auggie replies without remorse. "It was worse because you were watching me come down her throat– it was one of the most powerful orgasms of my life. I pretended it was your hungry little monster mouth sucking me down instead of Nina's eager hole."

"I wanted to be her," I whisper the truth.

"I know," Auggie says without a hint of arrogance. "I could tell you were imagining it was you, too. I was willing you to crawl to me... and I almost had you, Willow. I almost had you as mine. I wanted to kill Isis when she stood between us– Isis always tries to take what's mine..." Auggie trails off, lost somewhere in the past. "And I'll never stop trying to take it back."

"I wanted to crawl to you. I wanted to kneel at your feet and give you pleasure. I tried, but Isis stopped me. I'm sorry, sir," I cry, causing Auggie to soothe me with another pass over my hair.

"I wanted to be Kieren tonight as he ground you into the wall. If it was physically possible for us, I would've had your shorts torn from your body with my cock buried in your virgin pussy, fucking the hell out of you in Rush's main hallway. I would've rode your ass on all fours like a fuckin' animal. I would've made you come so hard your scream would have eclipsed the pounding music of the main floor. Controlled... dominated... possessed... owned." Auggie breathlessly pants. "There wouldn't have been one single cell in your body that didn't belong to me."

Auggie's fingers skim my hip, skate over my inflamed flesh, then slide into my shorts. I buck against his hand as it touches my bare flesh for the first time. I grunt like a wounded animal as a fingertip slips past my folds to slide over my sensitive flesh. My eyes pop wide in shock before they roll back out of pure ecstasy. My mouth drops open, releasing no sound. This is the first time anyone has touched me sexually, including myself. Auggie is the first, and it makes me feel special, proud... honored.

"Thank you," I pray reverently. I'm not sure if Auggie hears me or not, but the hardness beneath me pulses and jerks against my chest.

Roughly clearing his throat, Auggie tries to speak. "God, you feel like silk." He groans in awe. "So soft... untried... all mine. Say it," he commands. "Say you're all mine."

I try to say the words, but all that comes out is a wheezing gasp.

"If I share you, it's by my choosing. I'm not teasing, you let Kieren touch you and you'll regret it."

"Yes, sir," my voice breaks in fright. Here's a man I respect, trust, love even, and he's threatening me while touching my private flesh for the very first time. A tremor runs up my spine and works its way down to my fingers and toes.

"Good girl," Auggie praises, sounding relieved. "Willow, slide your tiny finger down to the well." Auggie's large fingertip dips down to my opening, causing me to gasp in shock as a pleasant sensation builds. "Scoop up some sweet honey with your fingertip, and then rub it… *right here*… until you come." His lulling, hypnotic voice purrs as his finger performs the act he describes, circling my engorged clit in a dizzying rhythm.

"Auggie!" I cry out as he rhythmically strokes my clit. He murmurs *good girl* underneath his breath.

Lost in the pleasure, the pain takes me unawares. I scream in agony as Auggie spanks me harder than all the other times combined. My skin is on fire, but my pussy violently contracts, causing moisture to weep out. I've never felt that before, the gush of arousal and the clench of impending release. The ache in my belly instantly feels better, like the pressure has been relieved. I whimper in thanks as he intimately touches me.

Auggie slows his rhythm on my clit, making slow sweeps of the swollen nub. His mean, spanking hand pries my fingertips from the sheet to settle them on the throbbing thing underneath my breasts.

It is *HIM*!

Auggie clenches my hand a few times in example, until I squeeze the muscle the way he wants. His pajama pants are in the way of me really touching him, but I marvel over the fact that my fingers will never encircle his girth. Auggie groans, so I know I'm doing it right.

We both moan together from our mutual pleasure. My eyes drift shut as my body builds with a pressure I've never felt before. The pressure promises to remove that ache that has plagued me all damn day. I wonder if this is how Auggie feels when he has to masturbate. How do you know when to do it?

A scream tears from my throat until I can't make any more sound. Massive amounts of air fill my lungs and release out in a torrent as Auggie spanks me with reckless abandon. It changes from a searing, burning agony to a pleasure so deep my womb contracts. My silent screams turn into guttural moans of pleasure.

"Good girls come for their masters. Come for me, Willow." Auggie enchants me with his hypnotic sex god tone. A firm pinch to my clit, combined with my puppet master's words, has me writhing as the pressure builds and builds. I fear I'll die if I don't find relief soon. I rest on the precipice of release, stuck in agony.

The cock is no longer a *HIM* now that we're personally acquainted. The cock's movements are sporadic beneath my squeezing palm, twitching and jerking with every pull of my hand. Auggie starts to cry out, and I realize I'm making him come. That knowledge slams my orgasm into me– my first orgasm ever. It's not flowing and pleasant, but violent in its intensity. It leaves me sobbing and breathless, hurting worse than the spanking, yet it feels better than anything I've ever experienced.

"From now on when I punish you, you'll love every agonizing second of it. You may even come without being touched sexually."

My shoulder is wet and sticky. I stare at it in awe– *is that from him? It has to be. I made him do that,* I think with pride. Auggie laughs at my gobsmacked expression while he cleans me up with his towel. Like a ragdoll, he positions me where he wants me– curled around his chest.

"Sex isn't always like this, Willow. This is play– it doesn't truly count. The first time is the hardest to deal with, not just physically, but emotionally too. Sex comes in many forms: playing between acquaintances, fucking between lovers, and making love between partners. What we did cannot change anything between us, Willow."

"What do you mean?" I mutter, praying that I misunderstood as my heart aches with regret. Was Auggie just teaching me, or was he using me? He just admitted that this wasn't reality by placing me in the '*play with your acquaintances*' category. Did he even want me, or was he just taking one for the team by removing my ignorance?

My innocence.

"When we're at the store, I want you to treat me as you always have. I'm your boss and you're my employee. The same goes for when we're in public or with your family– either treat me as your boss or your brother's best friend. But no matter what, you will treat me with respect, not the familiarity of a friend. Do you understand, Willow?"

Expecting warmth after our shared passion, I'm floored by the cold, emotionless calculation Auggie exhibits. It's so shocking that it numbs me to my true thoughts and feelings. No cuddling. No reassurances. No thank you for getting me off. Just a list of rules I have to abide by.

"Yes, sir." I whisper because I fear what my voice would sound like otherwise. No doubt it would be tear-filled. A soft hand lightly strokes my hair, Auggie's attempt at comforting me.

"When I allow you into the Playroom, or when I say we're playing, you will act as you did this evening– Monster or Good Girl." Auggie's tone changes from cold to light with amusement, as if he's holding himself back from laughing. "…And I will be your beast."

A gasp cuts from my throat when he says beast. How does Auggie know that?

"You said it underneath your breath at least a half dozen times, Willow. I'm not deaf, and I was beginning to wonder if that was what you were calling my cock. If not, then from now on I want you to call my cock Beast. Lord knows, Beast and I have a lot of work ahead of us before we can fit into your pinky-sized hole. No one but Beast is taking your innocence. We'll figure out the rules from there, but I will always be your first. Your first everything."

CHAPTER ELEVEN

My fingers tap with impatience to the beat of The White Stripes. Not that I'm truly listening to the music since all of my concentration is focused on my laptop. Excitement pumps adrenaline through my veins as I stand on the footrest of my stool, ass off my seat, leaning over the counter to get a better look at the website.

"C'mon, higher," I hiss through clenched teeth. My fingertips clench on the Formica countertop in anticipation. "A couple dollars more... just a little bit more. Momma wants it higher. Please," I beg the laptop screen as if it can communicate with me.

Lightning fast, my fingertip clicks the refresh button... and then again. *Click...* and again. *Click...* and again... Insanity... and again... until...

Three.

Two.

One...

"Holy Fuck!" I scream to the empty store and almost fall off my stool when my Converse slips off the footrest.

"Willow, what the hell is going on out here?" Barreling out of the backroom, Auggie frantically looks around Revamped for thieving Fairport residents stealing our used and slightly abused merchandise.

"Oh, nothing," I murmur nonchalantly. "The final auction just closed." I say no more and act unimpressed. I tighten my ponytail with a yank as I hop off my stool.

"And?" Auggie gives me a look that screams he isn't messing around because I just interrupted his creativity time. I grin at him, flashing all of my front teeth, and he raises a russet eyebrow in response.

"Guess," I tease playfully.

"I'll spank it out of you, Monster," Auggie threatens with the raise of his hand, and I hop back out of reflex. Arm moving as if to smack me, Auggie scratches his whisker-shadowed cheek instead, all the while smirking at me. "Just keeping ya on your toes," he taunts with a wink.

"I always feel so worthless," I reluctantly admit, but it's the absolute truth. "I always feel like I have nothing to offer anyone, so why am I here? Why do I exist?"

"Willow." Auggie sighs my name as he takes a step toward me. "You're making me dizzy. How did you go from shrieking obscenities to being depressive? Don't be so negative. C'mere."

"Wait up!" I hold my hand out to stop him from giving me a bear-hug. "I always dreamed of making someone proud. Well, I just realized I'd rather make myself proud. I think I finally found my niche."

"And here I thought the Playroom was your niche." Auggie teases me, lips quirking up slightly at the corners.

"I've done a lot of work on this stuff, Auggie. The first couple of auctions bombed, but I've learned a lot from that failure. Now I make sure to post them so they close at the right time of day, when the most people are surfing the site. I make sure the listings are as accurate as possible and tagged correctly. The pictures are the most important part, because people need to visualize what they're bidding on. I try to make the images look as professional as possible. So after all that hard work…" I trail off for dramatic effect.

Smiling, I make Auggie beg for it like he did to me last night. "And?" he impatiently prompts after a couple dozen heartbeats.

"And… I sold something you paid $12.95 out of pocket for $1,001.00," I announce.

I feel proud of myself– wickedly proud. I'm finally good at something, even if it's a crapshoot. Auggie's green eyes are huge and shiny. I'm not sure he believes me. I turn the laptop for him to take a peek at the screen. I smirk at his astounded facial expression.

"Jesus! How much did you profit this week?" Auggie's fingers pull through his reddish-brown curls.

"I only had four auctions. One we broke even on. Two we came out a bit ahead. Obviously the fourth did very well." I quickly tally a total in my head, always finding math to flow as easily as water. "Twelve hundred in profits, give or take a few dollars. I could do more auctions at a time, but I was scared I'd fuck up and bomb on twenty auctions. I didn't want you to kill me."

"Do as many as you're comfortable handling. I'll let you do as you wish with the stuff." Auggie displays total trust in my abilities, and I'm floored.

"Along with all the social media sites, I started a website for the store, and I have a few items listed on it. I thought about adding our inventory to the site so people could order online. The more collectable things I could auction instead."

Biting my lip, I gaze at the floor– I suddenly feel bashful, unsure of myself. I've never had anything to contribute before. It feels foreign to be good at something, something that would benefit Revamped *and* Auggie.

"Bring the site up for me to have a look– I'm not good at this kind of thing. I have a website for my illustrations, but I don't even know how to get to it." Auggie's eyes scrunch together, like he can't believe I have a clue about something when he doesn't. "Why are you so good at this?"

Flushing with a mix of pride and embarrassment, I hit Revamped's bookmark on the browser. I should probably feel mildly insulted because Auggie finds it difficult to believe that I could excel at something. But I'm not offended, or so I tell myself. He's known me since birth– I've never shown a proficiency toward anything. Snark flows out of my mouth to cover my embarrassment at the unintentional slight Auggie directed at me.

"Dude, the ten-year age-gap is pretty wide today." I taunt Auggie, elbowing him in the side. "Positively geriatric, old man. I've never known a time without internet. If you don't know how to navigate the web by first grade, you're never going to make it through school. A monkey could make a page."

I blink at Auggie while fighting the urge to sing '*neener-neener, I can do something you can't do!*' I don't stick my tongue out like a brat, but just barely.

"A good girl would run this website and the one for her boss's illustrations too. Perhaps later she will fix another one for me. If she's good, I'll give her a percentage of the auctions– a twenty-percent commission. If she's really good, that is," Auggie teases. "Since a monkey could do it."

"Really?" I squeak in excitement and give a tiny hop. Auggie nods at me, and then leans down to kiss my cheek– his lips are warm and moist on my feverish skin. "I'll try really hard to do it right." My voice quivers slightly from a mix of hope and trepidation.

"You're so young sometimes," Auggie says with affection. "I don't care if you fail as long as you try. Life is a continuum. You don't need to know what you're doing in five years, because you won't even be this version of yourself next month. You need to lighten up on this shit, Willow."

Flashing Auggie a pinched look, I show him how much I appreciate his mentoring at the moment. Obviously he ignores my attitude.

"If you enjoy pushing Revamped's merchandise, then do it any way you want. After the webstore is set up and running smoothly, I'll show you what I need on my other sites. We'll work from there." Fingers wrap around the end of my ponytail, and then tug playfully. "You don't have to constantly prove yourself. Willow, I've seen you at your worst and at your best."

Hands gripping my waist, Auggie sets me on the counter. I wait to get yelled at for being a bad toy, but he surprises me instead. He tugs the end of my ponytail again, then smiles down at me with sinister intent when the movement exposes my throat.

Auggie nibbles up the column of my neck, and a moan slips past my parted lips. I shiver from the feel of his damp flesh pressing against mine, breath skating across my skin.

"I spy with my little eye something that doesn't belong on this gorgeous expanse of flesh," Auggie says with a sing-song quality to his voice.

"Ugh!" A grunt of pain is forced out of me when teeth bite just beneath my ear, sinking in with a sharp sting. Lips creating a powerful suction, each draw of Auggie's mouth on my neck has me squirming around the countertop, trying my damnedest not to make pitiful noises of ecstasy.

"There." Auggie mutters with pride, leaning back to get a gander at his handiwork. "I covered up that little boy's amateur mark. No more Ren on my Willow Monster's neck."

"Asshole." Growling, I palm Auggie's forehead, then give a forceful shove. Of course, he doesn't move even a fraction of an inch.

"That's what I was just saying." Auggie smiles grandly at me.

"I was calling you an asshole, Auggie." I roll my eyes in disgust at his bizarre possessiveness. "I'm starting to doubt that you'd ever want me if someone else didn't. You just want to have all the toys, even if you don't want to play with them. I think you're marking your territory and nothing more."

I bait Auggie, trying to get him to admit the truth. Last night's words still echo in my mind, and they aren't a comfort. I don't want hearts and flowers, or a ring on my finger, but I don't want to feel used and abused, or messed around with to prove a point to someone else. My worst fear, last night was a pity fuck.

"You think very highly of me, Willow." Auggie murmurs, not sounding insulted at all, which frightens me. "...And of yourself."

Distracting me from my destructive thoughts, supple lips flutter against mine for the very first time– gentle and sweet – heartbreakingly tender. I scramble forward, eagerly fusing my body against his. Wrapping my arms around his back, I dig my blunt nails into Auggie's shirt to keep him with me always. I try to do the same with my legs around his hips, but he's too wide. I scowl against Auggie's lips when our bodies refuse to align.

Dang it! I hate being inadequate!

Auggie laughs deep in his chest, a pleasant rumbling that vibrates against my budding breasts, and the sound warms my blood. "Is this what you're wanting?" Firm hands grip my legs, fingers splaying around my thighs and butt, then he pushes my knees to my armpits. Leaning into me, Beast is pressed tightly between my spread thighs.

"Yes." I whimper as Auggie grinds Beast against my aching flesh in a practiced rolling motion of his hips.

"Missionary will never work for us, I don't think. We'll figure it out." Auggie teases, but it still stings.

Seeking Auggie's lips, I get lost in the rhythm of our connection, forgetting all the ways I'm going to disappoint him and all the ways he's going to destroy me. This kiss is different than our first. Hunger that Auggie has long denied pours from his invading lips. My jaw nearly unhinges to accommodate his wide tongue, because everything of Auggie's is two or three times larger than mine. He lets off just before I choke, gives me a second to regain my breath, and then repeats the thrusting motion, tongue mimicking the seductive roll of his hips.

Back arching, fingers gripping, "Don't stop!" I cry out as a familiar pressure builds.

Last night and this morning, Auggie made me masturbate while he watched. He wanted to make sure I did as he bid and that I was doing it correctly. I know what an oncoming orgasm feels like now, and I'd chase that building sensation to the ends of the earth.

"My greedy little Monster." Auggie groans against my lips, then he sucks my tongue into his mouth.

Refusing to be Auggie's passenger, I take over, doing as he did to me, penetrating his body and taking ownership. I don't fear suffocating him, so I don't back off. I advance, thrusting and exploring the depths of his mouth. Reveling in the silky slide of his tongue trying to capture mine, I go boneless when he sucks my tongue deeper into his mouth.

"Don't stop." Auggie groans around my tongue while aggressively twisting his hips, grinding Beast hard against my crotch. "I'm close, too."

My knees are pressed near my ears, with my fingertips roughly gripping and flexing against Auggie's ass. I try to pull us as closely together as humanly possible, fusing our bodies as one, wishing he was deep inside more than just his tongue in my mouth. Our movements rock the counter as our rough breathing permeates the air. Auggie eats my moans as soon as my throat releases the ecstatic sound.

Ding...

I freeze in shock. Caught in the moment, I'd forgotten where we were. Revamped. When Auggie turns me on, I see, hear, and feel nothing but him. It's past closing time, but someone just entered the store anyway.

"Shh... it's okay." Auggie murmurs reassuringly, but it doesn't help. "It's only Rob."

Stunned frozen, I do nothing as Auggie pulls away from me to stand behind the counter. Staring down at me with intense hunger, Auggie swears a litany underneath his breath and runs his fingertips through his auburn curls.

"Fuck..." Auggie sighs heavily. "I was a second from coming. I'm going to have a wicked case of blue balls after this." He kisses me softly, chuckling against my lips when I growl.

Slumping bonelessly on the counter like a ragdoll, my head lolls off the edge while my legs just dangle into nothingness. Rolling my eyes up to look at my brother, upside-down, I find Robbie's worried brown eyes staring at my face in shock from a few feet away.

"What'd you do to Willow? She looks enthralled or high." Rob shakes his head, knowing exactly what I look like when I'm high, then walks over to me. Brushing a few strands of hair off my forehead, he stares down at me with a weary expression.

"It's incredible– Willow's reaction to me is instantaneous." Auggie's arrogance knows no bounds. "Usually it takes a long time, or a lot of pleasure or pain to bring that out of a submissive."

"Stop," Robbie begs, looking faintly ill. "Please, just shut up– you know why listening to you gloat hurts for several disgusting reasons."

Bragging about his newest toy, Auggie doesn't hear what Robbie's trying to say. "Rob, I thought you were fast until Willow responded." Auggie issues a snort while patting my brother on the back. "It's fucking intoxicating. Your family breeds the best submissives."

Echoing my thoughts, my brother speaks for me. "Don't be an asshole, Auggie." Robbie punches his friend in the chest, and it wasn't a playful thwack. The hollow thud pushes a surprised gasp out of Auggie.

"I'm just being honest." Auggie growls in annoyance while rubbing away the sting from Robbie's punch. "Be thankful someone who loves Willow is taking care of her needs. Be thankful you came to me first, while you're at it. You both were highly susceptible to very bad dominants."

"Willow would've never known about this shit if you hadn't turned her on to it," Robbie accuses.

"Not true, blame Essie for bringing Willow to the club. I tried to avoid the inevitable, but the craving to be led runs in your blood." Reaching out so fast I can't track the movement, Auggie's gripping Robbie's shoulders in his big paws.

"I didn't turn you on to it– you turned me on to it. Remember, Robin?" Auggie stresses, and I struggle to wrap my mind around what's happening. "You were wandering until you found what you were looking for, and you found more than you wanted in return. Willow's just like you, Robin. She never would've enjoyed sex without the right environment."

"You're so full of shit, you get that, right?" Gobsmacked, Robbie and I have never looked more alike than we do now. "This territorial display is so obvious, it's ridiculous. If you would've stayed with the plan, Willow would've never entered the Playroom. But you had to get jealous." Robbie shakes his head back and forth with a disgusted grimace twisting his lips, all the while glaring at Auggie.

"You're going to bring up Ren right now?" Auggie challenges. "He wasn't in the plan either."

"Shut the hell up, Auggie. I don't want to know about Willow enjoying sex. For Christ's sake, yuck! No amount of bleach will ever clean the memory of you rutting on her tiny body from my mind. I'd rather watch Ren get his rocks off a billion times over."

"Look at that face, so beautiful and serene. Would you deny that face anything?" Auggie's fingertips grip my cheeks, and he makes kissy faces at me. "Willow wants me, Robin, so I'm going to let her have me."

Watching them with droopy, passive eyes, I realize I'd let Auggie kill me if he wanted. Nothing moves on me but my eyeballs, and I find my mental and physical state utterly terrifying.

Witnessing Auggie's euphoric expression, Robbie's mouth falls lax and his eyes glaze over like he just took a toke of Mary Prynne's finest. Snapping out of it, "I give up!" Robbie tosses his hands in the air. "You're not going to listen to me anyway, because you never do. Are you going to be at the Playroom tonight?"

"Are you going to be there?" Auggie counters.

"Yeah, where else would I be, dumbass? You know I keep Isis company while she's at work." Robbie tries to sound put out but fails. He looks thrilled for a chance to be around Isis. I don't blame him, because I have a scary girl-crush on her. I don't want Isis– I want to be her.

"Well, asking me if I'm going to be there is just about as stupid as me asking if you're going to be there," Auggie replies childishly, albeit cryptically.

"You're such a bastard when you have blue balls. Go rub one out, then we'll continue our talk."

Ignoring Robbie, Auggie interrupts him. "We'll both be there tonight because I'm rewarding Willow for her prosperous auctions. Plus, I need to see how she reacts to different stimuli."

I close my eyes as Auggie's big palm rubs my belly and chest in one motion. It isn't sexual. It reminds me of rubbing your pet's belly in contentment. If I could purr, I would.

"You didn't fuck her, did you? I'll keep my mouth shut about this, but I won't allow you to hurt Willow's insides." Robbie growls, then punches his best friend again.

I scowl when Auggie's hand ceases to rub my belly in order to latch onto the fist flying at him. Robbie's acting in a way I've never witnessed. My brother's usually calm and easy-going, and wouldn't defend his own honor let alone any of ours.

"No, not yet." Auggie sounds disappointed. "I have the same fears you have, Rob. Willow may not be my family, but she's been in my life as long as she's been in yours. That's why I need to see how Willow reacts to different *stimuli*." He says this in a manner that means far more than the words express. "Ren's out because he's a little puke sticking his nose where it doesn't belong, but that doesn't mean the plan isn't still happening."

"I don't like any of this. I know we all talked about it, but I have some serious reservations about–"

"It's too late now, Rob... and one more punch and we will see just how lenient I am not," Auggie threatens is a level voice that it utterly terrifying. "I've allowed several hits because Willow's your family, but do not forget who I am to you, Robin." Pure menace radiates from a usually cheerful Auggie, causing a shiver to run down my spine.

"What?" I ask when I finally resurface to reality. Feeling groggy, I sit up and notice how Auggie and my brother are locked in an intense staring contest. I don't know what internal struggle they have going on, but that stimuli comment finally clicks.

"You're not going to have sex with me?" I yelp in disbelief, so many emotions warring. "That's total bull-fucking-shit." Angry disappointment spews from my lips in the form of a string of profanity that would make a sailor proud. Auggie laughs at the mystified expression on Robbie's face from my bad language.

"Monster, as I told you last night, I'll be your first everything." Auggie tries to pacify me, but fails miserably. "I'll try not to hurt you, but we may have to have someone else be with you a few times until your body's comfortable."

"Different stimuli means somebody else, doesn't it?" I accuse, jumping off the counter in a huff. "What the actual fuck, Auggie? You want me to sleep with someone else? You're just going to pass me off to some buddy! What the fuck was that lecture about Kieren when this is... far worse," I bite out.

My heart beats double-time, waiting for Auggie's answer. Why would he want to share me? Then I remember what Auggie said last night, how nothing will change between us.

Auggie's just getting his rocks off by breaking me in, then he's tossing me away.

I stare at the floor so I don't have to watch my brother witness my humiliation. I thought there was something between Auggie and me– not a relationship per se, but a friendship at least. I guess I thought wrong, since Auggie's acting like the men he was warning me about.

"Trust me and be a good girl." Auggie coaxes as his palm runs over my back, trying to comfort and soothe me. I flinch away, stepping out of his reach. "Remember, you said you'd always listen to Mr. Kline." Auggie throws my own words back at me, and I can't argue with him or myself.

"I'm uncomfortable with this," Robbie hisses. "We should've stuck with the plan, where Willow chose which one. Malcolm was furious last night– *at you.*"

"Fuck Malcolm and his *plan.*" Auggie seethes like he's plotting a violent murder– rage radiates off of him in waves. "We're going with the one Willow didn't choose, because last night turned out so well, didn't it?"

"Yeah, I saw Willow enjoying herself until your jealous influence ruined it. If you would've just let it happen organically, instead of playing junkyard dog when they tried to visit her, none of this would be happening. But you had to be a selfish fuck." Turning to me, my brother tries to pacify me. "No matter what Auggie said, Kieren really did want to ask you out."

"Malcolm's plan was the broken leading the blind, and you know it would've been a disaster and only benefitting of the Masons. Rob, when you were sixteen, you were calling me Mr. Kline and begging Isis to fuck you."

"This isn't about me!" Robbie bellows, but Auggie ignores him as usual.

"Willow's your family, but she isn't a baby any more than you were at her age. You were a little slut at eighteen. You can't honestly think an inept boy could satisfy her… and you know how you Prynnes are, like Velcro, sticking to your first fuck out of a misguided sense of romance and love. Willow didn't need to hitch herself to that prick at the tender age of eighteen, not with how Masons breed like locusts."

"Yeah, so Willow can hitch herself to you instead, motherfucker," Robbie snarls. "You're channeling Malcolm's daddy something fierce lately. Man up and take your woman back instead of trying to shape an impressionable girl into the female image of *me*."

"Shut the fuck up, Robin," Auggie snarls, then restrains himself. "This is happening, so deal. If it bothers you so much, don't watch, or you can hold Willow's hand and tell her what to expect. You've been there before."

"Ugg, this is bad– just don't let Isis touch Willow. I want to vomit thinking of you and Willow, but Isis... Willow won't ever be ready for Isis. I'm not ready for Isis, and I've been obeying her for over two decades." Robbie grabs my coat from beneath the counter and hands it to me– time to go, I guess. I'm more than ready to leave this confusing conversation behind.

"It's been decided, and you already got your way. You were against Ren, too. You got your pick of stimuli, remember?" Auggie raises a brow, waiting for my brother to argue. "I have a few things we need to figure out tonight, so don't interfere," Auggie warns. "Are you here to take Willow home?"

"Yeah, Clover bitched me out this afternoon for over an hour. They're holding dinner on us even though tomorrow is Sunday dinner. You know how Clover is..." Robbie trails off.

I bet Clover yelled at Robbie for missing my birthday. If I didn't know how alluring the Playroom was, I'd be extremely pissed at Robbie too. After their bizarre conversation, I don't know when my brain will go back online where I can think clear thoughts again.

"I'll pick you guys up at nine, and then we'll go to the Playroom together. You'll both need to have three drinks in ya before I get there." Auggie's order turns ominous. "You'll need it– no pot."

CHAPTER TWELVE

Leaning into me as we sit next to each other at the dining room table, my nephew stares at the side of my face, inspecting me. "You look different." Seth whispers conspiratorially in my ear. Robbie, overhearing our exchange, laughs, and it startles our family.

I shrug as multiple sets of eyes stare at me in alarm. I look down at myself to make sure I'm fully clothed, then I run a hand across my face to make sure I don't have food dribbling down my chin.

"What?" I grumble. I just stop myself before I ask, *can you tell I've been messing around with two guys in the past twenty-four hours? One was my crush who tried to date-rape me, and the other is a decade older and changed my diapers when I was a baby. Both are up to something nefarious, but fuck if I can figure out what.*

Does sexual activity have a look or a scent? Because I swear my family notices the difference I didn't see when I looked in the mirror a half hour ago.

… Or maybe they spot my guilt and confusion.

Our family, formed entirely of Prynnes and Websters, surrounds the oblong dining table at my parents' home. Robbie acts like this is Sunday dinner, but he's the only one in attendance who isn't usually at our nightly meal. Every night at seven on the dot, we promptly eat a meal together: my parents, me, Clover, and the twins. Sometimes we even eat breakfast together, too.

Sunday dinner adds Robbie, Aunt Ana, Uncle Will, and Essie to our table, and sometimes Grandma Margaret. Mom welcomes any guests you can bring. She thinks it's a great way to be a matchmaker for her children. I don't ever want to relive those horrendous occasions where Mom drags home young men from church like cattle on an auction block. Clover has been exempt from the blind dates, claiming she's still in mourning, much to Mom's disappointment. But Essie, Robbie, and I are fair game for Mom's weekly matchmaking sessions.

Grandma Margaret lives across the street. Uncle Will and Aunt Ana live a few streets behind us in a nicer part of Fairport, where it takes two minutes on foot by cutting through backyards, versus a ten minute drive. Clover and the twins live right next door, only sleeping there because they're always over here.

Countless times I've ran over to Clover's house to have some privacy while everyone else was here. Our house is a big house, but not *that* big. When everyone is crammed in here, the walls begin to close in around me, and I begin to feel like a caged animal at the zoo. I always end up feeling trapped, antsy– ready to run as fast as I can.

When I was growing up, Sam and I used to sneak off to his and Clover's house. I was Sam's partner in crime because Seth was too little to do much more than drool and babble. We'd eat junk food and secretly watch the horror flicks Clover forbid. I miss my Sam time. My brother-in-law left a gaping hole in my soul, one I know will never be filled.

"How's school?" I ask Violet, voice genuinely polite. I flash my freshly painted nails at her, trying to be nice by using the gift she bought me. I already have plans for the ridiculous dress Clover gave me.

Head jerking backward, Violet acts like I grew a second head for talking to her. "I'm top of my class, and I was invited to join the Winter Court for the Junior High dance," Violet smugly baits me, as per usual.

I went to a few dances– Essie's dances. I never went to any of my own. Essie was three grades ahead of me, and I spent most of my time watching her make-out while I got shitfaced during drinking games. My social life died a quick, painful death when Essie graduated. After she fled for college, I spent my time taking walks with Seth and burning all my brain cells away in the hope I could forget how badly I missed Sam.

"I'm sure you'll be crowned Princess," I mutter sweetly, and I even mean it. Orgasms are terrific stress-relievers. Silence meets my comment and my honeyed smile. Everyone stares at me in confusion– that second head appearing again, and then a third head bores its way out of my chest like on *Aliens*.

I snort at the ridiculousness, and it sounds so much like Auggie that I laugh, highly entertained.

"What?" I mumble again, looking around the table at my family members.

I know what.

Since Violet could talk, it was cat versus... well... cat. Claws, fangs, and a whole helluva lot of hissing fits. When Violet was four, she was the same size as me at nine. When Violet was nine, she was bigger than me at fourteen. If I wanted to fight, I'd call her Violent Violet. If Violet wanted to fight, all she had to do was call me Seth. We both have permanent battle scars that we wear with pride. Violet broke my pinky by yanking it backward while we fought over a Barbie– it was her Barbie, and I was chopping its hair off with pruning snips. Violet tried to take the Tonka truck I gave to Seth– I broke Violet's thumb with the toy's dump box.

Me being nice to Violet is an anomaly.

"I'm an adult now," is my explanation. "I won't lower myself by fighting with a child," I murmur smugly, doing my best to look haughty– if one can look haughty while wearing faded jeans and an oversized hoodie, all the while putting off some kind of scent that screams guilt and shame for entering the Playroom.

I giggle underneath my breath at the rabid expression crossing Violet's face when the dig finally hits her. Violent Violet wants to erupt, and she's fighting its call.

"Willow," Clover chastises. It makes me laugh because she has nothing on Auggie when it comes to making me behave.

"Oh, fuck. I'm coming home more often now." Robbie snickers. "Zombiefied Willow was a blast, but this new version has teeth."

"Robbie, ya better hope I don't bite you next." I taunt, and he chuckles in response.

"Bitch," he mouths at me.

"Language," Clover hisses, fork clattering on the edge of her plate.

My parents are seventy and completely addled by a life of weed and delusions of grandeur. They sit with pleasant, oblivious expressions on their faces. Passive eyes watch us as they lift forkfuls of food to their lips. I love my clueless parents, but on more than one occasion I've dreamed of having actual parents. I could fuck on the table while eating a drumstick, and Mary Prynne would ask if I wanted seconds, while Dave Prynne would offer instructions on my fuckage.

Clover would have a stroke.

I have no clue how Clover was born into this family.

"Language?" Robbie mutters incredulously. "You're going to bitch at me, your brother? I'm almost thirty years old, sis. You should carry around some soap for your kids' filthy mouths and forget about what mine's spewing. Violet called me a dick when I got home, and I'm pretty sure she knows what you do with one, *Mom*," Robbie mocks Clover.

"Fuck it," Clover curses, causing my mother to laugh at her daughter's hypocrisy.

My sister offers us all a death glare as she smashes her linen napkin on top of her plate. "You guys are horrible. I don't know why I try to keep you all from turning into savages. It amazes me that the girls haven't killed each other yet. Rob, you'd probably sell tickets to the show. Animals," growls from my sister's pursed lips.

"You need to get laid– good and proper," is my solution to the stick shoved firmly up my sister's ass.

"Willow's right," Mom offers her two cents, and the table goes insane. "I'll bring home a nice boy from church this Sunday. It's high time you began dating again. The new pastor is single. Perhaps he would meet your stringent standards."

Milk sprays out of Seth's nose, and I thump him on the back as he chokes. Clover stands, picks her plate up, and then smashes it on the table, splattering mashed potatoes everywhere.

Our mother consoles Clover with words that bring flames to her pale cheeks and smoke to our ears. Dad and Robbie are laughing so hard tears are sliding down their faces and they're grabbing their bellies.

Blaming me for the shenanigans, Violet's fury erupts, and she screams vile insults at me: *cunt... little boy... skank... whore... Tranny...*

"See–" Robbie gasps out, leaving Dad to finish the sentence. "No need to worry about Violet hearing swear words, Clover. Violet knows a bunch that I didn't even know existed. What's a hermaphrodite? Is it some kind of rock formation?"

Clover glares at each and every one of us in turn, hands forming fists at her sides until her knuckles turn white.

Now I feel bad for saying what I did. Even when Sam was alive, Clover had a stick firmly planted up her ass. Now that Sam's gone, that stick is shoved so far up there, there's no hope of ever retrieving it.

"I think my work here is done." I grab my plate and make a run for the kitchen before Clover beats the shit out of me– she will if she catches me.

Violent Violet inherited her rage from her mother, and Clover makes Violet look like an amateur. Clover blackened my eye after I took Seth to an amusement park. Sure, I didn't ask first, and I called after we already got there, that way it was too late for her to say no. When we got home, I was two steps from the car door when Clover knocked my ass out cold. I also didn't have a driver's license yet, but Mom said it was okay to borrow the car.

I was only fourteen.

Clover rationalizes that since she's my sister, hitting me isn't really child abuse. She's only my sister when I'm in trouble. Every other time, Clover tells everyone she's my parent. In Clover's defense, I usually deserve the ass kicking. When I don't, it usually makes up for all those times I didn't get caught red-handed.

Running for my life, with Clover at my heels, I clumsily take the stairs two at a time, losing my sister to her exhausting fury.

Breathlessly gasping, I stumble into my bedroom while holding the stitch in my side. I try to shut the door but an arm reaches in and grabs my ponytail, making me release a blood-curdling screech.

"Dumbass, it's me, not the blonde mother lioness pacing the kitchen." Robbie chuckles as I let him into my bedroom. "Nervous?" He asks me as he firmly shuts my door, and then leans on it, crossing his arms over his chest, just to make sure Clover doesn't barge in.

"Nah– I'm not nervous. More like scared shitless." I pant, tugging on my earlobe to cease the ringing from the noise I released. "You?"

"Nauseous." Robbie rubs his flat tummy and smirks. "Mom cooked tonight, that has to be why. Too bad Clover didn't– I may have behaved for her food." He flashes a charming smirk, one that if deployed on anyone else would've been a panty-dropper.

"I wouldn't have. I've eaten their food for eighteen years. I can't boil water because they wouldn't let me try. Blame them if I ever have to cook you a meal," I warn, refusing to admit that I wished I knew how to cook more than a PB&J.

I self-consciously look around my room, trying to figure out how I can hide all my dirty laundry without Robbie noticing. It's like my dresser drawers and closet puked their contents into the middle of my bedroom floor. I quickly punt the dirty plate beneath my bed with my heel. Cake or pizza? It's too moldy to tell.

I have Clover's old bedroom, princess pink with furniture fit for a tween: a twin-sized four-poster bed that used to have a canopy until I tore it down, a vanity with stool, and a matching dresser. The bedding is the same bedding Clover used, pink gingham edged in eyelet lace. I made my room my own by covering up the pink-posied walls with posters featuring comic book characters and indie rock bands… and by leaving my dirty underwear and moldy snacks all over the floor.

I'm slovenly.

If Mom drags a Pastor-in-training home from church for her matchmaking shenanigans, I'm going straight to Hell. I break two or three commandments a day– at least. We all do except for Clover. Maybe that would be a match made in Heaven.

For a nanosecond, I feel shame over how I treat my environment– my room has never felt like mine –until I notice that Robbie doesn't give a shit. I'm his sister. He's lived with me, so he knows damn well I'm a slob. I shrug like I'm a bad-assed mofo who just doesn't care. Robbie laughs at me as he pulls my blankets flat, and then sits down on my bed.

"Well." Robbie sighs, getting comfortable. "Auggie and I will be impressed if you don't give us food poisoning." Robbie winks to lessen the dig. "On second thought, I'll cook for you instead. I make a mean pot roast. Clover used to let me cook with her before you came along."

"Not my fault, dumbass," I mutter affectionately. Leaning down, I hug Robbie because I have to, because he understands and gets me, and doesn't fucking judge. I burrow against his chest, curling my fingers in his t-shirt. Robbie isn't a big guy, so he doesn't intimidate me. He's just my Robbie.

"I… are you alright with me being there tonight? I won't stay away for you, but I'll try to understand your point of view."

"I don't want to see you that way, Willow." Robbie pulls away so he can look me in the eyes. "But no one on this planet understands why you need to be there as much as I do. It's weird thinking of the needs you have now, when all I see is a little shit running around causing havoc. Over that visage is the delirious look on your face at the Playroom, then the one you wore with Auggie tonight. It's discombobulating, but I'll deal, because I get why you need this."

Robbie pulls me closer and sighs. "I'm sorry I wasn't here for your birthday. I wanted to be, but I didn't want to admit what I've known all along. Since you've been working with him, Auggie's been telling me for months, and I just couldn't face it. You're a grown woman with grown woman thoughts, wants, and needs. You're no longer that pigtailed little girl who worshipped me."

"I'm sorry." I hide my face in shame, sniffling against Robbie's shirt. "But I feel like all I do is apologize lately."

"Don't be sorry, Willow, especially over last night. I can tell you were properly punished for your part in what happened with Ren. It's finished and never to be revisited. That's why we are wired the way we are. We can't handle guilt, so we need someone to absolve our conscience."

"That's for damned sure."

"C'mon, we gotta get downstairs before Auggie gets here. He'll kick our asses if we're late, trust me on that."

"Oh, I believe you– there's a bit of a sadistic streak in him." Even though I sound scared, a dreamy quality infuses my tone too. At the same time, my palm-marked ass elicits a burning flare over the prospect of being spanked again, and I don't know whether it's anticipation or trepidation.

"I'm still nauseous." Robbie pulls me away, closely watching my facial expressions. "Are you still freaking out?"

"Yup!" I chirp.

"Well, it's a good thing fear and illness turns us on then, or tonight would suck," Robbie mumbles sarcastically as I stand from the bed.

Ignoring the uncomfortable truth in my brother's words, I start poking around in my closet, noticing that it's nearly empty. Time to do laundry, I guess. "What do I wear?" I ask from the depths of my closet.

"What you always do," sounds muffled to my ears as I crawl around my closet floor, looking for something to wear. I wince when an earring pierces my shin. Staring down at the impaler, I smile. So that's where that went– I'd been missing my guitar-shaped dangling earring for nearly a year. I really have to clean in here someday.

"Auggie won't want you too dressed up. Just be yourself, Willow. No dressing like an amateur pole polisher. I hated seeing you looking like Essie last night."

"Ah-ha!" Triumph rings in my voice as I gather up my clothes and exit my closet. Robbie gives me an amused grin, lips splitting from ear to ear.

"I see rainbows, that cannot be a good sign," Robbie grumbles to himself, sounding a whole helluva lot sarcastic.

"Rainbows are a sign of good luck, I'll have you know." Smirking, I can't help but bounce on my heels.

"And under whose authority did you learn this tidbit?" Robbie arches a brow, somehow baiting me, but for the life of me I can't figure out how.

"I don't know," I say with a shrug. "I heard it somewhere."

"Word to the wise," Robbie drawls. "Unless it flows from Auggie's mouth, it's not true– at least not when you go to the Playroom. So rainbows will not bring you good luck this evening, little girl. They may get your assed tanned ten shades of Hades, though."

"Perhaps that's what I want."

"Oh, Lord," Robbie groans, covering his face with his palms. "Save me from curious little sisters and demanding best friends."

"Wait here. I need to take a quick shower and change. The hooch is behind the Iliad on the bookshelf. Don't start without me," I tease as I breeze out of my bedroom.

~~~

"You're a freak," I mutter to Robbie when I return. He's actually reading the Iliad. I can tell by the expression of concentration on his face: eyebrows knitted tightly together, lips pursed. Lounging on my bed with his ankles crossed, Robbie looks like he could wait forever in this position.

I can't make it a paragraph into the first page of the Iliad without conking out– show off!

Looking thoroughly put out that I interrupted his 'light' reading, my brother rolls his eyes up to meet mine. Narrowed brown eyes slowly enlarge until they nearly pop from his skull. Startled, the large tome slaps shut in his hands.

"Holy shit!" Robbie shouts when my clothing choice finally computes. He sits up and gawks at me. "Are you trying to kill Auggie?"

"Too much?" I ask innocently, posing.

Standing in front of my floor-length mirror, I gaze at myself. The pigtails are back, but I braided them at the nape instead of creating two buns on top. My favorite skin-tight jeans hide the pink panties with lace ruffles adorning the ass. My ribbed tank is light pink with rainbows printed all over it. I pull on my Chuck's over top of white socks that have lace trim. Even I'll admit that I'm pushing the toddler envelope with the socks.

"What's wrong?" I ask with false innocence while batting my puppy dog eyes. Essie said to never lose the innocence, even after I was experienced. I'm still innocent, but I'm proving I can act.

"You know damn well what's wrong." Robbie pulls the *99 Blackberries* from the shelf, then guzzles a mouthful. "Jesus, you really want this, don't you?" Robbie wipes his mouth with the back of his hand.

"And you don't?" I smirk at how uncomfortable I'm making my brother. He looks like he wants to jump out of his skin. Mutual genetics aside, I know I'm not his type at all. I have a feeling Robbie likes his women curvy and dominant.

"Fuck... Cheers to *like brother, like sister!*" Robbie takes another slug. "Good shit," he rasps roughly in appreciation as he stares at the purple-labeled bottle in his hand.

"Watch out. It really is ninety-nine proof." I offer as a warning as I snatch the liquor from Robbie like it's a prize. I guzzle three mouthfuls without coming up for air– a good two or three shots' worth. I no longer feel the burn as it slides down my throat to pool in my stomach. A second later, warmth radiates up and out, and I sigh in deep pleasure. Placing the bottle on the shelf with the Iliad as camouflage, I hide the liquor behind the snoozefest read.

Robbie gives me a strange look– that *do I know you? What have you done with Willow?* look.

I narrow my eyes as I say, "I've been drinking since I was younger than the twins. I don't do it often, so don't get alcoholic intervention disillusions in your head. When you look twelve and hang out with people way older than you, your options are limited. I was coveted as a teammate on drinking game teams while Essie's knees got carpet burn." I try to mask the pain in my voice, but some leaks through anyway. Thankfully, in a few minutes, I won't be feeling anything except the effects of the *99 Blackberries*.

My body glows as the alcohol flows through my veins. All right, I'll admit, I love that euphoric feeling. It's almost as good as taking a toke from a bowl– almost, but not quite –a close second.

"Okey dokey, smokey, let's go find me some freaks with jailbait fantasies." I flick my pigtails and try to look innocent, causing my brother to bust out laughing.

"Auggie is going to kill you," Robbie issues as a warning.

Ignoring him, I ask, "What's your appeal for Isis? I'm not saying you're not um… hot… if you weren't my brother. But what's her deal?"

Our eyes meet and flash away. I blush from discomfort, not embarrassment– that's a first. "I hope you never find out," Robbie mutters ominously.

We jog down the steps, only to find Clover chatting up Auggie at the front door. I don't like that calculated look in my sister's eye. I said get laid, not lay with my boss.

Auggie takes one look at me and backs up a step, ass meeting the front door. He appears frightened of me, like I'm the Antichrist. His throat contracts as he takes a hard swallow– my eyes seek the vein in his neck that is visibly pounding. I can almost hear his erratic heartbeat across the room.

Clover scowls at Auggie, then flashes me a look of confusion. Blushing so fiercely my skin prickles, I stare at my feet so Clover can't get a read on me. A throat clearing has my eyes flashing back up to meet Auggie's intense green gaze.

"Yeah," Robbie whispers in my ear. "Look farther south and you'll know why Auggie's face is drained of blood. You're pushing his control with the rainbows and pigtails, Willow."

Suddenly playful, but I can see through his act, Robbie pushes me down the last few steps, causing me to almost fall on my ass. Catching myself with a palm to the floor, Robbie's maniacal laughter flows down the steps and coils around me. Instead of getting mad that my brother is trying to embarrass me, I take it for how it was meant, teasing your little sister. I know Robbie is as uncomfortable as I am. Giggling with him, I stand upright, brushing imaginary dirt from my ass.

"Willow, get a grip." Clover bitches, looking equally embarrassed *for* me and *of* me, but disappointed mostly. "I don't know what's gotten into these two. They've been conspiring ever since they got home."

If Clover thinks Auggie will help rein us in, she's lost her ever-lovin' mind. He's our instigator.

"Auggie's gotten into us," flows as a naughty suggestion in my husky voice.

A slow smirk slides across Auggie's lips, signaling that I'm in for a world of hurt. A smile that is as anticipatory as it is predatory. A shiver rides my spine.

"Where are you off to so late?" Clover demands, eyes latching onto me instead of Auggie or Robbie. Clover has always treated Robbie like a brother. She still tells him what to do, but not like she orders me around. Hell, she's bossier to me than to the twins.

Unsure, Clover tucks a few loose strands of hair behind her ear, and I really look at my sister for the first time with clear, adult eyes. Clover would be really pretty if that bitch expression wasn't constantly pasted on her heart-shaped face. Clover and I do look just like mother and daughter: we're both short, with thick, straight hair, but Clover's eyes are blue to my brown and her hair is blonde instead of chestnut. Clover looks a lot younger than she is, maybe late twenties instead of mid-thirties. I can't imagine how pretty and young she would look if she wasn't stressed out and ornery– always angry and miserable.

I'm positive I'm the root of Clover's problems– there's that motherfucking guilt creeping in again.

I wonder what Clover looked like at my age. There are no pictures of her from the time she was sixteen until her wedding photos with Sam. Tenacious me, I've searched for years' worth of absent images. If Clover was small like me, then I'd hold out hope of looking like a woman one day. Clover and I have the same ass, but she also has titties like Essie. I'd be jealous of Clover if she wasn't my sister, and if she wasn't such a miserable bitch.

Attitude fortified by ninety-nine proof alcohol, I state, "Adult." I point at Robbie. "Adult." I point at myself. "Our sister." I point at Clover. "Goodnight. I have no clue when I'll be home, or *if* I'll be home." I'm a disrespectful shit, and Clover looks disappointed in me.

I regret being a bitch for the time it takes my heart to beat two or three times, and then the alcohol shuts the guilt down. But nothing stops me from feeling bad that Auggie sees me behaving like a spoiled toddler. There is too much history between Clover and me, and the mean words flow without thought.

Hell, I truly feel bad that I'm disappointing Clover again–maybe I *am* growing up.

Auggie picks up my puffy coat and holds it out for me as a signal to get my ass moving. I slowly walk toward him, half afraid and half exhilarated by the insane light glowing from his eyes. Shoving my arms into the sleeves, I pull my jacket on and start buttoning it.

Out of nowhere, huge hands grip my ass and squeeze, causing a gasp to wheeze from my throat. Bewildered, I watch Auggie stare Clover down as he releases a possessive warning growl.

A part of me is pleased that Auggie is taking ownership over me, but a very small part of me screeches from my depths, feeling disrespected and used. That tiny seed causes any pleasure I feel to shrivel up and die.

The look that flashes across my sister's face is murderous. I have no idea whether or not Clover is jealous because Auggie is touching me instead of her, but it's more like she wants to incinerate any body part of his that touches mine. They share a look that I can't comprehend, and I wonder if they've shared a history of violence, because right now, Clover is positively lethal.

"No telling Willow what to do anymore, Clover. If you have an issue, take it up with me. The same goes for your issues with Rob. Tell Dave and Mary that the three of us will be back tomorrow for Sunday dinner."

Auggie lets go of my ass and sets me near the door. It wasn't a sexual touch. He was placing his ownership on me in front of the one who by all rights already owns me.

"Both of you get in the truck. I said three drinks, meaning sips. Not get drunk." Auggie is thoroughly disgusted with us, and right now, I can't call this man Auggie. The furious, possessive, in control man can only be called Augustus or Mr. Kline. The guy I know of as Auggie disappeared when he began mentally sparring with my sister.

Ill at ease, unsure as to whether I'm flattered or pissed, I let the alcohol deaden my worry. I leave my home with Robbie at my side.

"We're so in trouble," I sing as I skip down the sidewalk.

"Yup, pain's a'coming," Robbie slurs, alcohol hitting him harder than me. "It's a good thing I'm a pain slut."

"Don't worry, Clover. When we return, you will find two very apologetic siblings at the Sunday table." Auggie's pissed off voice follows us to the truck. "I apologize for their disrespect. Don't push them anymore, and they will be respectful and polite. I can promise it." Auggie's threat lashes out and smacks us both on the ass.

"Well, do you get into trouble on purpose?" I ask my pain slut brother. I've thought of nothing else but being bad and getting spanked since last night.

"Sometimes," Robbie mumbles bashfully, looking sheepish and embarrassed. "If I do it too often, they deny me. Isis will humiliate me instead, and I hate that. Never let Auggie know what you hate, because he'll use that as punishment. He's not as scary as Isis, though."

"Good to know, brother." Tone eager, "Keep that advice coming."

Crawling into Auggie's truck, I settle into the middle of the bench seat with Robbie riding shotgun. The driver door being wrenched open has us both cowering in our seats. I sit like a good girl with my hands folded in my lap, waiting for Auggie to start the truck. He stares at us for what feels like an eternity. I don't have the nerve to look back at him. Finally after ten minutes, I look at Robbie in my peripheral and realize he's staring intently and dutifully at Auggie.

"Sir?" I say, chancing a glance. As if waiting for my undivided attention, Auggie yanks me into his lap and rips my coat open. Green eyes glowing in the dim of the truck cab, he stares salaciously down at the rainbows on my shirt. My nipples bead beneath his gaze as my breasts swell. Breathing heavily, my chest rapidly rises and falls like a lusty offering.

With a tug to my braids, my eyes connect with his. "Say it again," Auggie roughly demands in a gruff voice, sounding raw and raspy.

"Sir?" I meep out, somehow forgetting what the word does to the man.

"Monster is going to get punished something fierce tonight. I have to fuck something, and you better not freak when I do."

"Oh," tastes like bitter ash on my tongue.

"Willow, I simultaneously love and hate how you look like a little girl tonight. I've never been so horny in all of my life. I may fuck ten people tonight. You gonna be okay with that?" Auggie asks in challenge.

Trick question, that. Plus, I realize Auggie's manipulative powers have extended to causing me to think him fucking other people is my fault based on how I'm dressed. I haven't forgotten last night's conversation, so I know it didn't matter what I wore, because Auggie was going to get laid by someone other than me tonight anyway.

I lean against the steering wheel, breathlessly panting as my mind spins like a renegade hamster is in control. Images of Isis kissing Auggie, followed by Nina worshiping Beast, provide my answer.

I may be Auggie's, but he sure as shit will never be mine. I have to accept the fact that I get my rocks off by looking at him, touching him, and I'm not the only one who has that honor.

Mature Willow has to remember the advice Essie gave me last night when I said I'd never touch her sloppy seconds, mixed with Auggie accusing the Prynnes of being Velcro. I'm not going to fall in love with a fellow virgin, get married, and have a bunch of kids– ain't gonna happen. No way, no how. I need to grow up and realize everybody has touched someone else at some point, and it's childish to pout about it.

If I tell Auggie I'm uncomfortable with it, all he'll do is toss my ass out of this truck, and back to Clover I'll go. No more Playroom. No more Auggie in any capacity aside from being my boss. Beast belongs to Auggie, and I have no say in who he touches with it. But, if I'm smart and act mature, I can negotiate for my comfort and sanity's sake.

"I'm– yeah, I'm really good with that. Just please don't touch my family members, and you can fuck fifty people for all I care," I numbly negotiate. "Family will always be off limits with me. Auggie, don't shit where I eat," I warn.

I feel conflicted because I don't feel conflicted. Shouldn't I feel jealous or pissed off that my guy wants to do other people? Does that mean I don't care for Auggie? I'd love to think I'm so enlightened that I don't believe emotion and sex are linked, but I'm not. I'm an eighteen-year-old idiot, and I have no idea what the hell I feel.

Torn.

Torn is what I feel.

And slightly drunk– high on Auggie's power.

I'm also horny.

Drunk, high, and horny, that's probably why I don't give a shit about anything.

…and then I realize the problem: Auggie isn't *my* guy.

I remember Auggie's earlier comment about stimuli. He obviously doesn't want to be exclusive, so I'll make the best of it while I can. I have a feeling if I threw a fit, Auggie would drop me in a heartbeat. It hurts like a sonofabitch, but I'll see how I react when he touches someone else.

Curiosity eggs me on to touch someone else and seek out Auggie's expression while I do it.

I want to play with fire to the point where I don't care if I get burned.

My buzz is wicked, and I don't mean the alcohol. The kiss Auggie shared with Isis and that epic blowjob keep playing on repeat in my imagination. I'm not too proud to admit that I used both of those images when I got myself off in the shower just a half hour ago.

Staring at me, no doubt watching the emotions play out across my features, Auggie agrees to my terms. "Deal, but Rob's grandfathered in already." Auggie negotiates, no arrogance or cockiness to be heard. This is serious business to him— negotiating terms of play. "The only people of Prynne blood I will ever touch are you and Rob."

"What?" I ask, feeling foggy. "You've *touched* Robbie. I thought he belonged to Isis."

"What Auggie means is that it's too late between him and me," Rob reluctantly admits. A metallic sound startles me, and I look over to see my brother unsnapping the leather collar from around his neck. Robbie tosses it to me, but Auggie's the one who catches it.

Big hands stretch out the leather band and present the inside: **Mr. Kline's Good Boy** is branded into the leather. A fuzzy auburn brow arches at me, menacingly casting a shadow over his green peeper. My mouth forms a silent O as I realize what Auggie is to my brother, and a bunch of cryptic shit begins to make sense.

"I'm Robin's master." Auggie finally admits the truth. "Not playing around like we're doing, Robin is *mine*. Always and forever. I allow Isis to fuck him and play with him and beat him and love him. But never forget, Robin belongs solely to me," Auggie warns, sounding scary, obviously not happy that he has to share his toys with Isis. But Auggie loves his toy enough to make sure Robbie gets what he desires– Isis.

I have a feeling Isis is nonnegotiable. No matter how deeply Auggie brands Rob as his, Isis has to be included.

Reading me thoughts again, my boss is no longer the man I know– I don't know who the hell this man is, but Robbie surely does. Auggie's body tightly coils beneath mine, thighs strung as hard as steel. This persona is someone else entirely, someone I don't like. He's possessive and lethal. Quite frankly, he terrifies me.

I may shiver in fright, but my brother shivers for an entirely different reason I don't want to examine too closely.

"Rob found it humiliating to have my tag visible since he isn't gay. But the reason you started calling me Mr. Kline is because Rob was at a stage right then where he wanted to call me that. You were picking that shit up when you were a kid, and didn't even realize it." Amused, pride resonates in his voice.

Auggie leans over to snap the leather strap around Robbie's neck. He whispers, "Good boy," underneath his breath, then gently pats Robbie's hair. The beatific expression on Robbie's face that those two words elicit leaves me speechless– he's basking in the glow of Auggie's praise.

I begin to wonder if that's the same idiotic look Robbie keeps saying he didn't like seeing on my face. It's a look that has no name– a look filled with adoration, pride, trust, and lust.

It creeps me out, but there is a symmetry in seeing it shine from Robbie's eyes as he looks at Auggie after their shared history. Now I respectfully understand why Robbie hates that expression on my face.

Is my brother jealous of my attachment to Auggie?

I slide from Auggie's lap to sit between the guys while my mind spins in a billion different directions. "Fucked up," I whisper as Auggie pulls away from the curb.

"Like brother, like sister," Robbie gravely whispers back, not sounding happy about it in the least.

–*trying to shape an impressionable girl into the female image of me.* Words Robbie said earlier today repeat in a loop in my mind, followed by Auggie saying Rob was too embarrassed to wear a tag with Auggie's name on it because he isn't gay.

Am I a socially acceptable version of the one Auggie truly wants? Seth may be my doppelganger, but does Auggie see me as Robin's? If he can't have Robbie in every capacity, then he'll take the closest thing.

CHAPTER THIRTEEN

The cinderblock wall is cold at our backs, while the air around us is heated with lust. Rob and I sit like two bad toys put high upon a shelf, away from playful hands. All of our attention is focused on Isis and Auggie as they stand in the center of the Playroom, no doubt talking about Rob and me. I hope they are, at least. I'm not arrogant enough to think they haven't forgotten me, but they surely can't forget their little Robin. Sitting on the floor with our backs to the wall, my brother and I pretend we aren't being punished for a reason I've yet to learn.

We dutifully followed Auggie and Isis through Rush, not saying a word and getting glared at when we tried to stray off course– the bar and dance floor were calling me, and I could tell the thrumping music was having a similar effect on Robbie too. Bouncer Rory followed us the whole way, making sure Robbie and I didn't break free from the herd, effectively cutting off any and all escape. Winding down the labyrinth of hallways, Auggie and Isis led us into Rush's backroom, otherwise known as the Playroom. We were greeted by a dozen deviant revelers involved in sexual acts and simple conversations. Several people tried to engage us, only to be deterred by Auggie's audible growl.

Eager to join the fray, my hopes deflated when Auggie simply pointed to the spot we currently occupy. Slumping to the floor, Robbie instinctively knew to sit and stay like a good pet, earning a passionate, tongue-filled kiss from Isis and a pat to the hair from Auggie. I quickly followed suit, pouting when I was left out of all the fun because I didn't get an encouraging touch for my begrudging efforts.

I came to the *Play*room to play, not sit on my ass and chat with my big bro. I can do that at home, minus the live porn being acted out by Fairport's hedonistic denizens.

I know better than to make eye contact, because I'm not sure if I want to see our firefighters, police officers, and even the waitress at the No-Name in the throes of passion. My eyes are glued on Auggie and Isis so I can't discern who makes use of the Playroom. Knowing for sure would make walking down the sidewalk a new experience– an embarrassing experience. I shouldn't know what the Post Master sounds like then he comes– my sixty-year-old Post Master. But I give the man mad props for only playing with his wife. Mailman Pete is a faithful man, and his wife is a screamer.

Better yet, I don't want Pete and Rhonda, or grubby Jim from the gas station, or Mrs. Cleary– my seventh grade math and science teacher –knowing what I look like naked or sound like when I orgasm.

Shit!

I'm not sure I'm cut out to be a pet. I don't have an obedient cell in my body. Everything in me craves the freedom to run around and play, to explore, not be tied to my coop like a forgotten bitch.

I thirst to gaze around the Playroom and drink in every detail, to digest the sights and sounds of sex and play. But, as usual, Auggie holds all of my attention– everything else fades, becoming muted background noise.

Bored out of my skull, I try for small talk, safe topics that won't make my brother or me blush. I lean in and whisper to Robbie. "I'm *Good Girl* when I'm rewarded and *Monster* when I'm punished. What are you?"

Robbie's eyes are magnetized to Auggie too– he's hypnotized by the beast of a man, more so than I am. Rob doesn't even glance in my direction as I speak to him. I stare at the side of my brother's flushed face– pink high in his cheeks, a sheen of sweat glossing his forehead, mouth parted in a pant with beaded perspiration above his upper lip, brown eyes glittering and glassy. Rob looks as if nothing could stand in his way of being in the Playroom, and I forgive him on the spot for missing my birthday dinner.

Robin David Prynne is an addict– addicted to the Playroom, or Auggie, or Isis, or a combination of all three.

Moments trickle by where all sounds amplify: deep, pain-filled grunts, heady moans, and reverent prayer to a god who wouldn't condone the actions being played out before us.

I'm being jaded by the heartbeat. I can feel my innocence flowing from me in a steady stream, and I glorify in it.

We await our fate, and I seriously mean WAIT. It's been at least an hour as time trickled to a crawl. Abandoning the scene that holds my brother's rapt attention– because it seems beyond creepy to be engrossed by the same thing as your big brother – with longing, I watch two girls in my periphery. Well, not girls. Women.

A young woman is releasing happy barking noises while an older woman is tugging her around on a leash. That leash is snapped onto a leather collar, a collar not unlike the one circling Robbie's throat. The girl crawls around on her hands and knees, playacting a puppy.

The curious puppy sniffed me about a half hour ago. I petted her head, and told her she was a good girl too. I was surprised when Auggie didn't snap out a denial when these two new friends tried to interact with me, like he had the previous times. I assumed the older woman was important somehow, because Auggie gave her a respectful nod and left us alone.

Finally getting some attention, I relaxed as the puppy's master tugged one of my pigtails, smiling down at me while silently laughing. The woman evidently likes tails... Robbie liked the long length of fuzzy brown tail *a lot*. He was fascinated by how it was attached to the girl via her backdoor. Rob played with the tail the entire time he chatted with the puppy's owner, much to the puppy's delight.

I think the tail would be on my list of humiliations, and I'm never telling Auggie about it. My ass will forever be an exit.

"I'm Good Boy and Menace," Robbie finally supplies, absolutely no shame ringing out from his voice.

"Ah– way to keep it original, Auggie," I mumble, voice laced with affectionate amusement. "I guess he can't forget and call us something else since those names are so freakin' similar. Good Girl. Good Boy. Monster. Menace."

A disbelieving giggle flows from my throat, catching Auggie's attention. Green eyes snap out to touch upon my face like a physical caress. Somehow Auggie heard my teasing words.

"Don't push him, Willow," Rob warns abruptly in a raw voice I've never heard from his lips before. Knowing his best friend better than I ever could, even if I spent the rest of my years studying the man, Robbie stiffens beside me, prepared to save me from his master's wrath.

Powerful green eyes never leaving my face, Auggie rips his jeans open at the fly in one forceful movement, unleashing the Beast in a silent threat that makes me quiver in fright-filled anticipation. Long, thick, and rich with blood, I can practically see the veins throbbing in Auggie's dick. He's painfully aroused.

Like a predator stalking a poor, defenseless bunny rabbit, Auggie's got his sights set on me.

"Jesus," Robbie hisses. "I never thought I'd be having this conversation with you, Willow. There's no stopping Auggie when he wants something, and he's overpowered every fight I've given over you for the past few months. He outwardly challenged Malcolm over the plan last night. Augustus Kline is nothing if not persistent. You need to trust me on this, you don't want Auggie using that thing on you until you're fully prepared. There's no way he's fitting inside you yet. Take that advice from someone who's learned that lesson the hard way."

I can't concentrate on anything but the sight before me. I gape, eyes bulging from my skull, as I finally see the Beast in its magnificent glory. Seeing it within pajama pants as Auggie stroked himself didn't prepare me for the sight. Touching it above the fabric didn't prepare me for the reality of the Beast. Cock jutting out from the center of his body, engorged with arousal, with his heavy sac dangling between his muscular thighs, Auggie is the epitome of virile.

I feel impregnated just staring at the Beast.

I watch in awe as Auggie strips bare-assed naked without a shred of indignity. He stands with his arms folded over his impressive chest as he chats with Isis. It's like Auggie is the master of this realm, surveying his kingdom— untouchable and totally in control of everything within his boundaries.

Musclebound lord of the land, standing next to his raven-haired beauty, Augustus Kline makes us all feel unworthy in their presence. Robbie stares down at himself with a grimace pulling his lips. While the dominating power couple looks perfect, my brother's and my self-esteem shrivels up and dies a painful death. I can see the self-deprecating thoughts flashing across Robbie's face, and they mirror mine.

We Prynnes are not beautiful or tall or muscular… we're tiny and cute, and we offer no competition, not even against ourselves.

We were made to be someone's pet, whether we like it or not.

Isis looks at Auggie in appreciation, eyes taking Auggie in from his toes to the curls on top of his head. An amused smile twists the corners of her lips, but otherwise she's unaffected. After a few seconds of perusal, Isis meets Auggie's eyes and continues on with their conversation as if she isn't standing next to a naked and painfully aroused man.

Clearly, this isn't an unusual occurrence for Isis.

However, I am *not* unaffected. I quickly glance at my brother– Robbie sure as shit isn't unaffected, either. His earlier blush is now a smoldering fire licking at his flesh. Leaning forward as far as he can get from the wall without his ass moving from the spot Auggie placed him, Robbie tries to get the best possible view– or maybe he's trying to get as close to his master as he possibly can get without breaking free from the punishment wall.

"I call it the Beast," I murmur conversationally to Robbie, trying to break free of our master's capture.

A furious blush burns my cheeks. Okay, not the best way to get my mind off of Auggie… talking about his mammoth cock… with my brother. The brother I thought was as straight as an arrow– the brother who is obviously lusting after the same bit of dangling flesh that I am.

Get a grip, Willow!

I can't be in a lust-filled infatuation triangle with my brother and his best friend. I'll lose both Auggie and Robbie if it came down to choosing. Or is it a square? Beastly best friend, best friend with talons, my brother, then there is me– a nobody. Rob is just as enticed by a fully clothed Isis as he is with a naked Auggie, so why am I in this equation at all?

Insecurities coil in my belly and grow, feeding on my budding happiness. Small. Boy-like. Nothing about me is remotely womanly. I'm just a loser living with my parents, with no hope of a productive future. If Auggie has his pick between Isis and Rob, why would he ever need me? I'm not good enough for him, and I sure as hell could never please him.

Heart breaking, tears stinging my eyes, I swallow down my fears, telling myself that Auggie put a collar on my neck and invited me to the Playroom so he must want me here. But it's hard to swallow how my brother is obviously in love with his best friends, and I'm just an interloper, staring at them from the outside.

I'm confused.

I'm a pervert.

I belong in the Playroom.

I'm mystified, Auggie stands naked in the middle of the Playroom and no one thinks it's weird. If I stood up and stripped down, people would probably cackle and make retching sounds. But if everyone looked like Auggie, I bet there would be no laws for public indecency. Six and a half feet of pure muscle... and the Beast is proportionate.

Not noticing my emotional upheaval, Robbie finally responds to me. "Fitting," Rob muses over the nickname I gave Auggie's cock. "Well, in your case... it won't *fit*." He trails a chuckle at my expense.

Ignoring the obvious dig about my failings, I ask something I wouldn't have otherwise. "How big is it? I have nothing to compare it to." Curiosity gets the better of me. I lick my suddenly dry lips because nothing will drag my eyes from the Beast as it twitches and jerks beneath my gaze.

"Eleven inches. Don't get any ideas– it's not normal," Robbie warns, sounding self-conscious. His brown eyes finally flick in my direction, flashing me an earnest look. A split-second later, Robbie's gaze is glued back on his best friends.

"I have no idea what's normal for a guy, but even I know nothing on Auggie will ever be normal."

"Normal is almost half of that... *thing*. Half the length and width. Don't forget that, Willow, or you'll be sorely disappointed in every guy you ever touch. It was one of the reasons I put up a fight for you against Auggie. If you experience the Beast before anyone else, Auggie will ruin you for other men. Either because it hurts so much you'll never want a repeat, or because you'll think every man is built like him. Auggie is the major leagues, and you aren't even in the minors. You're still in T-ball."

"Great, I couldn't even be in Little League– you put me with the toddlers." I just stop myself from asking if Robbie is jealous and warning me off, or if he's just warning me for my own good.

"You have to learn to hold the bat first," Robbie says with a snort.

"Sports metaphor– *nice*... Um... yeah..." I stammer, having no reply to that. "Do we just sit here and wait until we're summoned?"

"Yup, we were placed here and we will sit here until told otherwise." Robbie dutifully sits like a good pet– a good pet I'll never be.

"That's going to get old fast," I whine as I shuffle around until I'm sitting cross-legged. My ass is falling asleep from sitting on the cement floor. "You know I don't like to sit around and wait."

"Patience is a virtue," Robbie chirps, all proud of himself because he finally got to use the saying, as if he's waited a lifetime to pull it out and this is his first opportunity. Robbie always says stupid shit like that.

"Yeah, for those who are too lazy to go out and take what they want. I'd rather not be patient. Instant gratification is a virtue– patience is martyrdom."

"Clearly, my marauding sister, we hear different things from the sermon as we share a pew at church," Robbie says with great amusement.

"*Clearly*," I stress while smirking at my brother. "A lot of the congregation hears something else entirely as well, since I see about a dozen of them engaged in sinful acts as we speak. What would Pastor Otis think if he walked in right now?" Eyes shining, I take in our organist playing a different kind of organ, with her mouth instead of her hands… and it's not her husband's organ– it belongs to the neighborhood handyman.

"Pastor Otis is ninety-three, and he can barely keep a cognitive train of thought. If you would've went to church last weekend, you would've heard Otis calling Martha a harlot, and you would've noticed the new Pastor sitting in the first pew. Mom was eyeing him, waiting to target him with some matchmaking at the Prynnes' Sunday dinner table."

"Oh, Lord," I groan.

"Exactly," Robbie draws out while laughing silently. Not a single Prynne would do well with a Pastor as a husband– we're either stoned or sexed.

"Anyway, get used to waiting on Auggie's whim unless you want to be punished all the time," Robbie mumbles grumpily, and then our eyes connect and we share a laugh at the possibility of punishment.

"Remember, if Auggie thinks you're getting into trouble on purpose, the punishment won't be pleasant and it will be memorable. Look at us, Auggie isn't tanning our asses right now or making use of our bodies. He's making us sit here like we're discarded and useless. I can see that you feel like shit, as do I. Hell, I don't even know why we're being punished, either. It's not always hot and sexy with Auggie. Beware, if you piss him off enough, he may lend you to Isis," Robbie warns with a shudder. "Or worse, ignore you."

"I need a drink." I sigh dramatically. "I'm bored. I swear the wait is our punishment. They want us to sober up."

"Yeah, the wait is our punishment. But for what? I haven't a fucking clue. Which pisses me off all the more. I swear that is Auggie's ultimate goal– testing the limits to my patience until I snap, and then he has a real reason to punish me. If Malcolm hadn't held me back last night, I would've decimated my friendship with Auggie."

"I'm not worth it, Robin... *I'm not worth it*," I whisper so softly I doubt my brother can hear me.

Lost in my insecure misery, a wet lick on my big toe has me gasping in shock. I look down, and all I see is thick, brunette hair blocking my view. On hands and knees, the puppy girl gives me another experimental lick, expecting to be kicked away. I wiggle my toes, giving her permission to play with me. She hesitates before she nibbles each of my little piggies. I groan, courtesy of the puppy's expert oral skills.

"Good girl," I breathlessly praise, wiggling around as her slick tongue hits a particularly ticklish spot on the underside of my foot. Lapping at my skin, the puppy leaves my toes saturated with sticky, hot saliva.

"I think my doggie likes you, little girl. She kept pulling on her leash, wanting to wander in your direction. Every little girl needs a puppy, don't they?" The older woman purrs down at me.

Rolling my eyes up, I take in the tall blonde who's in her forties. Contradictory to her role as the puppy's master, she's dressed in an old-school nurse's uniform that screams ironic. I'd bet my life-savings of four hundred and sixty-two dollars that this woman is a nurse by profession.

The naughty nurse-dog-walker has a pleasant, round face with her blonde hair razor cut to an edge at her jawline. A no-bullshit air wafts from her. She's a good woman if you don't cross her. Something inside me– self-preservation perhaps – informs me that I need to be respectful and we'll get along.

"That they do," I say, playing along. I use my innocence to my advantage. Twirling my pigtail around my fingers, I ask, "Can my dog be a Saint Bernard? I'm in need of some medicinal libations."

"Rob," the dog walker purrs huskily. "No doubt this exquisite creature belongs to you. She's as charming and naughty as you are. Naughtier even."

The woman's admiration and the puppy's ministrations remove all my inhibitions and insecurities. They make me feel wanted, not alone in my strange cravings. It's not entirely sexual–

a feeling of camaraderie, a place of belonging… and that is when I finally understand the reason for the Playroom.

The Playroom isn't about sex, or coming here to get off. It's about communing with people who get you– even the strange shit you're ashamed of and want to hide. This knowledge gives me the strength to be myself and not be ashamed of that wayward girl who doesn't know what she wants to do in the future, let alone tomorrow.

I feel at home, even if deep down I know that I'm going to disappoint everyone. Those insecurities are for real life, not play. The Playroom is about play-acting, stress-relief, and letting go.

"Can I rub your puppy's tummy?" I ask the lady, hope creating an upward inflection in my voice.

With a serious expression, the woman makes a twirling motion with her finger. The girl instantly rolls onto her back, offering up her soft belly. The puppy's tongue is hanging out and her feet and hands are curled in to resemble paws.

Playing with the girl will make the wait more bearable, and maybe the lady will give me something to drink if I play along. A bottle of water would feel fabulous wetting my parched throat. I have cotton-mouth after the three shots of *99 Blackberries* I guzzled.

"Who's the good girl?" I croon as I rub the puppy's soft belly. Not too thin or too chubby– just perfect. Soft like a woman instead of skin and bones. I like the velvety feel of her skin beneath my palms.

My eyes slowly rise from her belly, taking in the rest of her. Brown eyes bulging from my skull, as a curious warmth and pressure fill my womb, I notice the puppy's perfect tits jiggle with every movement of my hand on her belly. I gotta say, that lights my fire. I rub her belly more to make the tear-shaped handfuls swirl enticingly.

"What's her name?" I glance up to the lady.

"I'm Opal, and my puppy is Bethany," she says with pride.

"Oh, my God." A laugh of utter shock escapes my throat, jaw dropping.

I hadn't looked at the puppy's face because her tits were perfect. I slide onto my hands and knees to crawl around the girl until I'm near her head. A teasing giggle flows from my lips into the puppy's ear. "How's it going, Beth?"

Bethany smiles at me and winks. I can't believe she's the same girl who danced with me for hours last night. She isn't anything like the Beth I knew three years ago at school. This Bethany looks happy and content.

Bethany grins at me as Opal orders, "Puppies can't talk. Bark!"

Bethany lets out a happy sound, so I rub her tummy in reward. Well, pain slut and little girl are nothing compared to puppy. I laugh in relief that I'm not the biggest freak here– my brother already trumped me in that department, but I think Bethany wins the award for the most original kink.

Smiling, giggling, I feel Auggie's gaze searing a hole through me. I roll my eyes up to find Auggie staring at me with a tight expression. Unbidden, my eyes slowly lower until my entire view is of the Beast. As if sensing my attention, I watch the Beast grow, finding it impossible that the thick flesh could get any larger. The more I stare, the harder it gets, the more it throbs, the more intense the burn of Auggie's green gaze becomes.

I flush and quickly look away, breaking the spell.

Completely oblivious to my inner torment, Opal speaks to me as if my entire body isn't throbbing for Auggie. "You two can pet-sit while I get us some libations," Opal drawls as she walks away.

As soon as Opal is out of arm's reach, I take charge of the gorgeous puppy. If interacting with Beth gained my master's attention, what would playing with her do?

"Bethany, sit!" I call out, and she does as I ask.

Rob and I both turn our heads to the side in wonder as Beth sits on her heels, legs spread wide. Sitting is very exposing for our puppy. Beth's thighs glisten in the light, arousal impossible to hide as it dampens her flesh.

Awestruck, I've never even seen my own pussy up-close-and-personal, let alone someone else's. The puffy pink lips are swollen and wet, exposing Bethany's core. Impossible to look away, I watch as a rivulet of moisture is released from her body to slide over her pussy lips and backward to disappear between her ass cheeks.

An agonized sound is torn from my throat as I stare at Beth's pussy.

Do all girls' areas look as pretty and perfect as Bethany does? Do I have something else I need to worry about? Will

Auggie find me funny looking down there? I'm pretty sure I look different. Bethany's inner lips hang down a bit, whereas mine are nonexistent. I have no idea what is normal or not. Am I normal, or is Bethany?

… And Puppy doesn't have a hair on her.

Will Auggie think it's gross that my pussy is covered in hair? He had to have noticed last night. Why didn't Auggie tell me I was supposed to wax it off?

Fretting, I sink inward until all I notice are my rampaging insecure thoughts. I want to be in the Playroom as much as I want Auggie to be proud of me, want him to want me. I'm already at a disadvantage because I'm built like a ten year old boy. Will the only part that sets me apart from looking like a guy embarrass Auggie if anyone finds out I'm hairy and misshapen?

Heart pounding out of my chest, I'm rapidly approaching a panic attack.

"Beg," Rob orders with a laugh, finally joining in on our fun. Thankfully my brother's comforting voice brings me back from the brink of panic. I push my destructive thoughts away, because it's not my pussy on display anyway.

Too bored to be good, my naughtiness yanks the monster from just beneath the surface. I gaze at my brother, tempting him to join me. My hand slowly reaches for Bethany's breast, waiting to see if she objects. I softly cup Beth's abundant tit and she groans in invitation. Rob looks shocked– mouth gaping like a fish on land.

"Beth has two," I offer, eyebrow arching in challenge at Robbie. I'm not sexually attracted to girls, but breasts intrigue me. I think it's because I envy them. Since I don't have a nice set, I want to feel theirs.

"Monster!" Auggie's voice lashes out like a slap, shocking me.

My eyes instantly seek Auggie. He's not angry, judging by the way his green eyes are dancing with a feverish delight. He and Isis have another companion– Opal. The three of them laugh while I freeze like a thief caught in the act. My hand pulses guiltily on Bethany's tit.

"You're a bad influence. Rob's learned to behave as a good boy." Auggie calls across the span of the Playroom, sounding highly amused. His eyes glitter in the light and his teeth are blindingly white from his wide smile.

"Rob's probably more fun as the Menace," I breathe out the corner of my mouth toward my brother, never moving a muscle.

Monster's a bad influence. Rob heard me and gropes the puppy's perfect titty, too. Groaning deep from his throat, Robbie learns it feels good to be bad. Bethany practically vibrates beneath our combined touch.

"Oh, very nice, Bethany," I praise. "I'm jealous." Beth closes her eyes and takes anything I'm willing to give. Rob drops his hand as if burned the second he makes contact.

Good Boy's a bigger pussy than the one between my thighs.

"Bethany, let's walk you back to Opal." The puppy's warm, wet tongue licks my face in a long line from chin to forehead in response. "That's a good girl." I excitedly giggle as I wipe Beth's saliva off my face with the back of my hand.

"What are you doing?" Rob protests in a panic and tries to grab my hand.

"I'm not going to be sequestered all night with my brother. Auggie won't kill me if I go to him. Watch and learn– sometimes it pays to be bad"

I slip Bethany's leash over my wrist, then crawl to Auggie. I've been dying to get on my hands and knees and crawl to him since last night. Auggie's face lights up with lust while watching my ass sway as I weave closer to him. Sweat beads from his forehead and slides down his cheek. The Beast rises in a wave. Neither man nor beast is disappointed that I crawl eagerly toward them.

CHAPTER FOURTEEN

Curling seductively around Auggie's bare leg, I kiss his furry knee, winding my body around him from upper thigh to foot. Auggie's fingertips grab my braids, twisting my hair around his grip, and then he tugs until we have eye contact. With patience belying his obvious eagerness, his movements are unhurried. Auggie removes the leash from my hand and passes Bethany over to Opal without looking away from me.

I hold Auggie's vibrant, hungry gaze and flick my tongue out until it reaches the Beast's heavy sac. Hair tickles the tip of my tongue, causing Auggie to suck in a large gulp of air, then hiss it out in shock. Auggie's knees go weak, and he braces himself by clenching his thick thigh muscles.

"Naughty, naughty Monster! Don't tease," Auggie gently reprimands, looking a bit insane. Green eyes glassy, breath rapidly moving his chest to saw out between his lips, sweat coating his entire body, Auggie coils for attack.

"If you're going to do it– do it!" Voice dropping into a deep growl, Auggie practically challenges me to take him into my mouth.

Auggie abruptly releases my hair to wrap his hand around the Beast, fingers gripping and releasing in a massaging rhythm that has him groaning in pleasure. Auggie waves the Beast in front my face with a satisfied smirk flirting with his lips. His big hand wrapping around that thick stalk of a cock makes my mouth water. I go from cotton-mouthed to flooded and drooling in an instant.

"Suck it!" Auggie growls the command, blocking out the two dozen Fairport residents that will undoubtedly watch me give my first blowjob. If it wasn't for Auggie's commanding personality and my need to please him, I'd get to my feet and run as fast as possible. I don't know if I want this, but I know I want Auggie. There are too many people clamoring for his attention– I either act now or I lose him forever.

I struggle to obey, to reach him from my kneeling position. I crane my neck and try to draw the Beast down to my mouth with my hand. I marvel over the feel of his heavy weight in my palm for the very first time. Flesh on flesh. Hot and hard, my fingers don't meet around his shaft.

I try my damnedest to draw the Beast to my lips, but Auggie's too aroused. I stand and bend at the waist instead, struggling to meet his cock with my mouth. But no matter what I do, he won't budge. Auggie's cock is firmly pressed to his belly, like a steel rod jutted up against a cement wall. I have no idea what to do and get frustrated. My entire body flushes with crimson, skin incinerating. I feel ashamed that I'm inexperience and it's beyond obvious.

Everyone is witnessing my humiliation: the townies, my brother and Isis– all of them are pleased that Auggie's new toy is broken and disappointing as they try to earn their position as Auggie's favorite.

"Willow," Auggie sighs my name as if I'm acting like a child, and I envision the floor opening up and swallowing me whole. Auggie used my birth name, which means I'm so far beneath him that I'm no longer Good Girl or Monster.

Backing up a few feet, Auggie puts me out of my misery by lounging on long sofa that has no backrest, just a big rounded arm with a small curved back. I think they're called a chaise, but I have no clue about furniture. I do recognize it as a consignment item from Revamped. All I know is that it's the perfect height for me to reach the Beast from my knees.

Pointing at a spot near his feet, I quickly shuffle over, remembering the gesture from earlier when Auggie placed Robbie and me against the punishment wall. I kneel by the side of the chaise, and Auggie shifts until I'm between his spread thighs, just inches from the Beast.

Noticing my avid attention, Auggie strokes his cock, eyes never leaving my face. His huge hand engulfs the entire shaft and slides downward. Overflowing his palm, Auggie squeezes his balls and groans in pain. My eyes bulge in shock– that had to have hurt.

"A good girl starts here." Auggie patiently explains as he puts a fingertip on his sac. "And licks… and licks… all the way up to here." He draws the fingertip up the length of the Beast, his fingernail leaving a white trail on his flesh.

"Where would a monster start?" I say snarkily, and end up biting my bottom lip to stop a devious giggle from erupting. About two dozen sounds of amusement flow around the

Playroom. Auggie's deep chuckle nearly makes my heart burst with pride.

"At his asshole," Isis explains in a husky voice, but there's an underlying edge I can't understand. "But then again, I'm a very, very, *very* naughty girl."

"I'm a good girl," I chirp, not wanting my tongue anywhere near Auggie's hairy anus.

Auggie laughs deep in his belly, causing his stomach muscles to ripple and the Beast to jerk with excitement. "Isis, darling, this is a beginner's course in cocksucking. I believe you bypassed pro about twelve years ago."

"As if I was given a choice in that matter," Isis grumbles as a blush flashes over her pale cheeks. And here I didn't think the vampire lady had a drop of blood in her system, or the ability to be embarrassed.

Quickly leaning forward before my cowardice gets the best of me, I nestle my tongue deep in the thick thatch of russet hair, trying to feel the skin of his balls. Musky-scented, a warm smell that tickles my nose and explodes in my womb. Auggie exudes manliness.

Auggie flexes his hips, his fingernails digging into the edge of the sofa in a death grip. I'll have to remember how he likes being licked right there. It would be better if he was hair-free. Now I understand why Beth was hairless. A tongue to bare flesh is easier for the pleasure-giver. I wonder if it feels better, too.

I wet my tongue again, which isn't difficult since I'm drooling like a bastard, and slide it up the shaft of his cock. The Beast tastes salty, but the musky scent is stronger than before– I'm instantly addicted. The Beast's head is round and plump like a ripe, juicy plum. I flutter my tongue around it, pressing harder each pass, trying to figure out what Auggie likes best. When I flick the slit at the top with my tongue and follow down a small groove, clear stuff flows out the tip. I readily lap it up, and Auggie's hips go wild– thrusting into the air.

"Rob, hold my hands." Auggie's voice is deep and strained. "Hold me back."

In a lust-filled fog, I look around and notice that everyone in the Playroom has stopped what they were doing and is watching in thrall. The room's the size of Auggie's loft. It has beds, sofas, and some furniture I don't know what to call. The people are crowded around us in a swarm.

The girls' ages range from Bethany at twenty-one, all the way up to sixty-something. The men are older– almost all near thirty and up. I only see two boys close to my age. One is Kieren, who is leaning against the wall, blue eyes glowing with unleashed fury. He's angry to the point that Malcolm has a hand on his chest, holding him back for some reason. The other boy is Kieren's older brother, Devon, looking shocked and scared shitless.

I feel shy and embarrassed doing this with an audience, especially an audience of Fairport's most deviant. But it's knowing boys I went to high school with, boys I've crushed on, are watching that freaks me out the most.

Auggie gazes down at me with unending patience, as if waiting for me to bolt– expecting me to disappoint him by running. This was a test he wanted me to fail. If I run, Auggie wins. I'd no longer be a temptation. I'd be a coward who didn't prove she wanted Auggie enough to do as he bid. Instead of doing what Auggie truly wants, even though his vocal command contradicts him, I do the unexpected.

I stay.

The infectious air in the Playroom makes this feel natural. A thrill trills in my veins from just the thought. Devon never saw me as anything but a friend, while Kieren just wanted to use me as a cum-dumpster. Now Auggie is showing everyone in the room that a woman who looks like a prepubescent boy can be sexy and desirable.

"What's wrong?" Rob asks Auggie what I want to know too.

"I'm close to losing it." Auggie groans, the raspy sound pained. "You're the only one strong enough to hold my hands back, to keep me from shoving my cock down Willow's throat. You have a vested interest in me not hurting her on accident." Auggie sounds physically exhausted, as if he's fighting himself for control.

Rob holds Auggie's wrists, but turns his head away so he can't watch. Betraying his interest, Rob's brown eyes are turned toward us.

Wimp.

If you're going to do it, don't pretend.

Own it.

Blocking out everything that isn't the man lying on the chaise, I pretend Robbie isn't here… or the Mason brothers… or the townies… or the fact that no matter how experienced I'll become, I'll never be as good as Isis. At anything. Auggie will never need me like he needs his best friends. I'm just an interesting layover. A trinket. A toy to be played with until broken.

The only solace I have is that Auggie's reaction to me is as visceral as my reaction to him. Augustus Kline truly wants me– *he* wants *me*. I will appreciate the gift that is offered for however long I hold his interest. I doubt any other man will ever want me with the level of fascination Auggie is showing me right this second.

Proving how much I appreciate the beast of a man, I repeat what Auggie showed me. My tongue makes several passes, enjoying the feel of his silky skin against my flesh. I try to remember everything I saw Essie do when she would suck a guy off. The problem is that Auggie isn't a regular guy, and I only ever saw the back of Essie's head as she bobbed in some random dude's lap.

I open my mouth as wide as it will go, wishing I had a flip-top head like the cartoon dude in the Oral-B commercials. I only manage to get the plump head to slip inside my mouth, but there isn't anything I can do about that besides practice, since I'm unable to unhinge my jaw.

I lick and suck the Beast's head, making slurping noises. Drool slides down the shaft, looking glossy and inviting under the glow of the lights. Auggie moans, the sound reverberating down my spine to pool between my thighs. This moment is surreal, like anti-reality. I feel as if I can do anything without consequence, as if it truly doesn't count in the fantasy world known as the Playroom.

My skin prickles, tightening with awareness and quivering for attention. My blood rushes in my veins, heavy with endorphins. The buzzing sensation is stronger than taking several hits of weed: eyes glassy, pupils in pinpricks, skin sensitive to a level that I can feel the air waft around me. I worship Auggie's cock as if it's the mouthpiece of my bowl– the stronger the toke, the better the high. I can almost hear the rasp of a lighter as the muscles in my cheeks draw on the Beast, sucking the intoxicating high from its flesh.

Auggie starts to struggle, to pull his hands away from Rob. Jerking, thighs flexing and hips rising and retreating in a thrusting rhythm, he tries to feed me more of his cock. I assume that means

I'm not doing a good enough job since eight inches of the Beast are being ignored. I do what I saw Auggie doing this morning underneath his pajama pants. He taught me how to masturbate, and I do it just as he showed me. I watched him masturbate, so I guess the reverse would be true.

I suck on the Beast's head and run both hands up and down the thick, pulsing shaft. I can't wrap my fingers around his girth, but I try my best. I'm drooling all over him, but it helps my hands slide freely. I roll my eyes up to make sure Auggie likes it. He groans and stills when I look at him, blinking heavy-lidded green eyes.

Recognizing the power of a look, I can't tear my gaze from his. I coil the potency of my need for his pleasure and spill it out into him through my gaze. I've learned a few things in the past few days. A guy wants all of your focus on him at all times, as if he's the center of your world and you can't breathe without him. Auggie said as much last night. So as I worship Auggie's cock, my eyes never leave his.

Watching Auggie watch me suck him off is causing that ache in my belly to return with a vengeance. Intensifying to painful levels, I want to rub the ache away. But I can't take care of my own needs because Auggie's must come first. I need both hands on his cock to satisfy his huge shaft. I groan and anxiously rub my thighs together, but I only succeed in creating a delicious friction that feeds the ache.

This morning, just before Auggie came, he cupped his balls. I do that now, sliding both hands down to cup and fondle the furry, heavy weights, all the while furiously sucking his plum-sized cockhead. I hope it's the right time, because I can't keep up this momentum for much longer. My jaw aches worse than my belly, and my hands hurt from stroking. I'm scared that Auggie is too much man for me, or I'm not enough woman for him.

With a deep groan, Auggie floods my mouth the second I touch his sac. My name echoes hauntingly around the Playroom. Mouthful after mouthful, I try to swallow the viscous fluid that is equal parts sweet, salty, and bitter. It leaves a frothy taste in my mouth, similar to liquid soap. I can't keep up with the flow and it globs on my jeans and splatters the front of my tank top.

Little rainbows covered in cum: symbolism of Auggie raining on my innocence.

"Good girl," Auggie breathlessly praises. "No more, Willow." A full-bodied shudder arches his spine and rolls his eyes, just as his cockhead slips free from my numb lips. I sit on my heels and wait. I ignore all of the gazes warming my skin and focus all of my attention on Auggie. I know that's what he ultimately wants– Augustus Kline believes he is the center of our universe.

Sated on Auggie's pride in me, I patiently wait. It's a strange thing to feel pride over, but a feeling of accomplishment warms me. I, Willow the wayward, pleasured Augustus Kline with the beastly cock to a climatic finish. I gave my first blowjob. It's slutty and trashy, but I can't help the smile that stretches my cum-coated lips.

Twenty-four hours into my new drug of choice, and I'm already addicted. I'm addicted to Augustus Kline's approval. The thought of Auggie's disappointment makes me sick to my stomach.

You could hear a pin drop in the aftermath, not even the sound of my own heartbeat can eclipse the deafening silence of shock from the Playroomers.

Five heartbeats and one breath later... the silence ceases.

Kieren's furious curses and my brother's explosive torrent reach my ears. "I can't believe I just held you down so Willow could suck you off. Lord knows I love you, Ugg, but I don't think I'm perverted enough for you." Rob hastily whispers to Auggie, yanking away from him. "I'm sick of having to prove that you come fucking first. Yes, I mean that in any way you want to take it. You self-righteous prick!"

Towering over my back, Robbie gets into his best friend's face and spits his words in the form of age-old resentment. "Did I finally prove my fealty, Master?" Rob snidely whispers into Auggie's ear, but I can hear him perfectly. "Do you want the twins delivered at your doorstep on their eighteenth birthday, too? The instant you show any interest in them, I'm cutting your dick off." I wince at the violence in my brother's voice. "You're too cowardly to take what you really want, so you take anything that is a part of me. I'm done!"

Gesturing to an area I refuse to acknowledge– Rob's crotch –Auggie says, "Explain your current condition, Rob." Auggie responds in a voice dripping with indifference and sarcasm to cover either guilt or shame, I'm not sure which.

I understand Robbie's anger. It's a combination of outrage at Auggie and himself, and jealousy over the fact that Auggie wants my touch.

I feel sick.

"I know you don't want Willow. Even if she wasn't family, she isn't your type. You only have two types, if you can call *people* a type." The *Isis and me* hangs heavily in the air. We all know that's what Auggie's not-so subtly hinting at.

"I know you're turned on because you were reliving sucking this cock." Auggie grips himself and wiggles his flaccid flesh as explanation. "And wanting your cock sucked, just like the many, many times you refuse to admit out loud." Auggie sounds just as resentful as Robbie did a moment ago. "Fine, I get it, but I won't apologize."

"Of course you won't," Rob hisses. "So very like you– always right even when you're wrong."

Ignoring Rob's outburst, Auggie speaks over my brother. "I'll reward you for helping– pick someone out for your oral pleasure."

"Are you fuckin' shittin' me? Like that erases a damn thing! I'm scarred for life."

Auggie's eyes never leave Rob's face as he gauges my brother's reaction. "I can't change what just happened, or what's to come. I did it. I made you watch as a punishment for trying to deny me… and I wanted to do it. *Badly*. In fact, I want to do it again. I won't apologize, right or wrong. You can be a jealous shithead, or you can behave. It's your call. You know I don't negotiate sexual favors."

Rob's only reply is a furious glare that could melt fire. After enduring that look for more than two decades, Auggie doesn't incinerate.

"You have thirty seconds to decide, Rob. It's been what, three months since I allowed you to be touched? The pressure must be killing you."

"Yeah, asshole, because I put up a fight over Willow," Robbie snarls. "I didn't want you using her as a way to get to Isis and me."

Looking beyond guilty, Auggie refuses to meet my gaze. "Well, I will excuse your violent rages and outbursts due to sexual frustration. You now have seventeen seconds. Pick quickly before the offer expires, Robin. It may not come again."

"Ugg," Robbie cries out, looking devastated.

"Tick-tock… tick-tock… and Isis is still off limits. You both need to know your place."

"Go screw yourself!" Isis shouts. "Why are you airing our very personal, dirty laundry to the entire town? It was you who didn't want anyone to know you were shagging your best friend. You were channeling my father by saying it wasn't manly to make love to a man when you're a man."

Isis surprises me. She looks broken, like when a disillusioned child realizes the monsters under their bed aren't as scary as the real monsters shadowing as people. Shoulders slumped, hair hiding her face, Isis leans against Malcolm Mason while holding Devon's hand for some reason.

Upset, I tell myself what I just did to Auggie isn't the cause of their fight– it was just the catalyst.

"I decided it was time to allow everyone to know Robin has a prior claim on me. It was my way of apologizing," Auggie says, sounding exhausted. "I'm not changing for anyone, so stop nagging me like you're my bitchy wife, Isis."

"I hate you," Isis snarls.

"No, you don't. You just wished you did. You want what's mine, and I'm not giving him to you." Lips twisting into a nasty smirk, Auggie and Isis fight over Robbie like he's a toy they don't want to share.

What does that make me?

"Robin, please accept my gift as it was meant. Choose someone before my patience runs thin. But I'm not on the auction block," Auggie warns with complete and total arrogance. "It's been a long time, but I'll never forget. Willow sucks as good as you do."

…And with that comment, I hide my face against my thighs, wrapping my arms over my head to hide my burning ears. I'm so fucking confused that I can't form rational thoughts.

Rob looks at the floor in shame. Too spineless to tell Auggie to go fuck off so he can be with Isis… or is Robbie more like me than I'd realized. Maybe he's more wayward than I am, and he wants them both equally and can't pick. If he picked would he still believe patience is a virtue, or would he be brave and take what he wants?

I'm speechless. It's as if I just met my brother for the very first time after knowing him for eighteen years. I haven't been paying close enough attention to my family members if I managed to miss the fact that my brother is in love with his best friends.

We all wait in total silence while Rob's inner-conflict wars.

Apparently patience is not a virtue for Augustus Kline. "Three... two..."

"Master, will you ask if Opal is willing to suck my cock, please?" Rob rapidly, albeit respectfully, asks.

"Ah– you are definitely not Opal's type." Belying his words, Auggie's tone is cheery, evidently pleased with Rob's cocksucking selection. I knew Opal was important somehow, I just don't know how yet.

I'm confused, because Rob is acting like a whipped pup, and he won't even look at me. I grab his wrist to tug him down to me, trying my damnedest to get him to acknowledge my existence. When Robbie won't, I grip his chin with my fingertips and force him to meet my concerned gaze.

"Why won't you look at me?" I breathe in Robbie's ear. "Are you angry with me? Are you ashamed of me now?" It matters what my brother thinks of me.

"Didn't you catch what Auggie said?" Rob breathes back to me. His brown eyes hold humiliation, and I don't like seeing it.

"So?"

"Willow, I've had sex with Auggie– a lot of sex, every kind of sex in every possible combination imaginable. You just sucked his cock for Christ's sake– a cock that's been in every one of my orifices... and not just mine, but Isis's too, and the majority of the people in this room. Auggie's a slut, and he's using both of us. He's toying with us for his own amusement until he tires of us, then he'll use emotional extortion against us. If you don't believe me, ask Isis how long she's begged for me."

"Twenty three years, four months, and six days... fourteen hours, give or take a few minutes," Isis quickly tabulates. "Since I was five years old, if that clarifies it for you, Willow. Welcome to Hell, baby girl. I've been there since I met a fat, bossy toddler at the tender age of three."

"Fuck," Rob hisses as he runs his fingers through his hair out of sheer frustration. "I love Auggie, but I wish I didn't. I don't want to admit this because it makes me the world's biggest asshole. But yes, I'm as jealous as I am concerned for your wellbeing. That slut hasn't touched me in three years as he fucked and sucked his way through the Playroom like a brushfire fueled by lust. So here he is, playing with my blood instead of me.

Basically, Auggie is torturing me because you have a pussy and I don't. Got it? You're *my* female version."

"I–" At a loss, the word just hangs there without any real meaning, and it sounds like pure confusion.

"Let me explain properly, since you don't seem to fucking get it. Fairport is a conservative town– the only kinky fucks are clustered in this room right now. Since I was old enough to hold a paintbrush, I've been labeled a faggot, and no one believed I was straight. Bullied and bashed and beaten and harmed."

"Rob–" Auggie tries to comfort Robin, but his arm gets slapped away.

"I *am* straight, except when it comes to Auggie, but no one believes me. It's not me protesting too much. I'm small and artistic, so they assume weak and gay. That isn't a bad thing, but it *isn't* me. When people look at Auggie, they see the manliest of men, so he can't possibly love it when I fuck him– he buys into the bullshit too. But Auggie can get away with it, even as he's fucking anything with a heartbeat. The only derivative of *BI* people in Fairport know is bicycle."

Robbie grabs my upper arms and stares into my eyes, looking desperate and scared. "No one would ever understand who I truly am."

It matters to Robbie what I think of him too. It makes me smile and spill the truth. "Being ignorant and intolerant is shameful, Robin. It's not shameful to own your sexuality. I'm literally twenty-four hours into being enlightened, and I already know that if Auggie asks I can't say no. Who could deny Augustus Kline anything he wants?" I gaze at the sex god lazing on the sofa as he intently watches us. "Why is that shameful? Didn't you like it? I can't believe that Auggie wouldn't make it spectacular."

"God, you sound like Auggie's zealot." Robbie sounds exhausted as he draws the words out. "You really need to listen to yourself. Willow, it's shameful because there is toxicity when it comes to Auggie and me," Robbie hisses in my face.

"You should be proud that Auggie wanted to pleasure you." Even to my own ears, I sound like the zealot Robbie called me, but I can't stop the words from flowing. I sound like an addict speaking of their drug of choice.

"You're an idiot– go get your dick sucked by the dog-walker-nurse-hybrid." I push my brother away from me. "I know jack about anything. But if you like it– own it. Don't be a cowardly pussy. If you're not okay with what you want, then it's just another way to silently judge those who want what you want."

Auggie looks amused and proud as we have a sibling fight over him. It's more like the toys are lining up for their kid, and they're fighting over who deserves to be played with more. I guess it's more like a pet fight now. I was told real life doesn't invade playtime, so in the Playroom, Robbie isn't my brother but my fellow pet. Auggie's pet. Auggie likes his pets fighting over him, it seems. He's radiating pleasure like a warm summer day, and as sick as it sounds, I soak up his sunny warmth.

"Fine, Willow. You want me to own it? *I will*." Robbie's threat reverberates around the room, causing everyone to wince from the intensity. "Don't say I didn't warn ya!" He stands up and rips his zipper down. I breathe a deep sigh of relief that he has boxers on underneath.

"I got turned on by how aroused Auggie was by you. I'm proud to know that no one will ever get him off like we do. Is that what you wanted to hear?" Robbie asks in challenge, looking crazed and feral.

"It's not what I wanted to hear, but it's how you felt. So if that's how you felt, then great!" False enthusiasm laces my tone.

I want to end this conversation since Robbie's no longer whispering. Enraged, he shouts to the room. I guess Rob can pull Isis's tag off his collar now. There isn't a person here who doesn't know that Auggie is our master, that we share a lover– if you can call not touching someone in over three years a lover, and if sucking someone's cock makes you their lover. I doubt it very much, or every person in the Playroom would probably be considered Auggie's lover… and if that doesn't just make me feel special.

Special.

As in special school special.

"I'll remove the filter from my thoughts to my mouth– how about that?" Robbie challenges menacingly. "I'll show you how little I judge. Truth? I want Opal's lips wrapped around my dick, her throat milking the cum right outta me. It's been three months since I got off. Goddamnit!"

Holding my gaze, Rob starts to undress tantrum-style. Roughly tearing his clothing from his body, bitching underneath his breath the entire time. If a person can see red, Rob's experiencing that right now. I know he's not mad at me, but it's still awkward to say the least. I refuse to look away because he's daring me to. He wants to prove I'm as much a coward as the one I called him.

"Well, have fun with that. Opal sure does have a pretty mouth," I murmur jokingly because I doubt I can get any more uncomfortable. A few people laugh outright. A couple guys mock-cough into their hands. Auggie just watches us with a bemused expression, confused over our strange reactions to his manipulations.

Robbie strips bare-assed naked with his dick pointed at the ceiling. I try not to look at it, but that would make me a coward. He doesn't make me gag, so that's a plus. He's decent sized, I guess. His body is nice enough, too, in a lean swimmer kind of way. A Prynne will never be big, but Robbie manages to bypass geek and exude a strange mix of anger and lust. I can objectively look at my brother and understand that he would be desirable with his brown hair and warm eyes– when they aren't shooting sparks of hatred –and his skin is naturally tan instead of pasty white since it's the middle of winter.

Thank God, I feel nothing when I gaze at Robbie. No matter what, he'll always be my brother. That thought alone makes me feel better. I don't feel sick, and I don't want him. Neutrality. I just feel a sense of contentment that Rob's going to get his needs fed.

Rob grows a pair of metaphorical balls bigger than Auggie's impressive set, and pushes Opal to the nearest sofa. She yelps when he crawls up her body to mount her face. Shoving his cock into Opal's mouth while his hands seek out her blonde hair, Robbie displays pure sexual violence.

Robbie's angry at Auggie, or himself, or Isis, or me, or the world, or a combination of all of it, and he's throwing himself just like I would.

Like brother, like sister.

I've watched enough. Rob can't call me a coward now.

Where's my Saint Bernard? I need a drink.

Isis stands in the corner, laughing hysterically with Malcolm Mason– Kieren and Devon's dad. Their heads are bent closely together, both smiling and blushing at some private joke only they understand. I fear Isis is trying to distract herself from the fact that Robbie's mouth-fucking Opal. I feel sick about it and he's just my brother, not the man I've chased for my entire life. No, the boys I've chased since grade school are standing next to Isis with disapproving looks on their faces.

Malcolm and Isis are enjoying the strange dynamic between a brother and sister who like the same sick shit but are extremely uncomfortable because of it. I'm glad they're enjoying our discomfort. Malcolm Mason looks at me sympathetically, swats Isis on the ass, and then rumbles a deep laugh when she behaves. And here I didn't think Isis would listen to anyone.

Uncomfortable, and having no idea what I'm supposed to be doing right now, I do what I'm always supposed to do— look at Auggie. He looks back at me, smiling softly.

CHAPTER FIFTEEN

"C'mere, Willow," Auggie beckons with a curled fingertip. When I get within arm's reach, Auggie pulls me into his lap and pecks me on the lips, then he begins rocking me back and forth gently in his comforting embrace. "Robin needs to be punished for throwing himself," he murmurs against my temple.

"You should humiliate Robbie by making him wear a tail." I offer up as a solution, imagination running wild as I envision Robin and Bethany roaming together in the Playroom.

"Oooooo," Auggie draws out, the sound vibrating against the shell of my ear and reverberating down my spine. "You are a wicked monster. That is perfect. I knew I kept you around for a reason."

"And here I thought it was for my mad cash register skills and my ability to navigate the internet," I mutter lamely.

"I'm not using you, ya know? But maybe you don't." Auggie reads my mind, as always. "I could tell that's what you were thinking. I'm also not using Rob, or keeping Isis and Rob apart. Life is keeping them apart. You need to have faith in me, and don't let what you see or hear shake that faith. There are hidden, and often very private, meanings to everything an individual does, and sometimes they don't even know why they do what they do."

"I… I don't understand, Auggie," I reluctantly admit.

"It's because you're young, and everything is still black and white. By the time you're my age, and I hope you haven't seen or done what I have by that time, you'll bypass shades of gray and enter the world of Technicolor. There are a billion facets to everything, just as there are a billion truths to one simple fact. Hopefully you'll never have to understand what I'm trying to say."

"Good," I quickly reply. "Because I feel like you're speaking a foreign language. A language that suspiciously sounds like, *'sorry, Willow, but I plan on fucking you over, betraying you, and ruining your life. But I have a good excuse, honest.'* Does that sound about right?"

"Accurate but not entirely correct… and you sound so much like Rob right now. If I couldn't see him screwing Opal's mouth, I'd think you were him in my arms."

"Just what a girl longs to hear, how she's interchangeable with the brother that's ten years her elder," I grumble.

"I love your brother, so I'd say that's a compliment." The affection in Auggie's tone is sincere, as is the funny little quirk to his lips.

Shifting in Auggie's lap, I begrudgingly mumble, "I feel like a replacement part. How romantic."

"Try an upgrade," Auggie teases. "I traded in the old, broken-down device for one that doesn't throw shit-fits and whine about wanting to marry Isis. I'd say you're ten steps up from that, don't you think?"

"Jackass." I snort, trying hard not to laugh. Auggie is taunting me, trying to distract me from the scene I'm trying to avoid.

I feel at home in the Playroom, even with Robbie's exaggerated grunting. Opal's getting into it, so maybe it's not so exaggerated after all. The image of my brother's backside flexing will forever be imprinted in my memory– a scar I'll carry forever.

Avoiding the need to toss my cookies, I turn in Auggie's arms and bury my face into the side of his neck. Pretending we're alone at his loft above Revamped, I feather soft kisses on the creamy skin of Auggie's neck and shoulder. I linger on his freckles, connecting the dots with the tip of my tongue.

"Now this is nice," Auggie murmurs dreamily, voice slurred. "This little thing cuddles and kisses and listens and pays attention and trusts Mr. Kline in all things. It's easy to love someone who doesn't challenge you at every turn."

Auggie is praising me, but it somehow feels like an insult just the same. True to his assessment, I don't call Auggie out on the fact that I'll be easily forgotten if I don't draw attention to myself, and eventually he will grow bored if I don't challenge him. It's why Isis and Robbie still intrigue him after twenty-three years at his side.

I'm fucked in the head. A small part of me wants to rail against Auggie, but an even larger part of me is already addicted to his approval. One thing I do know is that I trust Auggie not to hurt me.

Looking into a pair of concerned green eyes, I decide I'll only live once. If this is a mistake, it will be worth it. I take what

I want without fear of consequence. I lean forward and attack Auggie's kiss-swollen lips. He moans into my mouth and opens for my seeking tongue.

I wiggle in his lap as my body ignites, flames of lust licking at my flesh. Auggie's huge palms massage my ass, fingers splayed from my hips to my thighs, one or two sneaking along the seam of my jeans. A brush against the fabric covering my clit enlivens me, makes me achy again. I guess horny is what you call it, but I think achy sounds sexier.

The more seeking, probing, Auggie's fingers become, the more my kisses turn aggressive. Gasping for air, I move from Auggie's breath-stealing lips to kiss along the thick column of his neck. I add mild suction to each caress of my lips, leaving my lasting mark. I glorify in the fact that my touch, my kiss, hitches Auggie's breath.

I may not challenge the man beneath me, but he challenges me more than anyone on this planet. I've never been challenged, given boundaries, or praise. I need Auggie to feel worthy, and his approval spurs me on.

My fingers slide along Auggie's jawline. His stubble abrades my fingertips but not nearly as much as my lips. Coarse auburn curls wrap around my fingers as I anchor him to my mouth, sucking, trying to bruise the flesh of his neck as mine.

I missed out in high school. I never made-out or played *spin-the-bottle* or *seven minutes in heaven*. I've never been on a date. I've never had a guy ask me out, if I don't count that disaster with Kieren and Essie. I missed out on so many rites of passage. But instead of giving those moments to someone unworthy, I freely give Auggie anything he wants for the taking. My lack of experience means I can give Auggie myself as a gift.

I traded a few stolen, awkward moments for pure passion that scorches your heart. Augustus Kline will either build me up or incinerate me. Either way, it will be worth it.

I unhinge, every inhibition I possess flows from me, leaving me susceptible to ecstasy. Writhing, sucking, succumbing, I give myself to Auggie. Sensing the change in me, Auggie takes over, dominating me with his kiss.

Auggie's satisfied, throaty moan gives me the courage to do things that I would've been too self-conscious to try days ago. "Sir," I whisper in Auggie's ear, testing to see if the word drives him wild. He doesn't disappoint as he bucks beneath me.

A surprised shriek is torn from my throat when Auggie flips me around on the sofa, my head bouncing on the cushion. Looming over me with a hungry glint in his eyes, his smile is more of a baring of teeth. My jeans are attacked. Yanking my zipper down, large fingers fumble with the tiny button. Auggie growls his impatience. When I'm unfastened, he yanks the denim from my body in one quick, jerking motion. My pants fly through the air to land in parts unknown.

Pride swells within me as I witness Auggie's undoing. Crazed, his mouth drops open when he finally notices my pink panties. His mesmerized expression brings on an infectious giggling fit I cannot suppress.

Green eyes slit in silent warning, stopping my laughter. "You're entirely too impressed with yourself," Auggie mumbles hoarsely. "Which is totally justifiable, Monster. If we were alone right now, I'd tear you to shreds with the Beast– I'd bleed you."

"Sir?" spills unbidden before I realize what I'm saying.

"Willow, don't push me. I'm barely hanging onto sanity." Auggie's words are tight with suppressed, violent lust. "I don't trust myself around you. The only reason I brought you here tonight was because I gave the order that they're to stop me if I take it too far."

Auggie firmly grabs my ankles in one hand and lifts until my feet are well above my head, leaving my ass exposed to his view. I slap my forearms against the sofa cushions, trying to hold my arms out to support the headstand Auggie places me in. Sounding like the beast I've nicknamed him, Auggie growls when he sees the lace ruffles across the ass of my light pink panties.

"I wore them just for you," I breathlessly confess.

"I will reward you greatly for your efforts," Auggie rasps out. His voice is deep and rough with promise.

With gentle hands and slow, practiced movements, Auggie arranges me until I'm sideways on the sofa. Lowering himself, Auggie sits on the ground between my thighs. Green eyes capturing my gaze, he slowly leans forward until his nose nuzzles the seat of my panties. The fleeting touch has me writhing in his grip, gasping with anticipation of what's to come.

Parting my thighs with his face, the abrading stubble adds a painful dimension to the pleasure, heightening it, flavoring it with an edge. A heady moan is torn from my throat when Auggie's mouth suctions to my inner thigh, lips parting and creating an inescapable seal. His tongue swirls in a rhythmic pattern that has me on the edge of bliss.

Leaning back, Auggie gauges my reaction, which is about as hot as I can become. A flash of trepidation crosses his face a second before, "Devon," is released from Auggie's throat.

I jump six inches only to freeze in shock. Devon's name is ice water dumped on the heat of my lust. The sound of Auggie's voice saying the name of one of the only friends I had in high school– the only friend I've ever had that wasn't related to me – snaps me out of my fog. My body strings tight and my lungs rapidly work to keep up with my body's need for oxygen as I slide toward panic.

Stimuli.

Auggie's different stimuli is Devon Mason.

Humiliated, I close my eyes in defeat. I already know what Auggie's up to and why. My mind and heart are conflicted: excited for the prospect of Devon, because I'll be seeing my friend again, and pained over the fact that Auggie is acknowledging that I'll never be enough for him. The only consolation is that I doubt any one person will ever be enough for Augustus Kline.

"Willow, calm," Auggie orders in a quiet voice while rubbing my belly in soothing circles. "Shh… what I do with you is wrong. But Devon will make it right."

"H-h-how?" I breathe, feeling betrayed and worthless. "How?"

"Trust me, Willow," Auggie practically begs. "Trust Mr. Kline in all things, remember?"

"Yes, sir." I relax my body the best I can, which is just shy of cramping my muscles. But nothing, no action or word, will relax my mind.

I watch warily as Devon approaches us. He casts a shadow because he's taller than me but still shorter than most men. Pale-skinned with jet black hair cut in a trendy, shaggy style, Devon doesn't look like he belongs in Fairport. Devon's blue eyes are so deep they appear blacker than his hair– eyes that always express his emotions. I know him well enough to know that he's extremely uncomfortable by the way his eyes are darkened with disapproval. I've seen those eyes twinkle with mirth as I was teased, glow with the buzz from drugs and alcohol, and pulse with the thrill of victory as we won a game.

Dressed in jeans and a t-shirt, Devon's appearance puts everyone at ease. He doesn't look cocky or arrogant like Kieren, and he also doesn't have that boy-next-door vibe. Devon is more edgy than traditional.

I was twelve, looking like I was going on eight, when I first met Devon at a high school party– a loud rager thrown by a guy Essie was giving head. I was only in seventh grade and Devon was a freshman. Devon caught my eye because he looked a lot younger than he was, just as I did. After I proved a worthy opponent at *Flip Cup*, Devon and I made instant friends– a friendship that only existed at parties. We never interacted elsewhere because of our age gap and lack of interlocking social circles. I lost track of Devon once he graduated and left Fairport. I listened for gossip, but the Masons are a secretive bunch.

Essie dragged me to every party, school dance, and football game she ever attended. She was scared to go by herself. Essie and Devon are the same age, so I got to know Devon very well at these functions. I used to play drinking games with him all the time since I was too young to enjoy the extracurricular activities that Essie excelled at.

Devon was popular, but never passed girls around like his friends. I never saw Devon with a girl's head in his lap. It surprised me when I noticed him in the Playroom. He looks comfortable here, though.

"Yes, sir?" Devon's voice is deeper than I remember, raw and gravelly. The warm sound trills down my spine, intriguing me.

"No need to act on formalities, Devon." Auggie smirks as if he holds a secret. "We've discussed this for months. First person you asked about when you moved back home was Willow… so here's your chance. Don't act all shy, boy."

Standing over us as I lie on the sofa with Auggie near my feet, Devon crosses his arms over his chest and gives Auggie a look I can't decipher. Devon doesn't say a word, but after a few moments of engaging Auggie in a staring contest, a blush slowly spreads over his pale cheeks.

Auggie chuckles, a deep, haunting sound that resonates from his chest. Ill-at-ease, Devon quickly glances over his shoulder, seeking out his father for protection against Auggie's newfound lunacy.

"Is this some kind of sick and twisted punishment, Auggie?" Devon gestures around the room to encompass all of the

Playroomers who are currently being held in awe by our tableau. "You know I only come here to desensitize. Everything about the Playroom turns my stomach."

"Dev–"

Not allowing Auggie a word in edgewise, Devon talks over him. "Haven't I been punished enough?"

"You're not mine to punish–"

"I'm no one's to punish," Devon calmly says while holding Auggie's gaze. "I'm my own man, and you know I don't enjoy power exchanges. So let's get this over with. I have to be at work at four in the morning."

"Eager, are we?" Auggie taunts. Answering Devon's shrug, "I just bet you are. Alright then... you may touch Willow anywhere above her waist," Auggie says with a smile.

"Auggie, cut the shit. What the hell is this really about?" Devon hisses angrily, showing Auggie no respect and no fear over the consequences. It shows a familiarity I didn't know existed. "I'm the least experienced person in this room to whore for you."

I gasp when the reality of the situation settles over me. What Auggie is doing is tantamount to auctioning me out– whoring me out for someone else to break in. It angers me as much as it confuses me. I have no idea what this all means. I just know that if I voice my objection, I'll lose Auggie forever. I know this is a test– a test Auggie wants me to fail.

I'm sick of failing. Sick of being the loser. Sick of being wayward with no direction in life. I'm sick of looking and acting and feeling like a child. I'm sick of no one expecting any better out of me, for always saying, *'It's just Willow,'* like that makes my failures less because I didn't try in the first place. I'm going to try from now on.

I know it's wrong to do this, and I wonder how Auggie can so freely share me. I wouldn't be able to share something that I valued because I'd want to protect it forever. Knowing this kills a part of me, how Auggie sees me as replaceable. But at the same time, Auggie makes me feel like a woman– a feeling I'd chase to the ends of the earth and back.

I want to be a woman.

Reading my pained expression, Devon tries to comfort me. "Sorry, Willow. I didn't mean that about you– the whore comment. I... I meant it as a verb." Devon steps from foot-to-foot in unease and won't make eye contact.

"I can tell you *really* like Willow," Auggie purrs suggestively, eyes darting to level on Devon's crotch. Out of respect for Devon, I don't move my eyes from Auggie's face. "Your father and Robin thought you and Willow could make instant friends. Well, your father wanted Willow to choose between your brother and you, but you know what I think about that. This is the only edict I'm not breaking for all of our sakes. This doesn't have to be sexual, but I'm sure it will evolve quickly."

I try to ignore the condescension leaking from Auggie's voice, but I can't. I barely breathe the words, "Auggie, this is your idea. This is what you want, so why are you being so nasty about it?"

I'm not sure Auggie heard me or not, because he doesn't acknowledge my words. Green eyes never leaving Devon's face, Auggie doesn't so much as blink at my words.

"I don't have to make friends with Willow because she's already my friend, and I would have kept in touch if it wasn't for you. Your stupid jailbait bullshit got on my nerves five months ago when I showed up at Revamped and you shoved me out onto the street, acting like an overprotective father with molestation fantasies. Kieren's been chirping Jailbait ever since the lecture, doing a daily countdown to Willow's birthday. We flipped a coin on who showed up yesterday at Revamped just to fuck with you. I knew Kieren would bug the shit outta ya more so than I would."

"Nice," Auggie and I say at the same time. Auggie, because he appreciates the deviousness. Me, because it makes me feel like shit, knowing that disastrous date from hell wasn't a date at all, just a way to stick it to Auggie.

"Ren said you stalked him down the street and nearly gave him a beat down. I wasn't aware there was a law against befriending a minor, and I would know. But Willow wasn't a minor as of yesterday, and then she shows up wearing a collar with your tag. Quite proactive, Auggie. Worried that someone Willow's age will steal her from you, so you give her to his big brother instead? Or are you worried Willow won't have enough daddy issues to put up with your bullshit?"

"I'm not worried," Auggie says with utter confidence. "I did what was necessary to keep you safe from our monster. Willow doesn't realize her appeal. I have triple your life experiences and

I barely made it through the months of June through December unscathed, or I should say with Willow's innocence intact. No way would you have succeeded, my man. You should thank me for keeping you a law-abiding citizen."

"Kieren's right, you're an arrogant ass," Devon growls.

"Don't be a dick," Auggie volleys back, finally getting aggravated. "I'm rewarding you and punishing Kieren at the same time, *prick*," Auggie twists. "Imagine the sting– Kieren's big brother gets to touch the pet he was explicitly forbidden to play–"

"You're not pitting me against my brother. Not happening, *prick*," Devon twists back. "Willow's no longer jailbait. You can try to manipulate her all you want, but eventually she'll see through it. If she befriends Kieren afterwards, I'm fine with that."

"Jesus Christ. I can never do right by you fucking Masons. Twenty-six years and the Masons still think they can yank my balls. I don't need to pit you against your brother. Neither of you shared your toys as kids, so I don't see you playing nicely as grown men."

"Willow's not a toy... and if you'd realized this, you'd understand why Dad had to drag Kieren from the room when you yanked Willow's clothing off."

Auggie's head whips around, and I follow the movement. Where Kieren and Malcolm were standing next to Isis is empty, with Robbie accompanying Isis in their stead. Auggie looks mildly confused, his face scrunching up while he shakes his head to and fro.

"Dramatic as always," Auggie mutters exhaustedly. "Sit on the sofa and make friends."

"As demanding as always," Devon counters. "In a hurry, Auggie? Worried Willow will pull out of her high and ask questions?"

"No, not worried at all. Willow will never question me. Now sit your ass down, or I'll find someone else to fill your seat. Someone the complete and total opposite as you: tall, athletic, blond, and fearless. Someone who is practically salivating for a taste of Willow, and would appreciate the gift as it was given. Someone Willow likes way too fucking much," Auggie snarls.

"I'm not jealous of him– I'm proud Kieren's my brother." Gingerly sitting next to me on the sofa, Devon gives me a sad smile. "I was going to visit you at Revamped on my next day off. But fate intervened, and by fate, I mean Auggie."

"Hi." Overwhelmed by bashfulness, I want to hide my face. My mind is spinning, unable to lock onto a lucid thought. I don't know why I feel so foggy, drugged. I hear their words but my mind computes it as a jumbled up mess– a mess of confusion, fear, lust, excitement, insecurities, and worry.

I feel ridiculous, lying half on and half off the chaise lounge with Devon sitting on the cushion by my head and Auggie kneeling between my dangling legs. My blush is furious and instantaneous. I don't know if I feel fevered or aroused as heat licks over flesh. Sweat beads over my entire body, slicking my skin.

Shifting on the sofa to get more comfortable, Devon speaks softly to me. "Hi, I'm only doing this for you, Willow. You need someone to protect you. So I hope you don't mind me hanging around for a while."

"I guess we could always play *Quarters* to pass the time." I joke to break the tension. But my heart is racing so fast in anticipation over what's to come, I'm sure a heart monitor would have me flat-lining.

"I've missed my Beer Pong partner. The frat boys were vultures, but not as good as you." Devon blushes again, then ducks his face to hide his embarrassment. "Now that I'm home, everyone is too scared to play with me. It seems my reputation as a lush, combined with my profession, makes people leery. When I show up at a party, they think it's a trap."

Before I can ask Devon what his job is, Auggie interrupts. "Okay, boys and girls." Auggie chuckles, deep and menacing, a sound that means he's proud of himself. "You seem friendly enough. I've screwed people without as much as a first name– you're reacquainted enough for now... I love corrupting impressionable youth."

"Word of advice, from what I've seen, Auggie doesn't know what the word foreplay means unless he's on the receiving end. Ya better hang on, Willow," Devon warns.

My eyes flick up to meet Devon's dark gaze. Concern shines down, and it frightens me. I'm not naïve enough to think that Auggie is going to give up on whatever quest he's on. But the determination in Devon's face screams that he won't be touching me inappropriately. Confused, my emotions war between insulted, relieved, and expectant.

"Uh!" I grunt when Auggie abruptly buries his face in my panties, picking up the foreplay gauntlet Devon threw down. Within one heartbeat to the next, Auggie owns me, dominates me, liquefies my mind to the point that all thought ceases.

My spine bows, arching my neck when Auggie licks the satin seat of my panties. Lapping at me in long strokes, I whimper and wiggle, either trying to get closer or farther away, I'm not sure which. Strong fingers grip my thighs and hold me immobile as his mouth relentlessly devours me through my panties.

Half embarrassed and half turned on by the fact that I'm sort of getting eaten out for the very first time while a crowd watches on. The kinkiness of it seems to fuel my conflicting reactions.

A small part of me is conscious of the comforting warmth near my head. I cautiously flick my gaze up to Devon, scared to see judgment shining out, and look directly into his heated blue peepers. Devon is reluctantly enjoying himself: lips reddened with lust and moistened by the tip of a pink tongue that keeps darting out, blue eyes now the shade of sunny skies, and the muscles of his thigh taut with anticipation.

For the first time ever, I feel powerful. Powerful enough to make a guy hot, and only a true woman has that effect on a man.

Always requiring my undivided attention, Auggie bites my tender flesh, teeth sinking into my labia through the thin satin barrier... and I forget all about Devon in an instant. Uncontrollably, I writhe and moan my Auggie's name in exquisite ecstasy.

Augustus Kline takes one more first from me, just as he promised. He owned my first sexual touch, my first orgasm, and now my first experiences with oral sex, both giving and receiving.

Distracting me from sensation overload, Devon massages my arms in a soothing manner, fingertips feathering along my skin. Bending down with his lips pressed tightly to my ear, he keeps whispering, "*You'll be okay*," over and over like he knows something I don't. He doesn't touch me sexually. Every touch of Devon's is the pure warmth of friendship.

I don't know what to focus on: the swarm of people watching, Devon's soft words and warm touches, or Auggie's tongue snaking underneath my panties.

All thought terminates when Auggie's hot, wet tongue caresses my naked flesh, drawing an ache to form in my belly.

He expertly licks my slit. My back arches when his mouth opens to suck on my lips, tugging them with his teeth. Proving his prowess, Auggie feasts on me without taking my panties off, keeping my private flesh for his eyes only.

Setting his lips to my clit, Auggie gives a forceful suck, tearing a deep moan from my throat. All inhibitions flee me. I don't care if I cry like an animal as I seek my pleasure. Within seconds into the sucking, the pressure builds and builds and builds, until my only thought centers on coming. I don't give a damn how loud my moans are or who's watching.

I just *need* to come.

My body ignites. Sparks fire up my spine as I near my crescendo. Unashamed, I beg and plead for the pressure to crest. The closer I get to the precipice, the more Auggie backs off– his tongue swirls slower, his sucks are lighter. Frustrated, I sing sweet nothings to Auggie, and even to Devon. Acting like Mr. Kline's wanton slut, I beg anyone who will listen– beg them to make me come.

Ceasing his assault on my screaming pussy, Auggie roughly taunts me, "Not yet, Monster."

Frustrated beyond measure, I yelp an unintelligible word that turns into a string of every profane word imaginable, much to everyone's amusement. Laughter fills the Playroom, teasing and taunting words warp into encouragements.

I don't know when I did it, but my fingers are fisting Devon's t-shirt, twisted in the fabric, stretching it until it's ruined. I loosen my grip and flash a wane, apologetic smile at Devon. As soon as my fingers are free from the shirt, Devon intertwines his fingers with mine, gently squeezing in reassurance.

Resting his lips against my ear, "You'll be okay, Willow," Devon gently murmurs, but his words belie the quiver in his voice. His hot breath flutters against my skin, causing me to shiver from the sensation. My ignited and then denied nerve endings scream in protest at the flutter of breath– it's too much but not nearly enough to get me off.

Devon lied his first lie to me tonight.

You'll be okay, Willow.

CHAPTER SIXTEEN

There are moments in your life that you can never get back– the tipping point. These are the moments you simultaneously wish you could change yet forever keep the same. These moments are the foundation of who you become. These are the moments in time when your older-self wants to transport back in time and scream *STOP* at your younger-self, and perhaps slap the stupid out of you while you visit.

You tell yourself pretty lies to cover the agony of betrayal. At some point, your future-self accepts reality as it is and no longer believes the lie. But in present time, the only thing that saves you from life's bitter truths is the lie you weave for yourself– the altered perception of reality that blinds you to the mistake you're making. It's a knife's edge that can either be wielded to protect you or cut you, and either way it alters the core of who you are, who you were meant to be, and who you become.

This is the first of those moments for me– the first of many.

Days, weeks, years from now, I'll wish I had analyzed what was happening and put an end to it. I won't regret, because tonight's actions, and those thereafter, led me on a path of enlightenment– a path I earned through mistakes. I'll forever rue my teenage ignorance in trusting when I shouldn't. As it is now, my mind is spinning, unable to light on one thought, let alone the dozens flitting around in a stew of confusion and unbridled lust.

"Are you ready?" Auggie asks me, smiling brightly to cover the unsure and worried expression that's trying to break free.

"What for… sir?" My voice quivers and finally breaks when I call Auggie *sir*. Devon's reassurances make me wonder why he's reassuring me in the first place.

"Would you like to lose your innocence in the Playroom?" Auggie coaxes me. I form a silent O and nod my head yes, knowing Auggie wouldn't have asked if he didn't want it. I don't want to disappoint him by denying it. I'm too scared and thrilled to think straight, let alone speak.

"It will be the worst sex of your life, I can guarantee it," Auggie promises. "It will hurt like a sonofabitch because of my size, but I have to be the one to breach you. I'll break through and stop. This isn't going to be sexy or romantic. After this, you can be with Devon if you wish. But no one else." Auggie practically snarls the words– the not so silent threat is directed to Kieren Mason.

It takes me less than a heartbeat to commit to the single-most idiotic yet brave act ever. "Okay," I meekly whisper as I hide my face against Devon's thigh. I may be feeling shy, but I just grew the largest set of balls on the planet.

No doubt sensing my bravado, Auggie rumbles an evil laugh, slightly off-kilter, and it terrifies me but I don't back down. This isn't how I envisioned losing my virginity. I never truly thought about it, at least not in the '*I can't wait*' sense. I just worried that no guy would ever want to do me, so I'd take the first one who offered to rid me of my innocence.

I was never a girly girl, thinking of my firsts. My first kiss. My first date. My first time. Prom. I never daydreamed of the day my dream guy would get down on bended-knee and propose. I never planned a fictitious wedding or named imaginary kids. Because I never expected I'd get any of that, and it would hurt worse to have a dream unrealized. Almost as bad as wishing on birthday candles, but I promised I wouldn't do that past my eighteenth birthday– the first day of adulthood.

I assumed I'd get taken in the backseat of a beat-up piece-of-shit car while parked in a field somewhere. Maybe some shitty eighties band crooning from the radio, mingling with guttural moans of sex from some guy Essie pawned off on me, with the sharp wheezes of pain from yours truly barely audible. Beer breath would fill my nostrils as some loser rutted on me without finesse. Loser guy's buddy would be screwing Essie on the hood of the car while I stared at the tears in the ceiling upholstery. I'd be numbed out from a combination of liquor and weed, dead inside.

Memorable, vaguely.

Regrettable, probably.

The Playroom. Augustus Kline. Unfathomable. Irresistible. A once in a lifetime offer.

I never dreamed of this because I don't believe in daydreaming about things that could never happen in reality. Not in a million years did I think I'd be in this situation. Yesterday morning when I woke up an adult, I thought the highlight of my birthday would be Clover's sinful chocolate cake, not that I'd be committing actual sins.

Nothing would ever be more memorable than losing it to Auggie in the Playroom with everyone looking on. No one will ever forget the tiny boy-looking girl losing her virginity to their sex god, that's for sure. I worry about how I'll feel afterward, though. Will I regret this? Only time will tell.

"Rob, you don't have to watch. I won't hold it against you. You can leave. Actually, I'd prefer it if you would. You can wait in the club or up in your loft– I'm sure that's where Malcolm ran off to with Kieren and Isis."

Like someone out of the Exorcist, Rob's head whips around to stare at the spot Isis was just occupying. He does it so fast, if I wasn't so petrified of what's to come, I would've laughed.

"I'm sorry, but I have to do this because Willow's running around like a cat in heat and I won't allow anyone to be with her before me. I'd do this at home, but I can't guarantee I'll stop before I harm her."

"I'll stay, and I'll stop you," Robbie states in a grave voice. Flashing me a wan smile, he tries to make light of this uncomfortable situation. "Willow was in the same tent with me when I lost my virginity. Thankfully sleeping and completely unaware, but fair's fair, I guess." Rob sits on the floor and leans with his back against the sofa, facing the wall. He can't even see us out of the corner of his eye. It's strange, but I find comfort in the fact that I can reach out and take my brother's hand if I get scared.

"I get the pleasure of devirginizing two Prynnes. Lucky me," Auggie jokes, but he looks tense. Devon lets go of my hands and lifts my head into his lap. He gently strokes my hair, calming me. I stare into my friend's eyes. I haven't seen Devon in years, but it feels like yesterday.

"You don't have to if you don't want to," I mouth to Devon. He responds by moving me farther into his lap, then continues to stroke my hair. I can almost see Devon's thoughts written across his face. *Willow, you don't have to if you don't want to, either.*

But if I want to make Auggie proud, I kind of do. I know Auggie wouldn't pressure me to do this. I take full responsibility for my actions. But I'm also not stupid enough to think that if I don't do this, Auggie will ever touch me again. I have a feeling he only plays, that Auggie doesn't do girlfriends, especially sexually inept ones. If you want a chance to be with Auggie, you do so on his terms and in his environment.

If I said *stop* right now, Auggie would take that as meaning forever. I'm intelligent enough to realize this, and free enough to say *go*.

Auggie holds himself above me on the sofa, letting just enough of his weight to fall so he doesn't crush me. The foot and a half height difference means my face would be in his abs. But he isn't ready for that yet. He wants to kiss me– reassure me.

The kiss is soft and loving. A brush of lips upon lips. Auggie uses his mouth to express his emotions for me. I fall into his kiss and the world dissolves, leaving just Auggie and me. My brain feels all the eyes on me. It hears all the loud, excited breathing and Devon's gentle words. It feels Devon caressing my hair and neck. The combination of these things flips a dozen switches in my libido. But my emotions only register Auggie and every inch of our flesh that connects.

Lost in our kiss, I barely feel the whisper of my panties sliding down my legs. Auggie presses my thighs tightly together and twists my hips until my legs are facing to one side yet I'm still on my back. The Beast nudges me from the back of my thighs, not the front.

Auggie kisses me harder– brutally pressing his lips against mine until I either open or cut the inside of my lips on my teeth. His broad tongue snakes into my mouth, delivering a sweet, musky taste that he licked clean from my cunny.

A snapping noise draws my attention, and then cold liquid drips down my hip and into my ass and slit. I groan and arch my back when the Beast slides silkily along my ass. I lift my eyelids enough to gaze down the length of my body. I'm twisted around so the Beast can gain access to my pussy from behind. Everything else is tightly secured by my thighs. My tank covers most of my front, and only a small patch of brown hair is visible between my closed legs.

Auggie uses his hand to push the Beast inside me. I hiss when he starts to slip inside– the burn of stretching flesh. I try to pry my legs apart so I can take him deeper and alleviate the discomfort. I instinctively know that once Auggie is firmly rooted, it won't hurt as much.

"No, Willow. Behave," Auggie breathes against my lips. "We both want to fuck each other. Your thighs are the only thing keeping us in control," he roughly gasps out, breath ragged.

"It feels good, though," I whine. It's a partial lie– it hurts like a bitch, but I need Auggie deeper inside me. I need to prove that I'm woman enough to contain him– to please him and relieve him.

"I know, my good girl. It feels too good for me." Auggie groans, the guttural sound causing a shudder to roll down my spine. "I'm about to come just from the thought, but it isn't going to feel good for you in a second. Keep your legs pressed together, or we'll both regret it when I have to take you to the emergency room. Right now, only a few inches will safely fit in your tiny pussy. I'm a good six inches too big for you. Behave," Auggie grits out. "This is beyond torture for me."

I take a deep breath and try to match Devon's pace, where his chest rises and falls beneath my head. I close my eyes and just experience, not wanting to miss a single detail: the shocked, heavy breathing of the Playroomers. The soft, repetitive fall of Devon's hand stroking my hair. The comforting warmth of Auggie's body cupping mine. The scent of my flesh on Auggie's lips as he pants against my temple. The hard muscle creating a burning sting at the entrance of my pussy, preparing to take my innocence.

This is memorable. I will never forget a single detail.

"Your cunt feels like a silk-lined inferno. You're scorching my cock with your heat. So soft." Shaking, containing a violent surge, Auggie rasps out between clenched teeth, "I have the power to let go and tear into you. It would be the most exquisite sensation– your flesh parting around my cock. The beast boring a hole all of his own inside your body. I'd make you mine in every sense of the word."

Auggie takes a deep breath, then I have to bite my lip to avoid screaming. The pain is searing as he rips through my unforgiving flesh. Tears slip down my cheeks as I silently cry. The pain goes away, but leaves behind an agonizing, stretching pressure. I want to tell Auggie to pull out, but my body wants him deeper.

Devon deftly wipes my tears away, causing my eyes snap up to his. Devon doesn't look at me in pity or judgment. No sign of lust fills his eyes, either. Only concern is reflected back at me. Devon gently squeezes my shoulders to relax me while flashing me a small smile, and I experience an axis-tilting moment. My life changes in an instant. Whether or not it's because Auggie is taking my virginity, or because Devon will undoubtedly be a friend for life, I haven't a clue. But something permanently changes inside me.

I whimper, "It's too big," when I can no longer endure the searing burn of my body stretching around Auggie's wrist-sized cock. The Beast is way too much for me to handle. I silently cry as my body screams its proof that I'll never satisfy Auggie on a physical level.

Failure.

Inadequate.

Not a woman.

"That's what I've been trying to tell ya." Auggie snickers in my ear. "Thank you for letting me do this for you, Willow. I'm honored that you trust me this much. This will be the worst sex my monster will ever have. I promise that Devon will have you all stretched out for me– you may never take all of me, but it won't be a battle."

"Thank you, sir." I mean it. I meant it when I said it to Robbie, and I mean it now. We should be thankful that Augustus Kline wants to pleasure us, even if it hurts.

The Beast starts to spasm and flex inside of my agonized pussy, and I whimper in pain. "Saying *sir* is a really bad idea right now, Monster. A bad, *bad* idea. I'm not wearing a condom, in case you hadn't notice. I wanted this to be skin to skin. No making me come by saying that naughty word," Auggie teases lightly. I ignore the amused sounds that erupt from the watchers. I'd forgotten everyone but Auggie and Devon.

Auggie pulls out slowly, and I whimper for a new reason. I fall lax and enjoy the pleasant sensation of his body pulling free of mine. I like skin to skin. "That's nice," falls dreamily from my lips, causing Auggie to snort. "Come back, and let's try again," I beg shamelessly.

"Um… It only felt good when I pulled free because your body was rejoicing that I left." Auggie chuckles. "Not until you've had more experience, Willow."

Devon rubs his hands down my arms and up my belly and chest, igniting my nerve ending with electrical current. I eagerly eat up the pleasure his warm hands massage into my muscles. Devon accidently hits my nipples and I moan. I sigh when his next pass respectfully avoids my greedy nubs. I arch into his hands, looking to repeat the sensation. Devon winks at me, but doesn't give me what I'm searching for.

"You're going to be a bad girl. I can tell." Auggie pats me with something soft. "Not too much. I thought it'd be worse. I've never taken a girl's innocence before." I look down to see red on the cloth and red on the tip of the Beast. Auggie wipes himself off, then pulls my panties up my legs.

"Okay, good girl, I need to fuck something now. You've been such a good girl that I want to reward you. So pick someone for me to fuck." Auggie slaps my ass so I'll sit up. Devon holds me up when I wince from the burn in the seat of my panties.

I slump back down when my legs won't hold my weight, and Devon readily settles me into his lap. I push down the jealousy and inadequacy that floods my system. If I want to be with Auggie, I have to take him without judgment or possession. He isn't mine, and never will be. I look at Auggie's offer with clear eyes and a logical mind. I realize the thought of having some control over who Auggie takes excites me.

The unsatisfied ache between my thighs makes itself known with a vengeance. Devon's body against the back of mine is too much sensation. I find my strength to stand. I peruse the room, looking for someone I'm willing to sacrifice to the Beast's pleasure.

"Really?" I mutter in shock. "Anybody I want?" Eager and excited, I look around the crowd as I lean my hip against the sofa.

"Willow, you're perfect. I can't believe you're excited about this. Any other female would be clawing my eyes out at this point, and then sheering my balls off to mount in a display case marked *rat-bastard*." Auggie shakes his head in wonder.

"If they de-nutted you, we'd all lose out on your expertise. I think the number one rule of the Playroom is that the Beast is sacred. Never harm the Beast."

"New girl is right!" is shouted from the crowd. "Only a dumb bitch would harm that piece of meat!" It takes me a moment, but I finally place the woman. It's the beauty– Nina the cocksucktress. I form an instant dislike to the woman, feeling the first trickle of jealousy as it enters my system and knots in my stomach.

"You all think too highly of me." Auggie tries and fails to sound modest. He's eating that shit up with a spoon, pale, freckled skin glowing with delight. "Good Girl, pick anybody– male or female. Whoever you pick can say no, so keep that in mind. Don't go creative monster on me and pick someone to punish." He huffs a laughs, giving me more credit for a devious mind than I deserve.

"Can I help you?" I ask, voice sounding squeaky for once, instead of throaty.

"Yeah, you can play, too." Auggie laughs at me, shaking his head again in surprise.

Robbie pops up from the side of the couch, looking like a deranged Jack in the Box: brown eyes popping from his skull with his hair sticking up every which way from running his fingers through it. My brother looks intrigued that I get to choose, like he never thought he'd see the day Augustus Kline would relinquish control, but equally leery that I'll punish his tantrum by choosing him. Something tells me every sexual or affectionate touch between the best friends was done in private and meant to stay private.

Devon slinks off the couch and ghosts away, scared to be in my line of sight, as if I'd choose him just to be a bitch. All the women eagerly step forward, trying to gain my attention, a few men, too. Nina's salivating– a wicked light radiating from her, as if this is a dream come true. All females are eager, except Opal. The nurse gazes at me in an *I dare you* fashion, with a threat of dismemberment if I go through with it. The rest hide behind pieces of furniture, or hightail it for the hallway.

My choice is obvious. I'll never be able to stand seeing Auggie with my family, but a friend is a different matter. I want to please Auggie and I want my friends to feel the pleasure I know Auggie is infamous for. I wouldn't know what to do with a stranger. I wouldn't want to touch a stranger, or watch one for that matter. Other than the actual choosing, I need to be able to watch, to touch, to feel like I have a choice. I need to feel as if I'm a part of this, so it won't hurt as much. I need to not feel sick inside.

My God, this feeling is powerful– holding the decision in my hand. Seeing the expressions of awe, lust, determination, and fright on the faces of the members of the Playroom. I could make someone's night... or ruin it. Is this how Auggie feels with every breath he takes? It's the most intoxicating feeling of my life, and considering I've spent the majority of my life intoxicated, that's saying something.

I feel invincible.

I respectfully gaze at the one woman who deserves it the most. Something about this woman screams trust. "Opal, can

Bethany play with Auggie?" I murmur in a shy voice, as a blush creeps up my face and prickles my scalp.

"Ahhh, the puppy," Auggie draws out. "I think this is more for you than me, Monster. Good choice." He praises me, but doesn't look surprised by my choice in playmates.

"Very good choice, little girl," Opal says with a smile, somehow sensing my discomfort. "You had me worried there for a second." Her lips quirk up and her chest moves, but the laugh is silent and doesn't reach her eyes.

Auggie slides up the chaise-sofa-thing, until he leans in the corner of the arm and small back-support. He holds my gaze, and I see a flash of fear. As if my opinion matters. As if he's frightened that he'll run me off by showing me the part of him most women would never accept. Something about that potent look, the blatant honesty, is a comfort. I relax, realizing that no matter what, even if Auggie breaks my heart, it's not the end of the world.

Bethany trots over on her hands and knees, pretending to be a puppy with her tongue lolling out, panting in excitement. It's beautiful, the way Beth accepts herself and her needs. I want to grow up to be confident like her. Seeing Beth infuses me with strength. I can do this. I can watch this and not have it shred me.

I'm torn between watching Auggie deftly roll a condom over the thick length of the Beast as if he's done it a billion times, which he probably has, and Bethany's perfect tits swaying as she crawls up the sofa.

"Puppies take it from behind, Bethany. Kneel on my thighs, facing Willow. You can't take much of me, either." Auggie controls us both as he sprawls back, looking like the sex god of the Playroom.

I feel better knowing I chose someone who's been with Auggie before, as if I made the right decision for everyone involved. I sigh in relief that I didn't disappoint by picking the wrong person. It's humiliating enough that I'm so dang inadequate I can't satisfy Auggie with my own body. How mortifying would it be to choose someone who couldn't either?

I watch in fascination as Bethany crawls over Auggie and places a knee on each of his muscular thighs. She squats her rear down, exposing her hairless, glistening slit, proving she is perfectly fine taking the Beast on. Beth raises a brow in my direction, silently asking permission, as if she can't quite believe I have the balls to go through with this.

"Since it can't be me…" I inhale a sharp breath as my inadequacies assault me. "I'd rather it be you than anyone else," I answer honestly. "You've always been nice to me, even when others weren't. You're sweet and friendly… and very pretty. It's okay."

Puppies don't talk in real life, but Beth makes an exception this one time. "Just remember that if you get pissed at me during or afterward, Willow– this was *your* choice. I'll say no if you think it will bother you. We don't have to do this at all. We could go share a burger and fries and laugh about these fools."

"If I get upset, I know it's all on me. I get it," I whisper. "Do you want to do this?"

"Willow, I'm fine with this. I've been with Auggie dozens of times. It's you I'm worried about, girlfriend."

I take a hesitant step forward, fearing my bravery will fizzle out if I think too hard over this. Auggie flashes me a look of surprise, as if he, too, thought I'd pussy out and run away, or scream obscenities while tearing his nuts off.

"Well, then. No sense in dilly-dallying." Auggie releases a manly laugh from deep within his chest that flashes lightning up my spine and shoots me right in the cunt. I've never heard anyone sound so sexual in my life. Auggie is relaxed yet filled with anticipation, eager to show me who he truly is, and that laugh is the epitome of the man. I press my thighs together, stemming the urges that laugh elicits deep within me.

"Okay, Monster. Kiss the puppy's teats while I seek my pleasure." Auggie is beyond amused, finding the entire scene entertaining as he directs us like characters in a play.

Walking on shaky legs, I crawl onto the sofa to sit on Auggie's thick thighs. Beth and I face each other, proving just how large of a man Auggie truly is if two girls can sit on him from hips to knees. Without hesitancy, I lift my palms, placing them on the soft, perfect globes of the puppy's breasts. I do as Auggie bids, experimentally squeezing and pulling at her nipples. I'm fascinated with this part of the female form. If I had big tits, I'd play with them constantly. I feel bad that I can't offer this fun to a guy.

Bethany's deep moan tells me the Beast is inside of her. I scoot back so I can take a look, and watch as Beth swallows half of that monster cock. The Beast slides in and out easily, each time adding more length that disappears inside Beth's pussy, and it comes back out shiny and wet. Before my eyes, Bethany's nipples get bigger and the little bead at the top of her pussy peeks out. She likes the Beast. I envy her– I wish I was her.

I feel Auggie's gaze on me the entire time, insisting I put my eyes on him, but I don't give him what he wants. We're playing with Bethany, and she should be the center of our attention. Not as Auggie requires, where he demands to be the most important person in our lives. I don't want to be rude, because if I look at Auggie, I'll be lost to him.

I palm and squeeze and weigh Bethany's breasts. She moans for me, arching her delicate neck and releases a throaty sound that is pure sex. I love how Beth reacts to my touch– it makes me feel warm and fuzzy, like I am good at something for once.

My mind keeps wandering to that swollen pearl. Auggie taught me that it gives the best orgasms, and sadly it's being ignored. Wanting to make Beth happy, I slide my fingertips down over Beth's soft belly, over her hairless mound, and I touch her clit with a fingertip. Bethany bucks wildly in response. A sharp grunt spills from her lips when too much of the Beast plunges deep inside her. I quickly back off, worried I'd done something wrong.

Shifting slightly, Auggie stabilizes Beth. "You can do that now, Willow," Auggie reassures me. "I have her hips. She wants you to touch her in any way you're comfortable. Trust me."

Trusting Auggie, I lean forward, taking the tip of Beth's breast into my mouth. I suck on Bethany's nipple and revel in the reaction it causes. Sexually this isn't doing anything for me, but it satisfies the hell out of me to give her such pleasure.

Bethany's breasts sway as Auggie moves her up and down on the Beast. It's a bounty I can't resist. I hinge my jaw open as far as I can until some of her tit is in my mouth, too. I suck hard, wanting to leave a mark. Bethany groans and eagerly presses my face closer to her. Bethany's breast is soft and squishy, tasting and smelling of lavender body lotion. I sink my teeth in, and a smile spreads my lips as she yelps.

My fingertip seeks Beth's clit again, and I do just as I was taught by Auggie. I go back to her opening for some moist slickness, but I get waylaid when I feel the Beast sliding back and forth. Auggie grunts when I caress his ball sac like he enjoys, cupping the hairy flesh in my palm and slightly squeezing.

I find a rhythm similar to the one Auggie's using, for my mouth on Beth's breast and my fingertip on her clit. Bethany starts to wiggle all over the place, moaning deeply, breath hitching, nearly sobbing in ecstasy. Seconds later, Beth screams out my name when she comes, not Auggie's.

My name.

Willow.

It echoes around the Playroom. I shouldn't feel proud of that, but I do.

Slumping forward, Beth hangs onto me for dear life, trying to catch her breath. I hold her, reassure her, and rub her back as she comes down from her orgasmic high. I bond with Bethany as if Auggie isn't still inside her body. What started as necessary sex turns to friendship.

"I won't tell Essie about this if you don't. Some of the stuff that happened tonight I want to tell her in private, okay?" I whisper to Bethany. "This is between us, okay?"

Essie and Beth were friends in high school, went to cosmetology school together, and now work together at the salon. I'm Essie's best friend, but cousin will always trump that, so that makes Bethany Essie's true best friend. I don't know if Beth would want Essie to know she fucked Auggie, or that she crawls around and playacts being a puppy. But I do know I don't want Essie to find out I lost my virginity from gossip. It's for me to share with her.

"Thank you," Beth says in obvious relief. She softly kisses me on the cheek in thanks, and I know I've made another friend tonight. I smile from the impossibility of living eighteen years with my only friends blood-related to me– everyone else was just an acquaintance. Tonight, I've forged real friendships with Devon and Bethany, even if they are freaky relationships. Nothing bonds people closer than mutual darkness.

Standing up on shaky legs, I wander away so Auggie and Bethany can have some privacy as they do whatever you do when you're done having sex. It's not anything I've experienced yet, so I'm at a loss of what to do next. Do you cuddle? Push the person off you and go shower? I haven't a clue, and I doubt I'll figure it out any time soon.

I hunt my jeans down halfway across the Playroom where Auggie had thrown them. I pull my pants on, feeling strangely exposed and raw. I notice that Rob and Devon are sitting side by side on a settee, both gazing at their fidgeting hands. That looks like the most comfortable place to be. I cross the room to join them.

Belatedly, I realize that not once during the sex act Auggie and I performed with Bethany did I look at him. It's the most disconnected I've ever felt. It should have bonded us closer together to share in such an experience, but it didn't... then I realize it wasn't a shared experience. Neither Auggie nor Bethany touched me in return, and the only place I touched Auggie was his thighs beneath my legs as I sat on him and his sac resting in my palm.

I learned a valuable lesson. What I just did wasn't sex– it was merely a body function.

CHAPTER SEVENTEEN

"Willow," Robbie greets me as my feet come into his line of sight as he stares at the floor. "Ya wanna get out of here before Auggie gets on us?" Rolling his sad brown eyes up to meet mine, he doesn't lift his face.

"Are we in trouble?" I mutter quickly, watching as Robbie's fists clench and release where they rest on his thighs. "Again?"

"You probably aren't, but I'm in for a world of hurt, and not the good kind," Robbie answers honestly. "Are you ready for step two in operation *make Willow an adult?*"

"I wasn't aware there was an *operation*," I tease. "Here I thought it was just a plan. I've been upgraded again, like a tropical storm upgraded to devastating Wicked Willow. I'll hit the Atlantic seaboard and wipe out half of Massachusetts."

Devon snorts, lips twisting into a smirk, but he doesn't truly laugh or smile. "I've got to find my family," he says as he stands.

"We'll join you," Robbie replies, and then he stands too. "I think it's high time Willow sees the real me, especially since we've screwed the same man now. I think in a perverse way, that almost makes us friends." I pretend I don't hear the pain, the jealousy, or the vindictiveness in Robbie's voice, but I'm not deaf or dumb or numb. I feel everything my brother feels and more. But mostly, I feel stupid.

"You were always my friend, Robbie. Hell, I worshiped you. I thought I knew you already, but even I will admit my head is always up my ass." I fall into step with Robbie and Devon as we leave the backroom of Rush, a.k.a the Playroom. I don't feel Auggie's eyes on me, so I don't look back.

"A predilection of being a teenager: head-up-the-ass-itis. It makes you unable to see anything that doesn't directly affect you. You need to require more of yourself now, Willow. We've all let it slide except for Clover, and watching you fight her tooth and nail made us keep our mouths shut. No more."

"You're mad at me now, too," I grumble as I look to the floor in shame as we walk the labyrinth-like hallways of Rush.

"No," Robbie says softly as his hand wraps around mine, lending me comfort and understanding. "I could never be mad at you. I'm just educating you for your own good." He releases my hand, pulls a key from his pocket, and then unlocks a door that lies just before the mouth of Rush's main club.

"I'm sure in your head, I still live in the city in that shitty apartment you visited once when I was in college. Proof your head is up your ass– I moved home. *Here*. Just before Sam died, because you all needed me. I come home almost every day to check on you all so there was never a need for any of you to enter my space. I didn't invite you to visit because I live above a club that houses a den of iniquity. Not a place for impressionable, naughty little shits whose other predilection is trouble. I'd rather cut my arm off than allow the twins here until they reach the age of majority."

"You live *here*?" I mutter in shock. My eyes widen as I take in Devon entering the doorway and marching up the narrow staircase like he owns the place. "You live at Rush? That would explain Kieren's baiting words last night– the douche!"

Robbie looks at me, eyes dancing with silent laughter, smiling at me like I'm being cute. "Where else would I be, Willow? Isis and Auggie lived here together, and I was drawn in like an idiot. The ass moved out a few years ago to live above Revamped."

"Why?" I ask as I follow Devon up the stairs. The boy must work out, because I don't remember him looking so taut. Damn. I try not to turn my head to the side to get a better angle of his flexing ass.

"Why Auggie left?" Robbie looks at me like I'm insane. "Self-preservation. The three of us sharing a single space was turbulent. Isis said the place was hers because she manages Rush, so she wasn't leaving. My leaving wouldn't solve anything since it was Isis and Auggie at each other's throats."

"Damn," I breathe in awe.

"As punishment for not declaring my undying fealty and leaving with him, Auggie hasn't touched either of us since. Isis has fun torturing Auggie by attacking him with violence and sex. When he wants more, she laughs in his face and retreats. Personally, I'm sick the fuck of the pair of them."

"I'm just a pawn in their game, aren't I?" I grumble as Devon holds a door open for me to enter.

As I walk past him, Devon breathes to me, "Most definitely."

"Um…" falls out of my mouth, making me sound like an idiot, as the scene before me stops me dead in my tracks.

The space is an industrial looking loft. The four walls are filled with living spaces sectioned off by furnishings. The highlight of the loft most certainly belongs to my brother, facing the windows is an artist's paradise with several works in progress. The most interesting feature is how the three bedroom areas are spread out as far apart as possible, as if the beds are magnetic polar opposites and cannot maintain the same space without imploding. The left-hand corner of the loft is hidden from view by a wall of paintings. Behind it, I assume lies the utilities: bathroom, laundry, storage. A high-tech kitchen for culinary creation, an office built to manage Rush, and an occupied seating areas also catch my attention.

"Cuddle party?" I raise a brow at the sofa in mystification. "Sorry, I forgot my pajamas at home."

Feeling as if I entered an alternate universe, I find Malcolm Mason wrapped around both Kieren and Isis, and all three of them seem perfectly comfortable with it. Isis is tapping on her cellphone and Kieren is chatting away as if we're all listening to him, all the while Malcolm stares off into space. Judging by the tight expression on his face, Malcolm isn't mentally present.

Devon's laughter flows to my ears as he ruts around in the refrigerator like it's his fridge. He yanks out a pizza box and grabs a few slices. "When Dad gets upset, he uses us as his security blankets."

"Nah," Kieren draws out, smirking his killer smile. "I say we're his living teddy bears." Shoving his father off, Kieren sits up on the sofa. "You're making me sweat– get off me."

"Okay…" I stand in the doorway, unsure what I'm looking at, or why. "I don't get it."

"My brother has an annoying coping mechanism, and we all suffer the consequences," Isis says, eyes never leaving the screen of her phone as her fingers continue to type a message. "I don't even know when he's touching me anymore. It just is."

My mouth pops open. "Brother?"

"You're still walking, so I assume the prick didn't screw you," Kieren says angrily from his position on the sofa, but he refuses to look up at me.

"He did," Malcolm gruffly answers for me. "Opal's texting with Isis. I've been reading their messages for the past ten minutes."

Like a violent breeze, Kieren rushes by, shoulder bumping me on the way. I stumble to the side, confused out of my fucking skull.

"Shit!" Devon hisses, tossing his pizza on the kitchen counter before chasing after his brother.

"Let them go," Isis commands Malcolm as if he made some indication he was going to follow. "If they go to Auggie, he deserves the ass kicking. My guess, Kieren's just running home to lick his wounds."

"I have a major case of head-up-the-ass-itis." I point at the side of my skull, wondering why I didn't figure this out earlier, but still unsure what I'm supposed to figure out. "What the actual fuck?"

"Let's talk," Robbie says in answer. "No one comes out on the deck. This is private, between Willow and me. Got it?" Robbie demands.

"As if I give a shit," Isis snarls, looking more feral than usual. Her dark eyes glow like angry obsidian as her fingers type so roughly on her cell that I worry she's scratching the screen.

"Yeah, ya do," Robbie and Malcolm say at the same time.

Malcolm gets up from the sofa and walks toward the kitchen area. "Pizza sounds good about now." Malcolm picks up the slice Devon was eating and takes a large mouthful. "I'll keep Isis from eavesdropping while I eat. But I'll warn you, Auggie's orgasm high will fade soon and he'll notice you're gone. This will be the first place he'll look, so I suggest you hurry up."

"This is nice– cold, but very nice," I ramble as I stand on Robbie's deck. "I bet you spend a lot of time out here." I huddle up to the railing and gaze out over Rush's rear parking lot. Music pours from the club, the bass a heartbeat of a sound, and voices flow up from the parking lot below. "It's pretty how the snow glitters from the street lamps."

"This is my thinking spot– no Isis allowed. But she's perfected the invasion by standing at the sliding-glass door and staring at me, waiting me out. It's creepy. That's why Malcolm's keeping an eye on her. She'd eavesdrop, and I don't want her to overhear."

"Why not?" I ask as I turn around to face my brother. I lean my back against the railing and face the sliding door just to be certain no one is listening. I can almost see the entirety of the loft from my position. Malcolm is carrying the pizza box around in one hand and a slice in the other, pacing the floor while Isis watches him like a cat after a mouse. I snort when Malcolm offers her a slice of her own pizza and a very large grin.

"Sometimes you need to vent about the people you love the most, and what you have to say will wound them if they ever found out. We all need someone to trust with these very dark thoughts, and I was hoping that person could be you, Willow."

"I'd be honored," I whisper, getting choked up.

Sighing heavily, Robbie stares me in the eyes, gauging my emotions. "I'm gonna need fortified for this conversation." He sneaks a peek over his shoulder, sees no one is looking, and then quickly rushes the length of the fifteen-foot deck. He crouches down and wiggles a cinderblock from the main façade of the building.

"What the?" My speech gets cut off when a bong materializes from the cubbyhole. "Could you get anything more obvious?" I chastise. "Didn't Mom and Dad teach you any better?"

"Well, I could always get my Hookah from the closet, but then I'd risk a night in the clink when Chief Mason arrests my ass for possession."

"Shit," I mutter with feeling. "You're fucking kidding me? Malcolm's a cop? Wait a minute… you have a freakin' Hookah? Dude, you're an idiot. Catch!"

"Swweeet," Robbie draws out in appreciation as he catches my bowl in his outstretched hand. A second later he catches the Altoid tin containing my stash and lighter. All of my winter jackets have secret hiding places for my recreational habit.

"Portability, my brother. None of that hydroponic bullshit, either. That's Mom's finest right there." I sound ridiculously proud of Mary Prynne's well-honed gardening skills. "I didn't even know you smoked anymore."

"Not often– only when I'm stressed," Robbie readily admits while packing the bowl with expert precision. Not often, my ass. "What about you?"

"Only when I'm stressed." I trail a giggle. "And I'm always stressed. I can turn any household item into a means to smoke pot if you give me two minutes and a lighter."

"Pothead MacGyver," Robbie teases, and then draws out, "Niiiiice."

"And that's why I think you're a moron for keeping a bong on your deck and a Hookah in your loft. Idiot. Isis's brother is the fucking Chief of Police? Fucking idiot."

"Auggie's right. You're a bad influence, Monster." Rob sounds so serious that I begin to worry, but then he flashes me a devious grin as he brings my bowl to his lips. The rasp of the lighter gets my blood pounding.

I watch in wonder, never having smoked with another person before. My habit was always private. I know exactly how Robbie is feeling this very moment. The way your blood rushes in your veins. The jitteriness of your hands. The calm that overcomes you just as you strike the lighter– its rasp a signal of the sweetness of what's to come. The heavy, powerful draw of your lips. The welcome suffocation as the potent smoke fills your lungs. The tightness, giving way to the need to cough– to breathe. The sweet surrender of relaxation as the drug slowly gushes throughout your system: arms and legs feeling heavy, eyelids drooping and fluttering… and then you just float in self-created euphoria.

Eyes cutting to the side, Robbie checks for watchers. Finding the coast clear, he offers me a toke. I shake my head no, wanting to be clearheaded for this conversation. "Keep it. It's yours. That will be a lot easier to hide than a fucking bong, Robbie."

I wait while Rob takes another hit… and then another. "My life changed the first day of Kindergarten," he says in a voice gone tight and rough from smoke. Robbie finally sounds like I do. "I was getting my ass kicked for having the name Robin. I was a cute kid– small and chubby-cheeked. Not quite as cute as you and Seth, but a close second. That was bad enough, until I went to school and was instantly bullied… by a girl."

I snort, trying to contain a laugh that is building. Robbie just shakes his head at me, rolling his eyes. He takes another toke while silently laughing at himself.

"My bully was bigger than me and scary mean. She punched me in the tidbits and I fell to the ground, crying while rolling around in the fetal position. She stood over me, laughing and pointing, and said she didn't think I had any balls because I had a girl's name. She was just checking… with her fist. Then she sat on my chest and tied a ribbon in my hair. I thought this strange creature was adorning me to look like a little girl– I was so very wrong. You know how Mom and Dad are. I had long, pretty hair, so the girl had a lot of hair to twist into her ribbon."

"Who was she?" I try not to laugh because I know Robbie got his ass kicked for years. He finally cut off all that pretty hair when I was a kid. Robbie let me hack it off. It was a disaster, and Auggie ended up shaving Robbie's head bald.

"Not yet," he says huskily. "It might be dark out here, but I know you're laughing at me– I can sense it," Robbie teases. "I was lying prone on the ground with her boney knee grinding into my crotch. I won't lie. She scared me so badly that I pissed my pants. I earned the nickname Pissy Pants Robin that day."

"Wow... just wow. Mom and Dad fucked you royally." I try my damnedest not to laugh, but fail. I cover my mouth with the back of my hand and end up making a choking noise.

"Laugh it up," Robbie taunts. "I was saved when a boy came running over and tossed her off me. She flew through the air and landed on her butt, then she started to cry. She wasn't hurt– she was wicked pissed. The two of them beat the ever-loving shit out of each other: black eyes, bloody lips and noses, ripped up clothes. I sat there in shock. Teachers tried to stop them, but they bit and scratched at anyone who tried to intervene. Finally a big kid from seventh or eighth grade ran over and stopped them."

"How? Why couldn't the teachers stop them?"

"No one could get close to them. They were fighting like wild animals. The big kid walked up, pulled his arm back, and punched the boy in the side of the head. I figured the big kid thought the boy was to blame. I was a coward and didn't tell him any differently. The big kid surprised me when he reached over and pulled the girl to her feet, then slapped her hard across the face. They both looked shell-shocked because he didn't pull any punches. It had to hurt. The big kid hauled the scrappers to their feet, pointed at me, and dragged all three of us to the principal's office."

"Did you get into trouble for getting beat up?"

"Nah– I found out that the bigger kid was the crazy bitch's older brother, so he didn't get into trouble for hitting her. My savior was their stepbrother, and he was in kindergarten too. I was surprised the lunatic bitch and the boy were both my age. I felt stunted next to them– they looked at least eight or nine, not five years old."

"What happened next?" I ask, intrigued. I missed out on Robbie and Clover's lives. They were just permanent fixtures in my life without having true personalities. The twins were raised as my blooded siblings, not my niece and nephew. The generation gap caused a major disconnect between Robbie and me.

"I cleaned myself up in the bathroom, but I couldn't get the crazy girl's ribbon out of my hair for love nor money. I yanked and yanked my hair, and it wouldn't budge. I knew I'd have to cut the ribbon out when I got home. I was just a little boy, so everything was so... scary and vivid, like the smallest things were the end of the world."

"Yeah, I still feel that way." I laugh without humor.

"No doubt," Robbie mumbles knowingly. "Man, I was so scared that I thought I'd pee my pants again. I kept looking around corners before I entered the hallways. I must have looked paranoid."

Pausing, Robbie takes another toke, closing his eyes and savoring the sensation. He gazes into the loft space and watches Isis and Malcolm chat for a moment. A look of serenity crosses Robbie's face as he turns to level his stare at me.

"I left the school by the back door, but somehow the boy knew I'd go that way. He was waiting for me, leaning on the outside of the building. When I saw him, I started to hyperventilate. I'll never forget that moment for the rest of my life. He shushed me, and then took great pains to remove the ribbon from my hair. Not one single hair was snapped– I'd never had anyone be so gentle with me. I can't explain it... I just felt safe."

Robbie's eyes are soft, his expression filled with a mix of awe, love, and adoration that even the blind could see. I no longer need to know why Robin puts up with all this shit from Auggie and Isis. It's beyond obvious now, even with my head-up-the-ass-itis.

"He took a friendship bracelet off his wrist, and then tied it around mine. The boy said, *'You're mine, and that means no one will pick on you again. Your name is Rob from now on, don't ever tell anyone it's Robin. Call me Auggie.'* I told Auggie that the mean girl would tell everyone my name. *'Leave Isis to me,'* he promised. Auggie walked me home that day, and every day after, with Isis by our sides."

"How the hell did Auggie know about that shit at five years old?" I yelp in shock.

"From his parents. Auggie's mom was Isis's dad's woman. Submissive in life. What they didn't see from their parents, Malcolm showed them. It wasn't sexual, just the levels of respect and what it meant to take care of another human being. John Mason was a real asshole– Malcolm and Isis's dad. He was also the only father Auggie ever knew. He was Fairport's Chief of Police– an alpha male, macho homophobe who liked his women submissive and quiet... and young."

"Little girl fantasies?" I whisper, feeling sick.

"Not in the sexual sense," Robbie admits. "It's the innocence. You haven't learned self-reliance and self-respect yet. No one has fashioned you in their image. Your thoughts aren't your own yet. It creates an impressionable canvas that someone can mold for their own purposes. While Auggie may not always have your best interests at heart, John Mason was just a domineering asshole who bordered on abuse. John's women didn't even realize they were being abused. They just saw it as obeying their man."

"I shouldn't be relieved that Auggie's fascination is over the fact that a girl like me is too stupid to know any better, but I'm glad it's not sick sexual shit."

"Me too," Robbie mutters quietly. "John Mason had all these rules men were to live by. You took care of the women in your life like possessions: mothers, wives, sisters, daughters, they are your responsibility until they marry. Your worth as a man hinges upon their happiness, or what you thought should make them happy. Malcolm doesn't quite think like that, but he's old-school for sure."

"Oh, I bet Isis just loves that," I say with a smirk in my voice. I gaze into the living area and watch as the brother and sister interact.

"Willow," Robbie draws my name out like I'm a moron. "Isis is gorgeous, intelligent, able to take care of her own needs, but she's Malcolm's princess. John Mason lowered his women so they would obey him. Malcolm elevates his so they know their true worth." Pointing into his apartment, Rob says with conviction. "That girl in there agrees with everything Malcolm stands for. The only men she's allowed to touch her are Auggie and me… and she made us earn it. If anyone disrespects her, she doesn't run to Malcolm, she takes care of it herself."

The level of respect and adoration in my brother's voice amazes me. Robbie thinks Isis is Malcolm's princess, but I doubt he realizes he sees Isis as his queen. "I totally pegged Isis as a raging feminist," I murmur to myself.

"Don't pigeonhole people, Willow," Robbie chastises me. "Isis just knows what she wants and won't accept anything less."

"Are you something she wants, or are you in the latter category of less?" I sound angry. I'm not angry at Robbie, though.

"I want to be happy. I want Isis to be happy. I want Auggie to be happy. I want you to be happy. It's not too much to want. I just know that it's not my place to make any of you happy. I learned a long time ago that what I want, truly want, will never work. Isis and Auggie fight over me and fight themselves. It took me years to figure out that they wanted me to choose so they wouldn't have to."

"But you can't," I whisper."

"No, I can't. They fought before they met me, and they will until they die. They are the male and female versions of one another. Hell, Isis even fights her own nature. She's a woman with a man's mind. She wants to be treated like that princess, but wants to own all those around her like a man. For some inexplicable reason, both Auggie and Isis see me as their *woman*. Huge ego boost, that," Robbie grumbles sarcastically. "I may be small, artistic, and cute. But as I said, that doesn't make me a female, and it sure as shit doesn't make me gay."

"I think I understand a bit how you feel, like how when people look at me, all they see is a little girl. You're not weak in mind, body, or spirit, so it's insulting that even your best friends see you that way."

"That ribbon– that friendship bracelet? They were tokens. Makeshift collars to bind me to them in ownership. When that bracelet frayed…" Rob yanks the piece of leather from his back pocket– his collar. "Auggie put this collar on me. So I ask myself, how much of this is about me, and how much of this is about them?"

I say the only thing I can think to say. "I'm sorry."

"I've asked Isis to marry me at least a dozen times over the past decade. The shit-fit she threw in the Playroom, where she listed the days lost over Auggie, that's all on her. When I ask her to marry me, she says she can't with the ghost of Auggie's shadow hanging over *us*. She wants me to choose just her, but she can't choose just me. Auggie, he'll never choose either one of us. It's not how John Mason, the homophobe, raised his stepson. Isis isn't a submissive, little female because of her drive and possessive nature. I'm not submissive at all, though they treat me as I am, but I also have a dick. Neither of us fits the rules Auggie was bred on."

"So I am just some replacement part," I stutter out, horrified.

"No, Willow. Auggie is a grown man, with grown man needs and wants and dreams. You just happen to fit all of the things he thinks he wants: a malleable woman who won't see his flaws, one that won't question him. A woman who will think of him as a god. You're someone he loves like family and can grow to love as a woman. He's fostering you to be his wife, and if you don't see that, you're blind. I get it. I may not like it, but I get it." Rob sighs, resigned.

"I don't like it, and I don't get it," I grumble.

"You're my family, Willow." Robin looks at me in a way he never has before, as if he's scared I'll hate him for what he's about to say. "It was me who demanded you befriend Devon. The *plan* was all me. Malcolm just wanted you to hang around his sons to see what happened– let nature take its course, so to speak. We all know what Auggie is up to, Willow. I have that possessiveness in my blood, too, ya know? I *am* a man, and you *are* my responsibility until you're married. My happiness hinges upon yours. I want you to pick a guy you like, live a little. Auggie was furious at Malcolm and me when we stepped in."

"What do you mean, you stepped in?" I ask when Robbie stops talking.

"Auggie and I fought from the second you started working for him, before even. I knew what he was up to. Auggie will deny it, so do not repeat this. But the bastard has been waiting for you since you could walk. I was jealous and angry and hurt and scared. John Mason has been haunting Auggie since he was a toddler, infecting his actions. It's subconscious on Auggie's part, but he's been crafting you since birth as his wife. The man has always known every move you've made. I thought it was sweet at first, another person having your back."

"What?!" I shout.

"I was the one who put Devon as the condition. Auggie could…" Robbie stumbles over his choice of words, treading lightly. "Be your first, but then he was to back the fuck off. I was the one who made Auggie see reason and wait until you matured. With Dad being busy and Sam gone, the responsibility falls onto me, like how you feel possessive over Seth. That will always trump boss, friend, or lover until you get married. Even then, your husband better treat you right, or suffer my wrath. I don't want you to get overpowered and trapped by Auggie."

"Like he trapped and overpowered you?"

"Exactly," Robbie admits immediately. "Just don't take this shit too seriously, Willow. You're still a baby, and I mean no insult by that. Experience life. Make mistakes. Make friends. Make lovers. Make enemies. Don't be someone's wife yet. Don't get trapped for life. Don't be someone's property– be your own. All I want for you is to be happy, to live life without regret."

"I want that for you, too," I cry out.

"Good." Robbie flashes me a sly smile. "So don't spit and sputter and get pissed at me, because I don't think you should be exclusive with a man who won't be exclusive to you," Robbie demands. "Even if you were to marry, Auggie wouldn't be faithful. I know it sounds like I'm coming from a place of hurt or jealousy, but I'm not. I'm warning you. I've thrown fits and beat the hell out of the man, but he's not going to change for anyone– ever."

"I try not to throw fits like you do," I tease, trying to lighten the mood since Rob looks like he's about to bawl. "I get it, alright? But picking out a boyfriend for me is crossing the line… tossing Devon at me." Furious, I shake my head in disgust.

"Not like that, Willow. Not a boyfriend. Not for sex. Friendship. It's like the bond between Auggie, Isis, and me. You guys need that. You can't have that with Auggie. Not that kind of bond."

"I don't know what you mean." I whimper out of frustration.

"Auggie, Isis, and I, no matter what, we're best friends. Yes, we've been lovers in the past, but not in years. It was a bond built on trust, trust in knowing them so well I can accurately anticipate their actions. Isis puts me first in all things. Auggie puts himself first in all things… and I just feel lost. But it somehow works. We may move on and marry other people, but that bond will never fade. Willow, you're going to need that kind of bond if you're going to survive Auggie."

"You can't just say, '*here, have some friends, Willow,*' like I'm too stupid to pick my own." Hurt, on the verge of tears, I try to hold myself together.

"Didn't you already pick them?" Robbie says knowingly, arching an eyebrow in my direction. "Willow, none of us are stupid. Other than this new fixation over Auggie, you've only had one crush in your life. If Kieren and Devon got any tighter, they'd fuse as one. It only makes sense you'd like them both. They are who you're going to need to vent to about Auggie." Robbie comes full-circle, back to where we began when we walked out onto the deck, where he said he needed to vent about Isis to someone.

"Not sex. I'm not saying you won't ever go there. I know how that can just overcome you, and it will be the best and the worst you've ever had."

"I don't want to talk anymore," I grumble.

"Too bad," Robbie states unequivocally. "We're talking. You look at Auggie like a Kool-Aid drinker at Jonestown."

"That wasn't Kool-Aid." I cross my arms over my chest and raise an eyebrow in challenge.

"See, smarty pants. You most definitely don't apply yourself if you know that little-known fact." Robbie challenges me back. "My point, you get this glazed-over look in your eyes when you gaze at Auggie, like a cult victim. I thought I'd give you some more realistic options that don't include marrying a misogynist and popping out red-headed babies before you hit nineteen."

"Realistic options?"

"The Mason brothers. I wouldn't touch *Date Rape* if you want to stay alive, though. That may push Auggie over the brink."

"What? Date Rape?" I try not to snicker at Kieren's new nickname. "What's Auggie's issue with Kieren, anyway?"

"Head-up-your-ass-itis strikes again." Robbie chuckles, looking slightly deranged. "Jealousy. Auggie's jealous. I was in that hallway, too, Willow. I saw what was happening. We all stood by and watched. We didn't intervene until you said no and Ren didn't stop… and we all could tell you didn't mean that *no*. If you weren't worried about disappointing Auggie, you would've done Kieren in a heartbeat. Holy chemistry, Batman, between you two. I get it. I was a hormonal teenager once. I was led around by my dick like it was a leash looking for its master's hand."

"I'm done talking." Voice tight with mortification, the words are propelled between clenched teeth. "D. O. N. E."

"I know the power a man holds over a woman." Robbie ignores me and keeps on talking. "A good girl will forge an unbreakable bond with the man who takes her innocence. She'll stick to him, even if it's not right for her. Auggie was willing to give you to anyone *but* the one you had a crush on… just think about that." Voice dripping threat and challenge, Rob stares me down.

"You're so full of shit," I snarl. "I could've done Kieren and never looked back. I'm pretty sure he was using my ass anyway."

"Isis was my first," Rob quickly says before I can say more. "Other than Auggie, Isis has never touched another man, and she never will– unless she meets someone who rocks her world and she marries the fool. That's how I know how a good girl thinks. One time is all it takes, whether on the floor of a hallway, in the backseat of a car, or in a bed."

Arms folded over my chest, I glare up at my brother. "I don't plan on marrying Auggie." I point out the fatal flaw in Rob's thinking.

Other than rolling his eyes, Rob ignores me. "Auggie and I know you *both*, Willow. I've known the kid since he was born, and Auggie lived with him. Kieren would've been an instant husband. Ren's a Mason, first and foremost, and you're *you*."

"You say that like it's a bad thing," I growl, eyes narrowing, so pissed off I'm not digesting Rob's words.

"If you'd had some romantic interlude with Auggie on your first time, you would've been trapped for life. Playroom–" Robbie snarls, pointing at himself. "Also me. I said I'd castrate Auggie otherwise. Clinical, no attachment deflowering. Now you won't be confined to a cage– imprisoned by whoever screwed you first, Good Girl."

Ignoring Rob's venomous admission, confusion spills from my lips. "I remember Auggie proudly announcing that he took two Prynnes' innocence."

"Auggie was the first guy I did. Isis was my first girl. Auggie and I took turns taking each other's virginity. Don't freak out on me, Willow. It wasn't about sex. It was about power and control. Giving someone your innocence is taken for granted– it's forever and you can't get it back once it's gone. It should be an honor, not something you throw away on someone unworthy. We agreed that the three of us would be each other's first. Isis made us promise to wait for her to turn sixteen. On her birthday, I made love to Isis, and then Auggie fucked her when I was done. They weren't getting along even then, but Isis wanted to be Auggie's first girl. It meant something to all of us."

"Wow..."

"Auggie can't be that for you, Willow. He's already been a teenager. He's a grown man in an adult world. You're a girl playing where you shouldn't. Play with Devon. Befriend Ren, and only fuck him if Auggie won't find out. Grow up before you try to take on Auggie, or you'll be lost forever, more lost than you are now."

"Kieren will just use me, and Devon just wants to be my friend. You have it backward," I try to reason with Robin.

"Kieren's a horny teenage boy. Yeah, he's probably dying to be inside you," Rob says with a shrug. "But he's Malcolm's son, raised on those same tenets passed down from his grandfather. I won't freak you out by telling you what I really think Kieren wants. It scared the fuck out of Auggie, as he saw his envisioned future slipping through his fingertips. Pretty sure Kieren is suffering from brain damage over the amount of beat-downs Auggie's given him over the years to keep him away from you. So maybe you better stay away from Kieren out of self-preservation." Robbie gives an evil laugh. "Auggie's not worried over Devon, so you can screw him until you're blue in the face without consequence."

"*This is fucked up, Rob!*" I rub a palm over my face, hating how my tone has taken on a whining edge. "I need to think."

"This *is* fucked up," comes roughly from the open sliding-glass door, where an angry beast of a man casts a shadow over us, looking and sounding betrayed. "Get your shit, and get in the truck. Both of you are coming with me."

"Fuck," Rob breathes out the second Auggie stalks back into the loft, where he begins a conversation with Malcolm and Isis. "Do you have any Altoids for real? Auggie is anti-drug in the extreme."

I take pity on Rob since he sounds petrified. "Here." I toss him a pack of Cinnamon *Ice Breakers* and a small can of spray. "That's deodorizer. It's scentless. Just spray it in your hair."

"Where the hell do you carry all this stuff?" Robbie sounds awed as he pops a mint and sprays his hair.

"Puffy coat. Even if I get hugged, ain't nobody finding my goodies." I trail a giggle, fearing it's going to be the last laugh for a while.

CHAPTER EIGHTEEN

The bumpy truck ride hurts like a bitch, smashing my abraded privates against the hard bench seat. I feel like I'm being punished– repeatedly –not going to Sunday dinner with the family.

Last night, Rob and I left the deck and entered into Hell. That is, if you call being ignored by Augustus Kline living in Hell. Hours later, disappointment and betrayal still waft off the man in waves. Robbie is being punished for the fit he threw in the Playroom and for spilling most of Auggie's secrets. I think I'm just being ignored because Auggie is upset and doesn't feel like talking.

Last night at Rob's place, Isis couldn't eavesdrop because she was chatting with Malcolm in our line of sight. What we hadn't realized was that Auggie had entered the loft and was leaning by the door, listening to the last half of our very private conversation.

We know everything Auggie overheard because they were the only words he's uttered to us in the past eighteen hours. Standing in the center of the loft, with Malcolm and Isis as his audience, Auggie succinctly listed everything we said like a lawyer giving their opening statements at a trial. When he was finished, he didn't speak again, no matter what we said or did.

Auggie then took both Rob and me back to his loft above Revamped. Furious with us, Auggie was still kind, leaving his bed for Rob and me to share. We tried to fall asleep, but it was impossible with Auggie pacing the floor while staring us down. Creepy.

Auggie has sulked since last night. When we got up this morning, Auggie made us go down to the shop and work even though Revamped is closed on Sundays. We worked on Auggie's illustrations website after we scrubbed and organized Revamped. Even while working, he said nothing, just grunted while pointing.

"How does the club work? I mean, is the Playroom even legal?" I ask Rob to break the strained silence. Auggie is just driving around town, going down street after street, instead of taking us straight to my house for Sunday dinner. I think Auggie wants me to flinch when he hits the bumps. The man is very creative with his highly vindictive punishments, considering my crotch hurts because of him in the first place.

"It's illegal, but Malcolm takes care of it on his end," Robbie replies quietly. "Auggie owns Rush."

"I did not know that," I drawl in shock.

"The Playroom has nothing to do with the club, so the legalities don't matter." Out of everything, this conversation gets Auggie's attention? Odd.

"The people in the Playroom are invite only– *by me*," Auggie stresses. "I'm not going to apologize for my *cravings*, or judge the people of this town for their own. We all needed a space to play so I decided to use Rush's storeroom until I could afford to buy a house. This works for now. We like to go play in the club to loosen up first. It's win-win."

Auggie slows down, running the passenger-side front tire directly over a pothole. I yelp in pain, trying to get my ass off the seat before the back tire meet a similar fate.

"What's the matter?" Auggie asks out of concern.

"I'm sore is all," I say lightly to lessen any guilt he might feel. In reality, I hurt like hell. But I'm not telling Auggie that. He'd probably never touch me again. I asked for it– I'll live with it. It's the price I would gladly pay a thousand times over to not be a virgin anymore.

"Are you bleeding?" Auggie accuses, and I finally get a clue. Auggie isn't ignoring me– he feels guilty. He's acting like he murdered my innocence. Poor bastard.

"No, I'm perfectly fine," I lie. I'm spotting a bit. But I think the issue is that the skin is rubbed off, like a brush-burn. Sex is the furthest thing from my mind.

"Alright then, I guess it's normal," Auggie murmurs as he pulls over to the curb, and I worry he'll make me walk instead of enduring the ride.

"That one over there." Auggie points to a massive three-story house with a mansard roofline. It's rundown and creepy in a gothic sort of way. "It's going for next to nothing. The owner just passed away. She was a ninety-nine. No one has taken care of this beauty in over thirty years. Combine that with the fact that she passed away *inside* the house, nobody wants to purchase it. I bid twenty grand on it yesterday. It's known as the neighborhood spook house. The kids won't even walk on the sidewalk in front of it."

Flashing an evil grin, Auggie loves knowing this house is creepy. A delighted glow shines from his green eyes. The wrought-iron hurricane fence surrounding the property is mirrored on the roofline. The pointy metal is foreboding. The siding hasn't been painted in decades, with no hint of its original color– it's gray weathered wood now. The house matches the era of furniture Auggie is obsessed with, but the house and furnishings do not match Auggie– strangest thing ever.

"It should close soon with no other interested parties, and it was willed to some distant cousin who lives across the country. They'll just want the money as fast as possible. I have to fix the place up, but this way I can customize everything. It will be nice not to live in the store's inventory loft and play in the club's storage room. Plus, I'm sick of paying for storage units."

"Wow," Rob and I say in unison.

"If you guys are good, I'll even let you have a floor. The top floor attic is for the Playroom. It has access to the widow's watch. The Spook House has a full basement, the attic, and two more floors for whatever. There are nine bedrooms in the place, so be good and I'll let you move in."

"Wow," I say again.

"It shouldn't be longer than a month before it's live-in ready. New rule is in effect as of last night. If you want to play at the Playroom, you have to work at the Spook House. It will be twenty-four-seven until completion. If they don't have the time to work, then they have to hire someone to take their place. If they don't put in twenty hours a week, then it's no Playroom for them."

"Do I get extra credit if I work longer than that?" I mutter snarkily, loving that my Auggie is back. Playful, smiling, and warm… demanding and commanding, no longer sullen and silent.

"You *will* live here," Auggie stresses, staring directly at Robbie, looking right through me as I sit in between them. "Absence makes the heart grow fonder. Make Isis miss you enough to marry you. Plus, after what I heard outta your disloyal ass of a mouth last night, you'll want to save your sister from my predatory ways."

Rob and I say at the same time, "Aug–"

Ignoring us, as usual, Auggie talks right over us. "So the twenty-hour rule doesn't apply for either of you. Rob, if you're not deep into creativity, you'll be at the Spook House. Willow, you will go to work, eat, and then go to the Spook House and work. I'll give you seven hours to sleep, and then we do this again– everyday until its completion. It will be in your best interest to make everyone work very hard on the house, because the more the Playroom minions work, the less you have to do. Your extra credit is that you both have a say in the design. I already have your rooms picked out."

Auggie pulls away from the curb and starts toward home. He doesn't ask us what we want, he just tells us. I guess that's what it means to be Auggie's property. I'm not going to bitch. He knows what he's doing.

Rob's stoically frozen like a stone. I stare at the side of his face until the corners of his lips quirk up. Yeah, Rob's not fooling anyone. He's fucking excited, too. Remodeling houses runs in our blood. My father put food in our bellies with the sweat of his brow. When Sam married Clover, he joined the family business too. I grew up being my dad and Sam's little helper. Mix our heritage with Rob's artistic side, this project is calling us like a moth to flame, just as Auggie knew it would.

"Like brother, like sister," I say underneath my breath, and Rob barks a laugh in reply.

I try to act normal as I enter my family's house with Rob and Auggie flanking me. I don't want to look like the girl who crawled around the floor in a sex den, gave a blowjob, and lost her virginity with the majority of Fairport's hedonistic denizens watching. I don't act like my brother and I are owned by his best friend, or that my owner gave me to another guy to play with. I'm not ashamed of the fact that Robbie and I watched one another have sex with people. But your parents just shouldn't know these private things about you. The dark perversions that dwell deep within your soul are for only the likeminded to know and understand.

The house doesn't even feel like I live here anymore. I've hated it since I graduated. I just live here in body, not spirit. Every time I walk through the front door, I feel like shit. Worthless. Deadweight. I'm an adult living with her parents when I should just be coming home to visit or to help out. I feel like a loser mooch. I'm not a part of the house, not like my parents. Clover and the twins are more at home than I am, and they live next door.

If I move into the Spook House, I know Auggie will make me work for my keep. He'll make me *work* for it, not *pay* for it. There is a distinction. Auggie makes me feel very useful, like I have a purpose in life. I need that feeling. I guess Robbie does, too. It's not about sex, either. Must be my parents raised us wrong somehow, or it's bred into us.

I run upstairs to change, avoiding everyone.

"Hey," I say to Essie, stopping in my tracks. So much for avoiding everyone while I wash the taint of last night from my body. "Give me ten. I've gotta shower." Essie never even looks up at me as I breeze by.

I find Essie lazing on my bed when I'm fresh from the shower and looking for something to wear. "I'm baaaacccckkkk…" I draw out when Essie ignores my presence.

Essie says nothing in reply. She just stares at me in contemplation while worrying her bottom lip between her teeth. She pulls a piece of hair from behind her ear and gnaws on the ends. It's a habit that she's tried to break, but it reappears when she's anxious.

"Well, spit it out," I coax Essie, knowing that the look on her face means she wants to talk.

"I went back last night. I saw," Essie whispers sadly. She nibbles on her hair and stares at me. I can tell she wants to cry. It breaks my heart that my best friend and cousin judges what I did last night. I know it's not normal, but it's *my* normal.

"What'd you see?" I avoid looking at Essie while I pull on a pair of knit slacks and a wool sweater. We have to dress nicely for Sunday dinner. I'm lucky they don't always manage to drag me to church beforehand. Essie still goes. She's in a pretty navy dress, pearls, and ballet flats.

I don't mind going to church, because I do have faith. It just feels strange to sit with my family when I disrespect them to their faces on a daily basis. I feel guilty about my behavior, but I still do it anyway. It's a compulsion. Pastor Otis would call me a harlot as he glared at me from his pulpit if he knew what I did last night. He'd cast Robbie and me to the pits of Hell. No more church for me. My faith is between me and God. I don't need an entire congregation judging me, too.

"I only watched for a minute, and then I ran out." Essie sobs, and I finally look at her.

"What minute?" I breathe so quietly I fear Essie can't hear me.

Unfathomable, I can't believe Essie is this upset with me. I'm the same Willow as yesterday morning. It's not like I killed someone. After all the times I've watched Essie on her knees with some dude's grubby cock between her lips, and once when she had one man between her lips and another one's hand up her skirt. I never judged her. I made sure it was Essie's choice and watched, and she was thrilled that I accepted what got her off. Now Essie judges me, and it's not even silent judgment. It's painted across Essie's features and boring into me from her penetrating, disappointed gaze.

"Did Auggie force you? Your legs were pinned down and Devon was holding your head. Everyone was watching. When I saw you cry out in pain, I ran away. I'm such a huge coward. I should have stopped Auggie. I couldn't believe that Rob was just sitting next to you... watching." Essie hides her face in her hands and cries for me.

"Essie! Essie, no, it wasn't like that." I hug her tightly. I shouldn't have thought Essie would feel ashamed of me. Oh, God, she blames herself.

"If that's all you saw, then you wouldn't understand. I wanted Auggie to do it. I wanted him to do it in the Playroom, and I was proud that it was him." I plead with Essie. I can't have her thinking she was a coward for leaving when she's totally off base.

"Did you like it?" Essie asks me, hoping I'll say yes.

"I didn't hate it," I drag the words out. "It was more clinical than anything. It wasn't about sex, not really. We can't have sex without Auggie hurting me. It was some guy thing over who got to pop the cherry. It must be a badge of honor for a guy or something. I don't know. But I wanted Auggie to be the one to do it. He just pushed inside me and slid back out. That was it. In the technical sense, I still haven't had sex yet. I guess virginity is tied more to who pokes you first than the actual act of sex. Let's call Augustus Kline the hymen destroyer."

My joke falls flat, hanging out there without a laugh. "Why can't you have sex with Auggie?" Essie scrunches her eyebrows at me, looking at me like I've lost my ever-loving mind.

"Ah... tiny hole." I make a circle using my thumb and index finger. "Versus an Augustus-sized cock." I part my hands like I'm telling a fish story. "I don't know much about sizing, but I assume eleven inches is monstrous." A pair of blue eyes the size of saucers gaze back at me, and I bust out a laugh.

"Surely you're joking," Essie draws out, denying that it's possible.

"I wish I was, or I wouldn't have to wait to fuck him. I guess I need practice first. I think Auggie's worried it'll never work right for us. We'll just have to do other stuff. Truthfully, I think Auggie's right. I've never felt so inadequate in my life, and that's saying something." I admit self-deprecatingly, then add sarcasm to the mix. "You know exactly how great I find myself."

I look at the clock on the wall. "Dinner starts in five minutes. We don't want to piss Clover off," I say to stop our uncomfortable conversation. Essie's my best friend, but I'll never be able to explain my feelings about the Playroom, or the dynamic between Auggie and me. She's never had an issue with body-image or sex, and she's always gotten what she wants, whenever she wants, and whoever she wants. Essie and I are cousins, and we may be friends, but we share no common denominators whatsoever.

"When isn't Clover pissed?" Essie grabs my arm so I can't leave yet. "Are you alright after last night? It was what you wanted, right?" Her concern warms me and simultaneously makes me feel guilty for not wanting to confide in her.

"Yes, it was what I wanted. I just wish I wasn't a freak of nature," I hiss angrily. "I'm not woman enough for Auggie, and I worry I'll never be," I admit before I can stop myself, and then I want to kick my own ass for saying the words out loud.

"Aw, Willow," Essie cries, pity lacing her tone.

"Forget I said anything." I quickly change the subject. "Auggie promised Clover I'd behave tonight, so we better get down there."

"What'd ya do?" Essie follows me out into the hall.

"During dinner last night, I told Clover that she needed to get laid. Mom agreed. Pandemonium ensued." I laugh as I jog down the steps. "I really need to start treating Clover like she's a human being."

"Then maybe Clover needs to start acting like a human instead of a buzzkill," Essie mutters, trying not to sound too much like a bitch.

The doorbell rings, and I run to answer it out of reflex. Flowers are thrust at me the moment the door opens. "Whoa…"

I take the bundle of flower shop daisies before my mind recognizes the guy standing before me.

"Oh! Hey, Devon, c'mon out of the cold." I gesture around the living room.

I give Essie a *what the fuck* look and she just shrugs back at me.

"Those are for Mrs. Prynne– I mean your mom... Um..." Devon stares at his shoes for a moment, and it gives Essie and me a chance to check him out. Devon's dressed in his Sunday best: charcoal gray slacks and a crimson sweater. Devon isn't blond and blue-eyed like Kieren. He has messy dark hair and light blue eyes. He's not much taller than I am, and lanky. He doesn't intimidate me like Kieren does. The quarterback was hot in fantasy, but scary hot in reality. His brother is more suited for me. Mr. Kline is always right. Well, in this case, my brother is right.

"How about we go give them to my mom," I prompt Devon when he nervously fidgets and looks at the floor. "She's in the kitchen with all the females in the family. Except us." I point at Essie, then back at myself. "We're told to stay away from the food."

"Only because they want it to be edible," Essie finishes for me. "I boiled a pot dry last time I tried to make Ramen Noodles... and the noodles were in the pan. Smelled like burnt hair for weeks. Mom nearly shit a brick when Dad threw all the Top Ramen into the trash. Said it was for my own good."

"Uncle Will bought five fire extinguishers, too," I add in while silently laughing. "Personally, I would've bought you a kitchen timer."

"... And a cookbook," Essie chirps.

"Yeah, that guy cookbook: *A Man. A Can. A Plan: 50 Great Guy Meals Even You Can Make*. I saw Dad eyeing that the last time we went to Barnes and Noble. I bet it was for you, Essie. I tried to tell him it was too advanced for you."

"Bitch," she replies with affection.

Ignoring our banter, Devon quickly says, "Auggie invited me today." Refusing to look up from his shoes, he doesn't see the look Essie and I share. "I hope that isn't a problem. Err... um– so how do you feel today?" Devon seems discomforted by his own question.

"OH! MY! GOD! This is beyond fucked in the head!" Essie shouts in awe when she figures out what's going on. She covers her mouth and runs from the room.

"You know how Essie can be," I say in response to her reaction, spreading my hands like *what are ya gonna do*? It's not every day the guy who emotionally owns you, who will deny he's educating you to be his wife, asks a guy to break you in for him. Actually, I doubt it ever happens.

We're making history here.

Fucked up.

I don't know why, but I give Devon a hug. My body moves on its own accord without a signal from my brain. I just find myself embracing the boy like a long-lost friend. I guess after last night, I feel closer to him. It's weird, and I can't explain it. I just missed the hell out of Devon.

"You smell nice," I breathe out against Devon's neck and he shivers. "Like snow... and you're so warm." I decide I like hugging him. He isn't that much bigger than me. When I hug Auggie, I feel like a toddler. Hugging Devon make me feel like I'm almost woman-sized.

Devon doesn't hesitate. His arms pull me closer to his chest and he sighs contently. He rubs my back in small circles and pats, causing me to melt into his embrace. God, he smells fantastic– leather and musk with a hint of vanilla. Memories of his smile and laugh pour into me from the past. He was always kind to me, truly befriended me– a gawky girl who was years younger and about as popular as pissy-pants Robin. We stay like this for far longer than we should.

"I heard Essie's exclamation when your guest arrived." Auggie says from behind me. Devon freezes, then instantly thaws. Must be Auggie isn't pulling his scary *don't touch my shit* possessive expression at the moment. I slowly pull away.

"Devon, you'll find Rob seated at the dining room table. He'll introduce you to the Prynnes and Websters as Willow's boyfriend." Auggie orders in a calm tone.

My palm quivers as I hand Devon the flowers. Devon smiles at me, and then leaves to meet my family. "My boyfriend?" I arch a brow in Auggie's direction. "Are you insane?"

"C'mere," Auggie commands, and then sits on the third stair step with his mile-long legs on the floor. He pulls me into his lap, and I know I'm about to get lectured when he sighs.

"Insane?" Auggie sounds extremely amused. "We both know I heard Rob's version of events. Mind you, they dramatically differ from my experience of those events. So I think we need to discuss Kieren and Devon. Your birthday night antics ruined a few plans of mine. Kieren ruined a few plans of mine as well."

"I hate how you all were planning out my life like I'm your own personal avatar on *The Sims*. You can't just form us with compatible traits and click on a bed. *WooHoo with Devon*. I'm a freewill player, Auggie. If that's what you have in mind, then just put me in a room and remove the door. I'd rather my character starve to death."

"Willow," Auggie draws my name out, trying like hell to suppress a laugh. "I love you. But you do realize I'm more creative than that, don't you? I wouldn't take your door away to starve you, Monster. You're far too thin as it is. I'd tell you to go swimming, and then remove the pool ladder. I'd sit back and watch you drown."

"Assmunch." I snarl, but I can't help smirking. "You're my kind of devious geek."

"And you're obviously mine." Auggie nuzzles the side of my head, sighing. "Kieren's a kid, a little whore. Truthfully, I hate his guts because he reminds me of myself at that age. So, no Kieren, unless he's just your buddy. I know the slut makes you hot– don't bother denying it. If I could create Kieren a ridiculously handsome yet equally stupid avatar, I'd name it Date Rape and trap him in a kitchen with a shitty stove and no smoke detector. I'd watch Date Rape burn to death while making a grilled cheese, all the while I'd be wearing a smile on my face. I may have done that this afternoon... several times over... for hours."

"I knew you weren't working– you have no clue how to run a laptop unless it's to play a video game. You're a demonic slacker, Augustus Kline. But enough with the death by Sim-ocide," I grumble. "Let's get serious, Auggie."

"A serious Willow? Hmm... that's a change." I move my elbow in preparation of assault, but Auggie shifts me to the side before I can make contact. "Okay, serious. Months ago, Devon asked about you when I came over for his *Welcome Home* dinner. He just got back from the academy and wanted to date you. I thought it best since he's a couple years older than you to wait until you were legal. It would look bad if a cadet was found with an underage girl. I don't think you realize that while you were crushing on Devon's brother, he was crushing on you."

"Why?" I mutter in shock, and Auggie laughs at me.

"Don't sell yourself short, Willow. Trust me when I say you're appealing." Auggie's voice dips low as he whispers the words into my ear. I stifle a shiver, overcome with the need to prove that I'm not addicted to his approval.

I fail.

Big time.

I melt into Auggie's lap as my eyes slip shut in pure ecstasy. Augustus Kline finds me appealing. "You're so full of shit," I say more about myself than him.

Ignoring the dig, Auggie keeps on talking. "Devon's quiet and smart. He wants to be your friend as a friend. But I know you and I know him– it wouldn't have stayed friendly for long. I'll let Rob take all the credit, but he's as full of shit as you're calling yourself." Auggie proves he can read my unvoiced thoughts. "I was fine about you and Devon all along."

"But not Kieren." I bait Auggie because I'm irritated that he finds me so transparent.

"Fuck. You. Willow." Auggie stares me down until I shrink. "My motives were pure, Monster. If I wanted you fucked and ditched, I'd be fine with Kieren. But I wanted you to know what it was like to have a real boyfriend. Devon's a really great young man, and I need you to see what it's like to date someone your own age, not a grown man who did this shit a decade ago. I don't want you to miss out on this stuff, and I don't want you saying it's not important. It's like a rite of passage in growing up from a teenager to an adult."

"I think I get it. You want someone to take me to the movies or mini-golf, because it isn't your scene?"

"Definitely not my scene." Deeply sighing, Auggie prepares to say something I most likely won't like. "Willow, I don't want you thinking I'm your friend, or God forbid, your boyfriend. It would be wrong." Auggie sighs again. "On so many levels, right now the age gap is far too wide. I find myself drawn to you for reasons Rob so nicely spewed last night. We aren't equals right now, and we can't be. You realize this, right?"

"I get it! I do! I know you're not my boyfriend, and that you don't want to be. I don't see you that way, Auggie. Honest," I protest in a panic. I can't have Auggie thinking that I see him as my boyfriend, because he'd drop me in a heartbeat. It's never crossed my mind. Our differences are too obvious for me to even contemplate Auggie as my boyfriend.

"I know that. I meant what I said. You're only eighteen. You will change from day-to-day. I'm not the same person I was last year. At your age, it's night and day from one month to the next. There are no guarantees that you and I will ever move in the same direction."

"I think I understand what you're saying, Auggie. Right now, people my age are learning to grow up: going to college or getting a job, looking for a place to live– exploring. You've already done that, and you don't want to repeat it with me. You're hoping I'll grow up, and eventually we'll be… evened out."

"Exactly, Willow. So that brings us back to the issue at hand. Devon. Date him, don't date him. Befriend him, or hate him. But give it a try. You guys have a lot in common, and I honestly believe you'll enjoy each other's company. I'm not *hooking* you up. I'm giving you a companion who's going through the same stage in life as you are."

"Okay," I breathe out. "I'll give it a try. For you, Auggie," I murmur, hating how much I seek his approval, but loving how amazing I feel when I receive it. It's twisted.

"Thank you," Auggie says, giving me a little affectionate squeeze as reward. "I also need you to understand that the Playroom and real life are separate. You can be committed to someone, yet all bets are off in the Playroom. Devon and Kieren have never played. I'm not Robin, leaker of all secrets, so I refuse to say why the boys go to the Playroom. I'll only say they're there to observe. Malcolm brought them in on their eighteenth birthdays, and they visit every Saturday night, and only watch what Malcolm approves."

"Why'd their dad do that?" I mumble.

"Willow," Auggie cautions. "Sometimes you're too much like Robin. If you want to know why, you can ask Devon."

"Shit," I mutter with feeling. "I'm sorry. I was more or less talking to myself out loud. You're right, as always, Auggie."

"Willow, I know you feel older than you are in your mind and younger in your body, and it's hard for you to come to terms with the difference. I had the opposite problem my entire life. I've looked like a grown man since I was twelve. But I am only twenty-eight right now. I'm not ready to get married or have a family, no matter what Rob thinks. Someday I may want that. But I'll never stop with the Playroom."

"You're trying to be tactful with your warning. You're saying no matter what, no matter who, you're always going to go to the Playroom. Which means you'll always want to do other people?" I hesitantly say, yet it comes out with more of a huge question mark at the end. It's what Robbie was not-so lightly hinting at last night... that Auggie won't change for anyone. You either take Augustus Kline as he is, flaws and all, or get the fuck out.

"The Playroom was something Rob, Isis, and I came up with when we were kids. So whoever I end up with has to understand that it's a permanent fixture in my life."

"I get that." I agree, but I don't know if I could live with it. Not that Auggie is proposing or anything. In a way, I think he's warning me off, or giving me time to come to terms with what I can and can't live with. He's being blatantly honest, which never feels good.

"Willow, you need to date boys who are in your stage in life. I'm buying a house, and I have a career. I own businesses. You still need to live to find out what makes you tick."

Auggie rocks me back and forth for a few minutes, and his sadness flavors his movements. I touch his face gently with my fingertips, enjoying the way his whiskers abrade my skin. "What's wrong?"

"Devon will be your friend for life. I'm just scared that you'll fall for him, and I'll lose you. We aren't right for each other right now, but we may be someday. I'd rather lose you than trap and suffocate you." Auggie kisses the tip of my nose, then sets me on my feet.

"Auggie–"

"Willow." The way Auggie says my name has me on high alert. Holding my gaze, he gives me the most earnest look I've ever witnessed. "Robin's perception of me wasn't entirely off base. Never forget that."

"I won't," I promise as I stand in my parents' living room, realizing this isn't the time or the place for such a life-changing conversation.

Stretching to his full height, Auggie flashes me a devious grin. "I have an announcement to make to your family. One that may get my ass kicked. So let's hope Devon's presence makes them think it's something it's not."

CHAPTER NINETEEN

"What kind of academy did you graduate from?" I ask Devon while we eat the huge dinner Clover prepared.

My sister may have a stick lodged in her rectum, but she's a mean cook. Today's Sunday meal is ham, scalloped potatoes, green beans almondine, and cranberry salad. I have no idea where Clover learned to cook since Mom is terrible at it. It must be Clover's natural-born talent. Clover would probably be happier if she cooked for a living instead of being Mayor Ross's personal assistant. I have no idea why she never went to culinary school. If I knew what I was good at, I'd grab hold of it with both fists and never let go.

Devon places his fork on the side of his plate, showing impeccable manners that are lost on my family, except for Clover, that is. "The Police Academy my dad went to. It's not far from here. But I had to board there because the commute was too far. It's the best Massachusetts has to offer. It spit out three generations of Mason police officers." Devon's smile is friendly and comfortable. I can hear the pride in his soft voice, and it makes me happy.

Devon has relaxed since he nervously arrived. Family is family, no matter whose it is. The family dynamic is always the same. I can tell Devon spends a lot of time with his own family by his comfort level with mine.

"I did not see that coming. A cop, eh? So much for drinking," I tease. "And other things," I mutter underneath my breath.

Devon moves a hank of hair off my shoulder and leans into me. "I think it's about personal responsibility. I don't drink and drive, and I won't let anyone else. But if they can vote or die for their country– go for it. I carry a badge and a gun and could die on the job. I should be able to relax responsibly in any way I see fit once I'm off duty." Devon's breath on my ear makes me shiver. He smiles knowingly as he sits upright.

"A cop's kinda... badass..." I draw out, thoroughly impressed. Devon smirks in response, but doesn't look away from his plate. I'm inexplicably drawn to the curve of his lips, and a fierce blush creeps over my cheeks. My eyes dart away and I busy myself with pretending to eat a green bean.

"I won't have a permanent position until the new year. Our county isn't very big, so a position is hard to come by. The Chief of Police is officially retiring on New Year's Eve. My dad's taking his job, not that he hasn't been the *unofficial* chief for a couple years now. So everybody's moving up a place on the ladder, with me at the bottom."

"Your dad will be your boss," I say in horror, causing Devon to laugh infectiously. I turn to gaze at the side of his face. I never knew a laugh could hold so much emotion, and make you feel those same emotions, too. Wild.

"Dad's been my boss since birth, what's the difference?" Devon shrugs as his blue eyes cut in my direction, seeing if I understand. "Dad will make a great chief, and the rest of the guys are awesome. It's all I've ever known." Devon bites a green bean in half and smiles to himself.

"But you like it though, right? It wasn't pushed on you?"

"Love it," Devon rapidly fires. "I'm good at it. It takes a certain personality to deal with the pressure. You have to constantly be in control and calm, be authoritative but nice. People skills are a must. Not only do you have to know how to read a person, but how to mediate and talk them down from harming themselves or others. In order to be successful as a police officer, the people have to trust you. Protect and Serve."

"I envy how you know what you are. I have no clue what I am," I murmur sadly as the same old feeling creeps over me– the worthlessness. I always hear the words *deadweight* and *loser* echoing in my mind.

Placing his fork on the edge of his plate again, Devon turns to the side in his seat and stares me down. "Willow, who says you have to have a label? I'm a cop, but that isn't who I am. When we're kids, we don't look at each other and say *student*. We see each other for our personalities. I have no idea why we do this as adults. Just be Willow."

"I–" Failing to come up with a coherent reply, something else entirely flows from my lips. "How come Kieren isn't at the academy?" I wince when I say his name, but my curiosity is stronger than my shame and confusion.

"Every family has a bad apple," Devon says ominously, as his eyes flick to Violet. I pegged myself as the Prynne bad apple, but Devon's cop instinct says Violet. Interesting. Perhaps Devon's *cop-dar* is malfunctioning.

"You know Violet? I wasn't aware twenty-year-old cops ran in the same social circles as thirteen-year-old princesses."

"Weston, my youngest brother, is in the same class as the twins. West wants to be best friends with Seth, but Violet won't let him. She won't let Seth have any friends that she doesn't hand-pick." Devon glares at Violet so strongly that she has to feel it.

"I'll take care of Violent Violet. Seth is my responsibility, not hers. We've fought this war since she could talk." We both glare at the sociopath in question as she sweetly talks to her grandmother, my mother.

I snort out a laugh when I realize Violet and I are playing the same game with Seth that Auggie and Isis play with Robbie. It truly is all about who owns Seth, like a prize, and it actually has nothing to do with Seth as a person. I'm ahead of the curve if I figured this out now versus when I'm twenty-eight and ruining Seth's life.

"So there are three of you..." *Whoa.* That house is full of testosterone. Mr. Mason isn't bad to look at either. I have plans for Malcolm, but I have to ask Seth first, with him being the man of the house and all.

"Four, actually." Devon smirks, his expression fond and filled with affection. "Rae is fifteen, and she and Violet *do not* get along." He stresses the *do not* heavily.

"Oh, no doubt. If your sister looks anything like your aunt, I bet she's gorgeous, and that drives Violet to see red. Teenage girls are so irrational."

"You're a teenage girl," Devon whispers to me like it's a secret, lips twisting up at the corners into a devastating smile.

Gobsmacked, I stare at his mouth like an idiot. "And what indication did I give you that I was rational?" I flirt back. "I assure you, almost ninety-nine percent of everything I do makes absolutely no freakin' sense."

Shocked, Devon cups his palm over his mouth and tries his damnedest to quiet his laughter. I can feel the eyes of every single one of my relatives lighting on us. Mom and Dad, Clover, Seth and Violet, Aunt Anna and Uncle Wil, Essie, and Robbie. Auggie is practically burning a hole into my forehead, trying to get me to look his direction. I love the power I hold over Auggie by withholding my gaze from him.

Leaning closer to Devon, I purr, "Don't say I didn't warn ya."

Coughing into his palm, blue eyes roll up and capture mine. "Irrational," he rasps. "Gotcha."

Sitting back in my chair, I open a new thread of conversation. "So… tell me about your dad. Is he single?" I ask with great interest, causing Devon to give me a look that screams extreme violence. It takes me a second, and then I understand the fury in his eyes. "Oh," my voice quivers with mortification, my earlier flirtatious bravado vanishing in an instant. Blush gone, and in its place I turn deathly pale.

"No… no, not *that*." I huff a laugh as I softly touch Devon's arm. Angry, his muscles are taut with tension beneath my fingertips. His eyes turn from light blue to as dark as Isis's obsidian gaze. "Not for me. I cap out at twenty-eight. As you've already figured out, even that twenty-eight thinks my cap is set too high– he's pushing for twenty."

Not finding my pathetic joke humorous, Devon grits out in a gravelly voice, "What do you want with my dad?"

"Jeesh, Devon." I roll my eyes. "What kind of person do you take me for? Never mind, don't answer that. Listen, I don't want to know anything about play. It's just… I may ask your dad for a favor."

"Favor?" Devon asks in a clipped tone.

I look at Clover and smirk. "It'd take a damn strong man to tame my sister, don't ya think?"

All of the tension bleeds out of Devon, and he slumps in his chair in relief. "Willow," he breathes near my ear. "That's a damn fine idea for all of them." Devon's eyes dart from the twins, to Clover, then back to me.

I know Devon's thinking of his little siblings, too. I don't know their situation, or if they have a mother or not, but I know Clover was born to mother. I can already see how Violet needs a man like Malcolm to make her behave. How Seth needs a father who will treat him as the special kid he is and show him what it truly means to be a man. Violet needs to make an attachment to someone who didn't share a womb with her. Clover needs a strong hand and an epic orgasm…

… And that's how you matchmake at the Prynne Sunday dinner table.

Auggie finally catches my eye, and I know he loves me looking at him. He looks satisfied, relaxed, and relieved. I pop an eyebrow in question, and his lips quirk up into a grin.

I was so involved with my conversation with Devon, I didn't notice how the table had fallen silent. Everyone is staring at me. I guess it's strange to see me so friendly and chatty with someone who doesn't have Prynne blood flowing through their veins. Clover looks awed.

"Do I have spinach in my teeth?" I bare my pearly whites at Devon and laugh. "I guess they find it weird that I'm talking to someone who isn't Seth or Essie."

Devon's hand snakes around my neck and his lips meet my ear. I love the fact that he's comfortable touching me without thought. I shudder as his lips flutter against the shell of my ear.

"Last time I saw you... it was at yours and Kieren's high school graduation. You looked like a walking pot-headed zombie: dull-eyed, dead-brained, lost... and today you look clear-eyed and happy. The difference is astounding. I'd love to take credit for it, but that bossy bastard with the shit-eating grin on his face is to blame. I'll make sure I add to your happiness from now on. I don't want Auggie to always get the credit."

My only response is to look at Devon with droopy eyes and a mouth gaping open, catching flies. Devon's aspiration is to grow up to be Auggie– no, Malcolm. I have no doubt Devon will achieve his goal.

Rob and Auggie are the only ones not staring at me. They chat like normal, discussing a mutual art project a local business commissioned. I turn to Essie, since she sits next to me and I've failed to acknowledge her presence until now. I mutter like that Kool-Aid drinker Robbie accused me of being. "Mr. Kline is always right. Never doubt Mr. Kline."

"I need a smoking hot Mr. Kline." Essie trails a flirty giggle that turns my stomach. My glare is instantaneous and combustible. I'll share Auggie with anyone but family– Rob is the exception. If Essie ever touches what's mine, I'll cut her hand off, and then shove it so far up her ass she'll be choking on it for decades to come.

"Someone *like* Auggie– not him. Jeez!" Essie scowls at me. "Possessive much?"

"Yeah, I guess I am." I offer as a warning, "I don't give third chances on the girl code."

"Girl code? Third chances? What happened to the second chance?" Essie looks confused for a heartbeat, and then she turns away from me when the implication finally seeps in. Yeah, I'm naïve but not fucking stupid. Even with everything going on around me, I never forgot how Essie failed to mention she was deflowered by the boy I called dibs on. How she failed to tell me for the past five years.

"You're already on your second chance," I whisper underneath my breath.

"Prynnes and Websters," Auggie says to gain all of our attention. "I have exciting news."

I'm thankful Auggie offered distraction. I'm in a strange mood: a mix of happy, sad, angry, and excited. Manic. In this mood, I don't know if I can control how I react. I was seconds away from verbally and physically ripping into Essie over Kieren, when I don't even know if Kieren's worth it. No one seems to think he is. Yet, what Essie did wasn't about Kieren– it was about Essie and me. The more I dwell on it, the angrier I become.

Auggie's words slowly filter into my destructive thoughts. "I bought a house today. The realtor called just before dinner. I sign the paperwork tomorrow."

A round of congratulations interrupts Auggie's speech. He smiles indulgently at my family, nodding at each in turn as they speak with him. After all, every member of my family, with the exception of the twins, has known Auggie longer than they've known me.

"It'll be a lot of work, and I'm in desperate need of Willow's help." Auggie pins me in his stare, effectively trapping me. "So Willow will be moving in with me… starting tonight." Auggie's announcement is laced with silent demand.

"Wait a goddamned min–"Clover tries to interrupt Auggie, but he keeps talking over her.

"Between working at the store and the house, there's no need for Willow to go back and forth. It'll be easiest this way. Besides, Willow and Rob will be permanently moving into the house as soon as it's livable. I bought the Spook House across town. It's huge, and I don't want to live alone– I need family to make a home. I practically stole it, it was so cheap."

Auggie laughs deep from his chest, that pleasant, happy, rumbling sound that I adore so much. Ear-gasm or not, I finally recognize Auggie's manipulative side. That laugh and every word from his mouth had a purpose of some sort, and they were wielded with expert precision.

"Are there even two bedrooms in the loft above the store?" Clover asks. My parents are grinning like fools, but not Clover. The calculating glint in Clover's eye screams her bullshit meter is flashing *warning- motherfucking warning!!!* Clover is a great mom when it comes to not buying into bullshit.

"Of course," Auggie purrs. "I wouldn't subject Willow to sharing a room with me. I'm sure Devon would take great offense, and Rob would kick my ass." Auggie lies smoothly, using humor to cover all the bullshit spewing from his lips.

Rob covers his mouth with the back of his hand, but his chest is rapidly rising and falling. I know he finds this hysterical, how Auggie is maneuvering all of us and we can't stop him– just as Rob had warned me last night. Robbie leans his elbow on the table and turns to the side, away from everyone so they can't read his expression. I want to find the situation as funny as Rob does, but for the first time ever, I feel sick over lying to Clover.

Clover deserves so much more than she receives. Rob and I are the worst siblings on the planet, and the crest-fallen expression on my sister's face says she knows we're all lying, and her arms are tied behind her back. She can't do a damned thing about it, and it's making her feel powerless.

I feel sick, like I'm not only betraying Clover but myself.

"Willow's been a huge help at Revamped. I'll need more of her time now that she's going to put our inventory for sale on our website. I don't think I could do it without her. You all should be very proud of our girl." Auggie announces in a voice filled with reverence.

That last phrase is what had the entire Prynne/Webster clan and Devon packing all of my belongings into the back of Auggie's pickup truck. It only took forty-five minutes to find everything that was mine and shove it into boxes. The entirety of eighteen years of living fit in the bed of a pickup truck– how depressing.

CHAPTER TWENTY

"Sapling," Clover sighs the nickname Sam gave me when I was a baby, sounding on the edge of tears. She pulls me back into the living room and closes the door to give us privacy. "I'm not going to stop you. Not only because I can't, but because you need to learn this the hard way. This is a mistake, and you know it."

"Please, don't do this," I beg, sounding desperate and hopeless. "Don't make me feel like shit. I'm sick of feeling worthless."

"You're *not* worthless," Clover growls, unleashing the mother bear that dwells deep inside her. "I'll murder the next person who says that, even if it's you." Drawing a deep breath, Clover centers herself. "I know you want me to tell you no, that you can't go with Auggie. I can see it written across your face, and I know it because I know you better than I know myself. But I'm not going to make this decision for you. It's time you grew up and lived with your decisions, even if they're piss-poor decisions."

"I know that," I spit out, my back bristling up, getting defensive like only Clover can make me feel.

"You're not fucking him, are you?" Clover sounds thoroughly disgusted. I flinch, knowing she'd be so disappointed in me if she knew what I did last night. "Willow, Auggie laying a hand on you is a crime."

"NO!" I plead innocent, covering my lie with great offense. "It's not a crime anymore, either," I mumble underneath my breath.

"As of thirty-six hours ago." Clover rolls her eyes, and she disturbingly looks just like me when I pull the same bratty maneuver. "How noble of Auggie to wait until your clock struck eighteen. No sense in lying, I know Auggie's touched you. The truth is written across your face."

"I'm going to have to work on my transparency, it seems. This is starting to get ridiculous." I try to use humor to override my discomfort, and fail.

Clover leans against the front door, arms crossed over her chest, and glares my ass down. I stare at the ceiling, the floor, my fingernails, anywhere but at my truth-seeking sister. Just one look, and she always knows if I'm lying or telling the truth. Clover has the uncanny ability to see straight to my soul– always has, always will.

"Willow, you have to be careful of men like Augustus Kline– men in general." I wince when Clover hits too close to home. "They'll twist you into knots as you try to please them. But the secret they will never tell you is that nothing will ever be good enough. *Ever*," she stresses. "Every time you bow down to them, they will ask more of you… and more of you… and more of you… until you're used up and nothing is left. One day, when you look into the mirror, you'll see what used to be Willow is now a shadow of what Auggie thinks she should be."

"I get it," I mutter stiffly. "I could see how you could lose yourself to a man like Auggie. The problem is how do you lose something you've never had? I haven't the foggiest of who I am, Clover." I hate how my voice dips down into whining territory.

"Just don't let Auggie tell you who Willow is– find her yourself." Clover breathes the last of her words while looking me in the eyes. My chest gets tight, panic threatening to overcome me. What I see mirrored in my sister's eyes frightens the hell out of me.

"I'm not saying this to be mean, or to insinuate that there aren't amazing men out there, or that you don't deserve one, or that Auggie is a bad guy. I'm saying this, because if it smells off, it usually is. You're still a child, and he's a grown man. A grown man who's obviously very proud of himself for pulling the wool over so many people's eyes. But I don't care if I insult Auggie. You come first for me, Willow, and it's my job to make sure you know you should come first for yourself as well."

"Then why don't you come first, Clover?" I don't give my usual attitude– I'm truly curious as to why Clover is giving me advice she doesn't take for herself.

"Because I'm a mother, and you're not. You have the freedom to be who you should be, not some man's ego boost, not your children's lifeline, not your parents' keeper. You have the freedom to work anywhere you dream, date whomever you wish, experience anything you desire. I'm locked in now, Willow. T. R. A. P. P. E. D."

"You don't like being a mother?"

"Being a mother is who I was meant to be, Willow. I don't regret a second of being a mother. My point is that until you become a mother, or take over the responsibilities of your family, you're free. You have no debt: financial, familial, or emotional."

"I think I understand," I say sheepishly, eyes darting away from my sister's gaze. She knows I don't truly understand. How could I?

"Willow," Clover says sharply to gain my attention. "Don't shit on the freedom I'm giving you."

"I–"

"You have an endless amount of potential. Intelligent, beautiful–"

I cut Clover off before she can finish. "I'm not beautiful," I protest, and fierce anger flashes across my sister's face.

"Willow," Clover chastises, annoyed as fuck with me. "I never want to hear that again. No worthless or ugly is to flow from your mouth or form in your thoughts. I'm not the most gorgeous person on the planet, but look at Mom, and Essie and Violet. They are beautiful ladies, inside and out, and you are one of *them*– one of *us*. Don't shit on your Prynne heritage with your insecurities. If one of us is disrespected, we all are. It's worse when you do it to yourself."

"I'm sorry–"

"Shush... I was dinky, just like you. Smaller even, until I had my first child. The hormones filled my body out. You'll look like me eventually."

"Clover?" I say her name as a question, because what she just said startled me and discombobulated my mind. "Back. The. Hell. Up. First child?"

Clover changes the subject before I can question her further and grasp the tenuous thread of truth she's trying to hide. "Addictive masculinity bleeds from Auggie's pores, but you're not ready for a man like him. I'm not blind. I'm a mom, and we have built-in predator radar. I see the way Auggie looks at you, like a man who's had a taste and wants you as his five-course meal. Auggie will consume you, and there will be nothing left to shit out when he's done."

"Clover, back up.... Wait, you have a wicked way with your words. Shit me out? Really?"

My sister smirks at me in exactly the same manner Auggie always does, like she can twist me up and mess with my head. "I have no doubt your affair with Auggie will be hot while it lasts, explosive even. But the only thing you'll have left when it's over is your scorched heart in ashes."

"You talk as if all men are evil," I say to distract myself from what Clover just said– her words are eerily close to the thoughts that have been rattling around inside my head.

"Sam–" Clover chokes on his name, looking pained beyond belief. I swallow a sob that's building– a sob that always tries to erupt when I hear my brother-in-law's name. For some reason, our mutual agony soothes my sister. "Sam was a good man, but it took a while to get to that place. Years. We all need to grow into a partnership. It was friendship, love, and trust. He was my best friend. I'm not pushing you to pick a guy at eighteen– I'm telling you *not* to. Just because I knew what I wanted at your age doesn't mean you will or should. Just play the field. I know Devon is Auggie's smoke and mirrors so we don't notice he's creeping into your bed. I won't lecture about sex. You're a grown woman with needs, but sex with Auggie will lead to a whole helluva a lot of pain."

The old Willow, or should I say my younger self, would've thrown a shit-fit and called Clover ten different variants of bitch. I shock myself by listening to her words, absorbing them. But even more so, I shock my sister by finally listening to her, respecting her.

Clover dabs a tear from beneath her eye. I'd always thought Clover frozen– an ice queen who felt nothing other than anger.

I was wrong.

"I'm not stupid, Willow. I know what's going on. I can tell by the mortified look on your face that you've already gone where you shouldn't. No matter what anyone says, you're not going to change your mind. You also know it will only lead to hell, but you don't give a shit."

"I've got to do this for me," I say without remorse.

"I know. My only advice is that I will be waiting right here for you when it wrecks you. I promise not to judge– I'll *really* try. In the end, I want you to remember that you never need a man to be whole. It's lonely, but you have us to hold you up. I need you to know this– Willow, you'll always have a home with me. I don't care what you do. No matter what, I'll make it better."

"Clover–" I choke on a sob.

"Now, stop that girly shit," Clover murmurs, sounding uncomfortable. "My sapling is made of sterner stuff. Go fuck up your life like a regular eighteen-year-old teenage idiot. Make stupid mistakes you'll regret until you die, and then come home when you've learned your lesson."

"I'd say you're probably right, but it'd feed your ginormous mother-ego. Plus, I was told that only Mr. Kline is always right." I try to make light of this dark topic. It's the first real woman-to-woman conversation I've ever had with my sister as equals. "I think my head would explode if you both were right at the same time."

"We've fought a lot, but it's only because we're so much alike." I give Clover a look that screams we aren't alike. At. All. She smirks my snarky smirk right back at me– motherfucker!

"You'll always be my sapling," Clover says the nickname in the same exact cadence Sam used. I sob, and cover it with a cough. "Go forth and fuck it all up, Willow."

"I'm sure I will," I grumble, but I cannot contain the naughty smirk that breaks across my face. "My fuck-it-up-ery is a requirement."

Clover steps to the side and opens the front door. "This is the last time you'll live here. Make your peace, and when you realize your mistakes and want to return home, don't use this door." Clover knocks on the door in a rhythm. "I want you to walk over there." She points toward the front of her house where the twins are standing on the porch, watching us. "Open that door, and finally come home where you belong."

"What?"

Pushing me onto the porch, Clover laughs the saddest laugh I've ever heard. "Go fuck it up. Be your imperfect self and make me proud."

CHAPTER TWENTY-ONE

Feeling more lost and set adrift than ever before, I stand on the sidewalk between my family's two houses and reflect back on the past few days since I turned eighteen. In some ways, I feel ancient since my alarm woke me on my birthday. In others, I feel even more naïve and innocent.

Almost three days ago, I was just a kid. I walked a specific path set out before me because I knew no other way. I'd wake up in the morning because I was told what time to set my alarm. I'd answer the alarm when it jolted me awake. I'd walk to work and do as my boss told me. I'd eat when Auggie placed whatever he wanted me to have before me. Then when I was told to go home, I went. When I got home, I did the same routine. Like a little lost sheep, I went from one keeper, Augustus Kline, to another, Clover Webster. I did this cycle, day in and day out, since I graduated high school. Before that, it was a similar cycle with Clover and my teachers.

Never have I had the power to be the one who set the cycle. The one who said when to wake, when to eat, what to do. Never. I'm at a precipice. I could allow Auggie complete dominion over me, no longer having the checks and balance of Clover or my teachers, or I could choose to be a part of that cycle and control myself.

I know I'm not ready to take care of myself entirely. Leaving home is like a rebirth. But I could be half of the cycle, trust myself enough to take over Clover's job. Someone has to keep Auggie from consuming me, and that person should be me.

Someday.

Someday when I'm wiser, older, smarter, more mature. Someday, I could control the entire cycle.

Someday, I could be free.

I gaze at the houses I grew up in. Clover is right— I grew up in both. I wasn't raised by a set of parents. I was raised by an entire family. My imperfection is a reflection of that upbringing. To find myself less because of it, is to find them less as well. I love my family too much to think so little of myself.

My family is scattered between two porches. My parents' porch holds the Prynnes: Uncle Will, Aunt Ana, and Essie join my delusional parents, who are waving like idiots. Clover's porch holds the small Webster clan: my sister and her twins, all three looking unsure of this new development.

Auggie and Robbie lean against the side of Auggie's truck, arms folded over their chests in identical gestures of extreme patience. Auggie looks exceptionally arrogant and proud of himself, truly like the predator he is, but I wouldn't change him for anything. Rob looks expectant, rolling his eyes at me and our entire family. He really expected Clover to stop this lunacy, and when she didn't, Robbie was lost as to what to do next. They're all waiting for me to say goodbye to my *boyfriend*.

Devon stands a few feet from me, looking on the edge of uncertainty. Training as a police officer didn't thoroughly prepare him for the madness of the Prynne/Webster clan. A fake smile is plastered on his face when he's not biting his bottom lip.

And then there is me, Willow the wayward. I just stand on the sidewalk as if lost at sea.

I know what everyone is waiting for– the goodbye kiss. It's a test. Auggie is challenging me with his stare. Robbie is egging me on with his cackle. Clover is begging me to end this farce by *not* doing it. And the rest of my family is waiting, thinking how cute it is that tiny Willow finally snagged herself a boyfriend. She's not the freak they thought she was.

I feel my age for once: a teenager with head-up-the-ass-itis, unsure and scared. Devon and I stare at our feet, silently willing my family to go into their houses when we both know they won't. Why is a goodbye kiss so difficult while they look on, but I can lose my virginity with an audience?

Fuck it!

I twist my fingers in the fabric of Devon's t-shirt and yank him into a hug, startling a surprised gasp from him. I like hugging Devon. I like hugging Devon because he doesn't want anything from me. He's not pressuring me, using me, expecting something of me I don't wish to give. I have nothing to give Devon, so he has nothing to ask of me. The only thing I can give Devon is friendship, and even then, he's not asking for it, demanding it. Devon patiently waits for me to give him anything I think he deserves.

I hug Devon because it's a comfort to know I can give as little or as much as I want, and take as little or as much in return as I wish. Devon won't judge me, no matter what. Gripping me back tightly, I know I'm as transparent as ever, that Devon can feel my tumultuous emotions.

This hug isn't as awkward as our first embrace. Devon is as warm and cuddly as before, smelling just as good, but his arms hold me like bands of steel. We embrace each other like we needed a lifeline, like we're holding the other together from falling apart.

"Thanks for coming," I breathe against Devon's neck.

"Thanks for having me," flutters the hair on the top of my head. I brush a kiss against Devon's sweet smelling throat and he shudders for me. Devon's fingertips dig into my back as he presses a kiss to the top of my head, and then he steps back.

I arch a brow in Devon's direction. "I guess I'll see you tomorrow sometime?" It's a question and a request.

"Yup, definitely. I think I have to buy some stuff at your store," he says with a wink. "Plus, I have a ton of hours to put in at the Spook House." Devon grins when he says the name, because of why he has to work there no doubt.

"Maybe I'll hook you up with my employee discount," I flirt back while rocking on my heels.

"Sounds like a plan," Devon says shyly.

Devon leans in and kisses my cheek so fast I don't even feel it. In the time it takes me to blink, Devon's already striding down the sidewalk. Turning to the side, he gives a wave to the Prynnes, and then the Websters. My family sings *Aaaawwwwww* really loudly and makes kissy noises in my direction. I blush fire-engine red and run to hide in the truck.

What took so little time to pack and load back at my parents' house, took three times as long to unload and *not* unpack. Baffles the mind. Ten times up and down the rear steps of Revamped while carrying boxes is a real killer on the thighs. Why ten trips? Because I was made to carry all of my own shit… by myself. I thought I was going to die from exhaustion, and then I almost went ass-over-tea-kettle on the last trip. I swear my feet grew with every step, and the stair treads shrank just to laugh at me as I stumbled.

My tiny pile of boxes sits in one corner of the loft, looking depressed in its own personal timeout. All of my worldly possessions take up less space than the weight bench they're keeping company. The only unpacking I've accomplished consisted of digging my toothbrush out and placing it on the sink in the bathroom area, and I made sure my clothes were on the top of the pile of boxes.

But there's a reason I'm not going *girlfriend* in Auggie's space. I assume when you move into your boyfriend's place, you nest a bit. Giggling while putting your panties in with his boxers, or hanging your clothing in his closet. The cutesy arguments that ensue when your guy thinks your shit is overtaking his– too much pink, too many pillows and candles. Vanilla or lavender is okay, but for the love of all that is holy, do not make the apartment smell like a florist shop. At no time should your feminine hygiene products be on display. Why do you have ten stuffed animals when you're an adult? Broadway Musicals aren't considered mood music– no way, no how. No, the complete works of Nicolas Sparks, both film and print, are not his idea of a fun-filled evening. No, he's not going to hide his porn... even when your mother visits. You know, the usual things new couples fight about. But I'm just assuming that's how it goes down because I'm not a girly girl and Auggie isn't my boyfriend.

In Willow reality, Auggie and I should be getting along fabulously since we're both freaks and geeks. We should be sitting on the couch with a bag of Doritos between us while we watch Adult Swim. But somewhere between when Auggie announced I was the most pivotal person in his life during Sunday dinner, and when the last of my boxes went into timeout, he got pissed.

Currently, Augustus Kline is acting like my prison warden.

None of my *move in* fantasies are going as envisioned. Not in my wildest imaginings did this situation come to mind. At all– ever.

Auggie is glaring down at the bottle of *99 Blackberries,* and its mate, *99 Bananas,* and their friends, *Sloe Gin, Butter Shots,* and *Hot Damn,* with a bemused expression. He has them on the countertop in a guilty lineup. I wait for Auggie to find a newspaper and thwack me while reprimanding *bad toy!*

"I see," Auggie slowly drawls out while folding his arms over his broad chest. "That you enjoy schnapps."

The Iliad, the Odyssey, and *War and Peace* are stacked next to the bottles. Auggie recovered the huge tomes while he was digging through my stuff as evidence. While I wasn't allowed to unpack anything once I carried all my shit up a flight of stairs,

Auggie was. He dug through my possessions as if they were his, removing any and all alcohol he came upon, along with the camouflage that had concealed them.

When we were packing up my bedroom, Auggie had pulled the books from my shelf and inadvertently discovered my stash. I received a furry red eyebrow raise that promised a wicked ass-kickin' the second I was alone with him. Auggie then went around the bookshelf singing *what doesn't belong here,* and choosing books he didn't think I'd read.

Auggie figured the epic classics weren't my type of reading material and chose those to pack. For years, I'd used the gigantic hardcovers to store my hooch out of sight. No one in their right mind would come into my room and pull them from the shelf for a little *light* reading. No one but Auggie.

"Yeah, I enjoy schnapps, but not all at once. I'd get sick if I mixed the flavors." Patting my belly, "Wouldn't want to get a tummy ache." I let the snark fly as I wander around the loft, knocking on the walls.

"What the hell are you doing?" Auggie demands grumpily as he keeps pace with me like an angry storm cloud.

"Oh, this?" I knock again. "I'm looking for that second bedroom and that other bed," I say to deflect the hypocrite from the mass quantities of alcohol he'd discovered. "I ought to text Clover a picture of our sleeping arrangements. She'll be waiting for Devon's fury and Robbie's fist marks to appear on your smug face."

As I spew utter bullshit, I make a mental note to hide the rest of my stash before Auggie searches all of my boxes. What's on the counter is only the schnapps. I also have mixers and their friends and barware. Either I'm meant to be a bartender or an alcoholic– it's up in the air at this moment in time. I'll choose alcoholic if Auggie doesn't stop parenting me. I'll need a drink to deal with his shit.

Underestimating me as usual, Auggie didn't realize I would never read the box sets *of Little House on the Prairie, Anne of Green Gables, and the Baby Sitter's Club.* Hidden behind those titles were the stronger liquors: whiskeys, vodkas, rum, and tequila. However, Auggie suffered a *geriatric moment* when he looked behind the *Harry Potter* series. I'm a geek. The fool doesn't know me as well as he thinks. I've read Harry four times over.

"HA! Pathetic try with the deflection, Willow." Auggie smirks, unrelenting. "We're going to talk about your alcoholism."

"Hold up, Hoss!" I put my hands out to halt Auggie's imminent lecture. "Most of the liquor is from when I was going to high school parties with Essie. I took a hiatus when she was at cosmetology school. I've behaved since because I didn't have anyone to drink with. I'm a social drinker, not a closet drinker. It's been... hmm..." I tabulate how long ago those binge-drinking, blackout drunks occurred. "I'd say, since well before I graduated. The first time I've had any of my stash in about five or six months was last night."

Body radiating tension, intently staring at me through narrowed eyes, Auggie judges my honesty. In this instance, I'm pleased that I'm so transparent. Satisfied that I'm not a raging alcoholic, liar-liar pants on fire, Auggie moves on with his interrogation.

"Is this the lot of it, then?" Auggie asks, gesturing to the bottles lining the countertop. He knows damned well it isn't, which is why he asks. Bastard is trying to trap me in a lie.

I sigh deeply, roll my eyes, and then decide the truth is the only way to go with Augustus Kline. I spend the next twenty minutes dragging the rest of my loot to the counter...

Auggie whistles sharply at the dozen bottles and their friends filling the small countertop island that bisects his kitchen from the rest of the loft. Auggie shakes his head back and forth in awe as he stares down at my shameful secret.

"I'm thoroughly impressed... and not in a good way," Auggie mumbles in amazement. "Monster, you have more booze than a frat house during rush week. It's inconceivable. The majority of your possessions is liquor."

The blush is instantaneous and furious. I burn all the way to my hairline. Auggie doesn't sound disappointed per se. He sounds baffled and impressed by the level of depravity I've possessed since an early age. Most kids my age are trying to figure out a way to get someone to buy them a six-pack of Coors, not have a fully-stocked liquor cabinet with mixers, barware, and accessories.

"Is this all of your shit?" Auggie asks, sounding skeptical.

Guiltily, I trudge back over to my pile of boxes and get to digging. I've never had anyone but Clover call me out on anything. I'd just mouth off, get slapped, and be done with it.

Auggie won't put up with my shit. I'm glad I wasn't born to a father like Auggie.

I find my princess jewelry box and pry the lock open with my fingernail. The ballerina pops up and makes me belt out a squeak and jump out of my skin. The metallic sound of the music box fills the loft like an air raid. I remove from the box what will undoubtedly earn me a gigantic punishment with a huge side of disappointment.

Palming my stash, I hide it behind my back as I shuffle guiltily over to Auggie. As of right now, I smoke a few times a week because I'm busy at work and with the family. But I used to smoke once a day while I was in high school. Every day like clockwork, I'd toke up at 4:20 on the dot. But there was a time when I was smoking four or five times per day, sometimes more, and it was the majority of my senior year. That period of time is what turned me into the zombie Devon called me.

The bowl in my hand is only the first of five I have in my possession, used to be six but I gifted Robbie my smallest and most concealable pipe last night.

Auggie's big palm is held out, patiently waiting. I drop my tin of weed and its buddy, my rainbow-swirled bowl, into his outstretched hand, and then I back up out of his arm's reach. Auggie stares at what I gave him, sadly shaking his head to and fro, before he gently places my pot stash next to my liquor stash.

"Is this everything?" he asks again, still sounding skeptical.

"Yes," I answer honestly.

"Are you sure?" Auggie tries again, not believing me, adding a raised brow for good measure.

"Yes." I nod my head.

"Remind me never to allow you to try hardcore drugs. I don't want to deal with a meth-head Monster. Where did you get all of this stuff?" Auggie's disappointed and it sucks. I hate the ache in my heart as Auggie looks at me like he doesn't know me, like he wishes he didn't know me.

"My parents." I mumble my family's greatest shame.

"You're fucking kidding me, right? Please tell me you're joking," he begs.

"No, my parents bought everything there. I didn't steal it from them. *I asked*. We went to the store, where I picked out what I wanted, and they bought it. They grow their own weed. Mom's a genius at horticulture. That bowl was a gift." I whisper as I point at my first pipe. I feel like a traitor betraying my family by letting out our dirty secret.

"You're joking. You have to be. They weren't like this with Rob." Auggie stands back and surveys the countertop of my bad behavior and vices.

"They weren't seventy with Rob," I state quickly, and the rest of the words tumble from my mouth before I can stop them. "Rob was probably too much of a wuss to ask," I mutter defiantly. "It wasn't my parents who treated Robbie differently than me, it was Rob who didn't act like me. That's the difference."

"How did you figure this out?" Auggie bugs out his green eyes in disgusted disbelief. "How did you know to ask them in the first place?"

"I have big balls," I say with as much bravado as I can muster. I laugh without humor, but Auggie doesn't join me. He just looks at me patiently until I spill my dark secrets.

"Every time I asked for something, it would magically appear. It's rather disgusting, actually, if I think about it now. But at first, it was fun and exciting. I started asking for bigger things, like borrowing the car at thirteen. Every time they said yes, I would up the ante on the next request. I've never heard no from them. I feel bad, but it's their fault. I was waiting for them to say no."

"So... let me get this straight," Auggie draws out while staring my ass down. That furry red eyebrow seems to get more menacing by the second. "You blame your parents for *not* saying no to something *you* asked for in the first place. Am I hearing this correctly?"

"I get that I shouldn't have asked. I get that *now*," I stress. "But if a twelve-year-old asks for a case of beer, you'd think she'd get told *hell no*, followed by an ass kicking. Didn't happen for me, and I didn't know any better at the time. I was a kid."

"*Obviously*," Auggie states snidely. "A kid who can't take responsibility for her own actions, places fault where it doesn't lie, and makes excuses instead of owning up to her actions. Yes, that sounds about right."

The *fuck you, Auggie* is on the tip of my tongue. With a surprising amount of control, I don't say it.

Auggie is right. Mr. Kline is always right.

But I still think my parents should've said no. I shouldn't have asked, and they shouldn't have said yes– we're both at fault.

I don't care if that sounds like an excuse or not. It's the truth, plain and simple.

"When I asked for the pot, I really hoped they'd say no. I didn't even want it. But instead, the next day, I found a bowl and a baggie of weed on my bed. I stared down at it in horror, shock, couldn't fucking believe that one of my parents gave me drugs– drugs that were placed on my princess pink bedding. I was so pissed off that they did it, I almost tattled to Clover."

I take a deep breath, reliving that moment in my memories, feeling every emotion I felt at the time. I almost felt betrayed by my parents. Any other child would've bragged to their friends about how cool their parents were. But I didn't brag for two reasons. One, I didn't have any friends who weren't related to my parents. Two, I was embarrassed and ashamed.

"I wanted to punish them, so I smoked it... and the joke was on me, now, wasn't it? The joke was that I liked it– *really, really, really* liked it. I was only thirteen the first time I toked up, and I haven't gone more than two days without a hit." I tear up at admitting how I may be addicted. "And those two days were *these* past two days."

Running the back of my hand over my face to trap the tears that are falling, I try to hide my sniffle in my sweatshirt sleeve. I turn away from Auggie, not wanting him to see me like this.

Ashamed.

Not broken, but slightly bent.

Lost.

"I haven't touched the stuff since I became an adult, and not out of any shame over using it. It's just because I haven't had the opportunity or the need. When I look at my parents, I don't see it as wrong. They are good people who happen to use recreational drugs. It doesn't make them bad. What makes it bad for me is that I feel bad about it."

I feel Auggie's gaze, but I'm too ashamed of myself to look at him. I'm afraid of what I will see reflected in his eyes. "I can see that you recognize that you may have a problem," Auggie murmurs softly, voice filled with compassion I don't deserve.

"I don't know, maybe?" I shrug as if it doesn't matter. "Maybe I just feel like weed was my first best friend, the kind that stuck around when the bad shit happened. I met my best friend when Sam was sick, and I half-assed think that's why my parents gave it to me in the first place. My own personal pacifier–

deadens the pain and misery of mourning as if the living are already dead."

"Willow," Auggie murmurs, and that one word is filled with so much pity that I fear I'm going to be sick.

"I don't think you understand the impact you're having on me– pushing Devon at me. I've never had any friends, not really. I've thought over Essie a lot these past few days. I'm Essie's best friend, but she's not mine. Or maybe she just pitied me enough that she kept me around like a hanger-on-er. Essie's friends were never *my* friends. I guess you could say, I bought their companionship. Essie's friends liked me because I brought whatever they lacked for their parties, be it drugs or alcohol. I'd drink and play games while Essie got shit-faced and fucked around with her classmates. When Essie's friends laughed, I always felt like I was the brunt of the joke– that I *was* the joke."

"I blame Hester for that," Auggie practically seethes, green eyes glowing with silent fury.

"If I'm to grow up and be a real woman, then I need to take responsibility for this shit, Auggie. I could've said no to Essie, just as my parents could've said no to me, but I didn't. And if I'm wrong when it comes to Essie, then my parents were wrong when it came to me. If Essie was wrong to treat me that way, then I was wrong to treat my parents that way. You can't have it both ways, Auggie."

I stalk away and crack the fridge open. I stare unseeingly into its depths, because what I'm thirsting for Auggie is guarding like a prison warden. Without a thought, my hand reaches in and grabs something wet. I open the bottle and drain it without ever tasting a sip. I don't realize I drained an entire Gatorade until I toss the container into the trash.

"Ever since Essie graduated, I've had no fun. I've pretty much been alone since I finished off my freshman year. Hell, even when Essie was here, right in my face, I still felt alone. I latched onto Seth because he does love me. He does want to hang out with me. I love the way he looks at me like I'm a freak, but I'm his freak. He's proud to hang out with me. So I've had to behave around him, because I won't allow this shit to rollover and affect Seth."

"That just proves that you think how you behave is wrong, doesn't it?" Auggie doesn't try to force me to look at him. He somehow senses how upset I am. Instead of pushing me, lecturing me, punishing me, making me feel like a piece of worthless shit– instead of treating me how I deserve –Auggie treats me with compassion and respect.

Auggie walks over to the cupboard, pulls out a few cans, puts a pot on the hot plate, cranks a can opener, and heats us up some SpaghettiOs.

"I need someone on this earth who believes in me. I need someone to think I'm special. Seth is that person for me. I can't let him know who I really am– how I get high and zone out. I don't show Seth that side of me, because I expect more out of him. He's better than that. If he sees me doing it, he'll emulate me… Seth is worth way more than that."

"Eat," Auggie orders while dumping a quarter of the contents of the pan into a coffee mug. He roughly shoves a spoon into my SpaghettiOs, then pushes it toward me. I take my mug and sit on the floor, leaning my back against the refrigerator. Too upset to eat, I just let the mug warm my hands.

"You haven't told me anything I didn't already know, Willow." Auggie stands at the counter, pot still on the hot plate, spooning SpaghettiOs straight from the flaming hot pot to his awaiting mouth.

My private thoughts just spill– I can't stop them. "My so-called friends have always been inappropriate. I guess I should thank you for forcing Devon to hang out with me. He's the closest person I could call a friend that wasn't entirely inappropriate, considering he's a cop now. He's not inappropriate, yet we met again in the Playroom years after getting wasted at parties."

Feeling sick to my stomach, the smell of the food making it worse, I angrily plunk my mug down next to me, trying to get way from its smell. I go on the defensive. "Ya gonna judge me for this shit, Auggie?" I ask in challenge.

I glare up at the display of my dirty little secrets. I want to smash the liquor bottles and scream out of frustration and pain, and then I need to take several hits of pot from my bowl to calm my ass back down from the epic shit-fit I threw.

"Jesus Christ," Auggie curses, slamming down his spoon, splattering SpaghettiOs everywhere. He reaches down, his big palm circling my upper arm, and he yanks me to my feet. Gently pressing the side of my face against his chest, he tries to comfort me. "I thought Clover was doing a better job watching out for you. I just can't see her not… *mothering* you."

"Clover did mother me– smother me," I breathe against Auggie's chest. "Never blame Clover, Auggie. I wasn't stupid. I knew when to strike. This all started when Clover was dealing with Sam's illness and death. I learned pretty damned fast not to request anything when Clover was in the house. My parents would rather indulge me to keep the peace and tranquility than deal with a real issue. It makes me want to puke that I did that to them. But mostly, I'm sickened over the fact that I used my sister's pain for my own gain."

"Not gain, Willow," Auggie murmurs, brushing a fleeting kiss to my hair. "You used it to escape your pain. Clover lost her husband, but she wasn't the only person who lost Sam. You all lost him, especially you."

"I know," I grit out tightly, trying to swallow back the sob that's building. "Auggie, I'm not a druggie or an alcoholic. I got that shit because I could. Yes, I enjoy it. But don't you see, I could never truly enjoy it because it's tainted. I got it for the wrong reasons. My parents smoke as a lifestyle choice. Other people do it for stress relief. Kids usually do it to rebel. I did it because I hated it, and now I fear I love it too much to stop."

"You will not drink or take drugs unless I okay it first," Auggie commands. "Holy hell, Willow," he sighs my name. "You are in desperate need of boundaries. It's no wonder you and Rob ended up my damned pets. You're begging for structure and guidance. What's surprising is that you and Rob take direction so well."

"Only from you," I admit. If anyone else told me I couldn't drink or smoke, I'd balk, sulk, and throw a shit-fit. I'd get slapped, and then do it all over again anyway. But for some reason, if Auggie says it, I know it's law. I'd rather break actual state and federal laws than Auggie's. I fear Auggie more– fear his disappointment.

Chuckling softly, Auggie's chest vibrates against my cheek as he rocks me slightly while cradling me to his chest. "That's how I want it to be," he whispers. "I want you to be the one person who believes in me, thinks I'm special, trusts in all I say and do. Never forget, Willow– Mr. Kline is always right. If you're unsure of what path to take, think to yourself *what would Mr. Kline do*? If you're still not sure, guess on whether or not you'll get an ass-kicking. If the answer is a definite yes, then don't fucking do it," Auggie warns.

CHAPTER TWENTY-TWO

Hours after showering and lying down to go to sleep, sleep evades me. I lay on my side, Auggie wrapped around my back like a living, breathing blanket. Unseeingly, I just stare at the clock on the microwave. I start to wonder if it's broken, the way the numbers never change. Did a minute somehow change to a thousand seconds?

My mind is a pool of confusion. There's no turning back. I did something irreversible, leaving home. Just a few days ago I was a kid, where people just told me what to do, and the only decision on my part was whether or not I did what they asked. Now that I'm an adult, I fear I'm just playacting at being a grown up. I'm not any wiser than I was on the night I went to sleep a seventeen-year-old girl and woke the next morning a legal adult.

"How sore are you?" Auggie asks in the dark quiet of the loft. He's curled around my back with my head tucked under his chin. "And never lie to me again." While the words said are a command, they are said in a soft voice.

"Just chaffed, I guess. It burns a bit," I murmur quietly.

A warm chuckling sound emanates from his chest, vibrating straight to my soul– a sound of pure unexpected delight. "Well, Monster, that's good to know. But I wasn't asking about your abused pussy." The laughter gets louder, Auggie shaking the bed with his amusement. I blush so fiercely I fear it'll never fade. "Well, I guess you assume I value your lady parts to the other parts of your body. Let me tell ya, I think all of you is delectable."

Auggie makes hungry noises and pretends to feast at my neck like a starving animal. A giggle flows from my lips, and I bite my tongue to stop it. Mustn't sound any more childish than I already do.

"Naughty, naughty girl," Auggie praises while hugging me closer to his chest. "I made you move your own shit so you'd get the impact of your decision–"

I cut Auggie off. "Decision? I wasn't even warned. I wasn't even asked. You took it upon yourself to tell my family I was coming with you, no questions asked. At what point did I get a choice in the matter?"

"You could've said no–"

"Oh, really?" I drawl out, and add a snort for good measure. "Are you high? You wouldn't have let me say no, not for nothing."

"Perception–"

"And only your perception matters, I suppose." I yelp out in pain as a sting radiates up my tender thighs into my ass cheeks. "Hey!"

"Cut me off one more time, and your ass will be in flames," Auggie warns, growling low in his throat, lips pressed to the shell of my ear. "Now, are you sore? Does anything hurt from dragging your shit up my steps?"

"The backs of my legs hurt, I guess," I mumble, confused as to why my mind is upset but my body is igniting at Auggie's threat of flames. "It's not horrible, just uncomfortable."

"Ugh!" I grunt when I'm tossed onto my belly. Auggie kneels next to me, his large hands attacking the back of my thighs. I wince when his fingertips start working on the knots forming in my muscles. It feels good, but it hurts more.

"Good girls get rewarded for their hard work, especially when they don't complain. Not one bitch came out of your perfect mouth. I was so proud. You were a trooper, exhausting yourself and not once questioning me."

I roll my eyes at the patronizing way Auggie is speaking to me, speaking to me as you would a child or pet. Maybe in another life, I would've punched him in the junk for it. But this is Auggie, and he's trying to be nice after being mean. Auggie's the type of man, when he offers you food and you don't take it, he'll never feed you again. I know better than to say anything, or he'll stop touching me.

Auggie's fingers tug on my t-shirt, giving me a hint. I scoot up, propping my elbows on the mattress so he can slide the material from my body. A firm hand presses into the center of my back, pushing me to the bed as soon as the shirt is pulled free of my arms. I groan deep from the back of my throat as nimble fingertips dig into the flesh of my shoulders, clenching and releasing in a massaging rhythm.

"My job is to take care of you, Willow. You're mine. I'll feed you when I think you're hungry. I'll let you rest when you're tired. I'll clothe you when you're cold. I'll keep you safe and warm and well fed. My job is to teach you, too. If the lesson leaves you in pain, it's my job to heal you. Now, don't be rolling your eyes at me again," Auggie warns. "No, I didn't see you do it. I just know you did, because I know my Willow Monster."

"Thank you," I breathe.

"It feels good to be appreciated," Auggie replies, sounding thoroughly amused. "Now... about that other pain I caused..." Auggie's hand comes into my line of sight as he reaches over our heads to the shelf built into the headboard. I can't see what he has hidden in his large palm, but his evil chuckle has me shivering in a mix of fear and anticipation.

Fingertips hook the sides of my boy shorts and slowly tug them from my hips. The material gets stuck on the swell of my ass, causing Auggie to groan. "Your ass is..." Auggie clear his throat. "Magnificent perfection."

Warm palms cup the back of my legs, running up my flesh, slowly parting my thighs. Auggie kneels between my spread legs, his knees widening me farther. "Gorgeous, Willow," Auggie murmurs in a voice gone husky with lust, and in this moment I do feel gorgeous.

Augustus Kline's lust makes me gorgeous.

"Oh, fuck." I groan as he manipulates my ass cheeks in his big palms, gripping and releasing in a wicked rhythm. Never would I have thought a simple touch would be so arousing. My breath catches in my throat. My body blooms for his hands– blooms for the man. Moisture wells inside my body and spills between my parted thighs. The moment Auggie hisses, I know he can see the reaction he causes within me.

Leaning forward, curving over my back, Auggie whispers into my ear, "You drive me insane with want. I have you spread before me... I could so easily take you like an animal. I want to. I want you. The only thing stopping me is *you– hurting* you."

"I'm sorry." I whimper, feeling inadequate. Ruined.

"No apologies," Auggie demands. His teeth press into my aching shoulder muscle and fiercely bite. I jerk in surprise, yelping. "I'll solve this tiny issue." Auggie giggles– he fucking giggles, the creepiest sound I've ever heard. "*Tiny*," he repeats the word that he found hysterical. "I'm about to change that word to *small*."

A warm palm slides between my belly and the mattress, pulling my body up off the bed until I'm on my knees and resting on my folded arms. My pussy is exposed, my small breasts hanging, sensitive nipples rasping against the sheets. Auggie directs me with his movements. Never telling me to do anything, he just places me how he wants me.

"Gorgeous," Auggie repeats, and I can feel his eyes searing, burning into my private flesh.

A surprised gasp spills from my throat when cold liquid hits my ass crack. The next sensation to hit my senses is the sound of a bottle squirting, and less than a second later cold lube floods between my spread thighs. The sticky liquid slowly slides down my ass crack to pool in the slit between my nether-lips, and then drips to the sheets beneath me. The cold sensation has lightning striking my spine, burning me to my core.

A shocked grunt escapes my parted lips when Auggie impales me with his middle finger and twists it in an intoxicating, circular rhythm. "Does this hurt?" With torturous slowness, Auggie slides his finger in and out of my aching pussy. He ends the slide with a twist of his wrist that has me quivering.

"Nah." I groan, drugged with pleasure. I pant softly, puffing bursts of breath from my lungs or I'd suffocate. "My God, don't stop." I lift my hips like a wanton slut. "That slippery stuff is amazing." Auggie snorts at the way my voice sounds– slow and gravelly deep.

"Tell me the second this becomes uncomfortable," Auggie commands me.

I begin to move with his hand, trying to feel more of him. I arch my neck and moan when he adds a second finger. The sensation changes when he spears me with two fingers and spreads them far apart inside of me. He pulls them out while they're still parted, and just as quickly, he closes his fingers and plunges back into my depths. He does this over and over. Each time Auggie widens his fingers farther apart on the exit. I whimper when it starts to hurt– sting and burn, stretched to my limits. Auggie kisses my neck to gentle me, but doesn't stop his assault on my pussy.

"A little more, Willow. I won't do it any wider than this. Just ride it out until it doesn't hurt." His voice is lulling and it soothes. I want to please him so badly that I gladly take the pain.

"Good girl," Auggie whispers as he pulls his hand away. I whimper because I was starting to enjoy it– the in and out rhythm was building a sweet pressure in my lower belly and I wanted to relieve it. Auggie hasn't touched my clit, and it's throbbing with ache. Each pulse screams its need for release.

"We're not done. Again, tell me when it starts to hurt." Auggie's words are laced with a threat of what's to come. I shiver in anticipation and trepidation.

A sound has me flinching– the sound of the bottle being squeezed. Auggie pours so much lube on me that I'd bet the bottle is empty. Auggie tossing the bottle halfway across the loft, into the kitchen, tells me I bet right. Empty.

Auggie's blunt-tipped fingers spread the slipperiness from my ass crack to my mound before slipping inside me. Sweat beads over my entire body as I move with Auggie, flow into his touch. My hips rock to grind on his hand. My clit is screaming to be touched. As if knowing the directions of my thoughts, Auggie pulls my hands over my head by anchoring my wrists together.

"No, Monster. All the pleasure you get tonight will be from me," Auggie purrs in warning. I whimper when he moves away from my back. The air feels cold in the absence of his hot body pressed along mine.

"Uh!" I grunt as thick, hot flesh slaps my left ass cheek, and then my right. Auggie spanks me with the Beast, the thwack of flesh on flesh reverberating down my spine. Rocking his hips back and forth, Auggie parts my ass cheeks with his cock and pleasures himself with the slide.

Leaning over me, rocking back and forth, Auggie nuzzles my neck with the tip of his nose and moans into my ear. With a swift shift of his hips, the Beast's trajectory changes. Auggie's cock slides slickly along my spread pussy lips, causing us both to moan in unison. I jolt in surprise when his bulbous head passes my engorged clit.

Pleasured out of my mind, all I can do is endure– moaning with every pass of his cock, and feeling pride that I make Auggie groan in response. I'm not an active participant, because Auggie wants me to be prone. Auggie wants to give, and for me to receive, and I'll take anything he's willing to provide.

"Don't stop," I groan when the length of the Beast moves over my clit in a tantalizingly long slide. His flesh is hard, scorching hot, and velvety smooth on my aching nub. The Beast sears me, burns me, consumes me, and I want nothing less than total annihilation. I can't stop the pulses that radiate from my core, not that I'd ever want to stop ecstasy.

"Don't stop this?" Auggie teases me as he flexes his hips in example. I sharply cry out his name when the flared head of The Beast strokes my clit. "Does my good girl ache for her Auggie?"

Her Auggie? *My* Auggie. The thought makes me light-headed with delirium.

"I ache so badly it's painful," I gasp. My knees threaten to give out, shaking, losing strength. Auggie's arm slides beneath my belly to hold me in place.

"Do you want me to keep doing this?" Auggie flexes his hips again, drawing his cock back and forth through my lips and across my clit. The Beast is so firm and wide that all of my flesh gets attention at once. The glorious sensation is too much to withstand without total combustion– I ignite in a flash-burn.

"I'm gonna come!" I shout. My nails bite into my palms, and the sharp edge of pain adds to the sweetness of the pleasure. I grit my teeth against the pressure of my release as I succumb to the ecstasy of Auggie's flesh gliding along mine.

"Or do you want the Beast inside you when you come?" Auggie breathes against the shell of my ear. His words leaving a trail of gooseflesh in their wake.

"Oh. My. God." I almost come just from his words alone. "Please," I beg shamelessly.

The Beast pushes until the tip parts my flesh. My pussy engulfs the head of the Beast, sucking him farther in. My muscles grip, refusing to release the flesh that we've longed to possess. I lift my hips wantonly, no longer retaining any form of inhibitions.

All I feel is *need*.

All I know is *want*.

All I experience is Augustus Kline.

I whimper when Auggie won't give me more– more of him inside me. "Please," I beg anew. "I need you, Auggie. I need to please you, too."

My pleading gets to Auggie, and he finally gives me what I want, what I need, what I'm begging for– the Beast. Auggie presses forward, as far as he did last night, and then slowly he adds a little bit more, and then a little bit more, until I can't take any more of him within me. It stretches me to the point of pain. I whimper from the burn, but I don't ask him to stop, because I don't want him to stop.

"Shhh…" Auggie croons to soothe me. "I'm just going to give you a few inches until you can painlessly take more. It'll start to feel good in a second after you've adjusted. We'll have to do it like this until you're ready."

I quiver as Auggie slowly pulls out and pushes back it. My body doesn't know what to think of the invasion. Every muscle in my body flexes in delight. My spine arches. My fingertips twist into the sheets, curling into claws. My toes anchor me on the bed as Auggie thrusts in jarring stops and starts. Pitiful noises spill from my mouth as I beg for more. He pushes in until I whimper in pain, and then retreats, only to go push past the point of resistance on the next thrust. I savor the prickly pain.

I look down the length of my body, needing to watch the Beast disappear and reappear within my body, needing visual confirmation that Augustus Kline is finally fucking me. I see nothing of the sort. It's too dark, too shadowy. What I do see has moisture flooding my cunt and a sharp groan yanked from my throat. In my line of sight, a heavy sac swings between my thighs, its hair brushing up against my pussy, tapping my clit. I arch my back, better positioning myself to take the pleasure. Auggie said I couldn't pleasure myself, that it was only his to give. My clit is dying for attention, and I make sure Auggie gives it to me.

Knowing my body is swallowing the Beast does wicked things to my nerve-endings. Just as I'm about to topple over the edge of climax, Auggie stops rocking his hips. The movement near my ass, the feel of flesh brushing against mine, hurts my ego as much as it brings me pleasure. Instead of fucking me, Auggie is stroking his length and allowing the movement to flow inside of me. His large, muscular hand strokes the Beast to climax, because I'm so inept, so inexperienced, so inadequate, I can't bring him to release.

Auggie picks up a hypnotic speed, and all I feel is his pleasure and my emotional pain. I hear my moans of disappointment and his guttural groans of ecstasy. But I can only focus on the fact that the only pleasure Auggie is getting is by the use of his hand and not my body.

Auggie kisses my throat, nipping my skin with his front teeth. I murmur *harder* when he sucks my neck, needing something to connect us together– needing something to grasp as an anchor. His breath warms my skin as he pants and moans.

"AH!" Auggie shouts as he pulls his cock from my body, pressing the length against my ass, sliding along my crack. His heavy palm wraps securely around my throat, arching my neck so that he can kiss my shoulder while groaning and gasping against my flesh.

Scalding hot liquid fires up my back before it finally comes to rest near my hairline at the base of my spine. Curled over my back, shuddering, the Beast jerking and spurting, Auggie comes *on* me, but not *for* me or *because* of me.

Augustus Kline educates me, but the lesson I'm to learn is lost on me. Selfishness? Inadequacy? Is the emotion you're to feel after sex worthlessness? In my deepest fantasies, the ones I refuse to admit, I'd thought I'd feel connected, loved, and sated. I thought it would mirror what my best friend gave me. A sense of being non-corporeal, floating– high.

I've never wanted to take a hit as badly as I do in this very moment. For the first time ever, I want weed to make me forget. But there's no waiting for Auggie to fall asleep so I can sneak off to get burnt. No, he made sure of that.

I was forced to flush my stash down the toilet. Auggie then made me drain every bottle of liquor, smash the bottles with a hammer, then dump them in the trash. He made me smash the shot glasses and throw the barware away too. But what hurt the most was when he made me pulverize my rainbow-swirled bowl. It was my first, the one that appeared on my bed after I asked– the bowl that had been by my side since I was thirteen. The same one I smoked, day-in and day-out, in the aftermath of Sam's death.

I cried as I destroyed my only true best friend.

… As I cry silently now. I've given and received oral sex. Technically, I've had sex twice now. Other than during my first punishment– the spanking –I haven't climaxed by a hand other than my own. Not once. Auggie didn't allow me to come when his mouth was on me. He hasn't allowed me to come during sex. Auggie said my pleasure was his to give, so he must not think I deserve it. Is it selfish that I cry over something so trivial when there are so many other things that merit my pain?

Biting back tears, I speak without thought. "Why'd you stop?" I ask in a soft, breathy voice.

"What do you mean?" Auggie has to clear his throat to be heard. He's sprawled on his back, one arm lying across his chest while the other plays with the tips of my hair. Auggie takes up most of the king-sized bed. As he does in our lives, Auggie is larger than life, dominating, not to be denied nor ignored.

Still lying on my stomach, hiding my nakedness, I feel stripped raw– emotionally bare-naked. So raw that I let my words fly. "I wanted you in me, moving inside my body, connecting with me. I needed you to come inside me, not spilling across my back and neck." I sound depressed, and hearing the desperation flow from my mouth sickens me. My emotions shouldn't be tied to an act with a man who said I wasn't his girlfriend. But then again, we both agreed Augustus Kline emotionally owned my ass.

"Willow, we can't do that," Auggie murmurs sadly as he rolls to his side. I feel his gaze sear into my cheek, the only part of my face that is visible– I don't give him the satisfaction by looking back at him. "I should be wearing a condom when I'm with you. I got taken up in the moment and lost my head. I apologize for that. You really should get on birth control for your own protection– accidents happen."

Auggie's palm lands in the center of my back, warm and heavy but no longer comforting. "I'm on the shot," I admit. For the first time, I'm thankful for my over-protective sister.

"What?" Auggie sits up abruptly, yanking me up with him until I'm sitting on my ass. Staring me down, Auggie reads me like a polygraph test. "Why the hell would you be on the shot already?" He hisses in anger, and I flinch back at the venom in his tone. "I know for a fact you were a fucking virgin. So please explain to me what need you had for birth control at your age."

"My sister got scared when I first got my period. As soon as I started menstruating, Clover took me to the doctor. I was fourteen– a late bloomer. No surprise there, right? Clover said I was extremely irresponsible, and she didn't want to raise any of my brats. Violet started her period early– she was only eleven. It wasn't much after I started. So every three months, Clover takes Violet and me to the clinic. She even watches to make sure we get the shot. Clover calls it a girls' day. She takes us to lunch and we get pedicures. The sisterly bonding kind of takes the creep-factor away."

Auggie bolts from the bed like he has to get the hell away from me or punch me in the face. Pacing in front of the bed like a caged tiger, he hisses, "I swear to God, your family shouldn't raise children. They'd destroy a fuckin' house cat!"

Stunned, I start to shiver, emotional overload finally overtaking me. I bite my bottom lip to stop my teeth from chattering. Auggie's skin takes on the hue of his hair– red with fury. His fists are clenched at his sides as he paces back and forth at the end of the bed. I worry that his anger will be directed at me next.

"I feel guilty for what I just did to you, and you're an adult." Fisting his hair, Auggie makes a frustrated sound, guttural and deep. "But to take a child, who should be playing with dolls, and make her get a shot of birth control is beyond fucking disgusting. What is that doctor thinking? The hormones can't be good for a growing body. I'd think you were stunted from it." Auggie gestures to my small boy-like body, causing me to flinch in shame. "But Violet is a normal-sized girl."

Auggie's harsh words lash out at me, smacking me in the heart, dissolving what little self-esteem I had left. In one sentence, Auggie insulted Clover and compared me to Violet, saying Violet's body is normal, making mine wrong. The sting takes my breath away, suffocates me.

"I'm sorry," quivers from beneath my breath. "I just did what I was told. Do you think it ruined me somehow? Shrunk me?"

"Motherfuck," Auggie hisses. He reaches over, picking me up beneath the armpits, and stalks angrily to the shower with me dangling in his huge hands.

"Willow, I'm not mad at you." Auggie growls, but his demeanor and actions contradict him. Shoving me roughly into the shower stall, Auggie gets in with me and turns on the water. Ice cold water sprays me, cleansing me of everything that was left of the sex we just had.

"It's not your fault." Fisting the soap, Auggie attacks my back like he wants to peel my flesh from bone, scrubbing me raw where he'd spurted on my back. "If Clover were to materialize before me right now, I'd punch her fucking bitch face. I want to beat your parents until they have a lick of sense, since they're usually senseless. I want to remove the twins from your demented family before they ruin them. You all need a fucking keeper. No wonder you and Rob always choose the wrong choices when they present themselves. The sheep were raising the wolves."

Auggie washes me roughly, like I'm a small child who is too stupid to do it herself. Instead of the way he always makes me feel loved and cherished, I feel belittled and judged: my family, my upbringing, my body, my soul.

Auggie sees me as broken, as something he needs to repair. What if he figures out there is nothing to fix, or that I'm irreparable? I curse my fucked up family and my freakishly small body. I can't even have sex right, and any moron can have sex. The man that I need to love and respect me has to resort to jacking off while inside me to get off. Unless my entire body grows several inches, we're doomed.

I'll never satisfy Auggie in any way– that's what Robbie and Clover were trying to warn me. Satisfying Auggie is impossible, and not because no one can. It's impossible because someone like me could never be enough. Not someone like me... *me*. We all know I'm not good enough for Augustus Kline, and by the way he's trying to remove any trace of his body on mine, he knows it too.

What Auggie needs from the Playroom isn't an issue for me. It's our time in private that I'm worried about. I should be able to make love to Auggie, and I can't. Eventually he'll find someone who can. I don't mean sex. I mean the act of connecting as human beings, of holding a conversation, of being comfortable in your own skin with another person. I have no delusions that Auggie and I are at that point right now– none whatsoever. Auggie only said that he thought we could be *someday*. That someday is never going to come to fruition, because I'll always be inadequate and inept– a woman's mind trapped inside a child's body.

CHAPTER TWENTY-THREE

It's late afternoon, and Auggie and I haven't shared more than a few words since early morning. I don't want to have a talk or a lecture. I miss goofing off with him. It's like *Invasion of the Body Snatchers* at Revamped. Auggie was a laidback geek who would play video games and tease me all day long, and now in his place is a... *dad*.

Auggie's been in a mood all day. He's working like a madman, trying to get all of the workmen and materials he needs for the Spook House. He left early this morning to sign the paperwork, and came back a homeowner. I didn't dare congratulate Auggie on his new purchase. I feared he'd punish me, make me scrub the toilets with my toothbrush or some other nasty task. He's been a monosyllable Cro-Magnon all damned day.

I found out the hard way what it means to be Auggie's live-in. As an employee, I was required to arrive at Revamped at a quarter of eleven to open the store. When I lived with my parents, I woke at nine in the morning and enjoyed a hot breakfast while watching the news with my dad, who would then walk me to work so we could chat. If it was a Saturday, Seth would join us with a feet-scuffing Violet tagging along. That warm and fuzzy feeling is not my life anymore. Amazing how fast your life can change, and I'm not entirely certain the change was for the positive.

After little to no sleep, my indentured servitude began. I was yanked from restless dreamland at six a.m., handed a brown sugar Pop-Tart (my least favorite Pop-Tart), and was pushed down the stairs. I've worked as much from the time I entered Revamped and turned the sign to '*Open*' than I usually do between the times I turn the sign to '*Open*' and shut the sucker off at closing. I'm now working three times as long and my pay-grade hasn't changed.

In that extra five-hour time period, I've organized fifteen more auctions of our more collectable items, and started the arduous task of listing every item in the store on our website. I was shocked to see we sold one of the items I placed on there last week as a test run. I already ran to the post office to ship it.

I found out one very annoying problem with my system. After placing the inventory on the site, a man came in and bought a few items. I then had to remove them from the site immediately. I found a fatal flaw in my system: what if someone purchases an item online at the same time I sell that same item to a customer in person? I don't have an answer for that, and I don't dare ask Auggie for help, not in his current mood. For now, I will just double-check before I sell it in person. If I goof, I guess I'll offer the online purchaser a refund and a discount on another item. There is a definite learning curve to this business, and I highly doubt my online sales will be that many.

"Eat." Auggie's voice startles me after hours of quiet. He pushes a peanut butter sandwich toward me and a bottle of milk. If I didn't already feel like a kid after last night, this meal would do it.

Not looking at Auggie, I mutter, "Thanks." I start shredding the crust from the sandwich. I pop pieces of crust into my mouth and try to keep the traitorous tears at bay.

Auggie pulls a stool over and sits next to me. Usually I feel comfortable around Auggie. Boss or not, Robbie's best friend or not, a few days ago I loved hanging out with the man. It was comfortable and companionable, and we had a lot of fun together. It's not the sex that's ruining it for me, or living with Auggie, or Auggie bossing my ass around– that's all par for the course. It's the hot and cold that makes me feel uncertain. It's the silent and not-so silent judgment that I've never felt before between us.

"I have to apologize for something," Auggie murmurs lightly. He reaches over, fingers clasping my shoulders, and starts to rub the painful knots away.

"What for?" I wipe my mouth, making sure I don't have any peanut butter on me. It would make me look even more juvenile than I already am.

"Many things. When I make a mistake, I will admit to it, and I will apologize. First, I feel like a dirty, old man for what we've been doing. Intellectually, I know it's not wrong, but I still feel guilty. I'm not ashamed that I want you. I'm ashamed that I took you without taking your feelings into account."

"I want you," I breathe out.

"I want you, too, Willow. *Badly*. But I've fucked up twice. I was inside you without a condom. Thank God your sister is a control freak, or we could have serious consequences. Last night, I wasn't quick enough and you got the first blast."

"I wanted you inside me," I murmur.

"I know." He sighs and closes his eyes. "Me too, but that's not the point. I did it without thinking of the consequences. After years of having sex in the Playroom, I've always worn a condom. I haven't had much intimacy outside of play. Rob is the only one who I've been with like that, and I can't get him pregnant."

"Oh… wow." I am utterly speechless.

"There is disease to think of, too. That stuff with Rob was before we were with anyone else. Two virgins can't give each other a disease. When Isis joined us, condoms were a necessity to keep Malcolm from castrating us. Once we started playing, we were always safe. I told Rob that if he ever messed up, I'd never do skin-to-skin again."

For some sick and twisted reason, I want to ask Auggie if Robbie ever messed up and does Isis count, because I'm positive my brother couldn't control himself around the woman. I know it's inappropriate, but I'm a curious person by nature. Auggie might get pissed at me if I'm ballsy enough to ask, but I know Robbie won't be. If I ask my brother anything, he'll happily supply the answer.

"I know disease was not an issue with you, because you were a virgin. I'm trying to stress that we have to take extreme caution when we play. So the fact that I fucked up that badly, twice in a row, disturbs the fuck out of me. You make me lose my head."

"Should I apologize for that, Auggie?" I mutter, but I don't sound defensive as usual.

"No, I'm just trying to explain that we need to act responsibly. It was just luck that you were already on birth control. So if you have sex with Devon, I'd prefer if you used a condom. But you don't have to because he's never been with anyone else."

"Devon's a virgin?" I sound utterly shocked.

"Not my place to give out that information." Auggie quickly backtracks. But it's too late, he already spilled the surprising truth. "If any of us are with other people, we have to be safe. We *must* be safe. Skin-to-skin should be private and between lovers. It's true intimacy and should never be during play. Do you understand?"

"Yes, Auggie, I've had the disease, birth control, and protection talk countless times. I understand what you mean. I get that it's more personal without a condom, and it's really fucking stupid to do this stuff without forethought. Don't be upset about last night. I can't get pregnant, and I want you inside me." I admit forcefully, getting irritated by the way he's speaking to me, like I'm a little kid and dim to boot.

I push the sandwich away and lean my head on the counter and just breathe. I understand why Auggie's upset. I make him lose his control and thought. I get it, because he does the same to me. But losing control or not, I can't deal with these mood swings, especially since they aren't *my* mood swings.

"Second, I want to apologize about having sex last night. We both wanted it, but I should've waited for your discomfort to heal. I wanted you so damn bad that I didn't care about consequences, pain, or your wellbeing. I'm sorry," he sputters before he can stop himself.

"I'm not," I state firmly in an annoyed tone.

"Willow, I'm not saying I'm sorry we had sex. I'm saying I'm sorry for being such an asshole." Auggie leans over me, kisses my neck, and hugs me from behind.

"Stop that, or I'll beg you to fuck me again," I tease, and I'm truly teasing. I don't want Auggie like that right now, not so soon. Not after last night. My emotions couldn't take it. I thought sex was about fun, and making love was about connection, and fucking was about passion. I didn't get any of those things. What I got was a big dose of feeling like shit.

"Nah… not happening," Auggie draws out, and I can hear the smile in his voice. He's pleased I'm back to flirting with him. Thank God, he didn't notice that I didn't mean it. "Monster, not until you heal up and experience it with someone else. Last night was beyond difficult for me." Auggie rubs my back, trying to lessen the hard truth of it.

"I'm sorry I'm a woman trapped inside a ten-year-old's body," I whisper. Tears leak out the corners of my eyes, and I rub my face on my sleeves to hide them.

"Hey," Auggie murmurs softly. He tries to comfort me, but it has the opposite effect. I just end up feeling pitied and worthless. "There's nothing we can do about this. Yes, you're freakishly small," he teases, laughing at me. "But I'm freakishly big. We make quite the pair, don't we?"

"I guess." I sniffle.

"You'll see, it won't be difficult with a regular guy. I can't take on a normal-sized girl, either. There aren't many who can take all of me. It's a joke how women say they want a guy with a big cock. Trust me, I don't get many repeat performances. I'm a novelty they soon regret. But you aren't, Willow. You have no idea how incredible it feels to be inside you, like a silk fist pulsing around my cock." Auggie clears his throat, because his voice gets thick with lust. "We will get this to work. Last night wasn't bad, now was it?"

Yes... "No, but you said we have to wait." I whine, needing a do-over to prove I can get it right.

"I'm afraid to lose control around you, Willow. I'm afraid I'll harm you. I promise the next time will be even better– trust me."

"I do." I look Auggie directly in the eye as I say it. "I do trust you."

Auggie smiles at me, and the warmth that glows forth is solar. "Third, I fucked up big time with how I spoke of your family last night. I apologize. I love your family– they're each incredible in their own right. But it's in my nature to protect you, and they've done some stupid shit. I'll try not to judge. I could tell I hurt your feelings. I didn't say anything to you last night or this morning because I wanted to process it before I spoke."

"It's okay," I mumble, feeling uncomfortable.

"No, *it's not*. Words have weight. I can apologize, but that doesn't take them away. I can say I didn't mean them, but you still heard them. Your mind is still haunted by them. It makes me sick that I hurt your feelings."

"You were just telling me the truth, Auggie. It hurt, but it wasn't a lie. Sometimes the truth hurts, right?"

"It wasn't my place to judge your family, Willow. I'm not your father, and you aren't my child– thank God. I don't want you to fear me, or think I'm disappointed in you."

"I don't think that's possible, Auggie. I'm so fucking scared you'll think I'm a piece of shit, I don't know what's up from down anymore."

"Get that outta your head, Monster. I want you to make mistakes so you can learn and grow. It's part of the process. I'll try to head the major mistakes off at the pass, though. I just can't stay on the sidelines and watch you fuck up."

"I like your advice." I sit up and eat the sandwich Auggie made me like I'm a good girl. I can't deal with any more of this conversation, so I make Auggie happy by eating the food he provided. Distraction effective, he steals my jug of milk and drains the quart in one long, continuous gulp.

"I'm a growing boy," Auggie teases. He smirks at me with a milk-stache, and then uses his forearm to clean it off. "I gotta get back to work." Arching a furry red eyebrow, he asks, "Am I forgiven?"

"There's nothing to forgive." I look Auggie in the eyes so he knows I mean it.

"Sure there is, but you're just blind to my faults." A bottle of pomegranate juice appears in front of me as if by magic. "This is for you. If I see milk, I drink it. You better drink that before I drain it, too."

I pop the lid and lick the rim of the bottle.

"Like that will ever stop me." Auggie's deep rumble echoes in my heart even after he returns to the back of the store.

CHAPTER TWENTY-FOUR

After the world's longest workday from hell, I'm testing out a *Mario Kart* disc on the *Wii*. Yes, just testing for the past half hour when the door dings. I glance over my shoulder, and get a happy surprise. My smile is huge as a small army of kids files into Revamped's small store space.

"Oh, wow! Hey!" I pause the game and gape up at Devon like a moron. I hop up from my nest and wander over to them, still grinning like a fool. So freakin' happy to have some friendly faces after the hellish night and day I've had. Too much emotional bullshit. I feel like Auggie is giving me therapy at a school of hard knocks– twisted bastard that he is.

"I'm trying a new tactic for later," Devon says conspiratorially, albeit cryptically. He has four teens following him– three look happy and the fourth looks murderous.

"You must be Weston," I say to the handsome thirteen-year-old standing next to his big brother.

It's uncanny how much Weston looks like Kieren, with his dark blue eyes and blond hair, and he's already a huge boy. Weston has an infectious smile and dimpled cheeks. I shake his hand like I'm an adult and he isn't nearly a foot taller than me already. He blushes and looks at the floor– so damned cute. No surprise Violet ran him off.

"I'm Rae." Violet's enemy says, holding out her hand for a shake. Violet isn't running this one off, that's for sure. Robbie said Malcolm treats his girls like princesses, and this one is throwing off airs like a reigning queen.

"Wow," I breathe. "You're really pretty." Long, tousled, dark hair and pale blue eyes– she looks just like Aunt Isis.

"Thanks," Rae says with confidence, as if everyone greets her with a *wow, you're really pretty* on a daily basis. "This place is awesome." A sultry voice purrs out of the young girl's throat. I shake my head as she wanders off to search the shop like she's never seen anything so fascinating. A gorgeous geek, who knew?

"Hey, turd, you didn't give me a hug yet," I tease Seth. "Don't you miss your auntie?" I yank Seth to me because I miss him something fierce, and he's usually a very affectionate kid. But right now he acts all tough in front of his friends, like I'm inconveniencing him with my touch.

"I missed you, too, Willow," Seth whispers to me so only I can hear. I snort when he squeezes me tightly for a nanosecond before stepping out of reach.

"You guys can go play with the game systems. *Test* out any game ya want. I need to talk to Devon in private."

"Ahhh!!!" Weston and Seth drawl out in unison, teasing the crap out of each other. They run off, horsing around: hooting and pushing, poking and tickling, taunt and cuss spewing– they pretty much act like me. Idiots.

"Not you." I grab Violet's boney arm and draw her flush to me. She scowls her sociopathic expression right back at me– the one that would bring a grown man to his knees. Well, I'm neither man nor grown, so it doesn't affect me in the least. The most disturbing thing is the fact that Violent Violet's *look* is the same one I deploy on unsuspecting victims.

"I don't like video games, anyway," Violet mumbles belligerently, lying her ass off. Violet is a closeted video game player. She pretends she's texting on her cellphone, when I know for a fact she's playing any game that ends in *Dash*. *Hotel Dash* is her current favorite.

Violet's scowl is making her look as uptight as her mother. While not as exotic looking as Raven, Violet is definitely a classic beauty with her chocolate brown hair and bright blue eyes. It's the constipated, pinched expression that makes her look like the raving bitch she is. Violet definitely gets that *look* from Clover.

"Listen," my fingers bite into Violet's arm as I hiss into her ear. "Officer Devon has a badge and a gun. If you misbehave, I'll let him use it. You may only get Juvie for misbehaving, but I bet there are a lot of your classmates in there that you've bullied, and they'd love to have you join them in their cage." I say in a voice gone deep and gravelly. It's my smoker's voice, but filled with menace. "Got it?"

"Yes, Aunt Willow," Violet replies smugly, not affected by my threat in the least.

"You don't have to actually commit a crime, you get that, right? I will frame you for one. I've been playing this game for three and a half years longer than you. You're just starting out–

a newb. I've reached expert level." I threaten Violet underneath my breath so no one else can hear me.

"I love you, too," Violet replies sweetly– her way of agreeing with me while telling my ass off.

"Good. Go play with them and be nice. I bet they'll even let you be Princess Peach." Violet strides away with her head held high and her shoulders back. She looks like she's holding a tiara on her head. Queen of Violence. *Mario Kart* is probably too mild of a game for her. I should break out *Gears of War*– the Lancer with its chainsaw bayonet is more Violet's speed.

"How'd you manage that?" I ask Devon how he corralled all four kids together as I walk us to the reading nook, trying for a bit of privacy.

I curl up in the front window seat, and Devon joins me on the small cushion. This is one of my favorite spots in all of Revamped. I love to sit in the window and watch the people on the street. Sadly, I don't get to sit here often since Auggie chains me to the front counter like a naughty pet.

When no screams of extreme violence fill Revamped, I look over to the video game section. I bark a laugh as I watch all four kids get along. All you have to do is give them a video game and everyone behaves. It's the United Nations for deviant youths.

"I saw the twins when I was picking the kids up from school. I thought it would be a great time to test the waters." Devon leans his back against the front window and clasps his hands over his chest. My eyes linger over the strain of his shirt across his pecs. I blush and look away when he catches me.

What the fuck is wrong with me? I get a taste for sex, and it's all I can think about. Thank God, only certain people affect me, or I'd be walking around in a perpetual state of heat. Of course, it could be the fact that I keep having sex without any relief. I comfort myself by letting that be the reason. Denied climax.

"After winter break, I'll be the Truant Officer for K-12. It's the grunt position. Busy work, not a full-time job. I'll have other duties. I may have fudged the truth of what the job entails, though. I think Violet's scared of me now. Good news!" Devon sings. "We have four more helpers tonight, because I told them if they didn't help, I'd stalk them for the rest of their school careers. Slave labor, gotta love it."

"You're a bad, *bad* man, Officer Devon," I tease, and then turn serious. "Can I ask you something personal?"

"I'll be an open book for you," Devon replies sincerely. I glance at the kids to make sure they're staying out of trouble and not listening in on our conversation.

"Are you okay with ya know… me and you? " I ask hesitantly. "I don't know what you're getting out of this. I know what Auggie expects, but what about you?"

All day, I've tried to push the thoughts away. I've felt guilty over how Auggie told someone to be my friend– worse, my boyfriend. I hate how it makes me feel worthless and used. The more I examine my relationship with Auggie, the worse I feel, and the more I want to avoid the thoughts because I'm not ready to accept reality.

What bothers me the most is that I don't want Devon to feel used or worthless. I don't want him to think all the things I'm thinking– how someone has to be forced to be your friend, forced to hang out with you. I also don't want to impose on Devon and make him uncomfortable. He has a family, a job, a life– he shouldn't have to babysit me, too.

I reach over and grasp Devon's hand, giving a little squeeze, so he knows I'm being sincere. "I want you to know that if you don't want to hang out with me, just say so. I won't be angry. I could lie and say I wouldn't be upset, but I won't. Just walk away, and I'll deal with Auggie. Don't do this for me. I'm not worth the hassle, Devon."

"No, I'm not fine with being ordered to hang out with you." Devon bites out fiercely, and I jerk away in surprise. I hadn't expected him to be okay with it– I just didn't think he'd be so angry over the thought of spending time with me. Devon turns his face away so I can't look at him anymore. His side profile shows me all I need to see, judging by his jaw clenching and ticking.

"I'm just so sickened over Auggie pimping you out, and I know for a fact he didn't give you a choice."

I pull my knees to my chest and hug myself. I thought Devon would understand and not judge me for something I don't understand myself. "I don't know what to say to that, Devon," I grumble in a stiff voice.

"What could you possibly say, Willow?" Devon looks at me, and I finally see the resemblance to Isis isn't only skin-deep. Those eyes are the same, turning obsidian when enraged.

"Auggie just brought me over, told you to accept me, and you did. Playing on repeat inside my mind is whether or not you would've gone through with it if Auggie had told you to fuck me."

"NO!" I shout, ten shades of Hades burning my skin. "Auggie is one thing. But even for him, I would never do that. What you must think of me?" I muse.

Speaking as if he didn't just deal me a fatal blow, Devon continues on. "So maybe I'm questioning the same things you are. Do you want to hang out with me, or are you doing it because Auggie said *sit, roll over, and stay*? I don't want my friends to *actually* think they are a dog. Playacting for fun is one thing, allowing a person to command your every move is another."

"It's not quite like that, but I can see where you'd get the impression. I'm working it out on my own." I mumble the words, feeling strangely ashamed in the light of day. "I asked about you, ya know? Everyone is tight-lipped in regards to the Masons." I chuckle to myself without humor, finally realizing why no matter what, no one would give me info– Auggie.

"Willow, what I want is my friend back." Devon grips my hand tightly, threading his fingers with mine. "The only reason I went to those parties was so I could hang out with you. I wasn't the most popular guest, being a cop's kid and all, with a legacy to uphold no less. They were scared shitless of me– still are."

"You?" I try to sound surprised as I tease him. "You? Devon Mason? Scary… uh, I call bullshit. You're harmless– a marshmallow."

Chuckling softly, Devon flashes me a smile. "I missed you when I went to the academy, and that's why." Devon points at my grin. "We have a lot of shit going down, and you're always trying to take the sting out of it."

"As opposed to screaming and crying? I'll take comedic relief to *that*," I stress.

"Willow, what's between you and me isn't about Auggie or the Playroom– you need to know that. I just want to hang out with the quirky girl who has the husky laugh. I refuse to have sex with you just because they say fuck her. I'd feel like a total douchebag. Also, I'm not pretending to hang out with you just to get into your pants, so it's easier on my conscience. I'm not that kind of guy. I'm fine with people thinking I'm your boyfriend because it's accurate– I'm a guy who happens to be your friend. The rest is our private business. But I don't feel right turning this into something more when you're obviously hooked on that arrogant assfuck. It's not fair to any of us."

"Okay," I mumble quietly. Devon's outburst shriveled up any reply I'd formulated. "Friends, then?" I hold my hand out to shake. "I could really use a friend about now."

"Friends." Devon agrees emphatically. He takes my hand and squeezes it instead of shaking. Warmth from his big palm causes me to shiver.

"Wow," I breathe, suddenly feeling scared to death.

"Well," Devon draws out while flashing me a smile– a perfect facsimile of Kieren's. It steals the breath from my lungs. Devon's smile is different in some ways. The emotions radiating from it are sadder, jaded yet innocent, less charming but no less captivating. "I better get the kids fed. They tend to get grouchy if they're hungry, like wild animals. I don't want to find out what a grouchy Violet and Rae would do, do you?" He shudders in horror.

"I've starved Violet before. She gets less volatile without sustenance. Too weak to fight back," I taunt, sounding serious. Devon looks at me like I've lost my ever-loving mind. "I'm not joking, Devon. *Really.*" I raise an eyebrow like Auggie does when he's trying to convince me to do something I don't want to do. Devon's eyes pop from his skull, and I know he's buying my bullshit. "Violet and I used to go on hunger strikes to get our way. They couldn't figure out how we weren't starving to death. Seth would sneak me food. I'm sure he was a traitor and fed his twin too."

"You guys are… insane." Devon sounds impressed, though. I'm lying out my ass, but he doesn't need to know that. If you can't mess with your friends' heads, whose can you? "What time will you be at the Spook House?"

"I close here at six." I answer as I hop up from the window seat. "So I'll probably get to the Spook House around a quarter after six."

"Well, that will give you a few hours of extra help. I have to have everyone home by nine. It's a school night. I'd be a shitty Truant Officer if I kept them out all night and made them late in the morning."

"Nah– it'd make you an evil one." I giggle.

"Don't give me ideas. I may use them." Devon laughs as he stands up from the reading nook. He surprises me by yanking my arm until my body is flush with his. Devon wraps his hands around my waist and holds my gaze. "Friends hug goodbye– I crave our hugs. You can thank my dad for my tactile dependency– cuddly bastard." His voice holds as much intensity as his deep blue eyes. I shiver and fall into his embrace.

The moment we make contact, my face buries itself into the side of Devon's neck– it's involuntary at this point. If Devon hugs me, I must breathe his scent deep into my lungs. Vanilla musk inundates my senses until I'm dizzy with bliss. The combination of Devon's scent and the warmth radiating off his body lulls me better than my drug of choice. My eyes droop shut and my muscles relax.

A giddy giggle has my eyelashes fluttering until I can hold my eyes open. Weston and Seth are giggling at us and blushing, while the girls roll their eyes in distaste. I ignore them, and bury my face farther into the side of Devon's neck until his black waves tickle my cheeks. I plant a not-so friendly kiss to the smooth skin where his neck meets his shoulder. He jolts as if touched by a livewire.

Devon's arms fully embrace me, one tangling up in the back of my hair and the other crossing over my back with his fingers gripping my hip. Our friendly hug turns into something more intimate than my two failed attempts at sex. I'm not filled with lust while in Devon's arms. I'm filled with contentment, closeness, connection. Auggie will scorch my heart to ashes on the wind, but I fear what Devon will be capable of if just a hug renders me into a swooning idiot.

One last squeeze, and Devon steps out of our embrace. Neither of us can look at the other in fear of what our faces will reveal. Devon clears his throat several times before, "Time to eat," rumbles out his mouth at the kids. Four heads pop up and look as one, like someone shouted *Beggin' Strips* to the family dogs.

"What's for dinner?" Weston asks. "Not spaghetti again."

"First one in the car gets to pick where we eat." Devon and I share a snicker. We only have one restaurant. The No-Name Diner. Running and shoving, the kids realize this halfway out the door.

"Well played, Officer Devon," Violet says with grudging respect, not falling for the trap the other three kids fell into. "No-Name it is."

"Later," I say in parting to the group. I start picking up the mess in the video game section so I can close Revamped early and get to work at the Spook House.

Forgoing the usual tunes flowing from the stereo system, I'm listening to Indie Rock on my iPod. I can only take so much discarded music. Testing out the CDs people bring in for trade-in at Revamped can get beyond annoying. There's a reason they're pawning them off onto me in the first place.

Being the best dang employee Revamped has ever seen, Auggie included, I've gone beyond the line of duty in the past twelve hours. I'm exhausted, both mentally and emotionally. What I wouldn't give for a meal of beer and pizza while watching *G4TV*, followed by a shower, and then lying in bed while getting baked. Drifting off to sleep without a care in the world sounds beyond decadent. I allow myself the fantasy for a moment, only to realize that was in another life. I'm no longer Willow the wayward. I'm Willow the responsible adult who has to go to the Spook House and work for another billion hours before I'm rendered unconscious by the Sandman.

"Are you going to the Spook House tonight?" Auggie asks me as I'm closing out the cash register, tallying up the receipts and praying they match the tape totals.

Auggie's been suspiciously silent, cold, even after our earlier talk. Auggie has stayed in the backroom, not saying a word to me– when he was inside Revamped, that is. He kept disappearing off and on all damned day, nowhere to be found when I needed him. I gave up on calling him on his cell phone when I had to ask him questions about trade-in values for customers. I'd call only to be sent straight to voicemail via that handy yet annoying '*ignore*' feature. When he did answer, it was with a grunt. I winged it, hoping I didn't rip off the customers. It would serve Auggie right if I accidently overbid their items. He should've answered his phone, or been in the store like he has been every day until today.

I never expected Augustus Kline to turn into an asshole of a man, but I guess I was wrong. The hot and cold routine is getting old, and it's only been one day.

"I believe it was *you* who said *I* had to be at the Spook House every moment of my time when I wasn't here at Revamped." I tease in a light voice, being snarky. "Guess where I'll be?" I smirk to myself, thinking all sorts of evil shit in my head.

Auggie's vibe is off. It has been since last night, and it worries me. His carefree attitude has changed since our relationship– if that's what you call it –has evolved from boss and employee to master and servant. I want my old Auggie back. I'd give anything to hear his growly bear laugh that always warmed my heart.

"I won't be joining you tonight at the Spook House. I have somewhere I need to be," Auggie mutters sheepishly as he ducks his head so I can't read his facial expressions. It's not like Auggie to be reluctant. If he means something, he says it, and he's blunt about it, too. Anger flashes through my veins as I realize what's making him behave peculiarly.

"Only one place would stop you from going to your new home to help fix it," I practically snarl. "So if you're going to the Playroom, just say it, Auggie. We're standing on the ground floor of Revamped right now, so I'm just your employee, right? If you plan on fucking off while I work all night, then just say it like you're my boss– no apologies. When you have to lie about it, it means you think it's wrong." My voice loses its anger as I speak. By the end of my diatribe, I just end up sounding exhausted.

I assumed Auggie would eventually have to go to the Playroom. I was expecting it, and I'll deal with the emotional fallout that follows. I assume that's the shitty hand we're dealt when we become adults. We're no longer allowed to throw a shit-fit when things don't go our way. What's pissing me off, is while I work, Auggie plays. While I try so hard, Auggie lies by omission.

"I don't think it's wrong. I'm just not sure how you'll feel about it." Auggie still won't look at me as he pretends to be busy scanning my receipts.

"Why does it matter?" I try to coax the truth out of him by seeming blasé about the entire situation.

"What do you mean?" Auggie *still* won't look at me, and it has a creeping sensation niggling at the back of my brain, like I'm going to be very upset soon.

"You're acting strange. You won't look me in the eye." I make sure Auggie realizes I'm not a total moron, or blind. "What I'm asking is why does it matter how I feel about you ditching work to go to the Playroom? You'd go anyway, right?" As soon as the words spill from my lips, I want to take them back. I realize I just inadvertently perfected the female trap men despise. *The damned if I do, damned if I don't.* It's the trap where either answer is the wrong answer. I'm so not going there.

"Yes, I would go no matter what. It feels weird. I don't know." Auggie sighs heavily, and runs his fingers through the wavy mop of his hair.

"I don't want to fight with you, Auggie, so I'm not going to. But you do realize that you just admitted you were going to lie to me about the Playroom, and go anyway even if it bothered me. That shit won't fly with me, Auggie. Not about the Playroom– the obvious lying and disrespect. I won't turn into a crazed female. That is not who I am as a person. Plus, that's not who *we* are together. This is whatever the hell this is." I muse, pointing between us. "Besides, next time I can go with you," I say, voice overflowing with hope.

"No, Willow, you won't be going back to Rush... or the Playroom." Auggie's voice deepens with command, and he finally looks me in the eye. I wish he hadn't when I see anger lurking in their depths.

"What?" I scrunch my face in confusion, tears threatening to spill from the way Auggie is staring at me. "What'd I do wrong this time? How could I have possibly gotten into trouble today? I acted like your fuckin' slave all damned day." I smash my calculator on the counter and start shoving the receipts into their folder– I'm done, closing up shop. I've got to get the fuck away from Auggie before I do turn into one of those women who goes postal.

"I set the rules of the club and the Playroom. You're not twenty-one–"

"Devon." I list off on my fingers as I hiss their names in a pissy voice. "Kieren. Essie. Not twenty-fucking-one yet!"

"My call. I never invited you to play. You invaded the Playroom when you entered Rush illegally. You're not going back." I flinch back as if struck with an open fist.

Auggie pins me with his furious stare, and I actually feel smaller than I am, about an inch tall, instantly causing tears to prickle the back of my eyes. With a handful of sentences, Auggie managed to tear any self-confidence I'd rebuilt and reduced it to shit.

"What the fuck, Auggie? What sort of sick game are you playing?" I hiss defiantly, trying to cover about a dozen emotions, and not one of them feels good.

"I'm not playing around, Willow. The answer is no. I'm not saying it as if I'm your father, because you are an adult. I'm not saying no as your boss. I'm saying no by the authority given to me as the owner of Rush and the creator of the Playroom. It is my right to deny patronage to anyone I see fit. No," Auggie states firmly.

"Understood, Mr. Kline. Crystal-fucking-clear." I yank my coat on and ignore the plethora of emotions screaming inside my brain. "I have to get to work– my second job I work for *you*. I'll see ya when I see ya," I mutter flippantly.

"Here," Auggie drops a set of keys into my hand. "Don't act out in retaliation," he warns. "The only person you'll hurt is yourself."

Auggie knows me too well. The old Willow would've acted like a brat and threw a tantrum, just like Robbie still does. But that Willow only threw a shit-fit when it was someone other than Mr. Kline telling her what to do. It disappoints me that Auggie doesn't know the difference. I was always so worried about how I'd feel when I disappointed Auggie, I never thought I'd see the day when he disappointed me.

"I take back what I said earlier," I admit sadly. I just shake my head over and over at Auggie for a moment. "I don't accept your apology. Obviously you didn't mean it. I guess I'm back to being too stupid to make a simple choice between A or B. Thanks for making me feel this small." I pinch my fingers together.

I run to my car. It's the first time I've ever driven it, and I don't even get to enjoy it. I don't know if I want to scream or cry. Auggie thinks I ran off because I had to pitch a fit like a spoiled child. That isn't the case. I just couldn't look at Auggie as he silently judges me, as he thinks of me as worthless, just as everyone on the planet does. I thought Auggie was different. I guess I was wrong again.

CHAPTER TWENTY-FIVE

I pull up outside of the Spook House, tears distorting my vision. I quickly reach up and unclasp my birthday necklace (collar) from my neck and toss it into my glove box. No Playroom? No need to tag my ass then. I was hoping for some privacy for a good cry, but that's not happening any time soon. Probably never. I may not be *that* type of girl, but I'm still a girl, and my feelings do get hurt.

No matter how dark it is outside, or how blurry my eyes are, the car idling at the curb isn't a mirage. Key in hand, I slowly get out of my car as Devon and the teen brigade spill out all of the doors of a squad car. Watching a grinning Seth and Weston and a glowering Violet exit the rear of a police car would've been hilarious if I wasn't on the edge of tears. I guess I can always wait to see it again when Violet gets arrested for assault and battery before she graduates high school. Probably, by then, I'll have matured so much I won't find it fun to gloat over her arrest. Pity.

I nod in their direction as I quickly cross the yard, mount the rickety front steps, and insert the key in the lock. This should've been an exciting rite of passage that I took at Auggie's side, not the feeling of doom that settles over me as the door to the Spook House swings open.

"This place is huge," Devon says in awe as he follows me into the house.

Earlier, I would've felt pride over the Spook House– a sense of ownership. But I can't now. That feeling was torn from me. It's Auggie's house, and I'm just his employee. I reason that every second of my time I work in this house will be rent for the future. My labor will not be like the rest of the Playroomers, where they have to work to pay off their sick membership dues.

I won't live off of Auggie. I will not take a handout from anyone that isn't family– they birthed me, they can feed my ass if I can't. Not Auggie. Never Auggie.

Auggie said his job was to house, feed, clothe, and protect me. That he was my mentor, teaching me lessons that only he could provide. I'm not some kind of worthless pet. The roof over my head, the food in my belly, the heat warming my toes, will be provided by me. I may not pay rent in the monetary sense, but it will be paid in full. I will pay for my room and board through manual labor. It's not like manual labor didn't put a roof over the heads of the Prynne/Webster clan for three generations. I'm just continuing the tradition.

Auggie can shove that master/pet bullshit up his ass, like it or lump it. I was only Auggie's pet in the Playroom, and since I'm no longer allowed inside Rush or the Playroom, it's reasonable to assume I'm no longer Mr. Kline's pet.

I never needed Auggie as my provider. If we're going the misogynistic route, I have a father and a brother, why do I need Auggie? I have two houses stocked with everything I would ever need. I didn't leave the safety of their love to be treated like a pet that wags her tail for any scrap you feed her. A few days ago, I would've run home to my family and used their shoulders to cry on, but not today. I made this mess, and I'm going to live in it. Besides, I can't go home because I'd look even more irresponsible and naïve than I already do. A few days ago, I wouldn't have realized I didn't need anyone to take care of me, because I have a job to pay for my own fucking food. I'm not eating out of Auggie's palm just because he gets off on it.

Augustus Kline either pegged me wrong, or I've changed dramatically in the past few days. Just because I work for Auggie, just because he's my boss at Revamped and the Spook House, doesn't mean he owns me. I allowed Auggie to emotionally own me, and when he disappointed me, he lost the privilege.

I don't trust Mr. Kline anymore.

When I entered the Playroom, and saw that beast of a man with the magnificent tattoo, he was a fantasy brought to life. I wanted to crawl to him, touch him, and worship him. But the man before me I didn't know. Fantasy. In reality, I just want *my* Auggie back. The man who kissed my boo-boos, who made me laugh when I wanted to cry. The man I wanted to make proud and feared I'd disappoint. The man who brightened every day. Not many can say they looked forward to going to work, but I could. I miss the man who made me want to be a better person.

It wasn't until it was too late that I realized Auggie was my *friend*, and you're not to know all the deep, dark secrets in the recesses of your friend's soul. Some things are best left a mystery. I wish Auggie would've stayed what he was for me, just Auggie.

This mistake can be salvaged. It wasn't the confusion of sex, or moving into Revamped, or being told that the Spook House was now my responsibility that ruined our friendship. It was Auggie himself who changed. He showed me one side, showed me the other, and then took both away, leaving a man I've never met before– a complete stranger who wants me to trust him and sleep in his bed.

I feel a billion years old tonight, and not as lost, and I owe that to Auggie. Only one thing will I allow from Auggie. Guidance. I've grown up enough to know that Auggie's advice is sound when it benefits him. So I won't discredit his advice. I'm smart enough to recognize that, even if Auggie thinks I'm not.

The lights in the Spook House flicker with a static hiss for a minute after I flip the switch. We stand in the two-story foyer that houses the staircase to the upper floors. I decide against going up the staircase just yet. I'm not sure it's structurally sound. I'll invite my father's crew over to test it out for me before I allow a Prynne, Webster, or a Mason to walk those stairs. The place is a disaster area. The elderly lady's furniture is still overflowing the house. Her distant relative had just wanted the cash and nothing else.

Idle hands are the Devil's playground. Time to make peace with my holy side and get to work.

I sigh dramatically as I turn in a wide arc. "Where to begin?" I mutter myself. "I guess we can't do the walls and floors if there's stuff on them. Dead old lady's shit first, I think."

"Motherfuck," Rae hisses. "We're just kids. You'd need a wrecking ball to fix this shithole."

"We need an exterminator, an architect, and a priest," Seth rumbles. "But since that ain't happening, we might as well wish for a million dollars instead."

"A priest?" I arch a brow at my nephew, and then scowl for picking up Auggie's annoying habit.

"Exorcism. We need to exorcise the spirit of the old lady who died in here." Seth proves he's a crafty little bastard with an angelic face by scaring the shit out of every female in the room. "Where did she die, exactly?"

"Let's just torch the place after the insurance kicks in." Violet offers her illegal two cents while standing next to a police officer dressed in uniform after arriving in a squad car.

"You inherited my balls somehow, girl," I say, thoroughly impressed with Violet's moxie.

"Officer of the Law." Devon points at himself. "I'm pretty laidback, but not *that* laidback. I might think Auggie is the biggest douche on the planet, but I don't want to meet his fists if I allow the girls to destroy the Spook House."

"I say we just get to fuckin' work," Weston says with an eager light glowing from his baby blues.

"I agree. I like you, kid," I praise Weston, reaching over and up to ruffle his blond hair. "Hell, you're all my new best friends." I only half-ass tease, which is pathetic. "Lesson learned: ya get what ya pay for. We'll begin by moving all the furniture from the front rooms to the back of the house. Let's separate it into three piles: one for a bonfire, a maybe pile, and a keep pile."

Without a single complaint, no bitching and moaning, no whining or feet dragging, the six of us get to work and prove the theory that manual labor is good for the soul.

An hour into moving ancient furniture, and we're all dragging ass. One benefit of hard work is that Officer Devon peeled his sweat-soaked t-shirt off, and I discovered that he isn't as lanky as he appears. His training has left him cut, and it's lighting my fire.

One downside to hard work is that boys like to emulate their hero. Weston and Seth are bare-chested, much to the disgust of every lady present. Sweaty, prepubescent boys are really gross and smelly. Some dumb-ass pheromone receptors in my libido find Devon's stink intoxicating. I'm the only one, though. Sweaty boys of any age think it's fun to shove their nasty armpits in girls' faces. Rae nearly puked when Devon did it to her. But when the sweaty cop did the same to me... I got achy. What the fuck is wrong with me? Seth's stink had me appropriately gagging my guts up, though.

I leave the bigger people to attack the furniture after I run out of things I can lift. I decide to start my renovation in the front corner of the house. It's the biggest room on the first floor. I think it would've been called the parlor when the house was built. The last owner– hoarder –used it for storage. Hideous pea-green carpeting is from wall-to-wall. I decide I don't need to be strong to tackle that monstrosity.

Home renovation is something I actually know how to do. Not a lot, but some. My father is a carpenter by trade, and Sam came to work for Dad after he married Clover. Seth and I spent a lot of summers and weekends playing little helpers. This won't be the first carpet I've torn up, but it will be the first I tackle without my father or Sam at my side. It's also the first time I've ever tried to pull carpet with a sob lodged in my throat as the happy, wistful memories bombard me.

As a big motherfucking, passive-aggressive hint, Auggie was nice enough to drop off a few buckets of tools by the front door. It's either that, or he came in here, took one look at the disaster the house was in, put his tools down, and gave the fuck up and left. I vote for gave up since Auggie is AWOL.

I grab a utility knife and crowbar, and attack the carpet with a vengeance. Pent-up frustration oozes out of my pores with every slash of the blade until I've cut the corner away. Old carpeting always has tack strips. You have to expose the strip to get your fingers under the carpet, and then pull like a bastard. Devon finds me when I'm in the center of the room, rolling the foul smelling carpet into a big tube.

"What's wrong?" Devon asks after he single-handedly tosses the roll onto his shoulder and dumps it in the foyer on top of the bonfire/garbage pile. I'm not sure how, but Devon reads my emotions like a Geiger counter measures radiation. Judging by the worried look he keeps tossing my way, he thinks my nuclear reactor is about to blow.

"I was told I wasn't a guest of the Playroom. My dubious invite was rescinded." I mumble hollowly as I attack the tack strips with the crowbar. One bright spot in my otherwise shitty existence, underneath that horrible carpeting is beautiful hardwood floors. *Will* be beautiful. Right now, they need to be sandblasted and refinished.

"What the actual fuck?" Devon asks in surprise.

"That's exactly what I said," I growl in frustration. "Auggie's there right now, most likely fucking someone. I don't know why he didn't just say the Playroom's his place to go to get away from everything, primarily me. We're together twenty-four-seven now. I'd understand. I'd like some privacy myself. Hell, Auggie owns Rush. He probably has actual work to do there. But instead of just telling me like it is, Auggie treated me like I'm a nagging wife." I get extra mean on a stubborn strip.

"Does it bother you that Auggie's playing right now?" Devon settles next to me on the floor and uses his strong fingers to pry up a tack strip. Showoff!

"Playing, such a nice euphemism for fucking some chick… or a dozen… at one time." I stop working and think about it for a second. Am I upset that Auggie is *playing*, or upset that he barred me from the Playroom?

"No, it doesn't bother me for some reason," is my immediate reply. I slump down on my haunches and get real. "Maybe a little. I'm slightly jealous because I'm not there and he is," I finally admit. "What bothers me the most is that I'm here after working twelve hours today, and he's off literally fucking around. My twins are taking up his slack. You and your siblings are doing his share. This shows me what my life would be like if I blinded myself to Auggie's faults– *this* would be my life," I whisper. "And by this, I mean being at Auggie's beck and call while he did whatever and whomever he wanted. Fun, huh?"

"Shit," Devon breathes out with feeling.

"Shit," I repeat as I wipe my forehead free of sweat with my forearm. "Devon, I'm scared that I may have made a mistake. I could pass the blame off by saying Auggie didn't ask me to move in with him. He just tricked my family into letting me go. I could say I didn't stand up at Sunday Dinner and tell my family Auggie was lying. They would've beat his ass if I had. All because I wanted my family to see how proud Auggie was of me. I could take the easy way out and run home to Mommy and Daddy with my tail between my legs and make Clover clean up my mess. But I need to require more of myself. I want to be proud of myself."

"I get that, Willow. I do. But is this the way to do it?"

I take a deep breath and decide to go for broke with Devon. "I know I'm not Auggie's girlfriend, okay? Any fool can see that. But what they don't see are his mixed signals, and they're killing me. Auggie says reality and play are separate. He made sure I knew I wasn't his girlfriend. Tonight, he told me I wasn't invited to the Playroom because he's my boss and the owner of Rush… so respect my authority!"

Devon starts snorting and covers his mouth with his palm. "I just heard Auggie imitating Cartman from South Park in my head. *Respect My Authoritah!* I even put Auggie in my uniform on the world's largest Big Wheel."

"You're such a geek," I mumble. But I start giggling, just as Devon expected. "Thanks," I sigh out. "I guess… after all that, after making all these unrealistic boundaries, why did Auggie have me move in with him? What's to gain from that?"

"Jesus, Willow. I have no idea. I truly don't, and I've known Auggie since I was born. He's an uncle to me– a very twisted uncle that I want to beat to death."

"I think you're gaining company. Won't be long from now, and a queue will form in that *kick Mr. Augustus Kline's ass* line."

"I'll let you be at the head of the line, but you'll have to stand behind Robin and Isis. I think they should be first, don't you?" Devon tries to sound light, teasing, but he's being serious.

"I just… why have me share and play in his bed if he believes play and reality are separate? Right now, I don't know what I am to Auggie. Am I his employee, roommate, or pet? All I know for positive is that I'm not Auggie's girlfriend. Everything else is a huge fucking contradiction."

"I'm sorry, Willow," Devon says in a strained voice. I don't dare look at him to figure out what that sharp tone meant. Maybe he thinks this is an inappropriate conversation between budding friends, and I keep going on and on. After all, Devon did just stress his relationship as a nephew to Auggie.

"I'm sorry. I shouldn't be unloading this shit on you. I'll figure it out somehow. Well, at least I know you're my friend because you want to be. I know two of those idiots out there are my blood. I know that I love this shithole and will try my damnedest to do whatever I can to fix it. That's good enough. I have friends, relatives, a roof over my head, and a job. Does it really matter what label I slap on Auggie when he doesn't want one?"

Deafening silence. Devon just stares at me like I'm a total stranger. Blank-faced. If crickets were in this house, they'd be chirping. "What?" I finally ask of the weird expression on Devon's face and his disturbing silence.

"I… I'm glad. Shit!" Devon curses underneath his breath, looking frustrated. "That came out wrong. Not glad. I thought Auggie and you were together-*together*. It creeped me out thinking that Auggie would want me to hang around you, that Auggie expected me to have sex with you, if you were together-*together*. I couldn't fathom wanting my girlfriend to hang out with some guy and fuck him. I didn't want to be the guy you used as practice," Devon grumbles. "Practice to satisfy that assfuck. It's beyond creepy."

"Yeah, creepy is one word for it," I draw out. "Disturbing is a better word. But, after all, we are in the Spook House right now.

Augustus Kline's new haunt," I ominously taunt, and then turn serious. "Devon, I don't expect you to do anything but be yourself. You're my friend, and I want to be around you. I feel comfortable with you– content. I would never treat another person as practice. Okay?"

"Okay," Devon murmurs quietly while looking at his hands. "We've got to go. I'm a bad Officer Devon tonight, and I've kept the kids out past curfew. When I drop the twins off at home, it'll look like I picked them up for a curfew violation. I should slap the cuffs on them for shits and giggles."

Devon and I share a good, long laugh at that, and it feels really good– almost innocent to be chatting and laughing about torturing my twins. "You'll give them some serious street cred, Officer Devon. Their reputations in junior high will be epic. Now I won't have to worry about my stoner-loner persona hurting the kids' reputation."

"Nah, they'll ruin it all on their own." Devon flows to his feet, and then reaches down to tug my ponytail. "I'll see you sometime tomorrow. I have nothing but time until I'm sworn in on the first of the year. Dad's just making me do a test run, driving around in the squad car while wearing the uniform. Showing me off is more like it. Fucked up."

"Your dad is an interesting character." I laugh, curious to know Malcolm Mason.

"Tell me about it." Devon acts put out, but the smile on his face screams of love and respect for Malcolm Mason. "So, anyway, I'll have time to put in some extra hours here during the day. Lighten your workload a little bit. See ya around."

The five of them disappear with a quick wave, leaving me all alone in the Spook House. I realize something, and I'm not sure if I want to cry or smile. Devon only touches me when Auggie is around. Devon really does only want to be my friend. Devon was only being touchy-feely because it was required for the part of boyfriend. When I gave Devon a way out, by telling him to just be himself, he gladly took it. I don't blame Devon, though. The ten-year-old boy-look isn't for everyone, especially when it's carrying some major baggage in the form of a six foot four, possessive, red-headed beast. It doesn't matter if Devon sees me as a woman or not. I'm just glad to have a true friend, one who isn't required by blood to like me.

Over the past few hours, I've fallen in love with the Spook House. The sense of proprietary connection I missed when I put the key into the lock appeared around room three of piss-stank carpeting removal. I know the Spook House isn't my house, but I can still take pride in it. Even if no one else on the planet knows I did it, I will know.

When someone says to Auggie, *"Wow, this floor looks fabulous,"* the Spook House and I will know who helped the floor reach its potential. Does it really matter if anyone else knows how it got there when I know? I'm not doing this for pats on the back. I'm doing it for the house.

"I looked all over for you." Auggie's quiet voice flowing from the dark startles the hell out of me, but I don't jump since I'm beyond relaxed from exhaustion. The tone in Auggie's voice speaks more than his words do. He's just as drained as I am. I hadn't heard him come in, and I have no idea how long he's been sitting on the floor, looming like an angry storm cloud.

So fixated on the task at hand, I didn't realize Auggie was before me. Auggie had spoken when I almost cut his boot with the utility knife when making a pass through the carpeting.

Attacking a stubborn tack strip, I studiously ignore the effect Auggie's presence has on me– the hammering of my heart, the sweat beading along my spine, the butterflies of worry and excitement in my belly.

"Well, you told me to go to the Spook House, and the Spook House I went. I guess the reasonable conclusion would be where you'd expect me to be– the Spook House." If my voice got any thicker with sarcasm, it would smoother me.

"I checked our bed first, hoping to find you resting. When I found Revamped empty, I then checked your parents' house. I was contemplating Clover's when I realized how stupid I was being, because you're a very stubborn girl when you're angry. Stubborn girls would still be at the Spook House. You're mad at me." Auggie doesn't *ask* if I'm mad at him, he states it as a fact.

"Probably the easiest thing to do was notice the car wasn't at Revamped, and then drive over here." Even to my own ears, I can't believe how the disrespectful words flow from my mouth. I'm being a bit of bitch. But this bitch is exhausted, so the filter from her brain to her mouth is nonexistent. "Auggie, I'm not mad at you. I'm disappointed in you." I brush my hair away from my face and sigh.

"What?" Auggie sounds surprised. His hand reaches out to grab my forearm, trying to stop me from prying up a tack strip.

The glare in my eye promising limb removal has his hand dropping within a heartbeat.

"Auggie." I slump to the floor and face him. "I'm at a loss. I don't know what's up or down with you anymore. Hot and cold. Hot and cold. My Auggie disappeared, and in his place is a stranger."

"I'm still here, Willow. You just didn't know me as well as you thought," Auggie replies immediately, proving he's not listening to me. In true Auggie fashion, he's not giving my words a real thought before saying what he wants to say.

"It wasn't a matter of knowing you, Auggie. It was a bait and switch. The man I knew for eighteen years isn't the man sitting before me right now." I point at the confused man who's confusing me. "I feel like I've aged ten years in the past couple of days. You've made it *very* clear that we aren't a couple, and I accept that. A week ago, I was an innocent seventeen-year-old high school graduate, living at home with my parents, and working for my brother's best friend.

"Willow–"

"Hold up." I raise my arm to stop whatever Auggie was going to say. "Let me finish, and actually *hear* me instead of thinking up your response. *Hear* me," I stress. "I don't expect you to change your life for me. I'm someone in your life, not a part of it. You don't need to tell me where you're going or why. I just don't want to be lied to."

"It wasn't a lie. I wasn't going to lie to you. I just wasn't going to tell you where I was going," Auggie rapidly spits his words, obviously still not listening to a word I'm saying, too self-involved with defending himself. Ironically, Auggie is acting how he accuses me of being: immature, bull-headed, acting as a child would while speaking to their parents. Caught. Confused. Lost.

"Lies by omission make me feel like an f'n idiot," I spit right back. "If I'm just an employee, then it shouldn't matter if you tell me where you're going or not. You shouldn't have to lie or lie by omission. If you don't want me to know what the hell you're up to, just say, '*Willow, it's none of your business.*' That's it!" I shout. "But know I have the right to say just that right back at your ass."

"No, you don't!" Auggie growls as he rises to his knees. He looms over me angrily, trying to intimidate me.

"Yeah, I think I do, Auggie. If you want me to act like an adult, then don't treat me like a child. I was stupid at first, I will admit. I thought you were my lover or my friend. But you've made it crystal clear that you're only my boss, someone who thinks he should own me lock, stock, and barrel. If you truly cared for my wellbeing, enough to want me to learn and grow and be happy, you wouldn't disrespect me by confusing me. You wouldn't make me feel like an idiot for not understanding the things I don't know because I haven't learned them yet. Don't make me feel worthless, Auggie. It goes against the mentor bullshit you're spewing."

"I…" Auggie gives me that *I don't know you* look and stammers. "Willow, I want you to be a kid. You need to go on dates, and goof off, and fuck boys your own age. I'm not for you– I'm a grown man. Even though your birth certificate says you're old enough to be a grown woman, you're not," he states as a fact, and I wince in pain.

"Harsh." I breathe deeply as my lungs fail to function from the cruel, verbal blow Auggie dealt me. "I know that I look younger than I am, and I act like it sometimes, too. But I'm not going to change my personality in hopes you'll like me, or love me, or respect me, or want me, or need me, or be proud of me. I'm Willow Aster Prynne, and that should be good enough."

"I never said it wasn't good enough," Auggie practically snarls. "I'm trying to help you reach your potential."

"Potential. I get that. But maybe, just maybe, you're doing a piss poor job of that by talking down to me and making me feel worse than I ever have."

"That's not what I'm trying to do, Willow. Even you are smart enough to realize frying your brain, pickling your liver, and sitting on your ass and doing absolutely nothing in your life is getting you nowhere. You might as well tattoo **LOSER** on your forehead. When I was your age, I was working my ass off. By the time I was twenty-three, I owned both Revamped and Rush. How can you live up to your potential if you're staring at clouds and drooling on yourself?"

"Nice," I mutter in appreciation as my face twists in pain. "You proved my point right there… way to elevate me, Auggie. You make me feel bad about who I am. Loser? Not a loser. Lost? Maybe. Not sure who I am yet? Most definitely. Maybe I'm just a late bloomer. Maybe you're the exception here, Auggie, knowing what you wanted to do and finding a way to get it. I have to know what I want before I can fight for it. But I'm not a loser, Auggie."

"Then don't act like one," Auggie snarls. Bending over me, doing a mighty fine job at intimidating me, I don't fall prey to his tactics.

"Instead of shouting loser, you could've told me I'm better than drugs and alcohol and being brain-dead. Then after you made me see the light, you should've showed me a different path. But nope, you just verbally assaulted my self-esteem, shredded my dignity and pride... nice."

"Am I wrong, Willow? Should I sit by and watch the girl I've known since her birth kill her brain cells, make herself stupid? I may be harsh, but perhaps nice doesn't cut it with you. You don't listen to your parents, your siblings, but you do listen to me. So harsh or not, it's working. You're finally growing the fuck up!" Auggie shouts at me, and then finally backs off. "I won't apologize for my methods because you are worth more than you've behaved."

"As much as I hate to admit it, I do trust your judgment. I think before I act now, when I used to do whatever felt good or bad. Now I think *what would Mr. Kline do?* and make the right choice. I haven't earned your trust yet. But I will, and not because I want you to like me. I'll do it because I want you to respect me. But maybe you need to realize, when it's all said and done, *I* might not like or respect *you* anymore."

I roll back to my hands and knees and grab the crowbar to get back to work. If this loser worked at Auggie's pace, the Spook House would still be in shambles when I'm an old woman and Auggie would be dead. Mr. Kline is blind to his own faults and hyperaware of mine. Maybe Mr. Kline should look in the mirror and see if he likes what he sees staring back.

"Willow, it's late. I wasn't being literal when I said you had to be here every waking moment. I thought you'd put in a few hours, and then go home to veg before bed. This is ridiculous— it's almost three a.m."

I gasp in shock at the time. I've been working at the Spook House for nine straight hours, a total of twenty-one hours of work today. While I might be exhausted, I feel enlivened. I realize that I've accomplished so much with my time, and it feels better than anything I've ever felt before. An orgasm has nothing on accomplishment, and Auggie doesn't give me either. This is all on me!

Secretly smiling to myself, I'm determined to work even harder. "I'll go back to the store when I'm finished with what I started." I jab the bar under a tack strip and pry with all my might. I wince when I get stuck with another tack. My hands look like I got into a fight with a hypodermic needle dispensary.

"Willow," Auggie tries again. If I hear my name one more time, I will either cry or hit him with this crowbar. One option sounds more satisfying than the other.

Auggie watches me work for a few minutes in silent contemplation. I really don't want to know what he's thinking. Right now, I just want to work in peace. I want him gone from my sight. He's too much stress for me to handle. When his mood passes, maybe then I can deal with him.

Out of the silence, Auggie's words make the pry bar slip from my hands. "Isis said Devon helped you this evening. I watched you two together at Revamped. It seems things are progressing nicely." He sounds pleased with himself yet worried.

I snort at Auggie's shitty matchmaking skills. I don't have the heart to tell Auggie that his quest to give Devon a girlfriend and me a boyfriend burned in flames. Auggie got his wish. I'm living the life of a teenage girl. The angst of having an idiotic crush on a boy nicknamed Date Rape, knowing he only wants in my pants, and my boss will murder him if he manages to do just that. A rekindled crush on a guy who only wants to be my friend, who happens to be Date Rape's big brother. And being in a hero-worship kind of love with the man who only sees me as Loser Girl.

"I'll be along in a bit," I say in dismissal. "It feels good to see my progress. It's not something I've experienced before. You'll see." I promise myself, not Auggie.

CHAPTER TWENTY-SIX

The dog has managed to slip her leash. Willow the wayward may be no more, but the adult Willow needed to get the hell out from beneath Augustus Kline's heavy, possessive thumb, even if for only a few hours. Unless it is a movie, or a burger at the No-Name Diner, or Sunday Dinner at my parents' house– all chaperoned by a Mason, Prynne, or Webster –Auggie hasn't let me leave Revamped or the Spook House.

As Rob so nicely said to Auggie earlier today, family trumps boss, and the boss wasn't too happy hearing the truth. When I left Revamped this evening, Auggie's warning was final and scary as all hell. "Don't fuck up, Willow."

In the past few weeks, I've accomplished more than I have in the previous eighteen years of my life. Revamped's website and auctions are gaining popularity and heavy sales, and the Spook House is starting to feel like a home instead of a disaster.

Thankfully Auggie has leveled out a bit, being more of himself: friendly, chatty, geeky, teasing, but still bossy as all get out. Auggie hasn't touched me in any way, not platonic affection nor lust-filled caresses. Creepy, he still makes me seek release every morning and night, and sometimes he asks to watch. While it confuses the hell out of me, it's taken a lot of pressure away from the situation. My Auggie is back for the most part, because he thinks Devon is my boyfriend in every definition of the word, and Auggie thinks wrong. Devon and I are just friends.

"When you said you gave Seth's ticket to Devon's best friend, I never expected this… I'd expected a man in blue, not a blue-balled asshat rapist-wanna-be." Essie murmurs in my ear with a snicker, followed by a disgruntled grunt.

The Revolutionary Road concert is tonight, and it was my ticket out of Dodge. If Uncle Will and Aunt Ana hadn't given me the tickets, Auggie would've put his heavy foot down. But family comes first, so I was allowed to leave the house like I'm a fourteen-year-old child, not a grown woman.

When I was given three tickets, I immediately gave my birthday gift to Essie and Seth. I was thrilled to have my best friends join me. Since then, Seth has abandoned me for a Boy Scout trip with Weston. I'm happy for the kid. He's acting his age for once. An indie band concert is not the place for the impressionable youth. I asked Devon to join Essie and me instead. Shockingly, Devon already had a ticket, but he asked if he could give my ticket to his best friend. I thought it was a fabulous idea, because if Devon liked someone enough to call them friend, then I was sure I'd like them too. Boy, was I ever wrong– or right, depending on how you look at it.

I join Essie in a long-suffering groan as Devon and Kieren approach the car. I'm worried about how this night is going to play out, and whether or not Auggie is going to be kicking ass and not bothering to take names when I get home.

I refuse to call Kieren Date Rape, because I know what truly went down that night– how I was screaming yes until after it got to the point of no return. I know I have the right to say no, and I did stop Kieren by a well-placed knee to the nads, but I don't blame him for being lost in lust. I shouldn't have allowed it to go as far as it had, so I'm partially to blame. I accept the responsibility for my actions.

"Hey," I mumble to the approaching Masons, and receive two very different results. Devon smiles warily at me, and Kieren flashes me that charming used-car-salesman/serial killer/heartbreaker grin. Shit! I like Devon's best friend a little too much.

I need my head examined.

Kieren's wicked smile is an indicator that he's going to be highly inappropriate. Essie high-tails it to the driver's seat to avoid whatever was going to come out of Kieren's naughty, filthy mouth. Not to be curtailed, Kieren slips into the passenger seat next to Essie and immediately starts to barrage her with smarmy flirting.

"Darling, I do believe you're hotter than you were when I was only thirteen. You've got nice tits now. Quite the cougar, aren't ya? Stealing little boys' innocence. Hester, you're a naughty, naughty girly…"

I wait for the greeting hug that never comes. In fact, Devon hasn't touched me in over three weeks, not since our third and last hug at Revamped. I miss our hugs. I miss the comfort and the connection. I keep the curse firmly lodged in my throat as I wordlessly walk around the car to sit behind Essie.

I silently brood about my man troubles as we ride to the concert. It's not like I have to keep up with the conversation. Essie is naturally chatty, as is Kieren. The car is filled with snarky chatter and sharp digs that have Devon snickering underneath his breath.

I'm officially a stupid-assed teenager with angst pouring out my pores, just as Auggie wanted me to be. I have a boyfriend who only wants to be my friend. A guy whose nickname is Date Rape intriguing the hell out of me as he flirts with my cousin. Lastly, I have a boss/roommate whose emotions run hot with lust and cold with loser.

Confused, that's what I am. Confused.

My eighteen-year-old self feels at least thirty as I work sixteen to eighteen hours per day– every day. I put in a good twelve hours for Revamped and another six or so at the Spook House. I work the store, run the website and auctions, and then I go to the Spook House and work until my body aches and I can barely keep my eyes open. In the early hours of the morning, I crawl back to Auggie's loft, shower, and then sleep like the dead, curled up on a sofa.

My work is two-fold. It feels so good to see a profound change in both Revamped and the Spook House. Both are changing before my eyes. I'm changing before my eyes– mentally and physically. My body is stronger from all the hard work at the Spook House, my mind is sharper from working on Revamped's future, and I feel at peace from accomplishing goals. The second reason I work so hard isn't because I want Auggie to respect me and pat my head for a job well done. I'm avoiding him. I'd love to say that I don't resent Auggie for barring me from the Playroom, for toying with my emotions, for making me want to better myself while making me feel worthless, but that would be a total bullshit lie. Being around Auggie is difficult. I want to be angry with him, but one look and I'm mush. I submit to his every demand, and I hate it.

Lastly, Clover's words about never being able to please a man like Auggie echo in my mind, and they sound eerily just like my own voice. It's not that I'm not enough for Auggie, or that no one is enough for Auggie. I'm beginning to wonder if Augustus Kline isn't the wayward one… lost.

Devon and Auggie have turned me into a confused girly girl. I constantly worry about how I look, what I say, and even the tone of my voice I use to speak. Hell, the less Devon touches me, the more I crave his touch. The firmer the friend lines are drawn, the more I want to cross them. The more Auggie coddles me because I ignore him, the angrier I get. When Auggie yells at me for acting like a brat, and for some reason the brat is coming out in full force, the more I want to fuck the hell out of him. The more I want to fuck Auggie, the more he treats me like a kid sister. I am an adult and have adult reactions, but when Auggie treats me like I'm a toddler, I throw a tantrum. It's his fault that my mind, body, and emotions won't line up. I'm a ball of frustrated confusion– I don't freakin' know what's up or down anymore.

"I'm sorry." Devon whispers in my ear, and I jump so high my head almost hits the car roof. He manages to get into my personal space and warm me with his body heat, but not even a brush of his clothing touches me. Devon's perfected this maneuver over the past few weeks.

"For what?" I murmur back. I push the friend lines by leaning into him and whispering so close to his cheek that my breath flutters back and warms my lips.

"For bringing Kieren. I thought you knew he was my best friend. I-I-I know Kieren treated you poorly," he stammers. "I promise Date Rape isn't the real Ren. I want you to like my brother, because if we're going to be a part of each other's lives, then you need to get along."

Devon leans away from me, like he can't stand to be near me, and the movement lashes out to sting my ego. So much for trying to flirt. I should've known better.

"I trust you. If you want Kieren to join us, then I'll treat him like I treat everyone else." Devon strings tight when I say that, and I can't help but laugh. "Devon," I chuckle. "I can't treat Kieren like a little prince. I won't be mean to him, but if you think I can contain my snark, ya got another think coming."

"Willow." Devon shakes his head and laughs. "I'll take that, I guess. It was more than I expected. You have a huge apology coming from Ren, and I want you to know it won't be bullshit. He really means it."

A snort erupts, and I roll my eyes. My bullshit detector is screaming at Devon. He and I have spent countless hours together every day for the past few weeks. I can read Devon, and he can read me. We both say stupid shit that offends the other on a daily basis, and we make no apologies for it. That's what friends do. If

I could only turn off my throbbing girly parts, then we'd be great...

With tears streaming down my cheeks, lyrics spilling from my lips, my feet leaving the ground in a rhythm with the beat, only to land again, I allow the music of Revolutionary Road to flow through me.

Revolutionary Road is an indie rock band whose roots are in New England. Their following isn't huge, but all their fans are loyal for life. Most follow them from venue to venue within a three-state radius. As Revolutionary Road tours around the country, they pick up new fans who stick to their area of the country. I feel proud of our home boys, being a witness to their dream realized.

This is my fifth concert. All five dedicated to Revolutionary Road and Sam. Sam was one of those fanatics who traveled around the area. He took me to my first concert here at Calico when I was twelve years old. Sam took me to my second concert that summer at the Fair Grounds, and my third the next summer when I was thirteen. Sam's final concert was mine as well. We stood here at Calico, just Sam and me and Revolutionary Road. Sam was gone less than two months later, and I never stepped foot onto Calico's property or attended another concert until tonight.

To this day, I get overly emotional when I hear one of RR's songs. I see Sam singing softly along with the band, and the contented smile on his face as his mouth twisted the lyrics. I miss those huge brown eyes that looked at me with affection, as if I could do no wrong. I miss the naughty smirk that would accentuate his chipmunk cheeks. I can still hear the smoky quality of Sam's voice as he sang to me. It's a bitter-sweet feeling. I have no doubt this torture was Uncle Will and Aunt Ana's way of trying to get me to let go of the mourning and move on— to release the bitter and embrace the sweet with my friends at my side. Not to overwrite Sam's memory, but to replace the sadness with remembered happiness.

Calico's venue isn't a big, fancy stadium in the middle of the city. Hell, it isn't even a fairground. We're in the middle of a field in the throes of a Massachusetts' winter. Believe it or not, Calico is a big venue that houses small, unknown up-and-comers and the huge mega-bands. Guitar riffs screech from the wooden stage–

the stage is so rickety, I'm waiting for it to erupt into a mass of rubble, but that's what's fantastic about Calico. Authenticity.

Less than a thousand hyped-up fans jump to the beat, and the frozen ground rumbles beneath our feet. Acres of people sing and dance to keep warm, but the majority use what I'm craving to keep their warmth and to dampen their inhibitions.

Not understanding I'm lost in the past with Sam in my memories, Devon keeps looking at me like I'm jonesing for some smoke, or thirsting for some booze. "Are you doing alright?" Devon has to press his lips to my ear to be heard over the band and its squealing fans. I shiver in delight because his skin is touching mine. Goosebumps break out and prickle my nerves, but I don't feel cold. Hell no, my body flashes hotter than the sun.

Clouds part and angels descend to the field where a group of rowdy music-whores worship their rock god, and it's all because Devon pulls my side against his chest and leaves his hot, moist lips where they rest against my ear. I bite my lip to contain the moan that's bubbling to the surface.

"I am now," slips out in a huskily purr before I can stop it. Devon's resulting chuckle vibrates my ribs. "I... mean..." I stammer. "Jesus, the smell is intoxicating. I really hate Auggie right now. *Willow, you're a teenager– act like it, but don't drink or smoke.* Fucking hypocrite! Teenagers drink and smoke. Auggie doesn't want me to act like an adult, because he'd have to treat me like one. But he doesn't want me to act my age, because that'd mean I'd be sucking on a bowl right now like a pot-headed fiend after harvest."

"You do realize my name is Officer Mason, right?" Devon snickers. "You just admitted to not one but two illegal activities: Underage drinking and the use of illegal substances."

"Oh, the smell," I murmur dreamily as I release a full-bodied shiver. My fingers clutch Devon's coat and twist, stopping myself from reaching out for the joint the guy next to us is passing around.

"Fuck," Devon breathes against my ear, shuddering.

"It was a mistake coming to a packed concert of drunkards and druggies. My people are calling me home, and I have to deny myself. All I'd have to do is ask, and it would be placed in my hand. Concert-goers are very generous with their vices. My sobriety is at risk just by being here. I hate beer, and even the smell of stale, cheap beer is making my mouth water. What I wouldn't do for half a dozen shots and three or four hits of Mary Prynne's finest."

"I don't know which is scarier, Augustus Kline or Malcolm Mason. But I'm not willing to find out," Devon says as his eyes latch onto the joint and follows it like a dog watching a stick in his master's hand. "At least Auggie doesn't randomly drug and alcohol test you like my dad does. The Chief can't have his underage cop son drinking and smoking. But… oh, my God! It smells so fucking fantastic," moans deep from Devon's lips and sends a quiver down my spine.

"We'll be good together," I promise. I firmly press my nose into the side of Devon's neck and inhale the vanilla musky scent. I nearly purr when it hits my system. Fuck drugs, a hit off Devon's neck is pure ecstasy. I've missed him touching me so much that my knees go weak.

"Okay, we'll call each other for support. But you do realize that if one of us falls off the wagon, we'll undoubtedly take the other with us."

"And it will be heaven until one of those bastards punishes us into sobriety. I think it might be worth it," I murmur dreamily.

"Ugh!" rushes out my chest when a solid body collides with mine. Large hands grip my hips and tilt my ass. I shouldn't be able to recognize the bulge grinding into my ass, but I do. I've only been in contact with two *packages* in my lifetime, and both are very memorable. I roll my eyes as Kieren molests me.

"Is our tiny brat cold? My brother isn't big enough to warm you up, darling," Kieren purrs into my ear while systematically dry-humping my ass. "We'll just sandwich ya until you're nice and toasty. Lean against me and we'll dance."

"Dance? Dance to the music, or your crotch? Toasty and warm, or dry-humped, Stud?" I drawl out breathlessly, and even to my ears I realize I'm flirting. "I'm not cold now."

"Get your dick off my girlfriend, Ren! Don't make me regret inviting you," Devon warns, but he starts chuckling at whatever expression is on my face or Kieren's, I'm not sure which.

Kieren curls around me from behind while pressing me against Devon's chest. I can't see either one of their faces. I can feel Devon's heart accelerate from where my palm is pressed against his chest and how fast Kieren is breathing by his chest against my back. I'm effectively pinned, and as strange as it sounds, I feel safe. I know Kieren is just teasing me. I'm not worried. It just feels nice to act stupid for a few minutes after being uber responsible for weeks.

"Girlfriend, Dev?" Kieren sounds disbelieving. "Interesting. I'm just showing Willow how a real man does it." Kieren chuckles near my ear as he rhythmically pumps his bulge against my backside.

"Fuckface, I believe Auggie already beat you to it. I was there, remember? You pussied out and ran off with Daddy and Auntie Isis." Devon tries to sound angry, but laughter keeps bubbling up.

I just stand there, pressed between them, and take it. I learned on the night of my birthday to just let Kieren do as he pleases. If you complain, you'll get something far worse than you're currently enduring, not that I'm complaining right now. The boys press me harder between their hard bodies and slap-fight around me, hitting each other on the top of the head and shoulders. The entire time, they keep spouting out hilarious insults and jabs, and actually praise the other when they spew a good one.

Laughing, I try to ignore the fact that as the boys struggle, I'm being moved around and Kieren's hard bulge has slipped farther south and it's pressing perfectly where it needs to be for optimum satisfaction. I'm hyperaware, but I doubt Kieren is since he's being distracted by insults and flailing hands. I tell my suddenly happy cunny to stop quivering with excitement. *Naughty, puss, that's creepy Kieren rubbing on you. Stop purring, dammit!*

"Fuckface? I said *real* man, Dev. Auggie's not the right man for the job, bro. He just popped and ran. Not cool," Kieren hisses, and the ferocity in those few words surprises me. Kieren sounds beyond angry with Auggie.

"Oh, and you're the right one?" Devon taunts. He picks me up off the ground and wraps an arm under my ass to keep Kieren off me. Which is a pity, because I was liking it way, *way* too much. "Stop grinding on Willow!"

"Either of us is the right man, but never Auggie," Kieren breathlessly pants out near my ear. "I'll flip you for Willow. I'd get a coin out, but then I'd have to stop touching her."

"Dude! I'm not a prize you flip a coin on. I don't care how hot you are, you're a fucking dick!" I snarl.

"Hot, am I?" Kieren purrs in a seductive voice filled with lust, and my face flames to cosmic levels. "I don't hear you complaining about my dick, sweetheart. You're liking it so much,

I can feel your cunny quivering with want." Kieren presses his hips to my ass as if we're the only two people on the planet, forgetting that Devon's arm is between our bodies, an arm that magically disappears in a heartbeat.

"Ren, you're a perverted motherfucker! Your dick touched my arm." Devon makes gagging sounds and dry-heaves. "Gross– you're hard!"

"Made ya move, didn't it?" Kieren sings arrogantly, followed by a series of wicked snickers. Kieren's hands drag me back up his body until we're perfectly aligned again. I try to put a damper on my mind and body. But for some inexplicable reason, I'm turned on by Kieren tonight. I don't know if it's him, or the fact that Auggie and Devon have been stringing me along for a few weeks straight. But knowing that I'm arousing Kieren is arousing me. My little boy body does nothing for most guys, but Kieren seems to genuinely crave it.

Shuddering, I have to put a stop to this madness before I come from Kieren Mason dry-humping me. "Dude," I shout at Devon. "You're just gonna let your brother molest the hell out of me while you watch?" I try to sound outraged, but my ragged breath catches in my throat.

"Willow," Kieren sings in my ear. "I'm not doing anything to ya that you're not enjoying. You're positively glowing with pleasure." Leaning in closer, lips tickling my ear, Kieren groans. "I wasn't teasing– I can feel your pussy getting ready to come for me."

"Keep telling yourself that, Stud." I protest as a wicked shudder rolls down my spine, but I don't try to get away or call Kieren off.

Devon's fingers seek my chin and tilt my face until he can gaze directly into my eyes. We hold each other's gaze for a few suspended moments in time. He flashes me a thrilled smile and snaps his fingers.

"Ren, set her down," Devon commands, and Kieren immediately complies. "You've got your jollies off enough for the night."

I stand on wobbly legs and look between the brothers– they share a secret smile I can't decipher. "I think I could actually... ya know..." Kieren whispers bashfully, but it carries to our ears. Kieren looks to the ground, and then his eyes snap back up to meet his brother's.

"Seriously? Are you sure, or are you just fucking with me to get my sympathy? Willow's my girlfriend, man."

"I'm not stupid, Dev. I know this is some fake boyfriend/girlfriend horseshit because Auggie demanded it," Kieren mumbles. "You seemed to forget a conversation we had years ago. The *Bro Code* seems lost on your ears, my brother."

I find it fascinating as the brothers silently communicate like I can with all of my family members. With just a look, you hear an entire conversation. There is a real bond, and even I can see betrayal screaming from Kieren's eyes, betrayal Devon dealt him, but it seems to be flowing both ways.

"Ren, Willow's a person, not a fucking object," Devon responds belligerently. "I won't treat her like a damn pet like that bastard does. If Willow wants someone, she has the right to choose for herself."

"I didn't mean it like that, and you know it, asshole!" Kieren growls, then stomps away.

"What the fuck was that all about?" I demand of the strange exchange they just had.

"You'll have to ask Ren. It's not just my story to tell." Devon thoughtfully cocks his head to the side, and a moment later he continues. "Well, if we ever get the balls to have that conversation, it would be best if it's the three of us. I don't want to subject you to the grisly details twice."

Devon tosses me a sad smile, and then stalks off after his brother. The crowd swallows around me. I can just make out Kieren's blond head above the crowd as it cracks backward from a well-executed punch. The dark messy curls that block my view inform me it's brother against brother for reasons unknown to me.

Confused.

I'm more confused than I was twenty minutes ago, which I thought was highly improbable until now. I breathe deeply and try to see the stage. The mass of writhing bodies blocks my view of the band, but the sound permeates my soul.

It's astonishing how I'm experiencing my birthday gift completely alone. A private smile tilts my lips. A month ago, I would've thrown a fit for Essie leaving me alone, then demanded Devon explain what the hell was going on. But I realize I'm not the center of anyone's universe. Their business is none of my business. I'm fine with being alone. I like me.

I just hope I don't fall victim to the crowd. Being alone is one thing, while being irresponsible at a concert is another. I don't want to put myself into a situation I can't get myself out of, so I shuffle to the left near a group of trashy-dancing girls who will buddy-up with me. I blend into the throng, and fall into the music. Friends or not, I'm here for Revolutionary Road and to reconnect with the memory of my brother-in-law, and for no other reason.

An hour into singing like a lunatic and jumping up and down with my new buddies, I notice Essie is right next to me. I turn to her and flash a smile. I can tell she's been with me for a while, but let me join the revelers in musical celebration. I grab Essie's hands and hop around until she giggles.

Sweaty in the winter air and parched from excessive screaming, I'd kill for a beer. But instead, I grab a bottle of water from Essie and drain it. That wicked bitch is nursing a wine cooler. I lick my lips and pretend my tasteless liquid is peachy goodness with a fizzy kick to the ass. The fact that I'd kiss Essie's lips to have a taste, screams that maybe I am an alcoholic-in-training. Christ!

I look down from Essie's shining eyes as she guiltily dumps her wine cooler, christening the ground with alcohol. Then she grabs her own bottle of flavorless wet and takes a swig. I contemplate lying down on my belly and lapping the divine liquid off the frozen earth. As I mouth *sorry* to Essie for being such a fucking buzz-kill, movement over her shoulder catches my eye. In an instant, all the blood drains from my face.

Essie turns slowly to see what caught my attention. I'm rendered speechless, but someone else isn't so lucky. "Fuck," is hissed near my ear. For the first time, I notice Kieren has been next to me for quite a while, too.

The final nail in the friend coffin is firmly tacked into place. A leggy blonde, with voluptuous curves and huge ruby-red lips, teases a fingernail up Devon's chest, and in return he gives her a roguish grin. When those perfect lips descend on his, I look away.

I swallow what little pride and self-esteem I have left and face the stage. I may not have mile-long legs and jouncing tits, but I do have self-respect. I won't throw myself at someone who doesn't want me, and I won't fall into the nearest pair of waiting arms to prove my worth. The new and improved Willow is smarter than that. I grab Essie's hand and avoid her crushed expression. I weave and sing to the haunting balled that Jackson Stone, the lead singer of Revolutionary Road, is belting out…

Revolutionary Road is finished for the night, but a couple of local bands are banging out a few tunes to soothe the savage beast. By *savage beast*, I mean the traffic jam in the parking lot. Calico is a great venue until it's time to leave. Add another two hours to your night trying to get out of the parking lot. Either you leave before the final act to beat the rush, or you linger after to avoid road rage.

"You!" is screamed at me as I'm sucking down a cigarette like it's the last breath of oxygen on the planet. Devon took Essie to the *port-a-john* at her request. No doubt Essie wanted to grill Devon on the bitch who's now pointing her talon in my face.

"Tina." My smoking partner groans.

I ignore the pair of them. I'm just thrilled to feel the sensation of nicotine infusing my bloodstream. Auggie can fuck off if he has an issue with cigarettes– I can legally buy them now. Next thing you know, the demanding fuck will cut my caffeine intake. I'll throw down if Auggie tries to take my *Amp* away.

At a concert filled with every drug known to mankind, Auggie's lucky I'm lucid. Ordinarily I use work to distract me from my addictions. Can't work. Can't drink. Can't get high. Can't fuck. I'm gonna smoke a cigarette, and apparently get my ass kicked by this *Tina* chick, if her glare is any indication.

"If Dev hadn't pointed this bitch out, I would've sworn she was Weston." Tina– Devon's lipsucker –insults me in the lowest form possible. After years of being called Seth, I'm about to fucking snap. One last drag, and my smoke is down to its filter. I drop it to the ground and grind my heel on it, pretending it's Tina's face under my heel.

"Ahhh…" I draw out menacingly. "I wasn't aware big tits were a prerequisite to be Devon's friend. I guess that makes you his BFF, sweetling."

A taunting smirk flirts with my lips. I'm so ready to brawl after all the shit I've dealt with since I turned eighteen. Fighting Auggie and weed cravings has had me more than on edge. I could use a release, and I'm okay with the violent kind. After all, this is what Violet and I have been doing since we were little brats. If one of us needed to feel better, we beat the ever-loving shit out of each other.

An evil smirk pulls my lips as I put my hands out and curl my fingertips in a rolling motion. "Bring it, bitch!"

Tina sputters in shock while Kieren throws his head back and barks a laugh to the sky. I think Kieren just moved up my friend list– it's a very short list, but he's no longer on the bottom.

"Your chest's so flat, do you even have nipples?" Tina snarls, confusing my *Bring it, bitch!* as an invitation to verbally spar, when I meant it in the physical sense.

I laugh, trying to say, "Is that the best you can do?" while Kieren murmurs, "I can attest to the fact that Willow's nipples are very, *very* nice."

"Devon will never want you. You'll always be Devon's little friend because he has a hero-complex. You'll never satisfy Dev like a real woman would. Fucking you would be like screwing their kid brother."

Ouch... Tina's assessment is too close to reality– the reality of my life. It can be applied to any male I interact with.

"Harsh, but oh-so true," I muse to myself. "Tina, I won't disagree with you. Yeah, I'm shaped like a kid. So what? I can't do anything about it. It doesn't make me a bad person. I'd rather live my life on my merits, not on how well my legs spread. Having a stretched out pussy isn't a badge of honor, and I bet yours is soggy and sloppy."

"I can attest to that, too." Kieren snickers. "Tina's cunt is like fucking a gallon jar of mayonnaise."

"Ewww..." I hiss. "Gross. I'm never eating mayo again, fuckwad. Kieren, this is a great reminder of why I'll never sleep with you. You really need to take greater care of where you stick your dick." Kieren's face whips back as if I hit him. So I say softly to remove the sting, "Keep it healthy, ya know?"

"I'm always safe," Kieren whispers back, looking kind of faint. Ill. "No one has ever touched *it* without a condom, even hands and mouths."

"Sorry," I whisper underneath my breath right back to him, feeling like shit. "I'm in no position to judge."

"Don't bother screwing Devon if you're not into my sloppy seconds," Tina brags condescendingly, and this time my head whips back like I've been struck. "Ren, don't flatter yourself. You were the worst lay I've ever had. You should stick to your innocent virgins. They'd never question your faking it," she bites out.

"Oh, I only faked it with you, bitch. Willow's right. Your pussy's so sloppy loose, I couldn't feel a thing, like screwing a filthy sluice pipe with a *Roto-Rooter*." Kieren makes a nasty gesture with his hands while shuddering in revulsion.

"It wasn't my size. It was yours." Tina verbally strikes in a way that disables every man.

"Oh, darlin', there's nothing wrong with my cock." Kieren hitches up his pant leg and tightly grabs his bulge.

"I can attest to that." I chuckle, and Kieren flashes me a surprised look, like he can't believe I want to be his partner in crime. That potent look infuses me with warmth, causing a shit-eating grin to spread my lips.

"Like you'd know the difference, little boy," Tina taunts me. "Who in their right mind would ever fuck you?" She arches a perfect eyebrow, looking just like Auggie for a split second, and stares down at me condescendingly.

Since I came to Kieren's defense, he comes to mine. "Oh, Willow's had a big one, alright." Kieren barks a laugh. "Anyway, Tina, Willow has your thong in a twist for a reason. I'm guessing it's a brooding reason who wears a uniform and can be a total dick. Quit the shit. You're scared Devon wants Willow for something other than a quick *fuck*, and we all know you'll never be anything other than a quick *fuck*." Kieren's lips pop every time he says the word fuck. "I also know what Devon really wants from you," Kieren say ominously, his voice twisted with anger. "And I guarantee it ain't that tainted cunt you call a pussy."

Before I can reason out what Kieren's hinting at– "Ah!" I yelp when my face and chest are drenched with stale beer. The skank threw her drink on me for Kieren's insult… *What the fuck, bitch?*

"Oh! You're lucky that didn't get into my mouth, skank. I won't lose my sobriety because some plastic whore tosses beer on me. If I fall off the wagon, it's gonna be for the good shit." I growl and flick my hand to get the metallic smelling shit off my fingers. "I'm going all out and springing for top shelf!"

Tina stares at me in shock. Evidently that wasn't the reaction she was expecting. "Fuck it! Being an adult is overrated, anyway!" I give Tina a half-second warning.

I fly at Tina like I've been doing with Violet since she could talk. I may be in the feather-weight class, but I'm a scrapper. I ride Tina's body to the ground while my fingers twist in her perfectly bleached hair. I wrap the tendrils around my finger and yank with all my strength. She screams bloody-murder like a little bitch, and erratically flings her hands around. Must be Tina was an only child. Anyone who has siblings knows how to throw down.

Just as I'm about to bash Tina's skull into the frozen ground, ball-catching hands pull me away. My fingers take the skank's fake hair with me, too. I stare down at the pieces of blonde weave wrapped around my fingertips in sick satisfaction with a shit-eating grin on my face.

"Jesus, Spanky. Where'd you learn to fight like that?" Kieren mumbles in wonder as he sets me on my feet.

"I'd avoid Violent Violet at all costs. Her mother and I taught her all we know. I can take down Auggie if I have a mind to," I brag proudly. "Sam wanted his girls safe."

Slightly out of breath, I feel exhilarated. Like a character in a black and white film, I'm in need of an after-sex cigarette– after violence, in my case. My fingers seek out Kieren's front pocket. He grunts when my hand accidentally brushes his erection– the boy must always be primed for sex. I chuckle as I pull the pack of smokes free from Kieren's too-tight jeans.

"Oh, that's smooth." I purr as I take the first drag to light my cherry. Shuddering in delight, I toss the pack and lighter back to Kieren, and he deftly catches them. Then I shock the shit out of myself. My hand moves on its own accord to palm Kieren's bulge. I tighten my fingers until he groans. "Bitch, don't ever talk about this cock again." My gravelly voice sounds possessive, slightly feral, and I don't know where the territorialism is coming from.

Owning the bulge in my hand, I squeeze harder until Kieren moans, "Fuck, please… more." He rocks into my hand, offering me anything I'm willing to take.

"Tina, as far as Devon and you… if Devon's that fucking stupid, I wouldn't want him to touch me. Hell, just looking at you makes me want to shower– twice –and take a course of antibiotics."

I take another strong draw off my cigarette and finally look to the eyes I feel boring into my skull. Essie and Devon stand frozen and speechless. I have no idea how long they've been watching, but it was long enough to see the majority of the action. I give Kieren's throbbing bulge another squeeze, then release him. Whimpering, Kieren tries to press himself against my back, but I step out of reach.

I walk over to the skank lying prone on the frozen ground. "Thanks for the drink," I say sarcastically. I turn on my heel and stalk back to the car. I decide right then and there that no man is ever worth fighting over. It's up to them to step in and end it. If Tina is Devon's chick, he should control her better than that. Defend or reprimand her– do something, anything but stand there and watch like a fucking prince while his brother tears the fighting bitches apart.

I'm Devon's friend, not his ego-fucking-booster. I won't fight over a man like a lion over a carcass. Even Willow Prynne has more class than that. But this fight wasn't about Devon for me. I was defending my honor, and as an added bonus, I was defending Kieren's as well.

"Can't a girl just go to a concert with her friends and celebrate the memory of her dead brother-in-law without getting fucked over?" Tears burn my eyes as I say this, but they never fall.

I look at Devon over the top of the car as I take another drag off my smoke. Frozen, he allows me to hold his gaze for the two minutes it takes me to finish my cigarette. He and I have our own silent conversation. It's one-sided, with me being the one who pours my emotions into my expression, informing Devon that I know my worth, and it's a helluva lot more than I've been getting from everyone. It's not truly a one-sided silent conversation. I just refuse to analyze Devon's expression, because I could give a shit less about anything he has to say at the moment.

CHAPTER TWENTY-SEVEN

I silently swear to myself as I try to find my way through the loft to the shower. I've got to get this beer-stank shirt off my body. The smell is making me sick to my stomach. Auggie usually leaves a light on for me to find my way across the space to the bathroom at night. But tonight it's pitch-black in the loft. So dark I worry I'll smack my leg into whatever furniture decides to jump in my way.

The slide of sheets and the click as the lamp glows to life are my only warnings. "I knew you wouldn't behave. It was a test, and you failed. Just as I knew you would." Auggie accuses from his position in the middle of his bed. His irate, cold and calculated voice slaps me in the face, and it gets my already rankled hackles up.

I immediately go on the defensive. "*Niiiiice...*" I draw out, seething. "A test where I was predestined to fail. I'm glad to see your faith in me isn't shaken, since I knew you'd automatically think the worst of me," I counter angrily. "Auggie, you're not my fucking dad, so quit fucking parenting me."

"What the hell, Willow? What's your problem?" Auggie abruptly lunges off the bed to stand in front of me. He leans his six and a half feet over me, trying to intimidate me into compliance.

"You want me to be an adult and make my own choices, yet you treat me like a toddler. At the same time, you want me to act my age." I throw my hands up in defeat. "Well, which is it, Auggie? Am I a kid who needs parented, or am I an adult who is supposed to make their own mistakes? You can't have both!" I shout into his downturned face.

Auggie stares speechlessly at me, totally thrown by my baffling behavior. I *never* call Auggie out on his shit. I never question him. I've never in my entire life yelled in Augustus Kline's face.

Auggie's eyes track my face, trying to figure out where this anger is coming from, trying to decipher my emotions. I was once called transparent by both Auggie and Clover, but not for a long while. My emotions don't cross my face like a ticker tape anymore.

I'm angry– furious. Just like Auggie, I wish I knew where it was coming from. I wish Auggie would tell me where this rage came from so I could deal with it, so he could fix it.

Ever so calmly, Auggie speaks to me. "Willow, I have to treat you both ways, because even though you're an adult, you're still very young and naïve. I want you to make *small* mistakes, while I stop you from making catastrophic mistakes that will ruin your future. You're addicted to alcohol and marijuana, and from what I smell on your clothing and hair, cigarettes too! Do you want me to stand by, so that in the future we have to toss your ass in rehab? Or when you're twenty and arrested for a DUI, do I bail your ass out of jail? Or when you're forty and coughing up a lung, do you want me to cry by your hospital bedside? Make smart choices, and I'll stop parenting you."

"I understand," I say just as calmly as Auggie was speaking to me. I walk away from him toward the bathroom area, effectively ending the interrogation.

Auggie's hand latches out to clasp my wrist, pulling me to stop. "No, you don't," Auggie murmurs. "I know you don't get it, or else you wouldn't have come home as I expected. Willow, I thought you were trying to avoid being a loser, but I guess I was wrong. Dumb choices everywhere– that's our Willow," Auggie sings sarcastically

"Dumb, *loser* Willow was under the impression she was making smarter choices, Auggie. I walk in here, wanting to shower after having a shitty night, and instead of asking me how my night was, you accuse me of breaking your rules."

"I wasn't accusing you of anything, Willow. I know for a fact you broke them." Auggie gets into my face and growls the words. "There is a distinction."

"Fuck your rules, Auggie," I snarl. "You think I don't get it when I'm the motherfucker dealing with it? I understand the no drinking, and if I didn't agree with it, I wouldn't have stopped. I know I could become an alcoholic. Hell, I think I'm already one. You think I don't feel the cravings? That gnawing ache, I fucking deal with it every waking moment of every day. It tickles my mind like an itch I can't scratch. I know this is mild. If I drink, it will only get stronger. I'll get more and more and more addicted, and when I try to stop, it will be like living in hell. So I don't need your judgmental, borderline abusive shit– I need some cocksucking support!" I scream in Auggie's face, trying to get him to back the fuck up out of my space.

"Support this, Willow? How was your night?" Auggie asks in a tone laced heavily with sarcasm, all the while tugging on my beer-saturated sweatshirt. I can see the silent judgment screaming out from his green, scrutinizing eyes.

"Fuck you, Auggie!" I scream into his face, vein throbbing in my forehead from the pressure. "I don't need a dad. I need a friend. I had a man I wanted to call dad and he died on me– that position will *never* be refilled!"

"Fuck..." Auggie sighs heavily as he drags his fingers through is auburn curls. "Willow–"

"I don't want your goddamned pity, Auggie!" I scream like I've lost my mind, mouth wide open, pouring vitriol and pain with my words. "Go the fuck to bed– I'm showering." I yank the saturated sweatshirt from my body and toss it at him. It hits Auggie's chest with a plop.

"I swear to God, Willow, I'm going to tan your ass if you keep this shit up. Calm your ass down and be reasonable."

"Reasonable? You want reasonable? How about you standing in front of me, tempting me with a punishment that would mean you'd actually have to touch me... that you'd play with me. I'm not invited to the Playroom, remember, *Auggie*? Reality and the Playroom aren't at the same time, either. Which means you can't punish me for reality, *Auggie*." I twist his name until it sounds a lot like *fuck you*. "Good luck with that shit, *Auggie*."

"Quit being a bratty fucking bitch, Willow, and grow the hell up. I can't take your fucking shit anymore!" Auggie bellows right back at me, finally losing his calm.

Like a switch being thrown, Auggie's anger deflates mine– my body loses its fight. I hang my head in shame. Clover's words rattle around my mind, but they're spoken in my voice. *No matter how hard you try, Willow, it will never be good enough for a man like Auggie. He'll want to control you, consume you, until you no longer exist.*

Feeling numb with shock, I just let the words spill without using the filter from my brain. "Thanks. I'm glad the truth's finally out in the open. Thanks for calling me a bratty fucking bitch."

Standing before Auggie, I strip down until I'm completely naked. Satisfaction slams into me as Auggie's eyes track across every inch of my exposed flesh. I strut over to the shower, feeling Auggie's penetrating gaze the entire way. Just as I enter the enclosure, I turn and look over my shoulder. Auggie stares at me with a gobsmacked expression on his face.

I hit Auggie square in the nuts. "I thought you'd like to know–" I give a heavy pause to make sure Auggie's truly listening. "Some skanky, crazy chick flung her beer in my face because Kieren insulted her, and then I kicked her ass for insulting both Kieren and me. No need to be concerned. I can take care of myself…"

I take my sweet-ass time showering while Auggie paces the loft like a caged tiger. When the hot water runs out, along with all of my fury, I give up and towel off.

I walk over to my bed– the sofa –and curl up beneath my fuzzy comforter. Wishing for the first time I was a stuffed animal lover, because I sure could use one to hug.

After Auggie rescinded my dubious invite to the Playroom, I refused to sleep with him. I was disappointed to see the relief in Auggie's eyes when I settled down to sleep on the sofa that night and every night thereafter– relief that he didn't have to tell me to get the hell out of his bed.

"We need to talk," Auggie says roughly as he drops to the floor near my feet. He sits on his heels, and then turns to face me.

It takes everything in me not to reply with *you think?* "You start. I think I can pretend to be an adult for a few minutes," I utter so sarcastically I manage to impress myself. "I don't know if I can, but I'll give it a try."

A long-suffering sigh expels from Auggie's lungs in a rush. "I'm so sorry, Willow. So fucking sorry."

"You say that so much, those words hold no meaning any longer."

As usual, Auggie plows over me. "I didn't mean to say those things to you. I don't know why, but our attitudes have been feeding off each other. At first, I thought it was just frustration– working the kinks out of finally having structure and boundaries. But now I realize you hold deep-seated anger and resentment, and I don't know how to help it."

"I don't need your help. Guidance? Yes. I don't know where I stand with you anymore, but I do know I don't need another father. I love my father, but he is sorely lacking in the parental department. Dave Prynne is the epitome of the perfect grandfather, though. Sam was my dad, and no one will ever disagree with that. I need to grow up, and I'm trying, but you parenting me is stifling my growth. I feel smothered, and if it was anyone but you, I would've rebelled by now. But you're getting me to that point," I warn.

"I don't know what to do, Willow! AHHH!" Auggie yells and pulls his hair in a form of self-torture.

"Truth?" I ask, feeling more like a woman than ever. This is the first time Auggie sees me as something other than a helpless child.

"Hit me," Auggie mutters, looking a bit insane with his hair spiking all over his head.

"I wish," I breathe out, trying not to laugh. "I just want you to be Auggie. I can tell you're struggling with what box to put me in. I'm not your girlfriend or lover. Everyone can see how you want to fuck me– even I can tell, so you know it's beyond obvious. Your problem is that you feel guilty about wanting me like that."

"I do struggle with leaving you alone, but not as much as I struggle with feeling like a perverted child molester for looking at you in that light," Auggie finally admits.

"I might look like a child with slightly stunted girly parts, but emotionally, mentally, and chronologically, I am an adult. That's my problem, Auggie. Treating me like a child hurts me. *Deeply.*"

"Shit," Auggie hisses with feeling. "I can't stop myself from being a dick around you. It just… happens."

"You bring that out of me, too," I say with a smirk. "So this is my major issue with you. You don't want me at the Playroom, so I'm not your pet. You want to order me around as your employee, but you want me to live with you. So what am I to you? I don't even think you know the answer to that question."

"I don't know," Auggie whispers, sounding as defeated and exhausted as I feel. "All I know is that I want you, and I don't want anyone else to take you from me. I'm confused."

"And you don't think I'm just as confused? I'm an eighteen-year-old idiot feeling her way through life. I just need you to pick where we stand. If you want to brother me, I'm fine with that. Just don't touch me like a man does a woman. If you want to be my friend, then don't parent me."

"I don't know how to do that." Auggie actually whines like a child, shocking the shit out of me. Lately, more often than not, I feel like I'm the one driving the bus around here–conversationally and emotionally speaking. Auggie has no issue giving out demands and telling me what he wants.

Sick to death of walking around on eggshells, I decide to end this farce. "Do you want to touch me, kiss me, and fuck me?" I ask in a voice filled with false bravado.

Green eyes bulge in shock. "You know I do," he hoarsely whispers.

"Well, wanting to fuck me narrows down our options considerably. I guess being my big brother is off the table then, so knock that shit off. You're my boss, so you can tell me what to do only when we're at work. You don't want me to play, so no treating me like a pet. You already told me I'm not enough for you sexually, or mature enough to be your girlfriend, so that's out. Friends, how about we just call us friends." I offer the only solution that makes sense.

Auggie stares at me for what feels like an eternity and doesn't respond. He gives me a blank expression and unblinking eyes. I don't know if I should take his non-answer as affirmation or rejection. The silence is deafening, so I go for broke. If Auggie won't talk, maybe he will listen and actually hear me for a change.

"Tonight was the hardest night I've ever lived through, Auggie. Tonight was for Sam. Revolutionary Road was his favorite band and Calico was his favorite place. No, Revolutionary Road was *our* favorite band and Calico was *our* favorite place. I went there to honor and remember Sam all the while dealing with teenage emotional horseshit in a place where drugs and alcohol run rampant. Mixing debilitating mourning with rejection, sexual confusion, and drug and alcohol addiction in that environment was the ultimate test. *I passed.*"

Auggie finally finds his voice. "Willow–"

And I shut him up. "I needed a shoulder to lean on when I got home. I needed you to listen and offer your invaluable advice. Instead, you judged me and fought me. You reduced me to something so insignificant, you made me feel badly about myself. I needed a friend when I got home, only to realize I don't trust you enough to comfort or listen to me. I don't trust you to be my friend."

"I'm sorry," Auggie mutters lamely.

"You can keep apologizing, but at this time, I don't trust you enough to believe you. I'm not the same Willow I was, Auggie, and I deserve the benefit of the doubt. I've *earned* the benefit of the doubt. I, at least, should be questioned before being attacked. Don't apologize to me again unless you know you'll never behave that way again. Otherwise, you're just spewing bullshit to get out of trouble like a fucking child. And yes, I just went there."

"Yeah, ya did," Auggie sounds impressed when I expected pissed.

"I don't care if you think you're the top fucking dog, sometimes you screw up and need to be punished, too. Maybe I'll call Chief Mason to kick your ass, or Isis. But, frankly, I'm sick of your shit, too."

"I fucked up– I get that." Auggie breathes in defeat.

"Ya think?" spills before I can stop it this time. "I'm sick of everybody's shit. I just want to go to work and ignore all you assholes. You've taken every outlet I have away. You showed me a taste of pleasure and dangled it like a carrot. Just like when I was little, you'd take the carrot away just as I'd reached for it, and then consume the fucker right before my eyes. No drugs, no alcohol– it won't be easy, but I'm trying. Smokes– fuck you. A cigarette was the only thing I could do to keep from toking up, so deal."

"I'll make a concession on that, Willow. But you need to slowly wean yourself off nicotine." Auggie tries to negotiate instead of demand.

"No." I deny him without any guilt. "I'll either smoke, or I won't, but it's not your call to make. Here is the list you've given me so far: *No Kieren Mason. No Alcohol. No Drugs. No Play. No Rush. No Playroom. No Sex. No Auggie. No Cigarettes. But feel free to work, work, work your ass off for me, Willow.* I'm eighteen, and you want me to act eighteen, but you leave me nothing to do that an eighteen-year-old girl would enjoy. So give me a dang break, Auggie, before I go postal on someone– mainly you."

"This new you confuses the hell out of me, Willow. But I think I'll like her once I get used to her," Auggie says with pride. For the first time tonight, he meets my eyes.

"It's called self-respect, and Mr. Kline taught me how important it is. Now, if only he'd give me some in return, our lives would flow smoothly."

"Sleep with me tonight." Auggie begs, reaching out to pull me from my nest on the sofa.

"No." I deny him, and it feels damn good. Empowering. Auggie flinches in response, and I momentarily feel bad. But then the satisfaction returns when I remember how confused the man makes me. "It's too soon, and not a good idea, Auggie. You need to figure out who I am to you. I can't handle you dangling that carrot anymore."

"No one said you couldn't have sex." Auggie adds, voice sad, as if he wished he hadn't offered that option in the first place and wants to take his words back. "I told you to play with guys your own age."

"Yeah, I'll do that," I threaten, and he winces. "Good night, Auggie," I say in dismissal. While watching him stand and walk toward his bed gives me some sick satisfaction, it breaks my heart even more. After Auggie gets comfortable on his big bed and flicks the lamp off, I say, "And by the way, I didn't even taste a drink."

CHAPTER TWENTY-EIGHT

As I've renovated Revamped's sales system and the Spook House, I've been renovating myself as well. A few weeks ago, my faulty online sales system came crashing down on me and I had to find a way to fix it. I went over to Fairport Community College, looking for a few evening classes in website design and business, hoping to avoid a catastrophe. Every class I browsed looked beyond helpful, and by the time I left the college, I'd signed up for a full course load for the spring semester's evening classes.

I haven't told anyone about going to college, fearing I'd fail out and be a laughing stock. I can see my parents and Clover going insane with happiness if I showed up and said I was a college student. Then in my mind, I see their disappointed faces and tears as I had to swallow my pride and tell them I flunked out of school. It's best that I'm keeping it a secret. This way, if I fail, I'll only be a disappointment to myself.

I've been working like a crazy person since, trying to get loose ends tied up at Revamped and the Spook House, so I'll have the time for school. Last night, I worked at the Spook House until it was time to go to work at Revamped. I didn't do it to prove I'm an adult, or to make Auggie proud, or to act as a martyr. I did it for me, and I feel fan-fucking-tastic... and dead tired.

Now, my only problem is how to avoid telling Auggie about school. I don't need him riding my ass about homework, or taking away my work at the Spook House or at Revamped. I can see Auggie lecturing me about concentrating on the task at hand, and I fear he'd take one of my current fixations away. I need the manual labor at the Spook House to keep my mind clear. I need the work at Revamped to keep my mind occupied on mental things. I'll need school to better myself for both. I decided I needed something that wasn't a vice to keep my mind off my other vices: drugs, alcohol, cigarettes, caffeine, sex, food. I need something to distract myself from all of those unhealthy things, so I decided to become a workaholic– working to better the

Spook House, Revamped, and myself. We all need to reach our potential, and I'm the girl to do it.

My only option of secrecy is to avoid Auggie in the evenings. He's usually at Rush from the time Revamped closes to the time Rush closes. While Auggie's not in the loft with me during waking hours, he'd still see my school books or me studying. I decided that leaving the loft and moving fulltime into the Spook House was my only way out. I'll study in the privacy of my own bedroom.

"I have a suggestion," I say hesitantly after several hours of Auggie staring at the side of my face. I've sat at the counter, working on Revamped's online sales for the past three hours with Auggie sitting on a stool, looking over my shoulder and not saying a damned thing. It's creepy and unnerving as all hell.

Sensing a change in me, Auggie has refused to work in the back of the store at all today. He's examined me, making sure I didn't metamorphosis into a spoiled brat monster by grabbing a bottle of whiskey, a bowl, and impale myself on his beast of a cock.

"I finished my bedroom in the house. It's out of the way, so it shouldn't be an issue with the rest of the remodel. It's the one on the second floor, all the way at the end of the house, facing the back lawn. Rob picked the master, and mine butts up against his, on the corner. Mom, Clover, and Violet helped me pick out some furniture, and it was delivered yesterday afternoon."

"You have no idea how proud you've made me," Auggie says, reaching over to rub my back. "I know I haven't been very involved with the Spook House, and I've left it all up to you."

"Yeah, not much help from your Playroomers, either," I grumble underneath my breath. Not a single Playroomer has helped, except for Devon. But Devon will deny his involvement in the Playroom as anything other than therapeutic– whatever that means. "If it wasn't for Dad and a few of his crew, I couldn't have gotten as far as I have. They taught me how to grout tile last night."

Auggie freezes beside me, and then says stiffly, "They haven't been helping?"

I snort– I just can't help the disrespectful sound that ejects from my throat. "Auggie, how can they help if they're fucking you all night long? I know you think they're multi-talented, but ain't nobody *that* flexible."

Auggie's warning growl makes me bark a sharp laugh, which only makes Auggie angrier. "I thought they were helping during the day. I assumed you'd set up some kind of schedule like you do with Revamped's shit. The house is really shaping up, so I figured you had a lot of help."

"Since I'm not a member of the Playroom, and I'm barred entrance to Rush, I'm not entirely sure how you expected me to contact these people. Run around town shouting *Playroomers! Get to fuckin' work, you lazy cocksucking deviants! Oh, Playroomers!* Yeah, I don't think so. My job is not to do your job, Auggie."

Sighing so heavily I swear he's counting to ten in his head, Auggie radiates fury like a volcano. I haven't been easy to deal with lately, as cravings assault me constantly. But Auggie hasn't been easy to deal with as he gets more confused by the day, which confuses me more.

I stopped being Auggie's Kool-Aid drinker. The less I get reprimanded for telling Auggie like I see it, the more I do it. I think I'm only one of a handful of people Auggie doesn't murder for shoving his shit right back in his face. I'll leave it to Auggie's Playroomers to stroke his ginormous ego along with his even larger cock.

"I wasn't aware there was a position that needed to be filled, so I'd assumed you told them the when, what, and where of the interworkings of the Spook House. My bad," Auggie grumbles, trying to rein in his temper.

I jump from my stool and pretend I need a drink from the mini-fridge. "I could say something about ignorance, but I don't want to get backhanded." I tease as soon as I'm out of Auggie's arm's reach.

"Bitch," Auggie hisses in appreciation. "I've created a fucking monster. You're starting to sound just like me, damn it!" My giggle has Auggie yanking me to his chest and cuddling me in his arms. He strokes my hair and sighs. "Mini-beast, you got some elves or some shit? How the hell are you getting so much done? I might not be helping at my house, but I check it out every single day. There's new plumbing in the upstairs bath, and new electrical wiring on the entire first floor. You're good, turning into the smarty-pants I knew you were, but you ain't that good. No one can learn that stuff from an *Idiot's Guide*."

"My dad donates his time in the evenings. We only use one or two of his men when it's a difficult job to tackle, which means I have to pay them for their time. Devon helps when he can, but he's now working fulltime for Fairport Police Department."

"You pay? Or are you taking it from my bank account?" Auggie asks, not sounding worried in the least. I have access to his personal accounts as well as Revamped's business account so I can pay the bills.

"Your personal account. I signed the memo *The Spook House* for your accountant. You're in luck you have me. If you hired Prynne Renovations, you'd have to pay them in man hours. I'm just paying their hourly rate under-the-table."

"I'd say it's because you're the owner's daughter, so Daddy isn't making you pay your share to the government. But I think it's because you're so cute." Auggie purrs as he runs his nose up the side of my neck. "...and snarly."

"Not as snarly as you," I point out as I wiggle from Auggie's arms. He's back to being affectionate– platonic –but after a few days of being treated like a sexual outlet, followed by weeks of a harsh freeze-out, being confused is an understatement. When Auggie touches me, I don't know if I'm to be the girl I used to be, the person he wants me to be, or the woman I am.

"What I wanted to tell you–" I draw in a deep breath and let it out in a big gust. "I'm staying at the Spook House. I want it to be my home." I started off my request meekly, but I ended it in a voice filled with confident strength that I'm not sure I really feel.

I learned a while ago, you can't ask Auggie, or you'll be denied. You have to *tell* Auggie, and hope to God he doesn't kick your ass. But sometimes the beating is worth it.

"It's already your home. As soon as it's ready, we'll all move in together," Auggie offers, purposefully avoiding what I really meant. "It will be nice to have Robin with us. You haven't lived with him since you were a tiny shit. He cooks almost as well as Clover. It's been so long since I've lived with him. I'm hoping Isis will thaw out and take the room I tried to give her– that will make Rob very happy. Living in the Spook House will be fun. You'll see."

Auggie strokes my shoulder, and I try not to pull away. I'm scared of how Auggie will react when I tell him I will *not* wait. I don't trust the manipulative powers of Mr. Kline.

Even more disturbing is the hidden meaning of what he just said, and how sad and miserable he sounded. Auggie misses his best friends so very much that he'd be willing to do anything to keep them. Am I in the Spook House as a lure to get Robbie there? Robbie would like to be near me, protecting me. Is Robbie the lure to get Isis there? Does Auggie miss them so much, he'll use me to get them all in one house?

Shit!

"You mistake what I meant," I slowly enunciate. "What I meant to say is, as of last night my bedroom at the Spook House is complete, and that's where you'll find me if you need me. I don't live at the loft. I never really did. I just crashed on your sofa. I think I've earned that room after five weeks of continual manual labor, Auggie."

"Why?" It's no longer just the *I don't know you* look– it's acquired its own tone of voice to go accompany it.

"As you said before, we have a lot to do at the house to complete it. I'm already there for most of the night. It would be easier on me to be able to crawl to bed instead of driving across town to Revamped when I'm dog tired. Besides, it's not like you're around in the evenings anyway. I know you have to be at Rush, so you won't miss me much. Nothing will change except where I sleep."

"Are you trying to punish me?" I can hear Auggie's teeth gnash together as his face flames red with fury. "Is this some kind of ultimatum? Are you giving me female shit about the Playroom?"

Auggie almost sounds like he wishes I'd throw a fit about the Playroom, like it's confusing him that I'm not. I figured out a long time ago, there is no future between Auggie and me. He's meant for someone else, and it's up to Auggie to figure out who. His future spouse can bitch and complain about his infidelity, but that person won't be me.

Since we set the boundaries of our friendship, I've treated Auggie with the same level of respect I give my friends. Unless it pertains to work, then Auggie gets his ass kissed by his dutiful employee. I've treated Auggie like a wild animal for the past six weeks. He's my boss when I'm at work, and my friendly roommate who wants to fuck me but wishes he didn't the rest of the time.

"Ha," I say without humor. "You're giving me too much credit as being a manipulative bitch. You think I'm jerking you around by your dick? Even if I was a woman in your eyes, I'd never do that to you, Auggie. I'd never manipulate you or control you. If you allowed me to twist you, I'd be disappointed in you. I don't want to see you as I do my parents. I respect you too much."

I look at Auggie's face and try to read him. I don't want him to see me as a spoiled brat who uses him. I've been ashamed of how I've treated my parents and Clover all these years. Auggie has to know I wouldn't do that to him. It's what I love about him in the first place. Auggie makes me want to be a better person. Someday, I hope to be strong enough for someone else to want to better themselves for me.

"I love seeing the changes in the house. Just that small bit I did overnight was a huge transformation. I don't want to miss a second of it. I want to be right in the thick of it and take pride in the house… and I wasn't being a sarcastic bitch about the club, Auggie. You own it. I bet you spent every night at Rush until I turned eighteen. I won't change your life because I'm in it. You'd just resent me for it, and it would ruin whatever we are to each other."

"I want you here with me." Auggie pleads. "I want you here with me," he repeats in a heartbreaking tone as I'm yanked into his arms. Immediately I'm engulfed by his addictive scent and scorching heat. I allow Auggie to hold me for what feels like hours, but it's probably just minutes. The only reason I know I'm crying is that my face is wet. Confusion muddles all my emotions.

The ding of the bell over the front door draws me away from Auggie– saved by the bell.

"My boyfriend's here," I manage to say without it sounding like a total lie. No matter what, my need for Auggie's approval is my driving force. I hate lying to the man, but I don't want Auggie to be disappointed in me because Devon and I are just friends. "Devon's here to help me move my stuff to the Spook House."

CHAPTER TWENTY-NINE

"So... college girl, eh?" I had to tell someone, or I'd explode, and Devon felt like the safest choice. We're having an indoor picnic on a blanket in the middle of the room that will eventually be the Spook House's living room. Right now, it's just a torn up mess with supplies scattered around.

"Yeah, I know it's probably stupid," I trail off, feeling unsure of my decision. Auggie always says I make the wrong decisions. It would've made sense to ask his opinion first, but I wanted to do something for me– 100% all me from start to finish.

"Nah, Willow," Devon says softly as he reaches over to tug my ponytail. "You're too hard on yourself. If you keep this shit up, you'll be burnt out before you hit twenty. Just do what makes you happy, and forget about that controlling bastard."

"I don't know where I'd be without that controlling bastard, Devon." That reverent Kool-Aid drinker quality in my voice rears its ugly head again. It's been weeks since I've heard it spill from my mouth. "I may hate Auggie's methods, but without them, I'd be that loser he likes to call me."

"Loser?" Devon snarls, blue eyes turning obsidian with rage.

"I was a loser– still feel like one sometimes, too," I mumble flippantly. "Forget I said anything." I grab a slice of pizza, once again wishing we had something better than the shit from the convenience store. "We're celebrating, remember? Celebrating me moving into the Spook House and my last few days before I'm chained to a desk."

"One day," Devon threatens, but I have no idea what or whom he is threatening.

"It's your deal," I offer as distraction. "You gotta give me a chance to beat your ass. Best two outta three?" I toss Devon the playing cards, scattering them everywhere, making him play fifty-two-card-pick -up. I chuckle when he glares at me while wearing a grin.

The front door opening has me stiffening. No one ever comes to the Spook House without my invite. My dad isn't due for a few days, and I didn't ask for any of the men from Prynne Renovations.

"Who the hell…" I breathe as I look over my shoulder. My eyes widen in surprise as a river of people flows into the Spook House. Chatting and laughing, the best of friends, they overflow *my* house.

"It's an invasion!" Devon laughs as he tosses his half-eaten pizza crust into the box. An army of Playroomers invades the Spook House. Playroomers from every walk of life. Young. Old. Man. Woman. I want to yell at them to leave my house alone, but then I realize it isn't *my* house. I shuffle the deck of cards, then slide it back into its box with too much force, tearing the cardboard down its side.

"I guess my break's over," I mutter grumpily. "This bitch never gets five minutes to herself."

I was enjoying my one-on-one time with Devon. We've been so busy lately, we haven't had much time to hang out. We packed my stuff up at Revamped, and then drove it over here. Devon helped me unpack my boxes and put my things away in my room, and now that we finally found the time to sit down to eat our cardboard-tasting pizza and engage in a competitive game of *War,* we're interrupted.

I was just starting to feel better, more like myself. I've had more fun today than I have in ages. For the most part, Devon and I avoided talk of misbehaving bosses and even more inappropriate so-called girlfriends. Auggie and Tina. Auggie's a subject Devon is reluctant to discuss, and Tina's a subject we've never discussed, ever after the concert.

The addition of the Playroomers draws my insecurities to the surface. Here's a group of people Auggie sees differently than me. He enjoys their *adult* company while relegating me to the likes of a child until it comes to working my ass off for *his* business and *his* house.

Seeing the Playroomers drives home the point that I'm not good enough, not even home repair as they invade *my* project! Can't Auggie see that this was for *me*?

"It's not my house," I breathe, trying to squash the tantrum-throwing child that wants to erupt. "Let it go, Willow."

"Are you okay?" Devon asks. Must be I'm being transparent again.

"Peachy," I lie poorly. "Just unexpected is all… after almost six weeks, ya know?"

"Oh?" Devon looks around, eyes narrowed in confusion. An annoyed expression crosses Devon's face, and then I feel *him* behind me.

"Willow," is breathed against the top of my head as his huge palm strokes my back. "I brought help," Auggie volunteers. "I didn't know they were being slackers. Every night I kept asking, and they kept shaking their heads like idiots, lying to me. You know how much I like being lied to–"

"No wonder you got people to leave their day jobs and families on a Saturday afternoon," Devon says, sounding awed. "What did you threaten them with?"

"You'll just have to show up to the Playroom later tonight to find out," Auggie drawls.

"Well." I hop up, needing to be away from both Auggie and Devon for different reasons. I'm transparent again, and I don't want either one of them to get a reading on me. "Let's see how much we can get done this afternoon." I sound chipper and perky. It's not all an act– the thought of progress trills energy into my bloodstream, even if it's not all *my* progress. I'm not so selfish that I don't want the best for the Spook House, even if someone else can provide the service.

Auggie's hand trails along my neck and down to my back. "The past few hours were lonely without you at Revamped," he breathes against my throat. His voice vibrates down my body, weakening my knees. I have to grip his forearms to remain upright. I nearly moan.

Jesus, this *no touch* shit is driving me nuts. So much temptation on my end, and no one wants me back. Between Auggie's hot and cold routine and Devon's *let's be friends* attitude, I'm running a lust-fever while my self-confidence shrivels up and dies. I'm not the flirty sort, and I've never been compelled to do it, but it's been an uphill battle to behave today. I've messed up a few times by accidently touching Devon, or innocently flirting. He's been a good sport about it, though. Devon just shyly blushes and looks away. I don't know the rules of this type of game. And now Auggie decides to turn hot on me. What the actual fuck?

"I… uh…" I clear my throat, hating how breathy and labored I sound. "What do we do first?"

"Demolition," Auggie growls evilly while flashing a naughty smirk and glittering green eyes.

"Fuck, yeah!" Devon grunts while he jumps to his feet.

Auggie and Devon actually fist bump– *FIST BUMP* –over the excitement of demolition. Grinning like fools while tossing information back and forth, they're actually aroused by the thought of ruining the Spook House.

I don't get men at all.

Alright, I change my mind. I love demolition. Twenty guys running around half naked, glistening with sweat and carrying sledge hammers is erotic as all hell. I don't even care that I'm ogling men who are almost as old as my father. Mailman Pete has a tight bod from all that walking he does on a daily basis, and his wife Rhonda is positively drooling as he swings a hammer.

It amazes me how ridiculous people are. I feel like I'm witnessing something from Animal Planet. Maybe a show on the mating habits of primates. It's January, in a house that's barely heated, and every Playroomer is stripped down to almost naked. The girls are running around in their bras and panties and the men are just wearing their pants.

Having worked actual manual labor since birth, I see how incredibly stupid they are behaving, childish even. Boots. Gloves. Jeans. They are not a fashion statement while working– they protect your ass from mutilating accidents. Plus, they keep the private bits warm when it's fourteen degrees outside.

I want to complain about how sexist it is that the women have to clean up the mess the demolition man are making, but I can't get my lips to form words. They're too busy drooling like Rhonda.

Ridiculousness aside, I don't mind watching the fools. The men are a nice view, and the women are too. But the men make me feel sad, and the women make me feel bad. Sad because I know not one single man is looking at me like they're looking at the female Playroomers. Bad because looking at the female Playroomers make me realize I'll never, ever look like them, no matter what I do.

I shut a part of my brain down– the part that is upset. This must be how men feel at a strip club, or watching porn. You know you're not going to get any attention from those you watch, but you can't look away. You know they'll never want you back, no matter how badly you may want them.

But regardless of how I look, they're still worthy of watching. Mesmerized, my eyes flutter between a compact cop wearing a pair of jeans and no shirt, and a gigantic illustrator who's still fully dressed. I see all the men, but those two eclipse everyone else. No matter how hard I concentrate on my work, my eyes still seek them out.

Auggie spends a lot of the time fending off the Playroomers. I watch with amusement as he flirts like a pro and flexes and bends to give us a show. Nina, the cocksucktress, is glued to Auggie's side, offering to fetch him this or that, to wipe his brow. Even going as far as to hold Auggie's bottle of water to his lips as he drinks. Nina is desperate in an eye-roll-worthy kind of way with her skank-o-licious behavior and white lace bra and panties that *accidentally* got drenched the last time Auggie took a drink.

What I didn't expect is the reception Devon is getting from the female Playroomers. I've never seen him flirt. Not even when we were at parties with a dozen drunken girls stumbling around and falling face-first into awaiting laps. Devon seemed indifferent to Tina's ministrations, other than a faint smile and a willingness to connect his lips to hers. Tonight, Devon flirts openly and confidently.

Devon flirting stings more so than Auggie's display. Auggie was meant to flirt and fuck. It's in his personality, and it doesn't necessarily mean anything. He's an equal opportunistic whoremonger. But with Devon, it has a purpose. He's selective, and he never selects me. It shouldn't sting, but it does. You want your friends to at least think you're attractive.

I watch as one of Bethany's friends– a little blonde girl who graduated with Devon and Essie –runs her fingernail down Devon's sweat-slickened chest and offers her damp finger to him. Devon playfully nips her fingertip between his teeth and laughs.

"Muhhahaaaaahhaa," I nastily mock underneath my breath, and start beating a wooden lath to bits against my plastic garbage can. Pieces ping off and fly around me like angry shrapnel.

"What's so funny?" Robbie asks me as he walks by, eyes cutting in my direction. I can tell he's trying not to laugh at my childish but slightly manic display.

"Me?" I point at myself, pretending I never said a word and Robbie's hearing things. "Not a thing. Not a fucking thing." I growl, breaking a wooden lath in half using my shin as a fulcrum point.

"No, what'd you say?" My brother asks again, not buying my bullshit. He stops in his tracks and flips around to face me.

"Nothing– I have nothing to say," I mumble agitatedly.

I ignore the ear-gasm of Devon's seductive man-laugh while he grips a girl's hips to pull her closer to him. I ignore the feverish light in Auggie's green eyes as he smacks a chick's perfectly rounded ass. Hmm... I guess ignore isn't the right word, considering I was completely captivated by it.

I'd love to turn into a petty bitch, but I can't, and not because I'm above that kind of manipulation. I'd love to flirt in retaliation, but not one of these twenty guys thinks Willow, with her ten-year-old boy body, is worthy of flirtation.

Where the fuck is Kieren when I need him– that assmunch is attracted to me. My eyes actually flick around the living room, hoping to find him. I feel bad instantly for wanting to use Kieren to get back at the men in my life. That would make me no different than these stupid fucks.

If I go without any longer, Kieren's going to move to the top of my menu– Auggie's warning of murderous intent be damned. I have needs. I might not look like a woman, but those same needs still simmer beneath the surface. Willow the wayward wouldn't have put up with this bullshit. One of these days, Willow the responsible adult isn't going to any longer either. I'll do something stupid, like find Kieren and fuck him into delirium. I'm no longer lying to myself– I know I'd like it just as much as Kieren would. So where's the harm in that? Auggie would render us both limbless if I so much as made a move on Kieren... there's the harm in that.

Staring at me as my emotions flash over my face like lightning, Robbie looks like he's either taking a shit or solving a Rubik's Cube. "Have you checked out the attic yet? It'll make a wicked Playroom."

Robbie doesn't realize he just twisted the knife deeper into his sister's back. "No," I murmur despondently, hoping Rob will drop this conversation. Praying he'll take a hint, I slump to my haunches and start cleaning up debris from the floor.

"Why not? It's perfect." He gives me that look– the one that screams *Willow's a dipshit*.

"I don't have an invite," I grumble, hoping no one will hear it.

"Silly, you don't need an invite to enter your own attic," Robbie says like I'm a moron. "Just walk up the steps and enter it. The door to the attic is right next to your bedroom door. You can't miss it."

"Robbie." I wipe away a few sweaty hairs stuck to my forehead. "You need an invite to your own attic if it's the Playroom. Auggie is serious about that kind of shit," spills out before I can stop it. I decide that working would keep my mouth shut. I pick up a lath covered in plaster and toss it into my garbage can.

"What are you talking about?" Robbie stills my hand by wrapping his fingers around my wrist so I can't ignore him.

With a sharp yank of my wrist, I pull my brother down to my level so no one can overhear. "Robbie, my invitation was rescinded. Well, I guess I was never really invited. According to Auggie, I trespassed. No Rush. No Playroom. No attic for me. I'm sure it's awesome, and that I'd love renovating the space. But I'm not going to torture myself with what I want when I can't have it."

"What? Are you being punished for something?" Robbie eyes me like I'm a total badass. "What'd you do? When in the hell did you have time to do it? Damn, you're a little rebel if Auggie banned your ass."

"Are you deaf?" I snarl, taking my hurt feeling out on my concerned brother. Feeling bad, I mumble an apology. "I didn't do anything wrong. Six weeks ago, Auggie told me I wasn't to set foot into Rush and he didn't want me in the Playroom. You get that? I'm not being punished for anything. He just doesn't want me!" I hiss out, doing my damnedest not to cry.

"I call bullshit on that." Robbie rolls his eyes at me, giving me my own look right back at me. "You guys have been going at it like monkeys since you turned legal." A chuckle rumbles up, and instead of the playful noise making me feel happy, it's a shot to the heart.

"Rob, I don't know why you'd say that," I whisper. "The only difference between me and a virgin is about a half hour of experiences rolled into one. I can assure you, I'm more innocent now than I used to be. No. All I hear is no. Kieren. Weed. Alcohol. Sex. Cigarettes. Rush. Playroom. Auggie. Devon and work are my only yeses."

"Ooooohhhh... I get it," Robbie draws out. "Auggie's giving you space while you date Devon. He knows you're a good girl, so it would hurt you in the long run if you played with him and Devon– confuse you."

"Rob, are you *high*? I just said Auggie doesn't want *me*," I stress the hell out of my words. "Devon is my buddy, nothing more. He's over there *playing* with that skank," I hiss, but the girl is as far from a skank as I am.

"Okay, now I'm really confused. So if Auggie isn't claiming you, and Devon is just hanging out with you, then it shouldn't matter. After we check out the attic, I'll take you to Rush tonight and you can blow off some steam. You're beyond stressing. You're just like me, Willow. We'll get ya taken care of."

"Robin!" I bark out, furious. "You don't get it. I just said I'm never allowed to go to the Playroom. The Playroom is wherever Auggie chooses it to be since it revolves around him. I'm not good or bad enough to *play*." My voice breaks, and I quickly brush away a betraying tear. "There's no blowing off some steam for me, Rob. Who the fuck would touch me? Auggie doesn't want me at Rush because he doesn't want to humiliate me– to humiliate himself. These people don't want someone like me. Age isn't the issue. Do you see anyone ugly? Do you see anyone who isn't desirable? Auggie said no to the Playroom because he's ashamed of me."

"Hey." Robbie tries to embrace me, and I step out of reach. "Willow." He tries again to pull me into his arms. "It's okay."

"Just don't tell anyone, alright? Nobody knows but Auggie, Devon, and me. I'm embarrassed enough as it is– I'd be humiliated if these people ever found out. I'm sure it's obvious since I haven't been back... since. Well, you know when. Maybe it wasn't memorable enough, and they forgot I existed."

"Doubtful," Robbie grunts. "Willow, come with me. We'll talk this out. I don't like that look on your face, or how you're talking about yourself."

Ignoring my brother's attempt at comforting me, the words flow unbidden. "It's difficult seeing everyone here, seeing them in the house I want as my own, and knowing it will never be. It's difficult knowing that I'm nothing to them. Invisible. If they start playing around with each other, I'll have to leave," I whisper. "I'll have to leave where *I live*. No matter how many hours I put into this house, it'll never be mine– I'll never belong here."

"What's going on?" Robbie pulls at my arm, trying to hug me again. "Answer me now. Where is this shit coming from? Who's making you feel this way?"

"Just forget it. Okay?" I reply weakly. I see Auggie making a beeline in our direction, and I start to panic. "I better go to the store and get a case or two of water. Wouldn't want anyone to dehydrate– their tits would shrivel up. I'll be right back." I make my excuse to bolt.

Mind not functioning properly, I aimlessly wander for a minute or two, trying to locate my car keys. When I find them in the pocket of my coat, I curse myself out for being so stupid, but I'm relieved I found my keys just the same. As I twist the doorknob to leave the Spook House, the door thumps closed.

I stare unblinkingly as a huge palm holds the door shut, cutting off my only means of escape. "Where are you running off to?" Auggie bends his six and a half foot frame over me, and places one hand on the doorknob while the other is near my head, effectively trapping me inside.

"Um– nowhere?" I stammer.

"Right answer," Auggie purrs near my ear, sounding menacing as all hell. "There are ten cases of water in the kitchen– as you already know, since you bought them yesterday. Why are you running off?" Auggie slides the car keys from my hand and pockets them.

I stand like a deer caught in headlights.

"You fucked Devon today, didn't you?" It's not accusatory, simply fact. I look at Auggie, dumbfounded, trying to process what he just said. "You're freaking out because you finally did it, aren't you? It's why he's so confident. Hmm… was it any good?" Auggie purrs while running his nose along the column of my throat.

"What? No!" I protest, on the edge of elbowing him in the ribs.

"Huh?" he grunts, sounding confused. "It wasn't any good? Are you lying to me? I have a hard time telling anymore." Auggie looks just as bewildered as I feel.

"You have a hard time telling if I'm lying or not because I never lie to you!" I sound so insulted that it stings my ears. "I didn't screw Devon today, or any day. Why would I lie about something like that?" I sputter. "Why would you ask me like this?" I gesture to being trapped and interrogated. "Just ask me, Auggie. Don't just assume you know every-fucking-thing."

"Devon's flirting," Auggie muses, mind calculating things I'll never fathom. "Why is he flirting?" Auggie ask quizzically.

"There are a lot of stunning women out there with hardly any clothes on, why wouldn't Devon flirt?" I point toward the scantily-clad women as proof. The only thing covered on one girl's tits are her nipples. Another woman's entire ass is hanging out as she strides around in a thong. These women aren't working on the Spook House, but they're working. They're the entertainment. They're here as an added incentive for those who are working to work hard and fast, or no more Playroom. Auggie's showing his members what they'll lose if they don't do their duty at the Spook House.

"Why isn't Devon flirting with you, though?" Auggie drawls as he grips my chin and tugs until I meet his scrutinizing gaze. He smiles down at me, evidently entertained with the dynamic between Devon and me. I'm not entertained. I don't find it funny at all.

"The better question to ask is why would Devon flirt with me? A question you have answered already. As you've told me a billion times over, just in case I could ever forget. I'm not a woman. I'll never be a woman, no matter how old I get. Augustus Kline, I won't embarrass either of us by taking my clothes off and flirting. I'll look like a toddler, and no one wants to see that. I'm humiliated enough wandering around fully clothed. I won't shame you or myself by acting sexual in any way. And I sure as hell won't flaunt myself when my brother's in this house. I finally get it, Auggie." I breathe out, on the verge of sobbing. "I get it, okay?"

I yank the doorknob with all of my might, my agony helping to infuse me with strength. For once, my size helps me. I slide out the six-inch gap between the door and the jamb, and run.

"Willow!" Auggie shouts, and I ignore him as I flee.

CHAPTER THIRTY

I lurk around the neighborhood for hours, waiting for the house to go dark when everyone vacates my space and goes to Rush. I hate having nowhere else to go. I can't even sit in my car because it's locked with my keys pocketed in Auggie's pants. I walk the streets for hours, upset on so many levels. A girl can only do so much. Maybe I should just worry about Willow from now on, and not what people think of her.

Christ, I'm thinking in the third person. Not good.

Teeth chattering in the single-digit temperatures, I keep moving to stay warm. After dark, I end up across the street, huddled on the porch of a property that's for sale. I've dubbed this place the Pink House because it's Pepto-Bismol pink. Even though it's in slightly better repair than the Spook House was when Auggie bought it, it's been for sale forever because it's so large buyers are scared to heat the monstrosity.

Someday, I'll have a place of my own. A home of my own. A business of my own. Kids of my own. Just something to call *my own*. I want total say in something that affects my life. I'm sick of feeling dependent on everyone. I wouldn't be huddled on an abandoned porch like a homeless person if my life didn't revolve around everyone else's bullshit.

My mind won't stop spinning, making me feel worthless, like that loser Auggie used to call me. I try to think of all the things I've done right lately. My work at Revamped, but it's not my business. My work on the Spook House, but it's not my house. My friendship with Devon, but it's tainted with Auggie ordering us to befriend one another. My lies to everyone over Devon being my fake boyfriend taints the friendship too.

My dark thoughts have me dreaming of rainbow-swirled ceramic and aromatic smoke, which makes me feel better. I'm stronger than my cravings. Even though Auggie told me to stop smoking and drinking, it was *me* who had to actually do it. I'm the one who takes it minute by minute, not toking up or downing a shot. Just as my going to college was for Revamped, but it's me who's going, doing the work, and will ultimately benefit from the knowledge.

See, Willow isn't all bad, is she?

Christ, back to that third person bullshit.

Finally I doze off, despite the cold. The past five nights of no sleep roll over me and pull me under. Seconds, minutes, hours later, I wake with a start, and see the Spook House is finally dark. I have no idea what time it is. I just pray that Auggie didn't lock the house. The Spook House, Revamped, my parents' and Clover's houses, and my car keys are on the ring he took from me. I was locked the hell out of everywhere.

I literally pray the entire time I ghost across the street and mount the front steps to the Spook House. "Yes!" I mock-shout in victory when the door opens with a twist of the knob. I tightly lock myself in and run to the shower.

Thankful for more of God's small mercies, no one touched the upstairs bathroom. I chose my bedroom because it's adjacent to the only free bathroom on the second floor. Rob's room has an attached bath, and Auggie shares a Jack-and-Jill with the bedroom that's for Isis. Until today, I was the one in charge of working at the Spook House, so I took it upon myself to make sure this bathroom and bedroom were completed first.

Chilled to the bone, I rest my forehead on the shower wall and allow the hot water to flow over my neck and down my back. I drain the hot water tank until it runs cold, but nothing will warm me, inside or out. I've caught a chill from being outside all night in the late January air. I can't stop shivering.

My frozen body is proof that Auggie is right– I make shitty choices. I should've manned up and come back into the house. I didn't need to be around the Playroomers. I could've barricaded myself in my bedroom. Another lesson learned. At this rate, I'll be wise before I make it to nineteen.

I startle in surprise when I enter my new bedroom. The mountain of a man lying in the middle of my bed is unexpected. I step backward, cowardly in retreat, hoping Auggie is asleep and didn't see me come into my room.

As soon as I move to flee, eyelids flick open and reveal captivating green eyes that make me feel a dozen conflicting emotions all at once. "Get over here and get warm," he gruffly demands while making my queen-sized bed look incredibly small. But then again, I'm used to seeing Auggie lying in the center of his bed fit for a king.

"What are you doing here?" My voice breaks.

"It's my house," Auggie says with a little laugh. The pleasant sound used to warm my soul. Now when I hear that laugh, it makes me think I'm the brunt of the joke. No, like I *am* the joke.

"No, I mean what are you doing in my bed?" I ask tentatively. Auggie looks and sounds and acts like the old Auggie, but I can't count on him to stay that way. He's in my space, the only space I have.

"Your bed is in *my* house," Auggie teases, and it makes my blood run cold. "Possession is nine-tenths of the law. This nice, new, cozy bed," Auggie says as his hands run up and down my new comforter. "Is sitting in *my* room, in *my* house. It's *my* bed now. I'm pillaging it."

I hate, *HATE*, how even though this is *my* bed, *my* dresser, *my* things, even though I purchased them, they aren't truly mine while they rest inside Auggie's home. I might work my ass off without payment, but that isn't any guarantee. It's not as if I rent this space and have a legal right to it through a lease. For the first time ever, fear freezes me. If I don't kiss Auggie's ass, I'll lose everything. My home. My job. Hell, I'll even lose my tenuous friendships.

"I don't want to be beholden to you, Auggie," I mutter stiffly.

Auggie abruptly sits up and glares at me. "What the fuck, Willow? You think that's what I'm doing. I'm just teasing you, for Christ's sake!"

"Why aren't you at Rush with the rest of your friends?" I demand, losing my patience.

"I was waiting for you." Auggie's voice and glare scream that I've offended him somehow. "You ran outta here like the Hounds of Hell were nipping at your heels. I tried to find you, but couldn't. So I waited in the one place I knew you were guaranteed to return. I was worried the fuck outta my skull– it's below freezing outside. Rob called your parents and Clover. I even checked in with Malcolm, wondering if you ran off with Kieren for the night. Hell, even Devon thought that's where you went."

"Devon's not my boyfriend," I spew. "I can't keep lying to you on that. It's the only thing I'm lying about right now. I needed to get that off my chest." I sigh deeply, feeling relieved. "Sorry to disappoint you, but we're just friends."

"What?" Auggie sits forward on my bed, legs hanging off the edge.

I lean against my bedroom door and decide Auggie and I need to have a talk. "I know you think you can play god, but you can't. Devon's just my friend. He doesn't see me that way. At all."

"You're kidding me, right?" Auggie arches his fuzzy red brow. The gesture always means he's either asking if I'm lying, or he thinks I'm being ridiculous. I'm pretty sure this eyebrow raise is a combination of both.

"Devon has a girlfriend. I saw them kiss at the Revolutionary Road concert– she's the one who insulted me, and then Kieren. She's the one who dumped beer on my hoodie, so I went postal on her ass. I didn't speak to Devon for about a week after that, and he's never mentioned it or apologized for her behavior. I don't like being lied to, either."

"Girl's name?" Auggie orders.

"Tina." I answer without thought.

"Not Devon's girlfriend." Auggie replies just as quickly as I had. "Dealer– Devon's dealer."

"What?" I gasp in shock.

"Not every delinquent drug addict has parents who grow their own." The insult to my parents is not-so silent in his voice. "If you're not Devon's girlfriend, then he doesn't have one. I can say with 100% accuracy that Tina is Devon's dealer."

"Devon's clean," I say with utter confidence. "He stopped using when I stopped. We're supporting each other."

"I told you I was proud of you, Willow, and I need you to truly feel it, know it, and absorb it. But not many people have your resolve. Tough love only works on those who respect the ones giving them the love. You respect me, and you respect yourself, so you stopped using. Devon might not respect Malcolm, or you, or whoever made him think he needed the change in the first place. Some people have enablers. Some people are just very weak. I'm not saying Devon is still taking drugs. I'm just saying the odds are pretty damned good that he is. If Tina's hanging around, those odds quadruple."

"How do you know?" I mumble, mind flitting around for the truth.

"I just know," Auggie growls, leaning forward on my bed, trying to get closer to me. "Now, why did you run this afternoon? Be responsible and actually tell me the truth."

"I know, Auggie." Sighing heavily, I slump against the door. "Okay, I get it. When I was showering, I thought about how juvenile I behaved, how idiotic. If I had a problem, I should've spoken to you, or went to my room. At the very least, went somewhere to cool off, preferably somewhere warm." I snort at the idiocy of cooling off somewhere warm. "I wanted to be alone... and it's just... you aren't that easy to talk to anymore, Auggie. I feel so judged."

"I'm not judging you," Auggie replies immediately without thought.

"Yes, you do. You always are– it's what makes you *you*."

"You need me, Willow. You need me to guide you," Auggie says without arrogance. "You don't have to admit it, or say thank you. Just *talk* to me," he begs– Auggie begs. Sliding to the foot of my bed, Auggie rests his forearms on his thighs and looks at me with sad puppy dog eyes, pleading with me to let him in, to be the girl I used to be. The one who trusted Mr. Kline in all things. The girl who always felt better when Auggie kissed her boo-boos.

"I'm failing you." A lump is firmly lodged in my throat, suffocating me. I slump to the floor to sit on the rug near Auggie's feet. I don't trust myself, or Auggie, to have this conversation if I sit on the bed with him. Somehow understanding, Auggie tosses me my fuzzy blanket to wrap myself up in.

"I haven't touched drugs or alcohol since you made me dump and destroy my stash." I look up and hold Auggie's gaze. "I need you to know that. I did it for you at first, but the craving taught me that I couldn't do it again. That's what stops me, not you. *Fear*. I'm afraid of who and what I'd become if I started again, and that fear outweighs the cravings."

"That's not failing me, Willow." I can hear the smile in Auggie's voice, but I can't look at him. I stare at my hands as they fiddle with a string on my blanket. "That's something to be so very proud of. The majority of all addicts fail. The fact that you've gone almost seven weeks and you've came to this fear conclusion is astounding. Jesus, Willow. In the last few months, Revamped is making ten times more than it did when I opened it. The Spook House is starting to look like a real home, and I owe that all to you."

"And I owe you for making me not a loser anymore," I whisper beneath my breath. "Think of the work I'm doing as repayment to you for making me want to better myself."

"Willow," Auggie says sharply, drawing my attention. I look up at him as he prefers. "If you relapse, it's not the end of the world. You work at Revamped, but not to repay me for shit. So get that out of your head. You are not *beholden* to me! I've been paying you for your time, both at Revamped and the house. Instead of managing my bank account, maybe you better manage your own. No matter what I pay you, it'll never be enough recompense. You are not a loser!"

"I was," I whisper, ashamed.

"No, you weren't. You could've *become* a loser," Auggie stresses. "Big difference. I was trying to show you your potential, not make you feel like shit. Obviously I'm not good at it, though."

"You're good at it," I speak up, the reverent Kool-Aid drinker tone is back in my voice.

Auggie laughs, and this time it warms my heart. "I'm glad to be appreciated. Now, why did you run? I could tell it upset you that I brought all those people into *our* home, but I did it for you, Willow. You need the help. You need to relax. You need a break. I was trying to supply those things for you. I get to blow off steam– do the shit that makes me happy. But hell, when was the last time you played a game, or watched television, or just sat and stared off into space? You need to slow down."

"I guess I lost that part of me while I was finding myself." I chuckle, and it sounds slightly manic. "If you ask me what I want to do, I couldn't tell you. But if you ask me what I need to do, I'd say I have to go seal the grout in the downstairs bathroom and strip the paint off the kitchen cabinets, and before bed I better check out Revamped's sales on the website. But if you ask me what I want to do, lately it's what I need to do."

"You'll burn out if you keep going like this, and then you'll relapse. You need to slow down," Auggie orders.

"I know, and I will," I placate. "The Spook House is almost finished– I think."

"It is– finished for *you* –because I'm hiring it done from now on. You go to Revamped and you worry about work. You're not to work here in the evenings unless it's small projects, like decorating or ordering furniture. Willow, this is a demand. It's non-negotiable. You seal that grout, and I'm kicking your sweet ass." Auggie points at me, sounding angry but he's grinning.

"Auggie," I cry out in alarm, shakes starting in. "I need it. I need it to keep me from the cravings."

"Do your school work," Auggie commands. At my look of shock, he grins. "Good Girl, while you're playing in my bank account, I'm playing in yours. When I checked to see if your paycheck cleared, I saw the tuition payment. That was the *I can't tell when you're lying anymore* comment earlier."

"Oh," I mutter, hiding my face. "I didn't tell you because I thought you'd think it was stupid or something... or you'd hate me when I flunked out."

"Too. Hard. On. Yourself," Auggie says slowly. "I want you to be a fuck-up idiot teenager, just not a drunk and high one. That's all. I know I've been mean and nasty lately, and it's confusing you. I apologize."

"Why? Why are you so hot and cold? I can't handle much more of that, Auggie." I tell him the truth that's been plaguing me. I fear Auggie will confuse me so much, I'll have to leave the life I'm building behind. The emotional stress has been worse than the work, and just slightly less stressful than the cravings.

"I'll tell the truth, but only if you assure me you're not keeping anything else from me," Auggie negotiates.

"I'm an open book. Transparent, remember?" I smirk.

"Not as transparent as you used to be," Auggie says, sounding annoyed. "Hot. Cold. I know you aren't for me, Willow. But I want you just the same. I've done some things out of jealousy– things to you. I've done things to push you away, and things to draw you in, and it's all because I'm conflicted. I'm doing my damnedest not to stand in your way of finding your own path, because I know if I asked anything of you, you'd give it to me without a struggle. If I said, *marry me, Willow*, you'd say?"

"Willow the wayward would've said yes in a heartbeat without thinking. The responsible adult Willow would think about it first." I answer truthfully."

"Good," Auggie says with a smile, proud. "But you wouldn't think too long. If I asked tonight, I'm positive I could convince you by morning. A few months from now, you might even say no. That's why I'm giving you space. Hot. Cold. Truth, I think that's why Devon's holding off on showing you how much he wants you. He's not sure if you like him or not, either."

"Why?" I twist out in confusion.

"Why?" Auggie barks a laugh. "Kieren. Fuck, the little douchebag scares me, too. That's why I said *no Kieren*. I didn't want a pregnant and married eighteen-year-old Willow on our hands. I gave you Devon as a friend because I honestly thought you guys could be friends, perhaps friends-with-benefits. You can't have that with Kieren or me."

"Why not?"

"Cut. From. The. Same. Cloth." Auggie enunciates, not sounding too pleased. "I could continue lying and say I didn't tell you that shit about Kieren to push you away from him. He was my competition. If you started dating him, you would've either become that loser I feared, or his wife. Kieren's a man who wants the same thing as me, and I don't want him to have it."

"You don't want me, but no one else can have me, either?" I bite out, sounding betrayed. "So you lied."

"Not lied," Auggie says without remorse, shrugging. "Embellished, perhaps. Does Kieren like you? Yes. Does Kieren want to fuck you? Oh, yes. Would Kieren leave you after the fact? No, fucking way. Do you like Kieren? Yes. Do you want to fuck Kieren? Oh, yes. Would you leave Kieren after? No, good girls stay even when they shouldn't. Would I have been important enough for you to respect and obey if you had a boyfriend almost exactly the same as me? No. Fucking. Way. Especially when I worry over your drug addiction, and Kieren is Devon's enabler. I didn't want Kieren to become your enabler too. Plus, I knew you and Devon would get along and support each other with your problems."

"I'm lost." I cover my face with my palms. "What the fuck is up from down anymore?"

"That's up." Auggie points at the ceiling, teasing me. "Unless you're in the Southern Hemisphere, then it's down."

"Motherfuck," I snarl.

"Exactly," Auggie laughs out. "Life's too short, Willow. Go with the flow, just don't let that flow pump drugs and alcohol into your system."

"What am I supposed to do now?" I stare up at Auggie, feeling more confused than ever. What he just said isn't even computing in my brain.

"Truth, don't fuck me or Kieren." Auggie laughs again, but it has a hysterical edge. "You're not for me. We wouldn't work out. But that doesn't stop me from wanting you, from trying to get you, from trying to keep you. The more you grow up, the more I want you. It's driving me insane. I'm a very highly possessive man."

"Understatement of the year," I say underneath my breath, causing Auggie to chuckle.

"You love me, you respect me, and you obey me because you want me to be proud of you. That's what you need right now. I'm very possessive over that. Kieren won't act like that with you, and you won't act that way with him– you'd be equals." Auggie rolls his eyes at me like that's a horrible thing. "You're not ready to be on your own yet. Either of you. No matter what you think, you need the voice of reason. Kieren has Malcolm, and you have me, as your voice of reason. If you two hooked up..." Auggie makes an explosion noise while gesturing with his hands. "Too young. Idiots."

"And Devon?" I croak out, not knowing what to think anymore.

"Older. Not an idiot. Not looking for a wife. Not a threat to my guidance. Feel free to play with Devon when you finally figure out he wants to fuck you as badly as you want him."

Reaching forward, Auggie tugs my ponytail. "...And Willow, it's okay to want to have sex with people for different reasons. It doesn't make you a bad girl, just a naughty one. But naughty is especially appealing in a good girl."

"You've lost your fucking mind, lunatic." Auggie is eyeing me like prey.

"I told you I've been bad," Auggie says, pretending to pout– manipulative bastard. "Very, *very* bad. You should've listened to Robin. Have I been working my ass off to make you my wife? Subconsciously, I'd say yes, as sick as it sounds. But I'm not good for you, Willow," Auggie warns. "I hope to God that's the one decision you don't allow me to make, because it would be the wrong fucking decision," he says, sounding unbelievably ominous.

"I... um... there's no possible reply to that," I stammer.

"Of course there isn't. I'm finally showing you the version of Augustus Kline that scares you– the predator. Rightfully scared, as you should be. Now, for your own protection and my sick need, Robin had the members of the Playroom move his shit into the Spook House after you ran off this afternoon. He wants to be with you, and as a side bonus, give Isis a kick to the ass.

And since I want Robin to be near me, the bad guy in me is very, very pleased."

"What have I gotten myself into?" I mumble, doubting myself, but not nearly as much as I'm doubting Auggie at the moment.

"So, let me prove how well I know my monster. Robin loves you more than anyone, thought I should preface this thread of conversation with that. With that saying, within five minutes of your departure– the five minutes it took for you to lose me. Pretty sure you were a track star in your past life –you sure can run for a smoker. Anyhoo, Robin was worried, so he narked your ass out by telling me everything you said."

"Of course, Robbie did," I draw out, not entirely too upset. Now I don't have to have this conversation twice.

"The Playroom ban was for both our benefits. It was for several complicated reasons. Reason one: Rush. In order for you to enter the Playroom, you'd have to walk through a club teeming with alcohol and drugs– a club you aren't old enough to enter, I might add. You're working your little heart out, no sense walking into temptation. Reason two: I was uncomfortable with you seeing me in that light. I'm not ashamed of what I want, nor will I stop, but I like you looking at me like I set the moon and stars. Reason three: I've been trying my damnedest not to fuck you for two reasons. See, very complicated." Auggie chuckles.

"I'm too small and I'm gross," I spew out the two reasons.

"Willow, cut that shit out!" Auggie snarls. "Say that again, and it won't be your ass I'm tanning later. I've never hit a woman, but when I hear that shit, I come close to being a woman beater. Got it?"

"I'm sorry, sir," I reply quickly, because Auggie looks close to losing his temper– a temper I've been testing for weeks.

"Yes, you're too small for the poundings I like to give. But I don't want to fuck the shit out of you in front of everyone, and then toss you off me like trash. I don't want to use you to get off, then discard you. I want to make love to you in a bed without witnesses… and that freaks me the hell out. God, Willow. You're wife material, not a whore. You should be treated with more respect than that."

"You think poorly of those women," I mutter in surprise.

"Yes and no," Auggie readily answers, not sounding guilty in the least. "Some of them yes, some of them no. Your girl Bethany isn't desperate– she embraces her needs without shame.

Opal is there because she enjoys the environment. Isis is there because Robin and I are, and she gets to release her aggression. Women like Nina are there because they're desperate to hook you with their bodies instead of their hearts. They don't realize a warm and willing cunt doesn't make a man take you as his wife– that makes you a perfect candidate as a mistress. My future wife will be someone I cherish with all my heart, but they will have to deal with the fact that I'll still hunt. I know you can't deal with that because you deserve more."

"Fuck," I say with feeling, the truth finally sinking in. "Yeah, I love you, Auggie. But no," I mutter emphatically while shaking my head no, over and over.

"Good Girl." Auggie praises, sounding disappointed yet happy. "That's why I'm avoiding sex with you. Good girls think sex means love and commitment. Even bad girls like Nina think this, and they use their bodies to get it. Hell, all girls think it, no matter how *enlightened* they believe themselves to be. It's written in your genetics. So if you aren't at the Playroom looking at me like I'm the only thing you see, then I can avoid sex with you. Later is going to be difficult enough."

"Later?" My eyebrows scrunch in confusion.

"You'll find out soon enough," Auggie purrs in anticipation. "I also don't know if the Playroom is the right fit for you. You really are a good girl. A one-man kind of woman. I think sharing and swapping would confuse you and make you feel badly about yourself. I think your insecurities mean you aren't ready, and that isn't a dig. We're all different. Hell, I'm a freak, you're just normal– normal is a good thing."

"I–"

"Don't deny it." Auggie stops me before I can get a word out. "So when the Playroom is up in the attic, you can join us if you wish. But beware, I doubt your psyche can take it." Almost in challenge, daring me to join in and prove him right or wrong.

"Can I just watch, and figure it out from there?" I negotiate.

"Watch away," Auggie allows. "You just might not like what you see... So back to Devon–"

"Did you start taking crack without me?" I tease Auggie about his abrupt shift in conversation. "Why are you being so forthcoming?"

Ignoring me, as always, he talks right over me without answering my question. "I want you to do the things I didn't get to do. Willow, I don't want you to have the same regrets I have lived with every day of my life."

"What regrets?" I'm starved for Auggie to tell me his secrets. He never talks about himself. He always worries about us first, and any glimpse into Auggie's depths is addictive.

"I've never had a girlfriend. I'm messed up somehow inside." Auggie taps his temple, and then the center of his chest, directly over his heart. "I don't see sex and intimacy as the same thing. The fact that you do is a good thing. My friendships provide that aspect for me. I see it as separate– friendship versus sex. Sometimes I mix the two together, but not in years… not since... I would love to get married and have kids someday, but what wife would put up with the fact that I don't see sex as cheating?"

"Wow," I breathe as every emotion inundates me at once.

"Yeah, wow… I realized a few weeks ago, I was pulling a *John Mason*. Well, I didn't exactly realize it until Malcolm, Robin, and Isis ganged up on me."

"A *John Mason*?"

"Yeah, Malcolm's father picked girls he could manipulate and control, and he taught Malcolm and me do to the same. Malcolm went the opposite direction, but it seems I'm holding latent tendencies. I feel ashamed of myself. I can't in good conscience take a young woman and twist her into something that fits me. I wouldn't respect her if she allowed it. I can't squelch another human being's freewill like that… and Willow, make no mistakes, I've been systematically doing that to you all along. No doubt it's benefitted your potential, but it doesn't make it right, and it doesn't take my shame away."

"Hot and cold?" I ask, realizing that's why Auggie's been acting bipolar for weeks. I want to feel hurt, but I don't. I finally understand. I think.

"Hot," Auggie purrs, eyes latching onto mine and not releasing me from their capture. "Very, *very* hot tonight. I didn't go to the Playroom because of you. I was worried about you– petrified, actually. You acted irresponsibly, so you have a punishment coming. It's *later* now."

"Punishment?" I swallow thickly. "What the hell did I do wrong now? I thought we were talking it out like adults?"

"Punishment? Fun? Release? Whatever you want to call it, you fucking need it. I *need* it," Auggie stresses. "Now!" he growls in warning as he lurches off the bed like a puma to pin me to the floor.

Lying on top of my body, heavy weight pinning me, Auggie grinds his beastly erection into my ass. The Beast is a threat of what's to come, and damned if I don't want to be the one coming. Auggie purrs in my ear– literally purrs, the sound reverberating down my spine. I freeze, heart pounding in my chest, sweat beading my skin. I don't want this. But, do I ever need this.

"Ground rules: I can't penetrate you– I just can't. I'd end up making love to you in this bed. Making love equals love, and I won't go into commitment territory with you. We're going to have some fun. Rule two: I don't want you feeling upset, so I'll only touch you like this tonight. I know you're not dating Devon, but it'll make you feel guilty just the same. So at the first sign you think there's more between you and another man, I'll back off. I respect you, and I assumed you and Devon were a couple, so I backed off. I'm not backing off tonight. Punishment time!"

Trapped beneath a panting Auggie, I gasp. "What'd I do?" My voice quivers with trepidation. "I thought we didn't play around." I use as a defense, knowing if Auggie asked me to touch him, allowed me to touch him, I'd say yes because I could do nothing less.

Curling over my back, pressing me into the floor, Auggie whispers menacingly into my ear. "The better question would be, *sir, what haven't I done? The answer would be, I'm a good girl gone naughty. Which happens to be what turns Mr. Kline on the most." Twisting the words as if he's speaking like a girl, Auggie taunts me. Beyond disturbing.

Crawling off me, Auggie gets on my bed, leaving me to breathe deeply once his weight is gone. I stifle a gasp when his hands close around my arms, fingers curling under my armpits. With a jarring yank, I'm thrust from the floor to the bed. Tossing me to the center, Auggie sits on my shins and smiles down at me, green eyes dancing with hedonistic delight. My heart pounds, anticipation curls in my belly to pool in my cunt, and adrenaline courses through my veins.

I don't know if I'm ready for a man like Augustus Kline, but I'm about to find out. Willow the wayward was reckless. The new and improved Willow is cautious, and Auggie scares the shit out of her, which brings a part of that reckless girl to the fore. She– *me* –wants to play with Auggie, longs to play with him.

Laughing, I taunt. "Let's see what ya got, boss man. Bring it!"

"Ohhh… I've created a monster." Auggie purrs, pride infusing his voice. "You're the mini-boss now." Chuckling that deep manly laugh that warms me inside and out, Auggie looks like the man I know and love and trust and respect. "I'm giving you an out," he says, sobering.

"An out?" I mutter, confused. I reach back to tuck my pillow beneath my head. I know Auggie could devour me if he wished, but I trust him enough to know he won't. I feel completely at ease in his presence– and highly aroused. Auggie's giving me what I need to let the stress of the past few weeks melt away, the insecurity and shame. Knowing Auggie wants to do this for me, it makes me feel more secure and sure of myself.

"I'm just letting you know you have the right to tell me no." Flashing a killer smirk, I know Auggie is going to say something that will be my undoing. "But you never will," he sings. "You're mine to savor for however little time we have left."

"You know me well, Mr. Kline." Auggie beams, because he can hear the smile in my voice. "But, I'm giving you an out as well. You don't have to do this because you want to take care of my needs, Auggie. Only do it if you really want me. I can't handle feeling more like an obligation than I already do."

That fuzzy red eyebrow pops up like a turkey timer. "Obligation? That implies I'm not getting anything out of this, and I assure you that I'm getting more out of our… relationship? Err… no, not relationship– partnership?" Auggie looks satisfied with his word choice. "I'm getting more out of this partnership. I get the satisfaction in knowing I helped create my own personal Willow Monster. So… circle yes or no if you like me." Auggie chuckles, pulling a joke from elementary school's past. "Yes or no, Willow? Play or no play?"

"Yes, please. As long as you don't wreck me," I readily reply, trying for nonchalance but failing. My voice cracks on *wreck me*.

"Wreck?" Eyebrow again– smirking like the devil he is. "If I break my toys, I can't play with them anymore. Now that would just be silly." Auggie teases in a childish voice.

"Do your worst;" I challenge.

My words have Auggie's playful demeanor evaporating in an instant, and it its place is Mr. Kline, the man who accepts nothing short of total obedience. Auggie yanks a ruler from his back pocket and waves it in front of my face.

His voice is deeper than I've ever heard, a twisted version of Auggie's sex god voice but with added menace. "What do you do when you need to talk, need advice, or feel insecure? You should seek out someone you trust– family or a mentor. But not my monster. No, my Willow Monster runs like a coward, like a bratty child."

I yelp out in a combination of pain and shock when Auggie brutally smacks the sole of my bare foot with the ruler. The sting radiates from the arch of my foot, up through my toes, and into my shin. I hiss out a sharp sound of pain from between clenched teeth. It doesn't make me angry as I expected. I know I need this to release the pain, the shame, the insecurity. I need to let go, and Auggie is giving me what I need while teaching me a valuable lesson I'll never forget.

"Willow, what happens when you make shitty choices, such as running out into the freezing night with no destination in mind?" Auggie grips my ankle tightly in his palm and swiftly smacks me three times. Tears roll down my face, but I don't cry out. I deserve this. I already knew I was being stupid. I need to be punished for it so I can move forward and grow as a human being.

"The ruler is to remind you of your measure and the rules. Your feet are being punished because you *ran* from the comforting embrace of those who are here to help you– me, Rob, and Devon. You should've ran to Clover. We are your community. Your support system. Seek us out. It makes us feel as worthless as you feel on the inside when you don't let us do our job."

"Shit!" I gasp with feeling. "You're right. You're always right. I apologize."

Ignoring my outburst, Auggie continues on with his lecture. "You're not alone, Willow. You are loved and wanted by those who cherish you– flaws and all. Let us do our jobs."

"I'll try," I cry out, hating how Auggie's lessons are always emotionally difficult. While I may feel better later, he makes me feel worse first. Guilt. Shame. Pain. If life was sunshine and rainbows, then ignorance wouldn't be bliss. But reality is harsh, and ignorance gets you hurt.

"I will never judge you, Willow. You can come to me for anything and everything. I may not enjoy what you have to tell me, but trust me enough to understand you. Your feet will remind you of this important lesson for days to come. Never forget it."

Latex gloves materialize from Auggie's back pocket. As he puts the gloves on, they make an ominous snapping sound that has me flinching and Auggie smirking. I wonder where Auggie found gloves that large for his huge hands. A second later, I realize I should be worrying about why he's putting gloves on in the first place.

"Umm... Auggie? Why?" I stammer as I begin to struggle– self-preservation winning out over my unfaltering trust in Augustus Kline. Latex-clad fingers bracelet my wrists, stilling me.

"Well..." he draws out while that eyebrow hitches menacingly. "Since you'd rather freeze in the elements instead of facing your demons, and without thought of the consequence, I think this will remind you to make the wise decision next time."

Materializing as if out of the ether, Auggie squirts something into the palm of his gloved hand. He squeezes the tube until it is empty. Tossing the tube over his shoulder, it clatters to my bedroom floor. I moan in bliss as Auggie massages the cream onto my feet, fingertips digging into all the achy spots. I've never had my feet rubbed before, and now I'm going to want it all the time. I groan, and then flex my toes, hoping he will continue. Auggie switches feet and smiles sweetly at me.

"This feels really good, doesn't it?" Auggie murmurs, sounding dreamy. His demeanor changes from soft and affectionate to calculated and brutal. "Wait... for it," he threatens.

Suddenly, one foot is icy-cold while the foot he's rubbing blazes with licks of fire. Each press of his fingertips drives the burn deeper. I whimper and whine and writhe on my bed. He smiles down at me knowingly, arrogance and retribution shining from his eyes.

"You're mean," I whimper.

"No, I'm teaching you a lesson you need to learn. You made me worry– you made *Robin* worry. No one is allowed to do that but me. You made me wait for you, and Augustus Kline waits for no man or woman. Worry and wait, I couldn't go to work at Rush and I couldn't vent my frustration at the Playroom. All of that is your fault, Willow. What am I, Monster?"

"You're Mr. Kline," I respond immediately.

"And what is Mr. Kline to you, Monster?" Auggie prompts.

"My master," I respond reverently, but silently add *right now*. Once this lesson is learned, we'll be back to boss and minion.

"And what do masters do, Monster?" Auggie prompts me again.

"They punish you when you're bad." I whimper as the hot and cold intensifies, simultaneously burning and freezing my feet.

"No." Auggie shakes his head. "Master– or mentor rather. They inspire. They teach. They comfort and love. They are the security blanket of their pet. They punish to drive the lesson home, to remove your guilt so you may move on and grow. What is a master to their pet, my good girl?"

"You're my world," I say without hesitation. Auggie's blazing smile pushes the shadows from the room.

"And you're mine. I'm a lucky bastard to have my best friend and the girl I'm growing to love as a woman depend on me, need me– it's the currency of a man. What would I be without people who count on me? No man is as blessed as I am."

Abruptly, Auggie drops all of his weight on top of me, forcing the air from my lungs and my lips to part. With a sharp protest, Auggie feasts at my mouth. His lips latch onto mine and demand a response. His body engulfs mine, takes me over until all I know is him. Finally responding, I swear underneath my breath when I can't wrap my legs around his back to draw him closer to me.

"Big motherfucker," I murmur affectionately.

"Toddler," he replies, chuckling. Auggie growls when I sneak a toe underneath his t-shirt and rub that heinous cream on his bare skin.

"Oh, how I'd love to bury the Beast deep inside you and come," Auggie breathes into my ear, causing me to shiver and squirm. "But that's against the rules... and you're not finished with your punishment yet." Auggie shoves off me to kneel on the bed. He gazes down at me in amusement, content and happy.

"What the hell is this shit?" I complain. I try to rub my feet on my blankets, but Auggie stops me with a stern look.

"Does it remind you of *Hot Damn*? When you down a shot it's *icy* and *hot*." I'd love a fucking shot of hooch to douse this fire. The bastard is giving me a double punishment– using the cold fire to inflame my feet while igniting my cravings.

Auggie's words finally click. "Icy Hot?!" I shout in outrage. "You sick bastard! How did you make one foot burn and the other freeze?" Auggie laughs at me as he picks my cold foot up and starts to rub. It inflames instantly.

"Oh," I groan. "Oh, God, please... no more, Auggie. It's torture!"

"You're going to sound like a bleating animal in a minute," Auggie threatens, flashing me a sinister smirk. He yanks off a glove and pulls something from his back pocket.

"What the fuck?' I grunt out in awe. "You got a backpack in your pocket, or some shit?" Auggie snickers at me and swats my foot with the ruler. I yelp when the fire intensifies with the thwack.

"That's sounds like a disrespectful brat to me, Monster. You're being punished right now, remember?"

"Sir, I apologize. But I can't even fit my cellphone in my back pocket, so how the hell are you pulling all this stuff out?" I try to sound rational as my feet throb and pulse with my heartbeat.

Auggie arches that dang eyebrow again. "Big ass..." he pauses for effect. "Equals big pockets."

I snort and it turns to manic giggles of hysteria. It's taking all of my obedience not to run from my bedroom and wash my feet in a bucket of dish soap.

Auggie snaps the other glove off and tosses the pair to the floor. "Open wide until I can see your pretty, pink tonsils," he orders mischievously. His green eyes twinkle at the expression of horror that crosses my face. I open like a good girl should, and close my eyes, awaiting my fate. Hard plastic knocks against my front teeth, causing me to wince. Whatever it is, the object is room temperature. I gag when my tonsils get nudged.

Eyes clenched shut, I shudder when Auggie speaks. "Slobber up your new buddy... make it nice and wet," he coaxes in a lust-filled voice. "This vibrator is your new best friend. I want you to use this to masturbate. It's not much smaller than a normal guy. You'll love it, Monster." Auggie's voice drops to that of the sex god. "That's a good girl," he croons as he slides the vibrator in and out of my mouth, showing me just how a guy likes his cock sucked. "I want you to do this twice a day. Practice before you get yourself off. We can't have you in the Playroom with poor oral skills, now can we?" The teasing lilt in his voice is at odds with the erection he's rocking against my thigh.

The instruction is taking away from the enjoyment I'm feeling. I want to concentrate on the feel of Auggie rubbing the Beast against my leg and the pressurized ball of heat building in my lower belly, but I can't with a vibrator shoved halfway down my throat. Puts an entirely new spin on the term blow *job*. But this is Auggie, and everything and anything he does with me, or to me, is with a purpose. He's not here to get me off, or seek his own release– he's giving me his valuable wisdom by teaching me what a real man wants.

"Ack!" I cough and gag, sputtering around the invasion as my tongue tries to push it out of my mouth. Every inch of the vibrator I push out, Auggie pushes back in twice as far.

"Breathe through it and relax," Auggie purrs hypnotically. "You can do it... Ah, now that's a good girl..." I melt into the mattress and allow him to fuck my mouth with a vibrator. His loud panting spurs me on, has my legs scissoring on the mattress as I suck off a hard plastic cock.

"What?" I slur drowsily when Auggie pulls the new toy from my mouth, spit trailing from my bottom lip to the plastic in his hand. I lift my heavy lids to witness a half-crazed Augustus Kline. He's staring at my mouth with his hanging wide open. I lick my lips to see if it has an effect on him.

"Behave, Willow," he groans. "You know exactly what you're doing to me, you naughty girl. You wouldn't want to witness what happens when I lose control."

With eager fingers, my pajama bottoms and panties are pulled down my legs and placed next to us on the bedding. Not feeling any insecurity, shame, or bashfulness, my trust in Auggie allows me to part my legs in invitation, exposing the core of my sex. Auggie's gasp of shock has pride filling my soul.

Heart pounding out of my chest, I get excited. Is Auggie going to make love to me? I know he said it was against the rules, but maybe this will push him over the edge. I'm not worried about turning into a possessive psycho-bitch if he penetrates me. I just want one time of having real sex with Augustus Kline in my lifetime. I have a feeling it's an experience on many a Fairport girl's bucket list.

"Auggie!" I cry out as the vibrator, slick with my spit, slides deep inside me with one well-practiced thrust of his hand. A taunting laugh flows around the room, echoing back to my ears. The stretched feeling of fullness after being long-denied is addictive. I'm lost in the moment. I shudder in bliss, amazed at the new sensation.

"Hmm…" Auggie licks his full lips salaciously. "This fits nicely," he purrs. "Very, very nicely. You'll enjoy a normal-sized cock without any issue."

"OH! Ahhh…" I yelp as the vibrator whirls to life. Vibrations radiate throughout my pussy, up into my womb, and ignite licks of pleasure along my spine. I wiggle on the bed, not knowing if I love the sensation or find it uncomfortable. Lost, fading, feeling high, I don't protest as Auggie pulls my panties and pajamas pants back into place. I rub all over the bed in need. My feet are icy cold, but my pussy is on fire.

"Don't let it slip out," Auggie warns, sounding highly amused. He gives a playful pat to my crotch while chuckles rumble from deep within his chest.

"No!" I protest as Auggie rubs my left foot until the burn returns with a vengeance. I can't concentrate on one thing: the burn from my foot, the cold from the other foot, and the buzzing vibration causing my sensitive flesh to well and weep.

"Look at me, Willow," Auggie commands. I flick my gaze to his, knowing how much he loves to have my undivided attention. Smiling down at me, all I see is Auggie's pride in me radiate from his eyes.

Hand slicing through the air, I have no time to prepare myself. I suck in a deep breath before the ruler thwacks my icy foot. I barely hold the pitiful sound building in my throat. He promised I'd bleat like an animal. Mr. Kline always keeps his promises. Mr. Kline is always right. Obey Mr. Kline in all things.

Jesus, Willow, don't be a fucking idiot– always do as Mr. Kline says, or suffer the consequences. What the fuck is wrong with my brother that this agony gets him off?

The ruler pushes the cold away and replaces it with the fiery lick of flame. It's the strangest sensation, the fire surrounded by ice. Hot and cold, just like Augustus Kline. How Auggie deals with his emotions, feeling as my feet do, is baffling in the extreme. This lesson gives me more insight into the man.

I fall into Auggie's green eyes and I'm captured, caged. My body is his for however long our eyes connect us as one. I give, he takes. He gives, I take. It's an endless cycle that is inescapable. Hit after hit with the ruler to the soles of my feet, I sustain the agony without crying out. The pressure mounts inside my womb and sparks down my spine, before it radiates throughout my entire body. I bite my lip to stop all sound. I'll prove Mr. Kline a liar– I will *not* bleat for him.

"Let go, Willow," Auggie coaxes, begs. His upper lip is beaded with sweat. Auggie's t-shirt is molded to the wide, perfect expanse of his chest. Auggie's working for it. He's working me. He's earning the right to hear me cry out in exquisite pain.

My fingertips flex on the sheets as I bite back a moan of pure pleasure. Every hit shoots pulses of electrical current directly into my pussy. I clench violently around the waning vibrator.

"Jesus!" I shout, head kicking back into my pillow as I writhe about. "What the fuck is wrong with me and Robbie?" Another smack to my heel and I barely hold back my climax.

"Robin taught me what he wanted, and I taught him how to take it. You should thank Rob for my expertise in this area of punishment," sounding deadpanned, Auggie winks at me. "I figured what works for him would work for you."

"I thought Robbie was a freak for being a pain slut." I groan when Auggie lashes me three times in quick succession. "Let's not talk of Robin– that's too nasty for this good girl."

Throwing his head back, Auggie releases a deep laugh that has a bigger effect on me than the vibrator thrust inside my cunt. "Willow, you're not a pain slut yet, and I'm pretty sure you never will be. You're being stubborn, making me earn your release. Jesus, you make me respect the hell out of you.

"Respect– who would've thought that?" I cry out, desperation thick in my tone.

"Yes, who would've ever guessed that?" Auggie muses to himself, sounding confused as usual. "Don't be stubborn by fighting me on this, Willow. I can't do this much longer without really hurting you. Let go and come for me, be a good girl," Auggie commands in his lulling sex god voice.

"Anything for you." I moan, and then I finally let go. I writhe as the force of my release screams from my body. It doesn't flow through me. It's wrenched from my core. Torn. I held it in too long, and now I'm suffering the consequences– another painful lesson learned.

I sob, whimper, and keen as my body seizes, muscles tightening and releasing in jarring jerks. I find no pleasure in my climax, only the release of pressure. My stress flows from my body via the scream from my throat and the wash of moisture from my cunt. The last sound I make before I bonelessly collapse to the mattress is the bleat of an injured animal. I didn't prove Mr. Kline a liar, and I hope I never do.

"Thank you." I whimper as Auggie pulls the now dead vibrator from my body. He rubs my tummy in soothing circles as tears dry on my cheeks.

"Pay close attention, Willow," Auggie commands as he pulls away to kneel next to me. "This is how I like to be touched," is said gravelly deep. His lust and need is so tangible, I can almost see it wafting in the air.

Auggie's palm strokes the vibrator, getting my sticky wetness all over his hand. His clean hand pops the buttons on his fly until the Beast is released, flopping out to bob before my very eyes. An expletive pops out my mouth when the sticky hand covered in my juices wraps around that thick, veiny length, and strokes.

Auggie bites his bottom lip, and then smiles down at me. His forearm muscles flex with every stroke. Long, smooth movement from the bottom of the Beast to the tip, where he twists around the flared, ruddy head. I lick my lips as I watch. It makes me feel incredible to know Auggie's using the lubrication released from my body to slick himself to pleasure.

"Fuck!" Auggie groans, arching his neck and closing his eyes as his hand picks up a brutal rhythm. The sound of flesh on flesh has my thighs clenching together as a new ache builds. While the pressure had been released, I'm not satisfied. "You make me insane, Willow. I don't normally pop so fast."

I know Auggie's going to shoot the second his free hand wraps around his ball sac. I lunge forward and latch my lips around the thick plum of his cockhead before he can stop me. I shove half of his cock down my throat. Stretched, choking, too large of an invasion, my body instinctively knows what to do after Auggie showed me with the vibrator. As soon as I swallow the cockhead past my tonsils, Auggie shouts my name and spurts hot streams of bitter, thick cum down my throat.

"Willow," Auggie groans my name as his fingers twist in my hair. My eyes bulge when he pushes farther down my throat. I breathe in and out though my nose, allowing him to take my face as he did the beauty kneeling at his feet in the Playroom. It doesn't demean me. If anything, I feel empowered by the knowledge that I'm giving Auggie immense pleasure. He floods my mouth with scalding fluid, and I either have to swallow it, or choke on it. Some of it spills from my lips and dampens my t-shirt.

Auggie collapses on his heels, losing all strength to stay upright. "I didn't hurt you, did I?" He sounds concerned with an expression of worry marring his face. He yanks his t-shirt over his head and wipes my mouth with it, dabbing away the evidence of his release.

"All's good," I slur out as I lick my numb, overworked lips. I dab the spots on my t-shirt with his, and then I crawl underneath my blankets, exhaustion closing in around the edges of my vision.

"No need to practice your oral skills, Monster. That was wicked, truly wicked. You almost took all of me," Auggie says in awe, eyes popping from his skull in shock. "Holy fuck, Willow!"

"Clover always said I had a big, nasty mouth. I guess this is proof." I smile up at Auggie as I curl around my pillow, snuggling.

"I like your dirty, cocksucking mouth. I plan on making it even dirtier someday." Auggie teases while reaching down to tuck the blankets under my chin. "Have you sucked his cock yet?"

"Auggie, don't!" I scowl up at him, then duck underneath the covers. "Don't ruin our moment," I grumble, sounding muted from the blankets.

"I'll take that as a no, then. Willow, I'm not ruining the moment. I want you to suck Devon off. I want to watch his face when you do it," Auggie utters eagerly. "You can't fake how you loved watching me fuck Bethany. It's exciting to see how the people in your life behave in such circumstances. It's fascinating."

"You know Devon isn't my boyfriend," I whisper from beneath my blankets. "We're just friends. I haven't touched him, kissed him, fucked or sucked him. I thought you believed me when I told you this earlier."

"Uh-huh," Auggie drawls in disbelief. "I believed you. I just think Devon's a moron for waiting for you to initiate. Pussy move on his part."

"Devon doesn't want me that way, Auggie," I snarl. "Drop the subject. It's like twisting the knife in deeper. I want to make you proud by doing as you wish, but I'm not going to force the guy to touch me. You made me feel wanted a few minutes ago, now you're shoving how Devon doesn't want me into my face and grinding the bastard right in."

"This is about Tina again, isn't? I told you she isn't Devon's girlfriend. Trust me," he demands, upset that I'm not feeling, doing, saying, and acting as he wishes. Augustus Kline is trying to form me in his image– his mini-beast or mini-boss. But I'll always be Willow. I own my actions, reactions, and emotions.

Yanking the blanket from my face, I glare up at Auggie, pissed that he won't drop it. Furious over how he ruined something that should've been a release of the stress, not leading to an even more stressful conversation. I just wanted to drift off to sleep, body filled with need but not sated, with my mind filled with pride.

"You don't know everything, Mr. Kline." I try to hammer home how he's not omniscient. "I saw them kiss, and Tina admitted they've been together. She was pissed at me because of Devon."

Auggie fists the sheet and growls, "Bull-fucking-shit! Tina is *not* Devon's girlfriend," he fiercely bites out. "Tina has fucked Kieren, but never Devon."

"You don't know everything," I repeat, feeling deflated in the face of such anger– Auggie is radiating pure, unadulterated fury.

"In this, I know it all," Auggie says, not sounding arrogant in the least. "Trust me when I say I know what I need to know about this subject. A kiss is just a kiss, but I know for a fact that that kid is still a virgin."

"I get how you and Malcolm are stepbrothers in a way, but no kid tells their father or uncle everything."

"No, they don't, but I have other ways," Auggie says, sounding insane. "I can guarantee Tina isn't Devon's girlfriend, fuck buddy, or even a friend. I hope to God she isn't anything else to him, either. But I know the shit Tina deals in, and it's much stronger than you could ever fathom. So stay the fuck away from Tina, Willow! I mean it!"

Auggie's entire demeanor changed when I brought up Tina. His jaw clenched, his teeth gnashed together, and his hands fisted at his sides. I can feel the fury and disappointment eating him.

"I'll stay away from Tina. I didn't like the skank at all," I growl, and Auggie flinches like I sucker-punched him. I give him an inquisitive look, and he shakes his head no.

"Trust me. Tina isn't Devon's girlfriend," Auggie snaps sharply. "So get those stupid-ass thoughts outta your head."

"It's irrelevant since Devon only sees me as a friend," I mumble in defeat.

"We'll see," Auggie threatens, a calculating glint shining from his eyes.

"Don't you dare force Devon to do anything!" I cry out as I pull free of my blankets. I get in Auggie's face and hiss, "Don't go to him and say a fucking word, Auggie! Devon's my friend, and I don't want him to be uncomfortable." I yank the two hundred pound man to the bed, lean over his chest, and growl directly into his face.

Auggie laughs up at me, looking delighted that I just flung him around and attacked his ass. He pulls me to his chest, arms wrapping around my back like a prison made of flesh and bone. "I don't force anyone. Ever. Sure, I'll take you past your comfort zone. Devon's just being a pussy, and needs to be prodded."

"No prodding. If Devon starts acting differently around me, I'll blame you and not trust it. Don't you get that? I want to trust whether or not Devon wants me for me, not because Augustus Kline demand it of him. So drop it."

"Dropped– for now." Auggie cuddles us together and sighs. "Sleepy time for the good girl."

I close my eyes, but I don't fall asleep. In this, I do not trust Augustus Kline.

CHAPTER THIRTY-ONE

What did I get myself into? I spent twelve years caged within Fairport Area School District– walking the halls like a prisoner awaiting release. So why the hell would I subject myself to FCC? FCC, otherwise known as Fairport Community College. Or as I decided to call it, Fairport Correctional's Cage.

In elementary school, the teachers thought I was cute and tiny, protectable. In middle school, the students thought I was tiny and the teachers no longer protected me. By junior high, I was playing in senior high, so I was invisible to the teachers and my fellow classmates. By senior high, my *friends* had graduated, so I was still invisible to those I never bonded with or made as friends.

I coasted my entire school career. I didn't apply myself. I did my homework for the following class during my current one and so on. I never, ever did a lick of homework outside of a school room. I never studied for a test. Basically, I just didn't give a flying fuck about anything. I'd love to say my loser attitude was obvious in my grades, but somehow– divine intervention, perhaps –I pulled all *A*s and *B*s and the occasional *C*. Never in my life did I fail a test.

I was that loser Auggie called me. This Willow, the current Willow, if she could go back in time and apply herself, we would've been on the honor roll every nine weeks. It's unfathomable, how I didn't give a shit and now I do. I wish someone would've strangled me– *made* me work harder. If I was pulling above average without trying, what could I have done when I tried?

… And now I'll never find out without a time machine.

I've been scared shitless for the past few weeks, awaiting this evening. My nerves were frayed and I was getting no sleep. I never wanted to get burnt more in my entire life. The sweet relief that only the nerve-deadening smoke could provide. I was at the point where I'd do just about anything to relax, so I could breathe deeply. The cravings were debilitating, but I persevered and stayed clean… and here I am at Fairport Community College.

I was scared of the college life. College is portrayed in a different light on television. We see huge lecture halls packed with hundreds of students and one scary looking professor commanding his students like troops for battle. We see the frat house parties and the stupid sorority girls getting used and abused from their own negligence. In my head, I have guys that look and act just like Kieren Mason playing the role of the frat boy, and girls like Essie playing the role of sorority bimbo.

I guess you only get that experience if you apply yourself and end up at a university– thank fuck!

But this is community college, in Fairport no less. Continuing education, they call it. While you can get an associates or bachelor's degree in a billion and one fields, the main reason anyone comes here is because their boss demanded it– *go get smarter, or you're fired!*

I'm not judging. I'm not here for a degree either. I may get one if I keep finding courses that pique my interests, but it's not my main objective. I just want to do better at my job, just like every other person sitting in this room.

I feel short-changed, though. All that fear and anxiety over nothing. They need to call Fairport Community College the *thirteenth grade*. I feel like I exited senior year last June and entered another year the following January.

I'm disappointed.

Standing at the threshold into hell, I find thirty-some desks in tidy rows with a lady standing at the front of the room for my *Intro to Website Development* course. I came here expecting to find professors, and lecture halls, and difficult subject matter, and I find… comfort in the familiarity.

Gazing around the half-filled class of less than twenty students, I try to see where I'd best fit for the next ninety minutes of my life. Everyone seems to be in the Generation X era, with a few Baby Boomers. Daytime classes must be for my generation. I see one of my fellow Millennials and breathe a deep sigh of relief.

Nerves, those pesky shits are attacking me again. I slide into my seat without looking at the guy I'm joining. Shakes, the movement always starts in my lips for some odd reason, and then it travels to my fingertips. For once it's not the addict that's clamoring. I'm just nervous of the unknown. I busy myself with yanking the course-required materials from my bag.

"Weeping Willow," a smoky voice says, startling me.

"Jesus, your voice is like an ear-gasm," spills out before the filter to my brain catches up with my mouth. "Shit!" I hiss. "Sorry, you should sing or something." Embarrassed– mortified –I can't look at my companion as he laughs that devastating *man* laugh that's always a punch to the cunt.

"Hey, how do you know my name?" I demand as I flip around to stare at the guy. Gobsmacked. I notice the mop of dark hair covering his face before anything else. Hair that would look feminine on anyone else seems to suit this guy perfectly. I just want to fist a hank and reveal his eyes.

"You don't remember me, I take it?" He chuckles. Doing a practiced move of his neck, he flings that hair and reveals the prettiest eyes I've ever seen– lavender. I didn't know eyes came in that shade, but this boy has them.

"Nah, I think I'd remember you," I drawl out. "God, you're too pretty to be at FCC."

Snorting, smirking, a dimple indents one cheek– just one. "Ah, you were too *stoned* to notice." Chuckling to himself, he says, "I made a funny. I'm Langdon *Stone*, and you are most definitely Willow Prynne. Mason's girl. We graduated together."

"Mason's girl? I guess," I mumble, wondering how many people know about my fictitious relationship with Devon.

"I can't say I'm not surprised. He talks about you incessantly, even carries a picture of you in his wallet." Smiling like a huge romantic, Langdon says, "It's really sweet. 'Bout time, too."

Confused beyond belief, I go with what I do know. "I don't remember you."

"I transferred to Fairport mid-semester of junior year. You were a bit out of it. Your eyes were only clear once in a while, and only for one reason," he says cryptically. Instead of trying to figure out what he meant by that, I get embarrassed that I was fried my entire high school career.

"I'm clean now," I mumble, not feeling pride over being clean when it means I have to admit to being a fuck-up in the first place. I don't go around screaming *I'm clean!* because I don't want pats on the back for fixing what *I* broke, especially when most people manage to stay in one piece. I feel like I should pat the backs of everyone who never did a drug– they deserve it. I deserve a kick to the teeth for being a fucking moron to begin with.

"I know." He tosses me a grin, eyes crinkling at the corners. "Mason tells me every day how proud of you he is. Like a broken record." Chuckling to himself, he arranges his hair with his fingertips– boy has great hair and he knows it.

Leaning into me, Langdon whispers conspiratorially. "I do sing. A relative of mine is kinda famous in these parts. But no one knows it, 'cuz I grew up in Washington State with my mom. I moved out east when my dad got sick. So… that's my story. No need to tell me yours, Weeping Willow. I know more about you than I do myself. Broken record, that is our Mason."

"I…" Speechless, I make a funny sound in the back of my throat. "Alright, you started it. Ante up the famous relative," I demand, earning myself another *man* laugh.

"Not on your life, girly." Langdon flashes me a charming grin that reminds me of someone, but I can't put a finger on it. "So I'm guessing you're here for the same reason I am– Lady Mason sent me."

"Huh?" I grunt in confusion. "Lady Mason?"

"Isis Mason," Langdon readily replies. "I only know two female Masons: Lady Mason and teacup Isis."

"Ah… those girls are something else," I trail off.

"Aren't they, though?" Langdon murmurs, voice filled with affection and appreciation. "When my dad got really sick, I took over the business end of things. That's why I moved here– Pop wanted me to have the shitty Stone legacy of a broken down business. Instead of staying in Washington and going Indie, I did the right thing and came home to Pop. I needed some direction since I found out he didn't know what the hell he was doing, either. I asked Mason since he's from around here. He said Isis came to FCC for help managing Rush."

"Wow, you're a talker," I blurt out, surprised that I found a cute companion who likes to chat. A *guy* who likes to chat? "I guess I did come here for the same reason, then."

"So… Augustus Kline likes his women to take care of his businesses. He likes to draw in his little room and make you girls do all the dirty work."

"You know Auggie?" Surprise is thick in my voice. This chatty dude sure knows a lot of everyone's business.

"Know *of* Auggie," Langdon stresses. "Women are disposable toys– all except Isis Mason, and from what I hear from Mason, you as well. That's why you're here, isn't it? Isis came to FCC to become a better manager of Rush, and you're here for Revamped?"

Blushing, I mutter, "I guess so. Auggie didn't send me, or anything. I took it upon myself. He's… an interesting man."

"A man Mason would kill in a heartbeat." Langdon looks me over, like he might want to help plan the murder. "All's good, though. I'm glad you're here with me. Mason's gonna lose his shit when he finds out."

"Indie?" I pull from the conversation, needing to avoid anything Mason or Auggie related.

"Keep up! The ear-gasmic voice, girly… Indie Rock. Famous relative, remember?" One lavender eye winks at me, and I know in a heartbeat he has a killer voice on stage– the charisma is just oozing out of Langdon's pores. "So, instead of that gig, I'm crunching numbers in a filthy office and trying to keep my dad's shit together. But that's what it means to be a man."

"Responsibility," I say while nodding my head in agreement. "I get it."

"I know you do." Dimple indenting his cheek, Langdon flips his hair again. "Broken record, remember?"

"Welcome to Intro to Website Development," the instructor squawks, and I'm instantly taken back seven months to my senior year.

CHAPTER THIRTY-TWO

Late March. Month four into the renovation of Willow the wayward. The former pothead, closeted-alcoholic is now in recovery, whatever that means, seeing how it's an uphill battle on a minute to minute basis to stay sober. My changes aren't obvious on the outside– it's all mental.

Revamped is thriving under my care as Auggie gives me more and more responsibilities so he can concentrate on his *art*. While I'm not a genius with a perfect G.P.A., I'm not flunking out of FCC. I made fast friends with Langdon Stone. True friends without any baggage– study buddies. The stress is less because Auggie is managing to maintain the mentor/boss persona without the hot/cold routine. We've leveled out at affectionate warmth. Lastly, Devon and I hang out as friends, and that is comforting without the pressure to make it more– even though I know Auggie still doesn't believe me.

I'm trying to be a better daughter, sister, aunt, friend, employee, and student. But mostly, I'm just trying to be a better person.

While all the changes are within me and not obvious, the Spook House is a different matter entirely. Standing on the sidewalk that leads to the front door, I just marvel over the difference four months can make, not only in a building but in a person.

I did that, I think to myself. While I may not have laid every tile, or sanded every piece of wood, I had a hand in making the Spook House a home. It doesn't matter if everyone who passes the Spook House's threshold congratulates Auggie on the renovation. *I* know *I* did it, and that's all the praise I need.

As sad as it is to realize that someday the Spook House will not be my home, that some other woman will be the lady of the manor, my imprint is on this house. Just as Auggie's imprint is on me. People can congratulate me on bettering my life, but Auggie will always know he's the tough love that pushed me forward, instead of staying in stasis or walking backward. So if I silently acknowledge Auggie's imprint on me, then no doubt he's acknowledging my imprint on his home... and that's good enough for me.

I smirk to myself as I gaze up at the monstrosity known as the Spook House. It truly lives up to its name: a gray Victorian-era building with a mansard-style roofline, adorned with wrought iron details. The building is dark, ominously haunting. Beautiful. The house is a bit like its owner: large, unique, foreboding strength, but filled with warmth and love on the inside.

In celebration of the completion, I wander around the property, inside and out– a walk down memory lane of sorts. In every room, I remember what I contributed, like refinishing the wooden armrests on the antique sofa, or choosing the wallpaper in the hallway. I find myself standing next to my bedroom door, in front of a door that both excites me and frightens me. I don't know if I'm meant for what's behind this door. I worry that the excitement is a remnant of my wayward self, and that's what frightens me most.

I feel him before I see him. "Hey," I murmur to my brother as I gaze at the door like it's going to eat me alive. Robbie rubs the back of my neck, somehow understanding my fears.

I'm thankful for these past three months. Robbie left home when I was only eight. For the first eighteen years of my life, I looked at Robbie in a hero-worship kind of way, never truly seeing the person. Months of living side by side– working together, laughing together, cooking together –we've gone from a brother and sister who were virtual strangers, to the best of friends. I respect Robbie, and I know he respects me. Just another thing I am thankful to Auggie. For without Augustus Kline, Robbie and I would've never created this adult bond.

"I can't believe we're finished." Robbie's tone takes on an upward inflection, a giddiness. My brother is radiating pure, unadulterated bliss as we stand in the hallway in front of the door to the attic.

"Finally... and the master and commander of the Spook House said it would only take a few weeks," I mock. "Auggie was off by a mile. Proof Mr. Kline *isn't* always right," I say while arching a brow in exactly the same fashion as Auggie, causing Robbie to sputter out a laugh.

With the cuff of my sleeve, I polish the plaque Robbie customized for me. He can paint like a master, but can't construct anything. I don't have a lick of artistic talent. However, I can wield a hammer with expert precision. Robbie and I are the perfect counterbalance for renovations. I tacked the plaque on the door to the attic as a house-completion gift for Auggie.

I breathe on the shiny surface and buff it to gleaming bright. "Perfect," Robbie preens.

"Perfect," I agree. I smile at the hedonistic scene with *Welcome to the Playroom* scripted across the top. There's no mistaking the three creatures in the scene as anyone other than Auggie, Isis, and Robin.

My fingers twist the fabric of Robbie's sleeve, pulling him up the stairs and into the attic– the attic that no one has entered but Rob, my father and his crew, and me. We designed every inch of the space, down to the two private bathrooms and the wet bar. I didn't want the naughty Playroomers roaming the Spook House, using the facilities as an excuse to snoop in our private spaces.

I wasn't sure what to put in the Playroom, since I've only been to the club twice. After exhausting internet searches came up empty, Robbie took pity on me. He brought me to Rush during daylight hours to have a looksee. I then picked his brain for everybody's kinks. Never experiencing anything Auggie described, and not wanting to either, I gave up and let Robbie have creative license on the toys and weird furnishings. It's definitely not something the inexperienced should tackle.

"Well, what do ya think, brother?" I flop onto the chaise, and it is in fact called a chaise lounge. I researched all this old furniture too– it was a must when reupholstering and refinishing it. I was sick of being ignorant. I haven't told anyone that I secretly study everything I can get my hands on, since they would assume it's because I want to mature into the woman Auggie needs me to be. But I'm doing it for myself. I love knowing all of this stuff, even if the added side benefit is it helps with my job. I'm smarter than the average eighteen-year-old. A lot smarter– but I'll keep that bit of information a secret.

"We're Prynnes, so obviously this is fucking wicked." Robbie smirks at our private joke. "Are you ready for opening night?"

Robbie is testing the waters on a subject I refuse to discuss. He wants to know if/when there will be an opening night, and whether or not I'll be there. Auggie said the opening date of the Spook House's Playroom was entirely up to me. He was fine using the storage room at Rush for as long as I wished. Knowing me better than most, Auggie can sense the anxiety I feel over the Playroom being in our house and in my face, with my reluctance to participate.

I don't answer yes right away, as I would have a few months ago. In reality, I'm scared shitless. The past four months of my life have been the best and the worst of my life. I've spent countless hours with Devon, building a relationship that nothing could break apart. I've built a different kind of relationship with Auggie, one no less strong. I've made sure to repair whatever damage my bad behavior had on my family. But other than planning the Spook House's Playroom, I haven't done one single naughty thing. I haven't kept up with my *practice* as Auggie demanded. My hand is the only one that has touched me sexually since January, almost three months ago.

I'm not perfect. I crave my smoke and hooch more often than not. Hell, as long as I breathe, I will crave its sweet release, but I'm smart enough to know the high never lasts. I know Auggie is scared that since the house is finished, I'll relapse into a bratty kid with addictive tendencies. Devon's scared I'll become the zombie again. Both men don't realize that I'm not that Willow anymore. I trust myself, even if they don't.

Willow the wayward would have blindly jumped at the chance to open the Playroom, to participate. But that Willow was an idiot. My insecurities have not lessened– if anything they have intensified. I won't make a fool out of myself. I won't shame myself, Auggie, or Robbie with my presence in a place I don't belong. I'm not hot or bad enough to be in the Playroom. No one wants to see a woman who looks like a pre-pubescent boy strutting around, and I don't want to demoralize myself by having Auggie make someone touch me.

So sex is the farthest thing from my mind. I have other needs and issues that come first: work, school, and addiction. I'll work my ass off at Revamped and study until my eyes bleed to occupy my addictions. I was wayward on my birthday, but today I know what I want and what I'm good at.

I've learned patience. I don't care if it takes me a lifetime to accomplish, I'll get there eventually. I have Auggie to thank for setting my path with his devotion. I have Devon's unfaltering friendship to be thankful for as well. But I think it was the house that did it. Watching the Spook House transform from something a wrecking ball needed to strike, to the showcase of the block, and knowing it was my hand that did the majority of the work.

I transformed with the Spook House.

I rebuilt Willow.

"I don't know," I answer honestly, albeit reluctantly. "I *loved* the Playroom and the thrill that fired through my veins when I entered it. I got hotter than hell when I saw Auggie dominating everyone in his path. But I'm scared, because I'm not that Willow anymore. I'm not ready, so I'm not ready to have it in our house, always in my face, taunting me like another insecurity. I won't know how I'll feel until I walk in here and watch. Best I can tell you is that I'll let ya know when I know."

"Take your time. Don't worry too much. You've got it flowing in your blood– the inquisitiveness and naughtiness. But I'm glad you didn't just jump to saying how excited you are. I've notice a huge difference in you, Willow. I'm proud of you." Robbie leans over and quickly kisses me on the lips.

"Ah– don't be doing that gushy shit. I'll cry like a total girl," I threaten as I wipe his slobber off my mouth with the back of my hand.

"Oh, anything but *that*," Robbie says in mock horror. "Don't be a dipshit, Willow. You know damned well we've shared the same set of lips. You've tasted too much of me already, I'm sure." He shudders in horror, and it's not feigned.

I avoid Auggie until he takes a shower and brushes his teeth after he leaves my brother's room. I don't know what they're doing in there, and I don't want to know. Most of the time it's drinking a few beers and bullshitting. The beer is locked inside Robbie's room, so I can't fall off the wagon. They go in there to relax in the evenings. But I know Robbie has needs only Auggie can fulfill. I also know Auggie isn't getting any needs filled from me. So when Auggie hugs or kisses on me, as he does to say good night, it skeeves my ass out.

"I'm pretty sure the Playroom isn't for me if the thought of touching Auggie makes me think of the hundreds who came before me," I mumble. "I mean, I know if Auggie belonged to anyone, it would be you. It just makes me feel... too traditional. Like a stick is thrust up my ass, making me walk rigid– a stick I named Clover."

"Willow," Robbie breathes my name on a sigh. "It's not forward thinking to believe in promiscuity and closed-minded to believe in fidelity. There's no higher wavelength of thinking you must transcend so it doesn't bother you to watch your partner fuck another human being. It's not right nor wrong to believe that sex doesn't equal love– it's individual in nature. I'm not saying there's only one person out there for each of us. I'm saying what some of the Playroomers do is their self-inflicted version of punishment. A curse. Others truly value the connection and intimacy between those they play with– that, in and of itself, is a relationship built on trust and common lusts. But Auggie isn't one of those people. You know damned well Auggie feels broken for his way of thinking, which means he thinks you aren't. So don't go thinking you're broke when there ain't nothing to fix."

"You can't blame me for feeling confused. I was a bratty rebel for the first eighteen years of my life. Who would've thought a few months later, I'd be moving toward becoming a good girl," I muse.

"You always were a good girl, idiot," Robbie says with affection, giving me a wink. "Maybe since you've already lived that way, you're wondering how the other half lives. I don't know. But what I do know, you won't have a mid-life crisis where you go out and get drunk and cheat on your husband because you got that out of the way early on. You'll have lived both sides, and found which best suits you, and you can do so without regret."

"Do you regret?" Spills out before I can stop it.

"Some of us are late bloomers," Robbie teases me and himself at the same time for different reason. Me: for my boy-body. Robbie: over the fact that at twenty-eight he's living like he's eighteen. "But some of us are waiting for the people in their lives to grow up. Just be happy your happiness isn't tied to another human being yet. It sucks."

"I'd ask if you're speaking of Isis or Auggie, but I don't think you know which either."

"Willow, someday you'll meet that person and you'll just know. It could be insta-love, or something that slowly builds over time. It will just feel… right. You'll find your center, your home– your true north. But I hope to God you don't have the misfortune in meeting two at the same time, two who want me to choose between them."

"You can't choose." It's a statement, not a question. "I'd say you're lucky to have their love, but we both know you can't choose Auggie, because no matter how enlightened he likes to pretend to be, he ain't that enlightened. But you can't choose Isis until you let Auggie go."

Looking emotionally tortured with tears in his eyes, Robbie whispers, "And that ain't that the goddamn truth, Willow…" the expression on my brother's face proves I've never been in love, and seeing how much agony he is in, I'm thankful over the fact.

CHAPTER THIRTY-THREE

"Happy birthday!" I sing as I breeze into the Prynne house.

It feels good to walk through the front door and experience a homecoming instead of dread. Before, when I lived at home with my parents, it just felt all kinds of wrong, like I wasn't meant to be here and it made us all uncomfortable. Now it feels right to come home. The guilt of acting like a little bitch is slowly being replaced as I behave, instead of issuing verbal assaults, and in Violet's case, physical assaults.

My prey runs up to me like a puppy dog with big brown eyes and a naughty smirk. Seth is so dang adorable. Another year older, and he's still as cute as a button.

"Willow," comes garbled as I grab Seth by his chubby cheeks. I lay a loud smacker on his pursed lips. He freaks out on me, swearing up a storm. A taunting giggle flows from my mouth. I yank Seth back and do what he did to me for years– I press our lips together and blow a huge amount of breath into his mouth until his chipmunk cheeks fill out. He turns bright red and laughs.

"Payback's a bitch." I say from experience.

"Yeah, well… so is the fact that the only girl I've kissed is my aunt," Seth grumbles while running the back of his hand over his mouth. Blushing cherry red, he's even cuter if that's humanly possible.

"Not true. You used to pucker up for all the ladies. Hell, you were so adorable when you would kiss random girls on the street." I tease him. "You needed a leash, running the girls down. You were a tiny ladies' man, stealing all those kisses."

"Nuh-uh," Seth protests in horror. "That so did *not* happen, Willow. I'd remember it."

Seth still looks like a little boy with his messy brown hair and big, brown eyes. He's my male counterpart. I guess I can see why people think I'm adorable, too. But I'm not trying for a cutie boy persona. I want to look like a sexy, mature woman. But I'm sure Seth wished he was manly, so at least I have someone to commiserate with.

"Dude, I'm not shitting you. You really did. You used to break away from us to track pretty girls down the street. You had a thing for the curvy ones," I say with a laugh, remembering Seth chasing big girls down the sidewalk when he was just a toddler. "As far as first kisses, it only counts when you finally kiss a girl you like. Let's pretend you haven't kissed Violet a billion times, either." I make a gagging sound. Looking around the living room, I ask, "Where is my violent birthday girl?"

"Twin!" Seth yells huskily. His voice is starting to change, and creepily, it sounds exactly like mine. I know Seth isn't a smoker, so it must be genetics. I ignore the fact that it's Sam's voice– the one I hold deep in my memories.

Violet floats in from the kitchen, and I decide on the spot that being fourteen agrees with my niece. Three years out of puberty, and she looks like a full-grown woman. I haven't seen her in a few weeks because I've been so busy, but I swear she gained another ten pounds of woman since then.

The twins' dad was model-worthy, and Clover has these crystal-clear, blue eyes that draw you in and never let you go. The combination of Clover and Sam is incredible. Violet looks more like her dad. I loved Sam like a father, and I miss him so fucking much I have a void in my heart. I think that's why I can't look at Violet, because she looks exactly like him. Violet is stunning, and I'll never admit it out loud.

"Hi, birthday girl." I kiss Violet on the cheek, and she freezes in shock. "You and I don't have to like each other, and we can't kill each other, but I love you, anyway."

Those vibrant eyes fill with tears, and I quickly look away. I don't want to get emotional. I found out that as you do manual labor, the only thing your mind does is think. I've thought and thought and analyzed myself for thousands of hours.

Violet has been on my mind often over the past few months. I now understand how I was been mean to Violet because she was her daddy's girl and I wasn't. Sam treated me exactly like Violet, but it didn't matter because Sam was Violet's dad, not mine. Jealousy– an insufferable Prynne trait. I took Violet's twin brother away in retaliation.

It doesn't take a psychologist to figure out that my bad behavior started with Sam's illness and subsequent death. It sickens me that I took advantage of our time of mourning. I can't change the past. I can't change the fact that I've addicted myself to drugs and alcohol. But I can change how I treat Sam's real daughter and his widow. He would be upset that I've been treating his girls like shit, and I would never upset Sam. Even gone, I want Sam to be proud of me. Until recently, Sam had nothing to be proud of when it came to me.

"Will you guys take a walk with me before everyone arrives?" I ask instead of order. "I have to talk to you both about something important." Instead of answering me, the twins walk over to the door and grab their coats.

We take the usual route Seth and I walk. The old bridge is about a mile from our street, and we use it to get down to the river. We like to walk along the shore and collect rocks and interesting stuff that washed up. Violet hasn't joined us in years, and I'm glad she's with us for once.

Seth chatters away, telling me stuff I already know since I see him every day. I don't mind listening again, because I know it's not for my benefit. Seth and Violet haven't been around each other much since Weston became Seth's best buddy. Jealousy is a real bitch. I smile as the twins bond over their conversation. You can't *not* talk to Seth. It's just not gonna happen. The day Seth Webster and Langdon Stone meet... no one will get a word in edgewise.

I close my eyes and tilt my head back, loving the warmth of the sun on my face, the sound of babbling water on the rocks, and the smell of spring in the air. I'm learning to appreciate the little things in life, so the big things seem more significant. There is beauty to be found in everything, even the sound of your niece and nephew reconnecting.

I sit on the shore and sort through rocks, waiting for a break in their conversation. I pass the unique pebbles to Seth and the pretty ones to Violet. At first, I was worried Violet would be mean and throw the rocks back into the river, like she did the last time we took a walk together. Last time, I got into an argument with Violet about something inconsequential, so she took our pile of rocks and tossed all of them into the river. We didn't invite Violet again after that. This time, she inspects the pebbles while wearing a slight, contented smile on her face.

"Originally I was only going to ask Seth, because he's the man of your house, but I realized that was foolish and antiquated." I receive identical looks of disbelief over my vocabulary. If you didn't know they shared a womb, that look would clue you in. "I've been studying," I defend. "Anyway, your mom is unhappy and grumpy. Clover's a grown woman, and she has needs."

"Gross," Violet hisses.

"Eww." Seth makes a puking sound.

"Yeah, it turns my stomach, too," I murmur, getting skeeved out. "But it doesn't change anything. I miss your dad something fierce, but it's been almost five years, and your mom has to be lonely. So I need your permission to send a guy her way."

Neither of them look pleased. I see their wheels spinning, and I smile because I finally feel like an adult. It doesn't get more adult than this. I'm asking my niece and nephew for permission to allow my sister to get laid.

"Look, we are bad…very, *very* bad to her," I stress, because no one in our family treats my sister with the respect she deserves. The twins are cold to their mother, and I used to be a nasty, foul-mouthed bitch. Rob talks to Clover every day, but he doesn't help out with our parents, leaving Clover to babysit the seventy-year-old, burnt-out children all on her own.

"Clover's hard to deal with, and controlling and borderline insane, but let's make someone else deal with her. Hmm?" I don't realize I'm pulling an Auggie– eyebrow raise –until Seth and Violet stare at me like I've been replaced by a doppelganger.

I'm met with deafening silence and identical looks of disbelief. I realize I really have to sell them on this. "A happy Clover would be nice to be around, I hope. Odd, but nice." More staring. No movement of any kind. Not even a blink. "Listen, kids, I need some cooking lessons and I don't want to do that with a frustrated Clover. Ya following me here, kids? Don't make me say it out loud."

"Who do you have in mind?" Violet asks primly, and I can tell the answer is pivotal to her acceptance.

"Malcolm Mason," I state quickly.

Seth lights up like Christmas and Violet scowls. Both of them realize that if it works out between Malcolm and Clover, the Mason kids would be their step-siblings. Yay for Seth. Boo for Violet. Fuck! Me! I just realized what this means, too.

Devon would be a step-relation.

Kieren would be, too.

Fuck. Me. That's borderline incestuous even without a blood tie.

"I haven't spoken to Chief Mason yet. Ya never know, Malcolm may say no. But I need your permission first before I go to the next step. So I just need a yes or no from you guys. But before you answer, I'll remind you of who we're hooking up here. Your mom isn't an easy woman to be around, and Chief Mason is strong enough to deal with Clover's shit."

...And that's how the Prynnes matchmake: tell them their mom is a bitch, and only one man can tame her... and you get two identical head nods for yes.

"We're good to go," I whisper in Devon's ear as we sit on my parents' sofa. I linger a moment too long for friendly as I soak in his addictive scent– *highly addictive*. I could eat Devon alive, but I don't think he'd like that very much. "Umm... I don't know if you realize this," I hesitantly begin. "But... um... I'm not accusing you of anything... but... um... you smell too fuckin' good, if you're following me here."

"What?" Devon turns to face me and his baby blues connect with my gaze. Looking innocent and confused, he waits for my answer.

Without blinking, I clear my throat as a craving from hell inundates me. My bottom lip starts to quiver to the point I have to bite it instead of speak. The hands start next– the shakes. My fingers curl into claws against my thighs. I close my eyes and breathe deeply, but that only accomplishes the opposite– it draws the addictive scent deeper into to my lungs.

"Weed. Mary J. Pot. Smoke. Marijuana." My voice is tight with need. "Dude, you reek, and I say reek in a good way– the too good for my control kinda way."

"Shit!" Devon hisses with feeling while running a hand through his dark hair. "I pulled over a pair of fuckheads going sixty-four in a forty-five this afternoon. When they rolled their window down, the smoke billowed out. I had to endure their *stink* the entire ride back to the station. You think you have the shakes right now, imagine being trapped in a car with a guy who had just been hotboxing."

"Fuck," voice shaky, I sound dreamy.

"Yeah..." Devon draws out, but his control must be better than mine, because he doesn't have a quiver in his voice. Maybe someday I'll be as strong as him. "Listen, I've got another shirt in my car. I'll go change it– that ought to help."

"I'm sorry." I apologize for making Devon go wash up, but it's either that or sit on the opposite side of the room from him. "Thank you."

"Not a problem, Willow." He gives a chuckle and tugs my ponytail before he gets up and walks away.

"I bet you wished you were how you used to be," Essie says as she plunks her ass down right next to me on the sofa. "Auggie's made you stuffy. You used to be fun."

The *fuck you* almost rolls off my tongue. "Well, it's a good thing I like myself just fine the way I am. Sorry if my addiction is cramping your style," I mutter sarcastically out of the side of my mouth, hoping no one can overhear.

"It's like you had a personality transplant," Essie spits back. "You're no longer my best friend. We don't talk. We don't go out. You ignore me. I miss my party buddy." Essie's voice twists with a whine.

"Maybe my eyes are finally open– no longer clouded by smoke. Maybe I realize you'd rather tempt me than help me. Misery loves company, after all. But mostly, I've been avoiding you because I was always there for you, but you were never there for me. Now that I'm putting myself first, you decide to pout instead of noticing my struggle. Instead of supporting me, you're trying to get me to crack. Best friend?" I scoff. "Best friends have each other's backs. They don't break the girl code."

"Kieren?" Essie scoffs, mocking me. "Does Devon know you're still hot for his brother?"

"This has nothing to do with anyone other than you and your inability to *see* me," I stress. "*Hear* me. Essie, you're treating me like I've treated the rest of our family. Like I was put on this earth for your endless entertainment, and for no other reason. I'm a goddamned person, not a plaything!" My whisper shout earns me more than a few confused and concerned looks from the Prynnes, Websters, and Masons in the room.

"Hmm… does Auggie know you're not a toy? I don't think he does," Essie sings, petty jealousy thick in her voice.

"I could've been his toy," I hiss into Essie's face. "But before I made that mistake, I found my self-respect. Whether or not Auggie and I ever hook up, it will never be just a fuck." I snarl. "Can you say the same thing of the guys you bang, Essie?" She flinches as if I verbally hit her where it hurts most. That's the bitch in me coming out to play– the foul-mouthed, nasty bitch I try to dampen down for all of our sakes. She likes to tell the brutal truth, no matter how much it hurts.

I instantly feel like a monster as tears well in my cousin's eyes and her bottom lip trembles. But then I remember eighteen years of Essie's selfishness. Eighteen years of being Essie's plaything, of being her source of entertainment when she wasn't otherwise engaged. I was always waiting around for when Essie needed me. The past four months, Essie has been AWOL from my life because my problems aren't her problems. But Essie's problems are everyone's problems.

"You're in for a rude, very rude awakening, baby girl," Essie threatens. She stands from the sofa and stares down at me, and I finally see the mean girl from high school shining out of her eyes. Essie's going to hurt me to make herself feel better.

"Go fuck yourself," I whisper fiercely. I don't mean it, but I want to hurt Essie as badly as she's hurting me right now. "That's all you're good at anyway."

"Isn't it interesting how our talents are complete opposites, cousin?" Twisting the evilest smile I've ever seen, Essie lands a fatal blow. "But then again, you're talentless… Yeah, I'm good with the guys because I'm *all* woman." Leaning down into my personal space, Essie breathes into my face. "Hmm… does twenty seconds of penetration even count as sex? Any attention Auggie ever gives you is for instructional purposes only. Including your little *ruler exercise.*"

"What?" I gasp out, shocked. Only two people know of that night. Auggie, and I haven't told a soul.

"Rude awakening, cousin. *Brutal*," is whispered as Essie slinks out of arm's reach.

I slide back until the sofa swallows me. I tuck my knees to my chest and wrap my arms tightly around them, hugging myself. I may even rock back and forth a bit, but at least I don't cry. I listen to my family around me and try to pretend I'm okay. I'm determined not to ruin the twins' birthday celebration.

"What's wrong?" Devon asks softly as he runs a soothing hand over my hair. He sits down, smelling fresh and clean, like lavender soap and fresh air. He puts an arm around me, so I know I must look like hell because Devon doesn't touch me normally. Damn, if I don't miss our hugs– they made me feel warm and comforted.

"It's nothing." I brush off what happened, because I don't know what just happened. Pasting a fake smile on my face, I say, "So, as I was saying… the twins are on board with operation *Get Clover Laid*. So you can talk to your brothers and sister, if you want."

"We're good to go. Ren's known since you first brought it up, and I talked to Rae and Weston already today. Ren's excited, but Rae and West are both *pleased*." Devon tosses me a devious smile that expresses that *pleased* has a very different definition than the one defined in any dictionary.

We watch in amusement as the four kids in question square off. The boys are ogling a catalog for dirt bikes– like Clover will ever let that happen. I immediately decide I'll buy Seth one for his next birthday. I may be a reformed brat, but I'm still me. I didn't have that personality transplant Essie accused me of getting. I can be nice and loving, but nothing's taking the devious out of me.

Violet and Rae are glaring at each other, sizing the other up. It's obvious to me they both know the other had the same talk today, and they don't like it one bit. If Violet is stunning, then Rae is otherworldly, and both are too intelligent for their own good. Nothing sane will come from pairing them together. As enemies, they will kill each other. As allies, they will burn the world to its core. Rae looks eerily like Isis, but she's a softer, younger version of her ball-crusher aunt, so Violent Violet better be scared.

"This is going to be interesting," I draw out, smirking as all the possibilities unfold in my mind. "They're either going to kill one another, or be as thick as thieves."

"After first blood is drawn, proving who's in charge, the girls will be inseparable. Rae always said she wanted a little sister, and now we can give her one. I love all those kids, but if they're busy with each other, I don't have to run their lives anymore."

"Kiss!" Essie shouts as she pops up from behind the sofa like a demented but pretty *Jack in the Box*. I jump several inches off the cushion and swear like a pirate. Fucking eavesdropping skank!

"Essie," I plead, sounding exhausted and defeated. This is her retaliation. Essie is calling me out on my shit– this fake relationship Devon and I have been hiding behind. She plans to humiliate me in front of our entire family and most of the Masons.

Essie knows how I feel about Devon. While I'm not exactly crushing, I care for Devon as human being. I enjoy his company as my friend. But I'm not blind to his charms and good looks. I feel a draw toward Devon sexually, but who wouldn't?

What Essie's trying to show our family is how everything I feel for Devon is unrequited. Petty jealousy causes Essie to twist that knife in my back even deeper. Hating the fact that I'm trying to better myself, Essie feels the need to knock me down several pegs, then smash my face into the mud.

Deafening silence, every eye in the room is boring a hole into my face as I try to figure out what to do, what to say... an escape route.

"Yes, kiss," Rae drawls, sounding just as sinister and bored as her aunt. Something tells me that Auntie told Rae that Devon and I aren't really together. The knowing look Rae throws my way screams as truth. There is a brutal honesty in all the Masons, like they go around policing all the lies people tell.

I look at Devon for help since we've now attracted the attention of every Prynne in existence, half of the Mason clan, and a gaggle of Websters. Devon looks at me with calm, blue eyes and smiles like everything's going to be okay. I can almost hear Devon telling me to relax.

At a loss, I lean in and gently brush Devon's soft lips with mine, hoping everyone will be satisfied with a platonic kiss that is far more innocent than the one I pecked on Seth's lips as a joke. A second ticks by where you can hear a pin drop in the room.

I start to pull away, but Devon's arms slide around me and tighten, drawing me back to his lips. This time, Devon kisses me back– a real kiss, not a brush of lips. I sigh into his mouth with a deep shudder, then melt into his embrace.

Every muscle in my body is strung tight to maintain my control. I want to devour Devon, but now is not the time nor the place, and I'd worry about his reaction. Devon has maintained the friend-zone since the summit meeting declared we were dating. In truth, I have no clue what the man thinks of me: friend, annoyance, potential fuck buddy, girlfriend material. I don't know, because we were told to hang out, so we did.

The longer the kiss lasts, the less I stress over it, and the more I want it to last forever. The fire inside me ignites into a flaming ball of need, craving Devon almost as much as I crave my addictions. Devon's lips taste sweet from the icing on the twins' birthday cake and his natural vanilla scent. My tongue flicks out, licking Devon's bottom lip to get a real taste of him, needing more– so much more. I gasp when the tip of Devon's tongue seeks mine out and strokes playfully, testing to see if it's welcome within the depths of my mouth. My fingers flex on his chest as I smother the moan threatening to spill from my lips to his. Devon tastes so damned good, so much sweeter than icing. I want to kiss him forever.

Reluctantly, I pull away with a whimper, then bury my face into the crook of Devon's neck. My skin prickles as the blood rushes to the surface in the most epic of blushes. I'm shaking again, every muscle doing a dance that has nothing to do with substance addiction and everything to do with a new need forming in my lower belly.

Stunned silence fills the room, but I'm not listening to them. All I hear is the rapid tattoo of Devon's heartbeat and his breath sawing from his lips. He's panting so hard that his chest is moving mine.

Devon hides his blushing face in my hair and breathes, "Jesus." His fingertips shake against my back, and it ripples up his arms to his chest. He's wrecked.

I fucking wrecked Devon Mason. Me? The boyish Willow Aster Prynne wrecked Devon Mason with just a kiss. I shouldn't feel proud of it, but I do.

I open my eyes to find Essie gawking at me in shock, shock I mirror. Everyone could tell that was our first kiss and it wasn't fake. By the time Devon's tongue touched mine, I knew two things at once. One, Devon doesn't see me as a friend. Two, until that very moment, Devon thought I only saw him as a friend. We're both thrown by the revelation, and need some time to regroup.

"Well," Essie says ten decibels too loudly. "That was… well, that was… yeah. Presents, we can't have a party without presents."

I mouth '*thank you*' at her because I'm still speechless. I shouldn't appreciate her diversion, knowing she was trying to humiliate me but failed. But somewhere deep inside Essie is the cousin who loves me– somewhere very, *very* deep inside, lurking behind the jealousy, immaturity, and pettiness.

Devon gives up all pretenses and pulls me into his lap and squeezes me tightly. Everything fades to black around me as Devon holds me close, filling me with comfort and connection. I hear the twins squeal as they open their gifts and the happy clapping of my family, but my sole focus is centered on Devon.

Over four months of angst pours out of me. I've tried to control myself around Devon, to contain my true feelings. It took a lot of work. On the back end of the angst was disappointment. I feared we were disappointing Auggie. Auggie's not dumb. He knew damn well we weren't touching each other. But Auggie is so diabolical, this was probably part of his evil plan. Devon and I are bonded tight through friendship now. Even if we try it as lovers and bomb, it won't matter. We will forever be close friends.

I place a gentle kiss to the side of Devon's neck and he jolts beneath me, arms flexing and releasing in a rhythm. Needing to distance myself from the heat that is building, I slide from his lap to stand on wobbly legs. I quickly toss a pillow on Devon's lap to cover up his very obvious reaction, not wanting this mortifying situation to become any worse. I scrub my palms over my face, trying to rub the embarrassment away.

It's been minutes since the gift opening concluded, and all eyes are on me because I've yet to give the twins their presents. Kiss or not, Seth and Violet are kids, and they have a one track mind when it comes to new shit, especially *free* new shit. I blush as I pull Seth's gift from beside the couch.

"Here," I mutter as I pass Seth his present. Seth's blushing as badly as I am. He eagerly tears into the paper, revealing the geology kit with over a hundred different rocks and minerals. I got him a gift card to the webstore where I bought the set so he could buy geodes and other goodies. But at fourteen, Seth's still a kid, so obviously he won't find that out until he opens the birthday card that he thinks is worthless paper. I'm placing my bets that Clover's the one who finally finds the gift card when she picks up the living room.

"Whoa..." Seth breathes out in awe, running his fingertips over the picture on the box. I chuckle when he leans in to kiss my cheek, but looks at Officer Devon for permission first. Men, they're eye-roll-worthy.

Violet is sitting silently next to her mother, as if she doesn't expect to get a present from me. She covers her sadness and disappointment well, I'll give her that. There isn't a gift left in the room, so Violet thinks I didn't get her one. Even Willow the wayward wasn't that big of a nasty bitch. The younger version of me would've given Violet something she wouldn't have had a use for or enjoyed, but not purposely denied the girl a gift. Violet doesn't trust this change in me yet, but I'll prove it over time.

While working my fingers to the bone, I had an epiphany. Instead of treating Violet poorly, fighting her, I should take care of her. I was raised as Violet's older sister, and I should be her shoulder to cry on, her rock. I was doing our family and myself, and especially Violet, a disservice.

What kind of person would I be if I wished this beautiful young woman pain and sorrow because it made me feel better about my own situation? It was these thoughts that solidified my stance with Essie, made me understand her and not want to be like her. Lowering another person will never elevate me– it just makes me a bitch. I won't continue the Prynne cycle of petty jealousy with my niece. I'm better than that, and Violet sure as hell is.

The feeling of responsibility I've always felt over Seth has now transferred to Violet. I want them to look at me how I used to view Robbie, and I want them to connect with me as I now connect to Robbie as an adult. To have them count on me, look up to me, is more potent than any drug I could ever take.

I pull a small velvet bag from my back pocket, letting it swing from my fingertips like a pendulum. "Put your palm out," I murmur.

Violet's palm shoots out before I've even finished my request. It takes everything in me not to laugh outright at how eager and excited she looks. I pull the stings on the bag and pour the contents into Violet's hand.

"It's too much." Clover whispers of the necklace I had custom-made for my niece. The pendent is a crystal violet with an amethyst in the center.

"My niece has expensive tastes," I muse. "Just like her mother." I snort at my sister's pinched expression. "Besides, I'm no longer a minimum-wage worker. My rent was paid through manual labor and I work off of commission, and since I work very hard…"

Lifting the hair off the nape of her neck, "Will you put it on me?" Violet asks quietly, almost meek. Her voice wavers from a multitude of emotions.

I fasten the necklace around Violet's neck and whisper underneath my breath into her ear. "I'll try to be a better role model from now on, but I ain't making any promises. I'll still punch you if I have to, maybe break a finger or two."

Violet huffs a laugh and hugs me. I look at my sister, and it wrenches my heart. Even when Sam was dying, Clover never cried. Right now, her eyes are misted with tears, and I vow to see her smile again.

CHAPTER THIRTY-FOUR

Seth and Violet, the birthday twins, got picks on what to do after their party. Seth wanted copious amounts of ice cream, and Violet wanted to watch a movie. We compromised by doing both in honor of reaching an agreement on hooking Clover and Malcolm up.

First we took the kids out for ice cream, which Essie insisted on tagging along. That was an exercise in patience I never want to repeat. Not the children fighting over whether or not they could eat a five-scoop sundae, Essie flirting with Devon. But my patience was truly tested when Devon didn't tell Essie off. He didn't flirt back, but I felt disrespected none the less. I chalked it up to our *relationship* being fake. Kiss or not, that ain't a commitment.

I wanted to be angry at Devon, but it was Essie who broke my heart. Yes, Devon and I could get together for real, and he could cheat on me with some skank, and that would be on Devon. But when that skank is your own cousin... cousin trumps everything. It becomes about Essie and me, and has absolutely nothing to do with Devon. The fact that this isn't Essie's first time at trying to snag the guy I like, screams of a desperation that makes me sick– what it must be like inside Essie's mind and heart.

To add insult to injury– or leading me unto temptation, depending on how you look at it –we then picked Kieren up along the way to the theater for a double-feature. I spent the next four hours sandwiched between a pair of brothers that made my blood race in my veins. During the movies, I kept my eyes glued to the screen because I feared what I'd do if I looked back at Devon or Kieren. I could feel their gazes on my mouth the entire time. For several, scary minutes, I thought their thighs pressing into my legs was pure heaven.

The sensation of uncertainty gave me a new appreciation for Essie. I can't judge her promiscuity in the face of wanting two guys at once for completely different reasons– I'll still blame her for being a faithless bitch, though. The rule may not be written anywhere, but it's just known that you never, ever go after your friend's crush. At least not without a deep conversation about who likes him more, or who he likes. You don't just do it behind their back… and try it again with the next guy, and the next guy, and the next guy. It's not possible to like every guy I've ever liked. It's obvious that Essie is trying to hurt me.

Devon is my friend, and I care deeply about him. I want him to be happy and healthy for all of eternity. We can sit in silence without an awkward feeling. When we see each other, it doesn't matter if it was five minutes or two weeks ago, we pick right up where we left off in our conversation. Our friendship is flawless, effortless. Our shared kiss was like warm bathwater, soothing and comforting and pleasant. I could sink into Devon's warmth and breathe deeply for the first time in a long time. I trust Devon.

Kieren, I don't know him enough to determine if he could be my friend. I do know I wish him no ill will. In the short bursts of time I've spent with him, aside from my torturous birthday night, I've enjoyed the hell out of his company. Our time together isn't without effort, because I spend most of my time trying not to look in his direction to avoid his pull. When he tells a funny story, it takes everything in me not to lose myself to laughter, but a part of me won't let go on principle. I do know if I let go, Kieren would combust me. The butterflies in my stomach and the flush across my flesh whenever he's in my vicinity screams that my hormones recognize him as something they want to experience. There is a magnetic pull Kieren has over me, and I fear the pull is in both directions. I don't trust Kieren yet.

So as I sat between the brothers, I didn't watch one moment of either movie. As sick as it sounds, I was weighing my options. Devon is effortless comfort. Kieren is messy chaos. How much of my thoughts and feelings are directed by Auggie, with his pro-Devon and anti-Kieren propaganda? How much of it is on me? Which one do I truly want? Hell, if I know…

I've never understood sexual frustration until I was placed between the pair of them. It was like dropping me into the fiery pits of a lust-filled hell. Ache is not a strong enough word. Torture isn't appropriate, either. Devon *and* Kieren were feeling it right along with me. The sexual tension was thick with promise, and almost as strong as a drug craving. The kiss I shared with Devon opened up something inside of me that can't be contained, and the pressure is reaching its boiling point.

I kept mentally repeating the mantra of *Mr. Kline is always right* on the way home from the theater. It was the only way I could keep my sanity. I shoved Kieren into the friend box and ignored my screaming, disappointed hormones. It was difficult, but it made more sense. I owe Auggie. I owe Devon. I owe myself to explore what Devon and I started four months ago and pretended was friendship. I can't risk that bond on explosive orgasms, and no doubt Kieren and I would be explosive.

Keeping the commitment I made is what differentiates me from Essie. I have to be able to sleep at night, even if I'm missing out on things that would be fun and exciting. Right now, boring is safe and exciting could spiral me down into addiction hell.

The ride home took an eternity as we had to make three separate stops for Essie, the twins, and the youngest Mason siblings. Devon even changed into his uniform so he could go to work after visiting the Spook House.

I wanted to touch Devon after we dropped off all the passengers, maybe hold his hand and see if I still felt that earlier connection. But Kieren insisted on coming to the Spook House, saying he wanted to see the renovations. I call bullshit on Kieren. He's up to something. His *used car salesman/serial killer/you know I have what you want* smile is tripping my *oh, shit!* radar.

After four hours of living in hell, I take a deep breath of chilly March air and sigh it out in relief. "I'm not buying what you're selling, Kieren," I mutter as I put my key in the lock of the front door at the Spook House.

"I love the gray siding," Kieren says, fingering the siding in question as he smirks at my discomfort. "You know I'd never lie to you, Spanky. No, I guess you don't. I keep saying it, and you keep ignoring it."

Freezing with my hand on the doorknob, I blurt out, "What are you getting at now, Stud?"

"Those you trust the most, lie the most. You're blind to Auggie, seeing him as a superhero– Batman or some shit. But even Bruce Wayne had his flaws."

"That's scary, Kieren," I mutter, experiencing all sorts of bad feelings, and they aren't directed at Kieren. I noticed that same look on Rae's face earlier, that *I don't lie* look. "The fact that you're getting on my same wavelength, with the comic book references to get your point across, scares the shit out of me."

"Ren, knock it off, okay?" Now Devon steps in to save the day, to stop his brother from telling me the truth, but not when Essie was whispering into his ear and stroking his arm.

"Those you trust the most, just might be pathological liars," Kieren says as he shoulder bumps me out of the way as he enters the Spook House. Yanking me into the foyer by a hand braceleting my wrist, Kieren presses his lips to the shell of my ear while staring his brother down. "Or they lie to themselves so much they don't even realize they're lying anymore."

"Thanks," is my half-assed reply, because I'm struck dumb by Kieren's proximity and the serious subject matter of his words. A deep moan hits my ears, streaks down my spine like a lightning strike, and pools between my quivering thighs. My legs turn wobbly and barely support my weight. The next moan is louder, and I want to crawl on the floor to join him.

"What's Auggie up to in there?" Kieren asks while pointing toward the living room. Amusement is heavy in his tone, and I instantly know this was a trap. Kieren timed this to prove that *my* Bruce Wayne was heavily flawed. What Kieren doesn't understand is that Auggie isn't *my* anything, and I've witnessed all of his flaws firsthand– repeatedly.

"I know that sound. Auggie's close to blowing." I chuckle at the guys' expression of disbelief over the fact that I'm not weeping over Auggie playing without me– he did it for eighteen and a half years, and he'll do it for the rest of his life. Same shit. Every. Damn. Day.

Kieren hoped to bait me to anger so I'd see his *truth*, and now Devon's worried I'll be upset. I've got no room to judge in this situation. I'm so goddamned horny, after months of nothing, I could fuck the hell out of both of them right here on the foyer floor if I don't get some relief soon. Auggie can screw a cheerleading squad for all I care, as long as none of them have Prynne blood flowing through their veins.

Prynne is a deal-breaker.

"Might as well get this shit-show on the road," I mutter as I walk toward our living room. "Who's the lucky lady? Hmm… the cocksucktress is always one of Auggie's go-to favorites."

"Cocksucktress?" Devon asks over top of Kieren's snort.

"Nina," I answer without hesitation, causing Kieren to bust a gut, which leads me to discover he possesses the punch to the cunt *man* laugh. Shit! Boy's got my libido wrapped around his dick. I'm screwed, and not in a good way.

"Well, that's something I never thought to see in my lifetime," pours from my mouth before I can stop it. It's like a car wreck. I want to look away, but I can't force my eyes to move. I'm pretty sure the image is fused on my retinas.

My living room is being used as a roving Playroom, because wherever Auggie plays is the Playroom. Siblings, Isis and Malcolm, sit on the settee engrossed with the show. Malcolm looks amused and slightly bored, while Isis has that *deer caught in the headlights* or *train wreck and I can't look away*, combined with the *I'm starving to death and I want to eat me some of that* look plastered on her lovely face. Malcolm's expression turns guilty when he spots us, but Isis just briefly stares up at us like we're interrupting her *fun time*, and then gazes back at the spectacle.

Auggie's lips are fused with someone of the Prynne bloodline, but Robbie was grandfathered in from the time he was in kindergarten. I'm not sure if I'm sickened, or extremely turned on by watching my brother and my boss make-out.

I've never seen guys touch before, not even in a porn movie. There is a ferocity, a brutal violence that is displayed when two men mash their lips together and grip and grope wherever their hands can reach. Primal. Auggie and Rob's kiss is just a kiss, but more intimate, raw, and real than when most people fuck.

"This isn't at all incestuous." I murmur sarcastically to Malcolm as I lead his sons into my living room, where their aunt is fascinated by watching her stepbrother and my brother tongue-fuck each other's mouths.

"I... Um," Auggie stutters when he finally notices us, sounding drugged on passion. His eyes clear, and then he looks so bashful that I blush for him. "Robin was telling us some good news, and we were overcome." I can only imagine what these four would find as good news. It was another meeting of the deviant summit.

I can't even look at my brother, but Auggie is as bright and shiny as a new penny. His green eyes glow with delight and his lips are ruddy from passionate kisses. I pretend the glistening on Auggie's bottom lip isn't my brother's saliva, since I want to keep my popcorn in my belly.

"Ah, I can see that." I gesture at Auggie's crotch where the Beast is throbbing inside his pants. "But not overcome *yet*," I stress, earning me a laugh that trails down my spine and lights my body on fire.

"It's nice to see you again." I say to the Masons, playing hostess in my own home. "Is this the first time you've been to the Spook House since it was completed?" I abruptly turn to Robbie, forgetting my earlier embarrassment. "You didn't allow them into our Playroom, did you? That's off limits until I say so!"

I close my eyes to center myself. These whiplash moods have been frequent and hard to handle. I must look like the chick from the *Exorcist*, with my head spinning around, going from polite to seething in a fraction of a heartbeat. Fucking chemical dependencies!

"Willow," Malcolm says calmly to draw me down from my mood swing. He chuckles that deep rumble he and Auggie are known for, and apparently Kieren as well. "This is the first time Isis and I have been here since you finished the house. No one will enter the Playroom until its grand opening."

"Okay, good. It's just that I want to be there when everyone arrives. I have surprises," I announce, sounding shy and uncertain.

"I'm sure you do." Malcolm chuckles again, like I'm the most amusing thing he's witnessed in a long while. "Well, we better get going, because Willow is right, this is a bit too incestuous for me. Children?" He stands and waits for his family to join him.

"I… I have somewhere else I need to be," Robbie stammers, blushing bright red– mortified. He turns and hightails it out of the living room before any of us can respond.

"I bet we all know what Robin's gonna be doing," Kieren teases, flashing that killer smile.

"I don't want to know," Devon mumbles. "Listen, um… Dad, I might be late for work, okay? I'll see you at the station tomorrow." A silent message passes between Devon and his dad, which has Malcolm smiling brilliantly at Auggie.

"The fuck! I'm sick of picking up your slack, shithead," Kieren growls. "It was your morning to feed the kids and make sure they got off to school. Now Jackson is going to have my ass for being late to work again. The world does not revolve around you, Dev! Get laid on your own time."

"I'll see you at home, son." Malcolm says over his shoulder as he leaves the living room, effectively shutting down whatever strife is going on between his sons.

Isis looks me over from head to toe and back up again. She smiles at me when she's finished. I'm not a fool. I get that I'm being pimped out somehow. Like Devon figured out we both want each other, and he's not going to hide it anymore. But I don't like feeling like a *sure thing* in front of the guy's relatives. I know I can say no, I just hate that everyone knows I won't.

"I'll give you thirty seconds– tops," Kieren growls. "If you can even go through with it." With a fierce glare at Devon, Kieren sulks off after his family.

"I'm not as broken as you, Ren," Devon mutters beneath his breath, but I hear it anyway.

I drop onto the sofa, feeling exhausted and confused. Sometimes I dream of running away and only interacting with two or three people who want nothing from me. It wouldn't matter if I was trapped in a cabin because of a blizzard, it would still feel like paradise.

Devon joins me on the sofa, and a sudden sexual tension flavors the air. I look at Devon, Devon looks across the coffee table at Auggie, who's sitting on the other sofa, and Auggie gazes back at me. The three of us freeze in indecision.

Do we talk about what we just witnessed, or do we pretend it didn't happen? Do I ask Devon what's going on between him and his brother? Do I go all girly and demand to know how Devon feels about me? Fuck if I know what we're supposed to talk about now– after all *that*. I fidget, waiting for inspiration to strike.

"I have to talk to Rob alone for a few minutes. I'll be back down shortly," Auggie warns, and then practically jogs from the room.

"Is *talk* a euphemism for fuck?" spills from my lips, and my palm flies up to catch it a fraction too late. "Oh, God, pretend I didn't say that. I don't want to know what Auggie is doing with my brother."

Devon turns to face me on the sofa, a smile lingering on his lips. "Willow, it's Auggie we're talking about here. He would've just said he was fucking Robin if that's what he meant. Not that I don't think they do that… I've heard stories." Devon shudders, and it piques my interest.

"Like what?" I smirk at Devon's aghast expression, and shift closer to him on the sofa.

"You really want to know?" I nod yes. "You're as bad as my dad. Curiosity can bite you in the ass, ya know?"

"But I still want to know," I chirp, snuggling closer to him. Devon's arm wraps around my shoulders, drawing me closer. A comforting warmth infuses me as we cuddle on the sofa.

Everything is a struggle on a daily basis: work at Revamped, going to FCC and passing my courses, fighting my addiction cravings, dealing with Auggie's demands and expectations, and trying to prove myself to everyone– especially to myself. It's nice to have something soft and warm to enjoy, even if it's just a simple hug. Being around Devon is effortless.

"Well, pray you never see Auggie and Robin with Isis, that's what I've been told. During my Malcolm Mason mandated visits to the Playroom, I've seen Auggie fuck just about everyone but those two. As for Rob and Isis– my aunt doesn't get sexual, and Robin usually doesn't unless Auggie thrusts some chick at him for his own amusement."

"So you've never seen them together, either?" I mumble, surprised. I know both Rob and Auggie said it had been years since they were *together*, but it's still hard to believe that the atmosphere of the Playroom wouldn't affect them.

"Was that the first time you've ever caught them together?" Devon looks at me with blue eyes gone wide with disbelief.

"Ah… no… it was indirectly. Every night Auggie comes to my room to say goodnight– make sure everything is okay, I guess. Our ritual is a quick bedtime kiss, nothing overtly sexual." I wiggle around feeling uncomfortable and huff out a humorless laugh. "Let's just say, one night I tasted something on Auggie's lips– something I never want to taste again. I went through a bottle of mouthwash and a tube of toothpaste. Now when Auggie comes to wish me goodnight, I give him my cheek."

"Your brother's–" Devon busts out laughing while clapping wildly. His exuberance echoes around the living room. "Oh. My. God. That is beyond disgusting. I'm never kissing you again!"

I tackle Devon to the sofa before he realizes what I'm doing. He tries to fights me off, but I can tell he doesn't want to harm me. We turn into a ball of giggling arms and legs as I try to get the upper hand. I grab Devon's chin with my fingertips and plant a big smacker directly on his parted lips. Laughter drying up the instant our lips connect, Devon issues a husky groan. His fingertips dig into my flesh as he grips my hips, yanking me as close as possible.

"You're awfully wiry for a tiny shit." Devon taunts me, panting breathlessly.

"Ohhh… I did it now," I draw out while laughing. "I just assaulted a uniformed police officer. Are you gonna arrest me, Officer Devon?" I tease while batting my eyelashes.

Devon goes to pull his badge from his front pocket, but it's missing. His eyebrows knit together while he pats his chest, looking for his badge.

"Looking for this?" I sing. I wave the flip-wallet that holds his badge. "Ya can't arrest me without it, can you? Oh, I know… I could arrest you instead."

Devon growls from deep within his chest as he tries to reach for his badge. A burst of giggles escape my mouth as I play keep-away. I shift until I'm straddling Devon's lap while facing him. I can't help but smile. It's been ages since I felt free, since I had fun, since I acted my age.

I hold the badge way over my head, and Devon keeps trying to reach for it but can't with me sitting on his lap. "Losing a badge is a big deal, isn't it? Your buddies at the station would never let you live it down. Especially when they find out a ninety-pound girl stole it."

"Willow," Devon cautions me, voice stiff with seriousness, but he's trying his damnedest not to smile.

"Let me play with your handcuffs, and I'll give it back." A seductive purr rasps from my throat as I negotiate. I get even more comfortable by sliding forward on Devon's thighs until we're pressed from privates to chests. A pleased smile spreads my lips– I can easily straddle Devon without any issue.

One of my insecurities burns to ash. Devon makes me feel like a real woman while Auggie made me feel like a child. It wasn't so much my age or inexperience that made it difficult, it was Auggie's size versus mine. While there is nothing wrong with that beastly man, I finally realize there's nothing wrong with me, either.

"Handcuffs?" I arch a brow as I flash Officer Devon Mason's badge. "Hmm? I'll let you keep the keys."

"Not likely," Devon replies gruffly. "I don't trust my tiny sneak. You'd cuff me, and take all of my stuff."

"That's why I said you could keep the keys," I tease.

"You were going to cuff me!" Devon shouts in mock outrage. He runs his hand up and down my back in a rhythm that has my eyelids drooping with pleasure. Never having had tender caresses, I sink into Devon and go limp.

"Kiss me," I purr. Devon's eyes dilate and his aroused body starts pulsing underneath mine. I slide my body over him until the only thing separating us is my jeans and his trousers. "Kiss me," I beg with a twist of my hips. Devon's lips part and his pink tongue peeks out to moisten them. The movement draws my eyes and mesmerizes me.

"Deal," Devon breathes. "I'm your willing victim. Assault me." I tuck Devon's wallet back into his pocket so his badge is visible. I give it a little pat and smirk at his awed expression. I then patiently sit in his lap like a good girl.

Devon's hand runs up my back to cup the nape of my neck. He pulls me down to his mouth and kisses me tenderly, a slow dance of lips brushing feather-light.

Devon kisses me differently than Auggie. I'm not comparing them– it's just obvious that Devon hasn't done this with many girls. It means more that this is new to him, too. I feel more confident around Devon than I do Auggie. Auggie's experience can be daunting and intimidating. Devon and I are on the same wavelength.

A tumbler clicks into place, and I instantly know what Robbie was trying to tell me earlier about the bond created between people who are either the same age, circumstance, or in the same stage in life. It creates a connection you can't obtain with anyone else, a level of trust– an equality.

"Your uniform drives me batshit crazy," I murmur against Devon's throat. I kiss my way to the V at the top of his collar. I pluck the buttons on his shirt, revealing the white t-shirt beneath.

"You like a man in uniform, do ya? Maybe cos-play is your thing."

"I assume your definition is vastly different than mine. Cos-play in my circles is dressing up for ComiCon." Devon barks a laugh at that, and I know he's talking about Nurse/Dog-walker Opal and her costumes. "This isn't about play, Devon. This is our reality."

Devon tremors beneath me, and then attacks my mouth. Clothing is torn from our bodies, some of it no longer in one piece. Feral noises rise from my throat as I assault my officer. He lets me do anything I please, and it pleases me to taste every inch of his chest. That damned uniform taunts me every single day as it hides Devon's chest from my view. I've missed the days of demolition where I got to watch Devon's chest glisten with sweat. The days when Devon would walk by, I'd catch a whiff of his scent, and then I'd go insane with ache. I've envisioned myself licking him from belly button to chin countless times, and dammit, I'm finally doing it.

Devon pulls me up until I'm standing over him on the sofa, my feet planted on the cushions on either side of his hips. He's eye-level with my belly and chest. The wild, hungry look in Devon's eye has me shaking uncontrollably. He does as I did to him. He leans forward slowly and places the gentlest of kisses near my belly button. My legs turn to jelly, and I barely hold back a whimper. When his tongue flashes out to lick along my stomach, I grip his shoulders to stay on my feet. Devon kisses and nibbles my belly, running his tongue, lips, and teeth over my nerve-heightened, sensitive flesh.

I squirm with every teasing caress of his tongue and wince with the sweet pierce of his teeth on my flesh. I grip Devon's shoulders so tightly my nails indent his skin. My legs turn to mush under his care. He licks me from my hips to my neck and back down again, until every inch of my skin glistens with his saliva. Devon bypasses my nipples on every pass of his tongue. Frustrated with need, I groan and growl and beg him to put me out of my misery.

"AH!" I huff when Devon's teeth graze my sensitive nipple. My breasts are always forgotten. Other than Kieren's obsession with fondling my breasts, and a few seconds of attention from Auggie– both times on my birthday –no one has touched them since. My entire body vibrates with need as Devon hesitantly nuzzles my breasts with the tip of his nose.

Losing the fight to stay upright, I collapse onto Devon and roll to lie on my back on the sofa cushions. "Holy shit," I breathlessly pant in awe.

Devon settles in the cradle of my thighs and kisses me sweetly. I marvel over the sensation of wrapping my legs around his hips and how perfectly we align. Devon's skin is so velvety soft and warm against mine that it heats me to my soul.

"I think I could love you someday," I breathe against Devon's lips and fight the insane need to cry. He shivers uncontrollably above me. I've never told a man I loved him, never felt the need. I don't know what type of love this is, but I do know I care deeply for Devon and it adds to the connection I feel at this moment.

In the deep recesses of my mind, where it was safe enough to think about the things I never thought to obtain, this is how I longed for my first time to be. I didn't want a clinical few seconds in the Playroom with Fairport's most deviant looking on. I wanted soft and comforting– connecting on a baser level.

"A part of me already loves you, Willow." Devon's blue eyes gaze down at me in a mix of honesty and fear.

Devon shifts his hips, and then his hand slides down between us to fist his erection. Cock in hand, poised to enter me, Devon freezes in fear when the reality that we're about to have sex slams into him. This is really happening between us, and it's not play. It's reality and it's irreversible. If we cross this line, we'll no longer be friends, no longer living a lie of a fake relationship. I was wrong when I was with Auggie– I want this –I want a boyfriend. I need fidelity and commitment and monogamy. It's how I'm wired, no matter how much I try to deny that side of myself.

"What's wrong?" I murmur softly. So used to the aggressive side of sex, I instantly recognize Devon's reluctance. The lust has turned to something else between us, and I'm scared it'll spook him and harm him emotionally somehow.

"I… I've never done this before," Devon says in a voice thick with shame. He hoods his eyes to hide his true emotions from me.

I lift my face to kiss Devon's cheek softly. "We don't have to if you're not ready," I say to comfort him. "I know how frightening it is. Hell, we don't ever have to do this. If you're not ready, you're not ready. I may not even be the right person for you. Today is the first time we've touched as more than friends, so maybe we're moving too fast. You won't hurt my feelings, Devon. I get that this is important."

Devon rests his forehead against mine, breathing hard against my face. "Willow, it's not you at all. I'm just scared. I want you so badly, it's killing me." Devon groans. His body pulses against my sensitive flesh to show just how much it's killing him. "I… I'm scared," his voice breaks.

"Devon, you have nothing to fear. You held me during my first time." I caress his cheek. I don't want to force him. His eyes are wild with fright. But I want him to know it's natural to be unsure. "I think we should stop, okay? Just hold each other and kiss, if you're up for it. If you feel this uncomfortable, then it's definitely not the right time."

"I…I…" he stutters.

"Devon." Auggie clears his throat. "You're safe. I won't let anyone hurt you again." I expect Devon to freak out when Auggie speaks, but he relaxes his muscles and collapses on top of me.

I've known Auggie was sitting on the settee since I felt his eyes on me when I stole Devon's badge. I've pushed his presence away, wanting this to be about Devon and me. I'd hoped Auggie would keep to himself, because I wasn't sure Devon would like him watching.

Devon's relief tells me he's known all along. I won't ask what's haunting him. I'll wait until he feels the need to tell me. Some things are private for a reason. I'll never push another human being to tell me their secrets, because it's none of my business, no matter how much I long to know so I can help.

"Willow," Devon moans my name in misery, and then he kisses me hungrily– gnawing on my bottom lip before his tongue plunders my mouth, seeking its pleasure from my tonsils to the roof of my mouth, and even underneath my tongue.

I gasp out in shock and my breath hitches in my throat as Devon flexes his hips and pushes deep inside me– deeper than anything has ever been within me. I moan at the intense fullness of having all of Devon's length buried inside me. We move together instinctively in a push/pull rocking pace that's as natural as breathing. Devon's lips find my arched neck and suck in a mind-altering rhythm that matches the sway of our hips.

Devon's fingers intertwine with mine, holding our clasped hands above my head as he thrusts steadily, setting a lasting pace. Every movement causes sounds of agony to spill from my lips. I shatter emotionally and reform from my childlike mentality to one of a mature adult. I finally know what making love to someone feels like.

Now I understand Auggie's reasons for his no sex rule with him or Kieren. If I would've done this with Auggie, I would've never fallen for Devon. I'd never have grown up. Auggie would have stunted my growth, forever parenting me while I accepted the role of child.

The Playroom is fun and exciting, but it's cold and clinical just the same. Auggie finds this level of intimacy with Isis and Robbie through their years of shared history and the connection that formed an unbreakable bond. Robbie wanted Devon and me to experience a similar bond.

I kiss Devon for all I'm worth. I bite his bottom lip until he opens for me, and then I thrust my tongue into his mouth in time with the rhythm of his pelvis grinding into mine. When he tilts the angle of his hips and arches his back, I combust.

"More," I beg breathlessly of him. Our bodies don't move as two people who are ignorant of sex. We move in sync with one another, instinctively knowing what brings the other the most pleasure. The roll of Devon's hips pushes him deep inside of me and grinds his pelvis into my aching clit. The pleasurable sensation is so intense that I want to weep.

"Devon!" I cry. My fingers tighten painfully around his as I fracture. Devon shudders above me and cries out my name.

Auggie promised he'd always be my first in everything, but he lied, and I'm thankful he did. Devon was the first man to make love to me, and he's the first man to come inside me– scalding hot liquid fires deep inside me with every pulse of his cock. My body clenches around him, milking greedily until he's empty.

Devon slows but doesn't stop for a long time after we're spent. He kisses me gently and murmurs words of thanks and devotion as we come back down from the high we entered through sex– a high more intense than the kind alcohol and drugs provide.

Devon laughs abruptly, and it stuns me. "I feel like a dumbass for waiting so long, letting fear control me. Damn... Willow," Devon draws out, sounding disbelieving. "Make sure you tell my brother I lasted a helluva lot longer than thirty seconds. If you could tell Ren that I was the best you've ever had, I'll be eternally grateful. I have a badass, cop reputation to uphold." Devon chuckles to himself.

"I'll tell Kieren you shoot rainbows out of your cock if it makes you happy." I giggle while Devon huffs a laugh.

"Go to him." Devon points his chin toward Auggie. "I'll cuddle up and watch." He smiles at me, silently telling me he understands that I'm conflicted about what to do now.

"No," I murmur, sounding sleepy. "He can come to us." I roll until we're spooning on the sofa and I'm facing Auggie. I want to feel violated that the man watched something so intimate between Devon and me, but fair is fair. For an odd reason, it felt right, like Auggie was lending Devon strength somehow. I always forget that even though they aren't blood, they are family.

"Auggie," I breathe as I touch his whisker-stubbled cheek with a fingertip. Auggie kneels next to the sofa, looking concerned yet curious. He casts a shadow over Devon and me in more ways than one. I want to be angry that he's infringing on our cuddle time, but I can tell he's truly concerned over something.

"Monster," Auggie mumbles affectionately. The deep rumble of his voice makes me so terribly sad, to the point tears sting the back of my eyes. "Are you doing okay?" He lifts his chin so he can look Devon in the eyes. "Your dad will chat with you about this– it's not really my place. But I'm here for you if you need me."

"Thanks." Devon gets more comfortable behind me, pulling my back against his chest. "I'll talk to my dad. It's... it's too weird to have that conversation with you, Auggie. Okay?"

"Okay," Auggie says with a nod of his head. Huge green eyes come to light upon my face. "Willow, are you okay? That was a little intense and... um... by now you've figured out there's some traumatic shit Devon's dealing with. I don't want you to think it's about you. You okay?"

"I think so," I stammer, mind still reeling as it tries to process so many conflicting emotions at once. "I... I... I get it," I say after several false starts. "I thought I understood why you and I couldn't be together before. I would say it out loud, how I was okay with you messing with me while still playing with everything that breathed. But somewhere in the back of my mind, there was a seed of hope that I was the special one who tamed the beastly Augustus Kline. You became a challenge instead of a human being for me. Sound familiar?" I ask, knowing that's how Auggie has always seen me while never truly *seeing* me.

"HA!" Auggie barks a humorous laugh. "This beast can't be tamed, no matter how incredible the tamer. It would've never worked between us, my good girl. Would've never worked." Auggie repeats this a few more times beneath his breath. "We're not compatible in any way, shape, or form. And this is not on you or me. It just is."

"The dynamic between us isn't the same as it is with Devon and me– hell, even between Kieren and me." Devon freezes like stone behind me when I say his brother's name, but the truth is the truth, no matter how painful it may be.

"We may care for each other, but it's not the way it should be. Auggie, I would've been dependent on you, and it would've destroyed us both. I don't know what the future holds for any of us. But I know you and I have no future together. I would've been dependent on you if we got married, because I see you as the one in charge. Auggie, it's obvious that you need someone who is your equal. No matter how much you deny it, you already know who they are for you."

"I'm not going there with you, Willow," Auggie says roughly, shutting off that topic of conversation, which pretty much proves the point I was making. Who would want their spouse doing that to them on a daily basis? They'd go insane and rebel, which would ruin any love they shared.

"You and I are obviously *not* equals in your eyes. Devon and I are equals right now because we're in the same stage of life. It's not about age. You and I may never be at the same stage at the same time. Devon and I may be at the same stage right now, but that doesn't mean we'll be in six months. I get it, Auggie. I get it. Thank you for teaching me this valuable lesson."

Auggie's deep sigh echoes around the living room, and then he gives me a brilliant smile filled with regret, pain, and sadness, mixed with a lot of pride and happiness. "Good girl, you've grown so fast, and it makes me proud. I would've loved to marry you and make ginger-haired babies, but I didn't want to raise the mother of my children as I raised our children. It would have been a disaster for all of us."

"I can think of several people who were ready to kill you if you managed to get Willow to that point, and they all had the last name Mason. But I know someone who would've probably killed himself if it had happened, and that would've ruined a lot of lives." Devon gravely responds to the very private conversation Auggie and I are having.

"And that's why I hate myself so much right now, Dev," Auggie replies, sounding just as grave and agonized. "Just a word of warning, I'll always be in your shit, Willow. I'll always try to control what you do, but I'll allow you to make your own choices and mistakes."

"A few months ago, I would've said yes to anything you asked of me. But now I can't do that, Auggie. Now I'll fight you tooth and nail if you get between me and something I want or need, even if I shouldn't want or need it. It's my choice from here on out how I live my life. I don't want you to be disappointed in me, but I'd rather you just respected me. Something tells me you don't respect women who let you roll right over them."

Auggie laughs, the sound rumbling out of his chest, happy and disbelieving. It's a true laugh that reaches his eyes and makes them twinkle in the light. The sound is a huge comfort to me for some reason. Auggie laughs for so long that Devon and I shrug and shake our heads out of confusion.

"Hell, Willow, I haven't a clue what I want in my life. But I have a feeling you'd tell me what you think I need if I asked. I'm not ready for a family at twenty-eight. I'm not ready to get married. I'm just now setting my life on the path I've set. You're way ahead of me if you know what you know at eighteen. You're no longer my naïve, sheltered, innocent Willow Monster."

"What now?" I ask in confusion. I'm lost as to why Auggie is acting so happy and sad at the same damned time. Manic.

"You and Dev should share your bed tonight. It would be nice for you to cuddle. Devon definitely needs it now." Auggie casts a worried glance at Devon, who's using me and my afghan as a security blanket.

"I should probably get to work. Ren was right. I can't keep leaving him with all the responsibilities of the kids. I'll work for a few hours and see the kids off to school," Devon says to Auggie, but he looks like he wants in my bed for a long night's rest.

"Malcolm will understand if you don't make it into work. I highly doubt Fairport will have a crime spree tonight. Just get home before the kids wake. Plus, you'd better pacify your brother. Ren's probably wishing your dick shriveled up, or some equally painful version of what he always shouts at me when I beat the shit out of him." Auggie laughs, sounding guilty while dragging a hand through his messy hair. "Anyway, I have some business that needs attended." Auggie's blush narcs on what business he's going to attend– more Prynne business.

"I'd kiss your mouth, but no." I kiss Auggie's cheek and push him away so I can stand from the sofa. "Tell your business good night from his sister." I wink at him.

As I gather up my destroyed clothing, I step on a pair of handcuffs and erupt into a giggle-fit. "Missing something?" I taunt. I stand completely naked in the middle of my living room with two guys watching me, and I'm not ashamed of it. They both look at me with similar hungry expressions, like they're a breath away from devouring me, and it makes me feel beautiful. I don't care if everyone sees me as a kid, these men don't, and that's all that matters.

"Oh, shit! Give those back," Devon pleads in a panic.

"You'll give the man a stroke." Auggie grabs the cuffs and tosses them to Officer Devon. "You don't use metal handcuffs when you play, Willow. They're cold and uncomfortable and they'll leave bruises. I'll show you the proper way sometime." His heated gaze says he looks forward to the instruction.

"Time for business." Auggie smirks and rubs his palms together in excitement. I groan and roll my eyes at how transparent he's being. Something tells me Devon and I won't be the only ones cuddling until morning.

"That man better not plan on instructing you on anything from here on out," Devon half-shouts at Auggie's retreating form. "No fucking way, Auggie. I'm not *that* liberated."

Auggie huffs a laugh as he disappears from the living room. His trail of laughter adds to his heavy footsteps on the stair treads. No doubt he knew the direction of my angry thoughts, and found them highly entertaining.

If Augustus Kline is no longer allowed to tell me what to do, Devon Mason sure the fuck isn't. There is a large part of me that is always going to rebel, and an even smaller part of me that will always long to obey Mr. Kline. If Auggie ever touches me again, it will be by my decision and my decision alone. If Devon thinks I'm that big of a faithless whore, then maybe this isn't going to work out between us.

CHAPTER THIRTY-FIVE

"Something happened to me and Kieren when we were younger," Devon whispers his explanation in the dark of my room. We've had sex three times, and each time he froze from fear. Devon was overcome with the shakes, his body erupted in sweat while his teeth chattered. He was cold to the touch. Damn near catatonic. Each time, the reaction was worse than the time before. It was bad enough, with the last time, I almost ran to get Auggie. After Devon calmed himself, he wanted to keep going, but I shut him down.

I stopped feeling connected to Devon through touch before we even made it to my bedroom. I started feeling like I was a therapist, and it creeped my ass out. One doesn't want to witness the man they're making love to cry or grit their teeth against a scream. It should be a pleasurable experience, not one of agony. I couldn't take it every time Devon's eyes got this faraway look, no longer in my bed with me but somewhere in a memory that's haunting him.

It wasn't selfishness that had me telling Devon I was too sore and just wanted to cuddle while we slept, it was selflessness. I didn't want Devon to go through the agony anymore. The fact that he was getting worse every time is what had me lying to him for his own good.

I feel guilty for the thoughts rolling through my mind, as if I should be putting Devon's emotions before my own. Obviously he's been through a traumatic experience that's still haunting him, and I feel like the world's biggest bitch for wanting to run as fast and as far as possible. If Devon had come to me through a conversation, I would've held him as he spoke, but he didn't do that. Devon used me through sex, never giving me any warning, and that doesn't make me feel special.

I feel used.

Maybe if I was older. Maybe if this wasn't truly my first time. Essie was correct– a few seconds of penetration may take your physical virginity, but it doesn't take your virginity emotionally or mentally. Maybe if I was worldlier, I would've handle this situation better, not been insulted and hurt. But I'm not worldly or experienced, and this *is* my first time. I have no idea what's traumatizing Devon, but he's traumatizing me right now, and I can't handle it.

Is it too much to ask for someone to be with me because they want me? Willow Aster Prynne is always being used as a placeholder for someone, or something else. Auggie wanted me as his ideal, not truly seeing me as he tried to fashion me into his image of the perfect wife. Now Devon is touching me as a way to conquer his demons. But I cannot conquer the ghosts from his past, only Devon can.

Is it too much to ask to connect with another human being on a different plane? I thought I had with Devon, but I was wrong. I want the passion I felt from Auggie, mixed with the companionship I feel with Devon, and I want it– *need* it –with the same man. I need that man to *want* me, *need* me, and *love* me as I would want, need, and love him, and I've yet to find this with anyone.

Can't I just have normal sex? Just once? Not be used. Shouldn't I be lying in bed after making love, feeling warm and replete? No, I feel more conflicted than ever before– more confused.

As much as I hate using this excuse, it's none the less true. I'm just an eighteen-year-old girl, taking it day by day. I can't be something for everyone. I just want to be me. I want to be selfish enough to ask for what I want, take it, and never relinquish it. Is that too much to ask?

Yes, I guess it is.

The kind, loving, caring person inside me smothers the part of me that is seething. "Devon, you can trust me. You can tell me as little or as much as you're comfortable with," I breathe to the man lying next to me in my bed. I'm thankful that my voice sounds kind and calm, reassuring. I'm also thankful for the shadowy room, because I fear the transparency of my expression tonight.

Truth usually bonds friends closer together, but I have a feeling this may tear us apart. It all depends on how long Devon has been carrying this debilitating secret, and how much it infects his life.

"I'm not ready to talk about it yet." Devon denies me access, and I feel sick inside because I'm relieved. "I just wanted you to know why my brother is an inappropriate ass and why I freak out during sex with you. I don't want you to think I don't want you, or you're to blame. It's just, I get hit with the memory every time

I get to that point. Ren can have sex without a problem, but he can't… shit." Devon hisses.

Understanding dawns. "I know that it's none of my business, unless Kieren wants me to know. I get how your secret is tied with his. I'll do my best not to question you. I won't turn into the type of girl who demands to know everything and throws fits, screaming how you're lying or don't care for me, because you won't empty your soul at my feet. I understand the need for privacy. I'm not arrogant enough to think that everything has to be about *me*."

"Are you sure you're a girl?" Devon chuckles, and the sound has me relaxing after hours of pure stress. "Because you just described my sister to a T. I'm pretty sure you act like Ren. He doesn't push at all."

Feeling uncomfortable with the fact that Devon just compared me to Kieren, I do what I just said I wouldn't. "Can you answer me this much? Why do you go to the Playroom?"

"The Playroom is Malcolm Mason mandated therapy. It's only for an hour or so on Saturday nights, and everyone there is on their best behavior during that time. It's why there is a set time, and Dad preapproves what we'll see– usually Auggie. Dad thought it would help to show us that sex doesn't equal pain and death.

"Pain and death?" I gasp out.

"Pain and death are a part of the secret I can't discuss without Ren. He's been pressing for all of us to sit down and talk it out– Ren wants you to know. It's me who isn't ready. I thought you should know that, Willow."

"That's fine. It's your call," I mutter quickly, unsure how I feel about that. "Is the Playroom helping?" I ask to cover up my conflicted emotions.

"Well, I'm obviously not as skittish." Devon trails a laugh, finding it funny how he managed to have sex two and a half times in the past few hours, even if it was with complications. "Kieren isn't as out of control anymore. He's calmed down a lot. Auggie was exaggerating Kieren– my brother hasn't had sex in months. Ren was with all those girls to prove something, and every time it got worse and worse. Now he feels helpless and worthless, maybe a little bit lost."

"I can relate," I mutter before I can stop myself.

"Ha!" Devon huffs a laugh. "Don't tell Ren that. He has it in his head that you're his salvation."

I dampen the flash of warmth that flares in my heart from those simple words. I can't go there, because it scares the shit out of me on so many levels. I roll on my side to face Devon. My arms find their way around his back, embracing him. I want to draw Devon's pain and fear away, because I care about him so much.

"I guess my drinking buddy was drinking his own horrific miseries away," I mumble to no one in particular, not to Devon or myself. "I drank and did drugs to forget Sam– forget losing Sam. These past few months, I've realized I should be remembering him. The drugs dampened everything good in me, everything good Sam inspired."

"Yeah, sometimes it's good to forget," Devon muses, but I no longer believe that. I think it's best to remember, or you'll never get past it. The secret is to not dwell in the misery. "Willow, don't let me freak out. If I get to that point and stop, make me keep going," he pleads with me.

A thought hits me out of nowhere, a thought that is a comfort to me. *There won't be a next time* flashes in my mind. I don't know if I could live through it, freak out or not. Until Devon can come to me because he wants me, not as a test of his endurance, then I don't want to go there. I want the intimacy of our hugs, our small touches, but I can't live through the dead in his eyes when he's inside me. I will forever be scarred by the glassy-eyed look of agony that shone down on me when it should've been a different look entirely– one filled with love and lust. Sex for Devon equals pain and death.

"Auggie knows what happened." Not a question– a statement. Auggie didn't watch us in the living room to get his rocks off. Auggie was there to push Devon when he froze. It was what the silent communication between Malcolm and Auggie had meant.

"Yeah, Dad, Aunt Isis, Auggie, and Rob are the only ones who truly know what happened. Kieren will never tell a soul without me giving him permission, and I don't know if I'll ever be able to give it to him. I like you, Willow, but some horrors you just can't put into words. I want you to know, and at the same time, I don't. I fear it will change your perception of me and Kieren." The desolate tone in his voice would bring me to my knees if I wasn't already lying down.

"I don't need to know if you don't want me to know, but I'll help you in any way I can." I nuzzle Devon's nose affectionately with the tip of mine.

"Thanks for understanding," Devon whispers sheepishly. "I guess we better got some shuteye. We have some matchmaking to do tomorrow." He rolls away from me, giving me his back, ending our conversation and any connection we still possessed.

I lie awake for hours, listening to Devon breathe deeply in his sleep. Months ago, Willow the wayward was filled with angst, crushing on a boy who she didn't think liked her back, and in love with a man who saw her as a girl. Today's Willow is closer to wise than wayward, but no less filled with angst.

If this was right– Devon and me –I wouldn't be lying here filled with reservations. I would be sleeping soundly and feeling content and complete. Instead, I feel more lost and alone than ever. Instead of needing the smoke to dull my perception, and alcohol to deaden my nerves, I feel the instinctive urge to run, run until I find clarity. Clarity is what I'm truly looking for, but have yet to find.

I have to live in the moment until I get my shit together. I fear Devon is no more right for me than Auggie is. One day, I will know what's best for me, but I'll be the one to find it. It won't be Auggie, or anyone else, thrusting at me who or what they think I need, as if I'm too stupid to make the decision on my own. Who, if not Willow, is best to make the decisions for Willow? No one. Until the day I know what's best for myself, I'm going to act my age and do whatever the hell I want, as long as it doesn't harm anyone else.

"Can't sleep," Auggie breathes into my ear. His fingertips ruffle my hair until he can see my face.

"I was missing you," I admit honestly. "Your advice," I tack on, because it's what I truly value in Auggie, and he knows it. "Why can't you sleep?"

"Missing you," he says, slightly mocking me, judging by the earnest yet amused tone in his voice. "I miss how you make me feel. Omnipotent. Once Rob and I are done playing around, it always turns awkward with things left unsaid. Lately, I can only cuddle with you, since you never ask for anything I'm not willing to give."

"Someday you should give in, Auggie." I try to impart some much-needed advice I know Auggie will never take.

"Someday, you should let go, too. You and I are more alike than I first realized. How's Devon?" Auggie reaches to move the hair out of a sleeping Devon's eyes. Auggie shows Devon as much tenderness as he shows me, and it finally clicks into place.

Auggie has been in Kieren's life longer than he's been in mine, and Devon's even longer. Auggie has known us all since birth. Out of the three of us, the Mason boys and me, I'm the youngest. This knowledge makes me love Auggie even more– this isn't all about my happiness and health. Auggie's doing his damnedest to make all of us happy, even if he's going about it the wrong way, while sacrificing his own needs and wants, or trying to at least.

"Devon freaked a few more times before I put a stop to the agony. I don't think I can go through that again, Auggie." I hold the sob that is building at bay, but the tears spill out, giving away my pain.

Auggie sighs deeply as he tugs me to the edge of the bed, then bundles me to his chest. "You never cry, so I'm assuming it was awful to witness, if earlier in the living room was any indication."

"We… three times… and each time was far worse than the time before," comes brokenly from my mouth. "I can't. I don't think I can go through that again, Auggie."

"I'm not asking that of you, Willow. What you did will help Devon. I promise you it will." Auggie runs a palm over my hair, trying to soothe me.

"Devon finally admitted that something happened to him and Kieren, but he wouldn't say what. I'm not asking you to tell me what it was, because it's none of my business if Devon can't tell me himself. But Auggie, tell me this, is he going to be alright?" My voice breaks. "I can still see Devon's expression of terror. It's not something you want to see reflected in your boyfriend's eyes while you're making love."

"Oh, my sweet Willow." Auggie murmurs as he rocks me like a small child. We both listen to make sure Devon's breathing is even and deep, asleep. "Eventually Devon will be okay. He did damn good tonight. I was worried it would be a total disaster. You see why we paired you together? Devon needed your innocent patience, and you needed his unfailing friendship."

"I get that, but it doesn't make me feel any less used," I finally admit, causing Auggie to gasp at the anger in my voice.

"It was wrong. I know it was– we all do. But when you love someone as fucking much as I love you kids, you want them to be happy," Auggie fiercely bites out. "You can't look at a virile young man struggling with something that wasn't his fault and not fix it. Tragic doesn't describe how it feels. Malcolm's their father. Isis their Aunt. I don't think you understand the gravity of my situation, the loyalty. Malcolm continued to take care of my mother and me after his father died, until my mom found my stepfather to take care of us. I was only eight, living with Malcolm and Camille when Devon was born, and was visiting on a daily basis by the time Kieren entered this world. This kid is a part of me," Auggie says, reaching out to touch Devon's cheek.

"I get that, Auggie, I do. But I would've rather had you tell me the truth, point by point, so I could've understood and made a conscious decision on my own. But you took that right away from me. Now I just feel used, unknowingly whored out, and tricked. The truth puts a tainted edge on everything. I was sacrificed," I choke out, feeling more worthless than ever.

"We weren't sacrificing you, Willow." Auggie whispers fiercely, shaking me. "You needed as much help as Devon and Kieren. Jesus Christ, do you honestly believe Robin would sacrifice you? Which means Isis wouldn't either, nor would I. You were a fucking zombie, hell-bent on ruining yourself… and now you're the one who has turned their life around the most dramatically. So no fucking sacrificing bullshit is to flow from your lips, or I will smack that ungrateful mouth!" Auggie whisper shouts, trying not to wake Devon.

Struck speechless, a wordless, pain-filled sound flows from my mouth, causing Auggie to squeeze me tighter and rock me. "Shh… it's not all that bad," Auggie purrs. "I know you care for Devon, and it was… odd yet nice. Just be happy Kieren didn't win the vote." Auggie chuckles against my hair.

"Why? Why are you all so against Kieren?" I finally ask the one question that has plagued me.

"Kieren might be two and half years younger than Devon, but he's stronger in all ways. Hard to believe, I know." I can tell by the tone in Auggie's voice that he's raising his eyebrow. "It's not that we love Devon more than Kieren. Devon was worse off, so he needed the help the most."

"You are…" An unintelligible word erupts from my throat. "Un-fucking-believable."

"With Kieren, nature will undoubtedly take its course. We had to make sure Devon was fixed before it happened." Pulling me closer, Auggie rubs his chin against the top of my head. "I'm sorry, Willow. Sorry if this hurt you, truly sorry. But I don't regret one single second of it."

"I don't know if I can trust anything anymore," I admit what has been lurking in the dark depths of my mind.

"I acknowledge that. I've earned that distrust." Auggie rocks me back and forth in a soothing rhythm, and begins to hum. Minutes tick by as he tries to comfort me. "I love you, Willow," Auggie breathes so quietly that I'm unsure if I heard it, or imagined it.

"I love you, too," I whisper back, not caring if Auggie's declaration was a figment of my imagination, or not.

In an instant, I realize there are different types of love. You love those you take care of, and those who take care of you– family and friends. But you fall *in* love with your partner– your equal. The words I just whispers to Auggie were familial in nature, said in the same context I would use with Robbie. Auggie feels like family to me now. While Auggie will always be hotter than fuck, he can never be for me what I need him to be...

I now doubt Devon could ever be that person too.

CHAPTER THIRTY-SIX

Standing on the front stoop of the Mason's brick, ranch-style house puts a smile on my face. The twins are radiating excitement like I dropped them into the heart of Disney World. I like Malcolm Mason, but I doubt the twins meeting him for the first time will trump my first encounter with the man.

"Malcolm's a little intense, okay?" I warn the kids, and they just shrug at me. "No, seriously, he is. That's why we timed it so he isn't here yet."

"What the hell are we doing here, then?" Violet sounds like a pissed off sailor in their Sunday's best. The girl has a thing for prim dresses and swearing– it's a confusing mix.

"Hold your horses. He'll be here soon enough," I say to calm Violet down before she explodes.

"I'm good with whatever," Seth contributes, always an easy-going kid. "West wants to show me his chemistry set." Smiling, chipmunk cheeks popping out, Seth looks as devious as he is sweet. "We're gonna either blow shit up, or melt it with acid."

"Disturbing," I mutter as Violet says at the same time. "Seriously disturbing." We share an identical pissed off look for being on the same wavelength. "It was an accident." I shrug it off as I press the doorbell. "Nothing to be concerned over," I mutter, because Violet and me being on the same wavelength is beyond disturbing.

"Hey!" I chirp as soon as the door opens. I stand on my toes and press a quick kiss to Devon's lips. Exaggerated protests fall from the twins' mouths. It was barely a peck– jeez.

"Come on in. I just ordered the pizza." Devon steps to the side and invites us into his house. He still lives at home with his dad. Chief Malcolm Mason is a widower, so Devon and Kieren still live at home to help out with Rae and Weston. Kieren was thrilled with our plan, because marriage is the only thing that's getting him out of this house, and all the responsibilities that go along with it– his dad's marriage or his own, I'm unclear on which.

I gaze around the sprawling ranch house. It's bigger than my parents' Cape Cod, and twice as large as Clover's tiny house, but Devon and Kieren still have to share a bedroom. The twins catalog every inch, determining if this is adequate for them. I grin at the idiots. Their house is really small– this would be a major upgrade, shared rooms or not.

Coming up behind us, Kieren's deep, raspy voice scares the shit out of me. "Jesus, kid, could you and Willow look any more alike?" Kieren says for the billionth time– every time he sees Seth.

The first few times, I thought it was meant as a dig, whether it was directed at Seth or me, I didn't know. But now I think Kieren really means it. Our resemblance is rather creepy.

"Ask me again when Willow finally grows some tits," Seth says snarkily, earning a bat to the back of the head, courtesy of Kieren's palm.

"Kid," because apparently *Kid* is the nickname Kieren gave Seth, "I never want to hear you talk about Willow's breasts again... and I'm one of the few who knows they exist."

"Um..." I stammer, embarrassed all to hell. "They don't need to know that. You make me sound like a skank."

"You made it to your age with only my brother and me touching you." Kieren leaves Auggie out of it, thank God. "I'd say that's–"

"Unfortunate." Seth snickers out while Violet says, "Shocking that someone wants to touch her."

"Don't get on my shitlist, Princess." Kieren warns while pointing his middle finger at Violet's forehead.

"Enough talk of my tits, or any other part of my anatomy," I grumble, blushing like a sonofabitch.

"Yeah, Ren," Devon stresses. "Don't. Start... again."

"Quit pissing me off, then, and I'll shut up," Kieren counters.

"Seth, ya gotta see my bedroom!" Weston yells as he barrels into the living room like a maniac. Kieren stops Weston in his tracks by resting a hand on the top of his blond head.

"No naughty shit while you're in there alone, and leave the door open," Kieren demands.

"I'm not a baby anymore. I'm almost fourteen, Ren," Weston whines.

"The door stays open, kid." Kieren drags his fingers through Weston's hair and grips a chunk. He pulls back until they have eye-contact. "Please," Kieren sounds desperate from anxiety.

This is a different side to Kieren, a side that reminds me of Devon when he freezes from fright. I shiver as realization dawns.

"I don't ever do bad stuff," Weston protests.

"I know that." Kieren ruffles the kid's hair into a messy blond haystack. "We're just keeping it that way. Run off and show Seth your chemistry set. Don't blow anything up."

The boys flee in a flurry of chatter, no doubt planning on melting things with acid since explosions are off their list. Kieren meets my eyes and shows me unflinchingly the depths of his emotions. He waits to see if I'll drop my gaze, and when I don't, he smiles at me. It's the first genuine smile I've seen from Kieren, and we started kindergarten together.

"Ya want a beer, Willow?" Kieren asks nonchalantly on his way from the room. I don't think he asked on purpose, but who knows with Kieren. I think it was supposed to deflect from the uncomfortable silence that descended on the living room.

I sit down on the sofa between Devon and Violet. "No thanks," I barely get out since I have to grit my teeth against the immense thirst that threatens to overcome me.

I reach over and grab Devon, pulling him into a hug, because I want to hug Kieren and make him better, but I can't without him being inappropriate. I catch Violet's eye, and I realize she knows more than I do somehow.

Kieren returns with a two-liter bottle of soda with paper cups resting over the top and one beer. "I'm shocked that the school drunkard didn't want a beer." Kieren smirks knowingly at me– testy bastard, always seeking the truth and making us admit it out loud.

My eyes fuse to the bottle, and my salivary glands start to produce in excess, to the point I have to continually swallow my spit. I haven't tasted, smelled, or seen alcohol since Tina the skank dumped her cup on me. Oh, I've wanted it, but no one would tempt me. Leave it to Kieren to be my biggest temptation in all things– my biggest test of resolve. My eyes glue to the perspiration beading on the outside of the bottle as it slides enticingly down the sides, promising mouth-wetting sweet relief from the thirst.

"Princess, did you know Aunt Willow was one helluva drinker in high school?" Kieren taunts my ass via my niece. Kieren has nicknamed Violet *Princess*, and he says it with affection, and not a thread of his usual snarky, baiting attitude. "And do you know who the runner-up for biggest drunk was?"

"Who?" Violet leans forward on the sofa, captivated by Kieren. I roll my eyes at the pair of them. Kieren's upset that I saw him smothering his baby brother with concern, and now he's retaliating.

"Our local hero, Officer Devon, was a big drinker until a few months ago," Kieren says, sounding borderline sarcastic. "Now he won't even take a sip."

"Whoa…" For the first time ever, Violet gives me the *I don't know you* look, and it's mixed with one I've never see before– *total badass.*

"I was never too fond of the drink myself. I'm good for a taste now and again." Kieren takes a hearty pull from the bottle, lips wrapping around the top. I watch in fascination as he swallows its fuzzy, metallic goodness. I imagine the liquid flowing down Kieren's throat as the muscles move beneath his skin. I lean forward and whimper a little bit.

I hadn't realize that Devon was cold-turkeying it too. I knew Devon was avoiding drugs and alcohol for his job, because Malcolm piss tests him on a weekly basis. But Devon's white knuckles and clenched fingers inform me Malcolm, Robbie, Isis, and Auggie performed an intervention on both Devon and me, and neither one of us even realized it.

"It's amazing," Kieren says in a taunting voice, "How difficult this whole sobriety thing has been for Willow, yet so easy for Devon. He doesn't get the shakes, or the sweats, or the cravings," Kieren draws out. "Odd… how very odd."

Devon's fingers clench on his thigh. What looked like a craving is in actuality Devon trying not to throttle his baby brother. Something tells me they've fought since Devon left the Spook House early this morning.

"I'd back off, Kieren. Right now you're holding the only drink in the Sahara, and it's been almost four months of extreme thirst." Malcolm warns his son as he stalks into the living room. None of us even heard him enter the house. Kieren looks spooked, like he was caught misbehaving.

Malcolm plucks the bottle from Kieren's hand and leaves the room as quickly as he entered. My eyes follow the bottle until it disappears out of sight into the kitchen. I meet Devon's gaze, and we share a guilty look filled with greedy thirst.

Violet sits next to me, awestruck as she stares at Malcolm, like she's never seen a real man before. Malcolm radiates this inner-power that's overwhelming, and Violet's used to men like my father and Robin– pushovers. Sam was somewhere in between in temperament, not that Violet really remembers her father. Violet and Seth were only eight when Sam died, that's why it's so important they have a father-figure in their lives.

"Raven!" Malcolm bellows down the hallway. "Violet's here!" he issues as an order to play nicely. He falls into a recliner and sighs heavily. Malcolm closes his eyes, looking worn out and exhausted. He runs a hand through his dark hair in a gesture I've seen both Kieren and Devon use.

Rae finally comes out of hiding, looking thoroughly put out because she was disturbed. Half of her dark hair is wavy and the other half is straight. Rae's hairbrush is clenched in her fist, in preparation for use as a weapon no doubt.

"Fine." Rae sighs heavily, just as her father had. "Make yourself useful and help me tame my hair." She leaves the entryway, knowing her partner in crime will follow.

Violet drags her feet and scowls at me, but she follows Rae without protest.

"I swear to God, if the next four years don't go by in a blur, I'm going to eat my service pistol." Malcolm groans. "I wasn't meant to have a daughter without a mother. I have no fucking clue what to do with Raven, and she gets worse by the second. If Isis wasn't breathing, I'd swear Raven was her reincarnation. And if my house wasn't filled with kids, two of which are recovering alcoholics, I'd drain a bottle of whiskey and sleep for a week."

"Now's probably not the best time to enact part two of the Mason/Webster merge," I whisper in Devon's ear.

"Mmm…" Devon murmurs, smiling. "I think we've been merging those two families nicely since last night." I blush bright red and look away. Devon tried and failed to get me to put out this morning when we woke for the day. We may have not had sex, but we did other equally fun things instead, activities that didn't trigger painful memories.

Kieren rolls his eyes at my embarrassment, and walks over to his dad. "Bad day?" Kieren asks Malcolm as he rubs his father's shoulders.

"The worst– a Domestic Violence case. I could deal with it if it wasn't for the added stress and annoyance of little old ladies calling every night, saying someone walked past their houses, or the neighbor kids are too loud. Bullshit every day gets in the way of the real crimes."

"Hey, I'm the one who has to deal with those old women, and they have roaming hands," Devon says with a shudder.

"No shit? The rookie gets the bad jobs?" Malcolm's incredulity is heavily laced with sarcasm. "At least they give you baked goods. All I hear is the bitching." Malcolm groans when Kieren hits a sore spot on his neck. "Ah," he says in relief. "Your mom always did this for me. Thank you, son."

"I remember," Kieren murmurs quietly. "That's why I do it."

I give Devon a look of confusion. *Is this how Kieren usually is?* I get a nod and a shrug in reply. Must be Kieren reserves his atrocious behavior for girls sixteen and up, and is pleasant to the rest of the population.

"So… Dad, Willow would like to talk to you in private," Kieren uses as a segue into our matchmaking plans.

"Ah, does she, now? What do you need, Willow?" Malcolm doesn't open his eyes or move away from his son's massaging hands. It'll take a lot to get Malcolm out of that chair.

"It's private, sir," I state bluntly. "We have an idea on how to solve your wife issues."

Malcolm growls at me, and Kieren has to hold him in his chair. I instantly seek Devon for safely.

"Girl, please, for the love of all that is holy, never say that word to anyone but Augustus. On second thought, don't say it to him either. That shit just creeps my ass out. Little girl, bad things happen when you say that word. Give me a moment to collect myself, and then we'll talk." Malcolm recloses his pale blue eyes and sighs. "Rub my scalp," he murmurs to Kieren. "Use your fingertips."

"Spill it," Malcolm commands the second we enter his bedroom. "I've known you little shits were up to something for weeks. We've been curious to figure it out. Rob and Isis have a pool going down at the Playroom. I'll find out in a few minutes if I'm right or not. I'd like the odds stacked in my favor."

"What makes you think we're plotting something," I ask meekly, scared shitless to be alone with this imposing man.

"Raven willingly hanging around her brothers and Violet was the tipoff. That girl is the biggest introvert I've ever met."

Malcolm leans against his footboard with his arms folded over his chest and his legs crossed at the ankles. I look him over. I don't know what Clover likes in a man. Her whole life was Sam. I'm hoping that finding the total opposite of Sam will eradicate any need of comparisons. I can't imagine how difficult it would be for Clover to be with a man who reminded her of her dead husband.

Malcolm has captivating blue eyes versus Sam's deep brown. His hair is black instead of Sam's chocolate brown. Sam's face was soft and kind, with big chipmunk cheeks. Malcolm's features are rugged and manly. Malcolm is very tall, well over six foot, but Sam was rather short for a guy. Malcolm looks his age of late-thirties, whereas Clover is like me and looks a lot younger than she is. I guess that would be a plus for Malcolm. I could see where they might find the other attractive.

"You finished checking me out, girl, or do you want me to take my shirt off?" Malcolm asks sternly in a gruff, husky voice.

"I…" I open my mouth and close it a half dozen times in indecision. I don't want to see Malcolm shirtless, but I kind of do at the same time. Is he really willing to do it?

Malcolm smirks at me and chuckles. I close my eyes to the sound that is so familiar to me. He laughs deeper at my reaction, and I shiver. I swear Malcolm and Auggie practice that laugh. I wonder at what age a guy goes from the boy laugh to the man laugh. I look forward to hearing out of Devon's chest what I've already heard from Kieren.

"You said something about a wife?" Malcolm arches a sinister black brow above his twinkling blue eye. Oh, yeah, Clover will like Malcolm. I see the resemblance to Isis and Rae. I also see where Devon and Kieren get their drool-worthy faces. "That's a big tipoff, which means I'll probably win the pool. We'll see, though."

"I've noticed how you're having a difficult time of it. Devon and Kieren have said so, anyway. Um… household stuff: kids, schedules, meals, bedtimes, homework. Ya know, the duties a wife and mother performs? I have someone in mind. She's a real good mom. She's the best cook in world. She's really prim and proper, and super clean– you could practically lick the floors. I don't know much more about her, because she's usually yelling at me, but I know she works hard and tries real hard." I bashfully look at the floor.

Malcolm laughs for such a long time, my toes curl in my sneakers and my hair stands on end. I have a feeling that laugh is the equivalent of me saying sir to a dominant male.

"Girl, I know Clover better than you do, and that is just sad." Malcolm shakes his head in amusement, but it causes tears to prickle my eyes.

"I know. I'm a bad person," I mutter shamefully. "I've been trying lately. I'm doing this to make Clover happy. I'm gonna ask her to teach me how to cook, so we can spend some time together. I mean, I don't even give a shit if I know how to cook or not, but it'll make her happy. I thought I'd have the girls join me, Violet and Rae. Seth already knows how to cook because he's glued to Clover most of the time." The more emotional I get, the more I tend to ramble on about inane bullshit.

Cooking, really? Like Malcolm gives a shit.

"I'm trying," I stress.

"Hey, now. Don't get upset," Malcolm murmurs to soothe me, but makes no attempt to touch me. "That's what kids do to their parents. My oldest didn't start seeing me as a person until they were teenagers. Weston's just getting to that point now, but I doubt Raven ever will. I'll just be her daddy for life, and that's okay with me. It's good that you see Clover as a woman rather than a mom." He pauses for a heartbeat. "I grew up with Sam," he admits reluctantly.

"You knew Sam?" I sound awed, like Malcolm just told me he personally knows Jackson Stone, the lead singer of Revolutionary Road. Malcolm smiles softly at me, like he thinks I'm being cute.

"Um-hum, I sure did. Sam was my partner in crime since we were little shits. I'll miss that pretty bastard every day for the rest of my life, as surely as you will. I know Clover real well, too. Well, not since she was younger. When Clover ran off to college, Sam and I got closer. Then life, careers, wives, and kids got in the way. Sam and I always stayed in touch, I just didn't have the backyard barbecue kind of lifestyle."

"So you'll do it!" I exclaim excitedly.

"I'll think about it." Malcolm replies cautiously.

"I know Clover can be difficult to be around, and that scowl makes her look grumpy. But she is the best dang mother, cook, housekeeper, and I bet Mayor Ross would give you a recommendation if you asked him about her work-ethic. Ross always says he can't work without Clover. I know it's hard to tell since Clover always looks so serious, but I promise she's kind and pretty when she's happy." I appeal in desperation.

"I know exactly how pretty Clover is." Malcolm laughs at my pathetic appeal that turned into insane rambling. Malcolm tips up my chin with a fingertip and looks at my face, eyes tracking every one of my features. "You look just like your parents," he murmurs as his hands move to hold my face between his large palms, as if I were made of spun-glass.

I freeze for a second, and then relax. Auggie and Robbie trust Malcolm with their lives, and he created all of those great kids. Malcolm won't harm me.

"You have your dad's hair and almost all of his features, even his mannerisms and voice. Your lips come from your mom... and your size." Malcolm muses in a lulling and hypnotic tone.

I'm not sure Malcolm's looking at me, or imagining someone else, because my mom has blonde hair and blue eyes, and is a normal-sized woman. Clover and Violet are the only ones who inherited my mother's blue eyes. The rest of us are all muted browns.

Malcolm drops his hands and steps back. I watch as his eyes clear from the fog of some distant memory. "Clover and Sam were very close. I loved my wife, but it wasn't the same for us. It sickens me how someone so full of life was taken in his prime. Sam was so vital and alive, and it was a huge tragedy for you to lose him. Sam loved you kids so much. That's why I said I'd think about it. I can't go caveman and walk up to Clover like it's the Playroom and take her. I have planning to do, but I want to do it."

"Are you going to have a difficult time because of your wife?" I'd asked Devon and Kieren whether or not their dad dates. They both said he uses the Playroom as an outlet, and that's it.

"It will be difficult because it's been seven years since I had to share my life with another person, taking their feelings and needs and wants into consideration. It will be hard to open myself up again."

"Yeah, I totally get that," I mutter.

"I know my boys keep secrets well. My wife was weak. No matter the support I provided, she wouldn't take it. Camille thrived in her misery, and blamed me. If Camille would've loved her kids more than her trauma, she would still be here today. I hate her so much sometimes, I would've kill her myself if she hadn't already done the deed."

I gape up at Malcolm in horror.

"I didn't mean that," Malcolm mumbles. "Yeah… yeah, I think I did," he finally admits. "Only a coward would leave their children. Camille left me four kids without a mother. She couldn't deal with her trauma, but she left two boys to deal with it alone. We lose someone like Sam who deserves to live, and a woman like Camille cowardly takes her own life. What a fucking waste," he hisses in disgust.

Shock infuses me. I stare at Malcolm gape-mouthed. The public thinks Mrs. Mason was killed during a home invasion, but clearly she committed suicide. I want to hug Chief Mason. I want to run to the living room and hold both wounded boys. I don't know what happened, but this is what plagues Devon and Kieren.

"I'm sorry, Willow. I shouldn't have said that to you. It's not your burden to bear." Malcolm sighs heavily. "I've never admitted that out loud. Please don't repeat it to anyone." Malcolm mutters listlessly.

"Okay." I swallow.

"I've avoided relationships because of this shit, having to explain the truth. Not many women would be willing to take on a man with four kids whose job is his life, but add on the reality of my dead wife… I'll go slowly with Clover. She'll probably turn me down, so don't get your hopes up." His blue eyes drill into my brown. "Thank you for helping my son. Devon was driven career-wise, but hopeless in everything else. You and he were both walking Zombies. You've been good for each other, so thank you." Malcolm clasps both of my hands in one of his and squeezes, and then leads me to the hallway.

"Wait," I say abruptly, pulling to a stop. "You picked someone for Kieren too, didn't you?" Malcolm's devious smile is his only answer. "Who?"

"No, Willow." Malcolm shakes his head and smirks. "It was easier with you and Devon. You were friends, and he had a crush on you. His issues with sex made his crush on you more important than the one you had on Kieren. We've carefully weighed every possible trait and chose for them. Devon and you were going to come in contact with each other outside of the Playroom, but your naughty detour didn't upset our plans too much. But if you knew who we chose for Kieren, you'd upset the balance by accident. Just allow nature to take its course." Malcolm pulls me down the hallway toward the living room.

"Answer this question at least. It better not be a Prynne," I growl at him.

"Girl, that wasn't a question." Malcolm smirks at me the same way Isis always does. I don't know if that means Kieren's match is a Prynne or not... and that was exactly the point of that devious smirk.

The second I enter the living room, I run up and embrace Kieren. It's a compulsion I can't stop. He tenses for a split-second, surprised that my arms are wrapped tightly around his back, and then hugs me. He's soft and warm, and feels just right. I'd do anything to make Kieren not act like an asshole, because in reality he is a very good boy.

Kieren buries his face in my hair, his breath warming my scalp. His arms fold around me, caging me yet protecting me with their strength. Kieren lets me hold him, comfort him, for a very long time. We stand in the middle of the Masons' living room, embracing, slightly rocking– neither speaking.

After a while, I feel Malcolm's sharp gaze pierce me from his seated position in his recliner. When I finally look up to meet Malcolm's eyes, he flashes me a Cheshire Cat smirk– ridiculously proud of himself. That smirk answers my earlier question.

The girl they picked out for Kieren was a Prynne, all right... Me.

A flutter of lips on the nape of my neck and a hand on the small of my back turns me into Devon's embrace. I close my eyes, feeling insanely guilty, because I don't know which pair of arms I truly belong, or maybe the guilt stems from the fact that I do know where I belong, and I'm too scared to admit it, even to myself.

CHAPTER THIRTY-SEVEN

I find myself driving Devon and Kieren around. For some odd reason, after we ate pizza with Malcolm, where the twins interrogated Malcolm and he interrogated them back, Devon and Kieren won't let me out of their sight. I'm just relieved that everyone seems to get along without too much bickering. Next step is luring Clover into our trap. Malcolm came up with a fun yet unconventional way to court Clover– he's going to play secret admirer. Whatever the hell that entails is anyone's guess.

"Tell me again, why exactly did I need an escort to drop off my twins?" I mumble in the dark confines of Robbie's SUV. The amount of kid shuffling I've been doing lately, meant I needed a bigger ride. My tiny Beetle only holds two people. Rob has an older Explorer that I use on days when it's more than Seth and me. Robbie doesn't mind, since he and Auggie pretty much made me their bitch anyway. I drive Auggie's pickup and Rob's SUV more often than my car. I'm the grunt– I play gofer. Whether it's teens or lumber, I'm always hauling something around.

"I thought we'd have some fun, Spanky," Kieren snarks from the backseat, but I can hear his heart isn't in it. In other words, what we're going to do will *not* be fun.

Spanky, that damn nickname stuck. Kieren was so proud of my badassery– defending his honor to Tina –he runs around town, telling anyone who'll listens. Half the town is now calling me Spanky, which makes walking down the street interesting.

The nickname takes on different connotations when it comes to the Playroomers. Bethany asked me the other day if my thing was impact play. I didn't know what the hell she was talking about, so Bethany laughed and spanked my ass. That light bulb moment made me realize how far out of my depth I truly am in the Playroom.

Kieren can be such a fuckface.

I ignore Kieren as I pull up to the curb outside of the Webster and Prynne houses, which isn't without great difficulty since he never stops chatting. I can't imagine Kieren, Seth, and Langdon in the same room– my head would explode. As it is, Seth and

Kieren keep volleying back and forth in their conversation, and I doubt either one is listening to the other speak.

"Seth, I'm picking you up after school tomorrow, don't forget," I warn as I put the SUV into park.

"I won't," Seth chirps from behind me, yanking my ponytail. "Night, Sapling," he sings as he hops out of the car.

"Great– see what you've done now?" I bitch at Kieren, meeting his mischievous gaze through the rearview mirror.

I'll never be Willow again. Now that Kieren's nickname stuck, everyone is calling me by something different: Good Girl, Monster, Sapling, Spanky. I just want to be me. Willow. Seth hasn't called me Sapling since Sam passed away. Hearing that word, said in affection, from a face that looks so much like Sam, is heart-wrenching.

"Shit!" I hiss when I notice Violet sulking to the front porch. "Wait up!" I shout at her as I struggle with my seatbelt. "Hey," my voice comes softer than I'd meant. I bolt across the front lawn and take the front steps two at a time. I'm out of breath by the time I reach the girl.

Lately Violet's feelings get hurt super easy. If I speak to her or don't speak to her, if I smile at her or don't smile at her, if I include her or don't include her. Basically, everything I do or don't do upsets Violet. No matter how big of a brat I am, I just can't gloat over Violet's jealousy anymore. I'm trying, but it's not easy to stop fourteen years of bad behavior in a few short months. I usually don't realize I've done something wrong until it's too late, and then I have to look at the girl struggle not to cry, which makes me want to scream… okay, it makes me want to cry a little bit, too.

I grab Violet's wrist, yanking her to a stop. Since she doesn't lash out at me, I know I've hurt her feelings– yet again. "It's not like that, Violet." I release a heavy sigh, sounding emotionally exhausted. "I'm not excluding you. Seth needs help with a school project. Ya wanna hang out afterwards, just us girls? We can watch a movie or something. Seth doesn't like a good romantic comedy."

"Neither do you," Violet mutters pointedly, but her pretty blue eyes don't look as sad anymore. "You guys love that sci-fi shit," she mumbles dejectedly.

After Robbie said some nasty stuff to me a few weeks back, I realized how bad it sucks to have your older brother tear you to shreds, even if they don't mean it. I'm still hurt that Robbie didn't go to my birthday party, and that was four months ago. I may be the twins' aunt, but we were raised as siblings. I took the leap that maybe Violet looks up to me, and I'm a shitty sister for not connecting with her.

"I've acquired a girly side recently." I flash a smirk, because it's the truth. Lately, I've been gushy and weepy, just like Violet. My emotions are all over the place, like if I don't figure out what the hell is up from down, I'm going to need medication. "I enjoy watching swoon-worthy hotties declare undying devotion to plain-Janes. I get to live vicariously, since I know I'll never have a guy go down on bended knee for me."

I'm overcome with shyness. I look at the ground, blushing, and twist my fingers together. I peek up and notice Violet is doing the same thing: blushing, eyes cast downward, and wringing her hands.

"I don't think that's going to be a problem for you, Willow… Okay," Violet mumbles underneath her breath, and then perks up. "It's a date! I'll have Mom make us some snacks. Red velvet cupcakes with cream cheese frosting? Homemade Chex mix with extra Corn Chex for you?"

Violet strides across the porch, and waltzes through the front door before I can reply. The screen door smacking the frame has me flinching. Movement of the curtain snapping back into place has me huffing out a gulp of air. Clover… she's been super emotional lately, too. Every time she sees Violet and me getting along, she gets misty-eyed. It's freaking me the fuck out, and I have a feeling Clover is altering mine and Violet's emotional climate. Clover's our cold-hearted bitch, and if she changes too, it will upset the balance of the universe.

"I'm glad you're finally getting along with Princess," Kieren announces from directly behind me as I'm belting myself back in. "She's a good kid."

Feeling off kilter, I lash out and wish I didn't as soon as the words leave my mouth. "Dude, do you even know our names? I think you nickname us something you can remember." I snort a very unladylike sound as I put the SUV into gear and pull away from the curb.

"Nicknames make a person feel special. I like you guys, and I want you to know it. If I didn't like you, Willow, I'd just call you *bitch*," Kieren snaps back at me.

"Sorry," I groan, feeling like that bitch Kieren just called me. "My mood swings are even driving me insane at this point. I'm debating medication if it doesn't even out." I feel the need to elaborate, "Doctor prescribed, that is. Crying Clovers and Violets tend to get me on edge. I think *SORRY* should be my first tattoo. Just tattoo the sucker right across my forehead. That way, no matter how far I shove my foot in my mouth, you'd know I was apologizing."

"Here's a novel idea," Kieren says, leaning over the back of my seat until he's whispering in my ear. "Think before you speak, and don't use hormones and cravings as an excuse to say what you really mean, but don't have the balls to own."

"Jesus, you really are the morality police, aren't you?" I stammer, shocked. "I get Auggie's comment about you pressing his buttons because you're so much alike."

"I'm nothing like that indecisive prick," Kieren snarls. "Auggie's buttons get pressed when you tell him the truth he doesn't want to swallow. He might give you good advice, Willow, but he sure as fuck never takes it. I don't like liars, excuse makers, or victims. They make me want to beat the ever-loving shit outta 'em." Kieren mutters as he sits back in his seat. "But you're forgiven, because I know you didn't mean to snap at me. I can only imagine what last night was like for you. Since my brother is too big of a pussy, I'll apologize for him."

Flipping around in the passenger seat, finger pointed at Kieren's face, Devon shouts, "Ren, shut the fuck up!"

Hoping to defuse the situation, I try to make a joke. "Where's this fun at, Kieren? So far this outing has been the emotional equivalent of water-boarding."

"Are you sure you want to do this tonight?" Devon's calmed down, and now sounds reasonable, almost pleading as he speaks to his younger brother. "Everyone is on edge. It's not a good time. We should wait."

"Stop dragging your feet," Kieren snaps, proving how on edge everyone truly is. "Willow, drive to Wreck & Ruin Repair on River Street. The loft above the service bay is my hidey-hole."

"Oh, my God! I'm a dumb cunt." I chuckle until I start snorting like a dipshit. "I get it now– you know a good mechanic. Christ, I'm an idiot. Your four-wheel-drive really went out."

"What'd ya think I needed the money for, Spanky? I needed to buy a part from our inventory. Jackson was going to let me pay for it whenever, knowing I was good for it. But I don't work that way. I had to buy it before I used it– only fair."

"How ethical of you," Devon mumbles underneath his breath, but thankfully I'm the only one who hears him.

"Yeah, I'm my good mechanic. Super-fast service with a smile." Kieren sings in a southern drawl and flashes me a charming smile as I look at him in the rearview mirror.

"Ren, don't ever pull that accent again," Devon taunts, finally lightening up. "It's not working for ya, brother. Stick with your Southie."

"Oh, don't make me pull out that Boston gibberish." Kieren snorts.

"Children, we're here." I pull up in front of Wreck & Ruin Repair. "Where do I park?"

Bookended by a pair of smoking hot Mason brothers isn't awkward at all. Nope, not at all awkward, or so I tell myself. In fact, all three of us are extremely comfortable lounging on the futon mattress amid Wreck & Ruin Repair's inventory of car parts… If you can believe that shit, then I'm a six-foot tall Barbie doll with double-D tits.

Kieren's hidey-hole is a small storage loft above the main service bay of the mechanic shop. The roof-pitch is its walls, with the opening looking out over the bay. A tiny ladder is the only access. No worries that someone will catch us up here, since Kieren dragged the ladder up, effectively trapping our asses twenty feet from the ground.

"So, is there a reason we're hiding out?" I fray the cuff of my sleeve to hide my anxiety.

Devon and Kieren stare each other down over the top of my head, no doubt engaging in a silent conversation I'll never be able to translate. Their tortured expression is so similar, it makes my heart race. I'm mesmerized as I watch Devon's jaw clench and release– I'm pretty sure I can hear his molars being ground down to nubs.

"I'll start, since my big brother seems to have turned mute," Kieren says snidely. "We're here because no one else is. Everywhere we go is filled with prying eyes and listening ears. I'm sick of being the Hedonistic Four's pet project. I think we should make our own little group. Spanky, I'd let you name it, but you know my nicknaming skills are unparalleled." Kieren's arrogance knows no bounds.

"Ren's my best friend, you're my friend, and if our matchmaking works, our families will be connected. You need the truth, Willow. I don't want any more secrets between us. Fuck." Devon jumps up to pace in a two-foot square of unused space. "Ren–" Devon's tortured gasp rips tears from my eyes. "Christ, I can't do it. I just can't! Don't make me do it," he pleads.

"I'll do it, then," Kieren mutters despondently. If it hurts me to watch Devon be so conflicted, I can't imagine what it's doing to Kieren to witness his brother unhinge right now.

"NO! I'm the big brother. I'm the one who's supposed to protect you, goddammit!" Devon screams bloody murder– a deep keen that draws a sob from my chest. Devon's words echo back, over and over from the service bay beneath us. Stunned by his outburst, Devon freezes, looking haunted by the past.

"It's been you and me, side-by-side, since I was twelve and you were fourteen, bro. None of that superhero bullshit outta your mouth again! This isn't just about you anymore, Dev. Willow needs the truth because she has to make an informed decision on whether or not she wants her family connected to ours. We have to tell her the truth. Now," Kieren demands softly.

Devon whips around to face us with salty tears drying on his cheeks. His blue eyes glow black with a wildness I don't understand. "I can't do this sober."

"No! No, fucking way. Not around me, and not around Willow, you selfish asshole. It's bad enough you have me taking your piss tests."

"What?" I shout. "What…" I whisper when the pieces finally click into place. Never having any symptoms or cravings, having no problem abstaining, and Kieren's digs about liars– how Devon smelled strongly like pot yesterday afternoon. "You're still using?" Body shaking, betrayal slamming into me with the force of a tsunami, I begin to cry.

"Willow." Kieren sighs my name while reaching over to hold my hand. "No matter what he's told you, or what excuses he will undoubtedly begin to make, Devon's never stopped– not one day."

"You can join me." Devon offers, eyes filled with excitement and hope that he can convert me back to the dark side. He pulls out a metal pot pipe from the inside pocket of his jacket, tempting me, but turning my stomach more so.

"You've got to be fucking kidding me…" I mutter in utter disbelief. "I didn't work my ass off for the past 119 days to stay sober, only to have a drug addict pull me back in."

"So high and mighty– judgmental. Willow, who could keep up with the impossible goals you've set? In the end, you're still a lost, little girl, just one who's no fun anymore." Devon's fingers shakes so badly he can barely hold the lighter as he tears out my heart.

"Wow… Fuck. You. Devon. You self-righteous prick." My voice quivers, breaking. I sit in shock, unable to figure out what the hell is happening as my world comes crashing down around me.

"Welcome to my world, Willow. The three stages of Devon Mason: the sober asshole, the tweaking bastard, and the high fucker posing as our local hero. You've only known the poser." Kieren gestures toward Devon, and then back to me, "Meet the tweaker. This bastard says horrific shit as an excuse to light up. The damage is already done, right, Dev? So you might as well just light up and do your worst, right? That's your M.O. You're a victim of the past, and you use my resentment as an excuse to do drugs to punish yourself. I agree with Willow. Fuck. You. Devon."

"Fuck you, too," Devon mutters shamelessly.

"You have no idea how selfish you are, or what I've had to go through because of you. You're blind. You run around as Dad's pride and joy and Fairport's golden boy, while you leave me looking like a loser. I'm the one feeding two kids three square meals a day, making them do their homework, making sure they get to bed on time. I'm the one who gives the hugs. I'm the one who has to go to school and beat the hell outta guys who hit on Raven. Now I'm taking care of the twins' issues too! Last week, West came home with a shiner for defending Seth, so I went to school and put the fear of God into three freshmen. Violet was getting harassed by some mean girls, so I sicced Rae on them— now *that* took a lot of convincing."

"Kieren, why didn't you tell me about that?" I ask, mind reeling from all the information spilling from Kieren's angry mouth,

"The kids needed muscle, not brains," Kieren mumbles to me, and then he turns rabid on Devon. "Every night, I have to sit at the kitchen table, and explain to two kids why their brother won't fucking eat, so he can feel the high better. I'm the one whose bedroom stinks when you pass the fuck out and piss yourself. I'm the one you manipulate into lying to everyone because the truth would kill them. I. Am. The. One. Who. Sacrificed. My. Future. So. You. Could. Have. One… and you throw it in my fucking face. Hell, you throw it away!"

"I didn't ask you to turn the football scholarship down so I could go to the academy," Devon says defensively.

"No, but I had to, because all the responsibility falls on my shoulders. With both of us gone, Dad couldn't do it alone. I didn't do it for you– I did it for our family. It's what a man should do. Here you are, Officer Devon Mason, living the life of a drug addict and a drunk, all the while arresting people just like yourself. Hypocrite. It's a spit in the face how you use our past as an excuse. I was there with you throughout everything, yet you're the addict and I'm the one taking the responsibilities for the pair of us."

"You're just pissed about Willow," Devon snarls. "Admit it. Finally admit it, Ren!"

"YES!" Kieren screams at Devon. "Yes, you have *my* girlfriend because *our* family gave her to you, you entitled prick! And you're fucking it all up instead of appreciating what was given. You are an amazing actor, I'll give you that. You have them all wrapped around your drug addict fingertip, thinking you're getting better, so they give you anything you fucking want while I get denied. Denied. DENIED!" Kieren's scream of frustration and agony would've brought me to my knees if I wasn't already sitting down.

Veins visibly pulsing in his forehead, chest rapidly rising and falling from breathlessness, I worry if Kieren doesn't calm down, he may cause harm himself. I reach over to pat his back, trying to soothe him.

"How do you think it makes me feel, Ren? How would you feel if Willow came to you only because Auggie manipulated her into it? How would you feel if you had to listen to Willow and Auggie talk about you while you pretended to sleep? How would you like to wonder whether or not Willow likes you for you, or because she's being brainwashed?"

"That isn't true, Devon," I say quickly, before anyone can stop me. "If you listened last night, then you know that isn't the case. You're my friend. I thought you were my boyfriend. I was *intimate–*" my voice breaks. "With you last night, and this morning you didn't seem to mind whatever you overheard. Repeatedly, I might add."

"You don't know the real me, Willow," Devon cautions. "But now isn't the right time to talk about this, because I don't feel like myself." Running a hand through his dark hair, Devon begins to pace the small open space in front of the futon again.

"Humph," Kieren grunts out. "Let me answer your earlier question. How would I feel about *insert your selfish, addict ramblings here?* Gee, I don't know, Dev," Kieren twists sarcastically. "Probably about as good as it felt to watch Auggie warp Willow's mind against me, but I'm okay with that, because it has helped Willow better herself. I'm guessing your wounds don't bleed as badly as mine– how would you have liked to lie in bed last night, knowing *I* was inside Willow. Hmm? It killed me." Kieren presses a fist to the center of his chest and releases a tortured sound.

Not knowing what to do, but longing to comfort the pain I hear in Kieren's voice, I try to give him a hug, which spurs Devon on when I hadn't meant the gesture as anything bad. When you feel someone's pain, no matter who it is, you should help them, or you're a horrible person.

"You always make everything about you," Devon mumbles, pointing at how I'm trying to comfort Kieren.

"What?!" Kieren shouts, sounding incredulous. "Fuck. You. Devon. There, now you have an excuse to toke up. So toke the fuck up, buddy," Kieren spits the words, filling his voice with humorless attitude. "C'mon, ya know you're gonna do it anyway. Punish yourself by punishing us– go on now," Kieren coaxes Devon to disappoint us.

Glaring at us as we sit on the futon mattress, Devon shows no shame or remorse, only desperation and need. The twang sound of the lighter flicking to life beneath Devon's fingertip brings memories of my wayward life to the fore. Devon takes a deep draw that lasts seconds. His eyes close as a full-bodied shudder waves through his muscles. Devon's lips flutter and his chest starts to protest as he holds the drug deep in his lungs, refusing to release its sweet relaxant.

Shaking, my fingers turn to claws and dig into my thighs. I clench my teeth against the need to beg Devon to pass me the pipe. A tortured sound expels my throat as I rock back and forth. The scent of marijuana fills the small space, luring me in as much as it makes me hate Devon Mason. Steeling myself against the insanity that is trying to control me, I remember all the events that got me to this point in my life. I've worked too hard to succumb.

"How dare you?!" I shout. "How dare you bring me here, and close me in without escape, and do the one thing I'm trying to avoid?"

The Devon I know peeks out of drug-clouded blue eyes, but only for a split-second before another person appears. The stranger wins out– the addict. "And you call me self-righteous? Your body will thank me for the contact buzz, even if you won't."

Wordless, I make a noise in the back of my throat that sounds like death. I try not to breathe the smoke into my lungs. I try not to smell the enticing aroma promising an escape from this hell Devon placed me in. But try as I might, it does no good. I'm a human being, a human being who needs to breathe in order to survive, and the entire area is filled with a plume of pot smoke.

"C'mere, Spanky." Kieren tugs me into his lap. He unzips his jacket and tucks me against his chest, and then zips his jacket, enclosing my face and shoulders. "There now," he whispers while rocking me back and forth. "The mean smoke can't get you in there. I'm so fucking sorry, Willow. I wouldn't have brought you here if I'd known Devon was gonna snap. I think last night was too much for him to handle, adding that to my pressure over telling you the truth. It's my fault."

"Mr. Responsible," Devon grumbles.

Blinded, nearly deafened, all I can do is shake as I breathe Kieren's warm scent deeply into my lungs. He holds me close, protectively, while trying to comfort me. *I'm stronger than my cravings* I keep repeating inside my mind.

"So I bought a few tickets to the Comic Expo in Boston next month," Kieren says to distract me. "I thought we could take the boys and see if we could find anything for you to hock on Revamped's website. That would be fun, huh? I'll have my buddy join us instead of Devon. I'm too pissed off at him to look at him at the moment."

I nod my head yes. If Kieren can pretend this isn't happening, then so can I. My fingertips curl against Kieren's chest and hold on, trying to anchor myself to something familiar.

"Ah, now that's better," Kieren murmurs. "Dev's back to being Dev again."

"Sorry," Devon's voice sounds distant and muted. "Jesus, I'm sorry. You know how I get. I haven't had anything in over thirty-six hours, not since just before the twins' birthday party."

"The only reason I don't go straight to Dad is because I'd rather have this Devon, the stable yet high Devon, versus the asshole who could verbally assault the kids."

"I apologized," Devon whines.

"Yeah, 'cuz that right there is good enough," Kieren says sarcastically. "You don't understand what you probably just lost, fuckface. Do you have any idea what you ruined?"

"Willow will hate me as much as I hate myself by the time we're done with the truth," Devon says defensively. "I can't do it. I'm too much of a coward. You have my permission to tell her everything."

Kieren unzips his jacket, letting me loose. I sit up on the futon and just stare at Devon. His familiar features are the same, but the man beneath is different, even though nothing has changed. What changed is my perception of Devon, because I finally see the truth I've ignored.

Devon abruptly turns, and nearly topples to the floor. "I'm sorry," is the last thing Devon says as he grabs the ladder, hooks it into place, and crawls down to the service bay. The back door smashes shut before I can even take a deep breath to reply to his apology.

"I better go after him," I say in a panic.

"No," Kieren grabs my wrist. "Let him go. Devon needs to be alone. He does this all the time."

"Is Devon going to be okay?"

"I don't know," Kieren mumbles sadly while shaking his head. "I think you knowing about the past, and Devon not having to be the one to explain it, will be for the best. Do you want me to continue?"

Unable to speak, all I can do is nod in answer.

"First, I want you to know I didn't bring you here to–" Kieren fumbles for the right words, moving his lips a few times without anything flowing out. "I didn't bring you here to show you how Devon really is. That wasn't my intention. I'd rather you saw him as everyone does. It kills me that you had to see him like that. It's not only Dev's dirty secret. It's not the family's dirty secret. It's *my* dirty secret."

"It's not," I protest. "That's like saying my problem was because of my family." Kieren just smirks at me as realization dawns. "Okay, probably being my supplier was part of the problem. I'll give you that." I laugh without humor.

"Exactly. I've known Dev was using since I was twelve. Maybe if I'd said something earlier, it wouldn't have gotten a hold on him, and he would be better right now. Now he's been using for six years, getting worse by the week, and I fear doing stronger and stronger drugs to get that same high. He has to have built up a tolerance by now. So I'm part of the problem. But no more. No more lying to everyone. No more taking the piss tests. Okay?" Kieren says like he wants me to back him up and make him stick to it.

"Okay," I agree. "That could've been me." Horror dawns.

"Nah– never," Kieren stresses. "Clover would've killed you first... or Auggie."

I snort a very unladylike sound. "True. Too true."

"I thought I was loving Devon by letting him do whatever he wanted– I thought I was being loyal by keeping my mouth shut. I was wrong."

"Tough love is called love for a reason. The *tough* is because they love you enough to do what's right, even though it's not easy. I get that now, because I want to track Devon down and beat him to death, and then give him a hug. I'm so ashamed that I did that to my family. I hadn't realized how awful it is to be on this side of it, not hazed by the drugs."

"Yeah, Devon's either drunk or high, having a fuckin' rip-roaring good time, while we're all miserable. It's not pleasant for the rest of us." Kieren takes a deep breath, as if remembering the worst times he's gone through. "It's not like we can drown the miseries Dev places at our feet by downing a bottle of Jack. No, because then we'd be no better than him."

I slide forward on the futon to rest my cheek on my knees. I wrap my arms around my legs and hold myself together. Several emotions are the strongest: a wealth of pride that I didn't succumb to the drug, fear and sadness over Devon's addiction, heartbreak that Devon lied to me, shame that I've behaved just like Devon, harming my family. But primarily, all I feel is mix of confusion and betrayal.

Kieren places a heavy palm on the center of my back. He doesn't rub– he just lets his warmth seep into my skin. "Second, you heard some private stuff that should stay private. I'm sure you and Violet fight, and what you say no one should ever hear. Right?"

"Oh, fuck yeah," I murmur. "We don't fight as often as we used to, but hell yeah. It was brutal, and the words cutting. I'd look like a monster if anyone ever witnessed it."

Kieren chuckles warmly. "Yeah, that was mild for Devon and me, very mild. Um… that stuff about you. Um… don't think I'm going to like, date rape you or something. I wasn't going to last time, and I'm not going to now. I didn't bring you here for this conversation, but I'll just put it out there anyway. Yes, I've liked you for a while. I liked you when we were tiny bastards, but then shit happened and things changed. Then when I got my shit together and stopped being a whore, Auggie was like a junkyard dog protecting your ass. It took me five months to get inside Revamped– countless lectures and beat-downs about loyalty and didn't I love Devon enough to understand he needed you. Never mind, I won't go there." Kieren starts to laugh, sounding manic.

"You did get into Revamped," I remind him, and for some reason I'm smiling.

"Yeah, I didn't think I would. I was shocked when I walked in and didn't get tossed right back out onto the street. It was like there was a protective shield on Revamped's door, and I'd bounce right off it if I tried to pass the threshold, and its name was Auggie." He chuckles, no doubt remembering Auggie doing just that. "Well, I did meet the street about five minutes later when Auggie was sitting on my chest, lecturing me. Fuckface is damned good at laying on the guilt. But then I got home, and found Dev passed out in my bed, and it pissed me off, so I found Essie to set up the date between us. Got the ass kicking of a lifetime that night…"

"Sorry," I mutter lamely. "You could say that night was a turning point in my life. By the next day, Auggie had staged a private intervention, and I haven't drank or smoked since. Sorry."

"What I'm trying to say–" Kieren makes a funny noise, and the hand on my back disappears. I look up to watch him run his fingers through his hair, like his dad does when he's stressed out or tired. "I'm not going to try to date you, or touch you, or turn you against my brother. I do like you, Willow. But my brother is my brother, and I won't do to him what he did to me. I want to be your friend. I can tell you anything and you'll understand. So, be my friend, Willow. It's what we both need right now. It's not complicated."

"Friends," I agree, reaching over to shake Kieren's hand. "Not complicated," I say, rolling my eyes. "I smell bullshit, but whatever. I get it. I'm not going to go from one dude, to the next, to the next, to the next. Ever. I can't start something with someone unless and until I finish it with someone else. I think what I need right now is to be with no one… after I talk to Devon, whenever that will be."

"Yeah, good idea. Just don't be too hard on Devon. Everyone is right for the wrong reasons. Dev didn't need you for the sex issues– he needed your friendship. If he'd get off that shit, maybe he could work through the past instead of masking it in a drug haze. I've had enough sex to know it just exacerbates the issues." Kieren shudders, revolted for unknown reasons. "Trust me on that."

"I'll take your word on that, being as my only sexual experiences were used as instruction and therapy, and the instruction was so I could get through the therapy. Makes a girl feel really good about herself, it does."

"Ah, shit!" Kieren breathes out. "I– that comment I made about Dev having sex with you last night wasn't out of jealousy. I was worried about how it would make you feel. I guess I should explain at least, huh?"

"Only if you want to." But what I really think is *only if you think I can handle it*. I'm feeling extremely fragile after everything in the past twenty-four hours already. I don't know if I can handle much more without fracturing.

"I guess you've figured out Devon and I have some serious issues with sex, but they're just symptoms of the past. I'm sure you noticed how Devon freaks just before he sinks into you, or when you moan a certain way. That's when he gets hit the hardest. I don't have those problems."

"So the rumors are true, then?" Involuntary, my eyebrow arches in what I've now dubbed *the Auggie*. "You're quite the stud," I tease, but there's an underlying edge of pain in my voice.

Kieren cuts his eyes toward me as he flashes me his infamous smirk. My heart is an idiot, because it starts to pound double-time when he smiles like that. "The amount of girls isn't because I'm a sex fiend. I was on a mission of sorts, and each girl made it worse. Well, I only fuck virgins for a reason, because

I've never gotten off." Kieren makes a whimpering sound that has me reaching over to rub his back.

"What?" I whisper out of shock, but the sound fills the space like a gunshot.

"I fake it," Kieren says with a shrug, shoulder muscles bunching beneath my palm. "You heard Tina. She was the only woman I was with that wasn't a virgin, so it was obvious. And never ask why I was with Tina, or I'll puke." Kieren shifts on the futon like he's going to be physically sick. "Everyone thinks I'm like this huge predator. I've been with a lot of girls, and not because I have a raging sex drive. I was looking for the one that I could get off with. A virgin doesn't know what they're doing, so they won't notice me faking an orgasm. Practice makes perfect, right?" Kieren mutters humorously.

"Jesus. Never?" The word is drawn out with shock.

"Don't worry, my equipment fires just fine, thank you very much. I just don't want to spend the rest of my life fucking my palm. Ya see, something happened, and when it's time to come, my mind flashes back. Once I go there, I *am* there. It's all I am. All I see. All I hear. All I feel. I'm no longer there with the girl."

"I'm surprised you keep trying, to be honest. I would've given up," I muse. My own sexual history sucks, but nothing like Kieren's.

"I still have the need, so I pick a girl out and I fuck them until they're satisfied, and then I fake it if I sense it will go wrong, or because I get bored and want it to be over."

"Oh, Kieren." I reach out to hold his hand, trying to let him know I'm listening and I'm hearing him. "That sounds so—"

"Lost? Lonely? Starved? I hunger for the connection, and my body wants the release, but it's impossible. See, I have the same problem that Devon has. A moan, a look, even the sound of ragged breath will flip the switch. Devon's a lucky fuck, once he gets going, he's good. But not me. I can't get there. Sometimes it happens with my own hand, too."

"I'd make it better, if I could," I say before I realize what I'm offering. "Shit, I didn't mean that the way it sounded. Sorry!"

Kieren gives me a look that screams he's pretty sure I meant it exactly how it sounded. "If you say sorry one more time, I'm gonna drag your ass to Axel's and get the word tattooed on your forehead," Kieren threatens jokingly. "It was your idea, after all."

"I'll pass." We share an uncomfortable chuckle.

"Ready?" Kieren asks while turning sideways on the futon so he can look at me.

"As ready as I'll ever be," I reply hesitantly.

"Well, here's the Mason history," Kieren begins. "Dad is a strong man, but he has his own demons he's fighting. Dad raised Isis, even when my grandfather was still alive. He tried to parent Auggie the best he could, too. Here Dad was, trying to walk in my grandfather's shoes while raising a little girl. So he met my mom, thinking she could mother Isis. Dev happened right away. Dad's old-school, so sex only in marriage." Kieren tosses me a look when I snort.

"Has no problem pimping my ass out, I see," I mutter sarcastically.

"Different rules apply to Devon," Kieren grumbles. "Mom was fragile, not all there mentally or emotionally, so she didn't turn out to be the mothering type. She needed to be mothered. Dad now had Isis, Mom, Dev, and me to feed, so Dad started working as an undercover cop in Boston."

"Whoa... no wonder he's so intimidating."

"Badass, right?" Kieren sounds just as awed. "Dev could never walk in Dad's shoes– the coward." He sneers, looking lethal. "So Dad only came home a few days a month. Those days were when Rae and Weston were made. Slowly Dad started coming home more often, and sticking around longer each time. For about a year he was always home, and then one day he didn't come back for three months."

"I can't imagine. I don't go more than two days tops without seeing every single Prynne and Webster, Grandma Margaret included." I shake my head, imagining how it would feel for both Malcolm and their family to be apart.

"Isis and Mom were fighting a lot about how Mom was... not right. So Isis sent the little ones to Mom's parents until Dad came home. Mom changed, became borderline catatonic. She said the loneliness and the stress of raising five kids got to her, but that was total bullshit. Isis, Devon, and I raised ourselves, and we all took care of Rae and Weston. When Dad came back, the kids came back, and he never left again. He started working for the local police department. But we never lived like a normal family. Mom didn't raise us. When I was ten, Isis moved out, leaving Dad to do it all. But when Dad was at work, everything fell on Dev and me, and Dad worked a lot. We needed to eat, so I don't blame him."

"That right there is why Malcolm needs Clover, and Clover needs Malcolm," I utter, never feeling more confident about anything in my entire life.

"Thank God," Kieren mumbles in a voice gone thick with emotion. He turns away from me so I can't see his face, then whispers his confession. "One night, our lives came crashing down. Dev was fourteen. I was twelve. Dad was called out to the scene of an accident, and the kids were at a sleepover with Isis... I can't–" Kieren stops, his silence screaming through the space.

"Are you sure you want to?" I curl up on the futon mattress and hug my knees to my chest.

"Yeah, I think I do. I've never said it out loud before. Okay, here goes nothing." Kieren drags in a heavy breath, fortifying himself to explain. "What we didn't know was that Dad had been working on a high-profile case, and the three months he was gone was because he was sequestered for a trial. I mean... Mom probably knew, but we were kids and didn't understand. Seven years later, the guys he put away came back looking for vengeance. Only they came back to us, while Dad was safe at work."

Kieren pulls me into his lap and hugs me fiercely– so tightly I can barely breathe. "We heard a noise. It was really late. Since we shared a room, Devon and I both bolted up at the scream. After taking care of the kids for so many years, we did everything together. Neither one of us could've seen what we saw and stayed sane if we hadn't been together."

Kieren takes a huge gulp of air and expels it out his lungs in a gush. His body shakes involuntarily as he takes a shuddering breath.

"Mom was held down in the middle of the living room, with a guy brutally raping her. Devon ran to stop him, but we didn't see the other two guys. I'll spare you the gory details. I'm pretty sure your imagination will fill in the blanks." Kieren recounts in an emotionless voice.

"Pan forward a few minutes, and Devon and I were duct taped to our dining room chairs– chairs that were placed front and center to the action. Three guys, one mom, and two kids who had to watch and listen. When Mom passed out, their attention was diverted to stealing anything that wasn't tied down. So if you want to know why certain noises and actions yank us into hell... there ya go."

"What happened to those men?" My voice cracks under the strain of my fury.

"Dad came home. They didn't notice, because by then, they were too busy looting the house. Mom was still passed out, but Devon and I were trying to break free. We were leaning over, gnawing at the other's tape. Dad walked right past us, and then we heard a series of pops. It's the best way to describe it. No yelling or screams, just... *pop... pop... pop... dead.*"

I jolt every time Kieren enunciates the word *pop*. "Your mom?" Malcolm's earlier words echo in my mind.

"Camille Mason was a weak woman. She blamed Dad for not being home, more so than the men who raped her. Mom was born weak, so she couldn't handle any stress at all. She had no self-preservation. She was the type of woman who would lie down and die of thirst when a cup of water was near her, all because she was too fucking lazy to reach for it. Mom's way of thinking was that someone should get the cup for her and put it to her lips, so she could drink. Mom thought the universe owed her everything, and that she didn't need to do a fucking thing but sit on her ass and wait for it, and by universe, I mean the rest of us. We were put on this earth to wait on Camille Mason. It was our fault if we didn't do *her* shit for her– *we* were the lazy ones. The most courage that woman ever showed was when she blew her own brains out by taking the most cowardly way out."

The bitter resentment, the anger, the ferocity Kieren expresses is at odds with the demeanor he shows the world. Kieren was always the jock, the one to make a joke or flirt. Kieren always appeared shallow, and now I realize his depth is endless.

"Willow, all my thoughts on my mother were formed long before she was raped. I don't blame her for that. I blame her for how she acted before and after. When you get bitched at for not answering the phone– a phone that was sitting next to her – because you're changing the diaper of her youngest kid, you tend to hate the bitch. Devon called Mom *Get Me* because everything out of her mouth started with *get me this or that.*"

"Selfish and blind, and now you're dealing with the same thing with Devon," I murmur to myself, earning me a silent head nod.

"Doesn't make them a bad person, just makes them hard to love. It was a struggle not to slap Mom when I was a kid. But I knew it wouldn't solve anything. Whether Mom was there or not, someone had to teach Weston to ride a bike, or kiss Rae's boo-

boos. So screaming at Mom would've only upset the kids. But Dev, I'm done. That passive behavior didn't help Mom, so I'm doing something else with him. I'm gonna call Devon out on his shit from now on."

"I'll help." I sound too eager, so eager it scares me.

"I'll be holding you to your word," Kieren warns. "My past is also why it makes me sick that Essie is going around calling my ass Date Rape– I know Auggie put her up to it." Kieren snarls. "You'd think witnessing what I witnessed, and not being able to have sex like a normal guy, would make that allegation fucking disgusting. Making fun of the survivor is a punch to the nuts. And I assure you, every girl I've ever been with wanted seconds or thirds. I'm not selfish, in or out of bed. Selfishness was worked out of me since the day I was born. I wouldn't know how to put myself first. Fuckin' Date Rape?"

"I'm sorry," I mutter instantly. "I'm at fault there, too. Not the nickname… the erm… indecision," I stammer.

"I don't blame you, Willow– I was outta my head that night."

"What happened next, Kieren?"

"Dad was under investigation for the killings. It took months to settle. While we waited on the verdict, Dad made us burn all the furniture, paint the inside of the house, and no matter how badly we wanted to forget, he wouldn't let us. Dad's philosophy is to exorcize your demons. But Mom loved her demons. She cradled them, and fed them, until they took her life. On a random Sunday night, the day before the official report was due to be released, Mom went to bed and… *pop… dead…* more furniture to burn, and another room to paint. Out of respect for my father and our family, the official report stated Mom was killed during the invasion, and my father was declared a hero."

"I… I…" I speechlessly try to come up with something appropriate to say, but nothing could ever change the past. "I have no words," I settle on.

"It's alright, Spanky. It was seven years ago. As horrible as it was, I'm just thankful Weston and Rae weren't home when the bad men hurt Mom and Dev– that they were so young when Mom killed herself. Mom offed herself on the other side of the wall from where we all sat watching *America's Funniest Home Videos*. The stupid bitch didn't account for trajectory– the bullet pierced the wall and went through the television. Mom could've taken one of us with her."

Kieren hauls me to my feet and embraces me. He's calmer than I'd expected. I would've run like Devon did. I see Kieren in a new light, and it shines a revelation on me. Adulthood isn't about age or intelligence, or even emotional maturity. It's how we react to the world around us. Kieren may act immature for the most part, but right now he is a grown man.

"I didn't give you the details, because Devon may want to someday. Elements of that night and the months that followed, belong to each one of us separately. I'm not sure if I can ever speak my parts, but I do feel better after giving the abbreviated version. Lighter, like the burden has lifted. Thank you for listening, Willow, and for not judging."

CHAPTER THIRTY-EIGHT

"Shit!" I hiss when I drop my keys on the porch underneath the doorknob. I hunt around in the dark, wondering why the porch light isn't lit.

Earlier, I wanted to run to Devon, but Kieren assured me Devon needed his space. I waited in the Explorer, ready to hunt Devon down, until the brothers were together at home, and then I spoke to each of them on my cell before I made my way to the Spook House.

I sigh heavily while I fish around for my keys. Emotionally and physically exhausted, I barely made it home in one piece. I'm not making light of the pain the Masons have been through, but it affected me deeply– drained me. A girl can only take so much shit at once. Hit after hit. I need a vacation.

I reach up to slide my key into the hole while crouching down. The door opens itself, startling the hell out of me. "Willow," Auggie utters coldly while glaring down at me.

"Auggie," I reply snidely. "Were you waiting up for me like a parent? I believe we've been over this before." Auggie steps over my back and shuts the door, so I'm trapped between his intimidating size and the closed door. I shimmy up, trying to avoid touching him as I stand. Auggie's size has never intimidated me before, and it won't tonight. The fact that Auggie's trying to use it against me, just makes him an arrogant prick.

"You need to leave." Auggie's voice is deep and frigid. Instead of avoiding my gaze, he won't look anywhere but my eyes. He doesn't even blink. His usually happy, seafoam green eyes burn me with glacial fire.

"Why? Do you have guests over? You know I don't care what you do in your bedroom, but the Playroom isn't open for business yet." I scowl up at him. How dare he ruin our Grand Opening?

"You broke the one rule I will not tolerate, Willow– I've warned you. This is reality, and there are no punishments strong enough to take away what you did tonight. I won't stand idly by while you ruin your life. I can't watch it." Auggie clips out in disgust and steps away from me, as if he can't stand being in my presence.

"What the hell are you talking about?" I whisper angrily. If I don't whisper, I'll fucking scream.

"You smell like pot. Did you think you could get away with it?" Auggie asks, sounding incredulous, all the while popping that goddamned auburn eyebrow of his.

"I didn't plan to get away with anything, Auggie, because I didn't do a cocksucking thing wrong. I was going to give you a play-by-play, because I needed advice and a hug. But you're doing it again, where I come home and you accuse me of shit without giving me the benefit of the doubt– without trusting me." I clutch my chest and pound my fist in time with my heartbeat, expressing pure frustration and heartache. "Remember the Tina incident? This is the same fucking thing!"

"There is never trust when it comes to an addict. Never," Auggie hisses. "Every word is a lie, especially the ones bracketed by *trust me*." Auggie has the audacity to make air-fucking-quotes as he berates me.

"Perfect, fucking perfect," I mutter, fed the fuck up with Auggie's bullshit. "I'd ask how you knew to stand out here and wait to accost me, how you smelled pot smoke on me from the other side of a closed door, why you were waiting, but I won't. I could tell you why I smell like pot, and it's not an excuse– it's just the fucking truth. But I'm a goddamned liar, eh, Auggie?"

"The only good reason to use marijuana is for medicinal purposes. Unless you were diagnosed with a rapid case of Glaucoma in the past few hours, I don't give a fuck what your excuse is," he seethes.

Auggie doesn't shout at me. He doesn't call me names. He's calm, collected, and in control of every cell in his body. He finds himself justified for his reaction. I'm fed-the-fuck-up with his bullshit parenting. He's the worst parent I've ever seen. Auggie says he's never trusted me. Well, I definitely don't trust him now. I guess we're even.

"Un-fucking-believable," I mutter as I stare up at Auggie. I hope my face is as transparent as it used to be. I want that motherfuck to see just how furious, betrayed, hurt, and disappointed I am... in *him*.

"As far as it being my call or decision, it's my call on whether or not I allow a lying, manipulative, untrustworthy, worthless, going-nowhere-in-life-addict loser into my home. Willow, I won't allow you to taint my personal space. It's my decision who I spend my time with. Who I build a life with. Willow, that person will not be you, because you're incapable of acting with maturity instead of illogical instinct. I want you to leave *my* house. Go home to your parents, to your childhood bedroom. If you behave like a child, you should sleep where a child sleeps."

Auggie gestures to a backpack– my backpack from when I was in high school –a child's backpack. The zipper is strained from holding most of my belongings. I bite back a sob. Everything I own fits into a backpack?

Un-fucking-believable.

Wordless... speechless... thoughtless... faithless... emotionless... numb... Auggie called me manipulative... untrustworthy... worthless... loser.

I stand before Auggie, as he finally breaks his trust. Not the trust he has in me, but the trust I have in him. Auggie thinks himself a mature person who reacts with forethought, yet time and time again he has to apologize for jumping to the wrong conclusions– for seeing me as the old Willow.

Fury slams into me and takes root. The filter from my brain to my mouth disintegrates. I release the pent up frustration I've been holding back for months. Years. A lifetime.

"You're kicking me out of the Spook House? The house I fucking rebuilt? You're removing me from my bedroom, where the furniture I purchased is located? Or are we doing that nine-tenths of the law bullshit you're so fond of again?" I stare Auggie down, unrelenting. "Thanks for proving my suspicions right, how nothing I do will ever be good enough, how working my ass off gained me nothing and you everything. No matter what, I felt like this anvil was hanging over my head, because I knew you could tear this house away from me with the raise of that cocksucking eyebrow of yours. Even if I paid actual rent, you'd still toss my ass on the street like trash. Thanks."

"Your defensive reaction is that of an addict. They always lash out, trying to manipulate you, trying to make you the bad guy, when all you're doing is respecting yourself. You booked your own eviction notice." Auggie shows no shame, and sounds colder than ice. "Loser potheads don't sleep underneath my roof, no matter what. You were warned." Arrogant and wrong, Auggie stands before me and folds his arms over his chest like he owns the world.

"Loser? What the fuck was ever wrong with being me? Nothing!" My scream pierces the night, hurting my throat and causing Auggie to flinch. Panting, breathless, it takes me several long seconds, but I manage to rein myself in. Auggie doesn't get to own my emotions, to twist them. "I've never had someone make me feel as infinitesimal as you, Auggie, and I don't mean my size. How can you tell me you love me, only if I'm one way, but not if I'm another, when I'm still me either way? That's not unconditional, that's emotional extortion, and that sure as fuck isn't love."

"Did I just say I didn't love you, Willow?" Auggie sounds superior as he talks down to me about something that should make a person feel good, not reduce them to something worth less than shit.

"Love? Actions speak the loudest, and apologies don't mean shit if you're a repeat offender, kinda like believing a lying addict. I can't believe your apologies– it would make me a fool."

"I won't be apologizing for kicking a drug addict from my home, especially when the police chief and his cop son visit on a daily basis." Auggie says with a straight face, causing me to bark a humorless laugh.

"That's fuckin' rich. Wow…blllliiind." I draw out. "I was just a kid, a kid who was trying to find her way. Instead of helping me, befriending me, you've judged me every step of the way. Ya know what, Auggie? I don't need to make excuses to you. I don't need to lie to you. Ya wanna know why? Because I *am* an adult, not *your* child. I don't need *you* to make *my* way through this life." I sneer, staring at Auggie like he smells like shit. "Even if you fire me, I'll find another job. I can assure you, I'll never starve. But Revamped might just flop without me– I can promise your ass that much."

"I'm not firing you. I'm getting you the fuck outta my sight before I beat your drug-addled ass to death." Auggie spits, "Looking at you is making me sick."

"Goddammit!" I shout, arms lashing out, feet stomping on the porch's wooden floor– my version of a mini-tantrum. "I like me! I like the Willow I've become. If you're too blind to see me for who I am–" I lean forward into Auggie's personal space and barely breathe into his face, "Then fuck you, buddy." I whisper, because anything more audible would cause an explosion inside of me.

I take a page from Auggie's book. I don't yell, stomp my feet, or throw a shit-fit. I walk over to the bag Auggie packed for me– the bag he packed like an overbearing, controlling parent. I turn to look at Auggie, really look at him, and show him my displeasure in what I see before me.

"I'm done. I won't stay and argue when I'm not wanted," I say, but not in defeat– intelligence. It's not cowardly to back down when it's stupid to fight a losing battle. "Don't bother apologizing for this again. In advance, I don't accept your future apology, and mark my words, you *will* apologize," I hiss directly into Auggie's face. "You'll never change. I evolve by the minute, yet you keep repeating your past mistakes. Auggie, maybe it's you who needs to grow up and stop acting like a know-it-all, petulant child who doesn't know shit."

I give Auggie one last withering look. The indecision that crosses his face vindicates me. I can already see the wheels turning in his head. *Was he wrong about me? Did he misread what I did?* On the heels of those thoughts, I can see the moment of revelation– the moment Auggie realizes he just fucked up epically, and this version of Willow won't back down. Nothing was wrong with the younger, more naïve version of me, except for the fact that she wouldn't have batted an eyelash at forgiving Auggie the moment that expression crossed his face.

Well, this bitch just became an independent adult, and she's going where she belongs. There's a pair of warm, welcoming arms waiting for her, and she's going to use them for the very first time.

CHAPTER THIRTY-NINE

I shower out of respect. I want to be accepted as I am, but you shouldn't come to someone for support and understanding smelling like pot. I'm sure it's in an unwritten rule book somewhere.

I haven't cried, or screamed, or made elaborate murder plans, or debated arson techniques, or executed the perfect heist by emptying Revamped's business account and Auggie's personal bank account. You really shouldn't piss off the person you added to your accounts, just saying. I could be taking that much-needed vacation as early as tomorrow morning at nine a.m. when the bank opens.

I'd love to be vindictive and spiteful, but it goes against what I was screaming at Auggie, how I'm a changed woman. Willow the Wayward would've grabbed Violent Violet and hatched a revenge scheme from hell. But that was the old me, and I don't want to be a bad influence on an impressionable child anymore. The new me will ignore Auggie, make him beg for my forgiveness, and then feel a sense of power when I don't forgive him… and then feel like shit for hurting his feelings… and then forgive him, and pray he doesn't hurt me again.

Tough love is dual-sided.

I'm not numb, and it's not because I took a scalding hot shower. I'm resolved. I know I'm right– I can feel it to my bones. I feel vindicated. I am proud of myself for not groveling to Auggie, begging him to allow me to tell the truth, and then doing my damnedest to make him believe it. As an adult, with a fulltime occupation, while going to college fulltime, I shouldn't have to defend myself or my actions to anyone. Even if I had smoked pot, it was none of Auggie's business.

Augustus Kline doesn't get a vote in my life– it's not a democracy, and Auggie isn't my dictator. It's all on me.

I can breathe. I finally love being inside my own skin. It's freeing. It's the taste of independence, and it's more addictive than any substance I could ever take into my body.

"Welcome home, Sapling," Clover whispers in the dark as I crawl across her bed, snuggle under the covers, and then lie in her waiting arms. I sigh as I hold her back– hold her for the first time ever. It feels good. Right.

Home.

"I know it's not much after everything, but I always knew you cared. No matter what, you'd always be here waiting for me. It was a comfort."

"That's why I'm here." Clover arms squeeze me tighter, like she either doesn't want to let go, or she's trying to hold me together, instinctively knowing I'm about to break.

"Listen, I know I've been a spoiled brat, and I need to apologize. But I'd rather show you I mean it, because saying it would just be empty words. You were right. I knew you were right when I moved from Mom and Dad's, but I had to at least try."

"Willow," Clover murmurs, sounding just as emotionally exhausted as I am. "Are you okay?" Hearing the crushed tone in Clover's voice nearly crushes me, too. But the lack of judgment makes me smile. She didn't say I told you so as I'd expected. No, Clover's first thought was of my welfare. Hell, she didn't even ask what happened. Clover may not be the best mom on the planet, but she's the one I crawled to when I needed a hug. She's the mom I pray will put the Mason family back together again.

"I'm just singed a little around the edges," I admit with a sharp laugh.

"Not burned to ash, I hope?" She plays along.

"Nope." I snort.

"Well, give it time. Once you sleep on it, you'll feel differently. Perhaps by morning, you'll be scorched," she teases, trying to lighten the dark conversation. "Don't lie down and die. Take all that pain, ball it up deep in your belly, and use it to move forward. I don't know what happened, and it doesn't matter. You can tell me, or not. It'll be the first conscious choice you'll make as an adult."

"Auggie…" I begin with my first choice, the choice to trust my sister. "He's the type of man who will control you, consume you, and nothing you do will ever be good enough. I know who I am, and who I was. Auggie made me feel badly about myself. He made me doubt my own judgment. He made me feel alive, sexy, and wanted for all of two seconds. But at the same time, he made me feel small, stupid, and worthless. Auggie inspired me and stilted me. He made me love him and feel loved. He made me hate him and hate myself. And Auggie did all of it because he thought it was the right thing to do. Will I forgive him? Yes. Will I ever trust him again? I don't know. I'll have to let ya know."

"Seeing as you're in my bed, I assume you're not at the Spook House for a reason. It's not hard to deduce that he pushed you out somehow, since I know you love that house because of all the blood, sweat, and tears you've put into it. You know and I know, Augustus will probably come to his senses and eventually ask you to come back. What will you do?"

"I don't know. If I do, it won't be how it was before tonight. There's this sense of security, a comfort that vanished when he did and said what he did tonight. I'd like to say it was my gullibility, but no. If I go back, I'll always feel... unwelcome."

"And no one should feel unwelcome in their own home," Clover whispers. Her voice is filled with a remembered pain over something I don't understand.

"Exactly," I respond, too scared to examine Clover's comment any further. "I've worked so hard, and Auggie's blind to it. All the progress I've made at Revamped, the Spook House, and FCC. I don't want a pat on the back, but some acknowledgment would be nice. I owe some of the credit to Auggie. I wouldn't have tried as hard without him pushing me. I know I'm not perfect, but I didn't deserve to be called a *going-nowhere-in-life-addict*. It's not true– not one word of that is true anymore."

"Well, if Auggie said that and actually thinks it, then fuck him," Clover bites out.

I huff a laugh. "That was my parting comment to the man."

"Atta girl," Clover praises. "Auggie would have to be blind not to see the difference in you. Perhaps he's too close and it warps his vision. Putting distance between you guys will cast you in a new light. He'll see what he's missing, because he'll miss you. Your presence fills a house– I bet you didn't realize this."

"Yeah, 'cuz I'm Mary freakin' sunshine, over here," I mutter while giving a dramatic eye roll.

"It's true. It's too quiet around here now. The first few weeks, we turned the television up to compensate. Violet was beside herself without her sparring partner." Clover laughs at me when I growl. "Willow, I'm very proud of you. I've been over-emotional lately. Losing Sam..." Clover's voice breaks, and that bursts my dam. I press my face against her soft chest and sob. Her arms tighten in a vise-like grip as I unleash all my pent-up emotions.

Fuck being scorched– I'm incinerated.

"Losing Sam was difficult," Clover chokes. "But seeing how it affected you, how it changed your course in life… that is what killed me. I had to be strong for our family, but I can't tell you the amount of times I broke down after seeing you high and drunk and belligerently fighting us. What killed me the most is how Sam would've hated himself for causing you so much distress. The past few months, it's like I can feel Sam smiling down at us in pride."

"Jesus, Clover." I hiccup on a sob. "Are you trying to kill me?"

Clover ignores me and continues to talk. "I've been emotional because it's helping me move on. If a stoned-out-of-her-gourd kid can turn her life around, then so can I. I love my family, but I want a new outlook on life. Maybe you can help me."

"I'll try, but I'm not making any promises," flows snarkily from my lips, followed by a giggle. Oh, Clover has a change a'coming– his name is Malcolm Mason, and I hope he lights a fire under her ass.

"Can I ask you something?" I've never heard Clover sound bashful. It makes me intrigued.

"I invaded your bed in the middle of the night. You can ask me anything you please. I have nowhere else to go. I was already coming here. But when Auggie told me to go home to my childhood bedroom, because that's where a child should sleep, I decided nothing would ever get me to sleep in that bed again. You know I'm stubborn."

"Extremely stubborn. Which one are you really with?" Clover's words flow rapidly, and they're so quiet I barely hear her. It's like she had to say the words before she chickened out.

"Fuck if I know," I bark out. "Neither. No one. Not Auggie for damned sure– never was with him. Thought I was with Devon, until he pulled this exorcist bullshit on me, lying bastard. He and I are in for a long talk tomorrow."

"How do you feel about them?" Clover shifts nervously around on the bed, indicating that her question makes her very uncomfortable.

"I do love Auggie, and respect him. But right now, I dislike him, and don't respect him. But that love is the same you'd feel for a mentor or brother. If I had a relationship with Auggie, he'd try to parent me, and I'd fight him tooth and nail."

"Yeah, I can see that," Clover says, and I can hear the amusement in her voice. "Rule number one in dealing with Willow Aster Prynne, don't push her. You must lead her." I growl again because she's right. "What about Devon? That kiss at the twins' party wasn't a friendly kiss."

"What an f'n disaster." I groan, pissed at myself for being so stupid. "I love Devon. I don't know if it's as a friend or boyfriend. I do know he's the first real best friend I've ever had, and I don't want to screw it up. But I fear he already did that himself tonight, because the best friend I have is not the real Devon Mason– the good parts are, I hope. I miss Devon when he's not around, and it would kill me to lose him."

"I think you kind of answered it yourself– your true feelings. You'd miss the friend, not the boyfriend... And Kieren?" Clover coaxes.

"You know about him?" I squeak, feeling guilty.

"I'm not blind, Willow. You've been fixated on the boy since grade school. If it wasn't for the shot, I would've been worried about you coming home some night, knocked up with Kieren Mason's kid in your belly."

"Seriously?" I grumble. "Give me some credit, Clover. I did say no eventually."

"Eventually?" Clover sounds hella confused. Glad the Date Rape story isn't making the rounds.

"Doesn't matter," I mumble quickly. "Kieren is a fuckhead, but he's growing on me like a disease. Love of my life– oh, hell no! Strike that. I'm not *in* love with him right now. Do I love Kieren as a person? Yes. I have an unnatural attraction to the guy for some inexplicable reason. If you can call inexplicable tall, blond, built, charming, and athletic... oh, and has a deep man laugh and a smile that makes my heart go all aflutter."

"Ah, good ol' hormones and chemistry at work, there." Clover's laughter makes me smile. Glad my problems are amusing to someone. "Not to worry you further, but some of that is probably what you're picking up around Devon. Chemistry-wise, the brothers must be similar."

"Great!" I sound thoroughly put out. "I suck at biology." I sigh heavily, confused all to hell. "I'm only eighteen. I don't have to make up my mind right now, and I won't be with Devon by default. Devon deserves more than being my second choice– he wouldn't be, but it'd look like it while Auggie and I are hating on each other. Devon hates himself, so I'm pretty sure he's incapable of loving anyone else. And Kieren, that just freaks me out on a level I don't dare visit anytime soon. Incinerate wouldn't be powerful enough to describe it."

"Are you…" Clover cuts herself off, and I swear I can feel the heat of her blush.

That blush is question enough for me– I put my sister out of her misery. "Auggie and I never really had sex. The man took my virginity in a clinical manner. I wanted it, so don't blame him," I add hastily before Clover decides to neuter Auggie. "We've never had real sex, and we never will. There are some physical issues between us." I snicker as I picture the Beast. "I'm okay with that now. I wasn't at first. It made me feel like shit."

"Physical?" Clover's curiosity would kill any self-respected cat.

"Ah, eleven inches… all I'm saying about that," I stammer, and now it's my turn to blush.

"*Fucking ouch!*" Clover curses the Beast, and it's the most hilarious thing I've ever heard.

"Say that to Robbie next time you see him. See how he responds. Bet it's not ouch." I snicker at Clover's confusion. "My real first time was last night with Devon, and I kinda regret it now. It was by my choice obviously. I just hadn't realized it would be so tortuous. I don't mean physically painful. It was mentally and emotionally taxing. I'm angry because I feel duped. Don't kill me for what I'm about to say."

"Okay," Clover sounds suspicious of me, as she should. "I'll try not to."

"Auggie made it sound like he wanted Devon to break me in so he could fit *that* in me, when all along he was instructing me so I could be with Devon, because Devon's fucked in the head when it comes to sex. So no more sex for me. I don't want it unless it's mutual with no schemes. I just want a guy to want me for me. I want a guy who I feel passion and connection with. Is that too much to ask?"

"No," Clover breathes softly. "That's not too much to ask. Can I tell you a story, Willow? It will circle back to what you were just saying about needing to be wanted. I have to add something before I tell you my story, though. I know you and Violet are hurt because I insisted on you both getting the shot, and I have a very good reason. But after what you just told me, I bet you're glad I put your naughty ass on *Depo*." Clover snickers, and it warms me. "Be careful, though. No birth control is foolproof."

I breathe a sigh of relief that Clover's okay with her sister's skanky behavior. "I'd love to get to know you as a person, Clover." The hitch in her breathing has my eyes watering again. I sniffle and wipe my eyes on her nightgown.

"So Mom and Dad are weirdoes– there's no denying it. In order for me to rebel, I had to be normal. I loved the structure of school, it centered me. I understand you better than you think, Sapling. I was tiny, smaller than you are. I also didn't have a lot of friends because I exceled in school. By spring break of my senior year, I was only sixteen, seventy-five pounds, and an inch shy of five foot. I was worse off than you. At least you had the badass, stoner vibe going on. They didn't make fun of me because I was invisible."

"No freakin' way were you smaller than me." I thump my head against her breast as example.

"Smaller– I only had a set of nipples and nothing else. I told you how having kids brought out any curves I have now. I grew two more inches by the time I turned twenty."

"So there's still hope for me yet," I muse, and Clover laughs at the yearning tone in my voice.

"My senior year was split between Fairport High and FCC. I met a girl at my afternoon college courses. Ginny. She was a few years older than me, but we hit it right off. In fact, we're still best friends to this day," Clover says with a smile in her voice.

"I feel like a little maggot right now, let me tell ya. The fact that I'm just now finding out who your best friend is." I shake my head in disgust. "I've been completely disconnected, and Kieren better book me a session at Axel. I'm getting that tattoo." I snort.

"What?" Clover yelps in outrage.

"Sorry, I'm just kidding." I chuckle. "It's a private joke between us. I was told to stop apologizing constantly."

"Oh, thank God." Clover sighs in relief. "Since you hate Auggie fathering you, your lack of knowledge of me is because you've resented me mothering you. It's fine. Now is the first time we could connect as something more– as women."

"I'm glad, Clover. I'm trying. Really, I'm trying." Getting the sniffles again, I distract myself with Clover's story. "Ginny?"

"So, Ginny. We talked in class for months, but we never got the chance to hang out. During spring break, I had time off, and she invited me to a party. It wasn't a college party or anything– it was her family, but they were young. The moment I walked into Malcolm and Camille Mason's house my life changed."

"Oh. My. God. You're being serious?" I bolt up off the bed and try to look Clover in the eye. The glint of blue is shining with amusement.

"Hell, yeah, serious as meeting the love of your life. Camille was Ginny's sister. Everyone was there. Augustus ran up to me like I was a celebrity, and dragged me around, introducing me to everyone– the little shit. Hard to believe I met your future boyfriend when he was twenty months old, because your child-sized boss introduced us." Clover teases. "And hottie Kieren was incubating inside his momma's tummy."

"Now you're just making shit up as you go along," I grumble and slap her in the arm.

"My hand to God, I've known those guys since I was younger than you... so we're huddled around a picnic table. Everyone was chatting and I'm listening. Auggie and Isis were next to me, fighting over who got to force-feed Devon pieces of hot dog, making the poor kid cry."

"Why does that not surprise me?" I mutter, but I'm smiling.

"Auggie and Isis fought incessantly. It took everything in me not to smack them, which thankfully Malcolm reached across the table and popped each one on the side of the head... So I was eating corn on the cob when I saw him– gnawing on it like an idiot, I was. I dropped my ear and splattered myself with butter, but I couldn't look away. He was the most gorgeous man I'd ever seen. I thought he was my age, those chipmunk cheeks made him look like a kid. I found out later, much later. Too late. He was twenty."

"Sam," I whisper in awe. Clover has never told anyone how they met, no matter how much we begged. Clover's giving me a gift, and it has to be killing her.

"There's something about instant chemistry that cannot be denied. We didn't talk. All we did was stare at each other while the party went on around us. Hours later, when I was leaving the bathroom– before I could even blink, I was pressed against the wall with a pair of luscious lips descending on mine. Sam was my first kiss, and minutes later in Isis's bedroom, he was my first. There was no thought. It was a compulsion that couldn't be denied. I didn't even know his name. I hadn't even spoken with him yet. I didn't regret it, but there were consequences to losing my virginity at sixteen, without protection, to a grown man whose name I didn't even know. Five weeks later, I was bawling my eyes out on my graduation day. I was pregnant. Instant chemistry can't be denied, but it's irreversible too."

"Clover!" I cry. "What happened?"

"First, I'll say this is why I put you girls on the shot as soon as you menstruated. It's a fairytale to think you'll fall in love first, and then decide to make love. My decision was protection against later heartbreak. It's possible to have your innocence torn from you, and you're the one left with the consequences. But sometimes you turn brainless and fuck against a closed door while your best friend's family is in the living room, and then again on the edge of the bed, and finish the round off bent over a dresser." Clover trails a laugh at the memory, and then turns serious. "I didn't want you to go through the agony of having your self-worth shredded."

Clover pulls herself up to rest against the headboard. She's silent for a very long time. I worry she's fallen asleep, but I see a sliver of blue peering at me.

"I told Mom and Dad, and then signed up for summer courses at college. I moved away to live on campus. I told no one but my parents and Robin. I didn't know what I was going to do, but it wouldn't ruin my life. It was a choice I made, and I would deal with it. The child wasn't a problem– it was just a new path I had to take.

"Only problem was that I underestimated what it meant to have a best friend. I didn't have one for the first sixteen years of my life, never going to anyone for advice and expecting none in return. So I was shocked when Ginny showed up months later, fed up that I was ignoring her, and she had a handsome man in tow.

"When you weigh eighty pounds, you can't hide a pregnancy, especially when you're six months along. Sam wouldn't leave me alone after that. An hour with Sam, was like a week with someone else, and he made sure to give me many, many hours to learn him. Sam was an open book."

"What did you do with the baby?" I regret the words as soon as they're spoken. Clover starts sobbing hysterically. Feeling helpless, all I want to do is soothe her, but I don't know how.

"Sam never forgave me for this, even on his deathbed. Sam said he'd love me for an eternity, but he'd never forgive me. Sam loved me so much that *he* did what *I* thought was right. I regretted it a billion times over for emotional reasons, but then when I truly thought it over, I would agree with my decision. I went back and forth for years, but I believe that once you make a life-changing decision, you better stick with it. I gave the baby up for adoption, and it nearly killed me."

"Why?" I breathe out in absolute shock.

"I was sixteen, with no way of supporting a child, and not experienced enough to keep it alive. I had never held a child, let alone changed a diaper or fed one. I didn't adopt the child out because of my schooling, or because I didn't love their father. I didn't want Sam to think he was obligated to marry me, but that didn't influence my decision. Willow, I gave my baby up because I wasn't ready, and I thought my inexperience would ruin them.

"Sam chased me for three years, trying to convince me I was ready. I was never ready, even when the birth control failed. I married Sam because I loved him, but mostly I married him because I couldn't give another child away, especially two. I loved my first child enough to let them go. But I was older, more experienced, but no less stupid when I got married and had the twins. At least I could protect them, provide for them, and keep them alive."

"I get it. I'm almost three years older than you were then, and I can't imagine having a child for at least a decade. You did the right thing, even if Sam didn't agree."

"It was an open adoption, and if you asked me right now if I regretted it, I'd scream yes. I've ached since I was sixteen... Willow," Clover leans in and cups my face in her hands. I stare at her in bewilderment.

"Willow–"

"I thought I heard voices." Violet interrupts as she scurries into her mother's bedroom. "You should've woken me– we could've had a slumber party!" Violet shouts with excitement as she tackles me from behind. "Did you get in a fight with one of your boyfriends?" Curiosity heavily laces Violet's voice.

I want to rewind and press pause at the moment just before Violet interrupted us. Clover was going to tell me something important, and now I'll never know. Clover talks to Violet, but even in the dark, I can feel her attention centered on me.

CHAPTER FORTY

"Not cool," Seth whines when Clover won't let him order a double espresso before school.

When I woke this morning, I was shocked by the thrilled reception I got from the Websters. Clover was humming, Violet was fluttering around the house while getting ready for school, and Seth wandered a foot behind me while chirping question after question, asking why I was at their house.

Since we all were going in the same direction at the same time, Clover decided we should leave twenty minutes early and pick up breakfast at our local bakery. As Clover's examining eye roves over today's selection of goodies, she keeps commenting about what she'd do differently. You can take the woman out of the kitchen, but…

"I'll have a double espresso and a white chocolate mocha. Can you write *hot chocolate* on the espresso?" A sneaky tone warps my voice. "Oh, and I'll take one of those lemon poppy seed muffins."

"I love you, Willow!" Seth shouts gleefully, and then he orders a sour cream donut.

"Order me one, too." Violet whisper conspiratorially in my ear.

"Another phony hot chocolate before Momma Bear notices." I snicker with the barista who used to go to school with me. I slide my debit card in the reader after ordering Clover a black coffee– boring!

"We're gonna get caught." Seth tries to guzzle three days' worth of caffeine before he's caught.

"We won't. Willow will get into trouble," Violet sings just before she burns her tongue on the hot espresso. Her pained pucker makes me unhinge.

"Oh, my God!" I tilt my head back and laugh at the ceiling. "Gotta love Karma." I sing in the same cadence Violet used.

I feel eyes on me– it makes my stomach clench. Revulsion. I close my eyes and groan. Only one bastard on this planet elicits that visceral reaction out of me. I'd know the sensation of that stare eating me alive anywhere. I slowly turn to look at him, just as someone else stands on their tippy-toes to kiss his whisker-stubbled cheek.

"Motherfuck!" I growl and receive a chastising look from my sister, until she sees the direction of my gaze. "You've got to be fucking kidding me."

"Don't go there, Willow." Clover warns, thinking it's a scorned woman tantrum about to burst from my mouth.

If Auggie is screwing someone, it's Isis's and Robbie's business, not mine. If they like being disrespected, great for them. This is *addict* business. I get tossed from the house I built because Auggie accuses me of smoking when I hadn't. Auggie says he won't allow a pothead under his roof, but he'll allow a hard-core drug abuser and dealer in his bed. As always, Auggie's space is sacred, but not his body. Hypocrite!

Getting into my face until we're forehead-to-forehead, Clover fiercely whispers so no one else can overhear. "Auggie's not worth it," Clover says, thinking the fury that is radiating from me is over the skank on Auggie's arm.

"I know he's not," I snarl. "Auggie doesn't see me as I am. That's why I'm angry. He doesn't trust me, so now I feel stupid for ever trusting him."

"As women, it is our duty to show self-restraint and dignity. Show Violet what it means to be a woman, and Seth how a man should treat a woman. My rule, ask yourself if you'd want Seth to treat a woman that way, or if you'd want Violet to be treated that way. If the answer is no, then the situation is unacceptable and the man is wrong. Don't allow yourself to accept this shit, and don't be this type of woman." Clover gestures at Tina.

"Oh, I could never sink as far as *that* woman," I twist out angrily.

"Be the kind of woman who causes a man to regret, because his juvenile behavior let you get away. Be Auggie's cause for change. Be your future husband's salvation. If he grows the hell up, then that husband may be Auggie, or it might not be. But it doesn't matter who you choose as your future, as long as you love them, you're happy, you're not stifled, and you're respected. Don't act like trash and feel like trash, just because a childish, selfish man is treating you like trash. Let it go... so what do you do, Willow?" Clover chants.

"I let it go," I readily answer. My heart is beating out of my chest. My breathing is labored and raspy from anticipation.

"Good girl," Clover praises, finally relaxing– relaxing way too soon.

"I'll be an adult," I promise. I narrow my eyes and give a mischievous smirk. "Or not. A few minutes from now, I'll let it go. After I say my piece," I toss over my shoulder as I cross the bakery.

Stepping right up to the happy couple, I flash a menacing smile. "Roving Playroom, Auggie? Or is this a breakfast date?" I sound pleasant and perky with my raspy voice, which seems to frighten both of them. I lean in and whisper loudly for all to hear, "Or are you making a buy?"

Staring gape-mouthed at me, looking guilty as all hell, Auggie is rendered speechless by my brazenness. I may not be the smartest, or the tallest, or the strongest, or the biggest. We all know I'm not the sexiest. But what I do have is a very, *very* large set of motherfucking balls.

"I'm shocked, since it was only last night we parted ways. I thought you were the loyal sort when living in reality," I mutter flippantly. "Obviously I'm not talking sex, since you use your body like a dive bar toilet. Rule Numero Uno is stinging the fuck outta me right now."

Auggie breathes my name, and it sends electrical current down my spine– *not going there. I'm pissed at him, remember?* Auggie pastes a friendly expression on his face and waves to my family, who are hovering a few feet too close to not be eavesdropping. When he glances back at me, his face is filled with remorse.

"This is Tina," Auggie introduces my replacement– his new brain-dead skank/pet project. Must be Auggie has to have a mission. His mission with me is complete now that Devon got laid good and proper. Auggie tossed my ass out and selected another wayward soul. Lucky for Auggie, this one has a big set of tits and a stretched out, beastly-sized vagina.

I mock Auggie by raising a patronizing eyebrow. "Oh, we've met." I drag the words out while nodding my head like a moron, while wearing a huge, happy grin. "Haven't we, Tina?"

Laughter flows from my throat when I remember what I said to Kieren– if he'd fuck that, I'm glad I never did him. Then I remember my thoughts on Devon– if he liked a skank like Tina, then he wasn't worth my energy. This applies to any man in Tina's orbit, especially Auggie. He should be better than this. Devon and Kieren are young, and we tend to do stupid shit as part of the growing up process. Self-professed, smarty-pants Auggie should know better by now.

I'm through with men. At eighteen and some change, I decide they aren't worth the trouble. Fuck the whole lot of them, and not in a good way.

Auggie looks between me and Tina with a quizzical expression on his face, and then like the sun parting storm clouds, his expression clears. He finally remembers how Tina and I know each other.

I move my hand slightly. Frightened, Tina rebounds several feet in fear. "Did I mention this earlier, Tina?" I stress her name. "Thanks for the drink."

I walk away with my head held high, humming my own badass theme song. My twins join me in tune while my sister tries to figure out why the fuck we're humming.

When Auggie finally shows up to Revamped, I mumble, "Last night's sales report," as I press the paper in his hand. Auggie's half an hour late, no doubt consoling his skank. Tina was looking mighty piqued when I strolled away.

"Willow?" is said in the *do I know you* voice, combined with the *I've never seen you before* look. I ignore Auggie, and yank my economics book from my new backpack– the *adult* Willow pack. I flutter the pages to this evening's lesson and get to studying.

"What's this?" Auggie asks while tapping my book with a fingertip.

I debate between two responses: *going-nowhere-in-life-addict's text book*, or *a text book, you fucking idiot*.

"College-level economics," I say politely without looking up.

I'm so pissed at Auggie right now, that if I look at him, I'll burn him with my eyes. He's lucky I came to work today. I debated on telling Auggie to shove my job at Revamped up his wide ass. Then I was going to sit back and watch everything I built crumble down around his ears… and then I felt like shit, because it would be what *I* built crumbling. I've worked too hard to allow Auggie to push me out. Revamped is mine now. I might not own it, but it breathes for me.

The Spook House was altered by my hand, but it will survive without me. Revamped won't. It's not arrogance– it's confidence. Just like I bet Rush would implode without Isis.

Auggie doesn't run his own businesses. He finds a woman to do it for him. Maybe Auggie's buying a drug den or a whore house next, and that's why he's now auditioning Tina for the role.

"Since when?" Auggie's voice sounds pained, and I have to close my eyes against the emotions threatening to choke me. "I knew you were taking a course on web design. I just didn't think you were going fulltime."

"It amazes me how you don't notice what I'm doing, or hear what I'm saying, unless it directly affects what you want. Did you fail to notice me studying? Do you fail to remember conversations we've had about school? Damn, Auggie, what do I get out of this partnership, other than a motherfucking headache?" My voice didn't hitch… Please, for the love of God, I hope Auggie didn't hear it.

"I'm sorry," Auggie whispers against my ear before he stalks away with his tail between his legs.

After spending twenty minutes I'm not proud of– bawling my eyes out in the bathroom like a total fucking girl, snotting all over myself, feeling sorry for myself –I pull up my big girl panties and let it go. Calmed, rational again, I'm back on my stool scrolling through online orders.

Lurking on the other side of the counter like a burly, red-headed Revamped customer, looking sheepish as all hell, Auggie stares at me, trying to gain my attention. I ignore Auggie, marveling at how satisfying it is, and roll my eyes inwardly. When annoying me into acknowledging him doesn't work, he tries talking again.

"How do you know Tina?" pops out of Auggie's mouth. His hand flies up, no doubt wishing to stop his verbal spewage.

I shut my laptop and finally look up at Auggie, glare rather. "I know you know how, Auggie," I utter slowly with a dramatic eye roll. "But I'll play this game of *I'm a deaf, blind, and dumb man* you've started. Do I issue points, or is it a winner/loser thing?"

"Willow!" Auggie barks, losing patience. "I fuckin' get it. I hear you talk, but I don't actually listen. I just try to figure out how to get what I want while you're talking. No need to smash it in my face. Just answer the question."

"Maybe I want to smash you in the face with a motherfuckin' baseball bat," I say snidely. "Give a girl some satisfaction, why don't ya, by grabbing the bat for me."

"Answer me," Auggie demands fiercely, fists clenched at his sides, eyes burning with hatred.

"Stay away from Tina, Willow. Stay away from Tina. I can guarantee Tina isn't Devon's girlfriend, dealer maybe." I say emotionlessly in a mock-Auggie tone. "Spark your memory at all?"

"Willow, excuse me, but my life doesn't revolve around you!" Auggie shouts, causing me to flinch and my heart to bleed. "I am a very busy man with a lot to do. Now answer the goddamned question. How do you know Tina?"

"Auggie, I don't expect you to do a damned thing for me, but I would've thought that conversation would've been important for several reasons." I barely breathe the words, since I'm on the verge of tears. I stand up and get a bottle of water from the mini-fridge to cover my pain.

"Do you buy from Tina?" Auggie bites out while I pretend to be extremely fascinated by my Aquafina bottle.

"No!" I yell, offended as all hell. "Today is day 120 of sobriety, assfuck," I snarl. "The only drug I've used was weed, and Mary Prynne was the only person I trusted enough not to lace my pot with shit– strong, highly addictive shit. After all, that's what dealers to do drum up repeat business. I've never taken a hit of anything that wasn't grown by Mom."

"Good ol' Mom," Auggie says sarcastically. He leans forward, elbows on the counter, and gets into my face. "Answer. The. Motherfucking. Question. How. Do. You. Know. Tina?"

Pissed and not intimidated in the least, it takes everything in me not to punch the arrogant bastard. But I've never hit a man in my life. I'd break a knuckle.

"Never, *ever*," I stress, "Disrespect my mother, Augustus. *My* mother," I repeat. "Is off limits, and above any judgment from a bastard like you." It's Auggie's turn to flinch, which makes me decide to put him out of his misery and actually answer his question.

"Remember the first time you failed to give me the benefit of the doubt, the night you accused me of drinking? Tina was the girl who threw her beer on me, after insulting me by flirting with Devon, saying that if Devon hadn't pointed me out, she would've thought I was Weston. Then Tina proceeded to tear Kieren's sexual prowess to shreds. Oh, and Tina said she'd fucked Devon. I shut her up by dragging her ass to the ground and ripping her hair out. Don't judge– I'm rather proud of it, immature as it was. It earned me the nickname Spanky."

I sit in an amused state of torment as I watch the emotions flash across Auggie's face: fury, confusion, pride, disappointment, back to pride. He struggles to say something, like it's going to physically kill him to speak the words. I wait with a grin plastered on my face. I'm glad I'm not the only one who deals with the agony of indecision.

"I'm sorry. I guess I don't make it easy to confide in me, especially when what you say doesn't sink in. I remember that conversation now. I was just so scared that Tina was your dealer– scared you were taking hardcore shit, and I'd have to get you clean... and wondering if I could actually get you clean and you'd stay clean. I can't do this anymore." Sounding desperate and broken doesn't garner any of my sympathy, Auggie's made his bed– so fuck him.

"I understand how leery people must be to trust an addict, but not once in four months have I given you a reason to doubt me." I ignore the fact that I'm on the verge of tears. "I used to wonder how long it would take for you to finally trust me, what hoops I'd have to jump through. I thought actions spoke louder than words, but you neither see nor hear anything from me."

"You have no idea what it's like to be me!" Auggie shouts. He stalks away from me, toward the front of Revamped, like he's going to flee, and then he returns as quickly as he left.

"No, I don't." I answer him. "But you also have no idea what it's like to be me. Seeing a real drug addict, and the lengths they will go to for their addiction, made me realize I was on the edge of addiction, but not quite there yet. I'll never take again, because I hated you being in control of me as much as I hated Clover telling me what to do. My life can go one of two ways: let the drug control me, or I control myself. Clearly, I won that battle."

"Seeing the real thing?" Auggie asks, brow furrowing with confusion.

"I can't confide in you, Auggie. You lost that privilege last night. I was coming home to ask your advice and get a hug... you're the one who threw that away– threw me away like garbage. I don't need you for anything I can't get from somewhere else." I shrug, like it doesn't kill a vital piece of me.

"I no longer feel the need to defend myself to you, because I no longer trust you. As is evident by the fact that you don't remember jack-shit when it comes to anything I say or do. So, good luck with that," I mutter as I stand from my stool, putting distance between Auggie and me before I beat the shit out of him.

"I was dealing with something last night. I knew you went off with Devon for the night, so when I saw him on the street, high out of his mind..." Auggie mumbles, looking slightly sick around the edges.

Auggie waits for me to deny or confirm his suspicions, and I don't give him the satisfaction. "If you know me so well, answer that question yourself," I coldly reply to his unvoiced question of whether or not I got high with Devon.

Auggie walks into his office, but stops and turns to face me. "Tina has some serious issues. We've been battling her addiction to heroin since she was fourteen. Weed is called a gateway drug for a reason. Tina even got our baby uncle hooked– Tobias. We've tried everything from beating her, locking her in the house, to half a dozen rehabs. Someday I'll get the call– Tina's dead. She's my... Tina's my sister. I'll take care of it," Auggie whispers as he disappears into the depths of his office.

Another sucker-punch to the gut. Just another day in Fairport for Willow Prynne. Auggie's revelation doesn't faze me, because I'm too numb to understand the gravity of the situation.

Holy fuck, I beat up Auggie's sister.

The last thing I hear as I bend to turn on some music is, "I'm gonna fucking kill her." I snort, turning the music up ten times too loud to drown out the emotions threatening to come to life inside me.

Her? Tina, or me?

CHAPTER FORTY-ONE

"Hey, Stud," I purr, leaning against the side of a sedan as Kieren rolls out from underneath the car on a dolly. He stares up at me with huge blue eyes, like I'm the last person on earth he expected to see. "Lunch?"

"With me?" Kieren asks, sounding skeptical while pointing at himself.

"Yeah, I thought we bonded over past torments while Devon got baked and bailed. Made a new club from what I hear," I say with a wink. "Still waiting on its name, though."

Kieren's face lights up like Christmas– God, he's beyond gorgeous when he's genuinely happy. "I'm still thinking on it. It's more important than a nickname. It may take a while." He shakes his head in awe while wiping oil off his fingers.

"Don't hurt your brain muscle thinking too hard," I tease. Kieren busts out laughing, the sound flowing over me and warming me from the inside out. The man melts my stress with a simple laugh.

Kneeling down to pick up his tools, Kieren asks me, "And what did I do to earn the honor of your presence, Spanky?"

"Ah– you were my second, no third, choice," I lie flawlessly. No need to feed Kieren's huge ego any further. "I couldn't stand being in Revamped for a second longer with Auggie sulking about. Devon's tormenting K-12 today, and I don't want to be around him until we have *the talk*, and everyone else I know is either being tormented by Devon, or working for the man."

Waiting, Kieren looks at me, catching onto my obvious lie. "All right, you were the first person I thought of as my lunch date. I wanted uncomplicated after last night," I honestly admit. "You promised uncomplicated friendship, remember?"

"That I did." He flashes me a smile as he shuts his tool box. He stands and leans a hip against the car. "It was a lot to hear at once," Kieren mutters underneath his breath. "I'm sorry."

"Nah, it wasn't so much Devon turning into Dr. Jekyll and Mr. Hyde, or your tortured past. I think I can wrap my mind around that. I need uncomplicated after the fireworks from last night and a few minutes ago. Auggie," bitterly flows from my mouth. "Let's eat– I'm starved."

"Stone!" Kieren shouts into the shop. "Lunch break. I'll be back when I'm back."

I blink as perfect hair and lavender eyes appear on the other side of the bay. Waving like a little kid, Langdon laughs infectiously. "Weeping Willow!"

"Hey, Lang," I say with a smile. "Motherfuck." Eyes bugging out of my skull, I finally get it. *Head-up-the-ass-itis* strikes again. I'd bet the contents of my bloated bank account that Kieren is the *Mason* with the picture of me in his wallet– the Mason who is proud of me and talks about me constantly. This Willow Prynne is Kieren Mason's girl, according to Langdon Stone.

"What?" Kieren looks at me as if I'm losing my marbles.

"Stone." I point at Lang. "Broken record Mason." I point at Kieren. "I get it. Football buddies, I bet. You guys don't use first names because Stone and Mason were embossed on the back of your jerseys. True?"

"I knew it!" Lang shouts, eyes turning more violet than lavender. "I knew you weren't sure which one I was talking about," he says cryptically so Kieren doesn't catch on. "I waited and waited for you to ask the name of my business, but you're always so damn cautious, not wanting to step into any shit. Welcome to Wreck & Ruin Repair, Willow. My failing legacy." Lang turns in a half-circle with his arms stretched out at his sides and a huge grin on his gorgeous face. "Nice, ain't it?"

"Wow… yeah, it is," I mutter, at a loss for words.

"See, Mason, told ya Willow would like our place. Go get some grub. I'll do Mickey's Dodge while you're out." Lang disappears as quickly as he appeared.

"*Our place?*" I ask, intrigued.

"Later– over lunch," Kieren answers while trying to clean himself up. I watch with an amused smile as Kieren cleans his face and hands with a dirty rag. Basically, he's just smearing it around.

"Ya got a little bit right here." I point to my chin to show Kieren where he's still dirty, and he tries to wipe it away. "No, ya missed it. Right here." I point to my cheek. Kieren gives me a peculiar look and scrubs at his face. "Here, bend down and I'll get it for you," I say in reply.

Kieren complies. I lean in, placing a hand on his shoulder to balance myself as he bends his tall frame down to my height. He flexes under my touch, and I chuckle. I draw Kieren's face down to me and his breath hitches. Needing some kind of outlet, I love the power I feel over Kieren now. I know I affect him as strongly as he affects me. No Auggie or no Malcolm telling us how we should feel. No expectations. Just us genuinely liking one another. It feels good– light. It washes away the darkness of the past few months.

I flash a devious smirk, loving how Kieren trembles beneath my hand. With a naughty snicker, I lick Kieren from lips to temple in a long line. He gasps the second my tongue makes contact, so I end up licking his front teeth. I giggle and hop back before he can react.

Kieren stands before me with a dumbfounded expression– blue eyes bulging, among other things. His cheeks burn bright red and he's laughing huskily. "Spanky, you did it now," he warns a split-second before he lunges for me.

"Oh, shit!" Lunging to the left, avoiding Kieren's hands, I start running down the sidewalk. The No-Name Diner is a block and a half from Wreck & Ruin Repair.

"Spanky," Kieren taunts from behind, not out of breath in the least, because he's effortlessly pacing me. "You do know what football players do, right?"

"Catch stinky balls and fondle them… uh, I'm mean fumble them." I giggle breathlessly over my shoulder.

"Dumbass." Kieren laughs. "I *ran* my team. But there are many positions on a team, all equally important. We make plays. We avoid being tackled. We catch footballs," he stresses the *foot* in footballs. "I had to learn every position on the team before Coach thought I earned the job of quarterback. But, Spanky, you know what I did the most?"

"Dropped the soap in the communal shower?" I snark.

"Run!" Kieren warns.

"Oh, fuck!" I shout, and start booking it. Even with my head-start, Kieren's gaining on me. No fair, long-legged fuckface. I crash into the diner's door just as Kieren catches me around the waist. He picks me up as I wiggle around, giggling like a little girl. He dumps me in the booth closest to the door.

"And we score!" Kieren declares to the packed diner, and no doubt everyone hears the double-entendre. "Touchdown,

Spanky!" he yells at me with a firm swat to my ass thanks to those huge ball-catchers.

"Don't push it," I warn with a grin.

"Aren't we playing?" Kieren arches a blond brow in a facsimile of Auggie's gesture. "Because it sure feels like we're having uncomplicated fun, Willow... and I think that's exactly what we both need right now."

"Not the kind of play you mean, Stud." I'm so lying to myself. I close my eyes and tell Kieren the truth. "I really like you, okay? But your brother is my best friend, and I don't want to lose him. I need Devon. I need to fix him somehow– figure out what he's missing, and give it to him." The pained tone in my voice echoes in my heart.

I can't lose Devon, too. I'm in denial with Auggie right now. I pretend what happened last night and this morning didn't affect me at a cellular level. If I were to analyze it, I'd be bawling my eyes out, snot smeared on my face, gobbling mass quantities of ice cream, while Clover looked on with concerned eyes. I'm not going down that road– I *need* Devon in my life.

"We're night and day, but why can't you be friends with me, too?" Kieren holds my eyes captive in his intense blue gaze.

"Because I want to fuck you," spills from my lips. Instead of regretting the words, a badass sensation flashes heat throughout my body. There is something about Kieren Mason that makes me bold– uninhibited.

"Hmm," Kieren purrs as he leans over the top of the table, trying to get closer to me. "That's a good thing, because I want to fuck you, too," he whispers, causing me to visibly shudder. "Repeatedly... and I'd bet my first born I would come for you."

I close my eyes and swallow a dozen times, because I really, *really* want to know if my sexually-stunted body could get Kieren off. It's almost worth all the angst to try. But not yet. Someday. Sooner rather than later if my begging pussy has any say in the matter.

"I won't use you like that, Kieren, especially after what you told me last night. I'm not saying Devon's my future, but right now he's my present. I'm not going to go there until he and I have a talk. I don't want to be Devon's girlfriend, but I sure as hell won't cheat on him with his brother while I wait to tell him that. Even after that, I don't think I can go there. I'm not ready to be burned a third time in such a short time."

"Good girl." Kieren praises me while flashing me a genuine smile that is more brilliant and heart-palpitating than his charming smirk. "I was testing you, and you passed with flying colors. But don't misunderstand me, I'd fuck you in a heartbeat, but not until you have no ties to my brother. I'm not Devon. I do have morals, ethics, and loyalty."

"Ouch," I mouth. "Harsh, much?"

"And you don't think the bastard deserves my resentment? I have a very, very long list in my head– a list Devon can never make up for. And you're on the top of that list. That right there is a deal breaker between brothers."

"I'm sorry," I mumble, feeling like shit.

"Ah, Spanky," Kieren sings, lightening the mood of our conversation. "Shall I book that session at Axel? I'm thinking we tattoo a K on the center of your forehead. But Auggie would probably castrate me if you did that."

"Auggie is irrelevant," I bite out, pain lancing me deep.

"Oh, yeah?" Kieren says, intrigued, as he points over my shoulder. "Does he know that?" I turn slowly to see Auggie across the diner, intently staring at us– jaw clenched, fingers fisted and white knuckled, eyes glowing a green flame. Across from him sits a properly cowed Tina with tear-stained cheeks.

"Oh, so why didn't you tell me Tina was Auggie's sister?" I accuse.

Kieren's face brightens and his lips curl into a cocky smirk. "Spanky, I was bragging about ya because I thought you were a total badass for beating the shit out of Auggie's sister. I think I fell in lust with you the moment you took Tina down like an injured gazelle– pretty sure I came in my pants a little bit. Now–" he waggles his eyebrows at me. "I think I'm taking your nickname away. It's not so badass if you didn't know."

"What can I get ya?" our waitress interrupts with a nasty, sneering tone.

"Coke, cheeseburger and fries." Judging by the waitress's scowl, I'll be getting some extras in the form of bodily fluids and hair.

"The same for me, Leila." Kieren bats his impossibly long eyelashes at her, and she smiles back at him in adoration.

"One of yours, I presume, Stud?" I say the second she's out of earshot.

"Nope, believe it or not," Kieren replies. "Not my type. So, why is Auggie irrelevant, and why does he look like someone killed his puppy?"

"Auggie doesn't have a dog."

Kieren snorts. "I wasn't calling you his bitch, Willow," he says apologetically. "What happened?"

"Somehow, with Auggie's Jedi mind-powers, he knew Devon was stoned and thought I would be too. Auggie was waiting for me when I got home. No explanation or excuses allowed. Auggie told me to leave the Spook House because he didn't allow potheads underneath his roof. He already had my bag packed, and it was waiting for me on the porch. Auggie wouldn't even let me past the threshold. Trust me, the conversation isn't worth repeating." More like I can't say the words without bawling my eyes out.

Clover was right, yet again. I woke up feeling scorched.

Kieren spends the next few minutes glaring at the man in question, while looking at me with sympathy and guilt. When our food arrives, I breathe a sigh of relief. Kieren's tension was ratcheting up by the second.

"Tell me the story about *our place*, please," I beg to distract myself from my painful thoughts. "What'd you mean by that?"

"It's a long story, sure you want to listen?" He sighs while swirling a fry in a pool of ketchup.

"Oh, I think I've got the time," I say, sounding amused because Kieren looks bashful for once.

"If you insist," says the boy who loves talking about himself. "You pretty much know everything about me now, Willow. So Stone shows up right around the time my life was shredded. I was the quarterback on our team and Stone was the running back, so we spent a lot of time together coordinating plays. We found out we had a lot in common."

The background noise of the diner becomes overpowering in Kieren's silence. I say, "Like what?" to get him talking again.

"Responsibility, whether we wanted it or not. I had to give a full football scholarship to state away because of the kids. I don't blame anyone. It was my choice to make– one no one asked of me. It's not like I was going to go pro, anyway. I chose my family over my dreams, and I don't regret it."

"But do you resent it?" I prompt.

"Sometimes," Kieren readily replies. "But not in the way you'd think. I gave up my dream so Devon could continue with his. So the resentment seeps out whenever I see Dev pissing on his dream, because he didn't have to work to get it. It was a given that he'd be a cop. Dad paid for the academy, and Dev had an instant job– nothing to strive for. I worked at football since I was eight years old. I earned my place as our quarterback, and I led our team to the state championship two years running. I earned my scholarship. So when Devon just... ugh!" Kieren makes a noise of pure frustration.

"I get it. I think I've been on both sides– too blind to realize I was fucking my family over, and then feeling responsible for them. So I understand both of you, I guess."

"Yeah, I can see that," Kieren mutters. "So Stone and I hit it right off. He left a life behind back in Washington, so he could take care of Jackson after his heart attack. I lost a football career and Stone lost a budding music career, and we decided to make the best of it. Jackson taught me mechanics while Stone tried to figure out the fucked up books– what a disaster. We did this for nearly a year. Then on the last day December, Jackson was in the office with a Notary, and he made us sign the papers before he would tell us what they meant."

"Our place?" I mutter, smiling, purely happy for Kieren.

"Our place," Kieren repeats. "It wasn't the life either of us had dreamed, but it was the life we were given. Jackson said he'd worked too hard and too long. The lazy liar. He's barely forty– his heart attack was from booze and drugs and fatty food on tour and women– hard living he doesn't regret." Kieren looks awed as he talks about the man.

"Jackson said Stone and I complemented each other in business like we did on the field. A team: book smarts and street smarts. Stone could be the paper-pusher with light shop skills, and I could do the difficult mechanics. He's even paying for me to join you and Stone at FCC next semester– mechanics courses. The tricky computerized parts are a real bitch on these newer cars. Don't get me started on Smart Cars."

"Wait..." I breathe, mind computing Kieren's words, but not for their true meaning. "Langdon Stone, right? Jackson is his father, right? That would make him *Jackson Stone*, as in *THE* Jackson Stone? Hard living? Langdon Stone of I inherited my voice from my famous relative? Jackson Stone of Revolutionary Road? Holy Christ on a crackerjack!"

Kieren's man laugh trills down my spine to pool in my groin. "Spanky. Spanky. Spanky. Do you live underneath a fucking rock? Of course Jackson's *The* Jackson Stone. Everybody knows that. Girly, you gotta start paying better attention. You're missing out on all the good shit."

Whoa…" I go into a trance-like state, marveling over the fact that I know Jackson's kid and I'm sitting with the guy he signed his business over to. "Whoa."

Breaking me out of my catatonic celebrity state, Kieren gets serious again. "Are you going back? Where are you staying? You can stay with me. Can you afford your own place?" Kieren fires off like an interrogator.

"I went to my sister's. I won't impose on you guys– your house is packed as it is. Plus, I'm sure Auggie put out word to your dad. I can't afford my own place, either."

"What do you do with your money?" Kieren scrutinizes me, and I know what he's thinking. Obviously I'm not spending it on clothes or makeup. Since all my shit fit into a backpack, I'm not spending it on stuff either.

"Tuition is steep, and I refuse to take the money from my parents. Most of my income goes to school, or into my savings, which is to pay for the next few semesters." I shrug, *what are ya gonna do?* "I'd rather invest in my future. Burns the fuck out of me that I put in four months of continual, round-the-clock manual labor, with nothing to show for it except sharing my sister's bed."

"That does suck. Oh, Stone said you were a smarty-pants now– always in competition with him over your grades." Kieren picks on me. "A smart girl would get even. Are you plotting revenge, or do you plan on going back?"

No need to ask, going back to where…

"Auggie hasn't asked me to, and I doubt he ever will. But if he did, I would go back. I've thought of nothing else since last night. I know it looks like I'm living off of Auggie, but I've put years' worth of rent into the remodel of the Spook House. When Auggie kicked me out, it hurt. Yes, it's Auggie's house, but he kept telling Robbie and me that it was *our* home. Auggie didn't mean it if something so little made him throw me out," I say in anger, and then whimper beneath my breath. "Just like those three little words, he didn't mean those either."

I stand from the booth, overcome with emotions. I've got to get out of here before I break down and look like a fool. "I'll catch ya later, Kieren," I choke out as I pull a wad of ones from my front pocket. I toss the cash on the table and turn to flee.

"No," Kieren whispers as he grabs my wrist. "Don't go all girl on me now, Willow." The concern in Kieren's voice draws tears to my eyes, but the smirk that follows confuses the hell out of me. He flashes a cocky grin behind me, and then pierces me with his calculating stare.

"Go out with me tonight, Spanky. If Devon's free, he can join us, too." It sounds like Kieren's speaking to me, but in reality he's speaking to the man who just placed a possessive hand at the small of my back. It takes everything in me not to jolt at Auggie's touch.

"We need to have another meeting, and this time we should play," Kieren suggestively propositions me, but his eyes are on Auggie. "I don't think my brother would mind. We all can agree you were mine first," Kieren directs at Auggie. "Or I was yours– we all know that. I called dibs, did you?"

I play along, but I'm slightly shocked at Kieren's words, because they sounded serious. Real. "Yeah, I think I'd like that," seductively purrs from my throat, causing Auggie's fingers to clench on my back. "We need to name our little group. It'll give you something to do while you're playing around with your monkey wrench."

Kieren's warm laughter bubbles up from his chest– I shiver a little bit. Kieren's starting to sound like Malcolm. He hasn't reached toe-curling levels yet, but he's pretty damn close to panty-dropping.

"I'll try not to strain my brain too much." Kieren chuckles. "I look forward to our evening. Meet us at our house at ten tonight."

"Will do," I say in parting, and walk away.

Auggie's hand drops from my back, but it returns before I get to the diner's front door. His large palm encompasses the nape of my neck, and his fingers circle my throat. He steers me down the street toward Revamped.

"Auggie, your touch is highly inappropriate right now," I warn. It's doing crazy-bad things to my emotions. I don't know if I want to bawl like a little bitch, or rejoice, because clearly Auggie is wicked jealous. If Auggie is jealous, then he thinks something of me other than the indifference he showed me when he booted me from the Spook House.

"The only time I have to talk to you is between here and the shop. No way am I letting go. You'll hear me out," Auggie threatens. To punctuate his point, his fingers tighten around my neck while his other hand reaches out to grip my hip.

"I can tell it's eating you alive that I won't let you control me any longer," I gloat.

"Be careful of Kieren," Auggie warns. "He leaves wreckage in his path."

"Don't overestimate him, Auggie." I sigh in displeasure. "Kieren's my friend."

"Don't underestimate Kieren, Willow, and he's not looking for a friend."

"Don't underestimate *me*," I stress heavily. "Like you always do. I see Kieren clearly for the first time. I see everyone clearly for the first time– *everyone*... You're blinded," I accuse.

Auggie's hand draws me to an abrupt stop. I recoil on my feet. "What?"

"Blinded? And I don't want to control you, Willow. I want you to be happy," Auggie murmurs.

"You're blinded by *your* view of everything, Auggie. Everything you see is viewed through your perspective, causing it to become skewed by your emotions, petty jealousy even. Something tells me you were a know-it-all at eighteen, as you are at twenty-eight. But how much growth have you done in that time frame? I think you've blinded yourself with arrogance and self-importance, and it's stunted you as a human being. One thing I do know for sure, you sure as hell don't see me clearly."

I shock Auggie by breaking his hold. While he stands in stunned silence, I walk back to work feeling free.

CHAPTER FORTY-TWO

Leaning over the counter at Revamped, Robbie gives me puppy dog, brown eyes and a pout, trying to get me to smile. "Let's do a game night tonight," Robbie says excitedly, and it twists the knife in my back– grinds that fucker in nice and deep. "Isis and Malcolm are coming over. We could play Euchre. I call dibs on you being my partner. Auggie can find his own– blood come first."

"I can't. I have plans with my friends," I mutter sadly.

I'm not sad that I'm hanging with my friends. Hell, I'm thrilled that I can finally say that I have friends, let alone say I'm hanging with them. I'm sad that I can't live in a fictitious world where I actually play with the Mason brothers. But this is reality, and I have to have a talk with Devon, and I hope Kieren will back me up. I'm also sad because I'd love to combine all of us and play a Euchre tournament, but I'm not allowed in the house where the games are being played. My age group would totally kick those old fogies' asses.

"Malcolm can bring his kids." Robbie actually whines like a little bitch. "No one is as big of a card shark as you. We always win together. Just you and me against the world, Sapling."

I cough into my hand, trying to clear my throat of the sob that stuck there last night and has yet to dislodge. "I have class tonight. We aren't meeting up until later." I try to dissuade him.

"Great! We'll do it afterward," Robbie says cheerily, as if I was somehow accepting his invitation.

Auggie's hawk-like stare drinks in our interaction. I've painted myself into a corner, and there is only one way out of it. "I can't." The venom in my voice causes my brother to flinch.

"Jesus, Willow," Robbie sounds hurt. "I just want to spend some time with you. Is that too much to ask? I haven't seen you much lately. I miss your moody ass."

In the face of Robbie's guilt, the only weapon at my disposal is the truth. "I want to spend time with you, Robbie. You can come out with us tonight, if you'd like. I don't know what we're doing. I guess just hanging out at the Masons," I say with a shrug, realizing all the Masons Robbie would want to see will be hanging out at the Spook House.

"I don't see why we can't all just hang out together at the Spook House. I was going to make burritos– you love my burritos. C'mon, you know you wanna," Robbie coaxes me, trying to charm me."

"I do want to," my voice breaks, mortifying me. "But I can't." I lean forward, not able to say the words very loud. "I've been banished from the Spook House," I mumble underneath my breath.

"What?" Robbie says, leaning closer to me. "It's your home, how can you *not* go there?"

"Willow." Auggie's tortured voice fills Revamped, whether a warning or not, I'll never know.

"I–" the front door smashes against the wall, silencing whatever was going to spill from my mouth. The bell no longer dings, because it falls to the ground broken.

"Augustus, you motherfucker!" Devon shouts as he charges across the shop. Devon's blue eyes are furious. His chest rapidly rises and falls underneath his uniform. I haven't seen Devon since he ran away last night. My breath catches in my throat. Devon finally looks like Officer Mason– he's aged years overnight, and he's wicked pissed, if not a little frightening.

"Ugh!" Auggie grunts as a fist connects with his jaw, dropping his ass to the floor. His dazed expression screams that Devon's training was well paid for. "What the hell, Dev?"

"Devon!" Robbie calls, and then lunges to yank Devon back from planting another fist to Auggie's face. "What the hell, man? Calm your ass down." Rob pants as he tries to contain a struggling Devon.

"How could you do that to Willow, you arrogant bastard? How?" Devon screams into Auggie's face. "If anyone needs to grow up, it's you!"

"Devon, please don't," I beg. "It's Auggie's prerogative. I shouldn't have told Kieren."

"Auggie's prerogative, really? Did he even let you explain before he kicked you out?" Devon pulls himself away from my brother and yanks his shirt back into place with the flick of his wrists.

"What's going on?" Robbie asks in a voice meant to soothe, but all it does is incite Devon.

"Auggie thinks I broke one of his rules. A rule he offers no second chances on, and I accept that. Whether I was a pothead in the past, or the present, doesn't really matter– Auggie said no potheads are to be under his roof. Once a loser in Auggie's eyes, always a loser. I've smoked, there's no denying that. It is what it is. Last night, I came home after talking with Devon and Kieren, and as a result, Auggie kicked me out of the Spook House. I accept responsibility for my past."

I can't look at my brother's crestfallen expression. I busy myself righting my stool from where it fell sideways during the commotion, and then I shut my laptop down. It looks like I won't be getting any more work done today.

"How could you do this to Willow, and just because of some pot? I didn't even hear her say she smoked any, did you?" Robbie asks, alarmed that he could be next if Auggie ever found out he smokes as a way to de-stress. "Willow grew up in an environment where it was the daily norm. My parents aren't violent criminals– they're sweet people. What's the big fucking deal?"

"Did you even let Willow explain? Did she tell you she didn't smoke any? Did she tell you I tried to tempt her, called her all these horrible names, and then smoked in front of her? Did she tell you I hurt her feelings and broke her trust? Did she tell you I was a pussy and ran away, and left my brother to tell her our past? Did she tell you I'm a drug addict?" Devon's shaky voice breaks from shouting his words through clenched teeth.

"Because I'm sure she needed to talk to someone about last night. Did you talk to anyone? Please tell me you did?" Devon begs, looking desperate and out of sorts. High or sober, this is not the Devon I've known for the past four months, or the tweaking Devon from last night– I don't know who this angry, pitiful person is.

"This conversation is over. The Spook House has nothing to do with anyone but Auggie and me. It's his house, and he has the right to decide who lives in it." I try to calm the situation. "As for what happened last night between us," I direct toward Devon. "We need to talk. I want to help you," I stress. "I *need* to help you. I can't lose you, Devon," I mutter softly, causing Devon to wince and turn away from me, but not quick enough to miss the guilt that crossed his expression.

Auggie sits on the floor where Devon's punch dropped him. A panicked expression mars his face as his eyes rapidly dart from person to person. Devon and Robbie take my lead when I sit back on my stool– they fall into the nearest seats they can find.

"Where are you staying?" Robbie whispers.

"Clover's," I reply, and at the same time Auggie says, "At home, *our* home."

"Don't," I warn Auggie, sounding emotionally exhausted.

"You're coming home. I've regretted it since the moment the words flew out of my mouth. I've been trying to figure out a way to fix this without looking like a sniveling coward. I was jealous and scared, and I acted without thought. I'd apologize, but you already said it wouldn't do any good."

"What do you have to be jealous over?" Devon's voice screams that he's the one who should be jealous of Auggie, not the other way around.

"Kieren?" Auggie tosses out like everyone should just know this piece of information. "No matter what I do, I'll look like a prick trying to control Willow. My hands are tied. I'm jealous Willow will start going to Ren with what I used to give her: comfort, security, advice– fighting her battles."

"I can fight my own battles, thank you very much," I mutter, but get ignored.

"But mostly, I was freaked out of my mind, thinking Willow would turn out like Tina, and then two of the most important girls in my life will be lost. Six years I've struggled with Tina– I'm exhausted. God!" Auggie cries, voice wavering. "I can't... I saw Devon and feared Willow was using again, and I snapped. The thought of Willow with dead eyes or worse... that I'd be waiting on *the call* for both Tina and Willow. I can't live through that. I can't."

"You're a stupid fucker, you know that, Auggie?" Devon laughs humorlessly. "Didn't you think for one second that ripping the Spook House from Willow would push her back into using? Fear or not, you're an idiot."

"Willow's stronger than that." For the first time ever, I think Auggie sees me for who I am. "My fear is irrational, built over years of lying awake in bed at night, of sitting in hospital rooms after drug overdoses, of praying Tina would die to put her out of her misery and ours, while praying she'll live forever... years of watching my little sister disintegrate– the only blood I have left. So if I decide to become fixated on what Willow's doing, who she's seeing, or what she's taking, then I will. It bothers me about Ren, and I own that."

"I'll agree on being jealous of Kieren for all of two seconds, but then I realized that I only want Willow to be happy– I want my brother to be happy. I won't stand in the way anymore. When Kieren told me about what happened last night, I thought to myself, *it's about time Willow sees Auggie for the immature bastard he is*. A second later, I felt bad, especially when Kieren said that you made Willow cry. That's what propelled me to punch you in your smug fucking face."

"You think I don't know I'm a worthless piece of shit? Ask Rob, ask your aunt, ask your dad– they'll agree with you. Willow's too good for me. She deserves a life like Clover and Sam had. You saw what this kind of life did to your mother. Do you want that for Willow? A controlling man will ruin Willow. I can't give Willow the life she needs. Kieren can't give her that life. But maybe you can."

"I can't!" Devon cries, his expression desperate. He composes himself and says, "I refuse to be a consolation prize. I don't know why you don't see me for the coward that I am, Auggie. I love you for always believing in me, but at what cost? I'm a drug addict, and I have no intention of stopping, no matter what Willow's planning to say to me tonight. Fair warning, I know it's gonna go something like this, *Devon, it's me or the drugs*, and I'm going to choose the drugs. I'm a coward who didn't take care of my mother and baby brother– I let us get hurt!" Devon cries out.

"Dev–"

"Auggie, no." Devon stops whatever comfort Auggie was going to give him. "No more commanding Willow to date me. Kieren shouldn't be told to shut up anymore. Willow should get a choice. From now on, Willow will only do what she wants. Can't you see she realizes that now?"

"Yeah, I saw it screaming back at me last night when I tossed Willow off my property like trash. Will it make you happy to know I threw up for an hour because I sickened myself so much? I know I fucked up! Help me fix it," Auggie begs.

"You're both wrong." I whisper so quietly I can barely hear myself. I can't take the strong emotions. I won't sit idly by while they fight, over me and for me. It's my place to stop this shit, even though I think both of them are fighting over something that doesn't have a thing to do with me. I think Devon and Auggie are fighting separate demons, and using me as an excuse to do battle with each other.

"I'm just Willow. From now on, I'll do whatever I think is right, and suffer any and all consequences of my actions. I grew up some more last night as I talked to Clover. Her marriage wasn't a fairytale, no relationship is, and I won't model my relationships after someone else's. You all just need to trust me to trust myself, or fuck off. Those are your choices, because everything else is *my* choice."

"I'm making a choice," Robbie announces. "If you can't live in the same house with someone who's smoked pot, then you better move the fuck out, Auggie. If those are your standards, then your world just shrunk by a lot. The Spook House is more Willow's than anyone's. I'm so pissed at you right now, I'd rather piss on you as soon as look at you!"

"I didn't want Willow to leave last night, and I still don't want her to leave. Come home," Auggie begs me.

"On two conditions," I negotiate, but I don't bother waiting for their agreement. "Rule number one, you can't kick me out for any reason. I'll leave the Spook House when I'm good and ready, and on my own accord. I don't want to feel unwelcome in my home, as I wait for you to give me the boot for some petty infraction that is completely in your mind.

"Rule number two, get the fuck out of my sex life. I'm not playing this game again, Auggie. Play is play. Reality is reality," I mock Auggie. "You pushed me at Devon. A boyfriend is reality, so be jealous all you want– it's your own damn fault. And don't think that it's escaped my notice how Devon's pushing me at his brother now because he's feeling guilty. This shit is all about you, and doesn't have a damned thing to do with me. Frankly, I'm sick of the whole lot of you.

"Wanna know what's pushing me toward Kieren? You all are. Kieren's fun, no commitment, no angst or judgment, no conditions, no pain or confusing emotions, no future or past or present. Uncomplicated, no strings attached *friendship*," I say pointedly as I look between the two men I love, the ones who keep fucking me over in every way that counts but the fun way.

I jump off my stool, grab my backpack and coat, and ignore their gobsmacked expressions. I get ready for my evening class while they nervously fidget in silence.

"After class, I'll come back home," I say emotionlessly to Auggie. "Partner, we'll kick their asses. Our allies will be the brothers." I kick Devon's toe while talking to Robbie. "Euchre it is... and I want burritos, and our sister and her brats. We'll have a tournament."

I flutter a brief kiss to my brother's cheek in parting. I don't kiss Devon or Auggie, because it's taking everything in me not to turn into Spanky, the badass ass-kicker. "Who knew?" I sing to my men. "Actions have consequences, and it's about time you paid your debts in full."

CHAPTER FORTY-THREE

"Why didn't Clover show?" I whisper to Robbie after the fourth win of the night. Rob and I cleaned house at Euchre. Too bad there were no prizes, because we would've won them all.

"Clover made up some excuse that she had a headache. Reality of it is, she wanted you and Auggie to find a happy-medium without her being involved. Truthfully, I think Clover didn't want to be in the same vicinity with Auggie. I'm having a hard time not kicking Auggie's ass right now, so I can image what would happen if Clover was within scratching distance."

I snort, and end up choking on a laugh when I envision a hundred pound Clover beating on the beastly Auggie. "Oh fuck! I didn't think of that."

"What's up with everyone tonight? I know why Auggie's acting strange– guilty bastard. But why is Devon avoiding you?" Robbie's one of the most perceptive people I know, nothing gets by him.

Devon showed up with Kieren about two hours ago, and has actively ignored me ever since. Devon said hello, to all of us at once, and then stuck to his dad like a leech. I'd be really worried, but Kieren's acting normal. I assume if one is having a problem, the other would show it. It's how the twins operate, and those brothers are close enough to be twins.

Even when it was Rob and me against Devon and Kieren at the card table, Devon didn't give me the time of day. He wouldn't look at me or engage me in any way. I tried to tease Devon, and he ignored me until Kieren elbowed him in the side, and then he only nodded in my direction. I tried to catch Devon's eye to see if he was sober, or crashing, or high, but I couldn't. The vibe coming off of Devon scares the piss out of me.

"Hell, if I know why he's ignoring me," I mumble to Robbie. "Last night, Devon and Kieren tried to tell me about the Mason past, but all Devon accomplished was pushing me away, and then running out. Kieren was the one who finally told me what happened. You know how men are with their pride," I say to put Robbie and myself at ease.

Devon is avoiding me, that much is obvious. If I'm honest with myself, he's avoided me since he ran last night. Other than a thirty-second phone call to check on his wellbeing last night, and his outburst at Auggie today, he hasn't spoken one word to me.

"You need to go easy on Auggie," Robbie whispers in my ear. "He's confused and scared."

"So am I, but no one is going easy on me," I say bitterly.

Robbie mutters, "Touché."

"Willow." Isis's seductive purr makes my skin crawl in on itself. "I need to speak with you in private." It's said as a request, but we both know it's an order.

I follow Isis from the living room. Both Auggie and Rob look scared to death to see us wandering off together. Isis leads me to the powder room, of all places. She shuts us in and leans against the door, effectively trapping my ass in with her. I'm going nowhere until Isis is ready for me to leave.

"I'm proud of you," flows from perfect, red lips. I blink up at Isis– stunned. "You've gotten yourself clean, you're educating yourself, just all-around bettering yourself. So I need you to understand that Auggie is screwed in the head right now. He's dealing with a few demons of his own, and he's using you as his security blanket. So don't fuck up all your progress by running off to Auggie's bed." Isis pins me with her dark, piercing stare, and I don't dare blink.

"I wasn't planning on it. If that bastard hit on me tonight, I'd just as soon knee him in the nuts than look at him. I'm not the same impressionable girl I was four months ago."

"Don't be too confident, Willow. I'm not saying you haven't earned it. But you still don't know everything that is going on around you. People do stupid shit, and sometimes they do the stupid shit to you. But it's never about you. You're in college now, you should be able to understand that." Isis teases, but there's an edge of malice in her voice, malice I don't think is directed at me. *It's never about you.*

"Fucking thanks for calling me a smart idiot at the same time. That's a real talent for sarcasm, ya got there." I give it right back to Isis, and she flashes a delighted smirk.

"I knew I liked you for a reason. You entertain me," Isis muses while tapping her red-tipped talon on her hip. "You're a young woman dealing with a lot of outside factors. You need to simplify your life right now. When I was your age, my life was just as complicated. I said the hell with all of the self-created bullshit my family was burying me under, and found my own path. You need to do this for yourself, and not feel guilty about it. They made their mess, and they *must* to be the ones to clean it up. Leave Auggie and Devon to their demons. Don't enable their piss-poor behavior, or shun them for their issues, and never, ever feed their demons."

"I don't understand," I reluctantly admit, feeling like a small child in the face of such an experienced, intelligent woman.

"I love Auggie as much as I hate him, which is way too much for my liking. Devon is my blood– I was the first person to hold him after he was born, and I named the boy. So when I tell you to keep your distance, know it's not for personal gain. I love your brother, Willow, and it would kill Robin to see you hurt. Auggie and Devon are fucked up right now, and all they can do is drag your ass down into Hell with them. Auggie will pull you in, then push you away– over and over. I would know. Only you're susceptible to drug addiction to cope. So don't let Auggie do this to you."

"I came to that conclusion a long time ago, Isis. I don't trust Auggie, because he can't trust himself at this point. He doesn't know what he wants any more than I know what I want."

"Actually, I think you know what you want more than Auggie ever will." Isis praises me. "I know about Devon's drug issues, and I'm not talking about smoking a little pot after work to unwind. I've known. We all have. We thought your sobriety would wear off on Devon, but all it created was a better liar– a better actor. I know what happened last night, before, during, and after Devon was with you and Kieren. Trust me when I say you need to brace yourself."

My heart starts beating into overdrive with premonition. "Just tell me," I breathe, voice quivering.

"Loyalty, girl. Malcolm Mason only has one rule. Family comes first. I can't tell you, no matter how badly I may want to, because I would be breaking that loyalty. But at the same time, I needed to warn you. Malcolm is my brother, and I'd give him the world if I could. But I've tweaked that rule of his. Family comes first, after myself, because family will drain me dry until there is nothing left but an empty husk. I take care of myself first and foremost, so I am strong enough to hold my family together.

Because if they drain me dry, I'm useless to everyone. You need to start putting yourself first, Willow."

"I hear what you're saying, Isis, and I fear what you're not saying. I hear the underlying warning that either Devon or Auggie is going to wreck me, and you're worried about whether or not I'm strong enough to sustain the hit."

"Auggie will subconsciously toy with you, but you'll always survive. What I'm telling you is that Devon *is* going to wreck you. You have to talk to him tonight, and know you can't give an ultimatum of *if you love me you'll stop using*. Trust me when I say that won't work. Devon's beyond that tactic. You need to go to Devon as a friend, and no matter what he says to you, don't give him an excuse to spiral into hell. Don't allow what he tells you to take you on the ride with him, either."

Trembling, I mutter, "You're scaring me, Isis."

"You need to be calm, rational, and understanding while under fire. You need to know that Devon does things as an excuse to use, and he's trying to use you as that excuse. Don't let him be your excuse. Show no weakness, baby girl. Repeat to yourself that no matter what Devon says or does, it's not about you. Whatever you do, don't fucking cry… and when Devon wrecks you, don't run to Auggie for comfort. Because he will manipulate you into his bed if you're not strong enough to remember who you are and who you want to be. Don't let Auggie and Devon turn you into who you used to be," is Isis's parting comment as she opens the powder room door and disappears down the hallway, leaving me speechless, stunned, and shaking.

Heart beating out of my chest, I try to be as strong and cunning as Isis. If Devon won't acknowledge me because he's avoiding our conversation, I'll employ another tactic, no matter how much it makes me sick to my stomach.

Isis put fear in my mind and heart, fear that I've already lost Devon. I may have come to the realization that I didn't want to be Devon's girlfriend anymore, but I want– no, *need* –to be his friend. I need Devon, and deep down I know he needs me.

According to Isis, I can't interrogate, manipulate, cry, or yell until Devon tells me the truth, and ultimatums and begging will only give him an excuse to take another hit. I try the tactic Isis uses on Auggie, a tactic I've witnessed firsthand. Seduction.

I'm sure I'll fail at the art I've never learned, but it's worth a try.

"Psstt… c'mere," I purr to Devon from the parlor's pocket-door. Uncertainty flashes across Devon's face before he masks it with a neutral smile. I've laid in wait for Devon to walk by on his way to the bathroom since his sadistic aunt left me alone. "Follow me." I crook my finger in a come-hither gesture, and then close us in the dark parlor when he follows.

I shove Devon on the settee and straddle his thighs. It feels so good to touch him after all the bullshit in the past twenty-four hours. I bury my nose in the crook of Devon's neck and inhale his luscious scent– leather and vanilla musk flows in my nose and gradually seeps into my pores. It infuses my system with a calm sense of serenity that I feel from no one else. I could fall into Devon's embrace for an eternity and be content, and that thought alone springs tears to my eyes.

Devon and I don't have an eternity.

"I've missed you, Devon," I breathe across his throat and he shivers for me. "I was worried about you. I know we need to talk, but I just need to feel you for a few minutes."

"Willow," Devon cries out in desperation. I take the sound as invitation and connect our lips. He kisses me hesitantly, as if the past few days since we touched intimately have put us back to where we began. I worry that the revelation of Devon's past makes him feel less of a man, that he thinks I judge him for his drug abuse. I don't want Devon to feel any more insecure than he already does. I show Devon with my lips, fingers, and even the rhythm of my body against his, that I find him all man.

Witnessing Devon this afternoon when he lost control and went after Auggie bruised me mentally and emotionally. It was as if Devon was a completely different person from the one I thought I knew so well– a deep-seated resentment was revealed that I didn't even know existed. I never want Devon to think that I see him as a consolation prize. His friendship was always something I wanted and needed, something I longed to feel.

A fluttering of kisses on Devon's neck turns into nibbles, and evolves into the sharp bite of suction from my flesh-starved lips. Devon's fingers are clenched on my hips, nails biting into the unprotected skin at my waist where my shirt has ridden up.

I feel crazed, desperate to maintain any hold I have over this man, but knowing it's too late. Our tentative connection has finally snapped. I feel nothing, no binding between us any longer, not even the tie of friendship. I lick my way inside the collar of

Devon's t-shirt, gently nudging it out of the way with the tip of my tongue. The taste of him makes my mouth water and causes a low moan to spill from my lips. I circle my hips in his lap as I feast on his flesh– devouring him, consuming as much of him as I can hold in my mouth.

"Willow," Devon says sternly, and it doesn't register until he pries me off of him. "Don't," he hisses and turns his face from mine when I try to kiss his lips.

"What's wrong?" I ask breathlessly. Rejection is flooding my system at a rapid rate, causing tears to prickle my eyes. *Whatever you do, don't cry*, Isis said. I breathe deeply while repeating Isis's mantra, *it's not about me*. But it sure as fuck feels like it's about me.

"We can't do this anymore, Willow. We just can't." Devon mutters spitefully as he yanks me back, until we're a good foot a part with me sitting on his thighs.

"What'd I do?" A stunned whimper flows from my lips.

"Jesus! You didn't do a damn thing wrong, Willow. We just can't go on like this any longer. I know you want to have a talk, and I know exactly what you want to say. Do you honestly think I haven't been lectured by my dad, Isis, Auggie, Kieren, and counselors since I was fourteen years old? There is nothing you can say to me, no advice you can give that I haven't heard before. Just as there is no ultimatum strong enough to get me to stop. Drugs are called a drug for a reason– drugs are my medication."

"I–"

"No," Devon denies me. "I don't need you to say I'm better than this, how I deserve better than this, how the past isn't my fault. Somewhere deep down, I believe that. I hope. I swear to God, if you say shit like, *but look at how sobriety is working out for me*, I'll punch your bragging mouth. Because that's what I hear. Your encouragement sounds like you're bragging, telling me how much stronger you are than me."

"Devon, that's not how I mean it!" I cry out.

"No, shit! But that's what the addict in me hears. Do you think the addict wants me to stop? If I stop, then the addict ceases to exist. The addict wants to live, and he lives through shutting down the voices in my head– the voices calling me a cowardly son who couldn't protect his mother and brother. And let me tell ya, Willow, I'd rather shut that noise up with drugs, than be a better person by being sober while living with the past for the rest of my life."

I try to speak but Devon stops me. "No," he demands as he puts a hand over my mouth. "I'm not kidding. I've heard it all. There is absolutely nothing you can say or do that will convince me otherwise. I love you, but I hate myself more."

"What are we going to do?" I mutter lamely, completely floored by how Devon shut down every possible method of communication between us. There's nothing I can say or do, because he won't allow it.

"There is no we," Devon utters coldly, freezing me with the edge of his tone. "There can never be a *we*. I'm not good for you, Willow. You can't be friends with an addict when you're trying so fucking hard to stay clean, so don't even try to persuade me otherwise. Listen, I don't know how to tell you this without hurting you. You're my best friend, and I don't want to lose you. I love you, Willow, but obviously not like a boyfriend should."

"I love you, too," I say in confusion. "I don't wanna lose you, either."

"I slept with someone else last night," Devon blurts out as if he couldn't contain the information for another second. I stare at Devon in the dark parlor. I can barely make out his features, but his face is imprinted in my mind, so there is no need for illumination. His behavior over the past twenty-four hours comes into sharp clarity.

"You cheated on me?" I mutter in shock, sounding numb and defeated. I'm thankful for the numb– I hug and cuddle the numb for protecting me through this agonizing conversation.

"How can you cheat on your fake girlfriend, Willow?" Devon snaps nastily. "There is no nice way about this. For fuck's sake, you've been with Auggie."

"I haven't been with Auggie in over three months, and I've never really *been* with Auggie. You're the only person I've ever been with," I blurt out. "You know we're not together."

"Yeah, my girlfriend is living in some sugar-daddy's house, sleeping in his bed, and she had the audacity to say to me, *we're not together*." Devon twists in a cruel tone while raising a brow, mocking both Auggie and me. "Oh, really?"

"What?" I breathe in stunned mortification, wanting to ask who this person is that's speaking to me this way. "What? Sugar-daddy? Sleeping in his bed? I haven't stepped foot into Auggie's bedroom since I wallpapered it. And there surely wasn't a bed in there at the time. The bed I sleep in I bought with my own fucking money!" I shout.

"It's not like I ever wanted you, or anything. Obviously I didn't even enjoy it, or I wouldn't have kept freaking out. You're not that great of a lay, Willow." Devon drones on like I'm boring him. "You have no tits– just touching your chest skeeves my ass out. Not once did I touch you there, did you notice that? It's probably why Auggie's never fucked you properly. I'm not sure how he got through your *instruction* while staying hard. You know I was just using you to get over my issues so I could fuck a real woman."

Devon hits me where it hurts the hardest, right in my insecurities with pinpoint precision. "Thanks for the practice. It was uneventful enough to make me comfortable for last night. I was with a real woman with big tits, a healthy ass, and skills– didn't freak out once, either."

A cold calm encloses me, protects me. I freeze my emotions while my mind explains what's truly happening to my breaking heart and shattered confidence. Without Isis, I would have fallen into Devon's trap. I need to send the woman an *Edible Arrangement* in thanks.

"Shit," I hiss with feeling when I realize Devon is doing exactly what Isis said he would. He's using me as an excuse to run off and get high: my anger, my pain, my betrayal, he will digest it as his own and use drugs as his self-prescribed punishment. "I know what you're doing," I mutter in a dead voice. "And I'm not falling for it. Are you through?"

Devon is confused that I'm not crying, screaming, or slapping him, as he predicted, just as he predicted with every other part of our conversation: from shutting me down at every turn, manipulating me into feeling humiliated and insulted, to breaking my heart by betraying me. All of it is a tactic to push me away so he can use it as an excuse for the drug addict to seek its comfort in a foggy haze. Once off course, the real Devon peeks out at me through tear-filled eyes. I'm not going to give him what he wants. Devon has lost me, but I won't tell him that, because I won't be his excuse to use.

"I'm being a nasty prick because I'm pissed at myself, alright?" Devon looks pitiful, guilty, and ashamed, and I know it's just another side of the addict coming out to play.

I freeze my face against the unamused smile that threatens to erupt. After dealing with Auggie for months, I can spot this type of bullshit– the reading between the lines. Devon shows me the depths of his manipulations. The old Willow would've not only bought it, but ate it right up, and offered to shit it out for him, too.

"I'm not even going to apologize for it. You *are* my best friend and I love you, but not like *that*. I'd love to say I don't feel guilty, but my name's not Auggie. I could make excuses and blame it on being high, or being upset that I couldn't tell you about my past. But the simple fact is, I'm a twenty-year-old guy, and I'm not going to spend my life being with the only girl I've ever slept with– that dream is fucking gone after last night," Devon hisses bitterly. "I'm not going to go to the roving Playroom and pretend that fucking random strangers isn't cheating."

"No, of course not. You're just going to go behind my back, and then spit it in my face afterward. Whether or not we're together right now, we were together last night. So no matter how you warp this shit into your favor, you cheated on me. You think the Playroomers are deviants, yet they have rules and guidelines they live by, especially Auggie. So while silently judging others on their actions, you're just going to fuck whomever, whenever, and wherever you please," I say snidely. "While in a relationship with someone who doesn't know you're doing it. That's loyal, ethical, and logical right there."

"Don't be bitter, Willow. It's unbecoming," Devon chastises me, and it takes everything in me not to punch him in the fucking face. "You'd screw Kieren in a heartbeat, and then go give Auggie a blowjob afterward… let's get real."

"No, I wouldn't. Auggie will never receive anything from me but sisterly affection. As for Kieren, he and I are both too loyal to you to do that, even if we wanted to. I'm done defending myself to you, because that's what you want me to do, so we won't talk about the real issue. This entire conversation is a diversion, and you know it. So let's get real, Devon. Why don't you tell me what the fuck is really going on?"

Blinking, a monster gazes back out of blue eyes that used to look at me with love, but now only hold pain and malice. "Details, sure, why not?" Devon replies flippantly. "I was walking down the street after running like a coward– high out of my mind, when two girls I went to school with pulled over to give me a lift. It was a two-seater, so one had to sit on my lap.

They were both drunk, but I didn't give a shit. I was a coward, and cowards just don't care. I immediately found out that the girl on my lap was only wearing a skin-tight dress with no bra on. I blinked and my mouth was latched on her tit– real tits, bitable tits –tits that overflowed my hands." Devon demonstrates their size by holding up his palms like he's weighing fruit. "Unlike your nonexistent– well, I won't do a disservice to breasts everywhere by calling what you have tits."

"Please, feel free to insult me while giving intimate details on the woman you betrayed me with," I utter in a dead voice. "It's your grave, get to digging."

"Amazing tits," Devon murmurs dreamingly. "And no panties, because before I knew it, my hand was between her legs. God," he purrs, tipping his head back as if in ecstasy. "She was hairless and wet. She wanted me something fierce, but not as badly as I wanted her. Before we even drove two blocks, she was already riding my cock– bareback. Before my high mind could reason out what was going on, the driver was out of the car, swearing at us while stomping away, leaving us parked it the middle of the street. We just kept fucking in the car while sitting on an empty Fairport street– stuffy, conservative Fairport. I won't lie to you, Willow. It was a thrill. A motherfucking high. It was the first time I've fucked anyone– I don't mean that pathetic excuse for what you and I did. I mean *fucking*. It was pure lust, passion, nasty and dirty– and I didn't freak out when I fucked her two more times, once in the front seat and once bent over the hood. Best night of my life."

"I... I..." All I can do is stutter in disbelief, while my eyes bug out in an attempt to hold the stunned tears at bay.

Devon blinks, swallows, and the addict disappears for a moment as my Devon reappears, looking slightly sick to his stomach. "Did I feel guilty at the time? Do I still feel guilty? Yes. I'm not a complete monster. But I can't change what happened. If I really loved you like I thought I did, I shouldn't have been able to do such a heinous thing– high or not, it's not an excuse. You might be able to forgive me, but I'll never forgive myself. I'll always wonder in the back of my mind if I was with you by default, because they asked us to date, not because we were fated."

"And now we'll never know," I whisper so softly Devon doesn't hear me.

"It was twenty minutes of my life. Twenty minutes that changed the path of my life. While my brother was tearing his heart out by telling you our shame, I was cheating on you. What makes it worse is that you called me right after. I'd just got done scrubbing my shame away, and you called, concerned over my wellbeing. That second was the lowest point in my life. After trying to go about my day without killing something, Kieren runs me down to tell me what Auggie did to you because of me. Yeah, I'm a fucking scumbag. Both of us irrevocably fucked you over last night, and in my case, I fucked you over like three times... or more. Sorry, I lost count."

I don't cry, or scream, or lash out. I'm numb. I'm speechless. If I could think, I don't know what would be running through my mind at the moment.

"When I punched Auggie today, I was punching both of us. Willow, do me a favor and never take either one of us back. Save yourself from our destructive patterns. My train wreck of a brother is barreling toward you right now. Get the fuck off the tracks before he destroys you, too. Meet some nice guy at college, fall in love, and make a life for yourself. I *want* to be your best friend. I *need* to be your best friend. But I'm not good enough to be your *anything*. Hell, a best friend wouldn't do the heinous thing I did to you last night. I could spend the rest of my life repenting for it, and it would never be long enough. You deserve better than a coward, and you deserve better than a controlling, arrogant bastard."

I crawl from Devon's lap on shaky legs, because I can't touch him a moment longer. I'm going to be sick– physically sick. "I could've forgiven you for this, Devon, because you're right. It was hypocritical to call it cheating when I covet Kieren." My voice drizzles out my mouth, small. Dead.

"Willow, don't! I was just saying that bullshit to make myself feel better, or maybe to make you hate me as much as I hate myself. I know you would never betray me. Trust me, I cheated on you in the most deplorable way possible." Devon's voice breaks as he hides his face shamefully behind his palms.

"What I was going to say was, I could've forgiven you if it wasn't for the disrespect and the delivery of this information. I understand– I really do. Temptation is a wicked mistress. I've been fighting it for months. Our friendship could've survived anything but this. What I can't forgive, and I'll never forgive, is how you broke the only rule I have. Essie," her name flows in a wheeze of despair.

"How did you know? Who told you?" Devon croaks out in a panic. He starts toward me as I back away from him toward the pocket-door.

"I didn't know. No one told me– you just did."

CHAPTER FORTY-FOUR

I'd gladly take death over this torturous agony. I don't know how long I've been curled up around the base of the toilet, heaving until I thought I'd see my organs lying in the bowl.

The past few hours, days, weeks, months, years, fall upon me and smother me. I don't know how to cope. I'm only thankful, that after witnessing the destruction known as Devon Mason, I have no need for a crutch to get me through the night.

Drugs ruin lives: the life of the drug abuser, the lives that are taken by the drug abuser, and all the lives around the drug abuser. Is it the drug, or the abuser that is a scourge upon their surroundings? Without the drug, would they still wreak havoc on their nearest and dearest and any stranger who got in their path?

The deep, lancing pain I feel is multi-faceted: betrayal, desolation, agony. Betrayal over all the lies and misconceptions. The entire friendship I built with Devon was a fallacy. Was any of it real? Thinking of Devon makes me sick– the loss of potential in the intelligent, giving, and loving man. Devon is a life laid ruined by his own hand.

In my head and heart, Devon and I were never truly a couple, so I could've rationalized the betrayal somehow. But in reality, we were together– had been together –so it was cheating. The pain that hits me the hardest is how Devon reduced our time together while hurting me as painfully as he possibly could, by tearing my femininity and sexuality to shreds. The lack of compassion and empathy and the need to harm me is heart-shattering.

My cousin– my blood –the girl who has been by my side since my birth, the little girl who played Barbies with me, the girl who I held through breakups with friends and guys, the woman who sits next to me in church, and then eats supper at our table, fucked my boyfriend in the trashiest, sleaziest way possible. In *my* car! Will Essie have the nerve to sit in a pew next to me on Sunday, and then look me in the eye across the Prynne Sunday Dinner table?

Isis said that everything people do *to* me isn't necessarily *about* me. This catastrophic event was about destruction for Devon: destruction of his life, his friendships, and a source of his happiness. But what Essie did was all about her *and* me.

Once makes sense if you fell hard for a guy, and the feeling was mutual. It would be selfish for the one who called dibs to pitch a fit when it was an unreciprocated crush. But Essie screwed a fourteen-year-old Kieren to stick it to me, which is obvious since she screwed the only guy I've called boyfriend last night. Who's next? Auggie?

What does Essie get out of this *competition* she's running in her mind? Is there a tally of who's better, and what and why? Like our DNA-created breast size somehow is more important than our intelligence, and a caring, charitable personality. Anyone can fuck– even insects do it. It doesn't make you a higher life form because you can spread your legs and moan. Whatever Essie thinks she won, was it worth the loss of her self-respect and me?

Essie, she is who hurt me the most. I'm not blaming the other woman for tempting the boyfriend to stray. Essie couldn't fuck me over without Devon sticking his dick where it didn't belong. I blame Essie, because this was a personal attack by someone who should've had my back in all things, like I've always had hers. What Essie did had to be the lowest thing you could do to someone… *again*. On the heels of that last thought, I find myself hovering over the ceramic bowl, heaving my heart out.

Who do you confide in when your confidant betrays your trust? You usually go to your best girlfriend to bitch and moan about your worthless boyfriend. But I can't do that since they both betrayed me. I can't go to Kieren, either. I refuse to drive a wedge between brothers. I would be just as low as Devon and Essie if I were to tattle to Kieren. I can't go to Clover– I've disappointed and hurt her enough. I can still see the pain in her eyes from this morning at the bakery. If I hurt, Clover hurts ten times more than me. I can't torture Clover by telling her how one of our own betrayed me. I can't go to Isis or Robbie or Auggie. I can't go to the twins because family hurt me– *our* family.

Alone.

I sob anew as a feeling of desolation descends upon me. Earth-shattering convulsions wrack my body as I come to terms with the fact that Essie betrayed me, forget about Devon. Essie. I whimper every time her name flows through my mind. The more

I try to avoid it, the more I hear it, the more I envision what happened in *my* car. The second Devon said a two-seater, I knew it was Essie and Bethany who picked him up for a ride. Essie borrowed my car yesterday afternoon to go to a party.

I really hate Karma. The bitch.

I must've been a mass-murderer in a former life.

Big hands gently pry me away from hugging the toilet bowl. I drift in and out of a delirious state of despair as I sway up and down with the movements of Auggie's stride. I'm nestled on the sofa and that big hand wipes the snot off my face. Moments later, a tumbler of something ice-cold and alcoholic is fitted into my palm.

"I can't," flows in a wheeze.

"Drink it anyway," Auggie orders roughly. "Down the hatch." He presses the glass to my lips and forces me to swallow it. My empty stomach tries to reject the bourbon.

A warming sensation chases the chill away, and it lowers my shields. "I need Mr. Kline, Auggie," I rasp out.

"And Mr. Kline will always be here for you, no matter how badly Auggie fucks it all up. Mr. Kline will hold your hand, just like he always had in the past," he promises, and for once his actions back up his words. Auggie wraps both of my hands inside both of his, holding me securely.

I stare at our entangled hands, unable to look at Auggie. "I'm lost, and I don't think I can come out of this in one piece." My voice hitches on a sob, followed by a bourbon-flavored hiccup.

"Willow," Auggie sighs my name. He kneels down on the floor until we're eye-level, then leans forward to pull me into an embrace, and I start to panic, heart going into hyper-drive.

"No," I hold my hand up to stop his advance. "If you comfort me, I'll shatter to bits," I warn.

"Did I do this?" Auggie asks with a shuddering breath. "I really want to apologize, but I've learned my lesson on that front. Instead, I'll just say I'll do my damnedest not to underestimate you again. Please don't cry," Auggie murmurs, a coaxing sound that almost has me hugging him.

"No." I shake my head. "This isn't about you kicking me out of the Spook House. I want to talk about that eventually, but I can't think about that right now. What just happened… it trumps everything else. No one could have foreseen this. I don't think Devon even saw this coming. It's bad, Auggie, so very bad."

"You'll get through this, just like you do with everything else. Willow, I believe you could survive a nuclear holocaust," he teases, trying to get me to smile through the tears that fall at a steady rate. Auggie leans in close, so his body heat warms the chill away. But he doesn't touch me anywhere except for my hands, for which I'm thankful.

"Auggie, I want to confide in you, but I don't know if I can trust you anymore, and that isn't just about you. My trust has been broken by just about everyone in the past few days. I fear I won't be able to trust anyone ever again."

"I know you think I judge you, Willow. Honest, I don't. I need you to know that you can tell me anything," Auggie promises. "It's the emotions that make me a ruthless bastard. Conflicting emotions make me do stupid shit. What happened between us last night was born of fear and little else. I knew I was being irrational, but I couldn't stop myself. That isn't an excuse, and I take responsibility for hurting you. But know I *hate* hurting you," Auggie stresses.

"Would you like to hear a day in the life of Willow Aster Prynne? I can give you a snapshot of the past twenty-four hours of my life, and then maybe you'd understand why you found me hugging our toilet while bawling my eyes out.

"One condition," Auggie tries to sound serious, but I can hear the smile in his voice. "Let me sit next to you on the sofa. This old man's knees aren't as they used to be. Hardwood is killing me." He groans exaggeratedly.

"Har-dee-har, Auggie. Old man at twenty-eight... get up here," I tug on his hands until he rises to his feet.

"Thank you, Willow." Auggie sits next to me on the sofa, but makes no move to infringe upon my personal space. He just sits patiently while holding my hands.

"Well, I thought everything was great. Devon and I were great. I was connecting with Kieren as a friend. The kids were all getting along, and Malcolm said he'd woo Clover. So Devon was worried that if he didn't explain the past, it would ruin our future together. He and Kieren thought I should know, that maybe it would influence whether or not I wanted Clover mixed up with Malcolm."

"That was a good idea. Sorry to interrupt," Auggie mutters when I give him a look. "It's important that you look out for Clover, Willow, that's all I was saying."

"We went to Kieren's repair shop because it was private. Devon was acting strangely. He started getting defensive and saying nasty things to me and Kieren. Devon said he couldn't go through with it sober, so he pulled out a pot pipe and tried to tempt me with it. I was furious, as was Kieren. I just didn't realize that our anger is what Devon intended. If we were angry, it gave him an excuse to dope up and run."

"You didn't smoke," Auggie mutters. "I'm not asking, because I know it here," he presses our hands over his heart. "I know you're stronger than that. I'm sorry Devon put you into that situation, Willow."

"Me too," I whisper. "After Devon ran off, Kieren told me everything. And by everything, I don't just mean about their past, but of how Devon has been hiding his drug addiction since he was fourteen. Devon made Kieren take his piss tests, and he also possesses the acting ability to win an Academy Award. Everyone is blind to the real problem, Auggie."

"I knew Dev had issues, but I thought they were mild, and I thought he was joining you in sobriety," Auggie mumbles, sounding shocked.

"Devon is a master manipulator. He pulled the wool over all of our eyes. But truthfully, I'm not the only one you owe an apology. All these years you've been treating Devon like a prince and painting Kieren in a bad light– even Malcolm has. You need to make right with that, Auggie."

"I never said Kieren was a bad guy, per se. I said I was jealous of the charming little fucker. Big difference," Auggie grumbles, looking shamefaced. "What happened next?"

"I left Wreck & Ruin and called to make sure they both got home safely. Since you were there, I have no need to repeat anything that happened at the Spook House. I fled to Clover's and we talked all night about a lot of important stuff, and then we talked with Violet. But what I didn't know is that when Devon ran, he ran into two girls. They picked him up, and then he fucked one of them," I admit numbly. "Several times... in *my* car."

I have to pause before I can finish. Auggie is staring at me with a blank expression and dead eyes. I think he's trying to either contain his shock, or formulate a reply. It could be that this is so out of the spectrum of Devon that it's mind-boggling.

"Congratulations!" I sing to Auggie. "You got what you wanted. I fixed Devon with my subpar sex and the absence of a pair of tits worthy of being called breasts. No freak-outs. Cured. Devon had no problem fucking a girl without protection, inside and outside of my car!"

"Willow– I… *fuck*," Auggie stammers, at a loss for words.

"Devon tore me apart emotionally, mentally, and sexually. He said horrific things about my lack of femininity by comparing me to the woman he betrayed me with. Devon had the nerve to say he didn't cheat on me. But in the next breath, he said that if he could cheat on me, then it was because he didn't really love me. Devon decimated our friendship because the addict in him needed fuel to spiral out of control. So Devon hurt me in every way he could contemplate. I'll never forgive Devon for fucking Essie in my car while his brother was emotionally bleeding out in my arms."

Auggie closes his eyes and slows his breathing. The only giveaway that he's upset is his hands pulsating in mine.

"I don't know what to think anymore, Auggie. I try and try, and it does no good. I love Devon. I want him to be happy, but I'm not sure that's possible. I'm not sure there is a fix to him. I guess that's how you feel about your sister. So all this time you worried I would turn out like Tina, having absolutely no faith in me, but all the while Devon skated beneath your radar."

"I have to think," Auggie mutters. He pulls his hands free of mine so he can rest his forehead in his palms. "I have to talk to Malcolm. Don't be pissed at me," he says quickly before I can balk. "The man needs to know what his son's been up to. You have to agree with that."

"I worry now that Devon has crossed this line, he'll never cross back over it. I fear the Devon we knew will be lost to his demons. I want to be sympathetic, but I can only be so empathetic when it comes to someone who betrayed me while trying to maintain my self-respect. I can't forgive this, and I shouldn't have to. I'm not perfect, but I deserve better than that. I'm not gonna lie to you, Auggie. I'm mad as hell at you, too. You broke my trust, but it's repairable over time. But I don't think this shit with Devon can be repaired."

"I don't know what to say." Auggie sighs as he slides to the floor to sit on his ass, cross-legged, in front of me. "I didn't foresee this as something that could possibly happen… not even in a million years."

"All I know is that I'm done with love for now. The thought of sex makes my skin crawl." I visibly shudder. "I'm just going to live my life and see where it flows."

"What can I do to make you feel better? I'll do anything," Auggie pleads. "This is partially my fault. I put you in this situation, tell me how to get you out of it."

"You know what's funny?" I snort, and Auggie smiles at me. "Kieren really is my friend, more so than the rest of you assholes. Kieren flirts like mad, but at least he's honest about it. Even when Kieren wasn't taking no for an answer, at a base-level, it was completely honest."

"I imagine we would be having a very different conversation tonight if I hadn't interrupted you in the hallway at Rush, if I hadn't tried to sway you from Kieren to begin with. I wonder where you would be today. Would you be sober? You just might be," Auggie says with a shrug. "But I do know that Devon and Essie wouldn't have had the ability to harm you if things were different. My fault. What can I do to fix it?"

"What I need from you right now is honesty. Honesty. I need Mr. Kline back, the man I knew before fear and shame clouded him. I need us to be how it was before I wandered into the Playroom. Sex, punishments, and emotions have fucked this up between you and me. I want to play video games with you, and make fun of the consignment items people bring into the store. I miss your comforting advice. We moved too fast. We went from boss and little girl to..." I wave my hand around, trying to come up with a word. "... whatever this is."

"Willow, I love you, so I'll do whatever you need me to do to get you through this."

"I'm a work in progress. So I'll let you know when I think of something that might help," I say in indecision.

"Good enough for me," Auggie readily supplies. "I have a piece of unsolicited and highly inappropriate advice. I know you won't ever touch that betrayer again, even with a diseased hand. I want you to know that it's okay for you to explore your attraction with Kieren. Don't do it to hurt Devon, but don't deny it to be stubborn, either. It's rather depressive to hear an eighteen-year-old woman swear off sex and love when it's her time to shine."

"According to Devon, the only shining this 'girl' should be doing is to shoes," I mutter. I try to hold back my cringe as

Devon's destructive words echo in my mind. I feel sick again. "Do people even shine shoes anymore? Silver? Eh, all I know is, I won't be shining poles with my humongous tits."

"Hush," Auggie cuts off my uncomfortable babbling. "If it happens, it happens. We both know why it would be a good idea with Kieren. You're right– I didn't see it until this afternoon at the diner. Kieren truly cares for you as a friend. I'm not telling you to go seek his ass out tonight. Just don't build up an impenetrable wall because one douchebag said some mean shit to you. Do I have to remind you that Devon is a drug-addled pathological liar? So if Devon's mouth is moving, he's lying his ass off. So why would you believe what he said about you? You are the only judge of yourself. Don't give Devon any power over you."

"I get it, but I'm not ready to be with Kieren. I may never be ready," I admit, sounding depressed. "But I won't close myself off because my cousin is a faithless skank and Devon is a dumbass."

"We're on the same page, Willow. Skanks and dumbasses, the whole lot of them… Now, I know you won't share a bed with me, and I also know you won't get a lick of sleep tonight, so how about we share this couch. I don't want you to be alone. Would it be all right for Mr. Kline to cuddle with you, Willow? Mr. Kline is starved for some comfort and affection," Auggie coaxes, looking like a gigantic, red-headed little boy.

I give a small nod of my head. "Thank you," I say meekly.

Auggie gets up from his perch on the floor and grabs my afghan. I want to forget the memory of Devon wrapped up in my blanket, and the same memory of making love to him for the very first time on this sofa. It's time to replace those memories with new ones– ones of Mr. Kline holding a more worldly Willow on this sofa while wrapped up in my afghan.

I curl up on Auggie's chest, and he wraps me up with not only his arms, but his legs, too. I'm cocooned in Auggie's warmth. "I have another secret," I confess. "Clover told me I have another niece or nephew, and they must be close to my age."

Auggie clenches me so tightly I can barely breathe. His body strings tight and starts to vibrate with an unknown energy. He's panting in my ear and his heart is hammering frantically beneath my cheek.

"What?" I mumble.

"Nothing… tell me more, please," he demands with forced politeness.

"Today I found myself looking around for them, trying to find a young Sam or Clover in the crowd. I think Clover was going to tell me who it was, but Violet careened into the room and interrupted us."

"I need you to make me a promise," Auggie solemnly says. "You need to make Clover finish that sentence, but promise that you'll wait until after you're feeling better from this latest upset. Promise me," he begs. Auggie's whole body is shaking so hard that it's vibrating *my* teeth. I said something that upset him greatly. Auggie must know who it is, and he's scared to tell me because it's Clover's responsibility.

I'd do anything to stop Auggie's anxiety, so I whisper, "I promise," in the dark.

CHAPTER FORTY-FIVE

"Who's on a diet?" Weston asks while tearing lettuce leaves to shreds like he's never ate lettuce, let alone handled it before.

"No one," I slur, confused. I flick my eyes around to everyone, begging for an explanation.

"I thought salad was for when you're on a diet?" Rae pipes in. She pops a cherry tomato into her mouth and bites down, giggling when it spurts her with juice.

I see a scary trend forming here. Kieren's on the other side of the counter eating olives like they're a delicacy, and Weston already ate an entire cucumber. Do the Masons ever eat anything green or fresh?

"Are you kids serious?" Clover asks in horror. I can see her wheels turning. She's already making meal plans for the Masons, and she'll force me to drop their food off on a nightly basis to ensure they get enough nutrients.

"Mrs. Webster," Kieren charms, flashing his *used car salesman/serial killer/you know I have what you want* smile. "They're just joking. They know what vegetables are," he directs at the kids in warning. "I cook our meals, and we always have a vegetable with dinner."

I can tell Kieren's lying, but it pacifies Clover. Kieren has that effect on the female population. The second Clover turns her back to face the boiling pot of water, the kids start snickering. Devon swats their asses, and they instantly shut up.

This is the first time I've seen Devon since that night. It's been two weeks of torture, and right now, I'm comfortably sitting in the seventh circle of Hell. I attribute my circumstances on Karma and my past life as a blasphemer. That's the only explanation I can come up with for having to deal with this shit. Since I haven't told anyone what happened, everyone thought it was a good idea to invite Devon to our first cooking lesson.

I've spent the last hour moving around the kitchen. When Devon moves a foot, I move a foot. It's been a beautifully choreographed dance to avoid one another. The kids have noticed, but it's Kieren who's the most suspicious– I can't freakin' tell him!

Halfway through transcribing the lasagna recipe, my squirrely niece makes a reappearance. The girl has been clinging to me like Saran Wrap all week. "Why are you so sad?" Violet murmurs softly in my ear.

"I'm fine," I mumble a reply as I write down the components of homemade tomato sauce. What's wrong with the jarred stuff?

"I'm used to bitchy and bratty, even Zombie, but sad is a new one. Did Devon hurt you? Want me to kick his ass?" Violet's blue eyes flash with anticipation as Violent Violet makes an appearance.

"I'm sad, but I'm better than last week. Next week, I'll be even better than this week," I reply, feeling a billion shades of uncomfortable.

"Good, 'cuz if you're unhappy, then Mom's unhappy. You know the saying? If Momma ain't happy, ain't nobody happy."

I snort and pull Violet into a hug. "You're fabulous, Violet." She hugs me back, beaming a smile at me. I catch Clover dabbing her eyes again. That woman has cried all week. Every time Violet turned into a creepy cuddle monster, Clover started misting. Violet looks at my face– studying me… *again*, for the billionth time this week. "You're creeping me out with that shit, girl," I warn as I step away.

"Do you love me the same as Robbie?" Violet asks out of nowhere.

"Yeah, why wouldn't I?" I scrunch my forehead in confusion.

"Do you love Robbie more because he's your brother?" Violet asks cautiously.

"Nope, I love him because he's Robbie. Same as I love Seth because he's Seth, and you because you're you. I have to love you guys. It's a prerequisite to family."

"But you don't have to like us," Violet sings, quoting me, like she's okay with that.

"Jesus, do you remember every nasty thing I've ever said?" I shudder, because I hope she doesn't. I was a vindictive bitch.

"Here," Devon breathes to me as he hands me a recipe card. Startled, I fly across the room like I was fired out of a cannon. Everyone stops what they were doing and stares at me. I can deal with Devon being in the same room as me, but not talking to me, or breathing on me, or touching me, or acknowledging me.

"Willow, ya got a minute?" Kieren requests politely, but it's at odds with how he wraps his hand around my wrist, and then pulls me from the kitchen. "What. The. Fuck. Was. That?" Kieren demands when we get to the hallway and out of earshot.

"Nothing." I turn bashful, scuffing my sneaker on the linoleum.

"We've hung out all week, and not once has Devon joined us. When I say your name, he runs from the room. But every night when I get home from visiting you, Devon interrogates me for the details. Out with it now, Spanky," Kieren demands.

I push Kieren into the bathroom and shut us in. I just need a hug. Auggie's held me all week as I broke down, which is usually between the hours of sleep and awake, while I hysterically bawl. I've avoided touching Kieren because the thought has tears prickling my eyes. One of the last happy thoughts I had of Devon was how I could spend eternity in his arms– that fizzled quickly.

I burrow my face against Kieren's broad chest and sigh in relief. Kieren's so damn warm and strong. He makes me feel safe and protected. "We broke up." I sniffle. "Pretty sure we'll never be friends again, too."

"Why, when, and how? And more importantly, how come I'm just now finding out about it?" Kieren's tone is accusatory, but his hands slowly slide up my back and begin to massage my loneliness away.

"Two weeks ago. Devon was the one who broke up with me. I won't tell you why, because even I have some pride I'd like to keep. To say the words out loud would make them real," I whisper against his shirt. I take a deep breath and give Kieren the true reason I haven't confided in him, no matter how badly I've wanted to over the past two weeks. "Kieren, if you want to know the details, then you'll have to ask your brother. I won't become a wedge between the two of you. I can't have you resent me, because I can't lose you, too."

"Willow," Kieren breathes against the top of my head. His arms fold around me, surrounding me in his presence. "Not gonna happen. I promise. Auggie?" Kieren jumps to the logical conclusion.

"Nope, Auggie is Mr. Kline again," I happily report. "And he's going to stay that way. No funny business. No more hot and cold. No mixed up emotions causing him to lash out. It's been refreshingly easy, actually." Even to my own ears I sound surprised.

"Really? Whoa…" Kieren squeezes me tighter. "You've had a shitty time of it the past few weeks, huh?" Kieren chuckles, and

I know I won't like what's to come out of his mouth next. "And Auggie's balls must be indigo by now."

"Fuckface," I say with affection. "It's not like that. Sex has been the furthest thing from my mind."

"I prefer *Stud*, thank you very much, Spanky," Kieren teases. "And Auggie is a dude. Dudes like it when pretty little things need us, cuddle up to us, and cry on our shoulders. It's what makes us men. Being a manly man myself," Kieren says, causing me to snort a very unladylike sound. "I *am*," he stresses. "As I was saying. Being a manly man myself, I know what it's like to hold you–" Kieren presses his hips forward and retreats the second I feel *it*. "I can guarantee Auggie's got a massive case of blue balls if he's been your cuddle buddy for the past two weeks."

Blushing a billion shades of Hades, I mutter, "Let's go back to the kitchen. I can't have our families thinking I'm an equal opportunity skank."

"If only you were skankier," he muses in disappointment. A split-second later, Kieren slaps my ass, and adds a fondle that makes it not so much a punishment but a thorough groping.

"My name's not Tina," I gloat haughtily as I reenter the kitchen.

"Oh, I'm so telling Auggie!" Kieren sings. "He'll be wicked pissed you called his sister a skank."

"Willow," Clover reprimands, and then I finally realize all eyes on me.

Shit, I'd forgotten about everyone else once I started bantering with Kieren, and his wink informs me that that's exactly what he'd planned on. I give Kieren a small smile of thanks and walk back over to my duties.

"Gross," Rae complains for the umpteenth time, grating on my last nerve. Apparently all the Mason men treat Isis and Rae like princesses, because as I've learned today, Rae has never cut up a vegetable, cooked a meal, or washed a dish– ever.

I've been in the Masons' home, and it's homey and well-lived-in, but very clean. I'm not sure who the housewife is in that family, but it sure as shit ain't Raven Mason.

"Little Isis, if you complain again, I'm gonna leave you to clean up all this shit by yourself," I warn.

My patience is wearing thin after Clover made us, not only cook the meal, but sit down at the dining room table and be subjected to etiquette lessons. The girls loved it, while the boys and I suffered in silence. Now we're stuck doing the woman's work.

"If you make a mess, ya gotta clean it up. The more you bitch, the more I want to rip your tongue out and stuff it up–"

"Willow!" Kieren growls as he tightens his hand over my mouth. "Yeah, when Dad hitches to your sister, you'll regret finishing that sentence. You can't threaten your family like that, Spanky."

"Um… what planet are you from?" Violet defends me. "If you can't threaten family, who can you threaten?"

"I'm taking back my vote, immediately. No way in hell is this sycophant going to be my new sister," Kieren growls in disbelief.

"They don't call me Violent Violet for nothing," Violet proudly announces. "And it's too late to renege. The box just arrived. Mom's at the door accepting the delivery."

"Fuck," Kieren hisses as four jubilated *Yay*s shout around the kitchen. I don't reply, because Kieren's hand is still over my mouth. Officer Devon doesn't reply, because I think I cut his tongue out and shoved it up his ass.

"What is this?" Clover asks as she walks back into the kitchen while carrying a box. She bites her bottom lip to contain her happiness– so cute. Who knew she'd love surprises? Clover sets the box on the counter and slices the tape with a knife.

"An apron?" She looks at us like we bought it for her, and we're the best kids ever. Seven noes are shaken. "*Lucky Four Leaf Clover's*?" She reads the apron with a bemused expression on her face. "*Bake me your best dessert, and leave it on the porch. I'll leave you another surprise too. Your secret admirer, Papa Bear.* Um… kids?"

"Not it!" I mumble behind Kieren's hand, and then give it a long, wet lick. Kieren groans, hand disappearing in an instant. He rubs his palm on his pant leg like he's trying to get the feel of me off his skin. I don't think he minded me tonguing his hand, since he's eyeing me like he's ravenous.

"Sorry, I was taken up with the surprise." Kieren mutters an apology for silencing me. He glances at his hand and smiles his genuine smile. Kieren slowly rolls his eyes up to meet mine, and the heated look his gives me hitches my breath.

"Mrs. Webster, we didn't send it," Devon's honest voice taints my ears, and it's filled with utter bullshit.

"Oh!" Clover yelps and slides the apron on. "It's nice," she purrs while rubbing her hands along the light green fabric. Clover took the bait– *Clover's gonna get laid... Clover's gonna get laid...*

"Um, Spanky?" Kieren chuckles while gripping my shoulders, giving a little shake to put some sense in me. Devon's hearty laugh stops me in my tracks. I was doing a jig to the *Clover's gonna get laid* chant, which apparently wasn't being sung silently in my head.

The door opening wipes the good mood from my face and from my entire being. "Seth, tell her to leave, now." I command in an icy voice that brooks no room for argument. The kid runs to the door to stop her, but Essie bulldozes right over Seth. "Get out!" I scream, charging forward like an enraged bull.

"Leave," I hiss. "Don't step foot over this threshold again, or next door, or Revamped, or the Spook House, or Wreck & Ruin. If I frequent it, you're no longer welcome there." I breathlessly pant out, sounding murderous. I'm a hairsbreadth away from snapping. The blue-eyed, brown-haired jezebel stands before me, and only our familial tie stops me from tearing Essie's betraying head from her faithless neck.

"You told her? How could you? You promised not to tell?" Essie's bottom lip quivers as she deals with her own tiny betrayal. Essie's eyes are pointed above me, no doubt at her new lover.

"Oh... Oh... that is fucking rich, coming from *you* of all people," I sputter as I walk away. Shaking my head in utter disgust, I grab the *Sharpie* I was using to make recipe cards off the counter. "Since the shirt I made you four years ago is long gone, this will have to suffice."

I pop the lid off the marker with my front teeth. I carve an *A* in the center of Essie's forehead in permanent ink, too bad it's not tattoo ink.

Everyone gasps, except for the young boys. Seth asks Weston in a confused voice, "The anarchy symbol?"

"Dipshit, you need to pay closer attention in English class," Violet hisses. "More importantly, you need to pay attention to your family history. Essie just earned her right to be named after her namesake– Hester Prynne."

"So fucking rich," I purr. "You're accusing him." I point at Devon, "Of betraying your trust. Are you fucking kidding me? You, who betrayed me, expected Devon, who betrayed me, not to betray you? You deserve each other." My voice is deeper than the level of Hell I'm currently residing in. I hadn't expected to be this angry. Heartbroken, sucker-punched, but not infuriated.

"Leave," Violet orders. "This is our house, and you're no longer welcome. I don't know why Willow isn't kicking Devon out, but there must be a reason. I can't kick Devon's ass. But you're family, and family is fair game. I have no issue with punching a bitch out."

Violet's violence is displayed in Technicolor as her elbow flies back, and none of us are quick enough to stop her. A jab lands perfectly on Essie's left eye. Violet hops up and down, flinging her hand around, while saying *oww, uh, oooo, owie.*

Essie runs away with tears in her eyes, and I feel bad about it. I don't want to, but after eighteen years of Essie being my best friend, I hurt enough for the both of us.

"Thanks?" I shake my head, not knowing what else to say.

"You're very welcome, sister," Violet says primly as she accepts an icepack from her mom. I look quizzically at Violet, but then my attention is diverted.

On one side of the kitchen is Kieren, Rae, and Weston, all with identical expressions of disappointed outrage, and on the other side is Devon. Devon looks like he's going to be sick. It's exactly what I didn't want to happen.

"No." I shake my head in denial. "Don't. This isn't about you guys as a family. It was between Devon and me, and no one else."

"And apparently Essie," Clover says snidely. She sounds so much like me that I snort.

"And your Beetle." Devon hammers the final nail in his coffin. "Mustn't forget that disgusting part of my shame."

"Why haven't you killed him?" Kieren asks in a surprisingly calm voice.

"I have my reasons," I mumble underneath my breath. I still love the scumbag, or it wouldn't hurt so damned much.

"Bro, you couldn't think of a worse way to hurt Willow? Perhaps buy her a puppy, and then kill it? Assault her mom? You could've crashed Willow's car into Revamped and destroyed her livelihood, I guess. Maybe burn the Spook House down while you're at it?" Kieren's level of sarcasm makes me proud.

"I did hurt Willow's car. I watched as she dumped five gallons of gas all over it and killed it with fire. But that was after she took a maul to the outside and a portable reciprocating saw to the interior. After Willow was finished, I reported it as stolen and said vandals destroyed it, so she could get the insurance money."

"Why?" Kieren and I say at the same time.

"I knew you wouldn't see me watching. It was my fault. I know you, Willow. You'd never touch that car again. I'll admit, it was interesting to watch Auggie help you," Devon answers me, and then turns to his brother. "I screwed Essie *in* Willow's car… *on* Willow's car. I think the only thing I could've done that was worse, was to literally *shit* on Willow."

"When?" Kieren whispers, but I can tell he already knows the answer by the crestfallen expression on his face.

"Don't," I warn, trying to salvage Devon and Kieren's bond.

But of course, the scumbag doesn't listen. "I did the worst thing I could think of because I'm a huge coward and you aren't. I betrayed Willow while you were telling her the truth of our past." Devon admits, sounding dead on the inside and perfectly fine with it.

I close my eyes as Kieren walks from the kitchen, and a second later the screen door slams shut behind him. "Well, it's good that we got our first family fight out of the way, don't you think?" I say cheerily. Clover looks at me like I've lost my dang mind, but the other five heads emphatically nod yes.

This is why Devon's still here. This is why I haven't screamed at him like I did Essie. Nothing will ever remove Essie's family status. But the Masons' connection to us is tenuous, still forming. I'll do anything for my sister, even if it means looking at the man who betrayed me and calling him family for the rest of my life. And it's why Devon is still standing here, taking all of our shit-stares and ridiculing comments. Devon's here for the wellbeing of our family… and for once, Devon isn't being a coward.

CHAPTER FORTY-SIX

"Hey, how was school tonight?" asks the man lounging on my bed, and I like the looks of him there. Dressed in jeans and a Henley t-shirt, Kieren's a boy-next-door wet dream.

Every night for the past six weeks, Kieren's been waiting for me in my room when I get home. We talk about our day, and then eat some snacks while watching shows saved on The Hopper. I was surprised to learn that Kieren's favorite shows were the same as mine. I thought he was bullshitting me, but after we quizzed each other, I found out he knew the finer details of the plots. I like this routine we've created. It's comforting.

"I'd ask how work was–" I toss Kieren a wink. "But I just made out Wreck & Ruin Repair's payroll, so I think I know what's going down at work," I tease. "I'd tell you how school was, but I'm sure chatty Langdon Stone will give you the 411 in the morning. So no need to go over the boring stuff tonight."

"I like a woman who gets to the point." Kieren perfectly executes the man laugh, and my knees go weak. "Go get ready. I'll be waiting."

I grab my nightclothes from the top of my dresser and make tracks across the hall to the bathroom. I marvel over how things can change in a few weeks' time. I took Isis's advice and got my shit in order, the rest of them can deal with their own. I'll help them if they ask, but it's not my job to make everyone else happy if I'm miserable.

Essie is number two on my list of shit I had to straighten out. I do my Prynne duty, but I don't interact with Essie at our weekly family gatherings. Yes, she sits in the same pew with me every Sunday morning. I don't speak to Essie, but that's a step up from decapitating her, I would think.

Clover and the family top my list as most important. While I can't make them happy, I can lessen their stress by not adding to it. Auggie understands when I leave Revamped to pick up the kids– Raven, Seth, Violet, and Weston –from school, or when I cut out of work entirely if they have an event I need to attend. Clover has a not-so secret admirer making her cook and bake, and as much as she says it drives her bonkers, she's loving it. As a way for Clover to get to know the kids before Malcolm decides to remove the *secret* from admirer, we do a weekly cooking lesson as a bonding experience. During these lessons is the only time I see Devon. I never speak to him or look at him.

Devon.

Devon can't use me as his reason to spiral out of control. I don't yell at him. I no longer cry over him. I show him nothing but polite indifference, and everyone knows better than to talk about him with me. But Devon didn't need me to push him over the edge, he toppled over it himself. Devon can barely hold it together during our cooking lessons. By the end of the two-hour session, he sweating profusely and shaking so badly he can't hold a conversation. He usually leaves early to get a hit of whatever he's self-medicating with these days.

Devon is now a real, honest to God, drug addict.

When you think drug addict, you envision the people in movies and television shows who steal from Grandma to their baby sisters, and sell the stuff at a pawn shop to fund their drug habit. These people are glassy-eyed, with skin the color of wet paper, dirty and unkempt. That is Devon these days. He can't hide it any longer. He can't lie his way out of it, and he can't act himself through it. So he's stopped trying to hold himself together in any way. He's embraced his inner-drug-addict and shows it to the world.

I never look at Devon. I never speak to Devon. I refuse to listen to anything dealing with Devon. All because it hurts too much to know that I've already lost him– we all have. This is how Auggie feels about Tina. There is nothing you can do, so you don't want to watch them commit a slow suicide.

The word *Devon* is no longer a part of my vocabulary.

In the absence of Devon is my family, my work, my schooling, my true friend Langdon, Mr. Kline, and Kieren. While Devon is a painful spot in my heart, I feel fulfilled and happy.

Mr. Kline is there for me in all things: he teaches me at work, he gives me advice, he holds me while I cry when *the word* re-enters my vocabulary, and he's helping me regain my feminine confidence with innocent flirting.

… And then there's Kieren Mason. He's the most stable person I know. He mourns, but he never shows it. Devon is Kieren's big brother. You look up to your big brother like a hero, and when that perception is crushed, it's devastating. I can pretend Devon no longer exists, but Kieren doesn't have that luxury. Devon is in his home, sitting across from him at supper– not eating –and they share a bedroom. Kieren has to lie in bed at night, straining to hear whether or not his brother is still breathing. The fear and pain I feel is nothing but a shadow of what Kieren, Malcolm, and the rest of the Masons are going through.

I believe Kieren and I share the highlight of our day. The two hours at night where we're just ourselves, seeking what we need from the other, while leaving everything else at the door. I once thought that I couldn't find a person who *got* me– a person I understood in return.

I was someone different to a whole slew of people. I thought I needed separate people to feed my needs: friend, family, confidant, or lover. But I always experienced a void. While with one, I missed the others. I felt alone, unfulfilled. Lost. I hadn't realized I could find all that in the same person.

I was wrong. There is someone out there for everyone, someone who doesn't want you to change who you are, because then they wouldn't fit you anymore. Kieren's unflinching honesty and loyalty is exactly what I need. Kieren's not my boyfriend. He's not my best friend. I fear that in my head and heart, I'm making Kieren my center.

We are stuck in a strange spot– both mourning Devon, to the point he's a shadow in our relationship. We're both unwilling and unable to move beyond the strict boundaries we've set. We can't stay away from the other, but we avoid any word that is attached to an emotion. While Kieren is a huge flirt, making sure I always know my insecurities are unwarranted where he's concerned, he never initiates anything outside of platonic affection.

Devon's harmful words struck, stuck, and wrecked me. It wasn't until a few days ago that I even felt a spark of desire. Auggie's tried to yank it out of me with his shameless teasing and flirting, but it was to no avail. Asked too many times to count, Auggie begged me to tell him what Devon said so he could fix it. Unless Auggie has a magic wand, I'm not growing breasts anytime soon.

Insecurities and negative thoughts aside, I'm almost nineteen years old, and there is a man lounging on my bed, who I've wanted since elementary school. The desire flared a few days ago in a mortifying way. I was snuggled up to Kieren, our legs entangled, and I hadn't even realized I was rubbing against him until I was about to shatter. I tried to stop, wanted to run from the room and hide, but Kieren didn't let me.

Rolling over onto his back, Kieren settled me over his hips until I was straddling him. Neither of us spoke as he gripped my ass and started rocking me against him in a way that was so much more stimulating than his thigh. It took less than thirty seconds before I was calling out his name and wrapping myself around him like a second skin. We laid there for several long minutes, panting, coming down from a sexual high. Kieren simply got up, went into the bathroom for a few minutes, where I'm sure he finished what I started, and then we watched an episode of *Game of Thrones* while eating Cheetos.

Not a word has been said, but the activity is now a staple between finishing one show and starting another. Whoever has the biggest balls of the night initiates the act... and I always have the biggest metaphorical balls. Kieren's too much of a gentleman, never taking liberties. I'm going insane, trying to figure out if he's not pressuring me, or just doesn't want me back.

Horny, achy, whatever you want to call the intense pressure of desire that is suffocating– I've never been so aroused in my life. The need for sexual release is almost a compulsion for me now. I don't want to watch any television tonight, and I don't want to rut while scratchy flannel pajama bottoms press into my cooch as I ride ridged denim. If I can't have bare flesh, then I'll improvise on the most pleasurable way to dry hump.

"Holy mother," I breathe as I re-enter my bedroom. "Those are some big balls you've got there, Stud." Both metaphorical and physical balls.

"Why, thank ya, twin." Kieren releases his laugh like a nuclear strike to the cunt. I grip the doorframe because my legs turned to jelly.

Swallowing a dozen times to wet my mouth, I try to regain my ability to speak. "You win tonight, that's for sure," I mutter as I look on in shock. I thought I was the crafty one wearing silk panties and a tank top instead of my usual pajamas. But Kieren? The guy is only wearing a pair of silk boxer briefs, and I can see everything, and everything is perfect.

"I know we don't talk about it." Kieren shifts on the bed, getting more comfortable by propping a pillow behind his back. "I know we don't want to talk about it. But it's not that I don't want you. I'm just not ready for sex after..." he trails off.

After Kieren's past with using sex as his drug, but never reaching the final high. After my history of disastrous sex with Auggie and Devon. Just the past and Devon is enough to scare anyone.

"I don't want it to only be about sex with us. It ruins too much shit. So these stay on." Kieren tugs at his boxers. "I figured if I was getting chaffed, then you had to be getting pretty raw down there." He laughs again, but this time it sounds unsure and uncomfortable.

"A little bit." Feeling bashful, I mutter while looking at the floorboards "Lights on, or off?"

"Um… I like looking at you, but I think having the lights off will be more comfortable for us to begin with. Maybe we'll move on to lights and sunshine when we graduate from dry humping to foreplay."

The last thing I see as I hit the light switch is Kieren's genuine smile– the one that warms me from the inside out. I shut the door and lock us in, even though it's unnecessary. Robbie, Auggie, and I have very strict boundaries we live by. We never enter a room if the door is shut. Hell, sometimes it's best to stick your head into a room before entering it, say the kitchen or the living room, because you never know when, where, or who is worshipping the Beast.

"Why am I nervous this time?" I murmur to myself as I crawl onto the bed. The other three times, I was calm as I straddled Kieren's hips and did nothing but selfishly ride to my climax. There's never any foreplay between us– no kissing, no fondling.

"Can we try something different?" Kieren asks hesitantly. He tries the *something different* before I can answer. Rolling over me, he settles between my thighs like we're having sex. Even with the foot height difference, we surprisingly fit well together.

"There's a reason I don't kiss you," he says in a husky voice gone deep. Somehow he reads my mind, sensing the lack of intimacy is bothering me. "It's not that I don't want my mouth on you. I… that's the one thing I held back from when I had sex. I never let anyone touch me without a condom, not hands or mouths. A mouth on mine." Kieren shudders in my arms. "So if I kissed you right now, I'd be inside you in a heartbeat. Not a good idea yet, Spanky. Never forget the hallway at Rush."

"Unforgettable." I huff out a laugh. "You weren't actually going to do me against the wall, were you? Wait a minute." I lean on my elbows, gazing up at Kieren with narrowed-eyes, as if I can actually see him. "Are you saying I'm the only girl you've kissed? I don't believe you." I sound highly skeptical.

"A few girls stole some kisses," Kieren says with a laugh. "You'd be surprised at how many quick hookups don't involve anything but connecting body parts. Now, if we're talking about feeding at someone's mouth like you're trying to breathe life into them. The first time I kissed like that was with you at Rush. And yes, I had my dick halfway out of my pants before you kneed me."

"I don't know how to respond to that," I mutter, at a loss for words. "The truth is that everything we did in that hallway was a first for me."

"I know," Kieren says softly. "I'm glad Auggie stopped me from screwing you in public, because it would've tainted whatever we're building right now. A man should take his woman to bed first."

"Kieren Mason, who knew he was so traditional?" I draw out while laughing.

"Hey, if we're still together a few years from now, having sex in our bed like an old married couple, I'm not against fucking your brains out against a wall. Any wall. How about this, if we're still together two years from now, I'm gonna fuck you in Rush, Revamped, Wreck & Ruin, and the Playroom. But other than that, yeah, this man is very traditional."

"And a Mason isn't a man if he doesn't keep his word," I quote as if I'm Malcolm giving a lecture. "Can I touch you?" I flex my fingers where they rest against his sides.

"Please." Kieren groans as he buries his face against my neck. He shifts his hips in a practiced maneuver that arches his back and grinds his arousal against my sex. "Fuck," hisses from his lips to vibrate against my throat. "Silk was too good of an idea. I'm not gonna last."

"What?" After years of wondering what Kieren's muscles would feel like beneath my fingertips, I now know– pure heaven. My nails bite into Kieren's flesh as I countermove my body against his. The powerful surge, the thrust of his hips, has the muscles bunching beneath my hands.

"Moan in my ear," Kieren breathlessly pants. The tickling of his breath against my skin has me quivering, but not nearly as much as the intimacy of his words. I lose myself in the trifecta of

Kieren: passion, connection, and trust. "I want to hear you moan for me, Willow."

An arm weaves between my body and the mattress, picking me up until Kieren and I are aligned differently. Our foreheads and groins are pressed together with Kieren's back arched high to compensate for our height difference. Overcome, I wrap myself around Kieren like I do during and after an orgasm. I cling to him, arms crisscrossed over his back with my fingernails digging into his shoulders, and my legs over his hips with my ankles hooked.

My panties are saturated, making the fabric feel like a second skin and causing the seat to move to the side. A gasp is torn from my throat when bare flesh slides over mine. I arch my spine and moan, "Oh, God!" when I realize what I'm feeling. Kieren's boxers have slid south and his exposed length is gliding through my slit.

Freezing, holding himself rigid above me, I know Kieren's looking at me, even though I can't see him. "You have exactly three seconds to say no," Kieren warns breathlessly in a tortured voice.

"Yes," I breathe in an instant.

Simultaneously, Kieren's mouth fuses to mine as his body slides deep inside of me. "Finally… yes," is a shuddery breath from his lips.

I lay stunned for less than a second to imprint the sensation of Kieren filling me for the very first time, and then suddenly something snaps inside of me. I finally let go. This isn't instruction. This isn't a pity fuck. This isn't me grasping at a thread of connection that's in my imagination, trying to make it more than it is. This is me, and this is Kieren, and goddammit, I just want him.

Everything becomes muted background noise to Kieren's ragged breath in my ear. The rasping sound trills down my spine and beads sweat on my skin. I luxuriate in the way his lips feast at mine, sucking the air from my lungs while replenishing it with his. Kieren thrusts me into the mattress, because he wants to be as deep as he can sink.

My hands glide down sweat-slickened muscles, beneath a swath of silk, to the swell of his ass. My nails dig in, wanting, *needing* him deeper inside me. It's a compulsion to have him as deep as he can go. "Kieren!" I shout into his mouth as an earth-shattering orgasm flows over me and rolls me under.

Holding me like he can mold our bodies as one, Kieren shudders in my arms as his release floods my insides, wash after wash flows into me. "Willow," he breathes my name, sounding shocked. "I couldn't stop. I was a dipshit for thinking I could control myself. I've been wearing jeans the past few nights as a barrier, but the moment I felt your bare pussy on me... I was lost."

"You came," I say in awe, otherwise speechless.

Groaning, Kieren moves to kneel between my thighs, but he doesn't pull free from my body. "Inside you," he rasps as a fingertip glides down my side, over my belly, and settles over my clit. "Do you need another? I like how it feels when you come on my dick." I can't see him, but I know damn well he's flashing that infamous smirk.

"You're really quiet," I tease. I follow Kieren's lead and start petting him back, stroking his strong thighs as we come down from our sexual high. "If I hadn't felt you come, I would've never known it."

"There are five people in my tiny house, and I share a bedroom with my brother. I didn't want anyone to know what I was doing when I went into the bathroom, or when I woke in the night to rub one out. Sorry, Willow, this man is a quiet one. I shouldn't mention the screamer," Kieren mumbles, sounding sheepish. "Dev almost gave me a heart attack the first time he putted off in his bed. I was a kid, and had no clue why he was moaning. I thought he was dying on me. That fucker can grunt like a wounded animal."

A giggle flows from me for a few seconds, until I realize I'm laughing about Devon, and then it dries upon my lips. I sigh wistfully, wishing an infinite amount of times that Devon was healed. "But you came?" I repeat.

"Let's see," Kieren sings. He reaches down to yank me up until I'm wrapped around him. He kneels on the bed with his softening cock still buried inside of me. "I told you at Rush and at Calico, and I told anyone with ears, how very much I wanted you, but my needs were ignored for the greater good."

"I'm sorry," I mutter, feeling heartsick.

"Not your fault. Also, tonight wasn't the first time I've came with you. Fourth time, actually. I'm quiet, remember?" Kieren whispers into my ear, and then he bites the lobe. "Spanky, did you think I was whacking off in your bathroom? I'm not that naughty."

"What were you doing in there, then?" I grumble, feeling like a doofus. Kieren's man laugh has me shoving him to the bed. I reach over and flick on my lamp so I can look at him while we chat. Kieren rests across my bed, looking relaxed and replete. I cuddle up to his side, curling around him like a well-contented cat.

"Five people in my house, remember? I was cleaning up my messy boxers, so I didn't have to walk into my house with a huge cum stain on the front of my pants. I'd never live that one down."

Flipping me over to the mattress, Kieren smiles down at me. My heart beats double-time, fearful of what he'll say next. "Sons of Anarchy and Cool Ranch Doritos?"

A smile pulls at my lips over the ease and normalcy between us. "I'll get the Coke from the fridge in the kitchen. My mini-fridge is empty." I hop from the bed and tug on my pajama bottoms. "I'll need a quick detour to the bathroom to wash up," I say sheepishly as I learn what goes up must come down.

Kieren pulls off his soiled boxers and tosses them into my hamper. I finally notice he has a duffle bag with some clothes spilling out. "Make it a Sunkist, and take your time. I'll queue up SOA." He flashes me a blinding smile.

CHAPTER FORTY-SEVEN

"Filthy cheater." I growl as I make a grab for the Nintendo controller, but Auggie pulls it out of my grasp.

"Ooooohhhh... I'm a cheater because you suck at Kirby's suckage." Auggie taunts me during our daily video game session at Revamped. "It's my turn– you killed the pink guy. Bad Monster." Auggie makes that delicious sound, and it nearly destroys me. I shudder in bliss, and it makes him laugh harder. A hearty, deep laugh centered in his chest– scrumptiously addictive male.

"I do not suck at suckage," I flirt back. I stand on the sofa so I can reach Auggie's outstretched hand.

"You're so tiny, Monster. You have to stand on the couch to reach my hand, and you're still a few inches shy." Auggie trails a taunting laugh as he plays keep-away with the controller.

"Dude, you're a beast– a foot and a half difference is *huge*," I taunt as I jump up to reach the controller. "You're a freak. Gimme." Intelligence finally returns in the absence of the man laugh, I tug the cord.

Giggling, I hold my prize like it's worth a million bucks. I drop down on the sofa cushion and restart the level since I killed poor Kirby.

"No." Auggie pouts. "I wanna cuddle for a few minutes."

Tossing the controller onto the sofa, Kirby is long forgotten. I crawl into Auggie's lap in a heartbeat. This is what we do– nothing more, nothing less. There's an ease between Auggie and me that wasn't there before. Not when we were Mr. Kline and Good Girl, or Auggie and Willow. These past few weeks have changed Auggie, too. Dealing with the stress of both Tina and Devon has taken a toll on him– it's like he's aged a millennium with the rest of us. I trust Auggie now, and he trusts me, and we live within the boundaries we've created. It's the structure I needed in my life.

"I was just picking on you, Willow. I like your tiny body. I don't see it as a little girl anymore. I need you to know that. What you said to me really struck a chord, and watching you struggle made me understand you better. I wish you'd tell me what Devon said that made you close yourself off." he tries yet again. Relentless bugger.

I curl up in Auggie's lap and rub my cheek against his vintage concert tee. A deep sense of comfort hits me out of nowhere. I have support in many forms– I'm not alone anymore. No matter what, I can find someone who's been there before me. Auggie's been dealing with Tina's addiction for years, and he's been advising the whole lot of us. If Auggie needs to use me as a living teddy bear right now, I'll gladly offer my services.

"Thank you," I whisper softly, and then peck a kiss to Auggie's cheek. "I've been doing my damnedest to move forward, all the while Devon is ruining himself on a destructive path. I want to help Devon, but not until I'm strong enough to face *his* demons. So thank you."

"What for?" Auggie pulls me back so he can look into my eyes.

"I just wanted you to know that I appreciate you and all you've done for me. I understand how painful this is for you, because we're all feeling it, too. Now you're dealing with it from two people you love. I'm thankful for your tough love, or I could've been a third person ruined to a life of drugs."

"Right now, I'm in that stage where I don't want to talk about it. It reminds me of mourning a loved one. All these people keep coming up to you, offering their sympathies and handing you mountains of food. The sympathies aren't a comfort– they're a constant reminder of what you've lost. Then you look at that food in your hands and want to puke. All you want to do is forget for five fucking seconds, but no one will let you. Sometimes ignorance is bliss. A smile. A laugh. A thought they don't occupy. And when you finally reach this special place where the mourned one has never invaded– *bam!* –some dumb fuck reminds you. In our case, the dumb fuck is still alive and tweaking right before our very eyes, and they're the one who interrupted our peace."

"You don't want to talk about it, I take it?" I say with a laugh. "I get it. Ignorance is bliss. Out of sight, out of mind. Out of mind, and you can get a good night's rest. Then some dumbass calls you up, asking if you knew Devon did this or that… there was a Devon spotting here. They want to gossip, and trash your family while they do it. I told a mother at Violet's school to mind her own goddamn business last week."

"Let's talk about something else then, hmm? How about you tell me how your nights have been?" Insert patented Augustus Kline eyebrow raise here

I blush like a sonofabitch, and then I roll my eyes as Auggie laughs at me. "I may or may not have had sex with Kieren last night. I can neither confirm nor deny reports. How did you find out?"

"Who do you think?" Auggie mimics my eye roll. "You share a wall with the queen of gossip. Robin ran and got me. We sat on his bed, straining to hear, but you love birds were too damn quiet."

"Kieren's a quiet one, alright," I mutter with a smirk.

"How was it? Which one of you initiated?" Auggie grabs my shoulders and gives a shake when I don't immediately reply. "C'mon, put me out of my misery. It's strange for me. The only other times you've had sex, I was present. Not knowing makes me curious."

"Well, aren't you awfully big to be a curious pussy cat," I drawl, and then decide to put the man out of his misery. "Okay, so it wasn't planned– *kinda* not planned," I tack on. "I hadn't felt like sex in weeks. Hell, other than a few times here or there, it's not like I'm an incredibly horny person. But holy Christ, the past three or four days, I've been running hot. All I had to do was think about Kieren, and I was ready. Put the dude in the same room with me… It's beyond embarrassing to say what started our fun." I breathe in deeply, and release the words like carbon dioxide. "Dry humping Kieren's leg like a dog."

I thought Auggie would laugh and make fun of me, but he looks more concerned than amused. Eyebrows knitted together, Auggie mutters, "You sound like you're in heat."

"I didn't say I was a dog!" I shout, more embarrassed than outraged. "I said *like* a dog, jackass."

Auggie tips his head back and releases that godawful man laugh. "I didn't mean it like that. Sorry." Chuckles continue to flow. "I meant how when a woman is fertile, they become wanton little things. It's biological. Isis stalks Rob and me around for a few days a month. It's the only time I find myself on my knees, being of service. She won't take no for an answer. No sex, not even with a condom. Isis isn't on any birth control– says it fucks her hormones up and makes her feel off. You're still on the shot, right?"

"Yeah," sounds a lot like *duh!* "Like Clover would let me forget. Why?"

"Did your stud wrap it last night?" Auggie asks, but he can tell by my facial expression that Kieren didn't. "Do you feel less horned up today?"

"Yeah, I got laid last night. I fed the beast so to speak," I say as a joke.

"Let's hope that's not true," Auggie mutters. He's about to say something else when Revamped's front door flies open, smashing into the wall.

"Willow!" Kieren shouts, looking frantic.

"What's wrong?" As I stand, I realize what this must've looked like to Kieren– I was sitting on Auggie's lap while we were talking. "This isn't what it looks like. Please, don't be jealous. We were just talking."

"It doesn't matter– I trust you both," Kieren says with the wave of his hand. "You need to come with me, your best friend needs you right now." Sounding impatient, he cups my elbow, trying to lead me to the front of the store.

"What do you need?" I ask, sounding panicked. I'm picking up Kieren's anxiety and it's suffocating me.

"Not me!" he snaps. "Devon needs you." Kieren chokes out despondently, and then begins to plead with me. "Please, my brother needs you."

"No, I can't. I can't see Devon like that, Kieren. It's killing me just thinking about it."

"Think about what you just said, Willow. You don't want to watch Devon spiral out of control. Remember how lost you felt when Auggie made that choice for you without the benefit of the doubt? He just threw your ass out of the Spook House and cut you off. We don't have to like what Devon's doing, but we can't abandon him. He's my brother."

"I can't!" I cry. "I want to, but I can't. What if seeing Devon like that makes me give in to my own demons."

"I'll do anything for Devon. I'd even ask the devil himself to help. I don't drink, and I can count the amount of times I've smoked on one hand. You understand the cravings and why Devon is being destructive. Please," Kieren begs. "Trust me when I say that seeing him like this will cure you, not tempt you."

"Go, Willow! Devon needs you." Auggie stands up and takes my hand, lending me comforting support. "I'll go, too."

"Good," Kieren hisses and I flinch. I'm about to ask what Kieren's issue is with Auggie, especially since he's been emulating him for the past few months. "Tina is there, too," he spits out, sounding thoroughly disgusted.

Auggie strings bow-string tight and takes a deep, shuddering breath. "I can't do it, then."

"If you can't, then how the hell can Willow and I do it? Tina's into bad shit, and she taking Devon down with her," seethingly hisses between Kieren's clenched teeth.

Kieren strides forward and gets into Auggie's face. His blue eyes are burning with hatred. He blames Auggie for his brother's current situation– he blames Auggie because Tina is Auggie's responsibility, like Devon is his. But mostly, Kieren blames Auggie, because it's easier than blaming himself– easier than blaming the person who's ultimately responsible.

Devon.

"Auggie, I get that you're sensitive to this because you've spent five years trying to get your addict sister to stay clean. It doesn't work– it never does… and each time Tina falls into harder drugs. You think this is Devon's future. While you may be able to stand back and just let it happen, I won't let my brother go down with Tina, dammit! Either get in the fucking car with me, or I won't speak to either of you ever again."

The front door wasn't locked, judging on how it opens with a sharp creak, courtesy of the toe of my Chucks. I wouldn't touch a surface in this waste dump with my bare flesh. Toxic to my olfactory system– the smell hits me first. The sharp smokiness of weed. The sour tang of sweat. The sweet scent of sex. Ammonia piss stench and the breath-stealing power of shit. The suffocating stink of burnt chemicals. The foul pungency of sickness –the drug den's bouquet welcomes me home.

Fairport is a conservative town, where you hide your bad habits and pray no one ever finds them. The low-rent section of town is tucked away from the church-going suburbanites. Devon and Tina's Technicolor dream ride vacation from reality is directly across the street from Rush. The irony of this is not lost on me, or on Auggie, as he keeps looking at his property and growling that his sister and Isis's nephew are pissing on their doorstep.

"Well, this was quite the party," I muse as I step over fallen partiers. I babble on, talking to myself. "If only the residents of our town could see their Officer Devon now. How they will love the local drug addict strolling the halls of Fairport ASD while influencing their little angels. Chief Mason will kill Devon as surely as look at him after this, after he makes Devon arrest himself that is. This cannot be hidden."

I pull out my cellphone and start capturing rock bottom, deciding I won't allow it to stay hidden. Maybe the best cure isn't to hide it, but to expose it. I take a few shots of the litter on the floor: half-dressed ladies passed out in their own vomit. A guy I've seen around town is lying on a pizza box filled with rancid food. And then there is Officer Devon...

Devon's slumped on the threadbare couch with Tina sprawled over his lap, and another woman's face resting in his crotch. All three are bare-assed naked and filthy– so filthy I can't find a clean inch of skin on any of them. The thought that they were touching each other sexually raises bile in my throat. I shake my head in disgust– I cannot believe this vile lump of humanity is the man I called best friend. I can't look too closely, or I'll be physically sick.

I snap pictures of the cluttered coffee table. I don't even know what some of the drug paraphernalia is that's scattered around. That's saying something, considering my education in five years of smoking pot on a daily basis and hitting parties where people were taking much stronger drugs. Speaking of stronger drugs, judging by the pallor of Devon's skin, he wasn't smoking weed last night, or the hundred nights prior.

It's afternoon, yet they are frozen in a drug-induced sleep. We could do whatever we wished to them, and they wouldn't know until it was well-past too late. Their stillness resembles the shroud of death. I never freaked, because the sound of Devon's labored sleep hit me as I walked in the front door. After months of hearing Devon breathe as we sat in silence together, my ears instantly tuned to the sound. If it wasn't for the song of Devon's breathing, I would've gone insane upon looking at him. He looks dead, and that's what's wrong with my companions.

Kieren and Auggie never made it past the threshold. They are frozen in a perverse state of shock as they look at their siblings from across the living room. I didn't freeze, because anger infused me with fire, lending me strength to do things I never would've thought myself capable.

"He's alive?" Kieren's voice is devastated– stunned. "Please, God, let Devon be alive," he begs underneath his breath, not knowing we can hear him.

"He's alive– they're all alive," I reassure them both. They sag against one another in relief. "Devon will wish he wasn't when I'm through with him, though," I whisper underneath my breath, and I know they didn't hear me.

I don't know if they're silently crying in relief and hope, or out of disgust at the situation Devon and Tina placed themselves under. But I turn away, giving the men the privacy to cry and retain their pride. I allow Kieren and Auggie to comfort one another, because I have a worse task to perform.

I yank my shirt sleeve down over my hand, never thinking I'd see the day where I'd need something to protect my skin before I touched someone's arm. "Track marks," I hiss as I drop the limp and lifeless, bruised arm. Thoroughly repulsed, I swallow back my vomit. "What kind of shit is your sister into, Auggie?"

Auggie doesn't reply, because he's still stunned stupid. It's not every day that you see your sister naked on top of a man who you thought was Captain Superhero. Auggie chose Devon over Kieren for me, because he thought he was the level-headed brother. Auggie couldn't have been more wrong, because those track marks are speckling the flawless skin of Devon's inner-elbow.

I grab a filthy, ripped sheet off the floor and toss it to Auggie. "Wrap Tina up and put her in my SUV," I order. Auggie unfreezes, and then has his little sister swaddled and out the door in a heartbeat.

I locate a cum-covered, felt blanket and toss it to Kieren. "You wanted my help, so help," I hiss nastily and instantly feel bad for taking my pain out on Kieren. By the sad smile he gives me, Kieren understands where my pain is coming from and doesn't take it personally.

"I'll take Devon's feet. I want nowhere near the top half of him." I point at the chest that used to turn me on as much as it comforted me. That musky vanilla scent I found as an intoxicant has long been replaced by the scent of illness. Vomit coats Devon from the waist up. His? Tina's? Whoever the hell the other chick is?

Kieren and I struggle to get Devon from the drug den, because neither of us wants to touch him. I grab Devon's ankles while Kieren's fingers ring around Devon's wrists. The blanket is barely covering Devon's waist, but neither of us stops to fix it. If the man was worried about his dignity, he wouldn't be here in the first place.

Devon doesn't look big in comparison to his brother or Auggie. But trying to carry deadweight without really touching it leads to a few nasty spills to the floor. Devon's going to have wicked bruises, and he'll deserve every single last one of them. It's too bad Devon isn't experiencing what we are: fear, misery, anguish, epic vileness. It turns my stomach– selfish scumbag.

I leave everyone else in the festering drug den– fuck them. They crawled into that disease-ridden cesspit, let them claw their way out of it. My charity begins and ends with our families, especially for self-created lowlifes. The best thing for them is to get caught inside their rock bottom. Maybe going to jail will be a wakeup call to their friends and family. Maybe by some miracle, it will be a personal wakeup call.

As soon as I get to my SUV, I make a not-so-anonymous tip to Malcolm via text message. I send him a picture of the coffee table with the caption: *Officer Dope Fiend was here*. No doubt Malcolm will be here in under two minutes flat.

A satisfied smirk flirts with my lips– it's too damned bad Tina and Devon aren't being arrested too. They should suffer the same consequences as the rest of their buddies. I don't want to ruin Devon's life. He might not care right now, but we do. I don't want Devon to use an arrest and the loss of his job as an excuse to spiral further down the rabbit hole.

I feel mildly at fault for this incident. Devon has been using our broken friendship and the reasons behind it as an excuse to abuse. Yes, all of that is his fault, but he no longer thinks clearly. Devon's view is tainted by a drug addict tint, and everything is painted in the flavor of his next high. There is no reasoning with a person who will twist everything you say or do, and somehow make it your fault, and they truly believe it. While I know I'm not really to blame, my warped emotions don't give a shit.

The drive to the Spook House is silent with the exception of the gale-force winds pouring in from every window. The stench is a mix of sewer, sickness, and a strange scent that I can only assume is the drug metabolizing in their systems and seeping out their pores. Devon and Tina stink so badly that Kieren's threatening to toss Tina from my car. The emotional climate isn't any easier to swallow. I thought for sure Auggie would crack a smile when Kieren said he was going to toss Tina, and wanted me to back up to make sure I finished the job the drugs started. But I'm not sure Auggie thought Kieren was joking, and neither was I.

I will never drink another drop of alcohol or touch weed for the rest of my life, and I'm proud of the decision. Every teen should visit a drug den before they attempt to take a drug– it'd scare their asses straight. It's an experience I will never forget.

I'm nominated the boss, because Kieren and Auggie are stunned stupid. "Auggie, take your sister to the first floor bath and scrub her until she's pink. Kieren and I'll take Devon to my bathroom."

Auggie runs with his sister in his arms. I'd love to ignore the tears falling from his eyes, but some things you just can't unsee. Kieren's no better off. He shakes so badly he keeps dropping Devon on the ground. The desperation in Kieren's eyes is killing me.

"What?" Isis shouts when she sees one of her nephews dragging the other by the wrists across the foyer floor. My inner-aunt erupts, and fuck if that isn't what brings my tears on. I couldn't image how I'd feel if it was Violet dragging Seth– death, I'd kill him.

"Isis, we need your help. Tina needs some clothes, and then I need you to get as much Gatorade from the fridge as you can carry, and then grab a bottle of pain reliever."

I give Isis something to do so she doesn't go crazy, lethal bitch on us. Isis's ebony eyes are enflamed, and I fear I will be the one burnt by them. If it was between her best friend, her nephews, or the girl with the very large target on her back, obviously I'd be the one Isis would lash out at.

"How long has Devon been like this?" I ask Kieren, even though I'm scared shitless to find out. Devon was dead-eyed last time I saw him, not that I was looking at him.

"I don't know. He hid it really well," Kieren mumbles hopelessly. "I thought Devon didn't want to hang out with me anymore because of–"

"Because of me." I grunt as we carry Devon down the hallway to my bathroom. Devon's hands limply drag along the floor. We had to switch our holds when we carried him up the staircase. Now Kieren's arms are hooked under Devon's armpits, and I'm hanging on to Devon's ankles.

"Yeah, that's what I thought. I'm not going to let anything come between us, Willow. Not even this. The handful of hours I spend with you at night is the only thing I do for myself. It's our *no Devon zone*, and I can just breathe and relax for a few stolen moments."

"Me, too. I get it. That's what Auggie and I were talking about earlier. I just… I don't want to come between you and your brother."

Kieren roughly rasps, "The only thing that can come between Devon and me is Devon."

"I'm so sorry," I mutter hopelessly, and I finally realize tears are streaming down my cheeks. "I'll do whatever I need to do to help you get through this."

"I know, and you already have." Kieren's voice is filled with so much emotion, so many unspoken words, that I really start to bawl.

"It been so difficult to be around Devon. Just looking at him makes me sick, furious and resentful. Some days it takes everything in me to stop myself from telling Devon to just get it the hell over with and shoot himself like Mom did. Suicide is the coward's way out, but this slow death is even worse, because Devon is forcing us to mourn the living. Devon's pretty much stayed on an even level of high for the past few weeks– more high than I'd ever seen but not quite at junkie levels. When Devon disappeared Friday night, and then he didn't go to work this morning, I got worried and started searching. A lot can happen in three days."

"Dump Devon in my tub," I order as I yank that vile blanket from his body. I want to bleach Devon, and then my hand, because that filth touched us. I shove the blanket in a bag and send it on its way down the dumbwaiter. I'm burning it later. "It's time we scrub the taint off Devon. But it's too bad we can't scrub it from his veins."

For the past hour, I've scrubbed an unconscious Devon. After I ran out of hot water, I allowed the icy-cold water to belt Devon in the face for a good twenty minutes before the scumbag came to. After four bottles of Gatorade and three trips to worship the porcelain god, Devon's finally cognizant.

"Eat it," I grunt as I toss a piece of dry toast onto Devon's belly. I nudge his foot with my sneaker, none to gently, I might add. Devon's stomach is concave– the stomach that was filled with good health almost two months ago when I kissed and caressed it. He's lost so much weight since his only need to survive turned to drugs. His skin is still tinged gray, even though he's now clean. I no longer smell the drugs working their way through his system. The hollows beneath his eyes scare me– such a strange color, bruise-like.

"Willow," he croaks out.

"Shut the fuck up, Devon!" I walk over to my bedroom door and lock it. I'm sure Kieren didn't know any better, but Auggie should've known better than to leave me alone with Devon. Auggie's taking care of his sister while Kieren and Isis were commanded to attend a family meeting– intervention planning, I presume.

I hop on my bed and straddle Devon's thighs. His body disgusts me, even after I scrubbed it raw with a back-brush and antibacterial dish soap. The body I had worshipped has been used and abused. The body I made love to for the very first time– his and mine –has been fucked every which way and without a condom. I wouldn't touch the dick that lies flaccid and sickly looking against his hip without proof of negative test results and latex gloves.

"You're going to listen," I demand in disgust. I grip Devon's chin with my fingertips and sharply dig my nails into his flesh. "Whether it's because of the past, or what happened between us, neither is good enough of a reason to be self-destructive, you selfish piece of shit. You will never touch drugs and alcohol for the rest of your natural born life. If you do, I won't intervention your ass, I'll kill you."

"Willow." Devon coughs and tries to swallow. I hand him a bottle of water and tell him to nurse it slowly. I don't want to have to drag him back to the toilet.

"I said that you're listening right now, Devon. You need to hear me, not think up an excuse. Bad shit happens every day to good and bad people. We victimize and we are victims. We deal and move on. What you're doing is cowardly, because you're doing it to yourself, simply because you can. It's selfish because you didn't have to see the terror in your brother's eyes when he came to get me, or how Kieren couldn't even walk because he was shaking so badly, or how Isis nearly fainted when she saw your gray skin and sunken eyes. I don't care if you hate me, or hate yourself. But you'll love them, goddammit!"

It takes me several long minutes to reign in my fury and aggression. I close my eyes against the need to pummel Devon's chest purple. I can smell his goddamned addictive scent again. It's wafting up and hitting me in the head like a ballpeen hammer to the skull.

I flick my eyes open to find Devon waiting to connect with me. Devon's fingers are less than an inch from my calves. I watch as one tries to inch closer to touch me. I shake my head no and simultaneously mouth *no!*

"Your pathetic behavior doesn't scream of someone who wants to fade into the background because they think they're worthless. It screams of self-importance, as if you think your wants and needs supersede all those around you. *Look at me. Breathe me. All your thoughts should revolve around me.* Like you're the only victim on the planet? Malcolm lost his wife just as surely as you lost your mother. Raven and Weston lost their mother as well, and Kieren... there is nothing you experienced that night that he didn't face beside you, so why do you get to check out and suck up all the attention and love and time and energy from your family– suck it from your father, aunt, and siblings? Why? Because you're more important, right? If you truly hurt, and you truly loved us, you wouldn't ever want us to experience the pain you're dealing out. You're punishing us to punish yourself, and that means only you matter, right?

"Why are you so important? What did you do to earn such greatness? You know what I see lying on my bed? Someone else, probably a professional, would say they see a lost little boy, and we need to tiptoe around the real issues and kiss his ass until he's healed. Well, this planet has billions of fucked up souls just like you, and I don't have the patience to walk around like everyone is a breathing landmine. All I see before me is someone who needs a verbal ass kicking for shitting on their family. No one owes you anything, Devon. At birth, you aren't popped out an instant superstar. You have to earn the respect, the praise, the love, and the trust. Maybe if you knew how difficult it was to earn it, you wouldn't so easily throw it away. Maybe you'd contribute to your family, so you all could share the burden, instead of being the burden.

"I'm going to tell you the shit your family is too scared to say. You're gonna die, Devon," I utter without a single emotion. "You're gonna die. We all are eventually, but you're killing yourself as surely as if you picked up a fucking gun and pulled the trigger. Do you get that? I bet you don't even give a shit right now because the real you is buried so deeply that it can't crawl out from beneath the drug haze."

I look nowhere but Devon's eyes. I try to see if the real Devon is tunneling his way to the surface. While glossy-eyed from the drugs, the tears falling express that maybe, just maybe, the real Devon can hear me… or it's just my naïve hope.

"People I loved have died on me. My grandparents left our family after living a fulfilling life. It was bitter-sweet, but just the continuation of the cycle of life. The one thing that led me to use is the one thing that made me stop. Sam's death had me toking up. If Sam were alive today, and I used him as an excuse to do drugs, it would kill a part of him. I was killing his memory," I barely breathe out as the shame of my actions suffocates me. I can barely breathe let alone speak.

"I watched a great man die– his body cannibalized from the inside out. Sam wanted to live, would've done anything to live," I fiercely bite out. "That man fought for three years straight– having chemicals pumped into his blood stream and suffering the horrific side-effects… and he suffered for us. Sam fought so we wouldn't be left behind without him, and his suffering was pointless in the end because he left us behind anyway. If I knew that was how it was going to end, I would've let him go as soon as we found out he was sick, because we all suffered right alongside him. I loved Sam enough to lose him earlier if it guaranteed he would've been pain-free. That, right there, is love, Devon.

"I'm not telling you all of this so you'll pity me. I want you to realize what you're doing to all those who care for you. Unlike Sam, you can heal yourself and live. But you need to make a choice. If you plan on killing yourself, just fucking do it. Don't make everyone suffer as we watch you deteriorate and die, or possibly take someone innocent with you. Don't leave that legacy behind.

"But first, you need to realize what you're leaving behind. You have the job you trained for, excel at, and can make a positive difference in our community. A family who loves you.

Friends who would face their demons by diving into a drug den to save your unworthy ass. I'll always be here for you. No matter what happened between us intimately, I'm still your best friend. I will haunt you until you do the right thing. I have pictures of you at that house, in my tub, and wrapped around my toilet. You're going to stare at them every day, just as we've had to stare at you every day. If I find out you've drank alcohol or took a drug, I'll release every damn photo to the public. It won't be because I want you shamed. It will be because I will have every eye in Fairport monitoring your every fucking move. I will hold anyone who gives you a drug personally accountable, and I will drop Chief Mason on their heads when I find them.

"You will be my new mission, and you know when I perform a job, I live it. I will do this to protect our family, so I never have to see the pain in their eyes again. I know you don't give a shit about yourself, but what about those kids you've helped raise since they were born? What happens when everyone finds out their big brother is a heroin addict? Go ahead and ruin your life, but don't ruin theirs."

"Willow." Devon desperately tries again.

"Nope." I toss the pictures I printed out a few minutes ago onto Devon's stomach. "I'm done talking. I don't want to hear the excuses you formulated while I talked. You will sit here for an hour with nothing but your immortalized shame. Then I'll listen to you."

CHAPTER FORTY-EIGHT

I hid from Devon like a coward. I just couldn't say goodbye to him. The finality would kill me. I never went back to see what Devon had to say for himself. It would've been utter bullshit with that toxic poison flowing in his veins, altering his thoughts and reactions.

Five minutes ago, I let Malcolm in the house to take Devon home to pack. I took one look at the devastated expression on Chief Mason's face and ran. I didn't make it very far before I slumped to the floor, sobbing my eyes out. I couldn't watch Malcolm beg his son to go to rehab. What if Devon said no? If he says yes, in less than a few hours, Devon will be gone.

This time, I ran to where I was taught. I'd learned my measure at the hands of Mr. Kline. I ran straight to him, knowing he will help me through this emptiness, just as he has for the past few months.

Never entering this room since its completion, it feels foreign to be standing at its threshold. Auggie's sitting upright at the head of the bed with a sketchpad in his lap. "I couldn't say goodbye," I breathe into the shadow-shrouded room. Auggie doesn't say anything. He simply parts his arms, waiting for me to fly into them.

"I couldn't say goodbye to Tina, either. I pushed Tina on the bus and turned my back on her until I heard the bus drive off. I walked away, never looking back," Auggie admits, sounding torn and filled with self-doubt.

I can't let Auggie hold me yet, not so soon after breaking down out in the hallway. I sit on the edge of the bed and take a deep, shuddering breath. "I don't really know you, Auggie. After seeing you every day of my life, I barely know you at all. We live in the same house, we work in the same store, and I know nothing of your personal life. I learned the same thing when it came to my sister, too. My ignorance makes me feel self-involved. I don't want to be that person anymore– the kind of person I accused Devon of being. So I'll be learning you from now on."

"It's the dynamics between child and adult. We're the same now, Willow. So from now on, ask and I will tell. I assume this stems from your curiosity over Tina. You didn't need to know what was happening with Tina, because I wouldn't wish that stress on another soul. But I realize I should've explained it to you as soon as I discovered your addiction to marijuana and alcohol. I realize I went about it the wrong way. I'm sorry, it's just that speaking of Tina is very difficult for me."

"Why? She's your sister. It's like she's your dirty little secret," I murmur, wondering why I've never seen any photos of her, or why he never speaks of her. But then again, Auggie is very direct– no talk of emotions. Unless it has a direct impact at the moment, Auggie is silent.

"Well." He tosses his sketchpad onto the nightstand. "I don't respect my mother, or the choices she's made. I love her, but I don't have a relationship with her. I don't tell my story, because the only part of it that I'm proud of is my connection to Malcolm and my stepfather– everything else screams of white trash. I'm ashamed, and I don't admit that lightly."

I crawl up onto the bed and sit crossed-legged in the center. I face Auggie, showing him there is nothing he could say or do to change my view of him. "You're your own man, Augustus Kline. But you're a hard man to know. Easy to love and respect, though…" I trail off.

"I feel like a horrible person, because I'm ashamed of my mother and sister. I've tried to help them, but their personalities defy help. My mom was young when she had me, only fourteen. I have no idea who my father is. My mom looks just like Tina–"

I grumble something not very complimentary underneath my breath, causing Auggie to huff out a laugh. "No, my sister is not plastic. I assure you, she is all real. Even the hair you tore out is naturally blonde. So, somewhere out there is a giant man with red hair and green eyes. Someone who screwed my mother and doesn't know I exist. This man isn't in Fairport– I've looked. My mother didn't grow up here. John Mason found her in a similar place to where we found Tina and Devon today, only I was there too. I was three years old."

"Jesus," I hiss, thoroughly disgusted.

"I told you– trash," Auggie says without emotion. "The police were called because a neighbor heard me crying. My mom was three years younger than Tina is today, only eighteen. She was found lying in her own vomit while I wandered around a drug den. John was a ruthless bastard, but the good side of him saved my life. He took my mom and me into his home. John told me to call him Dad, and he raised me until his death when I was eight."

"What did your mom do after that?"

"Malcolm was only seventeen when John had a heart attack. Police officers belong to a true brotherhood, so they took care of their own– Malcolm –and Malcolm took care of us. Isis, my mom, me, and he married Camille shortly thereafter, and she was pregnant with Devon almost immediately. It took my mom another year of living off Malcolm before she found another lowlife to shack up with, but only after she got pregnant. My stepfather is not Tina's father– we don't know who Tina belongs to either. My mother was with nine different men over the years before she married my stepfather. Patrick is a man similar to John Mason– a savior complex. Only it was too little too late for Tina, since she was three years into a hard battle with addiction when he came into our lives."

"What has been done with Tina so far?" I ask, sounding curious. Kieren said Tina was a habitual rehab flunky.

"At first, I lectured Tina to death, but that's hard to do when your own mother is taking drugs while you're bitching at your sister. Literally shooting up while I was screaming at them. I spent my early twenties sinking every dime of my income into rehab centers for both of them. But I wasn't Tina's legal guardian, so Mom would sign their asses out within the first seventy-two hours. I prayed they'd get arrested. Something. Anything." Auggie's voice warbles with suppressed frustration. "Finally, I just washed my hands of the pair of them. I had to live my own life."

"But you feel guilty, like you abandoned them–"

"No, I feel like they abandoned *me*," Auggie stresses while placing a closed fist over his heart. "Because they abandoned themselves."

No longer having the words to comfort an old wound that still festers, I crawl into Auggie's lap and give him the only gift I have. I allow him to use me as a human teddy bear. Auggie's thick arms surround me instantly and tighten.

"Willow, I will give you some hope over Devon. I believe that drugs were written in my mother and sister's DNA. It's why I've never touched any. It's why I only drink a beer here or there or a glass of wine at a restaurant. Devon's DNA is clean. He is medicating a horrific event– drowning it. Tina is just a drug addict, born a drug addict of a drug addict. My mother is clean *right now*, but for how long? If something happens to Patrick, Mom will still be a drug addict, but she'll be a user again, too."

"So you think Tina is hopeless?"

"Yes," Auggie breathes gravely. "I do. I could hold out hope that Tina learns to cope with what she is without thriving in it, but that is just the hope of a big brother who loves his little sister. I'm a realist, and I know it will take something profound to make Tina change. Mom met Patrick at rehab. He's her fucking counselor, for Christ's sake. Mom never came to terms with what she is, never found that profound moment. She just uses Patrick as her new drug– thank fuck!"

I quickly wipe a few stray tears away and clear my throat. "What's going to happen to Tina now?"

"Tina is a legal adult, and it's taken the past two years for Patrick to get power of attorney over her. The pictures you took today, Malcolm sent them to the judge, and it got pushed through. So when Tina gets off the bus, Patrick owns her. Tina will get clean, but she'll always be a drug addict. Always."

"So even though Patrick will make it better, you won't be able to relax, because if something happens to him, you're back right where you were a few years ago?"

"Exactly, that's why I never talk about it. That's why I pretend I don't have a mother, or a sister, or a father out there somewhere. It's already invading my thoughts, whether I'm asleep or awake, and talking about it just makes it worse without solving anything."

"Devon isn't my brother, but yeah, I have a feeling I'm experiencing but a shadow of your pain. I'm sorry you have to go through it, and I understand if we never revisit this conversation again," I murmur against his chest.

"Deal," Auggie accentuates with a tight squeeze. "Tell me something to get my mind off of…" at a loss for words, he settles on, "Selfish fuckheads."

I bite my lip, but it doesn't contain what spills out. "I want to open our Playroom."

"What?" Auggie squeaks in shock. He pulls me away from his chest so he can look down at me.

"I think it'd be safer. You wouldn't need to worry about someone from the club wandering in on the action. I know

Malcolm keeps you from getting into trouble because it's not legal. Plus, it would be the best gift I could give Robbie. He's salivating to use it up there."

"Are you sure, Willow? I assumed we'd leave it as it lies. I want you to know, that for as long as you live here, the Playroom can just be a room in the Spook House. I know it makes you uncomfortable now."

"I just want you to be happy–"

"Don't do this for me," Auggie warns. "I remember how you looked when you were staring at me that first time. I don't want to ruin it by never seeing that expression on your face again. I don't even mind that it will be Kieren you're looking at like that. I just don't want to ruin that for you."

"I won't know how I'm going to react to the Playroom until I walk in there on opening night. I'm sick of being scared," I admit softly.

"Scared of what?" Auggie asks cautiously.

"I don't know. I just am. The Playroom frightens me, so I need to conquer it."

"No," Auggie denies me. "Not for that reason. I won't let you open the Playroom if that's the case".

"Listen, I'm pretty sure I know how I'll react. I know I won't participate. But I'm not the only person who lives in this house– the world does not revolve around me. I'd rather have your sexual exploits contained to the attic, than worry about walking in to find some chick bobbing your knob in our kitchen... where I eat. It's gross. This way, if I feel like watching the Beast take on some beauty, I can sit in a chair and watch without feeling like a freak."

"You want to watch me fuck? Monster," Auggie groans, his breath shuddering. "I think you just made me come."

"You did not! You're making fun of me, aren't you?" I finally look up at Auggie and startle as his green gaze pierces me. He looks crazed. I gaze down, and sure enough, there's a damp spot on the front of Auggie's pajama bottoms. Auggie grips the sheets, knuckles turning white, as if my eyes are physically touching him. I immediately flick my gaze away, feeling slightly guilty.

"Monster." Auggie grunts, a shudder roiling down his spine. "You'll let me watch, won't you? I want to watch your face when Kieren enters you. I loved watching your first time with Devon.

Sitting in Rob's room, knowing you were in there with Kieren, and I couldn't see, it killed me. If I could watch, then I could enjoy instead of feeling insanely jealous. Please, let me watch," Auggie pleads huskily.

"Maybe," spills uncommitted from my throat. "It's up to Kieren. I still have to ask him if he wants to play, and I still have to figure out if I want to play myself."

Auggie turns off the flirt and becomes my Mr. Kline. "No pressure, Willow. If all you do is enter the Playroom and walk right back out, that's fine. You'll have faced your fears. If you decide to stay and watch, great. But you need to know it doesn't matter either way. We all like different things, and if it's not your thing, it's not."

"I worry that it's not, Auggie." I admit for the first time– admit I don't have the balls to screw someone and not have it mean something. I don't want someone to touch me who I don't have an emotional connection with. I just can't do it. "It scares me." Over the past few months, I've perfected the art of masking my emotions. Everyone called me transparent– easy to read. I allow all my emotions to fill my expression for the first time in days.

"Why are you scared?" Auggie brushes a fingertip down my face, no doubt startled by my intensity.

"I'm scared, that at eighteen, I already know what I'm going to want at ninety. I'm not petrified that I'm making a mistake. I fear that I'll be like your mom and sister– what if I lose this person, because there will never be another one like him? Irreplaceable to everyone in his life."

"Christ," Auggie utters in awe, green eyes going wide. "You're *in* love with him, and I kept getting in your way. I feel like such as bastard for everything." Auggie's naturally pale skin blazes to the same shade as his hair in the most epic of blushes. In almost nineteen years, I've never seen Augustus Kline blush. "I'll stop being inappropriate from now on. I want to kick my own ass for what I just said to you a few minutes ago."

"It's okay," I mutter, blushing too. "You're a shameless flirt– we all know this."

Auggie reaches out tentatively, as if scared to touch me now that I admitted the truth I buried so deeply. He cups my cheek and holds me captive in his gaze. "Willow, Clover survived. Who knows, maybe she'll fall in love with Malcolm. Sam isn't replaceable, but that doesn't mean Clover should live her life alone. If you lose him– you'll survive. You'll fall in love again, but it will be a different type of love. Like right now, you're in love with him, but you love me too– just differently. That's life, no sense in being afraid of it."

I take a fortifying breath. "I'm going to go tell Devon goodbye, so I can move on. I won't allow him to use me as his excuse, so I can't use him as one either."

Auggie's startled gasp is the last thing I hear as I run from his bedroom– run toward my fears, to conquer and overcome them.

CHAPTER FORTY-NINE

I take a deep breath of the crisp, four a.m. air and turn the doorknob. Here goes nothing…

The Masons look up at me as a unit with tear-stained cheeks and one with hope-filled eyes. Malcolm smiles gently and gestures for me to join them. My feet drag as I walk across the carpeted living room. I don't know if I can get through this.

"Kids, say your goodbye and give us adults some privacy," Malcolm orders Weston and Rae. He tacks on a, "Please," to soften the command.

I stare at the floor as I hear their sobs. *I can't do this* plays on repeat as the kids cry. Devon has been their rock since long before their mother died. Last night, their hero died as well. They will never glance at Devon with that same level of veneration as before. They're all sobbing for the same reason I'm silently crying– the Devon we knew is dead, if he ever really existed at all.

I can't do this… I can't say goodbye!

"Get well and come home to us," Kieren mutters roughly, and then chokes on a sob. "We need you, bro." *Fuck.* My body shudders from the sound of the brothers saying their goodbyes. My knees grow weak and try to give out as my best friends say their *I love you*s.

"Girl, Devon's gonna be fine," Malcolm murmurs softly near my ear. His fingers grip my arm so I don't topple to the ground. "We're gonna be fine, and you're gonna be fine," he stresses. I jerkily nod my head because I can't speak. I can't get my eyes to open, either. The only sound I hear is the pounding of my heart filling my ears. The thump-thump is deafening.

I swear at myself. I'd promised myself I wouldn't turn into a girl. I wouldn't bawl like a baby, or succumb to the need to plead and beg. I wouldn't pretend this is just a nightmare, as if I could wake and all would be right with the world– a world where an *I love you* could conquer anything. A world where that *I love you* wouldn't weaken you like the twisting of a knife's blade to the heart.

A tentative touch to my cheek has my eyes flashing open to meet Devon's watery blue gaze. "Willow," breathes hoarsely.

All good intentions dissolve the moment I look at Devon.

Fuck, I would've let Devon ruin me and asked for more just to have him in my life. If this goodbye doesn't kill me, eventually Devon will be the very death of me. I'd give my life to heal him.

Since I didn't pull away from Devon's touch, Malcolm releases my arm and stands next to a silently sobbing Kieren. It takes everything in me not to run to Kieren and comfort him– take all the pain away.

It's like the past few months have been a dream, a dream with ups and downs, and I awoke to pure misery. I'm surrounded by Mason men. Malcolm is doing his damnedest to appear unaffected, because his broken son is breaking the heart of the son who needs to be strong enough to take care of the kids lurking in the kitchen doorway.

In the face of their misery, I pull myself together. I'm not the girlfriend– I'm not even really the ex-girlfriend, so I don't get the luxury of falling apart like an irrational female. I'm the woman who is trying to blend our families together as one. Our family needs a mother and a father. Malcolm and Clover. But it needs a strength and a heart. Kieren and me.

"I can do this," I whisper underneath my breath.

Strong hands, trembling with weakness, slide around my waist and tenderly glide up my back, pulling me into his warm embrace. A sob is torn from my chest as Devon's scent hits me, the warm softness of his chest against my cheek, the feel of his hands cupping my body, the sound of his ragged breath in my ear. I tremble in Devon's arms, stars bursting behind my eyes, warning that a faint is on the horizon.

"Why didn't you come see me before I left?" Not an accusation, it comes out jagged and pained. "I waited. I know I don't deserve it, but I wanted my turn to speak while you listened."

"I couldn't do it," I grit out. My hands find their way to Devon's back to clutch him closer– I try to meld our bodies as one, not ready to let him go just yet.

"I couldn't listen to words from your drug-addled mind. They would've haunted me for a lifetime. What you've already said and done will never leave me. What I've seen will forever be a part of me. I couldn't add any more to it and survive."

"I deserve that. I... Willow, nothing of what I've done was about you. You need to know that at least. I loved you with all of my heart, but it was tainted by so many things. I just... fucked it all up. I need you to understand that I still love you more than I thought possible, but not romantically. Everything that happened, it was all about me– all of it," he grits out while shaking me.

"When you get home and you're sober, I want you to explain everything. When I said your words would haunt me, I meant when you come home you'll have a different set of words, not the excuses you would've given me last night. I don't want to spend a lifetime analyzing the difference and wondering which were the real Devon's words. I think rehab will be best for you, Devon. You need to work this shit out."

"What I've done was unforgivable. I feel like I'm living in a nightmare. When I see myself, this is not who I see. I... Oh, God." He sobs and clutches me. "What have I done?"

I find myself being the strong one again, holding Devon from tumbling to the floor. He clings to me, sobbing my name, sobbing all the heinous acts he's committed in the past few months. Many of the things are a revelation– I hadn't known most of them, and I don't know if I can shoulder their burden. I'm impressed he's still alive. What he did with Essie was mild in comparison to everything else. Devon confesses his sins to me as if I am a Catholic Priest.

Malcolm left the room after Devon admitted the second felony– no doubt a conflict of interest, as his boss and the Police Chief, but mostly, as a father. No one should know the dark acts their children commit while chasing their demons.

"I don't expect your forgiveness, and I don't want it until I earn it. Don't forgive me, Willow. The look you gave me in your bedroom, that look of disgusted disappointment. Even feeling as you did, you still helped me when I was thirsty by giving me water. Your hard words and generous acts were what made me say yes to rehab and actually mean it."

"Don't be a coward for once, Devon. Do the right thing. Don't be weak," I order harshly. Devon needs harsh to light a fire under his ass. I can even read a strung-out Devon.

"I needed to hear someone say I'm acting just like my mother. You didn't say it outright, but that was what your suicide comments were about. I know more than anyone what it feels like to have the center of your world just lie down and die, and I won't do that to my family. I needed that verbal punch to the gut you gave me, Willow. You're right, and you're absolutely amazing. Don't ever forget who you are, and don't ever let anyone change you."

Devon pauses, as if at a loss for words. We've said all we need to say. I have to end this before I beg Devon not to leave, beg him not to leave us. I love him and myself enough to admit that we're better off apart than together. Even if Devon comes home sober, two recovering substance abusers shouldn't cohabitate. We can't be friends for a very, very long time. We're toxic for each other.

Devon tried to warn me when he said, *if one of us falls, we'll take the other one down with us*. I remember thinking *it'd be a fun ride down*. It's almost as if Devon pushed me away by sleeping with Essie, so I wouldn't be around when he hit rock bottom in a drug den. He didn't want me to go along for the wicked ride. I am eternally thankful, because I can't guarantee I wouldn't have spiraled down with him otherwise.

"I guess this is goodbye." I whimper as I press my face into the crook of Devon's neck, deeply inhaling one last hit of his intoxicating scent.

"No, never goodbye, Willow," Devon objects.

"Yes, it's goodbye. The man standing before me won't be the one who returns. Whether or not you're sober, it won't be this version of you. In sixty days, neither of us will be the same version of ourselves."

"Fair enough," Devon agrees. "I guess this is goodbye, then. I know I never should've been your boyfriend, but I'll earn the title of best friend back. I promise you this, Willow."

"No, you can never be my best friend again, Devon– never," I harshly admit.

"What?" Devon cries, crestfallen. He tries to pull from my embrace, but I won't allow it. I cling tightly to him, never wanting to let him go.

"Friends come and go, and change as we change. But there is a group of people who will never give up on you, no matter what you do, how you act, or even how badly you hurt them– family. You've hurt me so much, yet here I am, saying goodbye to you. Devon, I guess that makes us family now. You have to love your family, but you don't necessarily have to like them. Right now, I love you as much as I dislike you."

I take one last hit of Devon's musky vanilla scent. I can't draw enough into my lungs to last a lifetime, because I'll never get enough of his intoxicating, comforting scent. The warmth I feel when I'm in Devon's arms will never be enough for me. But right now, even Devon isn't enough for Devon. He has to learn to forgive himself, and then to love himself, before he can heal and try to love anyone else.

I don't say goodbye. I kiss Devon's throat and he shudders in my arms.

Seconds later, I find myself on the floor, rough carpeting biting into my palms as my keening echoes around the Masons' living room. I feel so cold without him– empty. I'll never be warm again. How do I draw air into my lungs if it's not flavored in Devon's scent? How do you stop your heart from bleeding you dry?

"It's going to be okay. Go back to your rooms." Kieren chokes on a sob. "Willow will be okay. I promise I'll make her okay. Spanky… Spanky… Spanky…" Kieren repeats my nickname, trying to get me to respond. Arms slide under my knees and around my shoulders. Kieren picks me up and carries me through the house to the bedroom he used to share with Devon… until less than a minute ago.

Placing me at the foot of his twin-sized bed, Kieren kneels beside me. "I guess you don't realize how much you love someone until they're gone," I sniffle. "Devon is just my friend, someone who's harming himself. Clover," I sob. "She must feel dead inside. I lost the ideal of a friend, but she lost her husband, the father of her children. Devon will only be two thousand miles away, but Sam is dead– gone forever, never to resurface. I thought it hurt then, this is so much worse." I hoarsely breathe. "Like a fresh wound."

"I never went a day without Devon when we were growing up. I haven't slept alone in this room since Devon came back from the academy. When he didn't come home on Friday night, I knew something was wrong. I could just sense it. Willow, I spent three solid days and nights looking for him. The only time I could stop myself was when I was with you. I didn't tell you because I didn't want you to feel the terror I felt."

"Kieren." Pulling his head into my lap, I curl over his body and hold him closely. "Next time, you need me. Tell me immediately. I'm not fragile– I can take it."

Kieren wraps his arms around my legs, fusing us together. "Okay, I'll try to remember that," he mumbles against my thigh, and I can feel as much as hear his smile. "The only reason I'm not going insane is because I have two kids down the hall who are shattered by this. We're Masons, and we take care of our own. Rae and West are comforting each other because they know how badly I need you to comfort me right now. I have to stay strong for my dad, and sometimes I just need a few minutes to break down."

Silent, I show Kieren with my actions rather than my words that he can trust me enough to fall apart in my arms. We both know he's strong enough to put himself back together again when he's through. I hold him close, and I do the only thing I can, just be there for him.

"I know everyone always thought I was the fuck-up who tossed his life away by becoming a mechanic instead of playing college football. Officer Devon was our saint, and I could never compete with that. Not once did I resent my brother. But right now, what I feel is pretty close to hatred. Pretty close to how I feel about my mom."

"What's that saying? There is a fine line between love and hate. I know that feeling all too well for several fucktards... I'm being selfish, what can I do for you and your family?"

Kieren laughs deep in his chest– that dang man laugh. Even in mourning it hits me like a lightning strike. "Nothing, Spanky Absolutely nothing. All we can do is just go about our day as usual. The kids are going to school, and Dad will go to work when he gets back from the airport. I took the day off so I could do the usual household shit, though. You can't do anything for my family, but you can do something for me." Kieren flashes me a charming smile with tears drying on his cheeks.

"Anything," I breathe.

"Blow off work and have some fun with me today– even if it's just helping me with the grocery shopping. Auggie can have you back when the kids get home from school this afternoon." He takes a deep breath and sighs it back out in a rush. "I don't want to be alone. Entertain me, Spanky."

... *Entertain me, Spanky* echoes in my mind. At nearly five o'clock in the morning, I do the only form of escapism left at my disposal. Kieren and I need to get lost, fade into one another. I lean down and place a kiss to Kieren's whisker-stubbled cheek, slowly making my way to his lips. The kiss starts out innocent, a gentle, feather-light brush of lips, and evolves into something I've never experienced– explosive passion.

Hands fisting hair, fingers twisted in the strands, tears drying on cheeks, we move beyond mourning and coping. We seek mindless escape and end up finding one another. Suspended in anti-reality, a dreamlike haze, we frantically pull at each other's clothes– fingers tearing the fabric from arms and legs. The need to feel Kieren's skin on mine becomes a compulsion. A budding addiction.

Panting, Kieren trails his lips in a long line down my neck to my chest. His breath flutters out to tickle my nipple, freezing me with insecurity. I move to the side before his mouth descends, lips landing near the center of my chest.

"Hmm… interesting," Kieren muses a split-second before his hands hook beneath my armpits to toss me to the head of the bed. Slowly, like a predatory animal, Kieren crawls over me, hovering, and the only thing I can do is freeze like prey and wait. Holding my gaze, his blue eyes question me. "I've been staring at your tits for years– don't deny me," he demands, flashing me a smirk.

Wishing for the bed to swallow me, I mutter matter-of-factly, "I have no tits."

"I beg to differ," Kieren purrs. "I bet you don't even realize this. You always watched– years of watching me, and I loved it," he roughly rasps. "Here you were, walking around in these tiny tank tops with no bra on during gym class while getting teased for having no tits–"

I try to yank away, but Kieren's stronger than me. He leans down, resting his weight along the length of my body, pressing his cheek to mine so he can breathe his words into my ear. "You would get aroused as you watched me play. I'd turn to look back and your eyes would flit away, but your tiny, tiny tank tops always gave you away. I've been dying for a taste of your nipples for years. Don't deny me," Kieren repeats. "I won't take no for an answer on this."

"Can't we just pretend that breasts aren't important? We don't need foreplay. I thought the sex was fantastic without it," I quickly stammer, mortified and no longer wanting to be touched. "Here, let me take care of you." I make a move to stroke Kieren's length, but he grasps my wrist in his big hand and presses it above my head on the mattress.

"I'm speaking the words, but you're not listening," Kieren taunts, and then licks his bottom lip as if he's salivating. Flashing me a predatory grin, he moves faster than I thought possible.

"Fuck!" I grunt as teeth bite into my nipple and tug. The pain has a sweet edge that seems to explode in my cunt. Every muscle in my body goes taut in a second, sweat beads on my flesh as Kieren begins to suckle at my nipple. Kieren's lips open wide, breath searing my flesh, tongue teasing the tight tip of my nipple. Then he descends, taking my entire breast into the heat of his mouth. Hot, wet, and beyond soft, the sensation is mind-bending.

"I bet you don't realize your breasts are bigger than they were back at your birthday, and I would know, because I groped them no less than a hundred times on our date. I was a bit obsessed." Kieren sounds delirious.

"I remember thinking you couldn't have been getting much out of it." I pant, thinking to myself, *not as much as I'm getting out of your mouth on me.* "Stud, that feels incredible." I moan, fingers curling into claws against Kieren's hand. "Don't you dare stop."

Kieren's hungry growl vibrates my nipple as he suckles, and it nearly has me in convulsions. I thought my itty-bitty-titties were numb. Boy, was I wrong. My hand escapes the confines of Kieren's grip to slide down his hip and wrap around his arousal for the very first time. He jerks against me as I say, "Fuck, everything about you is so goddamned perfect, Stud."

"Talk like that–" Kieren pants in warning.

"Holy hell!" I shout as three, very large fingers spear my pussy and start thrusting.

Releasing the man laugh with deadly precision, Kieren finishes what I interrupted. "Talk like that will only get you more foreplay." Kieren slows his assaulting fingers and leans down to breathe on my wet nipple. I shiver from the dueling sensations. "Do tell, why is my cock perfect?"

"Well…" I swallow a dozen times, and when that doesn't work, I wet my lips with my tongue. "I feel a bit like Goldilocks: too hot, too cold, and just right. Please, stop laughing," I beg, shuddering. "It turns me on too much."

"Hmm, too big? No need to guess on who you're talking about there. Too small?" Kieren busts out laughing, not able to contain himself. "Good thing *Dopey, gimme your drugs* is on a plane to rehab right now. He might be insulted by that."

"Devon's not small," I mutter, mortified, skin blazing with a crimson blush.

"I know, but he's not just right," Kieren says in a voice filled with so much emotion that I get choked up. "As you know, my brother and I are exactly the same size, so what's the difference?"

I turn my face to the side and whisper bashfully into the blanket– good God, it smells just like Kieren. "He's not you."

Everything happens quickly. Fingers are pulled from my body, and the flesh I was stroking is taken from my hand to replace the fingers. A guttural groan is torn from my throat as Kieren slides into me. Kieren proves he's just right, and right where he belongs.

"It's about time you figured that out, Willow," Kieren rasps into my ear as he begins to slowly rock into me, barely moving. We shudder together, and then we release a sigh because it feels so right. "I don't care that you took a few detours. It took the pressure off of me to make everything perfect."

Shifting on Kieren's small bed, I wrap myself around him, just content to feel his warm weight holding me down on the bed. "Believe me when I say every experience was far from perfect. Most of it was clinical, instructional, or punishment, and none of it was romantic. I spent the time before, during, and after, feeling confused, uncomfortable, and insecure."

"Idiots," Kieren hisses into my ear. "One of them messed with your head over your breasts, didn't they?"

"You're the only person who has shown an interest in that part of my anatomy. I don't want to talk about it," I mumble, hiding my face in the crook of his neck. I will Kieren to drop it, to not ruin this moment. Whether we're teasing and flirting, or being serious, I love being around him. Everything else in our lives is difficult, and I don't want that shit brought into our *Kieren and Willow time*.

"This is supposed to be entertainment," Kieren says as he pulls from my body to kneel between my legs. He looks down at me, wearing nothing but a naughty smirk. "Let me guess, missionary position, and you've never been fucked thoroughly?"

With any other person, I would've felt judged. But this is Kieren, and he's teasing me, not making fun of me. "No comment," I say with a smirk, and then burst out laughing for some reason.

"Naughty Spanky, very naughty," Kieren purrs as he reaches down to flip me over onto my belly. "Gonna fix that shit right this second. My Spanky needs to be fucked like a bitch in heat. Up on your knees... mmm... that's a good bitch, Spanky." Large palms run along my back to curve over my ass. "You bent over on my bed like this is the hottest fucking thing I've ever seen. Your ass is perfect, so damn round. It's just begging for it."

Smack

"Christ," I hiss as a slight sting radiates across my ass cheek. "Gives a whole new meaning to my nickname. What'd I do wrong?"

"Not a damned thing, other than having a fine ass I wanted to watch jiggle," Kieren drawls in a lust-filled voice. A shudder rolls down my spine when scorching hot breath flutters against the sting on my ass cheek. A wet lick is my only warning– Kieren buries his mouth against my exposed flesh and feasts like a starving man.

I cry out, trying to crawl across the bed to get away from the most pleasurable assault of my entire existence. "It's too much... too much... too much..." I mutter over and over as Kieren licks and nibbles at my pussy. Teeth tug playfully at my lips, and then he seals his mouth on my clit and begins to suck. Hard. My spine bows as Kieren draws my release to the surface using only his mouth. Fingertips clench my ass cheeks, stopping my retreat while simultaneously opening me. Tongue piercing me where no man has gone before, an orgasm slams into me with the force of a head-on collision.

"Not alone in the house, Spanky," Kieren warns as a palm wraps around the front of my face, silencing me. Biting my tongue, trying to keep quiet, I quake in Kieren's embrace as he slides deep inside me from behind. The soundtrack of my orgasm is his punch to the cunt man laugh.

"Nothing feels as good as you coming on my dick," Kieren rasps. Gripping my hips, he picks up a frantic pace, causing me to grunt with every thrust, proving I've never been thoroughly fucked before. Kieren pounds me into the mattress, and all I can do is twist my fingers into the blankets and try to stay on my elbows and knees. Moving faster and faster, harder and harder, my teeth even chatter from the force of the pounding... and it's perfect.

Panting breathlessly in a passion-drugged voice, Kieren slows his pace as he speaks. "I think this is my favorite position—watching my dick slide in and out of your tight pussy with my handprint tattooed on your ass. Fuck…" he groans. "Time to switch it up so I don't come."

Pulling out of me, Kieren roughly flips me over onto my back. Blue eyes gaze down at me and drink in every inch of my body. The starved look on Kieren's face has me whimpering in need as my body releases a flood between my legs, preparing for more of whatever he's willing to give.

Standing at the foot of the bed, Kieren's expression tells me more than words ever could. "Keep looking at me like that, Willow, and I'll never let you leave this room," Kieren rasps out roughly.

"Funny, I was going to say the same thing." My voice is at odds with my words— I sound deadly serious. Kieren and I don't have to talk hearts and flowers, because words lie. Actions are truth.

"Now, I know you've never done this before." Kieren lifts me by the armpits. I yelp in shock, fusing myself to the front of his body, arms wrapping around his shoulders with my legs tightly gripping his hips. "We started out with you grinding on my cock from on top— hottest fucking thing was you riding my leg. I'll never forget that for the rest of my life." Kieren laughs, warming my heart, even though he's relentlessly teasing me. "We've done missionary, and now doggy-style. You're a tiny little monkey, so I think standing up will be fun."

Reaching down, Kieren shuffles around awkwardly until he can press into me. Jouncing me up and down, he tries to thrust in and out. I've never cackled in my entire life, but I do now. I tilt my head back and laugh like an insane person, releasing long guffaws. "I feel like a cocksucking Shake Weight."

Kieren wraps his hand around the front of my face, silencing me. "Not alone, Spanky," he warns again, and then giggles evilly into my ear. "Guess this won't work unless my goal is to make you laugh. Idea," Kieren sings as he strides across his bedroom to press me against the door. "I promised you a wall a few days ago. Since this tiny room is packed with furniture, the door will have to do."

"Oh!" I grunt in surprise. "Very good idea." I fall lax against the door as Kieren moves inside of me easily with long, hard strokes. "Ooooohhhh…" I moan, neck losing all strength, the back of my head hits the door with a loud thump. I giggle, waiting for Kieren to chastise me for being noisy.

"You like that, don't ya? I can tell. My Spanky gets all dreamy-eyed when she's getting close to coming," Kieren chants in a smooth voice. He bends at the knees in a movement that fully impales me, while pressing his pelvis against my clit. Even my nipples get abraded by the coarse hairs on his chest.

Kieren Mason owns every pleasure center on my body as he connects our lips, kissing me while slowly making love to me against the door. This man is complex: fucks me on the bed, makes me laugh while standing up, and then makes love to me against a door. What a contradiction Kieren Mason makes.

"Fuck *just right*. I'm sticking with perfect– your cock is perfect for me," is the last thing I say before I shatter. Speechless, mindless, I come so deeply, it starts in my toes. Tilting my head back, I release a moan so loud it rocks the door. Kieren smashes his lips into mine, digesting the song of my pleasure. For the first time ever, I hear Kieren come as he shoots deep inside me, and then I'm the one silencing him with my mouth.

"We're never leaving this room," Kieren gasps in a drowsy voice.

"Agreed–"

"Is Willow okay?" Rae says from the other side of the door, only an inch away. "Is she still upset?"

Speechless, I stare up at Kieren with eyes gone huge from shock, all the while he laughs silently. Taking a few gulps of air, Kieren tries to get out, "Perfectly fine. Willow's fine– not upset at all."

"Are you sure? Willow?" Rae sounds so concerned that tears prick the back of my eyes. I want to reply, but I don't know what will flow from my mouth if I speak.

"Rae," Weston's voice comes next, and this time Kieren just lets his laugh fly. "Get away from the door." The kids start going back and forth, bickering over opening the door to find out if we're okay. Weston's laughing for some reason.

"Do something," I hiss, since we're leaning against the door, still connected at the crotch.

Kieren does something– bribery. "There's a box of S'more Pop-Tarts behind the gallon jar of rice. Have at 'em. We'll be out in a few minutes to take you to school."

"What about Willow?" Rae's voice is muffled by the door. Weston's devious giggle is answer enough.

"I'm great!" I finally squeak out in a voice rough from sexual exhaustion. Kieren and I freeze until we hear their footsteps recede, and then we just stare at one another with wide eyes.

Blissed out doesn't accurately describe Kieren: blue eyes glittering with happiness, cheeks rosy-red, lips swollen, blond hair totally fucked every which way but Sunday, and neck covered in love bites. It will be beyond obvious for days to come what we were just doing.

"You have to hide your Pop-Tarts?" is the first thing that flies out of my mouth.

"Dad has a wicked sweet tooth. Plus, we had a junkie living here. Devon would go a week without eating, and then he'd empty the fridge and cupboards while we slept. The Pop-Tarts are mine. I have to hide them, or I won't get any. It's my go-to bribe... Today's grocery day," Kieren says as he sets me softly on my feet.

"Um... what am I gonna wear?" I mutter when I catch sight of my shredded t-shirt and cami. My panties are destroyed too, but at least my jeans are in one piece. Laughing, Kieren tosses me a t-shirt. "*Niiiiice,*" I drawl, as I tug the Wreck & Ruin Repair t-shirt over my head. "I'm so going to order Revamped shirts after this. Hey, why was Weston laughing?"

"He's fourteen," Kieren offers as explanation. I just think *huh,* rather than say it out loud, because I'm too distracted by the gorgeous sight of Kieren's well-formed chest. At nineteen, the guy is sporting more chest hair than Auggie at twenty-eight. Jesus Christ, Kieren's all man.

"Weston's moderately quiet in the bathroom, just fair warning." Seeing that I'm still *duh-ing,* Kieren puts me out of my misery. "Boys are perverts from birth. We don't grow out of it, we perfect it. I'm sure it was me who clued West in on what we were doing. I'm usually silent, and this time I wasn't. Rae's too innocent for her own good– super modest, so she's clueless."

"I find that hard to believe," I mutter as I tug my hair back into a smooth ponytail.

"She's sixteen, living with all men, and her only source of female advice is Isis. Isis, who is a ball-basher. I haven't seen my sister in a bathing suit since she was ten. Between Dad and Isis,

Raven will be a virgin on her wedding day– when she's thirty-five. No shit," Kieren stresses.

"Motherfuck," I whisper in awe. "Sucks to be Rae."

"Or it sucks to be Dad and Isis when Rae rebels." Kieren flashes a grin, like he's anticipating the fireworks. "Time for my motherly duties: drop the kids off at school, hardware store for Weston's science final– can't wait until school's out for the summer –bank, grocery store, home, laundry, vacuuming, dishes, make supper… and you're my tiny helper monkey today." Kieren teases while yanking my ponytail.

CHAPTER FIFTY

Today revealed to me what the future could hold. What it would feel like to be in a partnership. I showed Kieren how I knew every nook and cranny in the hardware store, and he showed me around the grocery store– role reversal at its finest. We bickered over canned versus frozen vegetables. Kieren is surprisingly stubborn, as I am. We butted heads for ten minutes, and he wouldn't even budge when I threw a frozen pizza in the cart to shut his ass up. I finally called Clover and had her lecture Kieren on how the nutrients are cooked out of canned veg, when I just think they taste like hell and didn't want to eat mushy canned green beans for dinner.

So now I find myself cooking for the Masons when I've never cooked for the Prynnes or Websters in my entire life. Growing up, Clover was the chef, and at the Spook House, Robbie is the cook, and I'm a well-fed girl. The only time I touch the stove is during Clover's cooking lessons.

Kieren wanted pasta for the billionth day in a row, but after some stiff negotiations– I had to dust the house, then give Kieren a handy-jay –we're having chicken fajitas loaded with vegetables. The Masons live on processed food, which I'm good with, but only after Clover and Robbie stuff me with nutrients and homemade baked goods.

"You have to promise me you won't get mad," Kieren murmurs in my ear, followed by a soft kiss to the nape of my neck. He slides his arms around my waist as I stand at the counter cutting up bell peppers.

"Hmm… let me think," I muse. I place the knife on the side of the cutting board, just in case. "Usually when someone starts a conversation out like that, it means I'm really, *really* gonna hate what comes next. Have some self-preservation, and don't fuck with a woman wielding a knife."

Chuckling in my ear, Kieren moves closer, spooning my back. "I like your spunk, Spanky. I was originally gonna call you Spunky, but I feared for the first asshole who called you spunk. I decided against having to go around punching anyone who called my girl a derivative of jizz."

"Jackass." I snicker, even as I shiver from hearing *my girl* out of Kieren's lips. "Out with it. Quit the charming, cuddly routine. I'm gonna really hate what you have to say, aren't I?"

"Yup," Kieren says with a *pop* sound. He steps away, out of knife's reach– smart man. "Dad invited some guests, and I added one to the list. Dad needed his security blankies around him now that Dev isn't here... Essie," Kieren mutters hesitantly.

"What. The. Fuck? Why?" I shout, feeling borderline deranged. I look down and realize there is a knife in my hand again and Kieren has his hands out, showing me he's unarmed. I turn back to the counter and start cutting. I put all my energy in perfecting the julienne cut on the bell peppers. Clover would be proud.

"Remember when I said Devon would never get between us, and you would never get between me and Devon?" Kieren slowly walks over the stove to attend to the sauté pan filled with chicken strips. He tosses me a cautious look because he's now within stabbing distance.

"The only person who can get between you and Devon is Devon," I deadpan, knowing where Kieren is leading with this, and not liking it one fucking bit. "Yes, I remember."

"It should just be between you and Essie. I don't want you and Essie fighting over Devon," Kieren says calmly, but I can hear an unnamed emotion in his voice.

I look at the side of Kieren's face, trying to get a read on him as he over-stirs the chicken. I dump the pepper strips and onion into the pan, and then I stare as he mixes it all together. "I'm hurt over Devon, but not because of Devon. If that makes any sense. It was the deepest betrayal Essie could deal, and it was just because she wanted to wound me. That's not jealousy-based on my part. It makes me feel like I have an open wound that you're poking by inviting her to dinner. But that's not what has me wanting to shit in her fucking food," I snarl as I stomp off to the refrigerator. I breathe deeply as I yank fajita fixings from the fridge.

"Then why?" Kieren asks softly, trying to calm me by not instigating a fight.

"Jealousy. You, fuckhead," I growl. "I called dibs on *you*, and then Essie went out and did *you*... and *you* did her... and I didn't find out until I was on our *date*. A date where I wasn't sure who you were paired with."

"I was there with you, Willow." Kieren tries to comfort me by rubbing my shoulders. "I'm sorry. Let me get this straight, you never knew about her and me, and Essie waited to tell you until we were all at Rush together?" Kieren enunciates slowly, as if he doesn't quite believe what he's hearing.

"Yeah, she would never tell me who she lost her v-card to, but she told me every single detail of every single guy afterward. She told me after we got into Rush." The tortured emotions of that night inundate me as if they are brand new. I wipe my eyes with a kitchen towel, and then continue to prepare dinner like I'm not feeling raw.

"I can tell you what happened, if you'd like," Kieren offers.

"No!" I bark out. "I've heard enough about Essie's glowing attributes to last a lifetime. I'll never erase what Devon told me. A girl loves knowing she was an uneventful, boring lay. How she was great for breaking in a guy for a real woman with bountiful tits, a great ass, and epic skills… how what's attached to her chest skeeves a guy out, because they're too small to be considered tits, and are a disservice to breasts everywhere… excuse me," I mumble, voice breaking. I grab the dishtowel as I make my way across the kitchen, hoping to escape to the bathroom and have a good cry at my own expense– for the billionth time.

Hooking an arm around my waist to stop me, "I don't think so," Kieren orders. He picks me up and presses me to his chest. It takes everything in me not to break down in tears as he tries to comfort me.

"Every time I see Essie, it's like a punch to the gut. If I don't see her, I can forget for a few minutes. But when she's near me, I can't help but see in her everything that I'm not. Forget I said anything. I never meant to say those words out loud."

"You never told anyone Devon said that to you, did you?" Kieren asks as he sets me back on my feet. "Did he say any more stupid shit?"

"Doesn't matter," I mumble as I head back to the stove to make sure our dinner doesn't burn. "Shouldn't matter."

"But it does," Kieren states. "So it was my brother who fucked with your head. This morning, when you froze on me, I thought it was Auggie for some reason."

"Devon couldn't help how he felt," I say to Kieren, and I truly mean it. "You can't want someone because you're told to want them. If my lack of breasts freaked him out, then they did. I can't do anything about it. It's not my fault, but it's not his either."

"First, I call utter bullshit on what he said, and not because you turn me on like crazy, or because I've banged you four times today. But because I know Devon was trying to hurt you as badly as Essie hurt you– the bastard," Kieren growls. "Second, Essie's miserable, so I wouldn't want to be her just because she has tits. They've been a hindrance her whole life. Third, I was with her when I was thirteen, younger than Seth and Weston. I was a little kid who didn't know shit, and neither did she."

"I didn't want you to know what Devon said. It's humiliating," I mutter underneath my breath. "But thanks for not oversharing the details. Those just… suck."

Kieren huffs a laugh, not sounding amused in the least. "Imagine three minutes of *what the hell are we doing?* Whatever Devon said to you, you got him off a shit ton, the f'n liar. Devon was ecstatic when he came home after being with you– kept gloating and giving details. I wanted to rip his dick off."

"Essie thanks you because you didn't," I mutter snidely, but then I giggle at the ridiculousness.

"So imagine you're Essie, who had a bad experience with me on the first time. That's a hard legacy to live down– so you and Essie are even when it comes to the Mason brothers. After Essie, it took three more years before I got the balls to try again... and then again… and again… and again, and then I grew up and stopped… and then I patiently waited."

I finally look up at Kieren, to find he's smiling down at me. "Waited for what?" I sniffle.

"Who, not what, and you know who." Kieren releases the man laugh as I scrunch my eyes together in confusion. "You, dumbass. C'mere and give me a kiss. It's been half an hour, and my lips are feeling lonely."

"You're right," I say before Kieren can kiss me. "It shouldn't matter what happened between anyone and Essie. It only matters why she did it when it involved me. And the only thing that matters right now is you and me." I get on my tippy-toes and press my lips to his.

Kieren makes a sexy growl sound in the back of his throat. He tugs me against his chest as he gives me a soul-stealing kiss.

I wrap my arms around his back, twisting his shirt with my fingers so he can't pull away. I open my lips, letting out a throaty moan, as our mouths duel.

"About fucking time!" Auggie's voice booms throughout the kitchen. Embarrassed, I hide my face against Kieren's chest, feeling his laughter rumble against my cheek. "I was wondering how much it would take to make a good girl misbehave. I thought if you told a kid not to do something, they'd rebel and do it anyway. So much for reverse psychology for this stubborn one. Willow has a horrible propensity to do as she's told."

"Maybe you should've just told Willow to go to Kieren, instead of telling her how naughty he was," Malcolm deadpans. His voice has me wanting to bury my head *inside* Kieren's t-shit.

"Eh," Auggie grunts. "I thought she liked naughty. Plus, I wouldn't have known if she was behaving or making her own decision. Tricky business when dealing with Miss Prynne. Don't forget that, Ren."

"You're so full of shit, Auggie." I blush ten shades of Hades, but I still face the three men who are releasing the debilitating man laugh. "I gotta finish fixing dinner. Auggie of all people should know not to distract me when open flame is involved."

"Remind me to always make sure you only have access to an electric stove," Kieren teases.

My vivacious cousin is pouting her bottom lip and staring straight into my eyes, trying her damnedest to get me to feel sorry for her. Essie is sitting across the dining room table from me, flaunting her gorgeous self. I'm not entirely sure how it's humanly possible, but her boobs look gigantic, and she's not even showing them off. Seriously gargantuan– like bigger than a D-cup on her hundred pound body. Essie's looking like she's gained weight, too. Ordinarily that would please me, but she looks even better with the additional weight.

Ugh! I feel like shit sitting across from Essie, like I'm beyond disgusting.

Apparently my scowl isn't warning her off, because she keeps trying to have a silent conversation that I keep ignoring. I hate how I can still understand her unspoken words. I haven't spoken since I sat at the table, and I haven't taken a bite of food, either. I sit with my hands folded in my lap, staring my cousin down, and Essie can't look away.

Curiously, I am not angry. My brain hurts like I'm thinking too hard. I'm trying to drill into Essie's mind to see what she's thinking, to figure out why she did what she did and how she feels about it. Yes, I could ask her outright, but she'd probably just tell me what she thinks I want to hear. On the back of my curiosity is guilt. *I* feel the guilt. No matter what Essie's done to me, I stooped to her level when I aired our dirty laundry in front of our family and the Masons. I shouldn't have used a permanent marker on her forehead. Like the Tell-tale Heart, I see a faint outline of the wicked A I scrawled on Essie's skin, even though it's not really there.

Kieren looks between Essie and me with a worried expression marring his handsome face. Kieren's been under so much stress that I want to stand up and hug Essie just to make him feel better. I'm trying for everyone's sakes, but it doesn't mean I have to be chatty with the woman. I just won't be mean and nasty.

"Willow?" Auggie nudges me in the arm, and I can tell it wasn't the first time he's said my name. His big palm cups the back of my head and gently shakes me back and forth, rattling my brain.

"Auggie?" I mutter without taking my eyes from Essie.

"Willow," Auggie heavily sighs my name with dramatic annoyance. "Willow, I was telling our hosts how we're having a party in the attic," Auggie says pointedly. "Robin said the time and date were of your choosing." He stresses every other word because Essie, Weston, and Rae aren't invited to our party, because they don't need to know we have an adult Playroom in our attic.

"Tomorrow night at eight," I say conversationally. I toss Auggie a pissed off look that only a female can pull off, and turn my gaze back to Essie. I smile as she swallows in distress. I'll give her bonus points for not fleeing in fear. I may be ninety pounds sopping wet, but Essie knows I'm capable of downing a grown man.

"Behave," flutters against my ears. "If you don't, I'll drag your misbehaving ass to Malcolm's bedroom and swat it bright red," Auggie threatens me– a true threat. His lips are pressed tightly to my ear so no one else can hear him. "I won't make it feel good, because I don't want to face Kieren's wrath. I will smack the nasty bitch out of you."

I smile sweetly, like I'm a good girl. "Go ahead and try it, Auggie," I utter defiantly. "I'll fight you back. Let's see how you like your huge ass stinging from my palm." I growl under my breath, holding his furious green gaze.

Apparently, I'm not as good at the whole *no one hearing* thing– every adult at the table starts snickering. Isis is actually crying, she's laughing so hard. I'm glad someone likes my moxie, because Auggie's gonna kick my ass now.

Now Essie is scared, seriously? She's not scared of the woman she scorned, but Auggie being furious has her cowering in her seat. Really? Auggie wouldn't hurt a fly, but he's gonna tear off my wings the second we're alone. I can feel my punishment in the air. Malcolm actually looks worried for me.

"I saw a delicious chocolate tart in your kitchen, Malcolm. Wherever did you get it? Did our bakery finally get a new pastry chef?" I ask pleasantly.

Well, it took Auggie's focus off of me, just as I'd hoped. Robbie, Isis, and Auggie are evaluating Malcolm. I can hear *is he seeing someone* directly from their thoughts.

"I should have thanked you earlier for bringing the tart. My apologies, Willow. Give my thanks to your sister." Malcolm turns it back around on me, making me look like I was fishing for gratitude. A smirk flirts with his lips– well played.

That notorious, ball catching palm is covering a different mouth, his own. Kieren's chest is heaving up and down as he tries to suppress his laughter. I growl at him– traitor. He's supposed to be my partner in crime. My expression only makes him laugh louder.

"What?" Auggie's eyes are on Kieren, but he's asking me.

"I have no idea," I innocently drawl. "Maybe the lack of sleep is getting to Kieren. But it could be that he isn't very bright," I dig and bat my eyelashes.

"Spanky," Kieren growls from across the table.

"Traitor," I sing as I stare at Essie– she wouldn't be here if it wasn't for Kieren inviting her. "Traitors." I reiterate– Essie could have said no thanks.

"If he doesn't do it." Kieren points at Auggie. "Then I will," he threatens to give a whole new dimension to my nickname.

"I'd like to see you try," I hiss, leaning across the table, getting in Kieren's face. "You know I'll like it." I sound angry, but I'm teasing him. Kieren barks out a laugh and mouths *later* at me.

"Enough!" Malcolm's hand slaps on the table hard. The silverware clinks and the glasses threaten to crash over. "Quit baiting all of us because you're uncomfortable," Malcolm calmly directs at me. "I understand it, Willow. I do. But if you don't behave, *I* will be the one to punish you for acting like a little bitch. It will be highly unconventional, and you will be very, *very* sorry. Do I make myself clear?"

I suck in a sharp breath while everyone stares at me in shock. I let it out slowly and say, "Crystal."

I guess that wasn't the reaction everyone thought I'd have, because every single last one of them is staring at me gape-mouthed, Malcolm included. I guess running in fear, or bawling my eyes out would've been more appropriate, but all I feel is calm. Malcolm is right– I'm being a little bitch because I'm uncomfortable.

"My apologies," I say calmly as I pick up my fork. I stab a bite of chicken, and then thoughtfully chew, thinking I could have seasoned the meat more. My only thought is how much I miss Clover– that woman can cook. She also would've high-fived my behavior in private, but chastised me just as Malcolm did in public. Feels like home.

"I'm sorry," Essie blurts, and it kills a part of me because I don't believe her.

"Excuse me," tumbles out of my mouth as I stand from the table. I don't know where to go, but I can't leave. I take a deep breath and walk toward the adjoining kitchen.

"Spanky." Kieren starts to stand, but I hold up a hand to halt him as I walk away. I need some space, and he knows it.

Work. Work has gotten me through a lot of tough times. The menial gives me time to mull over my thoughts, and the repetition is a comfort, effectively killing the anxiety I feel. Kieren and I made a mess of the kitchen when we were preparing the meal, and he's already so taxed, I decide to clean it up– all an excuse to hide out in the kitchen, instead of sitting at yet another meal with Essie on the other side of the table, while she stares at me with her guilty gaze.

Speaking of Essie's guilty gaze, I feel it searing me as I hand-wash the dishes. Somehow sensing she caught my attention, she speaks to me. "Why are you doing that?" Essie asks out of curiosity, but I can tell that wasn't what she wanted to ask.

I keep my back to her. "Even though we're guests, they were kind enough to feed us, so we should help out. Plus, the Masons work very hard, and today has been a trying day. I'm doing my best by giving them a break."

"You don't sound like you anymore," Essie whispers. She takes the dish from my hand, so she can dry it.

"Is that a bad thing, or a good thing?" I ask in an emotionless voice.

Essie stares at me for a moment, her blue eyes eating the sight of me being so close. "I think it's good." She decides, and nods her head. "You would've used a butter knife on me before. I'd prefer to live." She gives a girlish giggle.

"Well, I've went through a lot since my eighteenth birthday. The nineteenth is rapidly approaching. I don't think I can live through another year like this one. What else? I was adopted? An alien? Born a boy?"

"I'm sorry," Essie apologizes, and her pale cheeks burn bright red. I sigh, not wanting to accept her apology, but knowing that it's futile to ignore. I understand the Mason brothers wanting her. Essie's a better looking version of me. We share the same brown hair, and a similar height, but nothing else. She's bubbly and fun, while I'm snarky and sarcastic and turning more serious by the day. Essie's voice is soft, and mine is raspy. Her curvy hips, tits, and ass are a man's fantasy come to reality. Basically, Essie is the complete and total opposite of me. I can't blame them for wanting her– I want to be her.

I sigh again. I repeat the mantra I've used for the past few months. *Accept yourself, Willow. Like yourself. Love yourself. Be comfortable in your own skin.*

I like this new version of Willow, flaws and all.

"I didn't mean for it to happen." Essie starts in, and I want to tell her to grow the hell up. I realize, even though I'm three years younger than Essie, she hasn't grown up yet. Yes, she graduated from cosmetology school and has a job, but she still lives at home. Most likely she'll live there until she gets married. She'll have some babies and have a happy life, and I want that life for her. But she will be stuck in this mindset she's refusing to leave behind. I'm not judging her, but I want more for Essie than to be a forty-year-old woman who is stuck in high school. At the same time, I'm an eighteen-year-old who is acting like a forty-year-old. I shake my head. I *need* to find a happy medium, or I won't be happy, either.

"Why?" My voice sounds like a child's, and I hate it. I fear what Essie will say. "Why did you do it?"

"I don't know," she lies, and we both know it.

"How can you apologize, and say you didn't mean it, if you don't know why you did it in the first place?" I don't mean to sound like I'm whining, but it sure sounds that way to my ears.

"I don't know what you want me to say, Willow," Essie says, sounding defensive.

"How about the truth for starters." I sneer like a total bitch. "Here's my truth. It shouldn't matter who the guy is, or whether or not I'm in love with him, or hate his guts. You shouldn't have done it, because you are my cousin– the only girl friend I've ever had. It shouldn't matter if Devon didn't love me, or wasn't my boyfriend enough to be faithful, but it should've mattered *to you*," I pointedly stress. "You should've stuck up for me. We're family, and there is only one side to family– *our* side. A true friend will always hate the boy who will cheat on her friend. She's the one who tears the vat of ice cream out of your hands, makes you wipe your nose, and hands you the baseball bat. She then drives you to his car, and helps you vandalize the puke's ride. She sure as hell wouldn't fuck him! IN. MY. FUCKING. CAR!"

"It was an accident," Essie says gutlessly in the face of my outburst, completely unaffected by my anger. "Devon still loves you, Willow."

"Actually," I hiss. "Devon doesn't love me, himself, or anyone else, because he can't. Right now, that boy is incapable of loving anyone. The only thing he's capable of being is selfish. Devon hates himself. What he did with you was to punish himself– to prove he is as bad as he feels on the inside."

"How can you be so cruel?" Essie's eyes are wide in shock.

"Cruel? You mean like, *cruel*. Fucking my cousin in my car? Or *cruel*. Taking a three-day bender in a crack house? *Cruel*? This is reality. We don't live in some fairytale, Essie. Devon needed help. I'm being honest. He can't love me. He's too selfish to see past his self-hatred. You're naïve if you think you can heal someone with love. It's bull-fucking-shit. You heal someone with self-truth."

"I…" Essie's stutters again in denial, and I've had enough.

"I can see the excuses in your eyes, and I can hear it in your voice. Somehow you've rationalized that what you did was justifiable, or not your fault. Own it, Essie. You could've killed yourselves driving drunk and high– you could've killed an innocent family! You could've gotten STDs or pregnant... Hell, you could've ruined lifetime friendships and a real relationship– oh, that's right, you did do that," I mutter snidely. "But I owe you one debt of gratitude. You showed me who you really are, and brought Devon's problems to light."

"Will you ever forgive me?" Essie says, sounding pitiful, but it's all an act.

"Yeah, I will. The day you take responsibilities for your actions is the day I forgive you. Until then, it would be best if you stayed out of my life," I warn in parting.

I turn to walk away, and find myself facing a wall of flesh. Three solid chests are at eye-level. Malcolm, Auggie, and Kieren must've been worried I'd knife the traitorous bitch. Each has a different expression on their face: Kieren has watery eyes and a sad little smirk, completely floored, and Malcolm and Auggie look proud for some reason.

"I'm sorry!" Essie shouts. "I'm so sorry, it's eating me alive. Fine! I was jealous of you. You're the kind of girl a man wants to marry and have a life with. I'm the kind they fuck while cheating on girls like you. That's how men see me."

"First of all, not all men think with their dicks and cheat on their wives." Malcolm sounds thoroughly disgusted. "A real man wouldn't do that. So you're obviously screwing the wrong ones, my sons included."

"A whore is how you see yourself, so that's why men treat you like one." Auggie speaks out. "I'm a man telling you how men think, so you should listen. Women like you fill my Playroom. They feel like shit, they act like shit, so men treat them like shit. You tried to give me a blow job six months ago, and I threw you off me. By your definition of a man, I should've let you do it. I give a girl what she wants– disrespect yourself, and I'll disrespect you back. Respect yourself, and I'll respect you back. Here's a novel idea, don't fuck losers in cars, and then blame the loser. Blame yourself."

"What. The. Fuck? Are you serious? You tried to blow Auggie?" I don't know if I should be surprised or not. "Why?"

"I was proving my point. Men like Auggie don't respect women like me," Essie says, sounding disillusioned.

"You just proved *my* point with your circular argument, little girl," Auggie mutters. "How about you respect yourself? I'm not saying you shouldn't have sex at all. I'm talking about throwing yourself at men you don't even want just to prove you're wanted. Value yourself more than that. Your self-worth doesn't hinge upon whether or not a guy's dick gets hard when he looks at you. My dick gets hard while watching a *Taco Bell* commercial, and I don't plan on fucking my taco– unless it's pink –I'm just hungry."

"Pink Taco– it's the fourth meal." Kieren flashes a devious smirk. "I had some for breakfast this morning. But what do I know, I always get hard when I'm thinking about chocolate cake... I like cake."

Unfathomable. The male mind is unfathomable.

"I'm done," I bite out. "Essie, there is absolutely nothing you could ever say to redeem yourself in my eyes. You're warped somehow. I've been thinking a lot, and seeing things differently. You say you're jealous of me because of the type of woman I am... you didn't know that shit when I was a toddler, yet you still did little things to alienate me. I'm done with you and your brokenness. Maybe if there was a whore-rehab we could send your faithless ass to, we'd wait and see if you came back fixed."

"I need you right now!" Essie cries out, sounding desperate. "Please, Willow. I need my cousin. I've never needed you more than I do right now. I'll get on my knees and beg. I need you, Willow."

"*Now*, she needs me," I mutter sarcastically while rolling my eyes. "*Now*, she's my cousin. Why would you possibly need me? Do you want to get close to me so you can hurt me again?"

"If you don't think I understand the consequences of my actions, you're mentally insane. I don't know what to do, and I need advice only you can give."

Finally looking at Essie, I ask, "What could you possibly need me for?"

"I made a mistake, and I'll be paying for it for the rest of my life, and not just losing you, or having our family look at me like I'm a whore. I don't know why I wanted to hurt you, but I really, *really* did. I wanted to hurt you, and I ended up hurting myself."

"That right there makes me really, *really* want to help you," I mock.

Desperate, Essie cries out, "I'm nine weeks pregnant with a drug addict's baby, and goddamn it, I need your fucking help!"

CHAPTER FIFTY-ONE
Welcome to the Playroom

The butterflies in my tummy are fierce for such small, fluttery creatures. My stomach threatens to overthrow my good intentions and wrap me around the nearest toilet. I'm scared that I'm not ready for the Playroom, that I won't feel the flare of adrenaline and happiness when I walk past its threshold. The wait was too long. Perhaps I've lost that internal spark that fires for all things hedonistic. I'm still naïve, still too innocent to appreciate the decadence, or I've grown up so much that I'll find it beneath me. What petrifies me even more, is that I'll still feel that flare of wantonness. I don't want to *want* to be in the Playroom. Not after last night. I need safe, easy, normal.

I'm at the Playroom Grand Opening because it was a project I started, and I want to see it to fruition. I won't be playing, but I think I'll enjoy watching. If Essie's revelation didn't make me take note of how fucking stupid casual sex is, then I'd be a moron.

After Essie's pregnancy outburst, Malcolm slumped to the nearest counter, and I blew the hell up. Screaming at Essie for being a selfish bitch– couldn't she think of someone else for one freakin' second, and let the Masons have one day without dealing with a catastrophe. Mid-bitch-fit, Kieren palmed my face, told me to simmer down, and pointed at Essie's belly. *"That's our blood, so shut the fuck up and deal."*

I shut up while Malcolm and Auggie went into lecture-mode. Robbie came in and held our cousin. Kieren made a plan on how to *deal* with the shit-storm. Ever-responsible Kieren. His brother's baby is forming in Essie's belly, and since Devon is incapable of knowing when to eat on time, Essie's now Kieren's problem, which made it *my* problem– my *big* fucking problem.

Isis and I stood side-by-side with identical expressions on our faces– one that screamed *dumb cunt*. We looked at each other and said something along the lines of, *"That bitch needs a DNA test before I believe it."* Regardless of who the father is, that baby gestating in Essie's belly *is* my family– no DNA test required.

Work, the ultimate coping mechanism. While everyone hovered around Essie, giving her all the attention she was seeking, I grabbed a pad of paper and started planning the

Playroom party. Everyone was going to need an outlet after all that horseshit. The entire time I kept silently thanking Clover for taking me to the clinic like clockwork, and then I felt bad for calling Essie irresponsible when Clover had to hold my hand and drag me to the clinic every three months– it's not very responsible when your '*mommy*' had to make you go.

"I really thought I'd feel different on this day," I mutter to Robbie. "When Auggie said I couldn't go to Rush, I was crushed. It's like him telling me no made the need worse. When you and I started renovating the attic, I worried the appeal of the Playroom had nothing to do with the kink of it, and everything to do with Augustus Kline. Now I'm pretty damn sure that was the case, because other than making this special for you and Auggie, and finishing what I started, I don't want to go in there." I point to the attic door.

I pace a path in front of the closed attic door to my bedroom door, and finish the route past the bathroom… over and over. It's a few minutes until showtime. Every few paces, when my hand brushes my dress, I shake my head, feeling like an idiot. The frilly, pink dress Clover gave me for my eighteenth birthday is now six-inches shorter, thanks to the kitchen shears, and way too tight, thanks to my final growth spurt.

Kieren was right. For some inexplicable reason, my tits have grown– it's like I finally have female hormones flowing in my veins, just as Clover promised. I dressed the part of Playroom Hostess, and my host is laughing at me from his position against the wall.

Robbie is barely dressed, and nothing about that is laughable. Robin Prynne looks badass with a black leather harness crisscrossing his chest. The straps have metal rings swinging from them. The only thing hiding Robbie's nakedness is a leather loincloth. The thick leather collar at his throat is missing Isis's tag, but that's because it's now tied to his wrist by a blood-red ribbon– the first day of kindergarten ribbon.

"You don't have to do this, Willow. Didn't you learn anything from Essie? Sexy is for you to decide. Everyone in the Playroom is in there for different reasons. It makes Auggie feel ever-powerful. Isis and I like to goof around and gossip and make fun of the people– before and after we do our thing. Malcolm's there to connect with his '*friends*'," Robbie actually uses air quotes.

I've learned Malcolm doesn't believe in sex outside of marriage– someone better tell his sons that –and he only plays *handsies* with his *friends*. I've never witnessed it, nor do I know what handsies means, or who these friends are. None of my business.

"I fear I'm a one man kinda woman– one that likes to play in her own bedroom. Um, I'm not boring though, no matter what your rumor-seeking ears have heard." I chuckle to myself when I remember the *Shake Weight*.

"I've heard no rumors." Robbie pouts. "Other than you're finally getting it on with Kieren, which isn't a rumor, since I have eyes and ears." The eavesdropping old biddy smirks at me. "Is Kieren into the little girl fantasy, or something?" Robbie gestures to my ridiculous outfit.

"You're looking pretty hot in your leather, brother. I think you plan on getting mauled by Isis and Auggie." I give a curtsy and grin. "Nah, I'm being ironic with my hostess outfit."

My dress is light pink with delicate pearl buttons up the bodice. I added a wide ribbon as a belt, and used more of the same ribbon to tie my hair into two high pigtails. The skirt is so short, the tulle tutu is visible. The tutu is so short, my pink panties with the rows of lace covering my bottom are on display. White socks with lace trim and white patent leather shoes are covering my feet. I've dangerously entered toddler territory. I look like a reject from Toddlers and Tiaras.

Footsteps on the back staircase have my heart pitter-pattering inside my chest. Robbie flashes me a feral smile, and I pretend his loincloth isn't tenting from excitement and anticipation.

Auggie sees me first and stumbles. Malcolm rumbles a laugh and shakes his head at me. Isis looks impressed until she sees Robbie. I watch her expression go from mischievousness to a hunger so deep it makes my need for the drink look like a simple thing. One look, and I know Isis is insanely in love with my brother, and the smirk he tosses my way screams he knows it, too. Robbie winks at me, and puts Isis out of her misery by taking her hand.

The deviant summit members create a bottleneck at the top of the stairs. I only wanted a small audience for our unveiling, so I had the guys invite no more than twenty. After tonight, anyone they invite is welcome, as long as they don't enter the rest of our house. The Playroom's visitors enter through the kitchen, take the backstairs, ignore mine and Robbie's rooms on the second floor next to the Playroom's door, and then enter the attic floor.

If reality and play are separate, I don't want my reality to be interrupted by their play. No more knob-bobbing in the kitchen for Auggie. I swear that man has a mouth attached to his groin at all times.

"A gift for you," I say softly to Auggie as I point at the plaque on the door. He smiles brightly as he touches it. Auggie places a gentle kiss to my forehead in thanks, and then winks at Rob, recognizing his artistic contribution.

I shout grandly, "Welcome to the Playroom!" With a wave of my hand, I present the Playroom. I walk through the door and begin to ascend the stairs. After I enter the attic, I stand off to the side so I can watch everybody's reactions.

The gasps and intakes of breath are payment for all of our hard work. I smile and look at Robbie's and my creation. I wanted it to look like a high-class Bordello. The age of the house and the style of the furniture left behind inspired me. The attic of the Spook House is bigger than Malcolm's entire home. The mansard style roofline created some interesting angles to the walls. I built small partitions to create spaces rather than having one large room. A bathroom is on each end of the Playroom, with the wet bar bisecting the center.

Robbie painted hedonistic murals depicting all the kinks our players possess on several of the walls. I padded the rest of the walls, and covered them with panels of red velvet and black leather to resemble sofa backs.

I smile to myself as I walk to the wet bar. This is the biggest test of my entire life. I bite my lip to hold the saliva at bay that threatens to drool out the corner of my mouth. *You're better than this, Willow. Don't give in to temptation. You'd be no better than the hypocrite you called Devon and Essie.* I overpower my need by sheer willpower alone. Alcohol is a choice, and I choose me.

I love to drink, but I love playing barkeep even more. I put all of my energy into giving everyone else an exceptional experience. The Playroom is my gift to all of them. I pull a couple dozen champagne flutes from the overhead racks and pop the corks on several bottles of bubbly ambrosia. I gingerly place them on a tray for Robbie to distribute. I longingly sniff the opening of an empty bottle, enjoying the sting of alcohol in my nostrils. I quickly toss the bottle in the recycling bin before temptation overrides my willpower.

I remember to flick the switch on the sound system. I chose something diabolically arousing. It's not music. It's a heartbeat pounding pure bass. It speeds up, causing your heartbeat to match, and then it will drop to deathly slow. Overlapping the beat is the breathing. When the beat runs fast, the breathing hitches. I tested it out on Robbie. I had to leave the room after a few minutes because he had business to attend, as did I.

I reserve two glasses and fill them with sparkling cider. I keep one for myself, for obvious reasons, and deliver one to Kieren, for less obvious reasons. Yes, Kieren is underage, but the reality of it is, he hates the taste of alcohol. I also believe, after all the issues with Devon, Kieren wants to avoid addictive substances at all costs.

"Nice," Kieren purrs into my ear while wrapping an arm around my waist. He leans back to stare at my frilly-covered ass. "But I prefer my Spanky naked. Not into kid fantasies."

"Har-dee-har," I mock laugh. "Mr. Mason, I dressed this way to keep the Playroomers at bay, not draw them in like flies."

"I'd be careful, there, little girl. Some of those men are into that sort of shit. Auggie's probably creaming his pants." I shrug like it doesn't matter what Auggie thinks, because it doesn't. I tilt my head back, waiting on my kiss. Kieren presses his lips to mine. The boy truly is traditional, because he doesn't give me any more than a two-second press of lips.

"Friends," Auggie clears his throat. He's looking at Robbie and me with the now familiar expression of *I don't know you.* Auggie's beaming at us like he's the proud parent of a kid who cured cancer.

"I'm speechless and in awe. Now I know why you wouldn't let me in here." Auggie chuckles. "My housemates locked me out of my own attic with two padlocks. They each kept a key so I couldn't influence one of them to let me in." Auggie turns in a circle and smiles at each of us. "Welcome to the Playroom!" he yells with pride as he raises his glass.

We echo Mr. Augustus Kline, raise our glasses in salute, and then drain their contents.

I decide I was born to be a hostess. I love fluttering around, making sure everyone is comfortable and happy. Robbie's showing our guests to the surprises we created specifically for them. Isis is gazing at a contraption Robbie had me build. He sketched out the design, and then I built it. I had to have Dad help me with some of the intricate cuts and the pulley system, though. I was shocked when Dad grinned at the Playroom, and his expression changed to a kid wanting to play– the Prynnes are a naughty lot. The result of our project is a rack of torture I will never touch again. Isis is caressing a leather strap with loving adoration and a wicked gleam in her eye.

Auggie's sitting grandly in the throne we commissioned for him. Rough cut logs with a black leather seat and backrest, create the medieval throne fit for the Beast. He's grinning like an idiot, running his palms up and down the armrests, and rumbling the sexiest laugh I've ever heard. I couldn't love the man more if I tried, or the man who's making him laugh.

A Beast needs a place for his nearest and dearest. We know how much the mountain of a man loves chaise lounges, so we created two to flank his throne. I found one in the old Playroom, and one in storage awaiting sale at Revamped. I reupholstered the set to match the throne.

Malcolm and Kieren are sitting on one, with Opal and the cocksucktress, Nina, on the opposing chaise. The ladies are teasing Kieren, and the men are laughing at his mortification. Kieren keeps looking at me and flushing. No doubt our recent activities are the topic of discussion. No sex stays secret among deviant friends.

I was completely ignorant as to who would need what to fulfill their deepest, darkest desires, so Robbie picked everything out. Our twenty guests are spread out around the Playroom, chattering and laughing as they caress all their playthings. We did really good– everyone is thrilled.

My gaze seeks out our host, and I find Robbie being strapped into that contraption by Isis. The expression of ecstasy on his face is so private that I quickly look away and blush. Now that I'm not looking at Robbie, the soft alluring murmur of Isis's words fill my ears. Words I don't want to hear.

I concentrate on all the Playroomers. Opal, the dog walking nurse, is showing Bethany the special place I built just for her. This was the only area I specifically designed without Robbie's help. It didn't take much imagination as to what a pretty girl would want when she played puppy.

In the far corner of the attic, next to the bathroom, I created a Pet Area for those who like to playact as puppies. I'd asked if anyone is ever a cat, but Robbie didn't know either. He laughed maniacally and whispered *horsy* underneath his breath.

Since the attic isn't big enough for that stable Robbie was insinuating, I built a doghouse big enough for a person to stretch out inside. The door to the house is hidden behind it. I don't want anyone who isn't playing puppy to know the doghouse turns into a cage. I don't trust someone not to torture our pets.

A basket of toys and brushes is next to a huge pallet to sleep on. The pallet is cushiony and big enough to play on. Opal fills Bethany's water dish, and I watch in fascination as Beth laps the water up with her pink tongue. Bethany slobbers all over Opal's leg, and I giggle before I can stop myself.

I feel eyes on me when I laugh. I glance at the throne and chaises to my captive audience. All are looking at me for varying reasons. Auggie's looking aroused beyond belief. Kieren's making sure I'm still comfortable. Nina looks at me with curiosity, while Malcolm looks like I'm invading his sandbox. I wink at them, and then return all of my attention to the scene playing out before me. I swell with pride because I did a really good job– Opal and Beth love what I provided for them.

Opal pretends to toss a ball, and Beth's eyes track its arc. Opal shrugs, and then tosses the ball a few feet. The dog walker laughs delightedly when the puppy shuffles after it, swaying her ass in our faces. They play fetch for a few minutes, until Bethany starts to pant and keeps lapping at her bowl.

"Puppy," Opal calls, and Bethany trots over. "Lay on your belly, on the bed." Opal grabs a brush and waits while Bethany gets settled. "Good puppies get brushed. Doesn't that feel good?" Opal croons to her puppy, smirking the entire time.

Opal draws the paddle bush through the puppy's long hair, and then smacks Bethany's bare ass with the brush on the down stroke. Bethany's whimpering and wiggling around by the time her hair shines and her ass glows rosy pink.

Alrighty, then...

Not my thing, but a few Playroomers are edging closer. I don't want to be involved with puppy play, but it's interesting to see how people are intrigued by it. I also don't want to be involved with the sadistic shit Isis is doing to Robbie at the moment, either.

I look around for Kieren, but what I find isn't my man but my boss. I cock my head to the side and watch in sick fascination.

Every play scene is straight out of a psychological study. Does Auggie avoid the two people on this earth who love him unconditionally because he has mommy and sister issues? The ladies always bobbing his knob sure do emotionally resemble his mom and Tina.

Nina– the cocksucktress –is doing what she does best. She's on her knees, servicing our reigning king. Auggie sits in this throne with Nina kneeling between his thighs with the Beast shoved down her eager throat. A shiver of lust rolls over me, but not nearly as powerful as the need to want more than what Auggie and Nina are getting. It's clinical, biological– not at all sexy or intimate. There's more of an emotional connection between Beth and Opal, and their fun is platonic affection, than the sex act Nina is providing Auggie.

Right then and there, an epiphany strikes me, searing up my spine and exploding in my brain. This version of Willow isn't ready for the Playroom, and she may never be. It has nothing to do with maturity level or open-mindedness. Right now, I have what I want, and that's perfectly fine with me.

I don't know what the future holds for me. I don't know if Kieren and I will last a week or an eternity. But who the fuck cares? I'm only eighteen years old, and if I want to fall in love and get my heart broken a thousand times over, that's my prerogative. I'll angst my way through it, and learn something new every damned time.

I'm no longer Willow the wayward. I'm no longer just Mr. Kline's Monster. I stand next to Auggie's throne and put my hand on his shoulder. Auggie gives me a new look, one that professes I'm his equal and a very good girl…

I return the look with one of my own. I'll be *my* own Good Girl, thank you very much.

I do the best thing I could ever do for myself: mentally, emotionally, and for my self-respect and self-image. While the Playroom may provide consensual fun for many, healing for others, it *will* harm me. I grab Kieren's hand, and tug him after me toward the exit.

"We're not meant to be here." As I speak the words, I've never felt surer of anything in my entire life. "It's game night at the Prynnes. Let's grab your kids, and pick Lang up on the way by."

Kieren flashes me a relieved look, like he was waiting on my ass to make the decision to evacuate the Playroom. "Besides, we have two more years before I have to keep my word about fucking you against the walls at Revamped, the Playroom, and Wreck & Ruin. No sense in being premature." Kieren releases the deadly man laugh, and I quiver with lust. "What's the game tonight?"

"The Game of Life, and it's a good thing Essie will be there. We can load her car with pegs." Kieren makes a sound in the back of his throat, admonishing me for being a bitch. "I'll do my best by Essie, because it's the right thing to do. I promise. But I don't have to like it... C'mon, Stud," I say as I yank open the door to the stairwell.

I shriek as Kieren tosses me over his shoulder, smacking my ass until it stings. Snickering, he hops up and down singing, "Shake Weight... we're gonna play Shake Weight in your bedroom first. It won't take long– I'm fuckin' amped and ready to blow. I gotta smack a naughty little girl's ass, and then thoroughly fuck the good girl back into her. Shake Weight, Spanky! Shake Weight!"

I tilt my head back and belt out a laugh that echoes around the Playroom, and continues to echo as Kieren carries me down the steps to my bedroom. I made the right decision for Willow.

Kieren Mason is Willow Prynne's *just right*.

CHAPTER FIFTY-TWO

"Chocolate cake?" I arch an eyebrow at my sister. Every time I do the gesture, a warm feeling fills me– like Auggie himself is comforting me. "Out of all the recipes in the world, you thought I'd need this," I mutter incredulously. "Over say… mac 'n' cheese?"

"Who the hell is this secret admirer?" Clover bursts out in a panic, her hands gripping the edge of the countertop, fingers forming claws. "It's every day now. At first it was once a week, then every few days. Once, I didn't give him what he wanted, so it became a daily occurrence, with threats of several times a day. Naughty threats– explicit imagery sent to Mayor Ross."

I laugh. I can't freakin' help it. I get a stitch in my side from giggling. Lesson one, don't disobey a man like Malcolm, or you'll regret the punishment he uses to make you submit.

"Making a lot of donuts, aren't ya?" I snicker at my cop joke.

"Yeah, why?" Clover's blue eyes are so spooked, I want to tell her the truth. "That's the daily thing now. I have to give him donuts by five a.m. Now there are singular deserts too, like pies and shit."

"Just food demands?" I prompt, curious as to what Malcolm is up to. He stopped having us kids do his bidding. Now the rat-bastard is hoarding the baked goods for his addictive sweet tooth. Kieren caught Malcolm in the act of creating that *explicit imagery*. Malcolm isn't a quiet one.

"No, look!" Clover yanks me to the pantry and opens the door.

"Whoa…" I whisper in awe. "Why do you have professional bakery supplies?" The huge pantry is stocked with mixing bowls, pans, *Pyrex*, and utensils. It's impressive. I bite my lip against the smirk that threatens to erupt. I fall in love with Malcolm in an instant– he's the perfect dad to the perfect mom. Malcolm wants Clover to be happy, and the community would benefit from it, too. The message is clear: Malcolm wants Clover to quit her job as Mayor Ross's personal assistant and live her dream of cooking as her profession.

"I get something new every time. This morning it was a cake pan, inside a sturdy box, with a note attached. Here." Clover shoves the note into my hands. Her poor fingers are trembling.

Lucky Clover,

The lemon meringue pie was delicious. Everyone says your donuts are the best they've ever eaten. I agree, and I've had a lot of donuts in my lifetime. My newest request: This evening, by six p.m., I need your famous seven-layers-of-sin chocolate cake. I've heard a lot about this decadent dessert. In fact, someone very dear to my heart said it wasn't sinful at all, but pure heaven. You must teach Willow to make the cake. She is to make it all on her own, and her love is to infuse the sweet treat. Thank you for being so reasonable, Clover– I wouldn't want to miss out because you're being naughty again, or do you want me to send video to Ross next time?

I giggle into my hand. Nice way to threaten someone by thanking them– leave it to Malcolm. Smile dying on my lips, I close my eyes against the threat of tears. The Masons are flying to Arizona for a family weekend with Devon, to celebrate the midpoint of his therapy. This cake is Devon's birthday cake. He's turning twenty-one while sitting in rehab. Malcolm wants Devon to have a fucking cake made by me. Why? I surreptitiously wipe my eyes dry.

I'm surprised my sister's this daft. For the past two weeks, the only thing we've talked about is their trip and the reasons behind it.

P.S. No donuts until you receive your next gift ☺

P.S. Willow, I believe it's time you asked Clover what Violet so innocently interrupted months ago. I'll know if you didn't!

P.S. Clover, if she doesn't ask, you better borrow some of Willow's balls and tell her yourself!

Hugs, & thanks for the cake, my little ladies! Your secret admirer, Papa Bear

"Clover, you're kidding me, right? You have to know who the hell your secret admirer is!" I shake my head at her like she's an idiot. "I don't believe your feigned ignorance for a second," I warn while eyeing her suspiciously.

No one is that stupid! Donuts and Papa Bear, really? The fact that Malcolm doesn't want any sweets for a few days, because obviously he's going out of town with the birthday cake in tow, should've been a huge tipoff.

My P.S. was definitely from Auggie.

"I don't know," she whimpers. Clover sounds desperate, but this is for her own good. I think Malcolm's right. Clover would've run from him if it wasn't for his secret admirer extortion.

"Yeah, well, I do know who it is." I reach over and tap her on her round behind, teasing her. "It's slapping ya in the ass, Clover. Wake up! Don't ask, 'cuz I ain't telling ya. It'll be more fun watching you figure it out." I snicker.

"Willow, it's driving me crazy– insanity. You have no idea the things he sends me that aren't food related, but sometime they include the food he demanded. I won't say what he did to the donut hole."

"Oh. My. God." I laugh so loud I startle myself. After playing naughty games with Kieren for the past month, I can only imagine what his father is capable of dreaming up.

Clover sputters underneath her breath, words I can't make out, and starts grabbing stuff from the pantry. She plunks everything on the kitchen island with a loud bang.

"Not a word from me," I warn. "Teach me to how to bake a cake. Time's a ticking away. We don't want Papa Bear sending that video of him screwing a donut to Fairport's elderly mayor, do we?"

Seriously, what the hell is wrong with a box mix? Nope, we can't take the easy route. We didn't even use measuring cups. Clover made me weigh the flour on a scale– before *and* after sifting. No cocoa powder for Clover, either. We had to melt premium chocolate– she called it tempering. It's no wonder the cake is so decadent. It's probably why I've gained ten pounds in the last month. Half of Malcolm's dessert orders are going to the Spook House and directly into my tummy… because I nabbed them from the front porch before he could collect them. He almost kicked my ass last week over a dozen cheese danishes– tried to pry them out of my hands as I got into my Explorer.

"Clover," I begin as tactfully as possible. I do everything Auggie says, within reason. "I've been thinking a lot about what you told me. In fact, it never leaves my thoughts," I admit reluctantly.

My sister's blue eyes cut to the side, gazing at me with suspicion, and looking a little bit ill. Clover knows where I'm leading. She figured out what that part of the note meant, I'm sure. I can see it in her eyes.

"You said it was an open adoption?" I ask out of curiosity. I swirl the last of the chocolate rosettes around the outside of the cake. A groan is torn from me as I lick the chocolate ganache off my fingertip. "Divine," I purr. "Utterly sinful."

"Yes, it was an open adoption," Clover answers cautiously as she bundles the cake into the sturdy box that came with the pan and note. "I'll be right back. I have to put this on the porch. Watch." Clover smirks, looking a little bit evil. "It will be gone in under a minute. I don't know how they do it. I can watch and nothing happens, then I blink and it's gone. Usually the kids pester me and I miss the pickup."

I snicker while Clover takes the cake to the porch. No doubt it disappears while the kids pester her. I bet Malcolm or Kieren calls Seth and Violet to get Clover away from the front window.

I lean back against the island and cross my arms over my chest. "Reason I'm asking," I say to Clover when she returns. "Is that it's driving me crazy. I walk down the street, looking for someone my age. I look for your blue eyes, or Sam's chipmunk cheeks. I don't ever find them. I need to know if it was a boy or a girl. I need to know who it is, Clover. What if one of us hooks up with them? That would be incest!"

"No need to worry over that, Sapling. It will never happen." Clover takes a deep breath, holds it for what seems like minutes, until I worry she'll suffocate. She expels it in a forceful gust, and continues speaking. "A girl– a lovely, brave, bullheaded child who looks just like Sam, but has my body."

I stare speechlessly at Clover as she reins in her emotions. Tears are gliding down her cheeks, and it kills me. "You don't have to say any more. I can see how difficult this is for you to talk about."

"She has Sam's chipmunk cheeks." Clover smiles and wipes her eyes. "She has his hair and eyes. His gravelly voice, too. She has his unflinching honesty. Her words sometimes feel like a suckerpunch to the gut."

"She sounds like she could be my best friend," I joke to lighten the mood. A smirk flashes across Clover's face. It's so similar to my own that I join her.

"Undoubtedly," she replies. "Sam made me promise on his deathbed that I wouldn't keep the secret. Thousands of times I've tried, but the words would get caught in my throat. When she was little, Sam told her the truth. She was too young to understand, but it made him feel better." Clover closes her eyes. "I wasn't lying when I'd said Sam never forgave me. He wasn't being harsh. This secret hung heavily over our marriage."

"Why didn't you tell the truth? Why couldn't you do it for Sam?" A slight edge of accusation and fury lace my voice.

"I love our daughter more than I loved Sam. Sam was an excellent father, but I made a deal and I stuck to it. Responsibility is difficult, because you have to do what is right, even when you don't want to. I was one week from my seventeenth birthday when I had her. I couldn't take care of her. Hell, I couldn't take care of myself. I would've been a selfish piece of shit to take her from her parents, from her siblings, when she was three and I was ready to be a mom. I tried to take care of her the best I could. I failed more often than I succeeded."

"Who knows?" I ask warily.

"Everyone who is older than you." Clover freezes, waiting for my reaction.

"Mom and Dad know. Robbie knows." I accuse, and Clover's facial expression screams the truth. "Auggie?" Clover nods her head yes and closes her eyes. "The Masons?!" I practically scream.

Clover audibly swallows. "Malcolm and Isis know, but none of the kids do. Essie doesn't know, either. Essie was too young, but she's came right out and asked me before. She suspects the truth… Violet knows," Clover whispers. "She figured it out three months ago."

"Who? I need to know the truth!" I scream. "I need to hear you say it out loud!"

Naïve Willow is no more. I'm not daft like Clover. I don't need to have it smack me in the face to get a clue. I get it. I'd joked awhile back that I couldn't take any more shit. Well, I'm not an alien or born a male, but I sure as fuck was adopted… by my own grandparents.

I stare a silently crying Clover down. "Sam was right not to forgive you," I harshly growl. "Say it, Clover!"

"Willow, she's you. You're my daughter." Clover gasps, looking devastated and torn. "I'd give anything to hear you call me Mom and not have it be a snide comment."

"I can forgive you for this," I honestly admit, and my mother relaxes. "What I can't forgive you for is that I never got to call

Sam Daddy to his face. I never got to be a daddy's girl. For Sam, I would've been a good girl, Mom."

Thank you for reading **GOOD GIRL**. Don't miss out on what's to come…

GOOD GIRL, Willow's coming-of-age tale.
WILDLY WEDDED WIFE, Rory & Bethany's novella.
WIDOW, Malcolm & Clover's journey.
WANTON, Opal & Ginny's tasty treat.
WARPED, Devon, Essie, Kieren, & Willow's future.
COMING SOON.
WOVEN, a novellas with surprising narrators.
WICKED, a novella showcasing Auggie & Tina's parents.
WAYWARD, Auggie, Isis, and Robin's angsty emotional roller coaster ride.
…and many more to come.

ACKNOWLEDGEMENTS

A lot of work goes into writing a novel, and it isn't just by the writer herself. **My parents:** for their unconditional support. **My readers**: thank you for reading my twisted words and spreading my books to the masses. For without you, no one would've ever heard of my stories. My readers are my lifeblood. A shout out to the members of the **M&M of Restraint Group on Facebook**: thanks for the endless entertainment and inspiration. **Wicked Reads**: (in all its incarnations) **Angela G.**, thank you for taking over and making Wicked Reads better than I could have done by myself. & thank you for helping promote my work and the work of other authors. Angela? Have I told you lately how much I appreciate you? A huge thank you to the **Wicked Writer's Betas** for keeping me grounded and encouraging me to keep trudging along when I get frustrated. Your thoughts and observations are invaluable. ((Hugs)) Beta readers: **Kris | Suz | Darcy | Sandy | Di | Angela | Diane | Jacki | Linsey | Alexis | Billie Jo | Tassie | Caroline | Judith | Jodi Lynn | Jodi |** Someday, I'd love to meet you all in real life– it would be the experience of a lifetime.

ABOUT THE AUTHOR

Erica Chilson does not write in the 3rd person, wanting her readers to *be* her characters. Therefore, writing a bio about herself, is uncomfortable in the extreme.

Born, raised, and here to stay, the Wicked Writer is a stump-jumper, a ridge-runner. Hailing from North Central Pennsylvania, directly on the New York State border; she loves the changes in seasons, the humid air, all the mountainous forest, and the gloomy atmosphere.

Introverted, but not socially awkward, Erica prides herself on thinking first and filtering her speech. There are days she doesn't speak at all. If it wasn't for the fact that she lives with her parents, giving her a sense of reality, she would be a hermit, where the delivery man finds her months after expiration.

Reading was an escape, a way to leave a not-so pleasant reality behind. Reading lent Erica the courage she gathered from the characters between the pages to long for a different life. Writing was an instrument of change, evolving Erica into the woman she is today- a better, more mature, more at peace thinker.

Erica has a wicked mind, one she pours out into her creations. Her filter doesn't allow all of it to erupt, much to her relief. Sarcastic, with a very dark, perverse sense of humor, Erica puts a bit of herself into every character she writes.

I love hearing from readers. If you would like more information on release dates, works in progress, teaser chapters, and random bits of madness, please visit my Facebook Fan Page: https://www.facebook.com/thewickedwriter my website: ericachilson.com or please contact me via email: wickedwriter.ericachilson@gmail.com
DEVIANTS ONLY, if you'd like to join Erica Chilson's closed Facebook group, M&M of Restraint: https://www.facebook.com/groups/MistressandMaster/